GO TO THE WIDOW-MAKER

In the world of physical danger, says the author, love is for men; women are for sex. This is the central theme of *Go to the Widow-Maker*, a superb novel which propounds the theory that men of action can be slowly killed by twenty years of peace.

"James Jones has written himself a sure best seller ... raw, ferocious, uncontrolled ..." *Books of the Month*

"He cannot be faulted when he is dealing with the world of masculine action. The skin-diving scenes are exceptional by any standard—the lure of diving, the mental thrill, the physical sensations ..." *Life*

JAMES JONES

Go to the
Widow-Maker

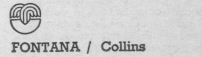

FONTANA / **Collins**

First published 1967
First issued in Fontana Books April 1969
Sixth Impression May 1973

© 1967 by James Jones

Printed in Great Britain
Collins Clear-Type Press London and Glasgow

The poem 'Harp Song of the Dane Women'
from Puck of Pook's Hill by Rudyard Kipling
is reproduced by permission of Mrs George
Bambridge and Macmillan and Co. Ltd.

Acknowledgment

With a special thanks to Clem Wood and to Carleton Mitchell for serious help on sailing data;

To my marvellous secretary Kathryn Weissberger for her devotion to the project and her great help in all the mundane things;

And to Monsieur Philippe Diolé, whom I have never met, but whose remark that 'more of our serious writers should look into this new undersea world' gave me the whole idea in the first place.

And of course, to my dear wife, Gloria, who helped, and whose faith kept me going through some pretty rocky times.

Special Note

This novel is a work of fiction, and any resemblance to any real people, living or dead, is completely coincidental, and totally outside the author's intention. The characters are not real people; they belong entirely to the author, who created them slowly over a long period of time, with a great deal of anguish and parental care, and also with a great deal of love. There is no town of Ganado Bay in Jamaica. There is no Grand Bank Island. There is no Island group called The Nelsons. There is no Grand Hotel Crount, and as far as I know there is no hotel at all on the seaward side of The Palisadoes spit. I think there ought to be one, though, and might be willing to invest with some far-seeing citizen who wanted to build one there. There is of course a town of Montego Bay in Jamaica, and I lived there for a year with a great deal of pleasure and of which year I have many fond memories, both of the time we spent there and of the many friends we made there But everything else, characters, actions, incidents, and the internal speculations of the characters, are all mine, and I am solely responsible.

AT SEA
ON BOARD THE PAQUEBOT
S.S. *Antilles*
26 JUNE 1966

Dedication

THIS BOOK IS DEDICATED TO MY DAUGHTER

Kaylie

WITH THE INFORMATION THAT THE REASON

HER FATHER NEVER TRIED TO WRITE

ABOUT A GREAT LOVE STORY BEFORE

WAS BECAUSE HE HAD NEVER EXPERIENCED ONE

UNTIL HE MET HER MOTHER

Harp Song of the Dane Women

What is a woman that you forsake her,
And the hearth-fire and the home-acre,
To go with the old grey Widow-maker?

She has no house to lay a guest in—
But one chill bed for all to rest in,
That the pale suns and the stray bergs nest in.

She has no strong white arms to fold you,
But the ten-times-fingering weed to hold you—
Out on the rocks where the tide has rolled you.

Yet, when the signs of summer thicken,
And the ice breaks, and the birch-buds quicken,
Yearly you turn from our side, and sicken—

Sicken again for the shouts and the slaughters.
You steal away to the lapping waters,
And look at your ship in her winter-quarters.

You forget our mirth, and talk at the tables,
The kine in the shed and the horse in the stables—
To pitch her sides and go over her cables.

Then you drive out where the storm clouds swallow,
And the sound of your oar-blades, falling hollow
Is all we have left through the months to follow.

Ah, what is Woman that you forsake her,
And the hearth-fire and the home-acre,
To go with the old grey Widow-maker?

RUDYARD KIPLING

ONE

On a hot February day, in the port town of Ganado Bay on the island of Jamaica in the Caribbean Sea, two white Americans stood by the side of an old, dilapidated hotel's deserted and dilapidated saltwater swimming pool. One of them, who (though he was of medium height) appeared short because of his blocky muscular build, was dripping wet. He wore only a tight, scanty, black European-type bikini, and he was, in spite of the profoundly burning tropic sun on his back, shaking so hard that his teeth chattered whenever he allowed his jaws to relax. He commenced to do a little dance, jarring himself down hard on his bare heels while the crotchbulge of his bikini jiggled alarmingly, without ever taking his anxious eyes off the other man standing in front of him. His name was Ron Grant, and with the possible exception of Tennessee Williams he was the most famous playwright of his generation, was judged just about everywhere also to be one of the two or three best playwrights of that generation, probably the best generation—because of himself and one other—since O'Neill's.

The other man was a veritable giant. At least six-foot-two, with an already enormous frame, from which suspended a huge belly, he was all over covered with inches-deep layers of muscle, the whole giving him the bulk—and the girth—of a minor mountain. On top of all this he wore an inch-deep layer of body fat like the blubber coat of some aquatic mammal, which hid all muscle definition and tied the enormity of him all together in one great mass while further increasing it. His tent-sized swimming trunks, worn hanging under the belly, were the long-legged boxer-type, and their loud Hawaiian print had been faded by the sun and the sea into a uniform blotchy yellow. Two snag tears showed on the front of them. Above the unbelievable expanse of chest and belly, attached to the front of a large-sized head, hung out a sharp-nosed face with furry eyebrows that met in the middle, two deep-set blackly burning eyes, and an expression of perpetual, malevolent impatience as if sitting tranquilly were painfully intolerable to him—an expression with which he gazed at the still dancing smaller man before him. The giant's name was Al Bonham and he ran a diving shop and underwater salvage business in the Jamaican port town of Ganado Bay.

. Under his gaze Grant the playwright stopped his dancing. Between them on the busted concrete pool-edge, from which tufts of unkempt grass grew here and there in the cracks, lay a glistening-wet aqualung tank and regulator with its mouthpiece dangling over the edge toward the water.

" Well, I think you're about ready," Bonham rumbled. He always rumbled, as if—or so Grant thought—he were trying to muffle the great power of his equally outsized voice to keep from frightening people.

" You mean, for the *sea*?" Grant said.

A smile like a cloud passed swiftly up over the great plain of Bonham's face revealing his bad teeth and disappeared into his hair.

" Sure, why not?"

" Well, I—Okay, if you say so." Grant had wrapped his arms around himself in an attempt to still his shivering and shaking, and was now slapping himself stingingly on both sides of his unusually broad back. " You understand," he apologised, " this shaking is not just because I'm nervous. I haven't got as much protection built on to me as you have. The cold always did get to me. I really get cold."

A transparent film seemed to pass over Big Al Bonham's eyes, and Grant knew him well enough to know by now that this was not due to any allusion to his protective fat. Instead it was his businessman's look, a businessman who has smelled a sale and does not intend to let the victim get away. Grant had seen it before.

" We got a foam rubber wet shirt back at the shop that belongs to Ali my helper. My stuff wouldn't fit you. You could wrap it around twice, and then some. But Ali might be willing to sell you his.—Or let you borrow it," he added, enigmatically.

" Oh, I'd be glad to buy it," Grant said quickly. " I'll need one in Kingston."

" If we ordered you a new one, it would take a month," Bonham rumbled stolidly. " Well, let's get into our pants," he said, and turned away to a concrete bench which like the pool-edge had part of its internal support iron showing. He picked up a grubby pair of rumpled ice-cream pants and began pulling them right on over his faded wet trunks. A huge, equally faded Hawaiian-print sport shirt lay nearby. After watching him bemusedly a moment (he had seen him do the same thing before), Grant followed suit and did the same.

As they walked wet through the decrepit, badly rundown hotel—which more resembled an over-large boarding house really, and was apparently customerless—the equally rundown Negro man at the desk (it was hard to tell if he was proprietor or clerk) exchanged a significant glance with Bonham, and the big man nodded. "Take care of it later," he said, clipped. Outside he stowed the aqualung in the back of the badly battered, barely creepable, wartime U.S. Buick station-wagon he had nursed over and then down the hill two hours before, and they started back up over and then down the hill toward the main town where his shop was.

Below them, on this particularly steeply falling hill road, wherever houses or villas or hotels did not block the view, the whole of Ganado Bay and the bay itself lay spread out before them. A Navy ship, a tender, was in from Guantanamo to-day, and the U.S. sailors' uniforms made myriad white bright dots in the dun colourless streets between the chipped, peeling, faded and almost equally colour-less red, yellow and purple painted buildings of the town.

"I could of taken you to one of the ritzy hotels on that same beach. I work them too. But I thought you'd want the privacy with nobody around watching," Bonham rumbled, "and knowing who you are. And, it's a lot cheaper for me."

Grant did not answer. The "hotel" had been plainly enough a dump. The day before they had gone to a some-what, but only slightly, better place. This one to-day was undoubtedly the cheapest joint in the town which could still be said to possess a pool. Indeed, it was almost one of those perennial settings of the Williams plays: hibiscus and other bright flowers Grant couldn't name growing on and almost hiding the crumbling walls and rotting trellises; grassgrown, anklebreaker sidewalks; two untended straggly trees: he half expected to see Blanche Dubois come out of the bushes in a disarrayed skirt leading Stanley Kowalski by the hand. Well, what the hell? Let Bonham make a few bucks off me.

Bonham was clearly feeling him out in some sort of way. The very first two days he had taken him to two of the ritziest hotels on the Ganado Bay beach. Then yesterday they'd gone to the cheaper place, and then to-day here. Each time Bonham charged him the same price, but had to pay the hotel manager less and so kept more.

But none of all that mattered. Grant was thinking about what Bonham had said about him now being ready to try the aqualung in the sea. He had been waiting, and in *one* way working toward, this moment a long time. His newest play, was all finished and received with great elation by his producers in New York, so he had earned this time off. A certain intensely warm feeling at the thought of the play, there, safe and sound and all *finished,* ran all through him warming and easing him all over. God, how did he know he'd ever get through it? and give it all he knew it had to have? How did you know you could ever do it again? You didn't. But he had. And this was probably the best of his work. So he had earned this. And fuck poor hotels. And fuck Art—" Art "—too, for that matter, he thought, and with this thought there arose also in his mind a sort of dark-dressed, spectral, mantillaed figure, with the gloom-sealed dark face almost hidden, standing on the church steps pointing. That was the way he almost always thought of her now. And to think he had begun *this*, diving, to get rid of her. That was a laugh now.

" I still think you're makin' a mistake to go on to Kingston," Bonham said. " I've dived both places. We got everything here they got there." This was not strictly the truth and Grant knew it; but he also knew Bonham did not know he knew it, and hated to think of losing such a rich potential customer. It was all such a rude jolt, elbow jab, from what he'd just been thinking.

Grant didn't answer for a moment. " Well, there's lots of other things involved, Al," he said fairly. " Besides just the diving."

" You mean that girl-friend of yours, up at the villa. You want to get away from *her*." Bonham said it very softly. There was a note almost of secrecy. Of complicity. It seemed strange he should say that just now just after what

Grant had been thinking. It was as though he had looked into his mind.

"She's not my girl-friend, she's my uh foster-mother," Ron Grant said, falling immediately into the old protection routine. "But uh well, yes."

"Oh, I'm sorry, excuse me," Bonham rumbled politely, but went right on anyway. "Even so I can't say I blame you. She sure is peculiar."

It was always that way. Especially around men Grant knew to be real men. None of them ever liked his mistress. "Mistress"! Jesus! The apologetic embarrassment had become as much a part of him as his breathing. "She *can* be trying," he murmured, conceded. He smiled at the giant. "Listen, when do you think we'll be able to go out to sea? Now that you think I'm ready."

"Go right now."

"Now!"

"Sure, why not?" That same smile that seemed so like a foreboding cloud passed up over Bonham's face again. It appeared to start at his heavy chin, pass up through his mouth with its bad teeth, then to his nose, eyes, eyebrows and forehead, warping and distorting infernally each in turn, before disappearing into his thinning hair. "That's where I'm takin' you right now." There was a pause, and the smile again, this time directed straight at Grant. "Might as well get it over with this afternoon as wait till to-morrow morning and think, brood about it all night." Eerily, he appeared to have looked—looked for the second time—right inside Grant's head.

After a moment Grant snorted. The half laugh did not lessen his nervousness, but it pleased him that he could do it. "Yeah. But you're sure you think I'm ready for that."

"If I didn't I wouldn't take you out. It don't do my business any good to kill off customers, or have dissatisfied ones."

Grant felt a slight chill pass over his shoulders. Also, he suddenly noticed that his crotch and the head of his peepee were beginning to feel scratchy from the salt crystals in his drying bikini. Rather furtively, he stole a hand down to scratch and adjust himself inside his seat-wet pants. Bonham did not appear to be bothered at all by his own. Perhaps because of this, as much as anything, Grant made no answer and they rode on in silence. They were now down the hill, moving slowly through the crowded streets of the dusty town, and the fresh-faced, so boyish sailor boys looked at them curiously and at the aqualung in the back. It was hard to believe he had once looked like that himself, in that same uniform.

More than fifteen, more than seventeen, years ago. At the shop, Ali, Big Al's narrow-chested, narrow-flanked East Indian helper, agreed bobbing and smiling to sell his foam rubber wet shirt to Grant for forty dollars, and Grant had a suspicion, more than a suspicion, that the shirt did not belong to him at all. Because he was so broad in the chest, it was an uncomfortably tight fit for Grant, and the green corrosion on the bronze zipper did not help in closing it. But Bonham managed. " Fits you fine," he rumbled and the deal was done. " Don't worry about it. I'll put it on the tab with all the rest." Grant nodded dumbly. It had all been done at the same time as Al and Ali were loading the gear and petrol cans for the dive into the station-wagon while Grant stood, as in some vague nervous apprehensive dream, watching them.

Bonham's shop was on one of those narrow, roughly cobbled little streets between the dock area and bay itself and the town's dusty, dirty little square called the " Parade " by the Jamaicans, after the British. Badly built out of poorly mixed concrete and cheap plywood, it was one of a block of buildings painted bright orange. Next door a native greengrocer peeled his cabbage heads and threw the rotting outside leaves into the street's deep run-off gutter. Inside, the shop itself was dominated by two huge hospital-type air compressors Bonham had brought down from the States. The other three walls were lined with aqualung bottles and regulators in racks. The boat was half a mile away, down at the bayside docks. Sometimes he docked her at the Yacht Club, Bonham said, where he was a sort of honorary member and had permission, but he hadn't been lately. Grant, feeling dimly that it was all strangely commonplace and everyday for such a momentous and wondrous occasion, piled into the broken dirty front seat with the diver and his helper and creaked away in the aged Buick slowly through the tiny sunburnt streets toward his first dive in the sea with an aqualung.

It had been a long hard road, in some ways. But Grant didn't want to go into that now. In the little boat (an eighteen-footer with a decked over cabin that was too small for anything but gear stowage), once they were aboard amid the dead seaweed, pieces of cardboard, old orange peels and other debris of civilisation that floated against the hull and the dock, he could see high up on the side of the hill above town the villa—the estate—where his " mistress " and her husband (and himself) were staying, visiting. He wondered if they were out on the patio. But even if they were, they wouldn't know Bonham's boat, or that Grant was on it going out.

"We know this area underwater like you know your backyard at home," Bonham said, like a pat spiel for nervous clients, from the helm as he peered out through the opened windshield. Ali had done all the casting off and they were now moving out into the bay channel, past the luxury hotels close on the right and so different from the dirty commercial docks and warehouses stretching around the curve of the bay behind them. The sun poured down on them making a strong light in the cockpit, and equally strong shade under the little roof where Bonham stood. It glinted off the water at them like steel points. The air had freshened noticeably already. "That's the Yacht Club over there," Bonham rumbled as he swung the boat away from it.

"Where are we going?" Grant asked. He knew the Yacht Club, had been there with his " mistress " and her husband, but he looked at the eighteen or twenty small sailing boats and launches tied fore and aft and swinging between their rows of mooring buoys. From the Yacht Club veranda someone waved at them gaily. Bonham's helper Ali waved back. Grant did not. Four days of training with Bonham had materially increased his sense of the dangers involved in diving, and the gay waver at the Yacht Club—who apparently thought they were going off on some kind of a happy sea picnic—had suddenly increased his irate nervousness and given him a gloomy sense of isolation.

"I'm takin' you out to one of the coral reefs," Bonham answered him from the wheel.

"How deep will it be?"

"Ten feet to sixty feet: ten feet at the top of the

reef, sixty at the bottom on the sand. Be just right for your first dive, and it's the prettiest reef this side the island."

That had to be a lie. Ocho Rios was supposed—" Are there any fish?"

" Hell, yes! Lots of them."

" Any sharks?"

" Sure. Sometimes. If we're lucky." The Navy tender, quite small as Navy ships go, now loomed up ahead of them in the deep main channel, appearing so huge from this close up that it filled the sky and threatened to fall on them. Bonham swung the boat slightly to pass it close by on his port side and increased his throttle. They were now out in the open bay. Bonham suddenly began to whistle merrily, if off-key, as if just being out on the water, headed for a dive, made him a different, happier man.

On the other hand, Grant was finding it impossible to put into words exactly how he felt, but which was mainly—if it must be said in one word without nuance—cowardly. He did not want to go on. He would give anything he possessed, not to. He had worked and planned for this, had dreamed of it—and for quite a long time. Now he realised that if Bonham's engine suddenly failed, he would not be disappointed. He hoped it would fail. He would be more than glad to wait, at least until to-morrow. Or longer, if it required repairs. And that was pretty cowardly. It was even pusillanimous. But he was too proud to say this, admit it out loud. " I was a little surprised at you taking me out so soon," he essayed, finally. "Especially after—you know—after what happened yesterday."

Bonham's bloodthirsty smile passed up over his huge face. " Oh, that happens to everybody. At least once. Usually more." Again as if he were eerily looking right into Grant's mind, he suddenly pulled from the drawer immediately in front of the wheel a half-full bottle of Beef-eater's gin (one of the two which Grant had bought yesterday), looked at it, and motioned with it to Grant. " Want a snort? No, you handled that very well yesterday I thought."

Grant took the bottle. Of course that eerie understanding undoubtedly came from so frequently handling people who reacted exactly like himself. But Grant hated to think he reacted like everybody else. Yesterday, which was supposed to have been his graduation day, during what was in fact supposed to be his graduation exam, he had made a serious booboo on the bottom of the pool. The result was that he had taken in a quick full-sucking breath of water instead of air from the tubes of the aqualung and, strangling and in total panic, had dropped everything and swum blindly and choking to the surface, clawing mindlessly. While he clung to the pool-edge desperately, strangling and whooping in terror to get air down his locked throat, Bonham standing just above him spraddlelegged in his sloppy faded trunks had thrown back his head and roared with laughter—a reaction which Grant when he finally could breathe again, though he grinned, found, if manly, nevertheless rather insensitive. Grant had always had this terrible fear of strangling, of not being able to get air. Also, whenever he looked up from the pool-edge, all he could see were those two huge oaktree legs disappearing into the gaping legholes of Bonham's trunks, within which he could see the shabby, ravelled, somewhat ill-fitting edge of Bonham's old jockstrap revealing a crescent shaped section of hairy balls, all of which he found embarrassing and distasteful.

The exercise he was attempting was not one he had not done before. He had already done it twice that same day, successfully. It consisted of diving to the bottom of the pool fully geared, divesting oneself of flippers, weight belt, mask and lung in that order and swimming back up; that was the first half. The second (after a few deep breaths) was to swim back down, near-blind because maskless, find the lung and clear it of water and then, once one was able to breathe through it again, re-don all the other gear and come up. Now, all this would be comparatively easy if one had attached to one's tubes a mouthpiece with "non-return valves" which did not let water get into the tubes; but Bonham insisted implacably that all his pupils complete this exercise with the old-fashioned open mouthpiece so that, to clear the lung, you had to hold it in a certain way with the air-intake tube up and the exhaust tube down. And then you had to exhale sharply all your precious air to blow the water out. That particular time Grant, hurrying, apparently had held the damned thing wrong, with the exhaust tube up, and instead of the quick relieving flow of air into empty lungs, he had sucked down water.

Standing in the boat cockpit, holding the gin bottle in his hand and looking at the familiar Tower-of-London-Watchman label, Grant could feel all over again the rush of water into his throat, his throat itself locking, the blind rush upward, and then the long-drawn-out process while hanging on the pool-edge of trying to get a tiny bit of air down into those heaving lungs whose heaving only locked his throat up tighter. Uncapping the bottle, he took a big swallow of the straight gin and waited for it to hit his stomach and spread out, warm and soothing. When he finally got his breath back yesterday, he had insisted on going back down and doing it again, right away, because he knew the principle from springboard diving that when you crack up on a dive, don't wait: go right back while your back or your belly is still stinging and do it again before time and imagination can make you even more afraid. Bonham had apparently admired him for that, and the second time he had done it perfectly, but that did not relieve his memory of the strangling terror.

Later, of course, Bonham had told him it happened because he hurried, that if he had tested it with just a little suction till he found water, he could have swum back up with his lungs empty: he had plenty of time. But for Grant it had required every last ounce of will he had each time to exhale into that tube down there. How could he have that much more control? Time, Bonham said; practice. And panic, *panic*, was the biggest danger, enemy, the *only* danger that there was in diving.

Luckily, Grant thought, last night he had not told his mistress or her husband about the little accident—now that they were going out. But then they did not even know that they were going out. Almost furtively, he glanced up again at the villa where they were up on the hill and still visible even from here, and once again that black-draped, mantillaed, half-hidden-faced image standing on the church steps pointing swam over him. Sometimes he positively hated his guts. Politely wiping the neck of the bottle with the palm of his hand in the time-honoured gesture of all bottle drinkers, he passed the gin back to Bonham at the wheel, grateful for the warming.

"Look!" Bonham rumbled, rather sharply. "You ain't gonna have to take your lung off down there out here.

Only the mask, like I told you. Outside of that we're just gonna swim around and look. I got this new camera case I wanta try out for a friend. So I'll take some pictures of you." It was a clear bribe. And as such, angered Grant a little. He didn't need bribes to do it, or anything. Bonham slugged down a healthy dollop of the gin himself, and then, after a hesitation, as if he were not sure he ought to do this in front of Grant, wiped the bottle-neck and passed it over to Ali—who bobbing and grinning took a drink himself and wiped the neck and capped it.

Grant did not fail to note the hesitation, or its meaning, but he did not say anything—about that, or about Bonham's rather sharp remark. He was, actually, after having looked up at the villa, at the moment much more interested in and concerned with himself. Why was he doing this? Reality? To find reality? Search out and rediscover a reality which all these past six or eight years and two plays he had felt was beginning to be missing from his life and from his work? Yes; a reality, yes. Because without his work he was nothing. *A* nothing. And work was vitality, vitality and energy, and—manhood. So go ahead and say the rest of it. Yes, reality; but also to search out and rediscover his Manhood. His Capital M Manhood, which along with reality and his work he was also losing. Yes, all that; and also to get rid at least for a while in a genteel way of his ageing mistress, the black figure on the church steps, whom he had once loved, but whom now he both in a strange way loved and did not love at all, equally and simultaneously, and whom he considered at least partially responsible for the loss of reality (and Manhood) that he suffered. Maybe he considered her. probably he considered her. *totally* responsible for the loss. But in the end he had not gotten away from her at all, because she had invited herself to come with him, along with her husband. Actually it was she who found Al Bonham for him! She had come on down ahead, while he was in New York, had looked up and had waiting for him a diving teacher she considered reputable.

And in the interim, during his " business " trip to New York with his newest, his latest play, something else had happened. Grant had met a girl.

Big Al suddenly swung the wheel hard right, and the little boat made a sharp turn to starboard and headed off in that direction. They were far out on the open bay now. Directly ahead a mile away was the jet airstrip, one of three on the island, almost touching the blacktop road that ran along the water's edge. " It's right off the end of the airstrip, this reef," Bonham said. " 'Bout half a mile out. I got two or three reference points I line up to hit it exact." As violently as he had made the turn, which Grant considered strangely unnecessarily violent, he suddenly cut throttle and Grant grabbed the gunwale to keep from falling forward, as did Ali. For three or four minutes Bonham jockeyed the boat backward and forward, peering down over the side. " There she is," he said. " My special spot."

Grant too looked over the side. Below him in the blue-green water yellow and brown colour-patches swirled and quivered under the water's wash. Just beside these, and as if he were standing shoetips to the edge of a vertical high cliff, he could now and then as the sea flattened catch a glimpse of clear sand far below, dark-green coloured through the surface. The sun hot on his back, Grant felt cold at the thought of being immersed in water which was not in a bathtub and whose lack of heat could not be controlled. " Let's get you dressed out," Bonham rumbled from just behind him, and began hauling tanks and gear around as if none of it weighed anything.

As he had before, Grant noticed that Bonham dropped his bad grammar whenever he was giving instructions. Now he kept up a running comment of instruction while the two of them, he and Ali, got the neophyte ready. Flippers first, then the mask spat upon, rubbed till it squeaked, rinsed and resting on his forehead, rubber wet shirt, weightbelt trimmed to exactly the right weight by Bonham, finally the tank, his arms through the shoulder straps, crotch strap attached to the weight belt. Grant simply sat, like an electrocutionee he thought, and let himself be handled. The running comment of instruction had to do with clearing his ears and equalising the pressure in them as he and Bonham went on down, and with what Bonham wanted him to do with his mask, which was to remove it when they reached the bottom of the anchorline, put it back on full of water, and clear it. Grant was to go first, swim forward to the anchorline, descend it ten or twelve feet, and wait for Bonham. Then last, the mask lowered over his eyes and nose, the mouthpiece stuffed into his mouth, and he was falling backward on to the tank on his back while faces and boat wheeled out of sight to be replaced by nothing but bright blue sky, what was he doing here? Then the water closed over him, blinding him.

Still holding the mask to his face with both hands in the approved manner to keep the fall from dislodging it, Grant rolled over quickly but he still could see nothing. He was now lying on the surface. Masses of bubbles formed by the air he had carried under with him rose all around him, blinding him even more effectively than a driving rainstorm would have done up in the air. He waited, vulnerable, what seemed endlessly but was really only seconds. Then, miraculously, everything cleared as the bubbles rose on past him, and he could see. See at least as well as he could on land. Maybe more. Because to his congenital mild myopia everything looked closer. It was supposed to. Snell's Law. (n Sin $a = n'$ Sin a'). Oh, he'd studied all the books—and for years. But this was different. Below him the yellow and brown patches were now clearly delineated fields of yellow and brown coral but in amongst these, invisible from the boat, were smaller patches of almost every colour and colour combination imaginable. It was breath-taking. And, as far as he could tell, there was nothing dangerous visible.

Tentatively, cautiously, for the first time since he'd gone under, Grant let out a little air and took a tiny breath. By God, it worked! He became aware of the surface swell rolling him and banging the tank against his back. Bending double he dove down to where there was no swell as Bonham had told him, and swam slowly forward along the boat's big shadow above him, toward the slanting anchorline. In the strange silence he could hear odd poppings and cracklings. With each intake of breath the regulator at the back of his neck sang eerily and gonglike, and with each exhale he could hear the flubbering rush of bubbles from it. Everything, all problems, all plans, all worries, "mistress," her husband, new girl, the new play, sometimes even consciousness of Self itself, seemed to have been swept from his mind by the intensity of the tasting of this new experience, and new world.

At the anchorline, after he managed awkwardly to grab it, he pulled himself down deeper hand over hand until his

ears began really to hurt, and then stopped. As Bonham
had shown him, he put thumb and forefinger into the
hollows in the mask's bottom and pinched his nose shut,
and blew. One ear opened up immediately with a loud squeak,
but he had to try a second and a third time before he could
get the other one completely opened. Then he pulled himself
a little deeper, feeling the pressure start to build up again,
and stopped again. Wrapping his legs around the line, he
peered at the diving watch Bonham had sold him and set its
outside bezel dial with the zero point over the minute hand.
Then he peered at the huge handsome depth gauge beside it
which Bonham had also sold him and saw that he was
eighteen feet down. On his right arm the enormous Automatic Decompression Meter which Bonham had sold him
still read zero; its nitrogen-absorption-measuring needle had
not yet even started to move. And so there he hung, having
let go with his legs and grabbed the line with a hand,
looking around. If Marty Gabel and Herman Levin could
only see him now! His nervousness had left him, and he
felt a kind of cautious rapture.

To his right and left coral hills forty and fifty feet high
stretched away in minor mountain ranges into blue-green
invisibility. Directly in front of him at the foot of the deep
end of these rounded ranges, a pure white sea of virgin sand
sloped away ever so gently out toward deep water. In
between the coral hills he could see down into channels
—glaciers; rivers—of sand which debouched on to the
vast sand plain. In these channels, varieties of brightly
coloured fish poked their noses into holes in the coral, or
rowed themselves gently along with their pectoral fins like
small boats with oars. None of them seemed to be concerned
with bothering any of the others, and Grant relaxed even
more.

Then, in the corner of his mask which acted like a horse's
blinders and cut his field of vision, he caught a flash of
silver. Turning his head he saw through the plate of glass
a barracuda which appeared to be at least four feet long.
It was about twenty feet away. Slowly it swam out of sight
beyond his mask and Grant turned again. This process went
on until Grant realised the fish was circling him. Regularly,
staring at him with its one big eye, it opened and closed its
enormous mouth, exposing its dagger teeth, as if flexing

its jaws preparatory to taking a bite of Grant. This was its method of breathing of course, he knew, but it didn't look nice just the same. Grant had read that in cases like this you were supposed to swim straight at them as if you intended to take a bite of *them* whereupon they would turn and flee and run away, but he did not feel very much like trying this. Besides, he was not supposed to leave the anchorline. On the other hand he felt he ought not just sit here and let the fish have all the initiative. But before he could make up his mind to do something, and if so then what, another figure swam into his mask's field of vision, further complicating matters till Grant realised what it was.

It was Bonham. Looking like some antennaed stranger from another world, which in a way he was, he swam down on a long slant behind the barracuda, leisurely beating the water with his flippers, his left arm with its hand holding the camera case stretched back at rest along his thigh, his right arm extended out straight before him holding the four-foot spear-gun. In the green water-air he was gravityless and beautiful, and Grant would have given anything to be like him. As he came on down getting closer, he stopped kicking and, hunching his shoulders in a strange way as if to make himself heavier, coasted down. Just as Grant saw his forearm tightening to squeeze the trigger, the barracuda gave an enormous flit of its tail and simply disappeared. It didn't go away ; it just simply was no longer there, or anywhere visible, with an unbelievable speed if you hadn't seen it. Bonham looked after it, shrugged, and swam on to the line.

There was a great paternalism, protectiveness, about Bonham underwater. He looked Grant over carefully, turning him about and inspecting his gear, then with a violent hand motion downward swam on down the line toward the bottom. Grant followed, his nervousness returning. Twice he had to stop on the line to clear his ears and he suddenly noticed that Bonham apparently did not have to do this at all. On the bottom, like some huge calm great-bellied Buddha, Bonham seated himself crosslegged on the sand, took off his mask, blinked blindly ; then put it back on and blew the water out of it by tilting his head to one side and holding the upper side of the mask. Then he motioned for Grant to do the same, as he had, upstairs, warned him that he would.

Grant had done this in the various pools, but down here (his depth gauge Bonham had sold him now read fifty-nine feet) he found it was more scary. It was all that water above you. Kneeling on the sand, he forced himself with the greatest reluctance to reach up and pull off his own mask. When he did, he immediately went blind. The salt water burned his eyes and the insides of his nose. He found himself gasping for breath. Bonham was now only one great blur to him. He made himself breathe deeply several times, and blinked. Then he put the mask back on and cleared it. Not as adept as Bonham, he had to blow several times to get all the water out. But when he looked at Bonham, the big man was nodding happily and holding up his thumb and forefinger in the old circle salute for " okay." Then he motioned for Grant to come and went swimming off six or eight feet above the sand. Grant followed, his eyes still smarting. He was ridiculously pleased. At the moment he felt very much the son to Bonham's massive paternalism. This did not irritate him. Instead, it gave him reassurance.

Bonham proceeded to point out the various corals. They were all very beautiful and interesting to look at—in a slimy, repugnant sort of way—but you could only look at coral so long without getting bored. Apparently fully aware of this, Bonham—after pointing out a number of varieties (including two which he warned Grant not to touch by wringing a hand and shaking it as if stung)—chose the exact moment of Grant's increasing restlessness to show him something else. At the end of the coral hillock they had been exploring he swam over to Grant and motioned for him to follow. He led him straight down over the steep side of the hillock to the sand channel bottom (here Grant's depth gauge Bonham had sold him read sixty-three feet), and there he pointed out two large caves. It was apparently true that Bonham knew this area like Grant knew his backyard. It was also apparent that he was conducting his tour and displaying his treasures one by one with the dramatic sense of a veteran entrepreneur.

To Grant the caves were both exciting and frightening. The one on the left of the sand channel went back in under the coral hill they had just swum over ; way back in there some hole running clear to the top of the coral allowed a shaft of sunlight to penetrate all the way to the bottom, illuminating greenly some strange coral shapes growing on the sand ; outside, its entrance was huge, not a real cave mouth at all, but more an overhang that ran almost the entire length of the side of the hillock. From under this overhang Grant carefully stayed away, as he looked. By contrast, Bonham had already swum on in. Turning his head, he motioned Grant to follow. Biting hard on the two rubber tits of the mouthpiece between his teeth, tightening his lips over the whole, Grant descended a little and entered. Scared as he was, it was magnificently beautiful in there. The ceiling was only fifteen or twenty feet from the sand floor, much lower than it had looked from outside. Several good-sized tunnels showing sunlight at their ends led off from it and looked safe for exploring. But Bonham was already swimming back out, motioning him to follow.

The other cave, across the channel, was really no more than a fissure, running maybe thirty feet up an almost perpendicular dead-coral cliff, hardly wide enough to admit a man, and it was to this one now that Bonham led him.

Gesturing Grant to follow, the big man swam up the fissure to a point that appeared slightly wider than the rest, snaked himself through, and disappeared. When Grant followed, he found he had to turn his shoulders sideways to enter. When he did, his tank banged alarmingly on the rock behind him. He remembered reading stories of fellows who had cut their air intake hoses on sharp coral, and who had barely got out alive by luck, superior experience, and by keeping their heads. Trying to keep his air intake hose (without being able to see it) somewhere near the centre of the cleft, Grant pulled himself along with his hands on the sucky, unpleasantly viscid living corals growing here. But when he was in far enough that he could no longer bend his knees to flutter his feet, the panicky breathlessness, the sensation of being unable to breath, to get enough air, which panic brings, and which he knew from before, hit him debilitatively. Stopping, he forced himself to breathe deeply but it didn't help. Suddenly his instinct was to throw off everything and run for the surface blindly, even though covered by coral rock, to get to anywhere where there was air. Instead, he reached out with his hands and pulled himself further in, trying to keep his movements slow and liquid, unviolent, though by now he didn't care whether the coral cut him or not.

Actually, he had only been inches away from freedom. The last pull with his arms brought him head and shoulders almost to his waist out into the open. One breast stroke with his arms and he was free, swimming almost forty feet above the bottom. Bonham, who Grant now realised had been directly in front of him watching and ready to help, had already rolled over head down and like an airplane in a full dive was swimming straight down toward the bottom, his flippers beating leisurely and slow, his arms holding camera and gun extended backward along his thighs to streamline. For a moment Grant was seriously angry at him, for taking such a chance with him on his first dive. Still breathing deeply, though slower and slower now as his heart and adrenal glands got back to normal, Grant watched in a kind of witless stupor as Bonham got smaller and smaller and smaller. A few feet above the bottom the big man levelled off over a huge coral toadstool and rolled over face up, and slowly sank to a crosslegged sitting position on it, his head back looking up, for all the world like some great, one-eyed humanoid alien frog from Alpha Centauri or somewhere. Still looking up, he motioned for Grant to come on down. Still staring, still breathing deeply from his fright in the narrow entrance. Grant suddenly realised with a start which brought him back out of his post-panic stupour that he was lying here all stretched out forty feet up in the *air* from this other man, relaxed, his arms out over his head like a man in a bed. Because it really could have been air. *Seemed* like air. The green-tinted water was crystal clear here inside, and Bonham by seating himself on the toadstool had avoided stirring up any sand clouds as they had done outside. For the first time with any real physical appreciation, Grant realised how delicious it was to be totally without gravity like one of the great planing birds; he could go up, he could go down, he could stay right where he was; in the strange spiritual excitement of it, his fear left him completely. Feeling ridiculous again because of his recent panic there, he glanced once at the narrow entrance fissure, then rolled over head down using exactly (though slower) the same body movements he once used to do a full-twisting half gainer, and corkscrewed gently down—relishing the leisurely control—into a vertical dive, his hands and arms straight back along his thighs palms up, his beating lazy and slow, as he had seen Bonham do. Only once did he have to clear his ears, and he did it now without pausing. Below him Bonham got larger and larger. Then, duplicating Bonham's manœuvre, he rolled over on to his back, exhaled and sank into a sitting position on the giant toadstool beside him, his knees clasped up to his chin. Unable to speak, or even to grin, he gesticulated wildly and waggled his eyebrows to show his enthusiasm. The big man nodded vigorously, then touching him gently, pointed upward, sweeping his arm across the view like a man unveiling a painting. For the first time since he had entered, Grant looked up.

What he saw very nearly took away the breath he had just regained. He was in an immense cavern at least sixty feet high, Apparently the bottom here inside was ten or so feet lower than the sand channel bottom outside. From where he sat at one end the other was almost lost in a hazy near-invisibility. In the dim ceiling a dozen holes allowed clusters of greenish sunrays to strike at varying angles across the interior until they shattered against the sand bottom or rock walls. Each beam wherever it struck against bottom or walls revealed weird outlandish coral sculptures. It was more than breathtaking, it was like having stumbled upon some alien cathedral on some other planet, which some other-world race with their incomprehensible architecture and alien sculpture had ages past built, decorated and dedicated to their unknowable God. Grant was suddenly frightened again, not physically this time, but spiritually. For a moment he forgot he was diving underwater in an aqualung. Was that some four-headed Great Saint whom they worshipped, there on the side wall? Was that seventy-eyed monster, all head and almost no body, resting on the sand floor, the Great Being Himself? And as always, when he found himself alone in an empty church—as he had when a boy, as he had when visiting the great churches and cathedrals of Europe and found one or another of them deserted—Grant felt himself beginning to get an erection in the dim stillness. Was it the privacy? Was it the quiet? Or was it the high-ceilinged dimness? Or was it maybe the nearness of God? The nearness of Unknowable? Embarrassed, he shifted away sideways, afraid Bonham might notice what was happening inside his tight, scanty bikini, and the feeling began to subside. Anyway he knew one thing for certain. One day while he was here in Ganado Bay he was going to come out here alone—come alone if he had to rent a *rowboat* and aqualung from Bonham's competitor—make a dive down here alone, strip off this damned bikini, swim around this cave stark naked with his erection, then sit on this toadstool and masturbate, come like a fury, and watch his milky semen swirl and mingle with the green water which itself swirled about his body with every tiniest movement.

Maybe he'd hire a non-diving native to handle the boat for him. The very secrecy of it, the native up there working the boat and him down here masturbating, made it a tinglingly exciting prospect. But, was this not a too-ambitious project for a neophyte diver just starting out: jerking off underwater? Well, he would find out. The idea of masturbating made him think of his new girl in New York. She, it had turned out, had loved that.

Bonham touched him gently again, on the shoulder, and Grant started guiltily. When he looked over, the other was motioning upward with one hand and beckoning with the other. When Grant asked "Why?" by shrugging up his shoulders and spreading out his hands, Big Al pointed to his watch. Looking at his own Grant saw they had been under thirty-two minutes, and could hardly believe it. And it reminded him of something else. During his last few breaths it had seemed to Grant that it was getting slightly harder to breathe each time, but the difference was so slight he had thought he was imagining it. Now he tried again and found it was distinctly harder to suck air from the lung. His neophyte's nervousness returned to him suddenly. But neither man had yet pulled his reserve valve! Grabbing his mouthpiece with one hand and pointing to his tank with the other, Grant made a heaving motion with his chest as if trying to breathe. Bonham nodded. But then he followed the nod by fanning his hands back and forth across each other in a gesture of "Take it easy; don't worry." Gesturing Grant to follow, and without pulling his reserve, he took off from the toadstool with a little leap upward like a bird.

But it was more like a foot-winged Mercury than a bird, Grant thought as he followed. He was no longer nervous. Underwater at least, he now trusted Bonham completely. Forgotten was the momentary anger at Bonham's having taken him through the narrow fissure.

Ahead of him Big Al swam upward on a long diagonal straight across the length of the green cathedral. He did not turn off to the right toward the fissure. Grant assumed, rightly, that there was another entrance—which made him feel good, because he had no liking for the fissure. As he rose on the long diagonal, the air in his tank expanded as the pressure lessened and it became easier to breathe and he understood why Bonham had motioned him not to worry. Only if they had had to descend again into greater pressure, he remembered now from the books, would they have needed their reserve valves. Grant remembered to exhale frequently as he rose to avoid air embolism and when, as he swam, he looked at his Automatic Decompression Meter Bonham had sold him it showed there was no need to worry about decompression. So they were leaving, or—rather—returning.

Ten yards ahead of him Bonham swam into and then out of some of the slanting rays of sunlight which crossed the cave, strangely bright and glowing when he was in one, almost invisible when he was in the darker water in between. Grant could not resist pausing and turning for a look back. He felt a curious sad tranquillity, toward all inevitability, because he had to leave. But when he looked, he found he was already forty-five or fifty feet above the bottom and the toadstool was no longer visible from here. With a second's tingling excitement in his groin he knew now more than ever that, eventually he would come back here and descend into that invisibility and sitting on that same toadstool looking up, masturbate himself. Play with himself, he added, in the jargon of his parents. Then he swam on.

Ahead of him Bonham had turned the corner into an alcove-cum-tunnel almost at the ceiling of the cavern and was waiting for him. Ahead at the end of it was sunlight, and together in this more than comfortably wide space they swam toward it, then through it and back into the world.

But the dive was still not over. Emotionally, it was, perhaps, but they still had to get back to the boat. Bonham did not even bother to surface and look around but (he really

did know this area like his backyard) struck off up and over
the coral hillock they had just left the insides of, and which
came to within less than ten feet of the surface. Grant
could not see boat or anchorline ahead, but Bonham was
obviously heading straight for them. Below them as they
swam were the tangled, trashy staghorn-coral beds—the
brown ones, their hunks of old fishing line caught here and
there, rusting beercans in the low spots—which marked the
hillock's crest. But now after the cave all that was boring.
It was hard to believe they had been inside this hill, and
that it was damned near entirely hollow. Grant's sadness at
leaving it—out here in the sunlit, brightly coral-studded, open
water—was slowly turning into a wild kind of elation.
Above him the surface was only a few feet away, and every
now and then—as in some silvered but unsolid mirror—he
could see himself or Bonham, grossly distorted, reflected
back from the underside of it as it moved. His air, without
his pulling of the reserve lever but getting harder and harder
to draw, lasted just exactly to the side of the boat. At the
boat he had a bad moment when, trying to shuck out of his
tank straps and pass the lung up to Ali, he went under
gulping seawater and almost choking; but then he was over
the side and in the boat safe from sharks, barracuda,
Portuguese men-o'-war, the bends, air embolism, busted ear-
drums, and mechanical lung failure. Why the hell had
Bonham tried to make it seem so hard? His elation continued to grow.

Behind him Bonham handed up his own lung easily and
smoothly, moved his bulk smoothly up the little ladder and
over the side and, dripping wet, started the motor. Ali ran
forward to haul in the anchor. Before Grant could get himself out of Ali's clinging wet shirt Bonham had sold him,
the diver and his helper were headed back to shore full
throttle like two men going home from the office, Bonham at
the wheel and Ali dismantling the lungs. In the west the
sun was still quite a few yards above the big mountain
that jutted out into the sea.

Grant's new elation lasted all the way back to shore. and
longer. It lasted through the Yacht Club and then to Bonham's
shop in the dirty old station-wagon, where they left Ali.
It lasted through all the drinking and eating they two did
at Bonham's favourite bar after that. It lasted, in fact,

until around two-thirty in the morning, when he walked half-drunkenly up the path to the villa where his "mistress" and her husband were staying, to go to bed. Then it completely disappeared, when he discovered his "mistress" was still up.

In the boat he had been shaking and chattering uncontrollably as he rubbed himself down with the towel Bonham thoughtfully handed him from the wheel. He had not felt unduly cold "downstairs," as Bonham called it, but up here in the air and speed-induced breeze he was freezing. When he had turned from the rail, Bonham had been holding out the gin bottle to him with one hand and wiping his mouth with the back of the other, the wheel's uppermost spoke held firmly in the crook of his arm. When the hand came away, the mouth was seen to be grinning widely over his bad teeth. "So you think you like it, hunh?" he demanded. "Well, that's only the start."

Vicariously, though he obviously had none of his own really, he was able to share Grant's elation. In contrast to Grant he had worn no wet shirt and had not towelled off and was letting the wind dry him, but he wasn't cold. Trickles of sea-water continued every now and then to run down his face from his hair as he spoke. He had ducked his head back into the water face up before climbing aboard, Grant had noticed, and the sea had slicked back his hair as well as any comb ever could, so that in contrast to Grant's wildly disordered hair he looked positively well-groomed. He could not stop grinning apparently, as he accepted the bottle back, as though he really did share Grant's enthusiasm, and Grant suddenly felt—(gratefully; though he did not know to whom, or to what)—that they two had established a rapport between them with this dive which almost no one— for instance Ali, a non-diver, or Grant's mistress, or her husband—could share who was not a diver himself. And maybe all of *them* couldn't share it, unless they had been down in the cathedral cave with Bonham themselves.

"Here. Have another one," Bonham grinned, extending the bottle after taking a second slug himself. "Warm you up."

It was the second of a great many rounds they were to down before the day, and the evening, were over. Grant was plain full of all sorts of technical questions, and he kept them coming one after the other. For instance, when Bonham had taken off his lung at the boat, instead of hanging on to the ladder and trying to keep his head out of water in the swells, like Grant, he had descended to ten or twelve feet, below the swell, and shucked his tank off over his head like a man taking off a sweater, while never letting the mouthpiece out of his mouth, and then had swum back up to the boat with it. Why had he done that? It was a keen trick, and had somebody taught it to him? And did Bonham have that much extra air left? because he, Grant, had been completely out when they reached the boat—unless of course he had pulled the reserve.

Yes, Bonham said, he had had more air left, because Grant didn't conserve his. " You remember when you went through that rock fissure into the big cave? You used a lot of extra air there because you got a little panicky. And probly a couple of other times. Like when you first went in." But that was nothing; after a while Grant would learn to save air both by relaxing and by never breathing until he really needed it.

As for taking the bottle off over his head down below the swell, it was just easier. No, nobody taught it to him. He thought it up himself. But probably lots of other divers did it too. Just because it was easier. " And in this racket, anything that is easier, requires less effort and energy, is the better way to do a thing. Simply because saving energy saves *air*."

" Well, what *about* taking me through that narrow place like that? Isn't that a pretty advanced manœuvre? for somebody like me? on their very first dive?"

Bonham shook his head no. " I don't usually take people through there in their first sea dive. I don't usually take them in that cave. That's true. But you're pretty cool. A lot cooler than you think you are, for some strange reason. Usually it's just the reverse. People think they're cool and they ain't.

" Anyway, I was right there watching. I could have got you out all right."

" Yeah, I *saw* that! *After* I got on through!"

Grant laughed.

Bonham grinned. He had decided, he suddenly interjected, to dock the boat at the Yacht Club to-night. He was getting bored with that crapped-up dirty commercial dock, even if it was closer to the shop. Something about his face, looking straight ahead out through the windshield, gave Grant a distinct impression that there was more to it than that, and that the something more had to do with himself, but Bonham did not admit more. Nor did Grant question him. And as they ran on in, his diction and his grammar began to undergo that peculiar change from educated and expressive to uneducated and laconic, which Grant had noticed now several times before. He was evidently preparing the personality he wished to present at the Yacht Club—for whatever reasons. When they came abreast of the Club, he swung the boat hard left at full throttle in that violent style of his, immediately and at once cutting throttle (as he had to do or crash), then skilfully and easily wove his way in amongst the small launches and sailboats to a mooring close to the dock. From there Ali rowed the two of them in to the long wooden dock in the bathtub-sized plastic dinghy which Bonham kept lashed down on the cabin roof, and returned for the tanks and regulators and to clean up. Bonham and Grant had already dressed on the boat, and went on to the bar. Bonham had covered his slicked back, thinning hair with a beat-up, old, but expensively made and very salty looking yachting cap bearing a crusted gold Captain's symbol, which he had pulled from the drawer where the gin bottle was.

Grant had been to the Yacht Club twice before, both times late in the evening for a drink after dinner, both times with his " mistress " and her husband. Both times he had found it nearly deserted and pretty dull. The only amusement was a European-type pool game with holes in the middle of the table protected by skittles which must not be knocked over, where for a shilling you could play for x number of minutes before the timer shut off and retained the balls. He and the husband had played. It was a pretty middle-class, pretty deadly place in a way which only certain British or British-Colonial institutions can be. Built modern of concrete in four stories (each with its veranda) up the side of a bluff from the water's edge to the street, it was much prettier outside than in, which was not saying much. Now, however, at the cocktail hour, it was cheerfully crowded with a hard-drinking crowd of local members, residents, and " winter visitors." Bonham knew them all, and he introduced Grant to all of them. Most of them were sophisticated enough, and had money enough, to spend a couple or three weeks once or twice a year in New York, be knowledgeable of American theatre, and so knew who Grant was, had heard he was in town, and were glad to have him down they said. Grant was personable and charming with all of them ; but he would much have preferred getting off in a corner and talking diving, to being Bonham's celebrity. This, however, was impossible since Bonham, after ordering the two of them drinks, was now engrossed in a conversation with two Club members about a 38-foot Matthews marlin boat which had been put up for sale over in Montego Bay. The gist was that Bonham, as he made plain in his deliberately bad diction and bad grammar way, wanted to buy it but was afraid it was not in good shape. The two Club members were assuring him that it was in good shape, that they had seen it, and then Bonham would only shake his head dubiously and it would all start over. When Ali came up from the boat and Bonham, after ordering them both still more drinks, sent him off on foot to go get the station-wagon at the commercial dock, Grant was glad. But by the time he got back, Bonham, after ordering them drinks a couple of times more, was heatedly discussing with the chairman of the PTA (of which organ Bonham it turned out was *vice*-chairman!) the meeting they were calling for next Thursday. And Grant was defending his old pal Tennessee Williams from three well-to-do ladies. By the time Ali had got the tanks and regulators loaded in the car, Bonham had ordered them one more round of drinks. Then Grant paid and they left.

Grant hadn't minded the drinking, or even the paying. He was a good boozer himself, and he suspected Bonham was short of cash. But he was still high with elation over his dive, and he wanted to remain up there with it. It was all very strange, and quite hard to explain, and the only way he could word it was that it made him somehow feel more *manly*. More *manly* than he had felt in quite a long time. And he wanted Bonham to himself to talk about it. Not about *that* part of it, but about the dive itself, and about diving in general.

"I didn't know you had any kids," he said across Ali

in the car, in an oblique reference to the PTA. "How many have you got?"

Bonham appeared suddenly to have become somewhat somnambulant, out in the air and the dark. "Ain't got any," he said, very shortly. "Wife teaches school," and he motioned vaguely upward with his head toward what appeared to be the left front corner of the car roof, but which was in fact the mountainside along which they were driving and upon which, high up, Grant knew there nestled a school. A ritzy one.

"I didn't know you were married," he said.

Bonham did not answer right away. "Well, I am," he said finally.

Grant hesitated delicately, then made his voice cheery. "Your wife's Jamaican?"

"Yeah," Bonham said immediately and without reservations. "But she's very light." He drove on a way before he added, "She's Jewish axshly. Mostly." Then after a moment he again added: "Columbus gave most of Jamaica to his relatives. So it was mainly them, the Jewish, who were the first settlers."

"I'd like to meet her some day," Grant said.

Bonham visibly seemed to settle stolidly into some protected interior of his nigh-immovable bulk. From it he spoke calmly. But it. his marriage, was plainly something he didn't like to talk about, or even think about, apparently. "Sure. You will. Some day. She's a great girl."

"I'm sure," Grant said. "You know, I couldn't help overhearing your conversation with those two guys at the bar about buying that boat. The Matthews. I don't mean to stick my nose in. But can you afford——"

Bonham snorted. "Shit, no. Wish I could. But I wouldn't buy that boat if I could."

"But then why did you——"

"Because you got to put on that kinda act, that's why."

"But surely those other two g——"

"Course they did," Bonham rumbled slowly. "They know exactly how much I'm worth. Just like I know exactly how much they're worth. And they know I'm not worth that kinda money." Then his grammar and diction suddenly got precise and educated again. "But that's the game. I pretend

I can. Because that's the way they all act. That's the way they function. And when I act the same, it proves to them that I'm like them. I'm normal. Then they'll accept me. Why do you think I joined that damned PTA? Hell, I joined the Rotary, and the Kiwanis, and the Chamber of Commerce. If you want to be a part of any social group, you have to join in their little rituals."

" I'm not at all sure it's all that easy," Grant murmured. " I wish it were," he added sadly.

But they had reached the shop. Bonham had already stopped the car in the middle of Grant's two sentences and gotten out, though pausing outside to listen to the end of it, and then began giving Ali his orders without answering Grant: everything was to be hosed down, fresh water, the regulators were to be laid out on the work-bench and stripped completely down and washed (Bonham always tore his regulators down after every sea dive and checked them he said, especially the ones used by clients), Ali was to be there at eight in the morning because they had a young couple wanted a pool checkout at the Royal Loggerhead. Under the necessity to work, or at least give orders to work, his earlier somnambulance, if that was what it was, seemed to have left him.

" I know a great little bar and restaurant where I hang out a lot," he said as he climbed back in and slammed the door. " It's not expensive and they got great steaks and a great bunch of guys hang out there. It's called The Neptune Bar. What do you say we go there and do some *serious* drinkin' and then have somethin' to eat? If you really want to talk divin', that's the place."

" Okay. For the drinks part, anyway. But I got to be back to the villa for dinner." He was supposed to dine at the villa with his " mistress " and her husband and their hosts the Count and Countess de Blystein, because there were to be two other couples, local " winter residents " (which meant they owned places), whom the Countess had invited for the express purpose (more or less unstated) of meeting Ron Grant. However, it was only a little after seven, and he could easily be back by a quarter of nine to change. Couldn't he? Of course he could. " Why not?" he said.

In the end, though, he had not gone back for the dinner, and had probably known in the back of his mind that he wouldn't. He had stayed with Bonham. It was probably a serious social breach, but he knew he could laugh the Countess—Evelyn—out of it. Not so his "mistress." She would be furious, not only because she loved showing him off, but also because she loved and adored the Countess and the Countess Evelyn's standing, while going to great lengths to pretend not to. But it had been the thought of her, as much as of the dull evening itself, which had been the deciding factor in his saying to himself what the hell? I'll stay out.

Down below in the cave during the dive, when he had gotten stuck on sex and the thought of his new girl in New York, his mind had automatically brought up his mistress too, the old mantillaed witch-mother image standing on the church steps pointing, as it had done for years. But down there, sixty feet underwater in a cavern and in a faceplate and aqualung, for the first time he had shut that off, shut her off, as if with a special new interrupter clickswitch in his brain. It was the first time this had ever happened to him, and it was a new sensation. Click-switch the witch. It felt almost exactly like the sensation he used to experience in a *physical* way when he would sit in the dentist's chair and have his teeth ground and would click a switch in his head and turn off the pain. He had learned to do that years ago when, after his first play was a hit, he had had his whole mouth rebuilt by a marvellous dentist but who did not like to use the old-fashioned impure novocain they were using back then. But it had never happened to him before with a self-inflicted *moral* obligation. Something somewhere in his brain had changed maybe? Afterwards, feeling around cautiously inside his head, he had tried to find what was changed and had failed. Everything had seemed to be stored pretty much where it used to be. He was not *really* in love with his new girl (or was he?) any more than he had been in love with a lot of other girls over the past ten years, and anyway Grant no longer believed in love; he was (as he well knew) at that age. So it couldn't be her, or could it? He was not, he was sure, a "changed" man because of a few lessons and one dive in the sea in an aqualung. Or *was* it that: *had* such a little bit of diving that quickly made him into a man again? (Again?!) Whatever it was, he just no longer gave a damn

about a dark-shrouded, mantillaed, hidden-faced figure standing on the church steps pointing. He didn't have to think
about her. He could just shut her off, and now he did not
want to unlock the switch until he absolutely had to.

It would be one of those long, conversational dinners, with
good food and good wine whose enjoyment would be cut
at least fifty per cent by the nerve-tearing conversational
necessities. Afterward they would play poker on the Countess
Evelyn's beautiful felt covered mahogany poker table and/or
backgammon on Evelyn's beautiful inlaid boards with ivory
counters. Most of them (all but his " mistress ") would drink.
Her husband would drink a lot. And so would Grant.
Grant was having too much fun with Bonham, and—also—
learning too much about diving and divers.

Grant had never seen anybody eat and drink as much
without showing it at all, or any after-effects of it. When
they first came in, Bonham had ordered a platter of six
superburgers, all of which he ate after Grant declined one
as they drank. Later they each ate a huge imported American
sirloin served with enough French fries to bury a battle-
ship. Between them, with only a very few drinks given
away here and there, they put away almost two bottles of
gin and innumerable tonics. And finally around two in the
morning Bonham had three more superburgers as a snack.
Somewhere along the line they were joined by two very black,
very handsome Jamaican girls whom Bonham knew, and
when he left with the handsomer of these he walked as straight
as a die. When Grant paid the bill, he found it was much
less than he had expected.

Bonham knew everybody in the place, of course. Mostly
they were a mixture of working people running from boatmen and fishermen, plumbers and electricians, all the way up
to small-fry white collar people who worked for the government, for local businessmen, or for the big hotels. Of the
two Jamaican girls who joined them one worked as a nurse-
technical assistant to a dentist and the other ran a gift shop
in the Royal Loggerhead. And yet in spite of so much
seduction talk to the girls, so many greetings, jokings, drink
acceptings (and offerings), the big man managed to impart to
Grant quite a bit of interesting learning about diving. In
the car driving over Grant had mentioned his notice of
Bonham's two distinct sets of language and diction. The

big man had only grinned and said, " You notice a lot, don't you?" That was all he offered. Here, in this place, he spoke a very carefully very low-class lingo, excepting only the times he was speaking seriously to Grant about the technical aspects of diving. He went into at some length the various aspects of his work as a real working diver, as contrasted to his teaching and taking out of tourists. The trouble was there just weren't that many working-dive jobs around all the time to keep you going. Grant listened, and kept nodding. And finally, when they had both drunk a lot and he had got his courage up high enough with booze, Grant got in his question about sex, about orgasm in the aqualung.

" Did you ever fuck anybody underwater, Al?" Both the girls giggled.

" Hell, yes!" Bonham said and put his arm around the ass of the nearer girl, who just happened to be the prettier one. "I would be willin' to bet that anybody who's ever done any divin' at all has screwed at least once underwater. It ain't hard. The ony thing is, one of you has got to hold on or you float right apart." He grinned. The two girls were fascinated.

" Well, how deep?" Grant asked.

" Oh, fifty feet. Seventy-five. Easy. Depth don't matter at under a hundred and fifty feet. Why? You got some ambitions?"

It was Grant's turn to grin. " Oh, well, sure. Naturally. Eventually. But don't you uh get out of breath?"

" Hell, yes. It's great." Here the girls both laughed out loud. " But that don't make no difference. Matter of fact, if you just roll over on your back so's your regulator's lower than your mouthpiece, the difference in pressure'll flush your lungs right out for you. All the girl divers I ever knew loved to get laid underwater."

So Grant had his answer. He *could* masturbate at seventy feet if he wanted. It was the increased breathing rate which comes with sexual exercise that had worried him. Relaxing, a little drunkenly now, he knew again that great private excitement of pleasure which always came with the rediscovery, the reutilisation, of the fact that the interior of one's own mind can always be kept secret, that nobody can ever really tell what you're thinking if you don't want them to. In happy silence, he sat back and looked around the bar at all the people who didn't know the interior of Ron Grant's mind.

It was only shortly after this that Bonham announced his intention of leaving with the girl whose ass his arm encircled. He announced it in a rather odd way, which was a sudden low pitched, bass giggle that erupted from him. " Me and Enid are gonna take off fum here in that goddam ole station-wagon of mine and go and park it somewhere in some glorious quiet canefield. Ain't we, sweetie?"

" Hell, yes! You damn right!" the handsome girl said. She was the dentist's assistant.

" You're perfectly welcome to come along," Bonham said. " Susie there would be more than glad to have you for her fella for to-night."

" I most surely would," Susie smiled. " I'd enjoy to know you a deal betteh, Misteh Grant. You're very famous in Ganado Bay. I'd like to love with you."

Grant shook his head. He liked her. She was just almost as good-looking and attractive as the other girl. There was very little to choose. But suddenly, working somewhere deep inside him, was the thought of his new girl in New York holding him back. Suddenly it was hard to believe it was only not quite five days since he had been with her. They had been together only a little over three weeks, and that was hard to believe, too. It was like some kind of talisman he had in her, that he would lose if he stepped out on her. For a sudden moment he thought of taking a cab out to the Royal Loggerhead or the West Moon Over and calling her. But the lousy phone service here took so damned long, at least an hour, and half the time the connection was so bad you couldn't hear or be heard except for a word or two. It would be more frustrating than good. And anyway what did he want to call her for? He begged off charmingly with Susie, not wanting to hurt or insult her, on the grounds of fatigue, too much booze, and a deep depression. To him it sounded lame. But if it was, Bonham came to his rescue.

" He's got something serious botherin' him, girls. I don't know what it is, because he don't talk. Maybe it's an idea for a new play. Anyway . . ."

Grant looked at him, suddenly remembering for the first time that the big man was married. Bonham drunk was very little different from Bonham sober. The only thing Grant could notice was that perhaps those blackly burning eyes burned a bit more blackly.

Bonham moved. "Well, since Ron ain't going, why don't you come on and go along with us two, Susie?"

"Okey," Susie grinned. "Why not?" She gave Grant her hand as they all got up. "It ratheh a shame, but we see each otheh. Maybe you be in a betteh mood Some Time." Then to the others she lapsed into the Jamaican patois, a—to Grant—, totally unintelligible, mumbled jumble of broad, flat vowel sounds, and whatever it was she said made the others both laugh out loud.

"What did she say?"

"She said it was very bad luck for her because you looked like a helluva good piece of loving for to-night," Bonham said; and Grant almost changed his mind about going. But he didn't; couldn't.

He watched them away, creaking off in the beat-up old station-wagon. Sounds of bright, rich laughter carried back to him from it in the night. He motioned for a taxi. The taxi deposited him, at his request, at the foot of the villa drive.

It was about a quarter of a mile up to the great house, uphill through the lush rich growths of special and rare tropical trees and plants which Evelyn and Paul de Blystein made a speciality of collecting. Grant walked it slowly under the hot burnished tropical sky, smelling the fleeting—fleeting because overabundant—flower and plant odours, thinking mostly about the dive he had made. The closer he came to the door, the more his elation turned into depression. Only one light was burning. In his guest-room he stripped himself naked, made himself a stiff drink at the little bar in one corner and climbed into bed with it.

Almost as soon as he turned off the light, his door opened softly and his mistress, his "mistress," came in: a flowing white shadow in the dark. *Hello, Lady Macbeth* he suddenly felt like saying, but refrained. In the image it was always black. black-draped, black-mantillaed, black-shrouded face, black-flowing, sleeved arm pointing: black of church, black of religion, black of guilt. Of course, if it were black now, he wouldn't see it. Or would he?

"You son of a bitch," she whispered.

Grant closed his eyes. " I made my first dive to-day."

" Do you know what you did to me?—To us?"

" I said I made my first dive to-day. In the sea."

" Evelyn was furious."

" I'll laugh her out of it."

She had sat down on the side of the bed and now smelled him. " And drunk, too!"

" Not drunk. Just high. Did I tell you, I made my first dive to-day."

" Until two-thirty in the morning? Hah!" The tone was ugly.

" We went out late. To a reef off the airport. When we got back, we went somewhere to have some drinks. And something to eat. And to talk diving. I forgot the time."

" Until *two-thirty* in the morning!" Tone uglier.

" I wanted to talk diving."

" I don't know what's the matter with you," the ugly voice said. " But something is. Anyway I don't like it. And I don't have to put up with it and I'm not going to. It must be some little pig of a whore, some cunt you picked up in New York. Is that it?"

For a moment Grant thought about telling her. But he stayed silent.

" It must be that. That's what it always is," the voice said. There was no give in it, no give at all. " Because that's what you always do. Every time you go. Some hot-assed little whore who wants to take you for everything you got. Everything *I* helped you to earn."

Grant didn't answer. Beside him the pressure of her ass on the bed went away. There was a rustle of clothing. The voice when it came was strident, harsh, loudly grating, though still in a whisper.

" Good will is worked out as qualifying the life of a group of Masters—(masters of their own destiny)—under the care of a Master of the Wisdom—(" Gnostic "). *The WILL-TO-GOOD is developed and understood in the groups of those of still greater attainment and is concerned with Purpose.* GOOD WILL has vision! Will-to-Good. *Then* you have Illumination."

Grant still didn't answer. " You know all that as well as I do," she said harshly. " I've taught you all I know." Her mules hit the floor. Then, naked, she climbed into the double bed under the sheet and lay beside him as stiff as a board. She was lying there stiff as a varnished bowstring waiting for him to screw her.

Grant didn't know if he could. In silence he finished his drink. Finally both pity and a terribly painful sense of how embarrassing it would be for her if he didn't, plus a vague moral obligation which he knew was ridiculous, plus the fact that she was a female, all came to his aid. God forgive me, he thought to his new girl in New York, *you* forgive me. Gracelessly, flat on his back, he groped at her crotch a little to aid him. Her arms above her head, she did not move. He rolled over on to her, stuck it in her, and pumped away until he came. As always, she neither raised her legs nor moved.

As he was falling into sleep, he heard again the rustle of clothing as she put back on her nightgown and her robe, then the soft closing of the door.

Awakened by it, he lay wide awake a long time staring at the ceiling and thinking about New York.

TWO

He had arrived there half-way between Christmas and New Year, and the holiday drinking season was on and going full blast in every Third Avenue bar and East Side cocktail lounge. It had snowed all the way through Ohio and Pennsylvania on the train and it was still snowing in Manhattan when his train from his hometown Indianapolis pulled into Grand Central. At six in the evening it was already dark, Christmas lights glistened everywhere, and people hurried into Grand Central station on their way home, or picked their way along the streets through the slush desperately looking for cabs. All of Grant's most horrible sentimentalities for Manhattan as well as his most rabidly hate-filled memories of it, this particular day called up in him. From the station he had taken a cab straight to his reservations at the New Weston at 49th and Madison. They would be pulling the New Weston down soon.

It was strange how later in Jamaica in February, so short a time after that day in December, *all* of his previous memories of New York—even those going back the full thirteen years he had known it—were now somehow tied up with the new girl he had met, with Lucky. Everything that had ever happened to him in that city had been reconstructed emotionally in his head to include the image of—a laughing 27-year-old siren from upper New York State named Lucky Videndi.

At thirty-six he should be embarrassed even to use such a phrase. But that was the way he thought of her. Lucia Angelina Elena Videndi. Even the memories of those very early, barren, broke days in New York and his life there right after the war, now seemed to include her brightening image, making everything seem less dark and awful, less bad than it actually had been. And he had never even seen her until a few weeks ago.

He did not meet her, actually, until January 10th—although he met some others. But those others . . .

In the nine years since his first big success Grant had been around a fair amount for a famous man. Especially whenever he came on to New York. In the faster sets of girls (he found out later from Lucky, who knew them all) he was known at the secret luncheon sessions as a very good lay and a better diver, but a man who did not want encumbering entanglements and might therefore be half fag. He was also the last of the unmarried writers.

But his real trouble (*Grant knew*) was that the terrible bone-cracking loneliness, the " Miseries," that he suffered whenever he was without a girl, and which drove him like a whipped horse, was strengthened rather than lessened whenever he dropped into sleep sated but not satisfied beside one of them. They didn't give a real damn about him any more than he gave a damn about them. That was his real trouble. That, and his sense of responsibility to his mistress. He didn't want to hurt her. However ridiculous that might seem.

But with Lucky all of that changed.

" You know what?" he said one afternoon in Florida, his head on her chest and his lips nuzzling at the pool of sweat that had formed between her magnificent rose-tipped breasts. He was already half asleep and he had a sense of revelation. " We're Hansel and Gretel, you and me. And the world is the woods."

" I've always thought of us as Clark Gable and Carole

Lombard," Lucky said softly, and took hold of his ears
with her hands.

"Maybe. To other people. And maybe they were scared
too. 'Let go my ears! I know my business,'" he quoted.
"Anyway I guess it's not just the world that's the woods.
It's the fucking Universe," he said, and rubbed his lips in
the delicious sweat on her chest.

"Don't think," she said. "Drink." He had glanced up
and seen her smiling.

It could have been her philosophy. In fact it was. When
Rocky Graziano's ghosted book had come out way back with
its horrible title designed for the consumption trade—for the
"assholes," as the Madison Avenue boys liked to say—
Lucky Videndi had taken it and twisted it to her own:
to read: "Somebody up there hates me." It made the rounds
from P. J. Clarke's to El Morocco, but she really meant it.
She was determined to extract every fleeting joy, beauty,
pleasure from her life that she could get before God or
whatever Monster it was Up There snatched it away from
her. She had also twisted for her own benefit Spinoza's
"Because I love God does not mean God must love me
in return" to fit the more modern age: "Because God hates
me does not mean I must love God in return." She also
said: "The reason there is so much divorce in America to-day
is because sex is not dirty enough in the home."

Grant found it all not only sane but encouraging. Especially
after his Middlewestern mistress's crazy occultism and yakking about moral responsibility. Because what Lucky said
was really the way he felt about the world, if he was honest.
Fuck responsibility. Write literature? Responsibilty to whom?
The inhuman race? Grant's youthful naïveté about the importance of literature had long since disappeared, buried
and suffocated to death by the new age's avalanche of mass
media propagandas and the people it created. The bureaucracy of Madison Avenue.

But when he used it back on her, Lucky surprised him
again. "People like you have to write literature," she said
in a sturdy way. Grant mocked her. "Yeah? For who?
The race?" Sturdily, she wouldn't back down. "For me,"
she said staring him straight in the eye. After a while she
added, "Anyway, you can't help it anyway."

He had met her the way he met all of his New York girls.

Some friend who liked them and wanted to do you a favour, usually a friend who had laid them in the past, arranged for a polite and proper introduction and then you were on your own. In the case of Lucky, Grant had gone out of loneliness over to Hervey Miller the critic's house in the East 60s. This was pretty drastic for a playwright even though Miller liked his work and had always given him good reviews, but the Miseries had tied him up in knots. He had spent the long New Year's week-end in Connecticut with his friend Frank Aldane the novelist and his family, where he had laid an ageing lady novelist who lived around there. No score. A good sweat but no score. Neither of them really cared. Then, back in the city, he had finally made it with the second of the two new secretaries his producer's office had acquired since Grant's last trip East. Again no score. All very friendly but no real score. He hadn't called her again. And so here he was at Hervey Miller's house all alone at five o'clock for a drink. And then Buddy Landsbaum had wandered in.

Buddy was a slightly older competitor in the theatre, and at the moment was collaborating with Hervey Miller on a film. What was more important for Grant, he was giving a party that very night in his hotel suite, a farewell party for the cast and crew of his last film. It was just the kind of party for a lonely writer, Buddy said when he heard about Grant's predicament from Hervey. But as it turned out, it wasn't. The five or six young chicks were there, as Buddy'd promised, but they were all interested in Buddy. They were all movie actresses and Buddy had just made one girl a star and gotten her a *Life* cover. The young star herself, who was present, worked hard and carefully to protect her interests. Slowly the five or six chicks wandered off and left—without Grant. They knew his name of course but he had never done any film, and they wanted film. Then the young star's husband came and collected her from Buddy. So after the last drunken technician left, Buddy and Grant sat down in the debris with the remnants of the whisky and got lonely drunk together.

They didn't really know each other well. Buddy was always off in Hollywood or South America or Florida, Grant was always home in Indianapolis with his unknown (but suspected) "mistress." Buddy it turned out was having his troubles too.

His second wife was costing him so much to divorce that he might not ever be able to marry again—even should he ever want to. In addition, her dress shop in Miami Beach had failed and he was having to absorb that. The young star he had made, and whom Grant had met to-night, was already beginning to dally her next producer-director, for her next film. When the whisky was gone, they went to bed. What was the point of Grant going back alone to the New Weston? It was in the morning, after they'd started off with orange juice and vodka, that Buddy thought of Lucky. Lucky Videndi.

" I don't know if I ought to introduce you to her, though," Buddy said after he'd promised to call her and had already picked up the phone. He put the phone back in its cradle. " You're one of those rough-tough brutal he-man types, and she's a very sophisticated, sensitive girl."

Grant grinned. He knew that a lot of people thought of him in that way, but he knew enough real " he-man " types to know that this opinion of him was comparative, very comparative. " Cut the shit," he said, " I'm no more of a brutal he-man type than you or anybody is."

" Well, you're not the type I—or Lucky either—would think of as a very hip, Ivy-League New Yorker."

" Aw, come on. Then what'd you suggest her for? Okay, then don't call her. And go to hell."

Buddy had a peculiar but very common look on his face. It was the look of a man who has screwed a girl and is vain of it and wants everyone to know, but at the same time is committed by his code of honour not to say so or tell. His eyebrows registered smugness, a little embarrassment and some chagrin, all at the same time.

" I don't know how to explain it to you, Ron. But she's a very special type of girl. She's not like most of the kids you and I run into in town. Hell, I could have put her into a couple of my films, groomed her a little, and made her a star but she said to hell with that. She thinks all actors and actresses are exhibitionist and stupid insensitive egos."

" She's right," Grant put in.

" So she works for us a little every now and then, in bit parts or doubling or as script girl, whenever she needs money. She's got her Master's in Political Philosophy. Her old man was the biggest bootlegger in upper New York State in the '20s and made a fortune. So she's . . ."

He stopped. His face wore another look, one of genuine puzzlement now, one which he had unintentionally talked himself into.

" She just had a rich young South American she was going to marry shot out from under her, so to speak, down there. You know the South Americans. That was a year ago. She's been working on a play since then. I don't know if it's good. She won't talk about it. She's been very low since her boy-friend got knocked off, says she's looking for a new relationship. I . . ." Buddy stopped again, and scratched his rumpled head, a different, deeper kind of puzzled chagrin on his face now. " Well, I called her up and tried to get back in with her," he said, " but she doesn't want any part of me any more. Says she's had me, up to here. That way. We're still friends, she still works for us sometimes, but that's it."

He looked at Grant with vulnerable eyes, his face puffy and his belly out from all the late nights and boozing. " This is all in the strictest confidence, Ron. But I had to tell you."

" Okay okay," Grant said. He suddenly felt sorry for old Buddy, who had not done a play in ten years now. " So call her or don't call her."

" And she's very beautiful," Buddy added. He drank off another half a glass of orange juice and vodka and then went back to the telephone. After he had talked to her a while, he put Grant on. The voice, coming through the instrument, sounded husky with a shy edge of wit and laughter just under the surface. She also sounded rather embarrassed, as if she were trying hard not to think of this call and introduction as a form of male procurement. After looking at Buddy, and receiving an affirmative nod, Grant gently and as charmingly as he could made a date with her that night. He was to pick her up at her place, it was over the liquor store and the only tenement on Park Avenue, she said.

" I just did you the biggest favour I could ever do you," Buddy said sadly as he hung up, and then carried him off to Faye Emerson's house around the corner where he pushed drinks on him all afternoon, then took him to a cocktail

party way downtown with Buddy's own date, all of it
as if now that he'd introduced him he was trying to get
him drunk enough and make him late enough so that Grant
would miss the date.

When he did arrive, he was forty-five minutes late and
more than a little drunk, thanks to Buddy. But he had
been emotionally turned on at the cocktail party by a good-
looking girl who wanted to make him (wasn't it always
that way? either drought or flood), and he could feel his
not inconsiderable charm working in him like a smoothly
purring well-tuned engine. (Ah, if he could only turn it
on and off at will!) After climbing four flights of narrow
stairs in the tiny building, he knocked and was admitted to
a delegation of four girls, three of whom seated on the
couch were obviously there to look him over. The prettiest
of the four, who had opened the door, put her hand out
and smiling nervously said, " Hello, I'm Lucky You're
kind of late. For a first date." He apologised. " I very nearly
didn't make it at all, by God!" he added. " I think Buddy
was deliberately trying to get me drunk and make me late.
So you'd be mad at me."

" I guess he's not above it," she said, her smile still nervous.

Buddy had told him she was beautiful. But that had not
prepared him for the kind of breathtaking beauty he found
himself facing. All he could think was, It's unfair, it's
unfair! It very nearly choked off and killed his smoothly
purring charm. Her shoulder-length champagne-coloured
hair was combed straight back above the smoothly rounded
forehead in a sort of lion's-mane effect. She had high slightly
prominent cheekbones that slanted her eyes the least tiniest
bit. But beneath the short straight nostril-flaring nose, her
mouth was her most attractive feature. It was wide enough
that it seemed to go all the way across her face although
it didn't, and the full sweet upper lip was so unusually short
that it appeared unable to cover a perfect set of prominent
upper teeth except by an act of conscious will on the
part of its owner. Below the long full lower lip was a tiny
cute jaw and chin that further accentuated the mouth. When
she smiled with it, even nervously like now, it not only lit
up the entire little apartment but appeared to radiate right
on through the walls into the apartments around. It was

typical of Lucky, Grant learned later, that she should consider her Italian nose her best feature and be embarrassed
about that exquisite mouth. But apart from her face, her
figure was enough to drive men mad.

Grant never was able to describe the why of her body's
beauty in words, even to himself. It had something to do
with the unusual width and squareness of the shoulders,
and the long line which tapered down from them to the
waist, to flare immediately into a pair of gorgeous, unusually
high-assed hips; and perhaps because above this width
of shoulder rode the slender neck and high small head of
a princess. Actually, she needed the wide shoulders to
support the big full globes of her breasts thrusting out in
the tight black dinner dress. Her calves were perfect,
and ended in strong delicate aristocrat's ankles and the
powerful feet of a pro dancer, which it turned out later,
she had been. In the tight dress there was suggested just
a hint of an equally powerful mons veneris. In her heels
she was just a hair shorter than Grant, and she stood very
straight, carrying her torso high off her hips, the slender
neck extended to carry the small head, in the manner of
a Jamaican woman carrying a market basket on her head.
She moved the same way. And icing all this cake together,
another indescribable quality, a reserved sexuality oozed
from her like her very own invisible honey. She was obviously
the doted-upon darling of the three girls on the couch,
to whom she now began to introduce Grant.

Grant was totally bowled over, but he managed to acknowledge the introductions. He had been out with several coldly
professional beauties over the years, but this girl was far
and away the most beautiful woman he had ever met,
and this included a few very famous female movie stars.
It would take him several days to separate the names of the
three girls on the couch. But he had always been bad at
names anyway.

Leslie Green was Lucky's room-mate in the apartment. A
small, pert girl with a good figure in crotch-tight green slacks,
raven hair piled up high on her head to make her look taller,
and a long haunted Jewish face perhaps a tenth as beautiful
as her pal's, she was obviously the self-appointed general
manager of Lucky's emotional life and the Leader of the
Delegation to Study Grant. Her snapping black eyes stated

unequivocally that she was not about to let Lucky not be appreciated. Grant felt that her eyes softened a little after she looked him over.

Mrs. Athena Frank was a blocky blonde girl with a square face somewhat marred by acne and a rather gracelessly lush, sensual figure. The introductions turned up the fact that she was a lawyer and Grant wondered uneasily if she were the official legal member of the team, the committee. Her open and belligerent hostility showed already, anyway, which way she would vote on the subject of Ron Grant, playwright.

Mrs. Annie Carler was a slender, fairly tall Jewish girl of about Grant's own age, with short tousled black hair and lushly dissipated circles under her eyes, much given to unconscious posturings of her long pretty neck and slender back into modern-dance, Martha Graham poses. With a sly puckish grin, she seemed to be enjoying the situation very much and appeared to be the most noncommittal of the three.

All three of them were clearly madly in love with Lucky, her wit and her beauty; and if there were any hidden jealousies in all this anywhere, Grant could not yet smell them out. If she had a big reputation going in Manhattan, and apparently she did, these three were going to promulgate it. And like any real queen, Lucky treated her subjects with dignity, and with a deep respect for their good taste in serving her. There was some small talk—in which Grant did not feel he came off particularly brilliantly—then she got her coat and they whisked out the door and down the four flights of narrow badly lit stairs out on to the nocturnal glories of Park in a winter snowfall. Rich people in dinner clothes and furs were getting into Cadillac limousines and taxis all around them.

"Well, do you think I passed inspection?"

Lucky gave him a sly crooked grin that made her blue eyes glint. "I think so." She looked at him squarely. "You're pretty famous."

He waited but she didn't say more. In the cab, glancing at her sideways, as she nestled that nosy, toothy, short-upper-lipped profile down into the collar of her coat, Grant realised with a start that he had never before in his life been so proud to be seen in public with a woman. And, especially after these past two years of hibernation and work in Indianapolis, with his " mistress " and his new play, it made his heart jump. In the past he had often looked with envy at the escorts of unknown, real beauties—of which there were few enough in this world known or unknown—the kind which made heads turn and tables buzz. Now he was escorting one himself. Settling back, he told himself this might turn out to be one of the great nights of his life.

It didn't. Though it started out well enough. He took her to the Petite Ange, haven of the sick comics after they graduated from Max Gordon's Village Vanguard, for dinner and the show. After a few drinks she loosened up and lost her nervousness and began to display that really penetrating wit, humour, and incredibly sexy charm Buddy Landsbaum had told him about. She was apparently an incorrigible flirt. But then, she was also so beautiful, so sexually attractive that for her simply to look at a man was enough. Grant had never sat in a nightclub so proudly, so self-content. Heads turned toward her, tables buzzed. The only trouble was that as she loosened up after a few drinks, Grant after a few drinks became quite drunk. All the drinks his old pal Buddy had pushed on him all day long, which drinks and other chicanery he had survived to keep his date, now began to catch up with him. The dinner and all that good food in his belly saved him for a while, but after the show they came back out to the lounge-bar to listen to the coloured fag piano player and drink and talk. Lucky was a little drunk herself by this time—but nothing like Grant.

Grant made his pitch for her there in the lounge-bar. With sly drunken shrewdness he had decided not to do it during the dinner and show inside. Too many distracting elements around. But you could talk while the fag piano player was playing; he was background. And he played a lot of love mood music, when he wasn't doing his funny numbers. So Grant had waited.

He had of course been making love to her as politely and charmingly as he could all during the dinner and show inside. Now for the clincher! The essence of his pitch was that he wanted her to come back to his suite in the New Weston with him, or, if her room-mate didn't mind, since he had noticed a soft bed in the living-room as well as twin beds in the tiny bedroom, he would be quite willing to go back to her apartment with her. Either way, he said, he intended to make violent love to her that night.

Maybe he didn't lay it on right. He had expected, especially after all his old pal Buddy had told him about her, that the result would be a foregone conclusion. He was astonished and shaken when she told him no.

"But my God! Why not?" he cried. "What's wrong with me?" He then discovered he had very nearly drowned out the piano player, who, being an old acquaintance from bachelor nights when the lonely Grant used to come in here and drink alone, looked over at him and winked.

Lucky had a hurt, embarrassed, but sturdy look on her face. "How do I know what's wrong with you? I don't even know you yet." She shook her pretty head and said flatly, "I never lay men the first date I have with them."

"But that's ridiculous!" Grant protested. During dinner she had been open and quite frank about all the men she had had in her life, though without naming any of them Grant noticed. She had claimed 400, though Grant suspected her of exaggerating to shock him, and now the thought of going back alone to that miserable suite in the New Weston after being titillated and heated up so by this exquisite female was enough to nearly unman him. Had he been more sober, he might have hidden it better. "That's . . . That's the same kind of rigid moral rule you hate the middle-class bourgeoisie for," he protested, lamely. What he wanted to say but hadn't the courage was If all 400 of them, why not me too?"

Lucky still looked embarrassed, and stubborn. "Well, maybe. But I don't care. I don't have to. And I won't." Then her eyes softened a little. "Anyway, you're getting pretty drunk."

"That's our goddam friend Buddy!" Grant cried waving his arm, and several people turned to look at him. He had been sweating all night in this smoky, overheated place, but now he began to sweat more in his excitement. "And because I'm shy!"

In an effect to calm him Roddy Croft the piano player had begun to play the famous, very popular theme from the film of Grant's first play.

Lucky was blushing. "People are looking at us."

"Hell with them!" Grant said. "Sons of bitches! What do they know about loneliness?"

"What do *you* know about it?" Lucky said sharply.

"I think you're nothing but a——" Grant started, but he couldn't bring himself to finish it, so he came at it from behind. "I hate cock-teasers," he muttered.

"And I think you're a boor!" Lucky said. "No girl would lay a man with such a rude, crude approach as yours!"

They were joined by the club's PR man, another old drinking companion from bachelor nights, who offered to buy a drink. He knew Lucky too, it turned out, from many dates she had had in the joint over the years. Grant thought to appeal to him, but wisely thought better of it. Instead, he began to brood. The PR man bought several drinks.

And that was the way it ended. His first date with Lucky Videndi. Nothing he could say would shake her. When they left at nearly four in the morning, Saul Weiner the PR man went with them, and Grant made his grand climax of the evening. The light snow had stopped and as they walked up Park toward Lucky's place Grant began to kick over the wickerwire wastepaper baskets along Park Avenue in furious, frustrated, outrageous protest.

"That's against the law," Lucky told him nervously. "It really is. They're very serious about it. You're liable to get picked up for it."

"Yeah? I hope I do! I hope by God I do!" he said and kicked over another.

At her door she shook hands with him. "Not only are you not a gentleman," she said in a sort of awed whisper, "I really think you're crazy! You're a savage gooff-off from the goddamned Middlewest!"

"You think so, huh?" Grant said. For one clear moment, one clear agonised moment that would forever stay burned in his head, he stared at her. Out from behind and beyond his large alcoholic haze, piercing into and through her smaller alcoholic haze, he tried to put into his eyes all that he really felt about her, and about himself, and about everything. He thought he saw that her eyes understood. But she was very angry. Then the cold dark New Weston suite closed its cloud back down over him and he turned away. Four hundred men! And she wouldn't even let him feel her titty! With the quiet, cynical Saul Weiner he walked to Reuben's, where he ate tartar steak he did not want and talked about things that bored him. When he staggered into his hairy furry old New Weston suite at six a.m., he found a telegram from his " mistress " who was at the moment in Miami Beach, which coldly demanded to know why her phone calls could never find him in and why he had not called or answered her wires. It was the third such in two days.

It also said that her husband would be joining her in a few days. Grant wadded it up and threw it on the floor. But he knew that once he sobered up the incredible, horrible, sick-making panic-guilt, she was somehow able to instil in him would return.

Carol Abernathy. And Hunt Abernathy, her husband. Grant could not say now, at this late date, which one of them he had really liked the best over the years.

Carol Abernathy. Wife of Hunt Abernathy. Head and prime-mover of the Hunt Hills, Indianapolis, Little Theatre. And also one of Indianapolis's most highly successful real estate agents.

When he was undressed and nude, and had with drunken care hung his clothes up neatly, Grant got the wool blanket off the bed and rolled up in it on the floor of the suite's living-room. This made him feel some better. The hard floor felt good. The double bed in the bedroom had a soft mattress and on top of that one of those European-type feather-bed comforters. The whole damn thing suffocated him, and he had taken to sleeping in the same spot on the living-room floor with the blanket whenever he was here alone. Also, that way, he did not have to think so much about the other half of the double bed being empty. He was lonely and panicky for so famous a man. Drunk in his blanket, he did some reviewing.

Up to the age of thirty-six, which was now, Ron Grant had never had what he considered a true love affair. As a result, he had come to believe no such thing existed—except in the movies of Clark Gable and Carole Lombard; and in that insane, complex, all-pervasive spider-web laid down over the entire American nation: the great American love song industry. Anything else was just kidding yourself. He had been considerably aided in this belief by his " mistress," who for reasons of her own never tired of stating it: *There is no such thing as love.*

Grant had for a long time strongly suspected that her reasons were entirely personal: if she could convince him there was no love anywhere else either, she could bind him that much more closely to her, because what would be the point of leaving her? She never let up on it. And he had to admit that up to now the theory had been just about 100 per cent accurate. Long and seriously deep were the philosophical discussions they had had about it.

However, he had been brainwashed like the rest of his generation by the great American love song industry, and he couldn't stop looking, stop hunting. His " mistress " considered this (and sometimes he agreed) a sin of ignorance. But he could no more stop hunting love than he could stop wanting to get laid well, which she considered a sin of indulgence. He had done a deal of hunting and wanting over their fourteen years. He had done a deal of hunting before that, for that matter. A great, great deal. All he wanted was to have just once in his life one love affair that was like those accursed Clark Gable-Carole Lombard films of his youth, that was all. He didn't even care if it lasted. After it, he would accept all torment—all the consequences, all the penalties, all the misery.

There were, in all, three love affairs he had had in his life. Innumerable liaisons; but only three love affairs, and not one of them a true one. The first two didn't even count really, since he had never fucked either of the girls. One was a girl in school, high school, when he was still too green to believe girls like doing it; she turned out a lesbian. The second was a big, lushly built, red-head Irish-American girl in Hawaii when he was in the Navy during the war, whom he never got any closer to than the grinding of his forearm on the outside of her dress against her enticingly protuberant mons veneris; she now had four kids. Neither counted. And then the third: his long, By God fourteen years long, affair with Carol Abernathy.

He supposed he had to count that one, since it had lasted so long. But it had certainly never been a true one, a Clark Gable-Carole Lombard one. As for the liaisons, both before

and during Carol Abernathy, some had been good and some
had been not so good. But none could be called love affairs.
A love affair, Grant had decided some time back, presup-
posed a need, an all-powerful, insuperable need—and not just
an insuperable, but a *happily* insuperable one—for whatever
weak, insecure reasons—of each party for the other which
superseded everything else in life. And if that happily
surrendered-to need wasn't there, it couldn't be a love affair,
only a liaison. And yet that need must be— . . . But that
was as far as he could take it at the age of thirty-six.

Carol Abernathy. Hunt Abernathy. When he had come
home from the Navy and the war to finish school and write
plays, he had thought the Abernathys both very glamorous.
The Hunts (from whom the Hunt Hills suburb got its name,
as had Hunt Abernathy himself) and the Abernathys had
been in Indiana since the days of Mad Anthony Wayne.
They had settled Hunt Hills. Carol and Hunt had been
1920s kids, flaming, him with a raccoon coat and Stutz
Bearcat, her with the cloche hats and titless dresses. When
Grant (who had read about them in the *Star* all his life) met
them at the age of 22, Carol was 39, Hunt 41. Now when
Grant was 36, she was 53. Easy to swallow, this fact
was hard to digest. It was a further irony that her name
happened to be Carol.

Born into a poor Tennessee hills family who had moved
north, she had met Hunt in high school. Later—so Grant
got the story from her (he had never talked of it with
Hunt!)—with him at college in Bloomington and her working
as a waitress downtown, he had knocked her up, paid for
her abortion after which she nearly died of infection, and
then, when more or less honourably freed, had come back
around and, because of some peculiar tortured sense of
chivalric masochism of his own perhaps, had married her.

She had been tolerated but never accepted by his family
and his country club, where she became known as The Madcap
Carol because of doing crazy stunts. He had never been true
to her. Having boundless energy, she had contented herself
with the social life, fashion and gay parties, but never
felt she quite made it. She had had three or four affairs around
the country club, one with a rich young happily married
doctor, the rest always with younger men who were poorer
than she and whom she helped to get started in some busi-

ness. Then she discovered literature and the theatre, began trying to write plays, and organised the Hunt Hills Little Theatre.

Hunt became the best golfer in Indianapolis if not in Indiana, general manager of the biggest brick making and lumber yard establishment in the area, loved cars, fucked many waitresses and low-class girls, and settled into being a serious heavy drinker.

When Grant entered the picture—though they went out together in public and gave gay parties at home—(she said) they hadn't slept together for years and Hunt had once seriously threatened to commit her.

It was such a banal story that it wouldn't even make a novel or a play. Grant's entrance into it had not made it any less banal. He knew of at least twenty childless couples scattered over the Petit Middlewest who had " adopted " a broke young artist or writer, who became a member of the family while he was also fucking the mistress of the establishment at the same time. About the only un-totally-predictable thing, which perhaps saved the story from total banality, was that Ron Grant through fate, luck, talent or all three, had become a world-famous playwright That, and the fact that Carol Abernathy, as she watched the years of Grant's and her ages mount together, began more and more to study Oriental philosophies.

It was four years after their affair started that Carol Abernathy began to frequent occult book stores. Their physical love affair (never very fulfilling sexually because after a very short time she would only do it one way, in one position) had rapidly waned as she occupied herself more and more with the spiritual side of things.

It was true that Grant had started having other women soon after their affair started (to be exact, one week after she started refusing to have him in more than one way, one position) but even so he could not believe he was *totally* responsible for what was happening to her. Carol, though, obviously felt that he was, that it was " his fault."

Through her occult studies she deduced that she had been appointed a sort of occult Master of Midwestern Artists, doomed by some unknown Karma to the great sacrifice of opportunity to create because of helping them. Under this concept her dictatorial tendencies emerged swiftly, since her sacrifice gave her the moral right to know what was best for more self-indulgent people. She made it plain to Grant that she now slept with him only so that he would not waste precious time from his Art chasing pussy. She even went so far as to tell him that a frustrated sex life was good for him, and all artists, all great men, because it allowed him —and them—to sublimate sex energy in work. And Grant at one point in his life with her believed, or tried to believe, it. After all there was a lot of truth in the idea. Look at Gandhi. And yet another part of him, the rest of him, which understood people surely but wordlessly, as would some languageless super-animal, knew it all to be a web of selfish, self-laminating, ego-perpetuating lies on her part. All she really wanted was to keep him like any woman wanted to keep any man, keep him and dominate him, be boss, make him pay. He knew all this and yet he didn't leave her.

Rolled in his blanket on the hard floor of the suite's living-room, Grant groaned in his half-sleep.

Carol Abernathy. Their first four months, most of which time they were separated anyway because Grant was still in the Naval Hospital at Great Lakes Station and still totally flat broke, was the nearest they came to a love affair. Using her husband's money, she used to meet him in Chicago and stay with him. Only some time later did he actually move in with them in Indianapolis, begin writing original one-acters for her Little Theatre, and allow himself to be supported by Hunt. This was after that disastrous year going to school in New York, after which his GI Bill ran out on him because he had only had his senior year left to do. She had visited him there too on Hunt's money, from time to time. But after that, having moved in with them in Indianapolis, instead of a love affair (even a bad one) it became like some crazy kind of unhappy marriage, with Grant not even having the public distinction of being anyone's husband.

Carol Abernathy paid him small sums of Hunt Abernathy's money for the one-acters. This with his tiny Navy pension gave him a little beer and pool money whenever he went out with the boys. But he was seldom allowed to by Carol, who could always threaten to throw him out, and sometimes did. For the rest—bed, board, books, cigarettes—

Hunt Abernathy paid. Grant could never understand why.
Except that he knew why. Hunt put up with her for the very
same reason he himself did: accumulated guilt. In any
case it was not a particularly manly way to live for Grant,
and his status could conceivably be termed gigolo or rich
lady's darling.

Later on, of course, after his first big three-acter became
such a colossal hit on Broadway, it was a lot harder for
her to hold him down. He had to go to New York quite
a lot. Carol Abernathy never went with him, though out of
politeness he asked her once or twice. She always refused.
Neither did Hunt go, who couldn't because of his job,
and who didn't give a good goddam about New York anyway.
And each time Grant went to Europe, he went alone.

But why did he always come *back*?

When the big money began to come in, Carol Abernathy
found for him (in her other capacity as real estate agent)
an expensive home right across the street from their own in
Hunt Hills. What was more, she got him to buy it. Grant
was aware that—in addition to being for his security, welfare,
quiet and peace of mind, as she told him—it also tied up
a big chunk of his sudden new income. And yet he went
ahead and did it. But of course at the time he had wanted to
do it.

Further, Carol Abernathy got him to invest an even greater
sum (over $75,000 to be precise, and most of it non-deduct-
ible) in the building of a brand-new theatre and grounds for
the Hunt Hills Little Theatre. By now, due largely to
Grant's first big success, the Hunt Hills Little Theatre had
quite a little group of would-be artists, novelists, playwrights,
designers and actors grown up around it. The new theatre.
grounds and living quarters caused an exciting little Arts
Renaissance in Indianapolis. But Grant also knew that besides
being for Art and the good of Art and that he owed it to
Art because he'd been lucky, as Carol Abernathy told him
(and as he himself believed, for that matter), the new Hunt
Hills Little Theatre tied up even more of his new money.
And yet he went ahead and did that too. But he had
wanted to do that, too. He allowed her to go on saying
in public that he owed it to her, for helping him.

Why?

That was nine years ago. And so far his share of all

spiritual profits had been, simply and solely, guilts—newer and bigger and profounder guilts: guilts as unfaithful lover, guilt as ungrateful son, guilt as commercially successful artist, guilt as a man who kept on repeatedly cuckolding his friend. My God, talk about Oedipus!

As Carol Abernathy in one of her better moments once chuckled and said huskily as they lay in bed, " Christ! You're the only man I ever heard of who got to live out his Oedipus complex!" Grant had laughed, at the time.

They began seriously the foster-mother routine for the first time when *Life* Magazine sent one of its hot-shot young feature writers out to Indianapolis to do an article on the hick playwright from some Indiana Little Theatre group who had come up with the biggest hit since *A Streetcar Named Desire*, and on the " strange Middlewestern housewife " who " dominated the Group like a dictator " and " ran the Group's affairs like a general." How they ever managed to fool the smart young *Life* Yale man Grant didn't know, but he suspected it was because not even a Yale man could believe a grown man who was fucking some woman would allow himself to be so bossed, so tongue-lashed, and so ordered around by her. But that was exactly his reason, once he allowed himself to be convinced by Carol that they seriously had to play mother and son or be found out, which—after all —would really hurt nobody but Hunt.

Naturally, the *Life* article made him look like a raving fag to the world. And from then on he was trapped in the role. A " mother "—dominated neurotic. His intention had been to protect Carol and Hunt—especially Hunt, who had come to be the biggest of his guilts. It was peculiar that there seemed to be no other choice. Either he shut up and let himself be a fag mother's boy to the world, or he told the truth and showed up his friend Hunt Abernathy as a cuckold—and, one made so by himself.

Grant never did know what Hunt thought about the whole thing. Whenever they two were together alone, they reacted and talked as though the *Life* article was right and they three were a family with Carol the mother, Hunt the father, and Grant the son—which, in one strange way, they really were. Only once did Hunt even obliquely mention any-thing about the whole business and that was one time several years after Grant's success when, after a terrible lovers'

fight with Carol, Grant had gone out and got drunk and
Hunt—not too sober himself—had come to find him and
bring him home. They two, both males—or both trying to
be males—had over the years formed an oddly deep, enduring friendship from opposite sides of this peculiar woman
who seemed determined (whether consciously or not) that
neither should ever be a man again. Driving along the darkened streets of downtown Indianapolis, lit only by the neon
of bars at this late hour, Hunt Abernathy had said, " Listen,
I don't know what this fight's about. But I want you to
know that, much as I've come to like you, even love
you, Ron, if it ever comes to a head-on collision, a head-on
break between you and Carol, I'll have to side with Carol."
—" Sure," Grant had said in a pained, subdued voice, " of
course."—" Because I think she's right," Hunt Abernathy
said. " I believe in her."

How had she managed it? It was incredible. For years
she had governed her every act by a double-edged policy
of declaring herself *arbiter morum* over the lives of her
husband and lover in order to " help " them, and also in
order at the same time to retain power over them both.
For years she had laboured—whether deliberately or not—
to instil sufficient guilt in them to bind both to her forever.
She had succeeded, apparently.

And yet of course it hadn't all been bad. Maybe that was
the trouble. Despite everything else, human loyalties had
grown—caused simply by the guilts, perhaps. Grant could
recall the time the three of them had gone out together
and celebrated his first sale of a Grant one-acter outside
the Hunt Hills Little Theatre ; some little summer theatre
in upstate New York had wanted to do it. When the first
big hit came, he had taken the two of them on a month's
vacation in Havana. What a time they had had. Hunt had
caught a marlin.

On the floor of the room in the New Weston Hotel the
rolled-up figure groaned again. If he could only just once
find one Carole Lombard. For one week. He would throw
it all up, throw away everything, success, money, talent even,
for one week.

Why then did he always come running back to Carol
Abernathy? Fear, that was why. Fear of being alone. Fear
that every girl in his life from now on would only be a

liaison; and that kind of bone-cold loneness he could not face. Terrorised and haunted and made cowardly by such thoughts, he preferred to run back to a little love which if it did not keep you really warm, at least did not let you quite freeze. Grant, half waking, remembered the crumpled-up telegram.

The reason Carol Abernathy was in Miami Beach visiting friends and on her way to Jamaica was because during the two years he had worked on his new play Grant had decided he wanted to learn skin-diving.

Reading M. Cousteau's book had started him off. He bought himself a little aqualung at his sport's dealer's, dove down thirty-five or forty feet into two murky Indiana lakes, saw nothing, and came back home with a serious external ear infection which it took six weeks to cure.

Indiana just wasn't the place for it. He bought more books on diving. And from diving he branched out into marine biology, underwater archæology, oceanography, marine geology. Sitting in his relatively safe vantage point of Indianapolis, Indiana, watching via newspapers he did not trust, the three colossal bureaucracies of the world wrassling each other for moral superiority and threatening each other with "retaliatory destruction," he studied the last frontier open to the individual, non-team man. He was writing a play about a languishing fourteen-year-old love affair which his agent, producers and director told him was almost certain to be a smash hit, and into which he was trying to put some sense of serious meaning of what it was like to live in his own terrified, terrorised time, and what that time itself was like when Presidents and Leaders and parliamentary bodies, and the vast anonymous bureaux and groups of bureaux their governments had created, could not influence —and could not even be held responsible for—what was happening to the world.

He promised himself that when he finished it, hit or not, he would take some time off and really learn this new world where it ought to be learned, in the tropics. At least it would be an antidote to world politics for six months or so. It would also be an antidote to Carol Abernathy. He told Hunt and Carol about it over dinner one evening in his house, in Indianapolis. This made it an occasion, because usually he dined with them.

Carol liked the idea. She liked it so much she immediately invited herself and took over the planning, suggesting Ganado Bay in Jamaica because they could stay with the Countess Evelyn de Blystein, who was the former Evelyn Glotz of Indianapolis before with her father's huge coal fortune she married the Count Paul, and whom they all had known for years and whom Carol and Hunt had twice visited in her Jamaican winter home. She would write her a letter tomorrow. The play would be finished in a matter of weeks, and they could leave before the real cold weather started.

Grant listened to all of this and said nothing.

Their plans, then—his and those of the Abernathys, after Carol finished with them—were that she would spend some days with friends in Miami and, leaving her Mercedes there, would then go on to Ganado Bay where she would stay with Evelyn de Blystein and where Grant after seeing his producers in New York would meet her, and where Hunt would join them for the six weeks of his annual vacation. Then, at their leisure (whatever the hell that meant, Grant thought sourly, because it was her phrase), they two would continue on to Kingston where he would take diving lessons from a European professional named Georges Villalonga he had read about and thus begin his diving career.

The thought of the diving excited Grant, but the thought of Carol Abernathy being there did not. Why then could he not tell her this? Explain to her that he wanted, preferred, to go alone? He couldn't.

His lady-love left first, driving her own little Mercedes to Florida, and leaving from her own house almost directly across the street from the house she had found for Grant to buy. (It required only a moment for him to slip across the street late at night, after Hunt was asleep; as long as he was always back in his own house some time before daylight. And Grant had always enjoyed being up at dawn.) With some part of all this in his mind he stood in her yard with Hunt as she left, waving. As she pulled away, she gave him a secret tender loving look, which lit up her dark brown eyes, and which also Grant noticed accentuated the petulant jowls on her jawline that she had been steadily acquiring over the past six or eight years because she felt he did not love her and because she was ageing. Then he went back across the street and spent five days going over the typescript of his new play one last time with a pencil, adding a word here, cutting one there, relishing reading over one more time his own finished work, which of course most of the time until now he had believed in despair would never be finished. There was always this sad feeling that once a play was done, and seen by the public, it was no longer his and he had lost it. Then he packed a bag and, after a last drunken evening with Hunt, left for the train possessed of a violent desire to get the hell out of Indianapolis and back to New York and quickly get laid, anxious to start living yet once again—which meant getting laid.

Again the figure on the floor of the New Weston suite's living-room groaned. Laid? Laid?

He was awakened by the desk clerk at eight-thirty with the information that there was a person-to-person call for him from Miami. He refused it, telling the clerk to say he was out, took a shower and shaved, and then, after hacking hard to get the cigarettes-and-whisky huskiness out of his voice, picked up the receiver and called Lucky Videndi.

THREE

Some time later Lucky told him that that very huskiness in his voice was what had sunk her, that the only reason she had allowed him to continue to talk at all without hanging up on him immediately was because the husk in his phone voice was so sexy and exciting that it startled and intrigued her into listening. "That was my bad luck," she grinned, running one hand lightly across his belly and then down into his crotch, kissing him in the centre of his chest. "My good luck!" Grant countered, and trapped her hand where it was with his own so she couldn't remove it, or stop what it was doing. "And it turns out it was only cigarettes and whisky!" she smiled.

Normally she didn't do things like that, grab him like that so often, and so Grant liked it. Usually she sort of waited, to be stimulated and then played upon, as though this was some woman's passive prerogative she could avail herself of if she wished to. Grant sometimes felt she saw herself as some sort of flesh and blood harp with somewhere deep inside secret strings that twanged, and that he himself was the harpist—a harpist—who literally twanged these strings. Like any instrument she had to be warmed up; then warmed, she could be played up, and Grant was dedicating himself to this art form. He had never had sex like this in his life, ever.

It hadn't been much of a phone conversation really, this time, not actually. Grant had apologised for his conduct the night before. Lucky had told him he ought to, but had not verbally accepted it. Grant had then suggested awkwardly (How did one ever disguise these things? they were always so blatantly obvious) that he might come over and look at her play for her. "At least I could tell you whether there's any hope at all or not for it," he added, because he wanted her to think he was serious about it.

"Thanks!" Lucky said sharply, then softened her voice. "But don't you have anything more interesting than that to do to-day?" Soft or not, there was a dangerous edge there, he thought.

"No, nothing. I got a date for cocktails, dinner and the theatre for to-night is all."

This was the *first* of the two new secretaries in his producer's office, the one he had not yet made because she first had stood him off and then departed on a January vacation. This date had been made before she left, and now Grant sincerely regretted it.

"I'm sorry about that," he hemmed, "but it's a date I——"

"Oh, that doesn't matter," the lovely low voice said airily. There was a pause. "Okay, come on over. I'm not really doing anything."

Like the other remark, just before, this too could have been an ego ploy with an extra meaning, a little dig. But he was soon to learn that Lucky incredibly, never said things like that. She always said simply and directly exactly what she meant, and so far from playing upon other people's sensibilities with double-extendre, she leaned the other way, almost too far, by ignoring sensibilities almost completely.

For a man used to the bitcheries of the average Middle-western country club woman, among whom his own " mistress " was a past master who would never give a phrase just one meaning if two or more were available, this was hard to believe and once believed harder still to get used to.

For example she had met him at the door, looked him over and said simply but forcefully, " You look like the wrath of God!"—" Well, I do feel a little rocky," Grant had grinned. " Some asshole drinking buddy called and woke me at eight-thirty." He was nervously aware he had just told Lucky his first lie involving his " mistress."

" Well I was still in bed when you called," she admitted smiling, quite clearly now aware of the lie, but then why should she be?

Anyway he didn't really care. Hell, not even his producers knew for sure about Carol Abernathy, although they might suspect what they wanted. He wasn't about to tell of her to some girl he had just picked up.

It wasn't really the most auspicious beginning in the world, but Grant felt fine enough to weather that because something good had happened to him on the way over from the New Weston.

He had decided to walk. It was only fifteen short blocks. And during the walk he had fallen in love again with New York, that was what had happened to him. It had been nearly eleven when he had telephoned to Lucky and by the time he had dressed, deodorised and scented himself for whatever might happen, it was almost noon. The sun had come out a little by the time he came out into the street, and while it was crisp it wasn't that bone-numbing cold the town had lots of the time in winter. Girls with their bare heads tucked down into coat collars and young guys in their almost brimless hats and narrow-shouldered top-coats were beginning to pour out of the mid-town offices for the long lunch, and Grant suddenly wanted to holler. He passed by Random House where he knew some people and made a mental note to call. He loved and liked these sharp, smart Madison Avenue cats and chicks, though he detested and deplored just about everything any of them did for a living—as, he knew, most of them said they did too themselves. They only did it to live and love in this town. And who could blame them for that? This town that was Number One Target, both propaganda and nuclear, to the whole fucking world. The feeling stayed with him, brimming up out of his eyes and grin, all the way up Madison and over to the Park Avenue of last night's holocaust. He noted the wickerwire baskets were all put back, now.

Actually he didn't know whether it was this mood that had him turned on and going so good, or whether it was some subtle essence extruding from under the exquisitely shaved armpits of Lucky. Maybe it was both. She had the ability to do that, to quietly and without pointing it somehow make a man feel more of a man than most of the time he was willing to believe he was. Whatever it was, he was male, vital, supersensitive, nearly omnipotent, gentle and because of it able to handle everything beautifully to-day. So naturally he was lying magnificently, about himself, about life, about work, about anything which contained no depression or fear or despair, which to-day was everything.

Later he was to think back in a nervousness bordering on collapse about how if he had been different that day, everything else might have been different too and he might never really have known her.

Her play wasn't very much, and he told her this with a rather blunt honesty. Then it turned out she was rewriting it to trim down and Hemingwayise the dialogue and it was the rewrite he was reading. When he asked for the old original, it turned out to be better but it still wasn't very good, and he told her so. There were some fine ideas and two remarkable scenes in the first act (which, shamefully, was as far as he got, and he didn't even finish all of that). Mostly it was the style, and that extreme selfconsciousness that came through and to which amateurs were so prone. But he couldn't really think about it much, or bother. He was too caught up and enraptured by her, and by himself even being there with her. Later, he noticed that while they talked on she had quietly and unobtrusively gathered it up and put it away.

He had been caught up again breathless by her beauty, and swept by it as by some violent storm. The moment he stepped inside. She was wearing a tight fuzzy white sweater over those magnificent tits and tight brown slacks that moulded into the crack of her ass all the way up. It was almost impossible to believe in that incredible rounded, flat-waisted, high-hipped ass. Half the time he didn't even know what he was saying really, but it seemed to be working apparently. Finally they walked down to P. J. Clarke's for a hamburger and beer lunch, and that was where it happened.

Grant was good friends with all the waiters and guys who worked at Clarke's, and the owner Danny, because this was another of his drunken-bachelor hangouts and they all waved and called out to him. But that couldn't have had anything to do with it. Maybe it was the two or three other couples scattered around at tables in the dim back room, all self-contained and complete and therefore throwing you into a closer intimacy, a neater rapport than you would have had at home in the apartment or on the street. That can happen sometimes. Anyway, over the hamburgers and two tall steins (which Grant augmented with a large bowl of chili) they were suddenly simpatico, together, a couple sealed against other couples, and finding they liked it.

Grant talked until he almost missed his cocktail date, and had to leave her at Clarke's and take a cab. He talked about himself with that freshness which only comes when one is with a new girl. All those things he had wanted to say about himself to someone for so long, but was too embarrassed. He talked about his life, his way of life, his new play, his earlier plays, about work in general, about his contemporaries and their work. He even talked about his ambitions, and whenever he mentioned Carol Abernathy and Hunt in talking about his life or way of life, he always referred to her as his foster-mother.—" Who is this woman, Carol Abernathy?" Lucky said once, her eyes glinting mischievously. " Are you her lover?"—" Are you kidding?" he said. " She's old enough to be my mother, actually." But everything else was totally the truth. And Lucky's warm eyes followed every gesture of his excited commitment and got warmer. When he put his hand over hers on the table to emphasise some point and then left it, she did not remove hers. Two days before he could not have talked to any girl like that, not without coughing and turning red.

Later on he wondered about this sudden spurting spout of honesty and freshness from himself. It was as though it had been backed up there behind whatever dam, waiting for some key that would open the sluice gates and then it all just poured out. So he was not incapable of freshness and reality after all. He decided that it must be that it had to be seriously a new girl, not a one-night quickie, and it must be at a time when one is not attached or in love with somebody else. Otherwise it was a pose, a game on both sides, and wasn't really fresh which made it stale and profitless. He had had that, too. But then . . . What the hell? He still didn't understand. He wasn't planning on marrying this girl Lucky.

It was Lucky who made him realise the time by reminding him of his cocktail date. Outside Clarke's there was only one cab around, and she made him take it. She could get home all right, she said. Pulling away from her standing there with those beautiful wide shoulders, Grant almost couldn't stand it. If it had been anybody but his producer's secretary, who was a sweet kid, he would have stood her up and gone back. As it was, all he could do was stick his head out and waving his arm shout over and over, " I'll call to-morrow! I'll call to-morrow!", and look back at this girl standing there who was in love with him, or soon would be. It was on her face. What a body, and also what sweetness, she had.

The marvel of the afternoon stayed with him all the rest of that day and the night, enhancing everything. In some peculiar odd way, almost before it even began to get itself started, he had divined that this was going to be the Clark Gable-Carole Lombard love affair he had always dreamed about. For the next two or three weeks he would be in town, before going back to Indianapolis and then on to Jamaica, he was going to show her such a time as few girls got to live even in this town. And after that, well she would be here and every time he came back to town he would look her up and take right up where they had left off. Maybe he could come to town oftener than he had in the past few years?

Grant was so happy that even the thought of his " mistress " could not make him feel hollow for more than a moment.

And the peculiar thing about the evening was that the producer's secretary, after having stood him off several times before, to-night after her cocktails date dinner and show, sensing his preoccupation and disinterest, offered herself to him practically on a platter.

It seemed nothing could go wrong for him, now. Then back

at the hotel in the morning, scrubbing religiously from himself any sign of last night before even calling Lucky, the phone rang and without thinking he picked it up and answered it while still towelling himself. The result was that, while panic attacked him with sickness in the stomach and goose-bumps on his bare flesh and the sweat began to run from under his arms down his bare flanks, he had to listen to a sharp, angry, virago, ten-minute lecture from Carol Abernathy in Miami on the subject of New York broads.

Grant was tempted several times to just hang up on her, but he could not quite bring himself to make so seemingly final a gesture. Naturally, oozing guilt in his panic, he became angry back at her. But underneath all of this old stuff, way down deep, was a new steadfastness in him. Totally selfishly, whether it hurt anybody or not and no matter what it destroyed, he was going to have his fun.

" I know exactly what's going on, you bastard," Carol's voice said clearly, sounding because of the excellent connection as if she were in the next room. Grant was immensely glad that she was not. " You've found yourself some soft luscious pussycat who is telling you how marvellous you are, what a great mind you've got, what a great lover, what a great talent, what a great *man*. And you're lapping it up. A piece of flufftail who wouldn't have looked at you before *I* made you rich and famous. It's what you always do. Every time you go. You weak pimp."

Grant didn't answer. Ruefully he wished it had been even half true those other times, what she said. It hadn't always happened. It hadn't ever happened—yet.

" Hello?" she said. " Hello?

" Don't you dare hang up on me, you son of a bitch," she said. She waited. " Hunt is coming down soon."

How could all this shit she said sound so sane out in Indiana, and sound so ridiculous here in the New Weston?

" I said, Hunt's coming down soon," Carol said. Again she waited. " Then we're going on to Ganado Bay. I want you to get your ass down here *now*, right away."

" I'm not coming," Grant said thickly.

" What? What? What do you mean you're not coming?"

" I'm staying here. For—for an indefinite period. Couple of weeks."

" Then *I'm* going without you!" Carol Abernathy shouted

threateningly, and hung up leaving his ear ringing from the broken circuit.

Grant had sweat so much that he went in and took another shower, though he probably wouldn't have noticed it if he'd had clothes on. Only then, after his hollow stomach and the nerves in his knees had settled down, did he feel up to calling Lucky. Whence this feeling all the time of getting caught, this fear of getting caught? That same figure. It was always that same figure: black-clad, mantillaed, dark-hidden face, standing on the cathedral steps pointing. Carol Abernathy couldn't do anything to him. If she had thought he would call her right back, she was wrong.

The warm rich voice was like a kiss in his ear. And what little she said said everything, and Grant knew he had been right about her face yesterday.

"Where've you been?" Lucky said. "I thought maybe since you didn't call you were on your way over already."

"I am now," Grant said simply.

On the way over he stopped off in some bar and had two quick, delicious martinis, savouring the quiet late-morning slack time of the bar, savouring the time he could afford to waste now, before going on to what he had waited for so long.

It always seemed to Grant afterwards that their two naked bodies had met in the centre of the room with a smack like the clap of two huge and irate, omnipotent God-hands summoning a recalcitrant Universal Waiter. But he knew that couldn't be true. She had had clothes on he was sure, and he certainly had to be dressed, coming in from the outside as he was. So there must have been some conversation, if only to fill up the time required in getting clothes off. But he couldn't remember. The most enduring image he had of that day was of himself lying on the living-room couch and Lucky astraddle him and kneeling over his face, then dropping like some stricken flower with the champagne hair falling over her face almost to those beautiful breasts as she cried out, and collapsing on him. It turned out that Lucky, either because of the way she was built or maybe it was psychological she admitted shyly, could have a real orgasm in only one way. And Grant, whose first play about a sailor's love affair with a Honolulu whore was more auto-biographical than generally supposed and who had learned his lovemaking in one of the toughest schools in the world, was her boy.

This did not for her however injure her need of and liking for simple sexual intercourse, and so it was growing scratchy dark outside the windows when her room-mate Leslie knocked discreetly on the apartment door. She did this because Lucky had taken the precaution of hanging a DO NOT DISTURB sign from the Beverly Hills Hotel on the doorknob outside. The knock came while they were eating, shortly after she had finished making scrambled eggs for them, standing nude in the dusk-painted, nearly dark apartment before the little two-burner hotplate of the efficiency kitchentte.

"Wait a minute!" she called and grabbing her robe from the bedroom threw something at Grant. "Here, put this on, Ron." It was a man's dressing robe.

Looking at it, Grant felt distinctly peculiar.

"It belonged to my South American boy-friend," Lucky said as if reading his mind. "He was smaller than you, especially in the shoulders, but you can get into it." Then she went to the door.

"Oh ho!" Leslie said as she came in in her brusque short-stepping little walk. Then she stopped. "My God, this place smells like the Bronx zoo!"

"Go to hell," Lucky said. Then she turned slowly, that sun-bright, wall-penetrating (and now beatific) smile Grant had noticed before shining on her face, stretching herself.

"I take it," Leslie said, "that you two have been making it together with each other while I have been spending the day in the office breaking my brains." She threw off her coat and slumped in the one big chair. "Well, it's only what I might have expected after the way she talked last night. You be good to her, you hear?"

"I intend to be," Grant said. "Hello, Leslie."

"He's built like a Greek god," Lucky reported. "A regular Greek god!"

"Yes?" said Leslie.

"You'd never know it to look at him dressed. We've got to see about getting him some decent clothes."

"I am not currently up on men's shops," Leslie said.

"Instead of those hick Indiana suits with the padded shoulders that he wears."

"Listen, now wait a minute," Grant said. "I bought that

suit at Broad-street's on Fifth Avenue." He had finished his eggs and was enjoying himself more than he could remember in a very long time. Maybe ever.

"Then they saw you coming," Lucky said.

"I think I am forced to agree," Leslie said.

"Absolutely," said Lucky.

"You think so, Hunh?" he said.

Grant grinned at her. Even though Leslie had come in Grant had hated seeing her put on the robe, cover up. Her body without clothes was even more incredibly beautiful than it was with clothes on it. The heavy beautiful slightly drooping breasts, that long lean line from armpit to the widely swelling hips, the high rounded bottom, the width of shoulder, not an ounce of age anywhere but not scrawny model-thin, not a bit of fat except perhaps the little delicious belly which wasn't fat so much as the way she was constructed and which she called her "baby fat," above the triangular bush on the protuberant Venus mound. And it was the most flexible female body Grant had ever come in contact with. She could actually put both feet behind her head at the same time if she wanted to. Grant sighed in the shoulder-tight dressing robe. Who *was* this South American guy, anyway? Even now this late in the day and after so many times, he wasn't sated and didn't want to quit.

"I'll have to take you somewhere to-morrow," Lucky said. "For the clothes. Hmmm. Where?"

"Not to-morrow," Grant said, "I've got a business lunch with my producer. Anyway, what I want to know is what are we doing to-night?"

"Whatever you want," she said simply. "Have you got a date?" she asked Leslie.

Leslie shook her head from the deep chair. "This is one of my boyfriend's nights with his wife," she said ruefully.

"Then why don't I take the both of you out somewhere to dinner?" Grant said. "Like Twenty-one or Voisin?"

"No, I don't want to cramp your style, you two," Leslie said. "You go out by yourselves."

"It won't cramp my style," Grant said. "I'd love to have you."

But the dark little girl continued to shake her head. "I'll make myself something and read a book. I got lots to read." Only when Lucky who, apparently, had waited

till she was sure Grant meant it and wasn't just being polite,
asked her, did Leslie change her mind and decide to go.
And so that was the way it started. Many of the nights
when Leslie had no date with her own boy-friend, who
was a small-time theatre critic on a Trenton daily but lived
in Manhattan, she would dine out with them but almost always
she came home alone earlier because she had to be at the
office by nine. Amiably and happily for her friend she
moved herself out of one of the twin beds in the tiny
bedroom and out on to the studio couch in the living-room,
as Lucky had done for her on nights when her boy-friend
came. She wasn't doing it for space she said since Ron and
Lucky invariably slept all night together in one of the
single beds, but for decency. She asked only that they let
her get to sleep before they started their action so she
would not have to listen and lie awake and be lonely.
Usually she was home and asleep before they got there.
The only drawback was she had to come in in the morning
to get her clothes and if Lucky didn't want her goddam
Greek god to be viewed in all his glory " and I mean all "
she said, then she better damn well wake up enough to cover
him up. If this arrangement was satisfactory, she would
request only that once in a while when her own boy-friend
came they would let her have the bedroom and sleep at the
New Weston. She was not very happy with this boy-friend,
he came around so seldom, and was going to have to quit him
and get a new one: there was really no future or happiness in these married men who remained devoted to their
wives while screwing you.

As a matter of fact, they slept at the New Weston quite
a lot, because they liked ordering breakfast and having it in
bed together.

As it turned out, they did not go to either Twenty-One or
Voisin that first evening, they went to the Colony—where
both girls knew as many or more people in the celebrity-
pocked crowd of diners than Grant did. They had been
room-mates all four years in college at Cornell it turned up
in the talk, to which Leslie had come from her hometown of
Toledo and Lucky from Syracuse, and had lived together
in New York the last four of the seven years Lucky had
been there. Leslie worked for a very big Hollywood-New
York publicity agency as an executive, and in fact personally

handled most of their star accounts. Lucky wasn't working at the moment. She had some money of her own, she told Grant, with an arch glance, and she didn't have to.

But it wasn't always to restaurants of the calibre—and expense—of the Colony that they went, as the days passed (at least for Grant) in a labia-pink haze of happiness. The girls knew a lot of excellent fairly cheap little French, Russian, Italian or whatever restaurants—such as Le Berry in the West 50s where a lot of show kids hung out and the French sailors off the liners came for the food—and after the first couple of days they started saving him money rigorously, especially Leslie. But what they saved for him on restaurants they more than made up for by what they made him spend on clothes, or at least Lucky did. Men's clothes, not ladies' clothes.

She had mentioned it that first afternoon with Leslie in the apartment, but it was really at Hervey Miller the critic's house that it started, as in a way their affair itself had—and, as in another way something else started there too, something sombre and dark and unhappy.

On the day he had first run into Buddy Landsbaum at Hervey's, Hervey had invited him to a cocktail party ten days hence. Back then Grant had mumbled "Sure, sure," but secretly—in the miserable "Miseries" state he was in—he had had no intention of going. Ten days later, with the smell of Lucky in his nose and moustache permeating him all over in fact like some delicious female cloud, he wouldn't have missed Hervey's cocktail party and the chance to show Lucky off to his theatre friends for anything. As they climbed the steps of the narrow brownstone with Lucky hanging tight on his arm and leaning a breast on him out here where nobody could see it, it seemed simply absolutely unbeliev-able that only ten days ago he had not known her, had been lonely and miserable, had been looking for some girl, any girl. Hervey was glad to see them of course although he didn't know Lucky, but when he saw Grant's face he beamed suddenly and looked genuinely, really happy for him. Buddy, he told them shaking hands, had departed for the West Coast two days before.

Lucky had been nervous about coming. "I don't know any of these legit theatre people," she said when Grant told her they were going. "They're not my crowd. Except

Buddy. And I didn't even know him when he was theatre, only in his films. I'm going to be on close display, aren't I?"—"I know," Grant grinned lovingly. But if she was nervous or shy, it certainly didn't show in the way she acted, or in what she said. It was, once again, so typical of her Grant thought.

They were sitting at one end of the long narrow living-room. Grant was sitting in a deep easy chair with Lucky perched on the arm just to be near him, and was holding forth to Hervey and a couple of others, a novelist and a movie critic, about the general shittiness of current American theatre. He was feeling pretty smug and self-satisfied, with his play done and this exquisite girl hanging on to him and on to his every word, and he was being really witty. Then in the lull that followed a laugh over one of his funnies, Lucky turned to Hervey and said in a matter-of-fact voice: "I'm in love with him." She didn't try to say it either quietly or loudly. It ran through the room and through that literary gathering. It had in it the quality that when she loved, it mattered, it was rare, and it counted.

"Well," Hervey said delightedly in his gravelly drawl, "well. Are you. That isn't too really difficult to see, my dear." He probably hadn't had that much openness in his house in months, and he grinned at Grant. "In my own way, I'm in love with him too, I guess."

Grant was embarrassed but it was a very happy embarrassment. He simply sat and grinned. Curiously, everybody in that end of the room was grinning happily too.

"Well," Hervey said. "You feel pretty good, hunh, keed?" Grant took Lucky's hand, aware the other end of the room was watching now, too. "I sure as hell do."

"Look at him," Lucky said in her best cultivated university voice. "Would you believe that under that ugly lumpy Middlewestern suit exists the body of a Greek god?"

Hervey was even more delighted. Letting his eye run swiftly over the room to check for audience, he said, "I know. I went swimming with Ron once at the YMHA pool to get rid of our hangovers." He winked at Lucky. "And perhaps the brain of a genius?"

"I wouldn't be at all surprised," Lucky smiled. Hervey had been totally charmed. "Where shall I take him, Hervey?"

"Take him? For what?"

" For clothes."

Hervey beamed. " Ahhh! Well, how about Paul Stuart? I go there myself. Sometimes. For things."

" Perfect," she said. " Why didn't I think of Paul Stuart myself?" And Hervey was recharmed.

" Hey! Hey! Wait a minute! I'm not all that bad!" Grant put in. " You Ivy-Leaguers!"

" Well, Ron," Hervey pontificated, " one's girl can sometimes bring up things one's friends don't feel free to . . ."

" I'm conspired against!" Grant grinned.

" You have nothing to say about it," Lucky said. " We'll go to-morrow." She put her fingers lovingly on the back of his neck just above his collar. " Look at that tie."

Hervey was captivated. Just about the whole of his cocktail party was listening now, and he decided this might be the high spot of his evening.

Grant saw it coming and played the straight man for him. " What's wrong with my tie?"

Hervey paused like the theatre pro he was. " Well," he drawled, " I can't do anything about the suit, Lucia. Ron's not my size. But I can certainly do something about the tie!

" Come with me," he said, and led Grant through the laughing party and up the stairs.

" That's certainly some girl you've got yourself there," he said as he rummaged through his tie rack.

" Isn't she?"

" Where did you find her? I've never even seen her before."

" Never you mind!" He smiled. " Actually, Buddy introduced me to her. The other day. She's an old uh pal of his." He didn't actually stumble over the word pal, but he felt he hadn't inflected it properly. He added, " A friend."

" Here we are. A nice brown-maroon and dark-blue stripe. That really is a terrible tie, yours. She's absolutely right. I mean that she really is *quite* some girl, Ron."

" I know," Grant said knotting it. " I'm going to *keep* this tie. A remembrance," he said grinning into the mirror. Behind him Hervey was studying him kindly, shrewdly, thoughtfully, thumb and forefinger to his chin. " And I think you should," he said. " I've known you a long time, haven't I, Ron? Not as long as your Mrs. Abernathy out

there in Indianapolis, but almost as long." Then abruptly
he turned away. " All the world loves a lover."

When they marched, chests out, back down and through
the party, there was applause and more laughter, and it was
then that Lucky, smiling and laughing with pride so much
herself that she appeared to be actually blushing, said to
Hervey the thing that echoed hollowly through Grant's
inner corridors and was to cast a faint but noticeably sombre
pall over the next happy weeks with her.

" I think I've decided I'm going to marry him," she announced to Hervey and the others around them.

" I can assure you that you could do much, much worse,
dear Lucia," Hervey grinned at her. He clearly had been
completely won by her.

Grant said nothing, her statement made him almost
blush with pride himself, but faint warning bells rang in
his ears dimly through the labia-pink haze in which he
moved. It was one thing for Hervey to hint vaguely
upstairs about Carol Abernathy, and quite another for Lucky
who knew nothing at all about any of it, to say what she
had just said. His old instinct to protect, so ingrained by
now that it amounted to a signal reaction almost, had
trapped him into that " foster-mother " routine so that now
his relationship with Lucky wasn't on his part an honest
one, and it wasn't fair to her. And as the days together
passed and as he fell more and more under her spell and more
and more in love with her, this initial dishonesty lent a
poignancy to their affair for him that at times became almost
unbearable. It also, curiously, gave him a vital tough
hard-to-catch male quality that enhanced their affair for
Lucky as well as for himself. Maybe if he'd been easier
to catch, she wouldn't have wanted him so much?

The problem was, of course, that he was going to have
to leave her. Sometime or other. This made the statues and
bare trees and open-air opera in the Park where they walked
on good days, the Zoo and the seals and the Cafeteria, all
much more lovers'-poignant, bittersweet and moving than
if they knew they were going to stay together and had set
up housekeeping somewhere. The same held true for the
joints they frequented. Like P. J. Clarke's, where they'd gone
that first afternoon, and now held a vested interest in.
Grant knew that certain people (many good friends of his

had this trait) actually required this sweet-sad, happy-tragic quality in a love affair for it to be interesting and fulfilling. And he found himself enjoying it too sometimes, as Lucky did obviously, sometimes. But at other times it was much too painful to be pleasant. And Grant had no wife to go back to, unless you wanted to count Carol Abernathy and Grant didn't.

That evening after Hervey's party which had established an even newer closeness between them, they had dinner at Billy Reed's Little Club in East 55th, a former hangout of Lucky's with some other boyfriend where she knew every-one and proudly showed Grant off, then he took her to a late party of literary and theatre folk on Central Park West in the Seventies. The cab ride through the cold Park framed with glittering buildings and signs, the (for them) lovers'-guide of the Mutual of New York thermometer, deepened the new closeness between them even more, and Grant caught the cab driver grinning at them in the mirror. All the world did indeed love a lover, it seemed, and this was a New York Grant had never known. In the apartment of the party high up on the West Side the downtown buildings were even more beautiful, and they stood at the window look-ing at it and sneaking a little hand-holding. Out there in the dark Park, Puerto Rican and Harlem kids might be right now beating some adult to death with bicycle chains, and Grant couldn't have cared less. Everyone to his own kind of fun. At home, half drunk and with a curiously communicated sorrow (curiously because neither of them mentioned it or gave any sign of it) they made love in one style or another with a strange hunger all night and into the dawn and the morning until Leslie got up at 7.30 and knocked to get in and get her clothes and then they had coffee with her.

Once she had got started with it, Lucky did not give up on the marriage thing she had started at Hervey Miller the critic's house. Yet she was never pushy with it, and Grant never felt cramped. Mostly it came in the form of jokes. Like: "You know, you have to marry me, Ron," she said one time. "I'm twenty-seven already, and you're about my last chance. And anyway, you're the last of the un-married writers except for the fags, and I couldn't marry anybody but a writer. Also, I'm in love with you." There was about her in this the same peculiar openness, frankness that he had noted in her in other things. There was also about her in this an odd and terrible sadness, as if she couldn't believe that it was not all too good to be true. And that sadness hurt Grant almost more than he could afford. She wasn't angry or demanding. She seemed totally helpless, totally at his mercy, and furthermore unashamed, uncaring about showing it.

He had told her about his plans to go to Kingston to learn diving (She had grinned, and said, " You don't need to learn diving, darling!") and it turned out that she knew Kingston very well, had lots of friends there, had stayed there often. Her South American boy-friend had used to stash her there for weeks at a time while he returned to his South American country to help make a revolution, " Oh, take me with you! I won't be any trouble!" she cried excitely. " I'll introduce you to everybody! I know wonderful places! I know Kingston like——" They were to have been married in two months when he went back the last time and got shot. " I can't take you with me," Grant said, almost automatically. Then he went on to explain how he had conceived this as a project to be done totally alone, how it had to be done alone, and studied, because he thought it might bring back a reality to his writing which he was afraid it was beginning to lose, that it would give him new material—new *thinking* material—for his work. He did not explain how it had also been half-way conceived as a means of getting totally away from Carol Abernathy for a while, or how Carol Abernathy had frustrated this by inviting herself along.

" Oh, you really must take me along!" Lucky said sadly and with the eagerness of a little girl. " I know it so well! I'd love to go back! I know the greatest hotel, the owner's a wonderful man, if it's me with you he'll give us a discount! I know so many places and things there!"

" I can't," Grant said. " I simply can't. I'd like to." Again she did not press. But she brought it up from time to time hopefully. And when she conceived the idea to marry him at Hervey's party, she tacked that on to it: they could be married in Kingston, at the hotel, her friend René Halder the hotel owner would officiate, he would love it. Grant could only smile and shake his head, and feel terrible.

She did take him to Paul Stuart. It was not the day after Hervey's party, but almost a week after. After a lazy morning in bed, after making love lazily twice with the bright winter sun streaming in coldly through the light curtains in the warm little room, while she squatted in the bathtub washing herself out for the second time and Grant stood leaning in the doorway watching her fondly, Lucky announced that to-day was going to be Paul Stuart day. So he might as well prepare himself, she grinned, and shook her ass like a wet dog and straightened up for a towel. Ron Grant playwright was going to buy clothes. They would have lunch at some nice mid-town restaurant and he could prepare himself with two or three but no more martinis and so would she, and then they would go to Paul Stuart's. No fucking around. Docilely Grant, grinning sheepishly, allowed himself to be led, and for it received what he could call, after thirty-six years of being alive, the most delicious afternoon of his life.

Lucky chose everything. She wanted nothing for herself. Indeed, there was almost nothing for ladies in the shop except a few scarves. The light of the love on her face for him was so visibly apparent that the clerks in the store fell in with the game at once, delightedly, and looked at Grant with envy. Even the customers who came in were delighted, and hung around to watch. When they took Grant into the little fitting room, Lucky went too. To fit Grant with a ready-made suit whose coat was big enough for his shoulders required that all the pants be altered and cut down. Lucky instructed them in this. And when the clerk was out of the little room, she was all over Grant laughing, kissing him and feeling him up in his shorts so that he had to be extremely cautious so the clerk would not see the more than half hard-on he was sporting. Laughing still more, she refused to leave him alone. The delighted clerk handed Grant a handkerchief for the lipstick on his face the second time he came back. " Compliments of the house, Madam," he said to Lucky. It was a scene from a Clark Gable-Carole Lombard movie of a happier time if there ever was one in life, and everybody was participating.

In the end they went out with two suits, a charcoal and a subdued brown stripe, a newly styled but still classic tuxedo, sundry knee-length black socks to replace Grant's

Argyles, narrow Ivy League ties, button-down shirts, handkerchiefs. Everything but underwear, in fact. Lucky extracted a promise that the altered suit pants would be delivered next day, and they took a taxi to the New Weston, an elevator to the suite, and fell laughing and loving on the bed—that big soft ugly bed that didn't seem so ugly to Grant any more.

The truth was he couldn't really believe that she was for real. If she was, why not take her to Kingston? Why not marry her in the hotel, go straight out to Indianapolis, straighten up affairs, come back here and pick her up. Better yet, why go to Indianapolis? He didn't have to. Take her from here and get on a plane and go straight to Kingston without even stopping in Ganado Bay. The truth was he was scared. First he was scared of the scene—or scenes—he would have to have with Carol Abernathy. Second he was just scared in general. It would mean changing, reorienting his whole life and his plans for his life. Yet he had always intended some day to marry. It was just that it was always off there in the future somewhere, vague and formless, not sitting here in his lap with its teeth in his throat. And yet—what the hell? What could Carol Abernathy do to him really? Point to the church?

It was a peculiar situation. Just because he was *not* married. Luck. Because in one way he was as free as a bird. He *wasn't* married, he *didn't* have to divorce anybody, or pay alimony, or dispose of any mutually held property. On the other hand there were fourteen years of a way of life, a manner of living (increasingly insupportable, it was true) behind him that it was difficult to uproot and wrench out of him. He was worried about money, for another thing. He had been spending much more this trip to New York than he had meant or intended to, more than he could really afford. And the way he was living with no investments or capital laid by, if each new play wasn't a solid hit—he was *broke*.

And what if this girl he was falling in love with *was* too good to be true? What if, like all the other girls he had fallen in love or nearly fallen in love with, Lucky turned out to have a set of complexes or a gross egomania she couldn't control? Or a megalomania like Carol Abernathy?

That evening after the Paul Stuart shopping trip they

didn't go out. They had drinks sent up, had dinner sent up, had coffee sent up, watched the Late Show and the Late Late Show, and made love over and over in that same peculiar hungry way they had the night of Hervey Miller's cocktail party. Grant's more or less definite date of departure was only three days off now, and they talked about this. " You talk about your search for reality in diving," Lucky said once. " Reality is me. Marrying me, taking our chances with living. Having kids maybe. Who might be morons. Mongoloids. Or geniuses. That's reality." Grant didn't answer.—" Maybe," he said after a while. " I know I love you." She was sitting nude on the bed with those supple legs clasped up against her chest, her cheek resting on her knee, looking at him. " But I don't believe in love," Grant said.—" Neither do I. I don't believe in love either," Lucky said. " It's funny, isn't it?" She did not move.

" I only know I have to be by myself, alone for a while," he lied, or half-lied. " I have to think a lot of things out." She still did not move, and her great blue eyes looked and looked at him solemnly. " Oh, I love you so," she said in a small voice like a little girl's. " I don't know what'll happen to me when you leave me." Two tears ran silently down her face. She continued to look at him. Then suddenly she threw back her head, sniffled, wiped her eyes and laughed a choked-up, lovely laugh.—" I'll be back in six weeks," Grant said painfully. Lucky had unclasped her knees and was sitting crosslegged.—" Ahh. But it won't be the same," she said. " Don't you see?" For answer, Grant took her ankles and gently pulled her to him until her legs fell over the bed edge. Then he knelt and kissed his way up both of them and buried his face in that delicious place where he sometimes would like, in such painful moods as this, or so he often told himself, to return completely. Above him, he heard her sigh.

He made no decisions. He postponed his departure date yet another week, rented a car and took her up to Frank Aldane's in Connecticut for a week-end.

FOUR

It would be a nice week-end, he told her. Secretly, he wanted to know what Frank and Marie thought of her. At the same time he knew beforehand, even to the phraseology his friends would use, exactly what they would say, and that it would be extremely cautionary. But he needed other opinions, any opinions. At the same time he was more crazily in love with her than ever, could hardly stand the thought of going away from her, and wanted nothing more than that his life continue day by day forever as it was going now. "I hate country week-ends," Lucky said. "I hate the country." But she knew she was being put up for inspection, and prepared herself accordingly without complaints.

Grant had already arranged one inspection for her. The day before Paul Stuart's had decided him to stay on another week he had arranged for her to meet his producers, agent and director for cocktails. From which meeting she had emerged with more than flying colours, with flying everything.

They met at Rattazzi's on 48th Street, a hangout of his producers because it was right across the street from their midtown offices, which were a little far uptown for Broadway producers but which for that very reason gave them a certain air they felt. Lucky had never been to Rattazzi's, though she often went to Michael's Pub a few doors away. Because he had a final conference with them that afternoon, he told her to meet them there at 5.30.

Paul Gibson and George Stein, Inc., had produced all three of Grant's other plays and had been with him as a gang, a rather bawdy gang, from the start. Big George Stein, massive, sorrowful, all the world's enduring and overpowering ills and sorrows stamped on his great kindly moonface like road directions on a map, was a perfect matching partner for the smaller, hard-eyed nervous bundle of bones and flesh which went by the name of Paul Gibson. It was hard to believe looking at the two of them that big

George was the tough hard mean-dealing businessman, and Gibson the sensitive, tasteful artist of the combination who could weep over some of Grant's scenes. They had plenty of other successes in the string, mostly in musicals, but perhaps for that very reason, plus the fact that Grant was their most successful legitimate theatre writer, he was a special favourite.

The director, a slightly older man named Don Celt, was the newest member of the group, having directed only one of Grant's plays before, the second, and had been suggested by Grant's agent Durrell Wood after they all read the first act sent in from Indianapolis. It was Gibson and Stein who had first suggested that Grant hire Wood, after the huge success of *The Song of Israphael*, the first play about the sailor and the whore. Wood was an old friend of theirs, and a perpetual enemy, and though they had chosen him now fought against them for Grant with a dedicated fury.

All in all they were a congenial, hairy, bawdy talking bunch, and Grant had been working hard with them on the script of the play all these weeks, in addition to his late nights and long mornings with Lucky. Usually they met for lunch to discuss and worked after, or met after lunch and worked through the afternoon till closing. Mostly the work consisted of trying to get Grant to change words or scenes for reasons of censorship or " business " (for business read " in good taste "), and also sometimes—this was rare—because of æsthetic or purely technical disagreements. If they were meeting for lunch, he would leave Lucky at 12.30 at the apartment, and then meet her for drinks somewhere as soon as he left them. It was the only time he was away from her. But now all that work was over, at least until such time as they began rehearsals, and he was only staying on now because of her.

He had told them all about her of course. In his happiness and relief he couldn't have resisted. And in fact Gibson and Stein had noticed the change before he told them, because all their secretaries began arriving on time and the office ran smoothly. Old friends now over the years they knew what to expect from Grant, and one unavoidable penalty of a Grant stay in New York was turmoil, inefficiency and late arrivals for work among the secretarial force. At least until Grant settled on to one girl. George Stein always accused Grant of suffering from satyriasis.

So it was pretty much an established pattern when Grant told them about Lucky. They expected it. George, his big moonface long-suffering of human beings as the moon's face itself, rolled his eyes over at his partner and made a slow-motion shrug. Both men had met Mrs. Carol Abernathy (taking the train out to Indianapolis expressly for that purpose), both had felt the lash of her tongue (and in the earlier days the power of her personality), both had kept their mouths totally shut about what they thought of Grant's relationship to her. They had also been introduced to quite a number of Grant's New York girls. They were totally unprepared for the entrancing vision of loveliness that came floating up to them in Rattazzi's, downed two hefty martinis, kidded them, spoke seriously and sympathetically to them about their boy Grant, and floated away again with a hammer struck Grant tightly in arm.

Of the four of them only Don Celt the director had ever even heard of her before. "Oh, sure," he said, in the office's bar-gameroom, when told they were meeting her for drinks. "I knew her out on the Coast, three or four years ago. Well, didn't really know her, met her a couple of times. Crazy chick. She's the one tried to run down Buddy Landsbaum with his own car one night. Damn near did. Would of killed him." Some look in Grant's eye seemed to warn him, and he seemed to sort of turn and run the ball along the sideline while at the same time trying not to step one of his feet out of bounds. "Uh, one of those crazy nights. Everybody drunk as hell. I don't know what the trouble—Yeah, I'd like to meet her," he said. "Again."

None of them knew what it was that she did to them. Least of all did Grant. It was as though she used some sort of ESP device, some sort of personal telepathy, which shut off and dazzled their eyes to everything but herself. For instance nobody knew what happened to her coat, or whether she even had one, or what colour her dress was. She came in, took over, dominated them, left them staring vaguely at each other, and took Grant away with her.

"That's some girl you got there, Ron," big George said with his sorrowful smile when Grant finally saw them again.

"She's a real beauty. Makes me wish I was thirty years younger."

"If you were thirty years younger, you'd be twelve," Grant said.

"Well, then twenty," George said.

"She's got class. Some kind of class," Paul Gibson said with a puzzled look, "that you don't see on a lot of girls in this town."

"Style," said the fastidious Durrell Wood, "is what you mean. Style."

Don Celt, still trying to move the ball forward along the sidelines without stepping out of bounds, frowned weightily. "She doesn't look at all like I remember her. She looks mellower now. That's it. Mellower."

Grant grinned at him viciously. "That because she's met me."

Anyway, they all thought Grant had done himself proud this time, and at the same time some curious delicate instinct made them refrain from kidding him about a new girl as they might be expected to do, as indeed they had done lots of other times in the past. It was about the most perfect reaction Grant could have asked for.

Lucia (he had taken to calling her Lucia a lot now, like Hervey Miller, as though Lucky was too crass and too New Yorkese a nickname now for the way he felt about her) Lucia had told him about the dress, her dress, right away after, as they walked away from Rattazzi's through the mucky sidewalks and slushy streets down 48th toward Park. "You were wonderful!" he said.

She laughed, with a sort of wild flashing glare. "Well, not really," she said modestly. "But I did have a serious decision to make. Knowing the way all those fink bastards——"

"Hey, wait a minute! They're not fink bastards!"

"(Of course not,)" she said parenthetically, "(don't you think I know that?)—Knowing the way all those fink bastards who step out in town while their wives stay out in Westchester County think about New York single girls. I decided I'd better dress for them. The trouble was, I only have two prim dresses. And one of them is sleeveless: Bare Armpits! But the other one is a little old and a little faded under the arms. Well, I decided to wear the one with sleeves and keep my arms down. And after I saw that gang, I knew I was right."

Grant had listened, at first delighted by the story, and then horrified at the direction in which it was leading her. " Oh, no! There wasn't anything like that in it," he growled. "They're not like that! They know all about you, how I feel about you, I've been bragging you up to them for weeks."

" Even so it's a hell of a thing to make a girl do and put her through."

" But that wasn't it, that wasn't it! I swear it wasn't!"

" Anyway, I did it for you."

" No! Please! Anyway, you were so magnificent I don't think any of them even saw your dress."

"What does that matter? It helped me get my con started. All of them sitting there in a row, waiting to inspect me. I bet I've fucked fifty men like them. Before I learned better. And every one of them scared to death."

Grant found there was very little to say to this.

" At least you're not scared, Ron."

" No," he said, hoping it was true. " I'm not scared."

" Their wives, their kids, their homes in the country. Inspecting me!"

" No, no! It wasn't anything like that. It wasn't an inspection. They're my friends! I work with them! I wanted you to meet them."

They had reached Park, and the wind came down it, biting in their faces. And now it was Lucky's turn not to say anything. Grant had never seen her in such a state. When she did speak her voice had an almost lowing quality, deep, reverberant, about it. " Oh, Ron. I love you so. You and your secret little inspection. Take me home. Take me home quick. Take me home quick and make love to me. Make love to me my way."

Grant thought later that he must have seemed almost to leap up off the ground. He moved that fast. But as usual whenever anyone really wanted one, there were no taxis immediately available. He came back to her and she took his arm. There was no anger in her now. Actually there had been no anger in her all along, it was something else. She hugged on to him and let him shelter her with his body from the wind. Finally, on the other side of Park, they found an empty cab coming down the ramp under the clock tower. In the cab they started necking hungrily, Grant not caring how much lipstick he got on him, with all the sweet hotness that belongs to youth and that before meeting her Grant had not felt for a long time, and Lucky grabbed his excited crotch through his trousers with one hand. But when they broke apart, she made him take her handkerchief for his face.

"Won't Leslie be home?" he asked, wiping.

"No, she's got a cocktail date with a new boy-friend. What she hopes will be a new boy-friend!"

Grant didn't answer, and the cab moved along past the snow-covered street islands. It had come into his mind while kissing her to tell her about Don Celt, his strange sidelines-running look when her name was mentioned, and his story about her trying to run Buddy Landsbaum down with his own car. Don had looked so peculiar. Could Celt have been one of her nameless 400 men too, like Buddy? Grant ground his teeth with a strange peculiar hate-filled anguish he had never felt before. He decided it was better not to say anything, not just now. And why had it come into his mind just when he was kissing her?

"You're such a stupid bastard really," she suddenly said lovingly. "You're so lucky to have——" She stopped.

"To have what?"

"To have me in love with you!" she said defiantly. "That's what!"

"I know it," Grant said humbly. Could she have divined his thought about Celt and Buddy? It was weird.

And he did know he was lucky. Nevertheless this did not save him from taking a fearful tongue-lashing from Leslie when she finally got home from her cocktail date. They were sitting together, already dressed again and having a drink together and warm and safe again, when she stamped in on her tiny feet in her tiny quick-stepping walk, and launched into him without preamble.

"Of all the goddam lousy chickenshit things to do! Of all the—That is the most goddam fucking insulting thing I have ever heard of. How *dare* you? Do you know who you are messing around with here? You are not playing around with some part-time call girl chorus girl from the Copa! You are having a love affair with *Lucia Videndi*, Ron Grant!

Making her come out and *display* herself and be inspected by your goddamned producers, to see whether they think you ought to go out with her or not! I don't care whether you're a big important playwright or not!"

There was much more in this vein before Lucky finally got her shushed up and stopped, with Grant trying to protest his innocence all the time. Then she went over and flung herself down in the one big chair and began to cry into a tiny handkerchief about the size of a postage stamp. "Goddam fucking men: Not one pair of balls down the whole of Madison Avenue. All of you. Men make me sick. Why oh why we even got to need you and have to have you—I just wish there was some other way for a girl to be happy."

"What happened with your date?" Lucky said.

"Nothing," Leslie said and shrugged. "Oh, you know. The same old crap. The same usual warm-hearted bullshit routine. I under*stand* him." She looked up at Lucky. "He's married too you know of course. I don't see why if they are all so goddam unhappily married so much all of them all the time, why did they ever get married in the first place." She wiped her eyes and nose—and became totally despondent. "I don't know," she said sullenly. "It isn't worth it."

"Ron's leaving, Thursday," Lucky said lightly. "That's four days from now."

"Oh, you poor darling!" Leslie cried, her eyes losing their dullness.

Lucky threw her head back, tossing her champagne hair, and laughed gaily though it clearly cost her quite an effort. She looked like she might cry but she didn't. "Four days is four days. Can be a long time."

Grant was hurting more at the moment than he was willing to invest. "Listen, you two deadheads," he growled at them, more viciously energetic than he meant, and both turned to stare. He softened his tone. "What's going on here, anyway? What kind of a morgue is this? Is this any way to spend my last four days in town? Come on, let's all go out and do something."

"You're absolutely right," Lucky said.

Leslie's eyes fired up again with indignant outrage when

she looked at Grant. "You really ought to take her with you! She knows everybody in Kingston!"

"I can't," he said. "I've explained it all before. I just simply can't." Stuart had made him decide to stay over another week, and coupled to the meeting with his producers, and then the week-end at the Aldanes' all three were enough to make him change his plans about New York.

He had intended, after his diving junket to Jamaica, to go straight back home to Indianapolis and start in work on another play (though he had no idea yet what subject it would be about), and try to get as deep into it as he could before he was needed for rehearsals on this one, on *I'll Never Leave Her*. (My God, he thought with despair, did you ever really call it that? Yes, you did!) Now though, he was coming straight back from Jamaica to Manhattan, to Lucky. Maybe he would take a small apartment, a cheap one, somewhere and try to get started on the new play here.

He told all this to Lucky, rather proudly, on Monday on their way back to the city from the Aldanes'. It was once again four days to departure time.

"All right," Lucky said calmly, without any great enthusiasm, "we'll see. It's all right. We'll just have to wait and see. How do I know what will happen in the next six weeks to change you? How do you know what will happen to change me?"

He was at the wheel. "You don't mean like—you would fall in love with somebody else? Do you?" Having to watch the road carefully, he did not look at her.

"I don't know," she said, with a sort of tired patience. "How do I know?"

"Well, if it is, it is," Grant said, vaguely but also stiffly, and braked slightly before swinging out into the second lane to pass a slower car.

"That's what I said," Lucky said calmly.

"Nobody's going to bulldoze me into anything," he said.

"Nobody's trying to," Lucky said airily, and went on looking out the window. She had, at the Aldanes', once again been her own unbelievably winning, too-good-to-be-true self.

It had been a lovely ride up there in the Hertz car, along the curving parkways, the fields all snowy but the roads clear and good, not much traffic. Frank had a nice old colonial house under big trees on the side of a hill, a guest-house, five acres of park-like woods they could walk through in the snow. They did not, however, do much walking. But they did do a lot of drinking. Lucky didn't like the country outdoors, and Grant discovered he was not equipped with the proper shoes and clothes for snow-walking. On the other hand, they both were properly dressed and equipped for whatever drinking might be done, and Frank Aldane was a big drinker.

Frank Aldane was a big drinker, but he took very good care of his health while doing it—as he did with everything. This was largely because he was a consummate hypochondriac. Six months ago he had stopped smoking because of the cancer scare. For two months he had been unable to write at all, but after that he had come out of it into the clear, clean-lunged and cured, and now buttonholed everybody that he could get to listen about how they must stop smoking. His intensity when making these speeches made his genuine concern for everybody that much more sweet, endearing. He wouldn't even smoke a pipe now, he said.

Among all of his contemporaries Frank Aldane was the one Grant valued most, both as a talent and as a thinker, the one he felt most drawn to. Although Frank was a novelist and Grant a playwright, they seemed to see more nearly eye to eye concerning the drift of the post-war world, and what was happening to America in it. They seemed to be trying to say and get noticed, each in his field, pretty much the same thing about this world—although in private they admitted to each other that it didn't matter much even if they did, would not make much difference.

Both men were deeply despairing-type personalities anyway but neither had sufficient egomania to try, like some in their generation, in every generation, to corner the market on despair all for himself alone. So they could talk about all this. Both believed that, given the expectable increase in government's control of the social body's functions and its mental attitudes, in order for it to perform efficiently in an ever increasingly complex industrial society, men of their type would be squeezed out of existence in a very short time, maybe fifty years, and they loved to discuss all this and elaborate on it gloomily when in their cups, which is what they did most of that week-end. Neither was in favour of this sort of human development. But neither had any answer to the problem since, as one of them was almost perpetually pointing out to the other, it was manifestly impossible to return to a more primitively industrial society and the taking over of men's minds was advancing at a vastly accelerated rate (compared to Rome, say, or the Middle Ages) because of both modern techniques in persuasion and advanced mass methods of what fools called " communication."

" Yes. Not only all that, we're in the Age of the Believer, Decameron," Frank hiccupped from in front of the great fireplace late on the night of their arrival (he adored calling Grant by his full first name, because Grant hated it). " The *real* Age of the Believer. Believers have always been dangerous. The most dangerous. But the various Inquisitions of the past have never had our means of communication, or the mechanical ability to employ our full saturation methods. *Or* the sheer bureaucratic political power of a modern great nation to enforce attention."

" I know it," Grant gloomed over his glass. " I know all that. In fact it was me who first pointed it out to you so succinctly. And there's no way out."

" *Or!*" Frank continued, finger in air, " the incredibly efficient means of industrialised destruction which the Believer can employ to destroy a segment of a society. I need not point out to *you* what happened with Hitler and the Jews."

" What happened with Hitler and the Jews has been grossly misunderstood by modern thinkers," Grant said.

" Exactly!"

" And not only *that*! It was not even a military function. It was a *civil* function! And there's no way out," Grant said again, hugging his glass, gloomily.

Lucky was with Frank's wife Marie in the kitchen preparing them all a 3 a.m. snack to kill hangovers.

" Don't be too sure!" Frank said, and laid a sly drunken finger alongside his rather shapeless nose there in front of his beautiful great roaring fire. " I think there is, finally, something that can be done."

" Then tell me."

" Not yet, not yet. I think I have to prepare you a little first. You're peculiar. But I'll tell you before you leave this place. That's a promise."

" Aw, fuck, come on. If you knew how depressed I get thinking about all this. I get so depressed I—That's the main reason I'm going away. Off on this diving business. Just to——"

" I don't see that that'll do you no good," Frank said with the air of a sage. " It don't make sense."

" I didn't say it did. I said——"

" Come and get it, or we'll eat it all ourselves," Lucky called to them softly so as not to wake the four Aldane children.

" On the other hand," Grant said, getting up to follow her, " this skin-diving stuff and underwater archæology and all that is the last frontier left to an individual to do individual work by himself and all on his own as an individual."

" But what the hell good does that do the world you and I're talkin' about?" Frank said following him. " And anyway!" he roared gleefully from behind Grant. " I think that you'll find that to really contribute anything to anything even skindiving will have to become—*bureaucratised, organised!*"

" Maybe not," Grant said over his shoulder mysteriously—with much more mystery than he actually felt. What he actually felt was depressed, rock bottom depressed.

" Aw fuck, come on! Look at fucking Cousteau," Aldane hollered triumphantly, following through the door. " He's made the biggest contribution made so far—with his *Organisation!*"

" The hell with Cousteau," Grant said glumly.

" Not so loud, Professor," Marie Aldane said to her husband from the kitchen table, and winked at Lucky.

" I saw that," Frank said.

" So did I," Grant said. He stopped before the table. " Look at my girl," he said spreading his arms, more to cheer himself up than anything else. " Ain't she something."

" She sure is," Aldane said with a lecher's appreciation.

" I think so too," Marie grinned, " and I'm a girl."

Lucky looked up at them and smiled, especially at Grant, and calmly went on eating. She was three-fourths drunk like the rest of them.

But it was all true. She had already seduced them both. By whatever alchemy or internal magic it was that she employed Lucky had once again, as she had done with the producers, completely altered her entire personality.

It was as if she had reached down inside herself with both hands and moulding her spirit as if it were pie dough, changed herself into some one else, a someone she knew with a shrewd psychology both the Aldanes would adore.

When they arrived just before dark and Marie showed them their room to which Grant carried the suitcase for her, she first put away all of Grant's things neatly, then put away her own, changed to a sweater and an old pair of slacks and came downstairs in old ballet slippers with her champagne hair tied back in a stringy ribbon, looking as if she loved and had lived in the country all her life.

It was an entrance calculated to sew the literary Aldanes up in a sack and deliver them at her feet from the very beginning, which was just what it did. But it wasn't only physical. She had made herself a country girl, like Marie. Leaving the men at the fire (a thing Grant had never seen her do anywhere before at any party or anywhere else: leave the men), she went out to the kitchen and began to help Marie and the coloured maid who were feeding the children their supper, all the time complaining laughingly how she was not a country girl, she was a city girl, she hated the country, all those trees!, she could not cook, and didn't want to learn, she detested washing dishes well, she would never do housework, she was a rare and delicate flower, and would be treated as such, if you hump them well that's enough, until she had both women laughing out loud.

At the same time she did as much work as either of them, tied on an apron, petted the children, but everything she told them was the truth and what was more they knew it was the truth.

That night was Friday. The next night being Saturday, they had a large bunch of people in and a big buffet for them, critics, newspaper writers, painters, an art critic, a sculptor, Grant's one-night-stand lady novelist whose recent book had lately suddenly shown signs of becoming a towering best-seller, all people who lived in the area. Now dressed to the teeth with full make-up and a simple sheath dress, and those magnificent tits and that high, back-switching ass below the champagne hair, Lucky had every man in the house breathing hotly through his nose and with one hand in his pocket to finger himself tentatively through the cloth. The art critic especially, an ageing and humorous egotist with a ragged white moustache and lecherous goatee, could not stay away from her and followed her wherever she went about the two large rooms filled with people. Even so, she made a friend out of his wife by more of her talk about the horrors of living in the country, and by calling him laughingly to his face a dirty old goat so charmingly that he was flattered and delighted. Grant had only to stand and beam, and the next day, Sunday, Marie received five phone calls about Ron Grant's marvellous new girl.

Saturday night after most of the people had departed, when Grant went out to the kitchen to refill his scotch glass and encountered Marie Aldane sitting all by herself over a large drink just giggling, he was ordered to sit down and was then given a ten-minute lecture on the reasons why he should immediately and forthwith marry Lucky Videndi, for good and all, without looking back, before some gentleman smarter than himself swept her, so to speak, out from under him. Thus he had the answer of one of the Aldanes. He never did find out why she was giggling.

Later on, when the two girls had given up and gone on to bed and the two drunk writers sat together before the fire, Frank was more circumspect. It was true that she had all the personal—*and* personable—qualities necessary. My God: an MA in political science! And a *wit* that couldn't be learned in *any* school. He wouldn't even bother wasting time going into her *physical* beauty and charm. But marriage was, or should be, for a long time. She had been on her own—*really* on her own, not by her family—around New York quite a long time; seven years was it? and that might indicate a kind of overly wild quality in her. And any girl around town that long had a tendency to get a little rumpled and shopworn which often made for neuroses later in her. Not so far as Grant was concerned, but as far as she was concerned inside herself. And after all, how long had he known her? only three weeks? She wasn't really a very literary type girl. And Grant had always been more a literary type playwright, rather than the Broadway type playwright. Anyway, after all, the clincher was that Grant himself was not taking her down to Jamaica with him like she wanted, but was going alone. Incidentally,

D

if Grant wanted to give him her telephone number he could look after her and sort of keep an eye on her while Grant was gone since he was going to be in the city quite a lot the next couple of months.

"Haw! None of that shit, you bastard!" Grant said. "Don't forget I'm comin' back in six weeks. You're on your honour."

Aldane sighed sadly. "Ahh. These damned honours of ours that we have." He stood up. "Well, we have a choice. We can go to bed, or we can play the Civil War records." For a moment he wavered slightly like the needle of some gauge, then came to rest fully perpendicular.

"No, not to-night," Grant said. "The way I feel, if I heard *The Yellow Rose of Texas* right now, I'd break down and cry again, like I did the last time."

"Then I suggest a nightcap, Decameron," Frank said heading for the kitchen. "What about her family?"

Decameron, Decameron! Grant thought with a sudden blind drunken rage. Boccaccio, Boccaccio! Once going to summer camp he gave himself the name Michael Jeremy Grant on the Application Form, and was very nearly disallowed for the season by the camp director until he agreed to fill out a new form. Very few people knew his real first name. And although *Time* magazine had once sent a researcher out to look it up amongst the birth certificates in the Indianapolis courthouse in order to expose it in their theatre section, very few readers remembered it. To the world and to readers of *Life* he was still Ron Grant. He had even legalised it. But not to yourself, not to yourself! As a very little boy it was Cam or Cammy. He still hated the superciliousness of grown-ups using a -y or -ie diminutive for youngsters. When he was ten or eleven for a year or two he was called Camera by his witty classmates. In high school where he just barely played football it was Deke which of course eventually, inevitably became Deacon and spoiled high school for him. At college he beat them to it and gave himself the nickname Ron, which seemed to work well with the girls—at least until he made the mistake of telling each new love his real first name, whereupon they would break into golden, joyous, sexless college girl peals of laughter. Apparently his father (whom he never knew well) had been one of those secret iconoclastic

Middlewestern scholars who believed in and loathed the general frigidity of the local females like Grant's mother (whom he never knew well either). But to name a defenceless kid Decameron was a low blow whatever the reason. Certainly it had contributed to his terrible and lifelong inferiority complex. Was it also what had made him so terribly oversexed all his life? Grant knew lots of people who didn't seem to give a damn about sex one way or the other.

" I don't know much about her family," he said. He discovered that he was now on his feet—had gotten up already —and followed to the kitchen. " I know her father was a big bootlegger, but he's dead. She doesn't seem to be on good terms with her mom. Uhh. She did say that when we get married, her mother would give us ten thousand dollars as a wedding present."

Aldane's head jerked up a little from the bourbon bottle he was pouring out of. " That's good," he said.

" I must admit that it impressed me considerably," Grant said shamefacedly.

" It never hurts a writer to have a rich wife," Frank said pouring now from the scotch bottle for Grant.

He was of course referring obliquely to himself, since Marie was worth something just under a million dollars. Grant knew the story of how Marie had chased him all over France one whole year right after his first novel came out, trying to marry him, and he kept refusing because her mother's family had had him investigated by a private detective when they found out she was in love with him. Aldane had had the upper hand ever since.

" You don't have to write potboilers, or for the movies," Aldane continued. " But then you as a playwright make a lot more dough than I do as a novelist. It's in the cards."

" If I do, I don't have any of it," Grant said ruefully.

" Maybe you should meet her mother," Frank said, and paused. " What's your uh foster-mother going to say about it? What's her name?—Mrs. Abernathy." There was, under that question, a serious note of secret interest.

" The same as any mother, I mean, any other mother. What the hell? That ain't got anything to do with it." Frank and Marie had always been content to follow his lead on the subject of his foster-mother, whatever gossip they may or may not have heard.

"Well," Frank said holding his glass up to the light and admiring it. Suddenly it fell from his hand and smashed on the tile floor. "Shit!" he said and turned to get another. "Well, as I was about to say, I enjoy, I might even say I *empathize*, with your affair, you and Lucky. But then, as you well know, that is my *goût*. However, *I* am a married man, and *you* are not."

Grant bent to brush splashes of bourbon from his pants leg and almost fell down in the glass shards. He straightened up smiling. "I tell you what. Let's sleep on the floor again and pretend we're boy scouts again. I got to do something. I'm going fucking nuts. You remember that crazy night?"

Frank Aldane grinned. Marie had found them in the morning snugly tucked under a big polar bear skin of hers on the living-room floor, fully dressed, peacefully asleep. "Not to-night," Aldane said judiciously. "The bear rug is being cleaned. Anyway, did you forget you've got Lucky upstairs?"

"My God!" Grant said, aghast. "I forgot! I actually forgot!"

"Take your glass with you," Aldane said.

Grant did. When he crept in beside her, she immediately snuggled up to him even though she was sound asleep, and he saw that she too was sleeping nude. He shook her shoulder gently.

"Do you think I'm maybe oversexed?" he whispered anxiously.

"Well if you are, so am I," Lucky murmured sleepily, "so it's all right."

"You don't care if my first name is Decameron?"

"I wouldn't care if your first name was Firestonetire," she murmured.

Grant felt an enormous relief flood over him, because of both points. "I'm glad these springs don't squeak," was all he said as he turned her tenderly on her back. But as he entered her, "Hansel and Gretel again," was what he was thinking.

"You drink too much," Lucky whispered sleepily and

kissed his ear as she elevated her hips and legs to receive him.

It was probably true he did drink too much. But it didn't seem to hurt him any. Yet. There was no getting around it, he was in love, and he was going to have to do something about it.

Sunday they all spent most of the day cursing Saturday night. In spite of that Frank Aldane did get set up and pursue his little indoctrination course which he had promised Grant, and he pursued it right to its promised end which was the revelation of his new panacea for America in a super-organised world. The " indoctrination " had mostly to do with a young lawyer who had been at last night's party.

" You met him. Do you remember him? Lester Horton. Did you get a chance to talk to him?"

" Dark and slight? Looked Jewish. No, not much. What's so important about him?"

" That young man graduated Harvard Law School with the next to highest grades ever taken. He now lives in Washington, where he is involved with the government. Not only that, he is a very close friend of the President."

" So?"

Frank's momentous pause was positively pregnant. " How would you some day like to be invited to spend a year, say, in Rio as the United States Artist in Residence in Brazil?" Triumph shone on his face.

" Well, I don't know," Grant said cautiously. " I never thought about it. You mean, it actually could happen?"

Frank nodded vigorously. " It could. That's Les's own project, one of the things he's working on for the President."

" Well, I guess I'd like it," Grant said still cautiously. " I'm not so sure it would be good for me. Or my work." He looked over at Lucky.

" I love Rio," she smiled.

" You been *there,* too?" Grant said sourly. She nodded, smiling at him happily.

" Under this administration," Frank said sententiously, " for the first time in American history it is happening that the artist and the intellectual actually can be active in Government."

" I guess that's true," Grant said. " But I worry about

an artist being committed to anything, any Administration, any nation even. You know how I believe that any artist who is really *engagé* to anything, any *politique*, any philosophy even, becomes *passé* and just about worthless as soon as the conditions which created his particular *politique* or philosophy change. Shit, look at all them Thirties writers!"

"Look," Frank said. "You're one of the few men of real integrity I know. Your first play was a huge success. All that fame, success, money never touched you. You, like me, know what the almost insurmountable problems are going to be to try and save any sense of the individual sceptic and free thinker in any future society which we are *already building now*; *to-day*."

"Aw, I'm too cynical," Grant said embarrassedly. "Nobody'd want to talk to me." He looked over at Lucky. "Anyway, I'd rather get laid."

"Well, it's what we have to do. It's our responsibility," Aldane said seriously. "These men want our ideas, for the first time in history, whether they use them or not. It certainly can't hurt. We must try to help."

"Can't you see that by it's very nature it can't work? The weight, the sheer mass, of any society is always unoriginal, unimaginative, conservative. The very things you and I, the artists, want to change about people to make them better are the very things people don't want changed. It can't be any other way. You and I are therefore *compelled* to address ourselves to unborn future generations."

"But now at least we can advise," Frank said.

"Aw, come on. Advise what? And `be listened to? Naw."

"Well anyway I gave ol' Les Horton your address," Frank said. "You'll be hearing from him."

"I ain't going to have any address for quite a while," Grant said.

"You're still determined to go through with this kooky diving business?" Frank said almost pedagogically.

"I sure am."

"What if you got *killed*?"

"It's not that dangerous."

"People do get killed doing it."

"I know, but not very many."

"You remember all what I've told you. Honour, you said! Honourably, we have to try. Think about it."

"Okay, I will," Grant said, glad to get off the subject. His depression of Friday night was returning, as it always did when he let himself think about the world and its future. He held up his left arm with his wrist watch on it. "Look! We made it! It's after five! What do you say we have a drink?

But in the car going back to the city the next day Lucky brought the subject up again herself.

"If what Frank says is true, you know you really do have to *try*. It's everyone's responsibility, to his society, to his *race*. Besides, I'd love to spend a year in Rio."

"We ain't married yet," Grant heard himself say. "And you lay off of me with your Cornell socio-political socialist ideas. I'm an artist, a playwright. I want to know what makes the well-springs of human character tick. Let the others save the world."

It was, he noted, as both of them had also privately noted only a little short while before, right here in this same Hertz car on this same highway, once again four days to departure time.

During those four days the closeness between them and the sense of poignancy in their love affair got stronger and stronger, like a musical note that is increased and increased in intensity until the glass is ready to tinkle and break, the ears to begin to scream. It was almost too much emotion to stand. Always before in Grant's New York affairs there had come a breaking point when it was over, finished, when he would know he was going to leave and go home. It coincided with the point at which he found that that particular girl's character flaws, neuroses, idiosyncrasies, or whatever, were in unequal balance to, too glaring for, any love from him. But this time there didn't seem to be any of that. He had started out (this time, too; as always) wanting not to hurt Carol Abernathy; and he had wound up at the end wanting not to hurt Lucky Videndi. Was this the basic choice of love: choice of who not to hurt?

Up to now they had existed in a sort of midtown lovers' vacuum which had nothing to do with either of their lives. Now their lives were starting to come back into it all and

take over, as the days passed and he did not postpone
again. She would go back to doing whatever she had
done before, being whatever it was she had been, and he
would also. You could smell it. There was that feeling in
the air.

Was it true, Grant wondered, the old saw, the old superstitious myth that said when a man found Something Good
and True he must give some token, make some gesture
of spiritual Commitment or he would lose it, lose it forever?
Certainly that feeling was strongly in him. But then he
had always been superstitious anyway.

He was still receiving phone calls from his "foster-
mother" in Miami. She had not gone on to Ganado Bay
after all. Most of these he refused to accept when he was
at the hotel, which was seldom now, usually only to change
shirts. But on the day when Lucky came to help him pack
to catch the evening train that night, perhaps because he
was so nervous and upset to be leaving anyway, the phone
rang and inadvertently he picked it up. Such a loud and
insulting volley of hysterical screaming and cursing came
out of the instrument at him, that he was sure Lucky
in the bedroom of the suite packing his ties must be able
to hear it. He made his voice guarded and low, and
answered in grunts and monosyllables.—Yes, he was leaving
to-day.—"And she's up there right now helping you pack,
isn't she?" the voice said incredibly. "No," he mumbled.
The voice went on. But underneath all his distress and the
submoronic guilts he could not seem to shake, another
emotion was rising in him: he was just getting a bellyful
of this; a hard, mean quality; and suddenly he just hung
up the phone, hung up on her, cut her off. He had never
done that in his life before.

Lucky was standing in the bedroom doorway, "Who was
it?" she said lightly. But some deep intuitive knowledge
shone powerfully on her face that she had understood it
all.

"Oh, just some guy," Grant said. "Come on, let's get this
over with and get the fuck out of here."

She didn't say a word and went back into the bedroom.
It was as if, by not retorting, she were deliberately putting
herself into the hands of Fate, whatever the odds, sealing her
bet for win or lose. When the phone began to ring again

just a few minutes later, Grant refused to answer it and became enraged.

"Goddam them! Goddam them! They all know I'm leaving! What the fuck are they all calling now for! I don't want to talk on the fucking telephone! I want to be with you!

"God!" he growled, with such a violent intensity that it surprised himself, "I *hate* packing! I *hate* it! I never *could* stand it! Come on, let's get out of this! How much time have we got?"

"About four hours," Lucky said in a strangely calm voice.

"Let's go over to your place, then." He put into his eyes that he wanted to make love to her one more time. Leslie wouldn't be there, was at work at her office.

"I'd rather not," Lucky said in a voice that was curiously decisive. "Let's go somewhere and have a drink or two instead."

She went with him to the train. He had checked his bags through early and then walked with her over to Rattazzi's, which had become a lovers' hangout for them since he first took her there and where they were known, and where they had four large martinis each, sitting at their own private little table in the back. So they were both a little drunk when they came back two hours later for Grant to board.

"I'll come with you," Lucky said in a still voice, "if you want me to."

"To where? Indianapolis!" It was an idea that had never occurred to him. Her jerking mind could not get used to it. Also, there was noise and confusion all around them, and people pushing.

"Sure. Why not?" she said. "I'll make the drive to Florida with you and fly back from there."

Grant could get used to the idea. He had never done things like that. But he had always wanted to. "Wait a minute," he said and climbed into the train to put his briefcase on his berth. He came back and hopped off on to the platform. "You haven't got any clothes with you. Anyway, where would I put you?"

"Haven't you got a house out there? You were telling me all about it the other day."

" Sure, but——"

" We could have a wonderful five days on the drive down."

From down the line the *All Aboard* call went.

" I've never thought about it," Grant said. " I don't—I can't——" He kissed her and climbed up on to the step, and there they stood, she on the platform with this strangely, incredibly forlorn look on her white face like some little lost girl, he on the step, looking at each other, waiting for the door to shut, the train to move.

" I can't take you to Jamaica," Grant growled. It had become almost a signal reaction.

" Send me back on a plane from Miami."

" Your clothes——"

" You can buy me a couple of little dresses."

" I don't know——"

" Please."

" All right then, come on!"

Lucky took two very hesitant steps forward. " But are you sure? I don't want to come if I—I won't push you."

" Well, I—I just haven't thought about——"

The door slid shut in front of his face. He stood looking out at her, an anguish bursting in him like a small bomb. The train began to move. She waved once, then dropped her hands to her sides and like that same little girl lost from her parents, she began to cry, then she disappeared from view, cut off by the angle of the glass. Grant felt numb.

That night he didn't eat but instead got drunk in the club car all by himself. When he finally climbed into the berth, drunk, it felt strangely empty.

FIVE

She didn't really know how she got back to the apartment but she assumed she took a taxi since she certainly wouldn't have ridden the subway. She had only ridden the subway five times in her life, five times in seven years in New York, and that was when she was doing that bit part for Buddy Landsbaum and Don Celt who were shooting it in Brooklyn.

She had ridden the subway to Brooklyn five times at four o'clock in the morning to do that job.

She didn't really know how she got home, or care, but she knew she had stopped crying right away. She hated crying, and she hated having people, especially strangers, see her cry. She was in a daze, that was the truth, a goddamned fucking daze. She had used up so much emotion in the past weeks, especially in the past few days, that she was as empty, and as ugly inside, as an old cold cream jar. An empty daze, and she didn't really come out of it until she climbed the ugly dirty stairs and keyed the apartment door open and saw Leslie there, Leslie and Forbes Morgan.

Tall, chubby, well-got-up Forbes Morgan. He jumped up off the daybed couch, cutting off in mid-sentence his conversation with Leslie. Forbes Morgan, her stud. Her friendly old stud. Her friendly old *ex*-stud. He had a very big thing.

" Oh, hello, Forbes," Lucky said lightly. " What brings you over here, uninvited?"

He came toward her, his chubby face wryly rueful, and looked at her, his eyes warmly searching her face for signs of —signs of trouble, she guessed.

" I have my little grapevine," Forbes said tenderly. " I keep tabs on you, even when I don't see you. He's gone?"

Lucky smiled at him. " He's gone."

" He's an oaf," Forbes said.

" I guess he's an oaf," Lucky said. She took off her coat, hung it in the bedroom closet, and came back and relaxed herself into the big chair which Leslie had tacitly vacated for her. " But he's also a *man*."

" He sure is that," Leslie said. " Whew!"

" And a very talented one," Lucky said. She was feeling bitchy, and ugly. She turned off her ears, and remembered the day, it was the Sunday after the Sunday they met, when he had spent almost the whole day from noon to nearly six o'clock in the evening telling her and Leslie and a couple of other girls the complex story of his new play. He had talked five solid hours, and had cried real tears at least four times. And had consumed more than half a bottle of whisky doing it. She had tried writing a play. And spent a year doing it. He was going to have a drinking problem some day if he didn't watch out. She turned her ears back on. "What?"

"I said we can't all be geniuses," Forbes said lightly.

"And I said I guess it's just as well!" Leslie said. She was trying to smile, and to get Lucky to laugh, and was not succeeding very well at either.

"I was down near 5th and 48th the other day, down near Gibson and Stein, and I saw him blowing his nose in the street," Forbes said.

"He says blowing your nose in a handkerchief blows the stuff, and the germs with it, back into your sinuses," Leslie said.

"Even so. But surely you don't like it?" Forbes said to Lucky.

"No, I don't like it much," Lucky said. Suddenly she laughed out loud. She was remembering her consternation the first time he had ever done that with her with him. It was that first day, when he came over and they walked down to P. J. Clarke's. It had certainly startled her, and embarrassed her.

Forbes had taken a stance in the middle of the room. "I guess you know I'm in love with you," he said dolefully.

"I didn't know," Lucky said. "I never thought about it."

"Well, I am," he said.

"Then I'm sorry for you."

"Don't make fun of me, Lucky."

"I'm not making fun of you, Forbes. I can hardly think at all."

"That son of a bitch. That son of a bitch." Forbes pursed his lips. "Then you're really in love with him?"

"I guess I am," Lucky said simply. "I can't seem to help myself."

"That hick! Well that's what I was afraid of."

Forbes Morgan. Old Forbes. He really did have a big thing. Lucky looked at him sorrowfully. She was exhausted. She felt sad for both of them, herself *and* Forbes. He was a nice boy but she had always told him she wasn't in love with him—or, well, if she hadn't told him, she had certainly given him enough signs along the way so that he ought to have understood that she wasn't. Looking up at him, she turned off her ears again. Forbes Morgan of the prolific Morgans. There were so many of the prolific Morgans now that being a Morgan hardly meant anything. Nevertheless Forbes stood to inherit a nice-sized little fortune when his old grandfather died just the same. She had even visited them up there in Connecticut with him one time, and last year, for quite a long time, Forbes—broke, without a nickel, with hardly a change of his Harvard-type clothes—had stayed here in the apartment with her and Leslie, sleeping on the daybed couch. She had taken care of him, fed him, kept up his spirits, fucked him, and finally had even gotten him a job because at just about that same time, when Forbes had moved in with them, she had met Peter Raven, and spent a crazy funny wild drunken weekend with him at the Plaza and then had started going out with him too at the same time. Peter Raven, who was married, and was another of those sons of old rich but now broke New England-Harvard families (*Les nouveaux pauvres*, she called them all). He was a top PR executive, and while she was going out with him, after much concentrated arguing, she had finally talked him into hiring Forbes in a good executive job. At one point Peter wanted to leave his wife and marry her, but she had gently without hurting his feelings talked him out of that. Neither man knew she was going out with and fucking the other. This was one of her own private little games, little jokes, that nobody knew about except Leslie and maybe Annie Carler.

"So how's the job?" she said, turning her ears back on again. It had been a big step up for Forbes, and the doing of it had been good for Peter's soul. She hadn't hurt anyone.

Forbes, who (aware that though she was looking at him she wasn't listening) had turned his conversation slowly around to Leslie, now brought his gaze back to Lucky. "Oh, all right, you know. It's fun work. And Peter's very good to me. We've become great pals.

"Listen, like I said a minute ago, if there is anything, anything at all I can do to 'ease your burden' as they say, will you tell me?"

"As a matter of fact, to be honest, there is something you can do for me right now," Lucky said. "You can go home and leave me alone. Maybe you guessed: I don't feel much like talking to anybody to-night."

Forbes's face expressed deep hurt. But he swallowed it down manfully. "All right, sweetie. I'll go right now. May I call you to-morrow? Just to see how things go?"

"I don't know," Lucky said despairfully. Forbes really did have a big one. Much bigger than Peter Raven's. Painfully, she wished Grant were here right now instead of him. "I really don't know. You must sense that I don't want to look at you right now." She felt if he didn't get out of here soon, she was going to start to cry again, and she didn't want to.

Forbes got his coat.

There was silence for quite a while after he left. But the growing pressure to cry began to subside as soon as Forbes was outside the door and was replaced by a deep sense of doom and gloom that was not entirely without its pleasant aspect. Doomed to gloom. They sat on in silence.

"Do you want to talk?" Leslie said finally.

"No I don't," Lucky said plaintively. "I really don't."

"Okay. Then we won't," Leslie said stoutly. "But let me ask just one question," she added eagerly. "Did he say anything about coming back to New York?"

"Yes. He's said that several times. He says he's coming back to me as soon as this diving junket is over."

"That's a strange thing, his feeling about this diving business, and how he had to do it alone," Leslie said.

"Yeah."

Leslie made a Jewish gesture, not quite a shrug.

"What am I going to do?" Lucky asked her.

Again Leslie made the gesture. She pouted out her lips. "I can't tell you."

"He's very strait-laced and very stern in *certain* ways, you know," she said.

"Well, naturally! He certainly is. Which is exactly what you want. Honey, I knew your father! Remember?"

"You know what the bastard had the nerve to ask me? It was yesterday at lunch, at Chanticleer, when he was already getting everything all ready to go, mind you. He said if we did get married, would I sign a waiver on his property and his income. One of those individual property statements, where he keeps what's his and I keep what's mine!"

"So what did you say?"

"I said certainly not. I wasn't marrying him as an investment, I was marrying him because I wanted to live with him the rest of my life."

"What did he say?"

"He didn't say anything. He thought about it."

"Well, at least he's thinking about marriage seriously, if he's thinking about his money."

"How do I know what that foster-mother of his will say that he lives with out there in Minneapolis?"

"Indianapolis, dear."

"Indianapolis," Lucky repeated vaguely. The silence reigned again.

"And fuck his money," Lucky suddenly said plaintively. "He hasn't got all that much money. My mother's got a hell of a lot more than he has."

"Which, I must add," Leslie said, "doesn't do you one damn bit of good."

"That's true," Lucky said gloomily.

Again the silence fell over them, each of them wrapped up in whatever special thoughts she carried.

"Do you remember how we used to talk, kid about him?" Lucky said finally. "Ron Grant, the last of the unmarried writers? How we tried to arrange plots for me to meet him?"

"We didn't really try."

"No, but we spent a lot of time laughing and joking about it. Ron Grant, the last gasp, the last chance, the last one left, for me to marry a real writer."

"I never thought you'd ever really meet him. Let alone really fall in love with him."

"I can't believe it won't happen," Lucky said, more to herself than to Leslie. "It has to happen. Why, it's like Fate. I have to believe it will happen.—If it doesn't happen," she said in a hollow whisper, looking over at Leslie with hollow blue-shadowed eyes, "I don't know what will become of me. I can't marry any of these people. I can't go back and marry some dumbhead from Syracuse."

"It's that kindly fatherly quality about him that sunk us all," Leslie said, "taking all of us girls out to dinner with you like he did, being so nice to us all. Remember the Sunday he told the story of the play? He really *likes* girls."

Lucky didn't hear this. She had lapsed into silence, turning off her ears again, and began thinking about that time,

the time when they used to kid about Ron as the last
of the unmarried writers. It was about a year ago, just
shortly before Forbes with no place to stay had moved
in with them. Grant was in town then, working with his
producers or something. He had even taken a hotel apartment somewhere, and was trying to write there. The grapevine had it that he couldn't be doing much serious work
what with all the heavy drinking and late hours he was
keeping, and apparently it was true because after six
weeks he packed up and went back to Minneapolis or
wherever it was. And it was during that time that he
started having an affair with an old friend of hers, Hope
York, a New Jersey very Jewish girl singer and dancer
who had never quite made it big on Broadway. She hadn't
seen or heard from Hopie in over two years when one day
she called and asked if she could come over. When she
arrived, it was to speak only about her love affair with
Ron Grant the playwright. She was madly in love with
him and wanted to marry him. But he wasn't having any,
and Hopie was afraid she'd botched it with her kookiness.
She was really quite kooky, and kept coming up with weird
wayout plots to pressure Grant or blackmail him into marrying her. She wanted Lucky's help. She did not, however
many times Lucky and Leslie invited her to, bring Grant
over to the apartment. She would not even say where he
was staying, though neither of them ever asked her. But
it was clearly a closely guarded secret. Hopie wasn't
about to set her competition up in business. So they never
met him. When he went back home to the Middlewest,
Hopie was distraught and beside herself for two months.
It was then that Lucky laughingly suggested that they all
get together with all the rest of the girls they knew who
qualified, and form a Writer Fuckers Club.

She sighed. Leslie, who knew well her habit of literally
turning off her ears when she was thinking, had lapsed into
silence too. And suddenly she thought of Forbes Morgan's
thing again. It certainly was a big one. Maybe the biggest
she had encountered. Except perhaps for Jacques the Haitian.
But it wasn't like Grant's. Nobody's was like Grant's.
Even though it was only normal sized. She guessed that was
love. It was so *pretty*.

"Remember the Writer Fuckers Club?" Lucky said, and

then suddenly she started to cry. She didn't cry like most people, with sobs and shaking shoulders and a screwed-up face, she simply sat motionless with her eyes wide open, breathing evenly but shallowly through a slightly open mouth, and tears ran down her face to splash on her lax hands in her lap, taking a large part of her eye make-up with them. She didn't know why she cried like that. She just always had. Maybe it was because she hated to cry so much that it hurt her more to do it. She felt totally helpless, unable to do a thing. She always had needed somebody to help her and take care of her. She always would.

When it stopped, she got up. Leslie had gone to get her a hand towel for the mascara, and fussed around her like some helpless mother hen. Lucky shook her head vigorously, splashing tears out to both sides with the swinging champagne hair. She had always hated being beautiful. People never liked you for you yourself alone, for what you were, but only for your beauty. It was one of the worst kinds of loneliness. That was why she was such an easy pushover for men so often. Oh, Daddy!

"I'm going to bed," she said to Leslie.

"It's only seven-thirty, honey."

"I don't give a damn. If anybody calls for me, I don't want to talk. I'm just going to stay in bed."

"For six whole weeks? Not again," Leslie said.

"I don't know. Maybe. Where's that book of Ron's plays and short stories he gave us?"

Leslie got it for her. "Can I fix you something to eat?"

"I couldn't eat anything."

"I wish there was something I could do," Leslie said.

Abruptly Lucky put her arms around her, and they stood together that way, hugging each other. "Ain't nobody can do nothin' for nobody," she said.

"Anyway, you know I'm here, sweetie," Leslie said.

"Aren't you going out?"

Leslie looked guilty. "I sort of had a date, but it wasn't sure, and anyway I don't feel like going out."

Lucky didn't answer. Later from the bedroom she heard Leslie's new boy-friend ring, come in, low voices for a little while, and then go out. She wriggled herself violently further down into pillow and covers so that nothing except her face and the hands which held the book were outside, uncovered. She did not want the cold air of the world to touch her, not one smidgen more of her than was absolutely necessary. Her two hands were a concession she had to make if she wanted to read Ron's book.

Ron. Ron. Ron. Names were so funny. They didn't mean a damn thing, until you met the people attached to them, and then they all seemed to fit and be exactly right. Ron Grant whom she had never met was one name, and Ron Grant whom she knew was a totally different name.

He wrote well. Even in his prose short stories. Which were strange introspective pieces almost without dialogue, as if he were deliberately trying to avoid the dialogue of plays. He didn't spend much time on delicate stylistic niceties but sort of bull-assed right through. But his sensitivity about the physical world and his perceptions about people were so incredibly sensitised that they were almost feminine, and they made you stop sometimes with a feeling of " Gee! I've felt that!"

She had never seen the first play, *The Song of Israphael*, which was such a colossal hit. She had not even been living in New York then, and was still in school. But whenever she did come into the city she avoided it simply because it was such a big hit, how could it be any good? Now she found that it was good. Very good. Grant's understanding of the whore amounted almost to empathy and astounded her—how could he know that much about women? —though when she thought about it, knowing him now, she did not see why it should. She read right through it without even a second's pause, thinking this writer was the kind of man one would like to know, until she remembered she did know him, and in fact had made violent love with him. When she finished it she put the book down and covered herself with the covers completely, head and all. After a while she put her head out and called to Leslie, in a plaintive child's voice.

" Do you think he might call me from out there?"

" Do you want to talk to him if he does?"

" Of course." She paused. " What time does the train get in?"

" Around noon," Leslie called.

She wriggled back down into the covers until only her face from eyebrows to mouth was outside.

"But I wouldn't get my hopes——"

"I'm not," Lucky said. She turned on her side and shut her eyes and began going back over the past weeks in her mind in luxurious, complete detail, recalling every happy second pleasurably, just as if everything were all right, and he was here, in the other bed there, beside her, sound asleep.

When she woke it was with a definite sense of loss. They had slept together so closely for so long that her body, especially her skin, began missing him, missing his skin, even before her mind was awake enough to appreciate it. There was that way he had of sleeping completely under the covers with his head resting on her flank and one heavy arm lying across her belly as if holding her down. She loved that feeling of being held down like that, by a man, by a real man. Authority.

When she opened her eyes finally, it was mid-morning and the cold heatless winter sun pouring in through the thin curtains carried a sense of autumnal stillness in the air outdoors and of a winter loneliness so deep that it froze to the bone. The same light had seemed happy and gay as long as Ron was still here. Staying under the covers except for her face, she reached out one hand, feeling for the telephone until she found it, and began calling people. She would not even get out of bed for coffee. Athena Frank, her lawyer friend; Annie Carler at home; Leslie at her office. As she talked she pulled lightly at her crotch hair with one hand, opening repeatedly the outer lips of her vagina ever so slightly. As she was so fond of saying at parties or wherever else she thought it might shock, her trouble was that at the age of eight she masturbated and liked it. At ten-thirty Forbes Morgan called her from his office, and she told him she was staying in bed and wanted to be left alone. He must already have been crying on Peter Raven's shoulder, because a few minutes later *he* called.

"You're really a cute little dirty rat fink, aren't you?" his voice came over the wire in that amused wry drawl he affected. "Forbes has been in here crying on my shoulder all morning because he's in love with you. It turns out he's been having an affair with you for almost a year."

"It was never an affair. We were merely sleeping together." But she didn't feel like playing sexy boy-girl games to-day.

"Sure. All during the time I was going out with you. I've lived in this town long enough that you'd think I'd smarten up. And not only that, you had the audacity to ask me for a job for him. And me, I gave it to him!"

"He needed the job. Are you going to fire him?"

"No. As a matter of fact, I couldn't fire him if I wanted. He's been promoted. Only the Big Man himself can fire him now."

"It was good for you to give him the job," Lucky said.

"Sure. It sure was. And the whole thing was *very* good for you, too. *Doubly* good, I might say, no?"

Lucky knew she was supposed to laugh here, but she didn't feel up to it. "At least I didn't tell your wife the story," she said tartly.

"No. That's true. I do owe you that," the amused voice drawled. "Only it might have been good for her. If you had."

"Listen, Peter, I don't feel much like talking," she said. The whole thing bored her, made her sick, even frightened her. She was tired of this life, and all these smart hip chic people who ran the nation's thinking for the advertisers. She simply couldn't go on like this. Not now.

"So he's got you over a barrel, the playwright," Peter gloated. "I hope he's as hard on you as you were on everybody else."

"You don't really mean that, Peter, do you?"

"No, I don't really. I hope Lucky has luck. Now go back to sleep. I'll call you maybe to-morrow."

She didn't even bother with saying "bye" as she hung up. Underneath everything else, under the electric skin contact she felt for Grant, under the deep passion of their actual lovemaking, below and under the deep desperation she felt about her life with him gone, was still something else. It was hard to even find words for it. Sometimes she wasn't even sure it was there. It was so deep down. Mainly it was a feeling, a superstitious feeling that she would be punished. Punished for what? Hell, take your pick. Anything. You could say punished for her "past." Whatever. A superstition that she would be punished by not being allowed to have Ron Grant, now that she had found him. She had heard the old soldier's cynical saying that "Whores make the best wives." And probably they did. Anything to get out of the profession. And she knew she would make Grant a good wife. But that superstitious feeling of getting punished was still there ; anyway, sometimes it was there. That goddamned fucking Catholic upbringing that she had tried and striven so hard to rid herself of ; superstition was still there.

If she didn't hate praying and the idea of praying so much, she'd by God pray.

His phone call came in just a few minutes before one. He had, he said, taken a cab straight home from the station and called her. When she heard that raspy, deep, husky, fatigued voice over the phone the pit of her stomach dropped completely out from under her.

" Get on a plane and come," he was saying. " We'll stay here in Indianapolis two or three days. Then we'll make the trip to Florida together. I'll send you home from Miami."

" I don't know how to get a plane ticket !" Lucky wailed. " I never know how to do anything like that !"

" Well—get Leslie to help you. I hate telephone conversations, damn it. I hate them. Nobody ever understands anybody. I wish you were here right now."

" I haven't got any money," Lucky was able to say finally, though it hurt her to.

There was a pause.

" Well, I'll send you a couple hundred bucks. That ought to be enough, hadn't it? I'll wire it. I'll send it Western Union. To your address. All right?"

" Yes," Lucky said. " Yes, darling. Anything." Her whole intestinal and pelvic area was melting into a frothy cream of butter. Her legs had gone too weak to stand up. She spread them apart and let herself come open. If only she could have him here right now.

" If only I could have you here right now," Grant's voice said. " Well, then, all right? Okay?"

" Yes, yes."

" Okay. Good-bye."

" Good-bye, Ron."

But neither one of them hung up. She could hear a sort of agonised breathing from the other end. Neither spoke.

" Good-bye again," Grant said finally, and the phone clicked dead in her ear. Tears brimming in her eyes, she put it back in its cradle.

She lay still for a few minutes thinking about him. Then she threw back the covers, and everything began to run too fast, like a movie film played at a speed faster than normal. At five-thirty in the afternoon she was at Idlewild boarding a plane. Somewhere in the confusion she had got stuck in her head that it was to Minneapolis, Indiana, that she was going. But fortunately Leslie, whom she had called and who had come home from the office to help her, had bought the right ticket and steered her to the right boarding passage. Because Forbes Morgan now had an old car, they pressed him into driving them out. The two of them waved her on board.

In such ways did people begin to change their lives, or try to. Change them upside down and all around until they didn't even look like the same lives. On the plane, she prepared herself for three hours of doing nothing but think.

Even while he was so sweetly and kindly driving her to the airport with Leslie, Lucky had nothing but contempt for Forbes Morgan. What kind of a man was it that would drive a girl he had been fucking and was in love with out to the airport to go and meet another lover? How could any real girl love a man like that? That was the trouble with all these people, they were all so kind and good and liberal and up-to-date and modern, they could no longer function as simple males. Victims of their own "liberal" propaganda. Treat girls as equals. But it wasn't only that. Underneath that was a still deeper, even scarier level: the work they all did in this hugely organised business of controlling the minds of the people for the sellers of products, whether in the advertising end or in the actual communication—TV, radio, publishing—had shrivelled their souls, if not their testicles as well, until each man became somehow less of himself than when he started, in some strange way nobody could define. This didn't seem to happen to the lawyers and accountants and book-keepers and simple office workers.

The diminishment seemed to take two forms. There were those who came to believe ardently in the stuff, largely junk, which they sold. And there were those who became totally cynical about it all. These were the ones who drove sports cars in rallies, flew their own planes, or became amateur bullfighters, or ski'd or mountain-climbed. All, both types, became ardent girl-chasers, even the impotent ones.

Perhaps the intensive, vicious competition had something to do with it, too. Even a man as highly placed as Peter Raven was afraid, knew he could be fired to-morrow if he fucked up on one single big account. And their manhood suffered. Like poor old Forbes.

Lucky remembered, by contrast with Forbes, the time Raoul had left her stashed in Kingston to go back into South America to mess around with his revolution he could not leave alone. It was like dope to him. After six weeks of it she had been bored, and had taken up with a handsome young Jamaican guy. Although he was really far too light to be called a black Negro (almost all the upper-class Jamaicans were mulattoes, quadroons, octoroons or less), and although his body hair, though kinky, was reddish in colour, Jacques still qualified sufficiently for her to be able to think of him as her " Negro lover." Anyway, æsthetically, their bodies were beautiful together in the mirror ; he was dark enough for that. In any case, whether Raoul had been told about it or had come back on his own and guessed what was going on, he packed her up and had her out of there back to New York so fast it made your head swim. She and Leslie had giggled about it for a long time.

What would Forbes had done? She was reasonably certain that Grant would never have driven her out to any airport to go off to another lover. Or would he? He seemed to keep sending her back all the time, sending her back to the apartment from the train, and now sending her back to New York from Miami. But he had called her to come out. She was pretty sure, if they really did make the drive to Miami, she could talk him into taking her on to Kingston with him.

And that myth about Negroes having bigger things than white men, if her Jamaican boy-friend Jacques was any example, was not a myth at all. By contrast, Raoul's had been very ordinary. They had giggled about that, too.

A hysterical laughter began to bubble up inside of her, rising out of her inability to cope with or accept appreciation of the awful suspense elements of this her life story—it was like spending a Saturday afternoon with *The Perils of Pauline*. When a man across the aisle tried to strike up an acquaintance, she closed her eyes and pretended to sleep, trying to keep from breaking out into uproarious crazy laughter.

Then, suddenly there rose up in her again the awful doom-gloom sense that she would be punished by not being allowed to have Grant. She could not open her eyes because of the man across the aisle, so she sat with it in the dark behind her eyelids, trying to make it go away.

He met her at the scary modern steel-and-glass numbered entrance portal as she came in off the field of the big new modern airport, and in the confusion of noise, flashing bright lights, shrieking conversations and reverberating footfalls in the hollow corridor there began for her a peculiar dreamlike sequence of unreality that did not leave her until she boarded the New York jet in Miami ten days later. In the confusion she was convinced for the better part of an hour, until Grant finally unconvinced her, that she was for some reason in a town called Minneapolis.

He took her right away upstairs to the handsome modern bar for a drink, where they sat looking at each other as they downed it. Grant was wearing levis, cowboy boots and a leather jacket. Then he drove her out to his home through the city. It was a much bigger town than Lucky, who had never been west of Harrisburg, Pa., except once to fly to California, had anticipated.

They spent three wonderful lovers' days there, in his house, never going out, cooking together, watching television, playing ping-pong or pool in the game-room, reading, making love. He had completely done over the old house and it had a huge stone fireplace, books everywhere on all the walls, glass cases of guns and fishing and camping gear. It very definitely bore the impress of his personality, and it constricted Lucky somewhat to see that he had very definitely built himself a very definite life out here away from New York.

Only once did he take her out. This was the third night when he took her to dinner at a fairly ritzy country club, which seemed pretty much like her hometown one in Syracuse and in fact seemed to be pretty much furnished with the same people—all of whom looked at her with surprise (and with admiration, she noted). Grant, as he introduced her and showed her around, seemed to be wearing a sort of subdued belligerence, as if he were doing something he did not particularly like to do but that he had promised himself he would do.

Then the drive began. It took them a full six days. Down through Indiana and across the Ohio at Henderson, Kentucky, where the snow slowly began to disappear and they began to be in the South. The close, fetid air of commingled lechery and hatred which became apparent to her as soon as they crossed the river affected her so strongly that it took her breath away and made her sick at her stomach, and the further South they got the stronger and more fetid it became. The cold and at the same time obscenely lecherous eyes of the tall paunchy men who looked at her lewdly made her skin creep. She _knew_ they hated all women. But when she mentioned this to Grant, he merely laughed. And when they stopped off at a few places to eat with people Grant knew, everyone was very nice. The women that she met seemed to her peculiarly two-faced in some mincing way, as though they all knew something about the men that they were not telling, something they did not need to tell because as long as they knew it and didn't tell it, it aided them.

It was the most Lucky had ever seen of the actual earth of the great nation she belonged to, and it all made her want to get back to New York as fast as possible and stay there and never leave.

As they drove, they talked and talked and talked. By the time they reached the Florida state line near Tallahassee they knew just about everything about each other. Grant told her about his "career" in the Navy during the war, and how he had gotten himself transferred from a nice safe clerical job at Pearl Harbour to duty on board an aircraft carrier which he was subsequently blown off of into the Pacific Ocean.

"My God, why did you do all that?"

He snarled. "I didn't know any fucking better. I wouldn't do it now. I was trying to escape from 'petty bureaucracy.' What I found was the same bureaucracy plus danger."

For her part Lucky told him about her horrible convent childhood, and how her father saved her from it. "He was really a great man. Even when I was only five he told me to listen to what they said, but believe what I wanted."

"Well, wasn't he a Catholic himself?"

"Nominally, yes. But he believed they were in business like everybody else. Like every idealogy." At which Grant roared.

Finally, after some hesitation and much prompting by Grant about the fact that she must have had *some* boy-friend before she met him, she told him about her stud Forbes Morgan, how she had gotten him a job, about how Forbes had driven her to the airport and how she felt about it. " I never was really in love with him. I never was *really* in love with anybody but you, that's the truth. Not even Raoul."

Grant listened politely, without anger, but there was such a strained look on his face that she decided not to tell him everything about Peter Raven, only that he was an admirer, another guy who was trying to make her.

Then it was suddenly late at night with the glow of Miami on the eastern sky as Grant herded the big Chrysler convertible across the ghostly, haunted Everglades toward it.

They had five further nights together in various hotels and motels along the road. They spent the last night in a middle-class motel across the Boulevard from the canal, and by noon the next day she was on the New York plane. She did not protest further. His face was set in a peculiarly stubborn way and she knew it would be useless. " I have some things to take care of before we can think of getting married, among them this diving business and the problem of courage." As she fastened her seatbelt and looked out the port she could see the tiny figure standing way off there on the ramp and knew that if he didn't hurry up he would miss his own flight to Jamaica. She was aware that people around her were looking at her, after the wild kiss of their farewell, and she set herself not to cry.

At Idlewild Leslie met her with a taxi and she went straight home to bed, and stayed there.

Only once in the next days did she get up, and that was when her uncle Frank Videndi, a big horse-player, came to town. Somehow he knew she was in trouble and took her to the Copa with a couple of his cronies. After Sammy Davis Jr. finished his performance he asked her what was the matter. So she told him.

SIX

The Abernathys had met him at the Ganado Bay Airport. There was no reason to assume they would not meet him, since he had wired them his arrival time, but when Grant saw them standing there together in the hot sun on the ramp he was disappointed. The muggy tropical Jamaican heat flowed into the big jet like a salty molasses as soon as the door was unsealed. Even the air itself smelled different, like holidays. But he needed more time. With a sinking feeling he felt that he *was* in fact sinking—sinking back into a rhythm, a part of his life that no longer suited or fit. After Lucky, after New York this time, everything was different. He could still remember how her plane had got off the ground and had so achingly disappeared northward in the blue Florida sky.

They even looked different. For one thing they looked years older. And for another, they looked to him now, suddenly, like exactly what they were: Hicks. Two hicks. And Grant realised suddenly that this was a thought he had been avoiding thinking for quite a long time. Why? Because he had thought it was too cruel a thought to admit, was that why? There had been a time, back when he first got out of the Navy and came home and first met them, that he had thought they were the two most worldly and sophisticated people he could ever meet. But they hadn't gone on! He had gone on, and they had been going on, for quite a long time now; he just had not found up to now an idea, a place to go on to.

He had had to force himself to get out of the seat to descend the steps into the heat, and when they waved at him—Hunt with his perpetually friendly way, she with that false smile he had gotten to know so well—he wanted to turn around and climb right back into the jet. Through passport checking, through customs, through the little glass of rum punch the pretty coloured girl from the Chamber of Commerce offered him, he felt as though he were leaning backward: moving forward while straining to go rearward; and then he was with them. He had had nothing at all to say.

123

And it had gone on like that for days.

It did not really matter that he had had nothing to say. Carol had immediately taken over and begun to run things. There was this diver in town she had found for him, his name was Al Bonham, and when they got his wire she had arranged for him to have his first diving lesson in a pool to-morrow. She would go with him, and learn it too. And she did. Fortunately, though she was a good swimmer, better than Grant actually, she proved to be totally unable to cope with anything having to do with a mask or an aqualung. She could not breathe through a lung mouthpiece under-water without choking, she could not let water into her mask and clear it underwater without choking. It was as if some terrible claustrophobic fear struck her that she could not control the moment she put her face underwater in a mask and she would stand up in the pool gasping and coughing, she who was always talking about "mind control," and after the first day she quit, leaving him alone and relieved with the big diver, Bonham. These were about the only times he was alone and away from her.

But before all this happened they had had their first conversation alone together.

She could not, naturally, say anything while Hunt was around. This was another part of all their lives together that Grant had somehow come to accept, and now no longer wanted to accept. But Hunt was playing golf to-day at the local club with Paul de Blystein and some other "businessmen" he had found around. He already had his clubs in the car with him. Grant had known a confronta-tion scene would be forthcoming, but he had hoped for more time. Apparently he was not to have it. Hunt had dropped them at the front portal (that was the only thing to call it; it was much too big to be called a door) of Evelyn de Blystein's huge magnificent villa and had driven off. Neither, of course, could she talk in front of Evelyn. But after the necessary fifteen minutes and two drinks of amenities and hellos; after giving his bag to the Jamaican maid to unpack in his room, he and Carol had walked down the hill through the unbelievably beautiful grounds to Evelyn's private beach and beach-house across the Jamaican "high-way" for a swim.

She did not say anything going down the hill, and she

did not take his hand as she might once have done under these same circumstances. Grant was grateful for that, but he felt it was all very painful.

"So," she said finally after they had crossed the road and were wading through the deep sand in the hot sun toward the beach-house, "was she a good fuck?"

"I don't know what you're talking about," he had said.

Carol snarled. "The fuck you don't!" It was like the face of some animal. "She was probably right there in that goddamned hellish New Weston hotel room with you all those times I was calling you, or trying to call you. I'm positive she was!"

Grant did not answer and plodded on. He had changed to what in the old days in the Navy at Pearl Harbour they had called a "gook" shirt and a pair of shorts and carried his bikini in his hand. In the pocket of the shirt he had put an undeveloped roll of colour film with a few shots he had taken of Lucky on the trip down. He owned an Exacta single lens reflex.

Actually, he had taken the precaution of removing the film from the camera and carrying it with him because he knew Carol Abernathy was not above blatantly and openly going through his things sometimes when he was not around and then daring him to do anything about it.

"What's that?" she asked suddenly. "In your pocket."

"Roll of film," he had said.

And suddenly, so fast and unexpectedly that he hadn't even had time to move, Carol had snatched the roll from the pocket, ripping the pocket slightly, and thrown it out across the beach into the sea.

"Well you won't have that!" she said viciously. "That much is gone!" She faced him defiantly, her head thrown back, as though expecting him to hit her or slap her, which in fact he had actually been thinking of doing.

Grant shrugged and made a face.

"I know they were pictures of her, it was pictures of her, wasn't it?" Carol demanded.

"Now you'll never know, will you?" Grant had said. He felt cruel. First red anger, then white fury boiled up inside his head, and he struggled to contain it. If she was following some planned campaign to go—get back—to what had been before, and he wouldn't put it past her to have planned it all, she was certainly going about everything exactly wrong. They were almost to the lovely little coral-stone beach-house. " I'm thinking of bringing her down and taking her to Kingston with me," he said with deliberate malice. He had no intention of doing that. But he didn't intend to take Carol either.

Carol stopped. " You won't! You'll not! You will over my dead body!" She was almost screaming and her fists were clenched against her thighs. " I didn't spend the best years of my life bringing you up and teaching you and making a man out of you for you to go off to Kingston with a little hot-assed floozy! I've got a big investment in you! I made you!"

Grant had stopped, too. The tropical sun broiled down on both of them. They had both been so nice to him really, had really helped him so much—Hunt perhaps because he was forced to by Carol, at least at first ; Carol because she believed in him and had been in love with him. He owed them a lot. But he didn't owe them that. The truth was that while he had gone on working and learning and growing, all on his own because they couldn't follow him, Carol had either given up or simply been unable to follow, and had moved on further and further into her lazy, easy-to-pretend-to-study mysticism. He had charge of his craft now. She worked by rote, chartclass ideas, usually ideas he had come up with, utilised, passed on to her, then abandoned for something newer while she clung on and on to them. And sold them like a philosophy to her little theatre gang.

" You'll get your share," he said thinly. " But you didn't make me." Stubbornly, like a man in a driving rainstorm, he had turned and plodded on for the beach-house.

It was that question of " courage," what he had said to Lucky that last day in Miami, though he was sure he had worded it so obscurely that she didn't understand and thought it applied to the diving. At least, he hoped so. He wasn't even sure that he wanted to marry her. Sometimes he thought he did, and sometimes he didn't. He didn't know, that was the truth. He was still afraid she was too good to be true. But that was beside the point of courage. He had to do something about this, and he had to do it soon. But he wanted to do it graciously, if he could. That was why he had made that point of taking her out to the Indiana-polis country club where he and the Abernathys belonged. If they hadn't heard about it in a letter by now, they would soon. Honour had made him do that, anything else would have been sneaking and anyway people knew he had her there anyway. What the hell?

He opened the door of the exquisitely appointed little beach-house, which appeared very dark inside after the bright sun outside.

It wasn't the first time she had acted this way. She had pulled the same routine before, over other women. She didn't like to sleep with him, but she didn't want anybody else to. What he hated was her way, her trick of always making him appear morally wrong. It was moral for her not to want to sleep with him; but it was immoral for him to sleep with anybody else. Christ, that shit went out with Queen Victoria. She didn't even believe it herself. Frustration and fury began to burn in him again. She couldn't believe it! How could she believe it, when here she was still married to Hunt and living as his, Grant's, mistress! For fourteen years! The irrationality of it was insane! Comparing Carol Abernathy with Lucky, there was no ground, no area—not by any possible stretch of the imagination—where Carol could even compete, let alone come off better. In the dim circular room he had begun to undress.

It was strange. Thinking back all those years to when it began, he did not even seem to be the same man. It hadn't even started as a love affair. It had started as a lark, not a serious " affair." He had been home on a short convalescent furlough from the Great Lakes Hospital and somebody had taken him down to their house. The war was not yet over even in Europe and she was entertaining all the wounded crapped-out vets, of which there was not such a huge pre-ponderance as later. Naturally there was a lot of drinking. She did not drink, but Hunt did and seemed to like getting drunk with the kids, who contrary to the mythology were not only not taciturn about their war experiences but in fact talked about damned little else. She was already inter-ested in " literature " and " the theatre " and he read her some of his young, bad poetry about being blown off the carrier into the Pacific and a couple of lousy one-acters, and the third time out he had made her. They were in her car,

driving home from somewhere in the afternoon. Hunt was in
his office at work, and they had driven out of town and
parked in a wood and done it for the first time in the back
seat. But for him it had been only a temporary lark, not
any kind of idea for a " permanent relationship." He already
had two girls going for him in Chicago, and was fucking
everything he could get his hands on then. He had been
too near dead too long, and he wanted everything he
could get. And he didn't care if everybody else felt that
way, either. There was a young Navy fighter pilot, a jg
named Ed Grear, who was home on leave too and hung
around down there, and who also had the hots for Carol
Abernathy. And Grant hadn't cared if he had her. Though
Grant was an enlisted man and Grear an officer, they hung
around a lot together, drinking, because they had played bad
football together in high school, and they had already
traded off two or three other girls in town. Carol had a
pregnant girl staying with her who was eight months along, a
distant relative from somewhere who had come there to
her to hide and have her baby, and she was one of the girls
they had traded off with. One night lying drunk on the living-
room floor and necking with Carol, while Hunt was drunk
in bed asleep, Grear (who was later shot down in the
Philippines) had passed by on his way upstairs with the
pregnant girl and Grant had signalled him to come back down
and switch places if he wanted to. Grear did come down,
but he didn't stay. Carol wasn't having any. She had seen
Grant signal, and while she said nothing then, the next afternoon (while Hunt was again in his office at work) her weeping
rage astounded Grant. He had had no idea that she didn't
feel as free and easy about it all as he did. It was an
episode she had never let him forget, and on certain occasions
recalled it to him as the basic cause for her later disinterest
with sex. She implied she had slept with several other men
besides him over the early years of their affair, usually in
deliberate revenge, but by that time Grant (who in his heart
could never be quite sure she wasn't also sleeping with Hunt
occasionally, too) didn't care, since he was reasonably sure
that if she did she still couldn't be giving very much away.
And yet he had loved her, later, loved her desperately. At
one point. If he was to be totally coldblooded honest about
it, and he wanted to, he had to admit that when he really

loved her was when the economic factor became involved, and they were supporting him. It was all so strange.

In the dim cool of the de Blystein beach-house he had looked thoughtfuly at the torn pocket of the gook shirt before he laid it aside. Carol had quieted down completely when she caught up to him and came inside. Silently, they undressed together like old intimates in the dim domelike room to put on their swimming suits, and she seemed quite friendly and kind. She actually talked and acted as if there had been no scene. That in itself was peculiar, wasn't it? he thought.

Then suddenly, standing nude in the centre of the dim room, she looked over at Grant and spread her hands. "Look at my figure," she said in a shy, half-embarrassed voice which carried a thin, and for Grant bitter, edge of hopefulness. "I lost a lot of weight for you I——" Then she paused, embarrassment on her face. "But my breasts got smaller. I don't know why. They never did before when I dieted." Her face was very vulnerable.

Grant was horrified by his own coldbloodedness, looking at her. He could not help but compare her to the beauty of Lucky, who not only had a lot of youth and years on her side but also natural endowment. Carol had been a beautiful, a very attractive woman when he first met her, but never anything like Lucky. And her breasts *had* shrunk.

"They look just the same to me," he had said, shaking his head. What else was one to say?

To his further horror, he saw a small smug self-satisfied smile of secretive triumph come over her face as she lowered her eyes and began to step into her suit, as if she assumed automatically that he really meant what he had said and therefore that she had won back everything.

"It wasn't really so much diet," she said primly, still looking down, " as worry."

It was a vast relief to get outside. In the eyecracking sun there was a lovely little sand terrace held in by a wall of coral-stone with steps down into the water. Back from the sand were two tall shady pines soughing in the trades breeze above a coral-stone picnic table, and on the sand itself was a tall royal palm. Evelyn de Blystein treated herself right with her money, and for a moment he envied her angrily. The water was green and ten or twelve feet

deep over a sand bottom running out a couple of hundred
yards past three big rocks to a reef so shallow the troughs
between the surface waves exposed it. It looked interesting
but he had no mask with him and anyway he didn't feel
much like exploring it right now. When he did swim out
to it and looked down through the sting and blur with un-
masked eyes, he saw that the entire reef as far as he could
see was alive with a forest of sea anemones waving their
tiny tentacles in the wash hungrily. He didn't want to get
into that, even with a mask. In amongst them he could
see here and there the long black spines of the black sea
urchins, *Diadema setosum*, moving pugnaciously about like
sharp black needles whenever something touched them. He
swam back to the little wharf, where Carol was. It was a
good place for a lazy, pointless, profitless swim. But it was
not to end there.

After showering, she had lain down nude on the big ample
oversized bed and called to him. Grant felt he could not
refuse her. It would be too terrible. Again he was struck with
horror at his own coldbloodedness as he went to her. Her
body felt alien to him as if he had never touched it before.
She must have sensed this. But if she did, she said nothing.

He slept with her only one more time after that, and that
was the night after his first dive in the sea with Bonham,
the day they went to the big cave.

He had no idea of course, then, that first day in Evelyn's
beach-house, that exactly twenty-one days later he would be
desperately calling Lucky in New York to come down.

But a lot of other things were to happen before that
occurred.

SEVEN

On his second dive in the sea with Bonham he shot his
first fish. Bonham had sold him a double-rubber Arbalete
which he also put on Grant's mounting tab, warning him
that until they went after really big fish he should cock
only one rubber. They went about three miles west along the
coast, where Bonham said there were *really* fish. " You'll

find spearfishin' a helluva lot more fun than just pokin' around on the shallow reef," he said with his bloodthirsty smile. A mile off shore there was a deep reef which was too deep for the native kids to spearfish, and since the depth was 75 to 100 feet neither of the other two pro divers in Ganado Bay took their clients there. Neither did Bonham usually, but since Grant was doing so well, he didn't see why he shouldn't take him. "You're lucky you catch on to things so quick." he rumbled.

Grant remembered that Bonham had said there were lots of fish on the "shallow reef" too, but he didn't say anything. Bonham appeared to be doing everything in his power to make sure his rich playwright stayed interested. It was only a long time later, when Grant knew a lot more, that he realised Bonham might have been pushing the safety factor to a fine edge by taking him so deep on his second day out. But by then it didn't matter anyway.

He never did know just when he began to feel at ease underwater. Suddenly one day it was just there: confidence. But it was certainly not on that second day, when he was at least as nervous as he had been on the first day.

Dressing out was more familiar now. So was the crashing fall over the side and under, and the descent. Poking his head around a coral hillock down on the bottom, he saw a large grouper (it turned out to be only 6 lbs) just sitting there in the water and staring at him. Pushing the spear-gun slowly forward until it almost touched the fish, who simply stared at him mildly if a little apprehensively with large liquid eyes, he pulled the trigger and put the spear through him just at the lateral line behind the head breaking his back. The fish hardly moved, but with the spear through him and the hinged barbs holding him securely he rolled his eyes and opened and closed his mouth in some silent fish's agony of his own. Holding the gun at arm's length and trailing the fish at the end of spear and double length of line, just in case there were any sharks or other predators around, Grant swam up with him feeling like a brute and a murderer.

But if he felt like a murderer, Bonham did not. He had towed along a small plastic dinghy in which to dump the fish (" Get them up and out of the water as fast as you can, and try for brain shots," he grinned; "it's the flappin' around and the blood spoor that brings the sharks.") and in it, by the time Grant got his one grouper, were already five fish larger than his own. And watching the big man from the surface, as he drove in viciously after still another, a large grouper, was like watching the predatoriness of some primordial sub-human hunter with his blood up going after a deer. It was a thrill, in a way, but it was scary.

When the big man surfaced with the new fish (a 15 pounder, it turned out), he was grinning that bloodthirsty, blackcloud grin of his. He went back down immediately.

Grant did not find it all that easy the rest of the afternoon, and in a way he was just as glad. He could not get the picture of that liquid-eyed fish gaping in agony out of his mind. And yet underneath all that, he discovered a savage joy in it, too. The savage joy didn't help him, however. He fired about six more times at fish and missed each time. The fish seemed to have a peculiar habit of flicking themselves away, with that incredible speed they all seemed capable of—if only for short distances, just at the exact moment when he pulled the trigger. Bonham seemed able to anticipate this and shoot a split second faster.

When they had finished and were running home with Ali the helper at the wheel and had gotten the gin bottle out, Bonham seemed peculiarly tired, even depressed.

" God, I love spearfishing! " he said with his thundercloud grin, leaning back against the gunwale after a pull at the bottle. " I didn't mean to run off and leave you like that." He paused luxuriously. " But you did all right by yourself, didn't you?"

" I got one," Grant said. " I loved it. But it seems kind of a shame, kind of unsporting, to shoot them like that, in a lung, with so little on their side."

" Are you kidding?" Bonham looked at him blackly, as if he'd been insulted. " We couldn't even get down to them there at eighty-five feet without a lung. That's why they're so unspoiled and easy. But they wise up fast. The word goes out that there's some kind of predator loose on the reef, don't ask me how, and they all begin to run. They communicate, don't ever worry about that. And anyway, if we didn't get them, something else would, eventually. That's the life of the sea. It's worse than any ' jungle '."

"It sure is. But I thought some divers could actually free-dive that deep?" Grant asked.

"Sure. And even more. You mean like the Pindar brothers. But they're specialists. In just that. I can do sixty feet, but I'm not sure I can do eighty-five. Anyway, why give them a break?"

He seemed totally disinterested in the fish, which now rode along behind them in the dinghy, and asked Grant if he wanted them. By rights they were his, since he was paying for the trip.

"Christ, we couldn't eat that many," Grant protested. "But I would like two or three good ones to take home."

"They're yours," Bonham said.

They would feast at the villa to-night, but not on bought fish, on fish speared by Grant the hunter. "I'd like to have the one I shot," he said with an embarrassed smile. It was the smallest.

Bonham grinned suddenly, and then displayed that surprising sensitivity Grant found him capable of so often. "Hell, take three big ones and tell them you shot all three. What difference does it make?" Or was it just vast experience.

Grant made an embarrassed shrug. "What'll you do with the rest?"

Bonham's eyes filmed over slightly. "Sell 'em. In the Market. If you don't want 'em. But understand that they're yours if you want them. Lots of times clients don't want that much fish, and then I sell them rather than waste them. Pick up a little change that way."

"I only shot one anyway," Grant said modestly.

"Doesn't matter. They belong to you. Because you're paying me for the trip, the use of the equipment, and the instruction."

Grant shook his head politely. He didn't really understand this big man. Yet. Bonham shrugged. Okay, then he'd sell them. He wasn't a bit above selling them.

Bonham, it appeared, was having troubles of his own. And after the question of the fish was settled, he discussed them with Grant on the rest of the run back in.

Unlike Grant, his troubles were not with women. The camera case he had tried out yesterday (the films of Grant weren't developed yet) had been designed and built by a friend of his here in Ganado Bay, an American, who was one of the best underwater case makers in the whole of the Caribbean. Bonham sold them for him in his shop. But they were expensive to make, because he worked only in the best plastic plate and did it all by hand, and he couldn't make very many except on order, and this limited Bonham's chances at sales. Most beginning divers couldn't afford to lay out that much for a case, especially if it also meant buying a new camera. Most vacationers already owned a camera, usually a model for which William had not yet designed a case ; and they usually didn't stay long enough for him both to design and make a case, thus losing Bonham other sales.

Anyway, in four or five days, he and William would be flying over to Grant Bank Island to test out still another new case which William had designed for the German Minox, and Grant was free to come on and go along if he paid his own expenses. The Minox case was Bonham's idea. They had found that lots of vacationers, at least those that began learning diving with Bonham, owned a Minox, either by itself or as a subsidiary to their 35 mm. And of course it was much cheaper, both camera *and* case.

" But why are you going to Grand Bank to test it?" Grant asked.

Bonham grinned. " Because a rich guy I know is stayin' there. And if it works, he wants to buy one right away ; that one. Camera and all." He seemed to pause, rather than to finish.

Grand Bank Island was a small coral and sand atoll located at the very southern tip of the Bahamas, about halfway between Greater Inagua and the Caicos a hundred miles to the southeast. That put it only another hundred miles from both Mouchoir Bank and the Silver Shoals. Shaped rather like an exclamation mark, it possessed one town at its wider end and a deep lagoon at the other where several ancient galleons were reputed to have sunk, although so far nobody had ever found any trace of them. It was three miles long, was covered with brush and a few palms and pines, was hotter than hell, and had one road which ran from the town, a wide-open free port under the Bahamas Commission, to its one moderately luxurious hotel which was situated on the lagoon. It had no air strip and could be flown to only by a flying boat service which landed on the lagoon. Grant had never seen it but he had read about it in several treasure-hunting-diving books.

" But that's not the only reason," Bonham went on finally. He paused again, and in the breeze that had dried them rubbed a huge hand lightly over his vast expanse of hairy stomach. " See, there's this great two-master schooner just been put up for sale in Kingston a few months ago. Sleeps six plus two crew, sixty-eight feet overall. The *Naiad*." He paused still again, and tried another tack. " See, I taught this rich guy—Sam Finer is his name—to dive last year when he was stayin' in one of the big beach hotels here in Ganado Bay. And he fell madly in love with divin'. So much that he's thinkin' of puttin' money into my business, just to have a good boat available for him whenever he wants to go on divin' trips."

It turned out to be a lot more complex than that as Bonham went on explaining, but the essential point in his trip to Grand Bank was to see Sam Finer about the schooner. Finer, who was not Jewish but a stocky little German (though that made no difference at all to Bonham), was from Milwaukee where he owned two good-paying bars as well as three tavern-hotel-fishing resorts up in northern Wisconsin. He spent his summers fishing in his own resorts and drinking in his own taverns, and he would eventually like to find something of the same sort to go into in the Caribbean, where he could spend his winters diving. Behind the bars and the resorts was something else about stone quarries both for cement and dressed stone which he owned. Anyway, he was willing—or just about willing—to put up $10,000 to go into Bonham's business here. However, as everybody concerned knew, $10,000 wasn't enough to buy and fix up a good boat big enough for two- and three-weeks diving cruises between islands. So in this connection, Bonham had come up with something else.

Grant thought he had never seen such unconscious hunger on anyone's face as appeared in Bonham's big mug when he digressed a moment to talk about the schooner before going on to his " something else " he had " come up with." Obviously it had to be totally unconscious hunger, or Bonham would have hidden it.

The something else was a potential partner named Frankie

Orloffski. Bonham it turned out had been born and raised on the South Jersey Shore, where he had sailed and fished all his life before becoming a skindiver after the war, and on a visit home to see his mother (a peculiar look came over his big tough mug when he mentioned his mother, whom he capitalised with his voice) he had met this Polack guy who owned a sporting goods and diving shop in Cape May. Orloffski also owned a thirty-eight-foot Bermuda cutter with which he was trying to build up a business of diving cruises, but it was tough sledding because even cruising as far south as Hatteras (which was really outside his comfortable range) the water was cold and murky, ugly diving water. Orloffski, when Bonham met him, was wanting to move south maybe to Miami. Bonham, who had spent two years trying the same thing in Miami, was able to tell him the Atlantic waters off Miami were not really much better than Orloffski's own, and suggested they might go in together in Ganado Bay, which was practically virgin territory compared to Miami or the Keys. They would have no competition, the single-master would make a good short cruise boat as well as a fine work boat for real underwater jobs, and if they could only swing the schooner through Sam Finer coming in on it they could cruise the Caymans and even beat up the Windward Channel to cruise the Inaguas, Grand Bank and the Silver Shoals, all really virgin territory. It would be the biggest charter thing on this island.

Bonham would put in his two small boats, all his gear, his building, his big compressors (the purchase and transportation of which was his biggest single investment, worth almost as much as the cutter), and last but not least his knowhow, the good will he had accrued here, and his already growing business.

Frankie Orloffski would put in his Bermuda cutter, and a minimum of $6,000 for running capital from the proceeds of the sale of his sport shop.

Hearing such knowledgeable business words and phrases come out of the mouth of the big diver made Grant feel distinctly peculiar, as if somehow he had not gotten himself outside the doors of Gibson & Stein after all.

Bonham had arranged for Orloffski to meet Sam Finer in New York when Sam was on a business trip and now

Orloffski and his wife (his girl really; since he was only living with her) were going to be in Grand Bank too for a few days spearfishing at the same time as Sam (and his wife), and they could all talk business over the bar. Apparently Sam and Orloffski had hit it off together in their New York meeting. The trip would be expensive for both Bonham and Orloffski, but Bonham had high hopes of them swinging the deal with Finer for the schooner.

" Of course, that won't take care of it all. We'll have to mortgage to get the schooner going. But at least we'll have it then. A year, two at the most, should pay it out in full."

Again that greedy, almost insane look of totally unconscious hunger—which would brook no interference, allow no stopping anywhere short of the goal: The Schooner—came over Bonham's cloudlike countenance.

He began to talk about it again. He had gone over her pretty carefully where they had her moored out at Sanderson's near Port Royal on the spit. Had flown down to Kingston especially for that. She had some bad dry rot forward starboard against the stem which might entail reinforcing the bowsprit or replacing it, and some of the deck planking was going bad near the stern, but she was in pretty good shape—very good shape, for a ship that had been owned by an oil company to take out executive week-end sailors. Of course she would have to be pulled and her hull gone over completely. There would be a good bit of yardwork to pay for. But . . . " Do you know what I could do with a boat like that?" he said almost viciously after a pause, staring pale-eyed off across the never-quite-quiet sea. " I could—I'd be safe the rest of my life Nobody could touch me. If I owned a boat like that. I hate companies. All they do is destroy. Destroy all the old ways and the old things. Destroy, and call it progress. They want to standardise everything and everything that ain't standardised they don't know how to handle. They gave her a very bad captain. A real bum. I know him. What did they care? They didn't love her, all they wanted was to take their fat asses out (with a captain to sail her) and play-like they'us sailors ridin' the bounding main. Impress a client now and then to close a deal." He turned to stare flat-eyed at Grant.

" He didn't take care of her at all. There was no need for
her to be in that kind of shape. But I'm sure her hull is
sound."

Grant didn't say anything. What was there for him to say?
He knew next to nothing about sailing.

What a crazy fucked-up world we live in! he thought
suddenly. Four men, four men from such widely separated
and over-industrialised places as New York, New Jersey,
Indianapolis, Indiana and Milwaukee, Wisconsin all converg-
ing on a tiny primitive grease spot of an island in the Caribbean Sea and why? To escape for a few days from the fetter-
ing conditions of their highly organised, boring lives—in the
primitive but now highly sophisticated sport of spearing
fish. And while doing this, they would be discussing and
planning ways to make money by bringing other people to it
and destroying the very thing they sought there. And behind
their trip, behind each pilot and hostess who would be
bringing them there, there stood the ranked rows of bureaucratic workers, stewards, clerks, handling tickets in triplicate,
numbered series of baggage checks to protect their luggage,
weights and fuel allowances and tonnages—all things they
all hated, but without which they would be unable even to
get to their primitive island. And behind these, all the
planning boards, engineering boards, air traffic control, the
towermen, the radiomen—almost all of whom would never
make the money to be able to afford such a trip themselves—
there.

And lastly, most amorphous of all because largest of all,
Government. Which none of them liked either, and were
all trying to escape (but which itself allowed them their very
opportunity to escape " But, mind you, for a few days
only!"), except that how can you escape from, or even
dislike, something you cannot see, or perceive with any of
your other senses. Shades of Frankie Aldane and his Harvard
lawyer friend!

He was rudely awakened from this pretty pointless reverie
by Bonham.

" You ever do any free-diving?"

" Well, you know. Not very much. Only a very little bit,
quite close to shore, in a lake."

" I thought maybe not. Well, you see, we're not taking
any equipment over with us. It'd cost too much overweight.

And anyway, we'd have to take a portable compressor since there's no facilities for refillin' tanks."

" You're not going to look for those galleons in the lagoon then?" Grant said, a little proud of his knowledge.

" Are you kidding? Hell, it would take Ed Ling and his Sea Diver II to even have a prayer of findin' them, and even then it would be luck. If they're there at all, which I ain't sure, they're under about twenty feet of sand."

Bonham hitched himself up a little higher on the rail and reached for the gin bottle. " No, here's what I was thinkin'. Since we can't afford to take equipment, and since you don't know free-diving, I thought if you'd be willin' to pay my plane fare and my room over there, I would take you in hand while we're there and teach you everything I know about free-diving."

Grant thought once again—with a little worry—about his steadily mounting tab with Bonham, and then turned away to smother a smile. " Well, okay. I guess that's fair enough," he said, looking off at the approaching docks. He knew he was being taken, but Bonham was obviously short of money, and he was really deeply excited about the prospect of the trip. Then suddenly there appeared before his eyes, like a colour transparency overlaid on the view of the dockage, a memory picture of Lucky standing nude in the little Park Avenue " tenement " apartment that first afternoon they had made love together, and the excitement about the trip fell down out of him leaving a sort of echoing hollow of emptiness and disinterest. He wished he had her here to go with him. The sun glints on the water, the fresh salt sea air, the movement of the boat and the beautiful whisper of the wash all were suddenly unadventurous and unspecial.

" It'll only cost you about fifty bucks all told," Bonham said.

" I'm not a very good swimmer."

Bonham wrinkled his small nose in the large expanse of his face below the clear, flat eyes. " That don't matter. With a snorkel and flippers anybody can stay in the water for hours.

" Meanwhile, we can keep on going out here the next few days, till it's time to go. Same price. I know where there's a good wreck—I mean a modern one—I can take you to-morrow if you want to explore it."

Grant nodded and left it at that. But the truth was he didn't feel like diving or doing anything with the thought of Lucky in his mind now. When Ali brought them deftly to dock in the messy tidewater, and they had climbed out on to the ancient wood jetty, he offered to take the diver over to the Yacht Club for a few blasts of gin.

But Bonham shook his head. "No, I think I'll stick around here." He was already hauling in on the line to the plastic dinghy to get at the fish. Native workers on the tottery old dock came crowding around to look at the catch. "Anyway, after last night," he said, looking up from the fish with his bent-jawed incredibly sanguinary grin, "I got to get home to-night and see my little old lady." He had not, Grant remembered suddenly, appeared to be the least bit hungover. He had already begun gutting the fish.

"I'll have Ali to run you up the hill," he called. "But first you got to pick your fish you want."

The Jamaican dock workers, all fiddling around with some small boat or other, had by now crowded up around him until their bare, greedy-looking toes were almost touching the fish, and Bonham suddenly let loose on them that thunderous voice Grant had always suspected him of having. "GO ON! GIT BACK AWAY FROM THERE, YOU BASTARDS, GODDAMN IT!" he bellowed at them, gesturing with the knife. The crowd moved back a reluctant two feet, grinning.

Grant, who was always overly polite to Negroes, was embarrassed but the crowd itself didn't seem to mind at all.

"Here, come on, Grant! Before these buggers rob me blind." But when Grant chose two of the biggest grouper to go with his own small one, Bonham shook his head and began instructing him about fish. "Those two there are mangrove snapper," he said, pointing with the knife to the two already gutted fish; "they're the best in the batch, take them." Beside them he laid Grant's now gutted grouper.

"But I like grouper," Grant protested.

"Okay, take this medium-sized one. Instead of one of the snapper," he added pointedly. "But not the big ones. They're grainy." He proceeded to gut the grouper.

While he talked to Grant, the crowd had begun to edge forward again, and one long slender adolescent boy with appreciably visible ribs had come forward far enough to

have one splayed foot on either side of the end fish in the
line Bonham had laid out on the pier. " GODDAMN YOU,
CYRIL, I SAID GIT BACK!" Bonham hollered, as the feet
slowly came closer and closer together around the fish,
and threw the knife which stuck in the wood pier six inches
from the fish's tail. Reluctantly the boy, his hands still
behind his back and still grinning, moved back away.

Grant had already moved away, still embarrassed. At
the car he threw the three fish in the back, their iridescent
colours now faded and gone as if they had dried up inward.

As Ali climbed in behind the wheel, Grant looked back
once and Bonham who had retrieved his knife, as if sensing
the look, glanced up and grinned and waved the knife at him.

Then they were grinding up the hill in the old station-wagon.

Grant the hunter was coming home with his catch. But
he would rather have taken a beating than go back to that
goddamned unhappy, miserable but beautiful villa where
he had to go, even with the fish.

Down below on the dock, Bonham watched them thoughtfully until they were out of sight.

EIGHT

The exquisitely honed knife cut into the last fish, at the
vent, easily and pleasurably and Bonham idly watched his
hands go expertly, knowledgeably and delicately about their
work as if his mind had nothing to do with it. He loved
his knife and always sharpened it himself, never allowed
anybody else to touch it.

The knife slid up the exact centre of the belly to the
chin as soft and easy as if moving through water, and the
slippery, slightly sticky guts slithered out on the dock like
prisoners released from confinement. This one had been
eating right good. Four completely whole shiner minnows
could be seen through the thin belly membrane. Bonham
slit the membrane and shucked them out. One of them was
still alive. Laughing, Bonham showed it to the Negroes,
who laughed too, and tossed it back in the water. " Lucky,"
he called. " He day no come up."

Automatically his fingers probed around inside the cavity

making sure everything was out. Then, pulling them out clean,
right up to the chin, he sliced all the guts off neatly at the
gill. In fact his mind was not on what his hands were
doing. It was on Ron Grant.

As he resharpened the knife on the big soft-Arkansas oilstone, he whistled inaudibly under his breath some idiot
tune.

You don't find a good easy touch like that every day in
the year. Most of them who got passionate about diving
didn't have the money to do more than take a complete
pool checkout and go out a couple times. And the ones
who had money never got interested. In his four years in
Jamaica, Grant was only the third. Sam Finer had been
the second. Last year. Then, this year, Grant.

He had been sitting in the shop with his feet up on the
desk. There was some rock'n'roll on the radio and he
listened to it picking his teeth, feeling the little wood instrument slide stealthily between two of his ivories searching
meat. He had sensed rather than seen the shadow fall upon
the open door up front, and sat up immediately and began
studying some regulator sales diagrams which lay on the
desk for that express purpose. He really knew them by
heart. Anyway regulators weren't all that much different
from each other once you understood them, except maybe the
Northhill, which only had one adjustable part compared to
the eight to seventeen of the others.

She was a tall broad, fairly, with her hair cut short around
her ears and back of her neck. Light behind her couldn't
see her face. Not a bad corpus, and she didn't have any
slip on. Kind of light in the tits department. And she
walked funny ; lumpish. Then he got up and she turned
and he saw her face and saw that she was old, fifty-three,
fifty-five. And there was something else. He at once didn't
like it. Smile—prissy ; and highly self-conscious. Pinched
in at the corners to make two sort of self-righteous jowls.
Was there a make there? Maybe ; it was too soon to tell.
But she was old enough he didn't really care.

" Do you teach skindiving? " Prissy voice, too ; self-adoring.

" I certainly do, Mam." He let his face open up in a
grin. " Especially to pretty ladies, Mam. That's my speciality." He especially made it flattery, and not any kind of
a make.

And a remarkable change occurred in her. The corners relaxed so the smile opened out into a real one, and her dark eyes opened more and got deep and friendly, had real warmth. That way she wasn't really bad looking, for an old one.

"Oh, it's not for me!" she said in some confusion. "It's for a friend of mine. My foster-son, really. Who is coming down. To-day. He wants——" She reached in her purse as if she knew just where it was and pulled out and held up a wire as if she needed it for confirmation, " —he wants to learn skindiving."

"Then you've come to just the right place, Mam," he said, putting heartiness in his voice.

Then a remarkable thing happened. For no reason that he could see the jowls clamped down again and the eyes got small and undeep again and the anxiety, or whatever it was, came back on her. Curiously, it even showed in the position of her back, which seemed to slightly bow itself suddenly. It was then that he knew she was crazy. Or awful close to it.

"We're staying with the Countess de Blystein," she said ; very prissy.

"I know the Countess," Bonham said promptly. "Not well, of course." He did. He had met her. Everybody in the town knew Evelyn de Blystein a little.

"Well, we are staying with she and the Count Paul. My husband, myself, and our foster-son. His name is Ron Grant. I expect you've heard of him perhaps."

"I think so," Bonham said. He had noted away the nominative pronoun error.

"He's a Broadway playwright. You must have heard of *The Song of Israphael*. It ran three and a half years on Broadway."

"I think so," Bonham said. "Yes."

"It was a very famous film. MGM brought it out. It won five Academy Awards."

"Yes. I saw the film," Bonham said.

Then he did remember it. He had seen it. About Pearl Harbour. About a sailor and a whore. He'd been in the Navy himself in the war, and he'd liked it. There was no bullshit in it. Or not much. But she was beginning to piss him off. Who cared? He smiled at her. " I remember it very well. I liked it."

"He's quite famous, you know." She didn't come out and say he was very lucky to have such a client, but it was implied.

"Yes, he certainly is," Bonham had said. "And what is your name, Mam?"

"My name is Carol Abernathy. And my husband's name is Hunt Abernathy."

"I see. Your husband's here?"

"Yes." She smiled that smile. "I think I told you that."

Bonham ignored that. "And will both of you be comin' along, too?"

"No, no. My husband won't. He's not interested. He's a golfer. But I thought I might come along the first day to see."

"You should try it yourself, Mam. You'll find it's very exciting," he had said, " and, I think, intellectually stimulating. The undersea life here in Jamaica is one of the richest in flora and fauna in the entire world."

The smile and the eyes had turned shy now. Vulnerable. "Well, I'm not sure I could do it. I'm an excellent swimmer, though."

"Anybody can do it. You don't even have to be a good swimmer. I start people off in a swimming pool," Bonham said gently, "for the first few days. Until I've taught them how to use the aqualung. It's much safer that way. And my way is to teach safely. Actually, I taught my own mother to skindive, and she is almost eighty. She loves it now." He kept his face completely open.

The woman was smiling ingenuously now, and the eyes and mouth corners were a bit more open. "Well, perhaps I will. Give it a try, I mean. To-morrow, then?"

"Be glad to have you, Mam."

"What time, please?"

"After lunch? Two? Two-thirty? Three?"

"Don't you have to let your food digest for four hours? Before?"

"Not in a pool, Mam."

"Very well, at three then. To-morrow." She offered him the tight prissy smile, this time, and turned to go. Then suddenly she turned back.

And her face astounded Bonham this time. It still had the jowly, pinched-corners, prissy look, but now the eyes had become like those of some very knowledgeable jungle cat. "There's just one other thing."

"Mam?"

"Ron—Mister Grant—plans on going on to Kingston to actually learn his diving, I believe. From a man named Georges Villalonga?" She pronounced it French.

"I know George," Bonham said. He pronounced it American. "But I don't think he's in Kingston any more. I think he went out to the West Coast to work for US Di——"

"Whether he's still there or not, I would like very much for Mister Grant to do all his diving here, in Ganado Bay." The voice still had its tight prissy sound, but now there was a very sharp edge to it, too. A very sharp edge. "I'd much rather he didn't go to Kingston at all." She paused. "Do you follow me?"

Bonham had stared expressionlessly into those eyes for quite a long moment. "I think so, Mam. You mean you'd like him to do all his learning and divin' here with me because you trust my ability. Well, I'll certainly try to help all I can." Then he made himself grin. "Naturally, I wouldn't like to lose a good, high-payin' customer to Kingston."

She didn't smile. "Good. We understand each other. Good-bye." And she turned and stumped—lumpish—herself, in that peculiar prissy bent-backed walk, out the door.

"Mrs. Abernathy!"

She turned back in the doorway.

"Would you mind telling me who sent you to me?"

"Why, yes," she smiled. "The manager of the Royal Canadian Bank." She turned and left.

By now he was absolutely certain she was crazy. Just how or in what way, or why, he didn't know enough to know. Things a guy had to do to make a living. That kind in divin' you had to watch very carefully. Be prone to panic. He hoped she didn't go. But maybe the guy—the boy-friend?—wouldn't want to go either if she didn't want to go. Some were like that. Damned women. Well, if he watched her close. He hated to lose two customers right now. Or even one.

Letta's salary was hardly keeping them going this month. And this was February.

Well he had a pool checkout at the Royal Carib this afternoon. One unwealthy tourist.

Probably, he thought as he had gone about getting the
gear ready at the back of the shop, this Grant would turn
out to be some kind of half-fag, highfalutin' snob type. If
his gir—if his foster-mother was any good example. Well
there was no accounting for tastes. As the old woman said
as she kissed the cow. But why didn't she want him to
go to Kingston? If they didn't get so terrible bad he
couldn't stomach it, he could do it. For the money. That
kind, the richies, always wanted the top luxury treatment
and anything else made them turn up their noses. He would
give it to them, if he had it. If he ever got it, ever got a
chance to get it.

Deliciously—but with a grinding jealousy of acquisitiveness
—he let himself dwell as he worked on the *Naiad* and his
trip down to Kingston to look her over. There was hope
there. If he could ever get her.

You met all kinds of kooks in this business. That dame, for
instance. He was pretty damn sure this Grant would turn
out to be a highbrow prick.

The weight of it on his broad back had made the tanks
heavier as he carried them out of his old station-wagon to
go the Carib. That and the fact that he knew he'd have
to do it. For the money.

And just think, some day they would all be dead.

The sudden thought opened up a hollow in Bonham, of
amazement, disbelief, fear and depression. What he'd like to
do this afternoon was go out and kill himself a shark.
Whenever he got to thinking of his own eventual, inevitable
death, and sometimes it lasted for days, the only thing
that could snap him out of it was to get Ali and the boat
and go out to his "Ol' Shark Hole" where there was
almost always one or two hanging around and diving down
deep and viciously with his fury and his fear spear himself
one of those evil foul-smelling bastards with a killing head
shot, a six or seven-footer Blue or Tiger or shovelnose. Even
if he didn't make a killing brain shot and had to cut the
line, he'd get himself a hell of a ride out of it. And they
weren't going to do anybody much good after that with
a spear through their head from top to bottom through both

jaws! Their brothers would take care of them down the line!

Suddenly he wanted very badly to go. He didn't take any buddies or his customers on these expeditions and usually went along, with just Ali. Ali thought he was nuts. But it cleansed you and fixed you up, took everything bad away, everything. After that he felt like a man again. After that, a man didn't have to worry about getting laid.

But he had this pool checkout to-day.

God! how Letta hated it. When he went shark shooting. Screamed like a fishwife. At the thought of his wife another hollow opened in him, but this one was of a different kind, too painful to bear, much worse than the death depression, and he suavely covered it over with a layer of something else, so it would not appear to be there. He had gone back to thinking about the *Naiad*, and about the equipment for the pool checkout.

But as it turned out Grant was not a snooty type at all. Just the opposite, he was a very regular guy. Almost too regular a guy, if that was ever possible. And Bonham, who was much more worldly and sophisticated than he was ever willing to let anybody know—just as he never let them know about his university education—especially people he had to do business with—found him curiously naïve, even boyish, for someone who had made as much money and acquired as much fame as he was supposed to have done—as he obviously *had* done.

Well, maybe that was what artistic talent was. He didn't know. What he didn't know about artistic talent was just about everything.

He had taken them out to the Royal Carib that first day. So *he* could work them in with his one unwealthy tourist, a nice young insurance man from downstate Illinois who was staying there, fortyish and beginning to go to fat, the kind of customer he was more used to handling. He would be able to afford to go out twice to the shallow reef and poke around before he went home to tell his pals at the country club about his skindiving experience. And this way he could work in three paying lessons all at once and save an hour to spend on his constant cruising of the other hotels. He had to drum up more business. The insurance man's good-looking wife only watched. Bonham had tried, but she was too scared and he couldn't talk her into a lesson.

That the boyish playwright was Mrs. Abernathy's lover was clear from the start to Bonham's jaundiced but unjudging eye. Didn' make him no nevermind. Fortunately the woman camped out at the start. She couldn't learn to clear her mask even sitting down in the shallow end of the pool. She panicked every time. And when he halfway through got her to put the lung on and lie on the bottom at the shallow end thinking that might help, she couldn't do that either. He hated to lose the money, but at least now he wouldn't have to take her out and watch her closely all the time.

Grant, on the other hand, was good. He was completely brave, although for some reason he didn't seem to know it. He caught on fast, and he caught up with and even surpassed the insurance man, who was on his third day, by the end of the lesson.

The second day he took them to the West Moon Over Hotel, because he had to take the insurance man, who was leaving in two days, out for his first dive on the shallow reef in the morning. The West Moon Over was the ritziest and most expensive hotel in Ganado Bay, and for this reason Bonham didn't usually take people there for lessons unless they were registered there. But he figured a little publicity couldn't do any harm. So he stopped by in the morning and told the manager who he was bringing in. Naturally they were glad.

The pool was deserted when he gave Grant the lesson and quite suddenly, after he was all through with what he had to do with mask and lung and looking relieved, Grant began to do springboard diving. They had a regulation three-metre board at the West Moon Over (the only one in town except for the Country Club) and Grant just up and climbed it—and on his first dive did a beautiful, absolutely letter-perfect pike forward one and a half. Then he seemed to get caught up in the emotional spirit of it, Bonham sensed (perhaps because the pool was deserted), and began to do all manner of things: a beautiful layout full gained to which he added both half twist and full twist; back one and a half tucked; flying mares, which was a layout swan held halfway down and finished off with a tucked front one; and then he finished it all off with two full-twisting forward one and a halfs. Bonham thought he had never seen anything so beautiful, absolutely beautiful.

The woman had come along to watch the lesson, but she didn't seem to think anything very much of the springboard diving, or of any sports, Bonham decided—any sports which she could not do herself, he guessed. Luckily she didn't come any more after that second day, and the men could be alone together.

Bonham had been around pools and swimming all his life, and had actually swum backstroke for both his high school in Jersey and for the University of Pennsylvania. He knew what that kind of near-letter-perfect three-metre board diving entailed. The high degree of nervous and muscle co-ordination to start with, and then the work. The literally hours and hours and hours of constant practice, over and over and over, the hard falls and faulted dives that landed you flat on the water on your back or on your face. It was then that he began really to admire Grant for the first time. He did them absolutely beautiful, and he was beautiful doing them. Never mind the intellectual, playwright horse-shit.

Bonham had always loved springboard diving, and had always wanted to do it himself. But he had always been too big and too heavy for any regulation board. But he knew what it entailed. He had always secretly cursed his own huge and broad-assed build, and Grant up on the board was absolutely beautiful with his tiny hips and the very wide shoulders and muscled, well-turned legs. It was a shame he wasn't just a little taller all over and he would be a perfect physical man.

When he surfaced laughing after the last dive, he congratulated him, but not warmly. He made it very casual.

"You're pretty good."

Grant had grinned shyly and swum over. "I used to dive for a Navy team at Pearl. And then I just always sort of kept it up. I like it because it's exciting and—well, it's a little dangerous. You *can* get hurt. And I guess I like that."

"Sure," Bonham grinned, "that's the spice. It's the same with the aqualung and with spearfishin'."

They had seemed to exchange a secret glance of special understanding, of complicity even, which the woman—if she noted it at all—did not acknowledge.

To-day, squatting on the jetty with his now gutted and
freshly washed-down fish, and still whistling to himself inaudibly and almost tonelessly, Bonham thought back again
to the physiological revelation he had had of Grant that
day of the first spring board diving. Playwright or not, intellectual or not, Grant was an athlete with an athlete's basic
outlook, and Bonham understood athletes. He was one.

That was why it was peculiar to see him with that peculiar
woman. It had never occurred to him before, he didn't
know why, but now he began to think of Grant coming in
on the buying of the schooner. It might be a very good
idea. He didn't know how much he was worth of course,
or how much he would be able to put up. But anything would
help. As far as that went. The woman of course would be
against it from the word go. And she was clearly very
involved in his life and decisions. How to handle her?
He would have to think about that.

Tossing all the fish into the big string bag he kept for
catches, he walked back off the dock and up the little rise
to where Ali would return with the car. It was too soon to
tell, really, about Grant. But if he kept up to that basic
athlete's outlook he had shown with the springboard diving,
he would come along and come up to snuff. Too soon to
tell. But Bonham would know more about that after those
four or five days over in Grand Bank. Almost certainly he
would *have* to acquire the passion for diving and spearfishing,
given his personality. He didn't know anything about sailing.
But he could learn. In some ways he speculated that Grant
would make a better partner, and a better friend, than either
Sam Finer or Orloffski.

Bonham had his reservations, which he had not told
Grant, about both of them. Especially Orloffski. Orloffski was
a crude, cocky, loudmouth, stupid insensitive brute. Smaller
than Bonham, he was nevertheless strong as hell and built
like a pro football player, and he was a more than adequate
spearfisherman and diver. But he was a lousy sailor. Bonham
had been out with him on the cutter up in Jersey, and while
Bonham knew quite well that he himself could handle the
schooner all alone, he had watched Orloffski sail and knew
equally well that Orloffski could never handle the schooner
by himself, though Orloffski loudly claimed he could. In
addition, Orloffski was a pretty big drunk. Though they

were all somewhat of that. But Orloffski was bad. And Bonham also suspected that he was some kind of a psychologically compulsive thief. That was a lot against. Still, what he was contributing to the deal was considerable. So considerable that the deal could not be swung without him.

Sam Finer on the other hand was very smart. And tough. He had come up along some very hard tough route, and his grammar was as bad as Orloffski's, but he was a smart businessman. " Bars will always make money, Al," was one of his theories, " because people will always drink." He knew nothing at all about sailing and admitted it. He was willing to serve as lowliest crew. And diving and spearfishing he adored. And he had the hard cash. But he was a very bad drunk. Worse than Orloffski. Because when he got drunk, he wanted to fight. Most of the time. And he was a mean fighter. Bonham had already bailed him out of three or four scrapes that might have gotten him killed, or at the least sent to jail. His wife would be coming down with him this time for the first time (they had only been married a couple of months), and Bonham had never met her. Sam had met her in New York on a business trip, Bonham thought he remembered. Wasn't she a model?

Well, we will see. We will see. This first general meeting was going to be very important he knew. Very imporatnt. He could feel his hands begin to sweat.

Oh, that ship! Oh, that ship! If he could only get his hands on her! Get her, and sail her, and pay her off. So he—so the corporation (but of which he would be both President and Captain)—would own her! He could take her anywhere in the world. He could sail her to Cape Verde and the Canaries and take her in the Mediterranean, if anybody wanted to go there.

And from there he could take her right on around the whole damn *God*dam world, if they wanted to go! A free man, in a free ship, and nobody to tell him one damn thing this or that.

Well, they would see next week. He could hardly wait, and at the same time he hoped next week never came.

It was good that damn woman, that Mrs. Abernathy, wouldn't be around either. Over there maybe he could talk some to Grant without her influence bein' around all the time to offset him every night at home.

NINE

On his third time out with Bonham Grant speared his first sting ray. And quite erroneously at least for a while—he decided he had reached a plateau of some kind.

They had gone out, this third trip, to inspect the wreck Bonham had told him about the day before. It lay just off the western end of the harbour mouth in about fifty feet of water. Apparently it had happened during the war Bonham said, when this freighter, a sort of modified Liberty ship carrying American war supplies for somewhere had tried too late to get out of Ganado Bay Harbour ahead of one of the rare hurricanes that hit Jamaica. It had sprung a leak due to heavy seas, been abandoned, and then had been washed on to a reef there by the winds, where it broke up and sank. US Navy divers had salvaged what was salvageable in her, and the rest was still there broken into huge chunks scattered across the quiet sand.

They had not meant to fish particularly but had taken the spearguns with them anyway since as Bonham said you never knew when you might see something either good to eat or exciting to try. That was exactly how it turned out.

The smashed and broken ship, parts of it lying as far as sixty and a hundred yards apart, filled Grant with a nervous awe for what the sea could do, for what power it could have when really agitated, as he lay on the surface in the lung looking down at it. Impulsively and a little fearfully, he raised his head and looked up into the world of air: the sun was shining brightly, glints of it sparkled cheerfully off the water, the wash rolled him gently and almost lovingly, the air was soft. Rolling over to the right he surface-dived and planed straight down not bothering with the anchorline in his new-found familiarity with the lung. On the quiet sand bottom, which registered fifty feet on the depth gauge Bonham had sold him, the light was almost as bright as it was up in the air.

They had only brought down one gun. It was Bonham's, a triple rubber variety with a stainless-steel spear which

Grant didn't know the name of, and Grant was carrying it. Bonham carried the same still camera he had brought out with them the first day, an Argus C-3 in William's plastic case, which Grant suspected Bonham was in the process of trying to sell him. He took a few shots of Grant inspecting various huge chunks of the wreckage and was just in the process of motioning Grant to come over and exchange gun for camera so he could try it out himself, when he looked down at the sand and motioned Grant violently to come. When he did, Bonham descended a few feet and pointed at the sand.

For several long moments Grant could see nothing. Lying side by side, their shoulders touching occasionally, he looked down over the end of Bonham's pointing, agitated finger and stared and stared. Finally he saw the thing. Buried in the sand which faintly outlined its form with only the top of its head and its eyes actually showing, was a small sting ray a foot-and-a-half, two feet across. As if in some peculiar way sensing it was being observed with malevolent intent, the ugly little thing heaved itself out of the sand and began swimming slowly away like some delta-shaped airplane with flappable wings.

Agitatedly, Bonham motioned for Grant to follow. Grant nodded holding up the speargun questioningly, but Bonham shook his head as if it was hardly worth a spear and the subsequent reloading, and drew his knife and glanced at Grant. Grant touched the heavy hilt of his own big knife strapped to his calf which Bonham had also sold him, and finally shook his head. He felt ashamed and cowardly, but he didn't know enough about it, about how to go about it. Agitatedly, Bonham thrust the camera at him and took off, swimming slightly upward.

Again Grant became aware of the almost rapaciously sanguinary quality in the big diver, as he watched. Everything in the sea was his enemy, would hurt him, even kill him if it could. And he in turn would kill it, damage it, destroy it every chance he got, and give no quarter or mercy. Grant watching him felt as if he were looking back through misty æons of time at the history of his race.

Swimming slightly upward, Bonham levelled off about six feet above the ray. It didn't take him long to catch it though he didn't appear to be swimming strenuously. Then

from above it he dove straight down. His knife was held
in his right hand with the butt buried in his palm and
the fingers extended along the hilt. The grip made Grant
think of a matador holding banderillas. Just above the ugly
little creature he braked, levelled, then dipped down with
incredible delicacy and stabbed the knife squarely into the
head just behind the eyes, wrenched it free and drew back.

The little fish, fairly struck, flapped and bucked and
lashed about with its poisonous barbed tail ineffectually.
In three seconds it was dead, and turned belly upward floated
gently down toward the sand. Above it, motionless, his
body in an odd indefinable posture which communicated
intense satisfaction, Bonham watched its death throes, then
sheathing his knife came swimming back to Grant. He paid
no more attention to the quarry. He could not grin in the
aqualung, but he smiled with his eyes and wiggled his eyebrows
with an innocent, totally unselfconscious pleasure in the
killing which Grant suddenly realised he himself would
never be able to achieve during the run-out of his life no
matter what he did. He felt his hero-worship for Bonham,
and his envy, growing. Casually the big man took the
speargun and motioned that Grant should try the camera out
and take some shots of him on the wreck.

It was only two or three minutes after that that they saw
the big ray, and Bonham galvanised into action again.

Where it had come from Grant couldn't tell. Not that it
mattered. Apparently it had been in among the reef hillocks
behind them where the big ship had ground itself to pieces
and which rose to within ten feet of the surface, feeding or
playing games, and was now off across the rippled sand
toward deep water on some private mission of its own. He
had no time to think more than this when Bonham from
thirty yards away was suddenly beside him wrestling the
camera from him and thrusting the speargun into his hands.
Agitatedly he motioned for Grant to go and get it. As
Grant started off, he repeatedly stabbed his forefinger into his
mask squarely between his own eyes while with his other
hand he held up two fingers. As he swam away Grant
nodded vigorously. Between the eyes and two inches behind
for a brain shot, sure, he knew all that, he'd read all that.

Following Bonham's method, he swam slightly upward to
get above the fish. Two of the gun's rubbers were cocked,

he noticed, but only vaguely. Because by then something had come over him and he was excited in a way he had not been excited since the war, and then only a very few times. It went from his chest straight down into his balls and sent tingle after tingle of electricity through them. His scrotum contracted. He remembered a bicycle race he had won at the County Fair when he was in high school, when he hadn't cared what happened to him or if he died. It was like that now. He was going to chase this fish, catch it, kill it, destroy it, and he didn't care what happened to him.

Four to four and a half feet across, it was more formidable looking than the little one. From above, as he started his dive, right arm and gun extended before him, kicking softly, like Bonham, he could see the long poison spine a third of the way back along the undulating tail, with its bone-white recurved teeth from which the skin sheath—integument, the books called it—was missing because of use and wear. This one was an old toughy. Okay; good! The spearhead hit him squarely between the eyes, went on through and smacked into the sand. Swimming back away, Grant pulled until the hinged, spoon-like, unsharp barks held him snugly. It wasn't a killing shot. Damn! Damn! Down below, the ray was kicking up a cloud of sand against the bottom. Grant swam him up a little. At the other end of the fourteen feet of spear and line the rising ray whirled and gyrated. Grant waited, fascinated. Spontaneously, he drew his knife. But the fish made no effort to attack him. Maybe he would wear himself out? But swimming him toward the dinghy was like trying to run with a kite against a heavy wind. What do we do now? How'll we boat him? What about sharks? He looked around for Bonham. Here I am, Bonham, attached to this goddam thing!

The big diver, who had been taking pictures of Grant as he swam down and shot, took one more picture of him holding the wildly gyrating ray and then swam over and calmly motioned him over toward the top of the reef. Inside his mask Grant could see that he was laughing.

The reef was a hundred yards away and by the time Grant got there, puffing and blowing from hauling his underwater kite, the ray had worn himself down a lot. When he whipped at all it was feebly. On the very top of the reef ten feet below the surface Bonham motioned what he wanted him to do. Following the silent instructions, Grant stuck the spear-head firmly into some soft coral and holding pressure on the end of the spear backtracked with his fins so that he was head-down at an angle, plenty high enough so the spine on the whipping tail could not touch him. Swimming around to the front Bonham put his left hand forward cautiously and grasped the wing just beside the head. His hand appeared to stick there when he did. Then, with his knife held the same way as before he stabbed for a spot two, two-and-a-half inches behind the eyes. The first try missed and hit an eye of the still moving fish. The second connected. The ray quivered. Taking the butt end of the spear, Bonham swam him over to the dinghy and boated him at arm's length with a long swing up of the spear, not unlike a farmer forking hay on to a wagon. It required a considerable amount of strength to do it, and the dinghy sank visibly under the weight. Grant felt his hero-worship growing even greater.

But the next development surprised him. Bonham calmly proceeded to give him a lesson on how to take the lung off over his head underwater without letting go of the mouth-piece. No sharks had appeared Grant noted, nor did Bonham seem worried about them. When he took the tanks off over his head underwater as instructed, he sank six or eight feet but with the mouthpiece still in his mouth he was able to breath easily and swam right back up where, grasping the ladder, he reversed the bottles and handed them up to Ali by the yoke.

In the boat after he clambered in and slumped back against the gunwale Bonham began to roar with laughter as he reached for the gin bottle.

Ali, after helping them in, had gone back to staring at the dinghy. "My God!" he said. "You guys crazy!"

"Here!" Bonham said, still roaring and holding out the bottle. "Slug it! You earned it!"

"What are you laughing at me for?" Grant said, thin-lipped. He was furious. He would not touch the bottle.

"I'm not laughin' at you," Bonham gasped, and roared for a moment. "I'm laughin' for you. You're gonna be all right, boy! You're gonna do just fine!"

Grant resented the "boy." "You think so?" he said thinly.

"I know so! I'll bet money on it! *Cash* money!" Again he laughed, roaring. "You were all ready to go for him with that knife if he came at you, weren't you?" he waggled the bottle. Reluctantly Grant took it.

"I didn't know what else to do."

"You could of cut the line," Bonham said. "Why didn't you cut the line?"

"It never occurred to me," Grant said wonderingly. "Anyway, cutting the line wouldn't have done any good if he was going to come for me."

"That's right! But most people would've cut it. In a panic. Rays never go after people after they're hit. Neither do sharks. Or anything else, except moray eels. They will." He had about stopped laughing, but he snorted again shaking his great head, before accepting the bottle back from Grant.

Grant, somewhat mollified now, mollified in fact to the point of shy embarrassment by Bonham's openness about his courage, had drunk deep from the gin bottle, and the straight gin warmed and burned in his belly pleasantly, heating up and dissolving the knot of cold fear that came when he contemplated what *could* have happened. He felt happy inside, down there in his belly where the gin was, but he was curiously depressed too. It was then that he knew he had reached no "plateau" after all.

"He would have died anyway, wouldn't he?" he asked. "If I had cut the line? I mean, soon enough that we could have got him?"

"I dunno. Probly," Bonham said, inhaling deeply after a generous helping of gin. Again he snorted out his laughter. "If you didn't look funny, you two, out there horsing each other around on the opposite ends of that speargun."

"I wasn't at all sure I could hold him," Grant said. "But he pooped out pretty fast."

"Most fish do. They ain't really built for long-term endurance. And they panic."

"What do you think he'll weigh?"

"I don't know. Eighty-five? A hundred? Maybe more." He turned his head, without moving his big arms stretched along the gunwale. "Ali, get that damn thing up here and let's see what he looks like."

"You know how I hate those damn things, boss," Ali said in his East Indian accent. "Those damn devilfish."

"He's dead. I promise you. And he's no devilfish. If he was, we wouldn't get him in this boat, I guarantee you. Every ray's a Manta to these guys," he said to Grant. "Go on, goddam it!" he commanded, "git him up here!"

"I couldn't even lift him, boss," Ali said.

"GO ON! Get him up. I'll help you."

Gingerly and reluctantly Ali drew in the painter till the dinghy was alongside, and got a long-handled gaffhook into the head. It was completely true that, at least in that awkward position with no purchase for leverage, he couldn't lift it. But with Bonham helping with another gaff they managed to slither the slimy beast over the side into the cockpit.

"He'll go more than a hundred," Bonham said breathing heavily. He stood looking down at the animal (Grant couldn't think of it as a "fish") whose spread-out wings nearly touched both sides of the cockpit. "Evil bastards!" he said finally. Working carefully, he first cut out and laid aside the stinger. It measured five and a half inches. "Make you a good trophy, after I clean it up for you. Like ivory. Make you a good toothpick!" he said, and roared. "Sure," Grant said. But when he bent to inspect it, Bonham called out, "Careful! That spongy tissue on both sides in them grooves is what generates the poison. It could still hurt you." He tapped one of the wings with the flat of the knife. "You see this here? One of the best eatin' fish there is, these wings. I'll cut them out for you when we get back in and you take them home with you to-night and don't tell them what it is, and they'll swear to you it's the best red snapper they ever ate. I'll bet you a hundred dollars on it.

"Okay, come on, Ali. Let's get him back in the dinghy. Wait a minute!

"You want me to take your picture with him, Ron?"

Grant did, but he was embarrassed, and also his depression was still there, had come back. His depression had been growing steadily. "No. No. I guess not. You got one of me with him underwater, didn't you?"

"Yeah, but it may not show his size."

Grant shook his head. "I guess not," he said, and as they got the gaffhooks into the beast again, he moved forward to the wheel dashboard to get out of their way. And when Bonham came back to start the engine and run them back in while Ali began washing down the slimy cockpit in the sun, he moved over and stood alone, looking out the half-open starboard windshield.

Why was he depressed? This was what he had come down here specifically to do. And already, on his third day of it, he had had a sort of minor triumph, spearing a hundred-pound sting ray. Nobody could say that wasn't at least somewhat dangerous. Then why so depressed?

Was it because he hadn't done it all alone? Certainly he wouldn't have done it if Bonham hadn't pushed him probably; and he might never had boated it if Bonham with his experience hadn't been there to help. Though he might have alone, because it was pretty obviously dying by the time they got over to the reef.

There was still in him a great excitement of triumph over having speared and battled the ray like he had, and over having felt his blood get up the way it had—to where he didn't really care about anything, anything but the kill. He was sort of proud of that. Bonham had even thought him brave.

Why couldn't he feel happy about it then? The excitement over the ray remained, although it was a dense, uncomfortable, not at all pleasant excitement. And yet, underneath that, there was a deflated feeling of: "If this was reality, so what?"

He had come down here seeking a reality. A reality of manhood. A reality of courage. What? Who knew? A relief from a feeling that life was too soft. Anyway a reality he felt was missing from his life, and from his work, and for a long time. A reality Carol Abernathy was at least partially responsible for the loss of, with her peculiar and domineering ways and coddling.

He had speared a big fish, and *they* had killed it, and what remained? What remained was to have your picture taken with it like a tourist (which was why he refused). What remained was to run it in to the dock and hang it on a block where the awestruck dockworkers—and maybe even a few whites—could admire you while you bragged. Like Ali. That was what remained. And yet he wanted to brag about it. This was *reality*?!

Ali, on the other hand, had his own reality. He thought they were both crazy. And who was to say he wasn't right?

Then there was Bonham's reality. Bonham leaped at a

blood challenge. It was as simple as that. And thought no
more about it. Grant's hero-worship for the big diver went
up another notch. His love for Bonham had been increasing
ponderously in three days' diving, Bonham's careful care
of him, his accurate and thoughtful teaching, his so obviously
serious mentorhood, who wouldn't fall in love with all of
that?

It was said in the rich international set in Switzerland where
Grant had visited a couple of times, that everybody falls
in love with his ski instructor. Or, in Manhattan, with his
analyst.

But the real truth was—the Grant reality was—he was
still the same sad Grant. After all of this. That was the
real truth. Nothing had changed. Because he hadn't liked
it. He had done it, but he hadn't liked it. He had hated
every moment of it, actually, and would hate it again to-
morrow. The thought of Lucky swam up into his mind.
He much would have preferred to be in that tiny Park
Avenue apartment fingering that lush body beside him and
snugly watching the cold winter sunshine outside the window,
and he almost hated her for that. The only thing that had
really changed was that next time he would know better
how to handle a big ray—and maybe he would shoot better!
He could see it down the future, fifty rays, a hundred rays,
until he became bored with knowing and shooting rays.
And he would still be the same scared Grant.

Well, if he did more and more dangerous things, sharks
maybe, maybe then it would be better.

Sharks. Did sharks worry about whether they were brave
or not? They did not. They were in fact about the most
cowardly creatures on God's earth. Only when they had
a wounded sitting duck to feed on, were they brave. Only
then and when they had *their* blood up—"mob feeding
pattern," the scientists called it! but why not call it "war"?—
in which in their frenzy they would eat a wounded brother,
a life preserver, a stick of wood. That was reality.

His arms folded tautly across his chest, his jaw muscles
tight, he stared out at the still dim but swiftly approaching
shoreline, and a hot fury rose up in him, so furious and full
of frustrated hate and loss, that he wanted to turn to Bonham
and ask him to go back out right now and look for something
else to hunt, something good this time, maybe sharks, some-

thing really good. He looked over. Beside him at the wheel Bonham was whistling happily.

" See this!" he grinned, and leaned over the wheel to pick up from the dashboard the sharp-pointed sawtooth spine carefully by its butt. He held it up, and suddenly he seemed to take on the stance and look of a professional high school studyhall lecturer (which he has probably done some of too, Grant thought; for free; for the Chamber of Commerce and business goodwill). Grinning, he intoned: " This serrated barb with its own built-in poison-creating tissue attached has not changed, evolved or regressed in over sixty-eight million years. Imagine that? *Can* you imagine that? The venom it creates affects the vascular system and causes swelling and violent cramps and, if the victim's abdomen has been punctured, may even cause death. This is the kind of wound it makes," he grinned, and propped his foot up on the helmsman's chair behind him to expose a corded scar two inches long on the inside of his right heel. " No dramatic attack and defence. No terrifying underwater battle simply stepped on him in the sand bottom of a lagoon in waist-deep water, and was laid up for three weeks." He tossed the spine back on to the dashboard amongst the disarray of tools and heavy leather gloves and took his foot down.

" Now he tells me!" Grant said with a bitter grin, made tougher and more bitter by his feelings of a moment ago. " Thanks. Thanks a lot." Curiously, the tough reaction made him feel some better, though deep down the depression stayed.

" Not at all. You're welcome," Bonham grinned. He picked the stinger up again. " Primitive man throughout the world has been using these spines for needles and spear tips since before the dawn of history." He turned it back and forth between his thumb and finger for a moment. " End of lecture," he said and tossed it back. " Yes, sir, we're gonna work all right together! Really all right!"

It was, or so Grant felt, a considered compliment. " What about sharks?" he asked, to cover his pleasure. " Don't you ever worry about them? Don't you ever keep an eye out for them?"

" Keep an eye out for them all a time."

" I mean, I thought once something was wounded and there was blood in the water . . ."

F

"Well," Bonham said expansively and rubbed his stomach, "you got to know your waters, and your terrain. Tide's important. With that ray now it was incoming tide and I was watchin' all the time, but there's almost never any sharks around that area. I don't know why.

"If you want to go someplace where you'll see sharks, now, I know a couple places. One of them, you'll see all the sharks you'll ever want to see."

Grant felt a small drill of excitement, an unwished-for and curiously unpleasant excitement, bore itself into his lower abdomen. He didn't answer.

"Yes sir! We're gonna get along really all right together!" Bonham said happily, and began his happy whistling again.

It was curiously odd, Grant realised suddenly, and another indication of that peculiar, almost-feminine sensitivity Bonham could evince for so seemingly extrovert a man, that he had strictly and without talking left Grant completely alone all that time he had wanted to be alone. Could he have known it was depression? Almost certainly not. He thought it was a pleasant savouring of the experience.

But if Bonham was happy over the bag and over the total results of the day's dive, he was taken aback and thrown off his stride when Grant told him that Carol Abernathy wanted to go along with them to Grand Bank Island.

Bonham's face got long, and his eyes flat. "Well, Christ!" he rumbled. "What'll she do? I mean, there isn't much there, you know. There's just this one real hotel, and the town. A real drunken port town. Two fleabag hotels, and ten bars in it. I wouldn't even stay in the town myself. And all we'll be doin' is divin'." He was trying hard to cover up his displeasure. "She don't dive. What'll she do with herself?"

Grant was staring off through the starboard windshield. "Says she'd sit in the sun. She likes to swim. She swims very well you know. Better than me. And then there'll be the other women, won't there?"

Bonham seemed to sense the implacability, though of course without knowing why. "Sure. But Orloffski's wife—his girl-friend—is a pig," he said unequivocally. "So is Orloffski for that matter. And she drinks like a fish. Mrs. Abernathy doesn't drink, does she?" he said politely.

"No," Grant said.

"And I've never met Sam Finer's wife. I don't have no idea what she's like." He shifted his stance behind the wheel. "I'm not tryin' to be a wet blanket, you understand. But there won't be much to do but dive. Dive, drink, and eat fish.

"And this isn't just only a diving trip, you know. It could be a very important business thing for me too."

"I understand," Grant said. "Well, she'd like to come," he said.

"Then it's okay by me," Bonham rumbled.

Grant nodded and gave him a smile, though he could feel that his own eyes were flat too. "Thanks." Then he shrugged. He wanted to take away some of the sting of forcing him. "She says she'd like to see the place. Who knows? I don't know why."

"I said it's okay by me. It won't make that much difference, I guess." He occupied himself with the steering.

Grant nodded again. He hadn't told him all of it of course. He couldn't. Not without telling him a lot of other things. He wished, suddenly, that he could tell him all of it. All fourteen years of it. Bonham would be a good confidant, he thought. It was the first time he had ever really wanted to tell anybody, he realised.

It had been a terrible night, last evening. But every night was a terrible night now. He was finally convinced that she was really crazy. But it was only part of the time. Just the same, this of course stimulated all sorts of frenzied, frantic guilts. Or was she just pulling that, to create exactly that effect? How did you know?

God, the guilts! Everything went back such a long way. When was responsibility fulfilled? Ever? They had really helped him so much. *She* had helped him so much. Even artistically, back at the beginning. Though that ended six or seven years ago. Even before the financial help became unneccessary. How much of the rest of your life did you have to give up for that? All of it?

Before dinner—at cocktails—it had started. It wasn't what Carol said, because Carol said almost nothing, but the air was so stiff it was like everybody was breathing overbeaten meringue. Evelyn of course could carry anything off, an atom bomb in the yard wouldn't shake her, and she was plainly, and quite frankly, intrigued by what was going on.

At dinner she was positively twittery over the fish—twittery in a social, keep-the-evening-going way that let you know cynically that none of this reached her soul; or, "meant a goddam fucking thing," as she would say, "who're you?" It was positively the best fish she had tasted in Jamaica, Grant's snapper. And her people get hers right off the deck, not at any goddamned Market. Of course by the time the French chef, imported by herself and Paul from Paris, got through with it you wouldn't have known it was fish, though it was delicious. Fish, *fish*, had to be cooked in cornmeal in a crusty black skillet on a swaying boat by a dirty Cherokee squaw and eaten crowded in with fishermen, Grant who had once worked on a fishing boat in the Keys at Marathon believed. He remembered suddenly the weeks, months, when Carol had come and visited—visited? come and stayed with him! lived with him! cooking, cleaning, marketing—when he was rewriting, rewriting hopelessly, the first big three-acter, *The Song of Israphael*.

Jesus!

And after dinner it was no better. Evelyn had asked some people in for poker, the almost-young couple who half owned and wholly managed the exclusive West Moon Hotel, and a couple of almost-as-rich-as-herself British friends who had driven over from Montego Bay for the night, expressly for the poker. They were all tough players. And Grant loved to play with them. But that night he couldn't. He was half drunk but the air was still too stiff. Hunt, three-quarters drunk, had determinedly stayed downstairs and played though he wasn't a good player. Evelyn was an excellent player, when she had the cards, but when she didn't have them she couldn't throw in and stop betting hoping to draw out, and could lose a bundle. Still she could afford it. Everyone waited for those nights, even the rich friends. But Grant couldn't stand it. He had excused himself and gone upstairs. Carol followed him.

"Don't you think that's a little unwise?" he asked as she came into his room. He had made himself a hefty drink and rolled up with Sir Algernon Aspinall's *Pocket Guide to the West Indies*.

"Probably," she said. "I don't care. That Evelyn knows everything about everybody in the whole world." Then suddenly her voice broke tragically. "What do I care about anything any more?"

Grant read.

"Come on down to our room," Carol said. "I want to talk to you. Seriously." She swept out.

He had put the book away and followed. She was being a woman to-night. Instead of the teacher-mentor-Master, who worried about careers. Hell hath no fury like a blah, blah, blah. He felt he knew every routine so well now. Still, this act was better than the other. Then his callousness made him feel guilty

He had told her all about the proposed Grand Bank trip the night before, after Bonham first broached it to him. He had not even said that he was going, only that he might, and she had said practically nothing about it all and had shown little interest. So when she suddenly, in Hunt's and her room, said that she would like to go along with him, he was surprised into asking, "Why?" It was exactly the wrong answer.

"Well," she said, smiling softly, and tears welled up behind her eyes, "it's probably the last trip you and I will ever make together anywhere. And I would kind of like to have it. Sort of a nice way, you know, of saying good-bye."

Grant had exploded. "Oh, Christ!" Such an unfair way to take advantage.

"A woman knows when she's no longer wanted," Carol said hollowly. Resigned sorrow had claimed her.

"So does a man," Grant said thinly.

"But a woman, being what she is—more intuitive, more dependent, more forced to take the second place—knows it sooner than a man, I think."

This kind of thing could always drive him into a frenzy. "Look, goddamn it! You've always said yourself someday I'd have to get married. I've heard you say it! I've heard you tell your friends—tell Evelyn—back home that some day you'd have to pick out a good wife for me! Jesus!" Aware how ridiculous what he was saying was, he still couldn't stop it. "Well, how about letting me pick out my own goddamned wife? What's wrong with that? Even a thirty-six-year-old boy like me ought to have that right!

Jesus!" he said again and clutched his hair. How could he get mouse-trapped into these things?

"But I never meant it," Carol said. "That was just glib talk. I never thought it would really come about.—I guess one never does, does one?"

"Aw, come on! Come off it! Are you kidding?" Grant hollered, waving his arms. "When I'm fifty, you'll be nearly seventy. You took your chances!"

"I know," Carol said. "I'm asking you humbly, please take me with you on this trip. Please let me go. A parting gift. A farewell trip together. For a nice memory."

"All right," Grant said thinly. "But on those conditions.—As long as it's all right with Bonham."

"It'll be all right with Bonham," Carol said with a sharp smile. "As long as you're paying his plane fare and his expenses."

Once again she had startled him. He had never ceased to be amazed by her. "What about Hunt?"

"Hunt understands me very well. Better than you do," Carol said sadly.

"I'm sure he does," Grant said. He wanted now only to get out of this. "Okay. As long as it's okay with Bonham. And on those conditions. Your own conditions."

Carol Abernathy nodded. But he already knew somehow that she didn't really mean it, or mean to stand by it, or even believe it. Jesus! "Thank you, Ron," she said abjectly, and then she sighed. "When is your new girl coming down?"

"That's none of your business," he said, furious again. "I don't know yet. Not till after this Grand Bank Island trip anyway."

"And you'll take her on to Kingston with you?"

"That's my intention. Yes," he said cruelly. "Why not?" But he still didn't really mean to.

"I hope you'll both have a very good time," Carol said. "Just promise me one thing. That you won't marry her until you know her better. You do owe me that. After all these years of helping you with your work and your career."

"Oh, Jesus!" Grant cried, clutching his fists in his hair again. Such abject self-abasement, even when this patently false, destroyed him.

There was a big Empire desk in the room, which Evelyn

had had moved in so Carol Abernathy could do her " work " and " correspondence " with the Little Theatre Group, though they all knew tacitly (except possibly Carol) that it was pretty much of a joke, and in front of it stood a large heavy modern metal executive's swivelling office chair. Grant, standing by it and looking around like a child who has been tricked by adult illogic and cunning into giving up his most cherished flaws, to find something to vent his frustration on, reached out his foot and kicked it with all his strength, banging his toe painfully in the soft, rope-soled shoe. On the bare tiled floor the chair shot across the room on its rollers to where Carol was sitting on the dressing-table stool and struck her on the ankle. The reaction from her was immediate and startling.

Yelling " Ow ! " automatically, she leaped to her feet, put her foot on the stool to rub the ankle, and eyes blazing almost sightlessly hollered, " You struck a woman ! You hit a female ! You *struck a female* ! "

" I didn't ! " Grant protested. He felt like wringing his hands. " I didn't ! I kicked the chair ! The chair hit your ankle ! But I didn't mean for it to ! " During this idiot speech he had become almost pleading.

" You hit a lady ! " Carol yelled right on nevertheless, her dark eyes blazing sightlessly and insanely. " I always knew you were a mean, evil, degenerate brute ! "

And at this moment Evelyn de Blystein came upon them. There was a discreet—but not so discreet as to be unheard and unnoticed—knock on the door.

" May I come in ? "

" Of course ! " Carol cried, still almost yelling, and sat down. The door had already opened.

" What the hell are you two doing, for God's sake ? " Evelyn said in her deep whisky voice. She had a seamed, tough, cynical businesswoman's face with knowing hooded lids. They made her look wryly sated as if she had seen everything and been amused by it all. And she loved that role. But if this attitude was also her act, there was enough truth behind to give her a certain style. " All that racket ! Having a fight ? Good ! Tell me !

" I came to see how you were, dear," she said pointedly, looking Carol straight in the eye.

" We were arguing over this man Al Bonham," Carol said,

her face still angry. "This idiot here has fallen in love with him, and I'm trying to tell him he better watch out for them. They're going to try to take him, I'm positive!"

Grant listened, astounded. She had leapt into this consummate, absolute lie like a running broad-jumper without looking back, utilising her anger from before as if it were some kind of tool. And it appeared to be enough to convince Eveln, the cynical Evelyn.

"Well, I don't know him very well," she said with a gravelly wryness. "But I can look him up. I don't see how he can take you for much, anyway, though. Some diving equipment. Some trips. Surely you can afford that."

"How about a share in a schooner?" Carol said.

"Ah!" Evelyn smiled. "That's different! I would certainly look at the schooner first. *And* at the corporate structure."

"That's what I've been telling him," Carol said, nodding.

Grant was still flabbergasted into speechless fury. "I'm not in love with him," he was finally able to say. He could feel how sullen his face was, but he couldn't change it. "But I do think he is a superb diver, and I trust him. At least in diving."

"I've heard that," Evelyn said. "I know he's pretty well liked by the local businessmen and their goddam fucking Chamber of Commerce." Quite suddenly, she yawned. "Darling, do come back down," she then said to Carol. "Do you feel better now? I want you to tell the Rawsons about your Little Theatre Group in Indianapolis."

"Not me," Grant said quickly. "I've got a lot of reading and studying to do if I'm going to make this trip."

Evelyn smiled slowly at him, in silence. She hadn't asked him. "Carol?" she said in her raspy voice.

"I think I will come down," Carol said. She stood up, drawing herself up with brave but weary gallantry, and threw her head back. "My headache's better. Maybe I'll even have a drink!" she said with flirtatious gaiety.

"Good!" Evelyn growled. "I'll even make it for you. With my own little lilywhite hands." She looked at Ron once, a hooded, enigmatic glance.

Grant had followed them down the hall to where they turned off down the grand staircase. Neither of them had looked back, and he was supremely glad.

" You poor darling," he heard Evelyn say as they descended.
" You really do overwork yourself, you know. With all your
correspondence to those Theatre Group kids of yours."

" I know," Carol had answered, and her voice was suddenly full of tears. " But I don't know what else to do.
They all depend on me so."

But after he got over his fury and irritated disgust, he
thought it really would be a good thing to take her. Whether
she believed in her " last trip, parting gift " conditions or not,
he did. And taking her over there would be a good way
to show her that. That he was quitting, that he was free.
Whether he ever married Lucky Videndi or not. The final
pay-off, so to speak. The final kindness.

But how did you explain any of all of that to a man like
Bonham? Grant looked over at him again at the little
spoke-handled helmsman's wheel under the cockpit cabin roof.
Bonham would kick them both in the cunt and just up and
walk out. Grant coughed and lit another cigarette. The
big man was not whistling any more, and set-faced and
flat-eyed was consciously occupying himself with the steering. They were back in the main channel now, coming up
on the looming Navy tender which was still in port. Then,
as Grant was looking at him, he turned his head toward
Grant and smiled. Something had suddenly perked him up
a little, and when he spoke Grant realised with consternation
what it was.

" I just had an idea. I think I'll dock her at the Yacht
Club again to-night and then we can have a few gins at the
bar to celebrate."

Coldbloodedly and implacably, he was going to get every
bit of good and valuable publicity out of his playwright and
his playwright's ray that he could get. And before Grant
could say anything, or protest, he had swung the little boat
in that way, cutting back the throttle.

Why, then, didn't he protest? Bonham would have, if he
felt anything that strongly. They could still have come back
out, and gone on to the small-boats, fisherman's dock. But
Grant didn't. Why? Well, for one thing he knew that
Bonham needed the publicity, or anyway could use it.
Who knew, it might get him another customer or two? But
he had not anticipated that Bonham would actually go
through with the whole Big Deal production routine of it.

Bonham, did, however. The Yacht Club veranda was quite crowded, with both members and tourists. And when they saw the big ray, they all began to pour down on to the dock. Bonham made sure that they did. After docking, he got a gaffhook lashed to a quarter-inch manila line into the ray's chin, and carried it all the way up the dock on his back to the hanging rack where they hung the marlin during the marlin fishing tournaments. He said not a word, didn't grin, and—at least to Grant's eye—appeared to stoop under the weight of the fish a little more than was absolutely necessary. And when the crowd began to mill around them, he answered their questions matter-of-factly and laconically. In the end Grant posed for about twenty photographers with it.

"Yes," he could hear Bonham say over and over. "Yeah. Speared it, killed it, and brought it in. All by himself. What? Three days. Three days' diving, with me. Yeah. That's right."

Once he managed to get in a flat-eyed, conspiratorial wink at Grant when nobody was looking. Grant could have killed him. While enjoying a certain small fame and notoriety as a well-known and successful playwright, he had never had the opportunity to complain about the kind of fame that goes with being a movie star, say, or a politician, and he did not have the professional know-how, nor was he used to posing for photos. Some were tourists who knew his name and were also somewhat skittishly interested in skindiving. Others were Club Members who wanted him and the ray to add to their albums that they kept of the marlin tournaments each year. You couldn't really be angry about it. But it embarrassed him.

As the spectators continued to mill around, Bonham got out the official Club scales, had the results witnessed, got the thing down flat on the wood jetty, and began filleting out the wings. The meat was beautiful. And there was more than enough for all three of them. Ali who hated rays unfilleted turned out to love their meat. Bonham gave him ten pounds to take home to his family of six. Grant got eight pounds and refused more, and there was still more than ten pounds for Bonham himself. And with Grant's permission he gave five pounds to the Club Secretary.

In the end there were many gins consumed at the bar, and

for once Grant could not pay. It seemed everyone in the place wanted to buy them a drink. So he was a little loaded when Ali in the old station wagon dropped him off at the grand porte-cochère of the villa.

He went straight to the kitchen. Bonham had thoughtfully, with no more communication between them than a wry knowing look, sliced up Grant's chunks, utilising the grain of the meat, to look like snapper fillets. In the kitchen, where the French chef (" Lucky Pierre," he was called by Evelyn and Paul) was waiting for him, he formally and dramatically turned over the fish with a somewhat malicious pleasure in the coup he and Bonham were putting over on the silly females—and silly males—of this ritzy household. Lucky Pierre assured him they would have it for dinner this night.

Hunt and Carol were out on the big side veranda which overlooked the bay and harbour on the left of the point where Evelyn's private beach lay below the smaller front veranda.

Hunt, in a wicker chair, was holding a drink, a large highball glass, and staring pensively and rather sadly out over the harbour toward the big black hill in the west behind which the sun had by this time disappeared in a golden haze. What was he thinking about? Grant wondered suddenly, was he wondering, or worrying about, all this trouble that was going on? His square-topped grizzled head with its thinning hair turned in the chair as Grant came out, and he looked up with a warm smile. Carol was reading and did not look up.

" Was that your boat we saw? The little white one that came in a while ago?" Hunt asked.

" Yeah. We put in to the Yacht Club," Grant said.

" That's the one! We saw it come in. It looks pretty seaworthy." A ridiculous phrase, but the crows-feet around his eyes were wrinkled with affection and interest. Hunt knew nothing about boats.

Grant shrugged. " It's a good little boat."

" So? How did it go?"

Grant shrugged again. " Pretty good. I speared a sting ray. And some snapper for dinner." He gave him an affectionate little slap on the shoulder. " But I'm still scared." He turned away.

"Shit, I'd be terrified!" Hunt Abernathy called after him, pride in Grant in his voice.

Carol hadn't moved or looked up, and from over his shoulder Grant said shortly, "Oh, by the way, Bonham says it's all right about the trip to Grand Bank," and went to wash up for dinner.

TEN

It was a trip marked for disaster from the start, and Bonham was right. But it did not seem so the morning of its beginning, as the little eight-passenger seaplane whirred in from Kingston in the joyous sub-tropic sunshine and bright blue sky, landed on the sparkling waters of the bay, and taxied over toward the Yacht Club where the four passengers were waiting for it on the veranda. It was such a beautiful day to be going anywhere. And the barometer was up and still rising Bonham said, which would mean good sun and quiet water in Grand Bank for spearfishing.

It was nine-thirty when the plane arrived. Bonham had arranged for a Club dinghy to row them and their gear out to the plane, and the four of them stepped into it lightly, happy and laughing in the manner of carefree people any- where going on a vacation, waving gaily to Hunt up on the veranda who had come to see them off, as the Club's peon rowed them out.

Grant and the Abernathys had risen early and breakfasted on Evelyn's terrace in the fresh early-morning sun. When Hunt had gone to get the car, Carol in her gentlest and saddest mood had made Grant a secret little speech. She understood that of course he had a right to marry; anybody of his choosing. She had always expected it would happen some day, had anticipated it, and she wouldn't have it any other way. It was only fair to Grant. And now she meant to make this last trip together, even though they weren't lovers any more, something they would both remember with fondness and lasting friendship. What she hoped to accomplish by this, Grant didn't know. But the result of it though he hid it was to irritate and nettle him exceedingly, especially since Hunt reappeared just then with the car so that he was unable to make any satisfactory reply. But she appeared to mean just exactly what she said. At the Club, where they met Bonham and William, the five of them had played the European-type pool game awhile, laughing and roaring over Carol's inadequacy at it, then had sat on the veranda in the sun, Grant, Hunt, Bonham and William the underwater-casemaker drinking Bloody Marys on Grant's tab. Carol a British bitter lemon. She could be witty and great fun when she chose to exert herself at it, which had been less and less over the past years, and she made quite a thing over her awkwardness at the pool game. Too much, perhaps. But she was being a top sport, and thus Grant's legitimate pity for her and his guilts over her both increased. He needn't have worried himself, though, because on the plane, once they were aboard, everything changed.

Even before they were strapped in, she appeared to have suddenly taken a peculiar and personal dislike to Bonham, which she manifested by seating herself as far away from the big man as she could get, and then just sitting there with an air of tacit disapproval for Bonham which made itself felt all over the plane. After they were airborne, racing and bumping over the quiet bay to get the lift, and had unstrapped themselves so they could move around, she ostentatiously hauled out two of her mystical books from her big catch-all purse, and stayed in her rearmost corner seat studying them. Grant, who had felt it was only polite to sit with her during the take off, now felt obscurely irritated and moved forward with the two men. There was no rational explanation for her to change so suddenly. Irritably, Grant stayed forward with the men and left her alone.

Bonham, who with his animal sensitivity felt the change too, countered in his own way, which was to pull out a bottle of gin, laughing and roaring in a deliberately vulgar way.

The tiny plane (actually it wasn't so tiny; it only seemed so after the big jets everybody was so used to seeing and riding) of course had no stewardess. But Bonham was prepared for that too, and when he hauled forth his gin—a bottle for which, surprisingly, Grant had not paid—he also brought out of his faded duffel bag several bottles of Schweppes. "We ain't got any ice!" he shouted ebulliently. "But what the hell! We can all pretend we're British!"

Carol Abernathy of course didn't drink ; but when Bonham politely offered it to her, she primly refused even the plain tonic water. This did not bother Bonham, or William, one bit ; nor did it much bother Grant, though he was embarrassed for her. They had all had three Bloody Marys apiece at the Yacht Club, and they settled down to the warm gin and tonic and the exchange of diving stories to see them through the boring trip.

And that was the tone the whole flight took, the rest of them drinking and talking, and trying to ignore the unpleasant presence of Carol Abernathy who continued to sit screaming silent disapproval forward at everyone from the rearmost seat.

By the time Grand Bank Island hove into view off their starboard wing and the little seaplane sat down in the bright sun and sparkling water near the shore to taxi toward the hotel dock, they were all well on their way to being crocked. With William it didn't matter so much, William wasn't going to go diving for the rest of the afternoon. They were. Or so Bonham said.

Grand Bank Island was just about exactly 365 British statute miles from Ganado Bay as the crow flies. However, for safety's sake and because of the ban on flying over Cuba, the pilot had routed them via Cape Dame Marie and Cap à Foux in Haiti. This added a hundred miles to the trip, but it kept them near to land in case of trouble. Cruising at 90 miles an hour, allowing for wind drift, it was a five-and-a-half hour flight.

Normally the little plane was handled solely by its captain/pilot. But this time he had brought along a friend of his, a professional diver from Kingston whom Bonham knew, who also flew and had come along as co-pilot just for the ride to Grand Bank and some free spearfishing. The pilot, a South American who ran this flying-boat service for a big Venezuelan airline while waiting for assignment to jets, was also an ardent spearfisherman ; and both men had brought their masks, flippers and guns with the intention of staying the full four or five days and spearfishing, rather than wasting the gas to return to Kingston and then come back.

Once they were up and cruising, the " co-pilot " had come back to sit with them. He was a stocky, small, sandy-haired American with pale eyes and blond lashes named

Jim Grointon. There was clearly no love lost between him and Bonham. They were competitors. But both men carefully kept their mutual antagonism within strictly limited civilised bounds, as if by some previously agreed-upon armed truce, and each pointedly made a point of not competing in telling bigger and better diving stories. Just the opposite, both leaned over backward in their modesties.

When Bonham went up to sit with the pilot, who had said he would let him fly a little in level flight, Grant talked to Grointon.

Jim Grointon, it came out slowly from both Grointon and William—like pulling teeth from Grointon ; more effusively from the praise-filled William—was about as famous in The Trade as Villalonga, della Valle or the Pindar brothers. He owned his own boat in Kingston, which he had designed himself and had built there, a sort of sleek long catamaran which he could convert into a diving platform with a huge retractable waterglass for diving parties, and powered by two huge outboards. He specialised in free-diving and hardly ever used the lung any more, though he kept them for clients, and could do a hundred to a hundred and ten or twenty feet free-diving.

" Just holdin' his breath!" William added unnecessarily. " Just think of what that means! A hundred and twenty feet below the waves! You know how far down that is? With no aqualung nor nothing!"

Grointon smiled shyly, but not really shyly. He was obviously a hero of William's. He did very well in Kingston, had a lot of diving clients who came back to him year after year, and was content to stay like that for the present.

" But it gets pretty boring, you know, after a while," he smiled at Grant. He had a strange smile with his pale eyes and blond lashes, a totally self-centred, non-caring, self-absorbed one, but with a strange secretiveness tucked away in it somewhere. There was almost an Irish cop quality about him. " Most of my clients just want to piddle around on the shallow reefs, spear a few parrotfish. There's two or three wrecks for them to explore with aqualungs. After a while I get to feeling like a bus driver taking people over the same old route day after day.——

" And that's not why I got into this stuff in the beginning." He paused again. " And it's why I came along on this trip."

"Why *did* you get into it in the first place?" Grant asked.

"Oh, adventure. Excitement. Danger. Taking chances. There's no frontiers any more. The Caribbean, and maybe the Pacific, they're the only frontiers left. It makes you feel you're alive." Grointon raised his pale eyebrows. "Like it was in the war. Have you ever felt as alive since the war as you felt during it?"

"No, I suppose not," Grant said.

"Well, that's it, you see. Course, I'm lucky, I guess. Because I seem to have a natural talent for free-diving for which I don't really deserve any credit."

"What *were* you in the war?" Grant asked.

"Merchant Marine; and then Coast Guard. I made the Murmansk run a couple of times." He grinned. "Course, if diving was as dangerous as the war, I wouldn't be doing *it*, either. Not voluntarily."

"Still, people get hurt."

"Not very many."

"I'd love a chance to get to see you make one of those deep dives," Grant said. But he didn't really care. Instead, he was strangely resentful.

Grointon smiled his strange pale smile and shook his head. "You won't. You probably won't even see me and Raoul. There's a big ethical question involved, and this is rather a ticklish situation. You're Bonham's client, and he's coming to meet other clients. I can't do anything that might make it look like I was trying to horn in on his customers." Suddenly he shrugged, very muscular shoulders rippling under his clean white T-shirt. Again he smiled that smile. "So you won't see much of us. I shouldn't have come at all. But when Raoul asked me, I couldn't resist. I've dived off Grand Bank and Mouchoir Reef. There's some good stuff around there, if you know the spots."

"What do you mean by good stuff?" Grant asked.

"Oh, manta ray. Shark. Big jewfish."

"How big is big?"

"With jewfish? Oh, four five hundred pounds." Grointon smiled again.

For some reason Grant felt distinctly uncomfortable. The little "Irishman" was bragging without bragging. Grant reached for the bottle. "How about a little drink?"

"I can't. Not while I'm 'working'," Grointon smiled.

" But if you ever get down to Kingston for any reason, and want to go out, I'd be glad to take you out. You ever do any free-diving?"

" No. I never really did any lung-diving till I hooked up with Bonham."

Grointon nodded, and looked at him both appreciatively and speculatively. "You've got the chest for it." Then he grinned, an open honestly cynical grin very different from his smile. Grant liked him again. "Understand, I'm not trying to rob Bonham's customers."

"Okay," Grant said. " I understand. You sure you won't have one little drink?"

" Sorry. Really can't while we're flying."

It sounded smug to Grant. Still, he knew it was the truth. Under no such compunction himself, he made himself another, rather defiantly. He wondered what other conversation he could make with this strangely reserved and yet unreserved man.

" You know, I've read all your plays," Grointon said. " I think they're great. And I mean really great. You got the Navy and the war-time Navy man like none of those novels about it ever did."

" Well, thanks." Embarrassment. Exactly the same embarrassment he had felt exposed to the cameras of the Yacht Club members with the big ray.

" It that your mother back there?" Grointon asked suddenly.

Grant looked up from the gin bottle with which he had been pouring. My God, did she really look that old? " My foster-mother," he said.

" What's eating on her?" Grointon asked bluntly.

" Oh, she's just in a mood," Grant said, and looked back down at the Schweppes bottle he had exchanged for the gin bottle.

" Well, I guess I better get back up front," Grointon said in a peculiar voice. When Grant looked back up, the diver had a friendly smile on. " I got a couple of course checks to make in a little bit," he explained in what Grant felt to be an overly warm way.

But maybe that was just himself. He watched the too stocky but heavily muscled back walk away from him forward. Like most average athletes who were never really great

at anything, he had always secretly admired superior athletes
and at the same time disliked them too, perhaps because he
envied them. He turned to William who was sitting beside
him and asked which of the divers was the better one.

"Well, they're different," William said. "You know?
Old Jim Grointon's one of the best free-divers and spear-
fishermen in the country. That's sports. You know? But
Al Bonham is one of the best working divers anywhere.
Underwater salvage, pipe-laying, cutting and welding, demoli-
tion and blasting, he's tops at them all. It's just different.
Ya can't say which one's better."

It turned out as they talked that it was Bonham who had
talked William into selling his little shop in Miami and coming
down to Jamaica. Bonham had promised him they would
clean up. So far they hadn't. But there was still a big chance
they would. William couldn't really complain. With a wife
and four kids he could live half as cheap here as in Miami.
They couldn't of afforded no maid in Miami! William it
turned out was no diver and had never even been in a
mask, except once in a swimming pool, let alone no aqualung.
It was dangerous, people like Bonham and Grointon who
done it were crazy anyway, and William would not be caught
dead underwater. All he wanted was to make a big clean-
up down here on his cases with Bonham like Bonham had
promised him. And if Bonham ever got this schooner thing
off the ground, they would.

When the big diver came back from the cockpit to concentrate on his drinking and interrupted this explication by
roaring with laughter at William, Grant found himself
looking at the big man with a new eye and in a new light.
The new light was William's information. It took a certain
amount of something peculiar—what? moral irresponsibility?
—to get another man to throw up his security and go off on
a goose chase (with wife and four kids!) when you weren't
even sure you could deliver and back up your promises.
And in the back Carol Abernathy still sat screaming silent
and self-satisfied disapproval at everyone from her lonely seat.

They circled the hotel once, everybody looking down at
the sprawling buildings and the docks and at the manager who
came running out waving his arms. On the dock there
was a group of four white people in swim suits and three
coloured in clothes who also waved their arms at them.

As they touched down and taxied in, a good-sized dinghy put out from the dock to take them off, and when Bonham with his stormcloud eyes now slightly drink-glazed offered his aid to help her climb down, Mrs. Carol Abernathy accepted it primly with a prim squeezed mouth. Grant could have booted her in the ass overboard. Suddenly he giggled to himself.

When it came his turn, he saw that the two men in trunks and floppy hats in the boat, who were busily stowing gear and passengers here or there to keep the dinghy balanced, could only be Sam Finer and Orloffski by Bonham's previous descriptions. Orloffski with a bullet head and butch haircut could indeed have been a guard on a pro football team, and anywhere but around Bonham would have been a big man. Finer was small and swarthy, deeply tanned, with a noticeable paunch but with broad strong shoulders. His eyes appeared as hard as two rocks, but surrounding them was a curiously weakly mobile face. Grant shook hands with them, his hand getting badly squeezed both times, and introduced himself, before sitting down where he was told to sit. They were having a great time being boatmen, it appeared; but they had not known that Jim Grointon and Mrs. Abernathy were coming, so their boat didn't really have enough room to take everybody.

" That's all right! Don't worry about us!" Grointon called cheerfully. "We'll make out all right! Me and Raoul have to secure the plane, first, anyway!"

Raoul, Grant thought, and a memory of Lucky shivered through him for the first time in maybe half an hour. He felt a double twinge in his gut, one for the absence of Lucky and one for the existence—former existence—of *Raoul,* her *Raoul.* What the hell was he doing down here in the Caribbean with all these professional outdoor types anyway?

It suddenly arose in his mind as a curiosity that while he had thought often of Lucky, he had not thought about sex or had a hard-on (except in the morning) for the past five or six days he'd been diving.

It was the last he was to see of Grointon or Raoul really, until the next evening when they returned with a mess of smaller fish, and one six foot ten inch ground shark

Grointon had taken all alone. A considerable prize, at least to Grant's eyes.

On the dock they were introduced to Finer's and Orloffski's wives. Finer's wife was beautiful. And with a guilty start, when he looked into her eyes as they shook hands, Grant was suddenly sure that he knew her from before in New York. But he could not remember for the life of him whether he had fucked her or not.

Bonham had told him Cathie Finer was a New York model, good-looking, red-headed, and that Finer had met her on a business trip to New York two months ago. But that was like introducing somebody to a New York cabbie and asking if you had ever happened to ride with him. The odds were . . .

Cathie Finer's lovely grey eyes appeared to be pleading with him in silent appeal to keep his mouth shut.

This was not their honeymoon he remembered Bonham saying, which they had spent in Miami Beach, but was by way of being a second honeymoon, and was the first time Sam had intrdouced her into his skindiving world.

Then, as he was afterwards shaking hands politely with Orloffski's sloppy (not fat; but with loose flesh hanging out all over) loudmouthed " wife," he remembered.

It was a couple of years ago, when he had been in the city and was hanging around with another novelist (not Frank Aldane) and his sort of " midtown " Village set. The novelist had introduced him to this girl he had been taking out, a favour from one artist to another, at a Saturday night party. They had spent a hard-humping, do-it-every-way, love-sweaty week-end in her drab but not unpleasant little flat—which week-end, because she was not working the first part of the next week, lasted from Sunday through Wednesday. He remembered she told him no one had ever gone down on her pussy so beautifully. But the week-end, though they both tried hard, had given neither of them more than a pleasantly sexual week-end so that they parted wistfully as friends. He had seen her at a couple of other parties afterwards. That was Cathie Finer.

Grant had once several years ago casually picked up a copy of *Playboy* and discovered to his delight and astonishment that the Playmate of that Month was a young female poet he had only a couple of months before spent another such hard-loving New York week-end with; and this experience was rather like that one: He had studied the nude photos of her carefully and with lascivious possessiveness. His ego was so thrilled he wanted to run out into the streets of the Hunt Hill suburb of Indianapolis with the magazine and start accosting friends with it. Lamely, and belatedly, he realised his local pals would probably think he was lying, and if they didn't would not care, and anyway would wonder what importance any of that had to them. It was a very frustrating kind of triumph; and so was this.

Nobody seemed to have noticed anything, and Grant next shook hands with the hotel manager.

He hardly glanced at Cathie Finer again. He did not want to hurt Cathie's marriage, he did not want to hurt Finer, most of all he did not want to hurt Bonham's chances of selling Sam Finer on the schooner. Of all the places in the world to run on to somebody you had laid!

He shot a quick glance at Carol Abernathy who, in spite of her vaunting of her much-publicised feminine intuition, seemed not to have noticed anything either. Immediately he was disgusted. They weren't even lovers any more. What a powerful force was habit.

The diving boat, an even larger dinghy than the one that picked them up, had already been prepared for them, (Finer and Orloffski had had it out all morning with their ladies, in fact) and Bonham, Finer and Orloffski were already fussing with it. Hotel houseboys were there to look after their luggage. All they had to do was change to swim suits and take off.

Cathie Finer and Wanda Lou, which was Orloffski's girl-friend's name, had decided they would not go along on this short afternoon dive, having had too much sun already during the long morning, and they were telling this to Carol Abernathy behind Grant. And at this point Carol decided she would not go out either but would stay back at the hotel with the "girls" she said. She seemed already to have taken a great liking to Cathie and her sensitive eyes and face.

But when Grant merely nodded and didn't say anything, Carol called him over to one side. "You're really going? Without me?"

Now what? he thought. "Of course I'm going! That's

what I came on this trip for, was to dive." He thought
perhaps he might have swayed a little. He was drunker than
he thought.

"Well, then don't expect me to look after your luggage
and lay out your clothes for you," she said viciously, "you *or*
him!" She jerked her head toward Bonham.

"I don't expect you to do *any*-goddam-thing!" Grant
almost shouted. He was suddenly dangerously angry, and
trying hard to avoid a public scene. "The houseboys are
supposed to do all that. He just told us," he said more
quietly.

"I just want you to know that you don't need to expect
any help from me for anything, on this trip," Carol said with
a mean smile.

"Okay! I don't!"

Bonham came over to them then.

"Ron, the manager wants to know about the rooms,"
he said in the slow calm immutable style he employed when
teaching. "William's payin' his own way, and he's got
a little room up in the back, cheap; he knows the manager
from before. Mrs. Abernathy will want a room by herself
of course, but there's no reason why you and me can't bunk
up together. Save you the price of one room."

For a moment Grant couldn't think, didn't even hear, he
was still so angry. "Okay," he said shortly. "Fine. Sure.
Why not?" He was thinking that bunking with Bonham would
certainly save him from any chance of being importuned by
Carol Abernathy's coming into his room at night and what
was more, she would know this.

"All right," Bonham said. "I'll tell him. Shall we go
and change?" His eyes were still glassy from the gin he'd
drunk. But he was gently and deftly elbowing Mrs. Abernathy right out of the play. It was what Grant would have
liked to do, and in the same way.

"Sure. I'm coming," Grant said, and turned on his heel
and left.

The hotel was constructed of separate, chambered annexes
around a central dining hall and bar. In the room he flung
himself down stretched full length on one of the twin beds,
and confessed how drunk he was. "What I really feel like
doin' is laying right here and going to fucking sleep."

From beside the other bed where he had started to undress

Bonham laughed. "Well, that's up to you. But since you're payin' anyway, you ought to go. As an added inducement, I can tell you from experience the best way to sober up now—*and* to avoid an early evening hangover—is to go diving with us." He swayed a little himself, as he got out of his Jockey shorts underwear.

"And besides, I'm scared."

Bonham laughed. "There's nothin' to be scared of."

"I'm scared anyway."

The room was cool and dim and quiet, shaded from the eyeball-searing sun of the lower Bahamas by the vine-trellised walk-way outside the windows. Bonham didn't answer.

"In fact, I'm always scared when I dive. Didn't you ever notice?"

Bonham still didn't answer. It was just exactly as if Grant had not spoken, and for a moment he wondered if he had. He forced himself to get up on to his feet. "Well, then I guess I better have another drink right now. If I'm fucking going."

Bonham's laugh boomed. "Now that's a *sensible* idea!"

Grant undressed languidly, feeling lazy and used-up and beat, while Bonham waited.

"You're still new at it, you know," Bonham said as they walked back under the shade of the trellises. It was Grant's turn not to answer. When the sun hit them, it was like a physical blow. The women had disappeared. And Finer and Orloffski were waiting on the dock impatiently.

"Come on! I'm burnin' my goddam mother-fuckin' feet off standin' here," Orloffski said in his blunt, brutal voice.

"Where's your Jap slippers?" Bonham asked pleasantly.

"Anngh," Orloffski answered.

All of them except him wore the Japanese-style shower clogs, made in America with sponge rubber bottoms and the hard rubber coming up between the toes, and which in fact Bonham had recommended that Grant buy for himself in Ganado Bay. "Gook boots" they had used to call the real ones, the straw ones, back in the old days at Pearl, Grant thought.

"His fuckin' broad stole 'em off him, Al," Sam Finer said in a curiously thin, high voice for such a chesty man, "that's what."

"She did no such a goddam thing," Orloffski cursed.

"He lost one this morning on the boat," Finer grinned. Bonham shoved them off.

It was perfectly true that the diving and the swimming sobered them up, and in some mysterious way of its own precluded a hangover. And when they came back in, Grant felt much better physically. But that was just about the only good thing about the entire afternoon.

In the first place it was too late, when they finally got started, to go down around the point to the so-called "lagoon," or to any of the other good spearfishing spots. So instead Bonham had run them straight out past the now-anchored and deserted airplane, almost a mile out from the hotel dock, and here he anchored them. The water was no more than fifteen feet deep, a flat sand bottom with almost no coral, and consequently almost no fish, and it appeared to run straight out to sea indefinitely at that depth. In fact, Bonham said, they would have to go out miles and miles in that direction to find any deeper bottom, almost to Inagua. Currents had made it a sort of dead area, piling up sand to make an uninhabited bank. But Bonham, it became immediately clear, didn't care, because what he meant to do was to concentrate on Sam Finer and the little Minox camera and case he had brought over for him. And that was what he did. "Practise staying down as long as you can," was all he said to Grant, and then he disappeared with Finer. If Finer liked the little camera, he said, he would give it to him.

Sam Finer appeared to be a pretty good sport. But of course he had been diving all morning, too. And he did have the camera to play with. He was the only one of them who had any real diving gear, having at great expense flown down a Scott Hydro-Pak with three filled sets of double tanks, since filtered air was not available on Grant Bank. In the boat he put this on, aided by Bonham and Orloffski, even though the depth was only fifteen feet, and leaped over the side. To save air he breathed only through the snorkel-like "air economiser" on the side of the full-face mask. Bonham, using only a snorkel, went with him and handed him the camera. Orloffski, who was no good sport at all, took up his speargun and grumbling and cursing over the bad bottom went trudgeoning off by himself. In the water no more than twelve seconds, Grant suddenly found himself totally alone.

Fifteen feet was no deeper than the deep end of most swimming pools, the bottoms of a number of which Grant had prowled around holding his breath. It wasn't even deep enough to bother clearing your ears. It certainly was no way to go about learning something about real free-diving. And most swimming pool bottoms were more interesting than this. At least there you could pick up hairpins and a marble or two. A few needlefish torpedoed themselves along behind their long thin snouts here and there, a few tiny, brightly coloured sergeant-majors explored the sand or the grass. That was all.

Angry over the attitude of Carol Abernathy, angry over how much he was spending on this trip, angry over the free-diving lessons Bonham had promised but wasn't giving, he swam around the area near the boat, saw and explored his first sea hare which he had read of but never seen and which looked like nothing so much as limp pie dough folded into a tart, watching with a kind of awed distaste the brown ink that spilled from its brown interior as his poking speartip tore it open, practised diving down to the sand or the sea grass and holding his breath, until bored to death he began to expand his circles and move away from the boat. When he did, he saw out at the extreme limit of his visibility Orloffski going after a fish, and swam over that way.

The big Polack had found a small thinly growing patch of coral. A fish-stringer was tied to his bikini and on it were several small parrot-fish, none of them a foot long. As Grant swam up, he went after another one. The man who looked like a pro football guard went after these small creatures with the same viciousness with which Grant had seen Bonham go after larger fish, only more so. With brutal, animal, totally selfish single-mindedness he dived down on another little parrotfish as Grant watched, and speared it just as it started to run. He now had six. Grant waved to him and swam off, back to his boring round. He didn't have the heart to shoot the dumb, adenoidal-looking little fish, and wondered if he was weak. Mostly as he dove down and lay on the grass or sand holding his breath, he thought about Cathie Finer, and about how strange it was that after knowing her that one time and then never seeing her again in New York, he should meet her again in God-forsaken Grand Bank Island in the lower Bahamas, where her new husband was perhaps about to go into the schooner business with his new friend and diving teacher. Thinking of Cathie also brought him back to thinking wistfully of Lucky. He wondered if Cathie knew her? When he heard Bonham yelling in his full bull voice from the boat, he motioned to Orloffski who was still further out, and swam back to it.

It turned out the camera was busted. Not really busted, but the push-and-pull cocking mechanism which William had designed and built for it was not functioning properly and had gotten worse and worse until they could no longer cock the camera. Bonham had called them so they could go back in and he and William could work on it for to-morrow. The usually impassive Bonham looked highly irrit-able, and when Orloffski swam up with his string of little parrotfish and made as if to pass them up, he bawled, " What the hell are you doing with those goddam things?"

" I hadda have somethin' to do to pass the fucking time," Orloffski said in his brutal way.

" Then throw them the goddam hell away!" said Bonham. " What do you want me to do with them?"

" Don't give me orders. Maybe some of the niggers'll want them," Orloffski said bluntly, and instead threw them into the boat.

Treading water as he watched this small bucking of heads, Grant noticed something that he had observed before but never really noted: he had never heard Bonham used the word " fuck " in any one of its many forms. He used it a lot himself, and so did most of the people in his more or less sophisticated world, though not with the totally vulgar brutality of Orloffski, and you would have thought Bonham would use it too. Saying nothing—and doing nothing, except to note that Sam Finer was carefully studying Orloffski with his rock-hard eyes—he climbed up into the boat.

" Go on ahead. I'll swim back," Orloffski said. " Prob-ably won't see nothin' but it won't hurt to look. Throw me your stringer." Bonham tossed it to him.

The boat began to move away from him, and Grant watched his head get smaller and smaller behind them until it disappeared. They were pretty close to a mile from shore, and he would not have liked to stay there like that, without even a companion, to swim back alone. Even though the depth was only fifteen feet a shark or two could come cruising by any time. It didn't seem to bother Orloffski. When he reached his room, he showered to wash all the dried salt off him and lay down on his one of the twin beds and immediately fell sound asleep.

It was while Grant was asleep, when Bonham was returning from William's room to wash his grimy hands after working with William on the camera case, that Carol Abernathy stuck her head out cautiously from the door of her own room and stopped him in the dim hall.

" I want to talk to you a minute, Al, if I may."

Bonham stopped and stared down at her anxious, dark-eyed, and now conspiratorial face. He had had enough trouble to-day already, with the damned camera not working. " All right, Mrs. Abernathy. What is it?"

" Come and walk over to the dining-room with me." She moved her head toward the next door. " Ron is sleeping." She was already dressed for dinner in a flowered print frock.

Bonham took a moment to decide. He hadn't been too upset by her so obvious dislike of him to-day on the plane, but it certainly hadn't made things any pleasanter. " Okay."

" I expect you've been wondering why I acted so strangely to you to-day on the plane," she said as they came out into the trellised walk-way. It was almost dark now. Soon the manager and one houseboy would be starting up the big outdoor gasoline-driven auxiliary generator in order to carry all the extra room, hall and outdoor walk-way lights. It would continue to chug noticeably amongst the insect noises all through the rest of the night until the last one went to bed, when the watchman would turn it off till the next night.

" Well, no. Not so much," Bonham said. " It seemed sort of strange and sudden after the fun we'd all been having at the Yacht Cub, though."

She nodded, a fast, primly eager nod. " I had a very special reason." She did not continue and waited, but Bonham would not respond.

" You see," she went on finally with a sly look, leaning toward him, " I have reason to think that Ron might be thinking about wanting to put some money into this schooner deal of yours."

" You know about that?"

" Oh, everybody knows about that."

" I don't think they do," Bonham said bluntly.

" Well, then, maybe Ron has told me. Does that matter?"
Bonham shook his head.

" Well, in any case, I think it would be a very good thing
for Ron if he did do this. He could put up five thousand,
even ten thousand dollars, if he really wanted to, you know.
And I think it would be good for him."

" Then why——" Bonham began.

" Because that's just the way he is," Carol Abernathy
said, obscurely. She went on. " He does just the opposite
every time of what I want him to do. Therefore, my plan in
being unkind and rude to you was all done in order to
push him the other way. If Ron thinks I like you and would
like to see him put money into your boat——"

Bonham's nerves jangled at the way she called the big
schooner a " boat."

" —then he would automatically refuse to do it. On the
other hand, if he thought I was dead set against you and
your project, he would be much more inclined to want to do
it with you.

" Now ; don't you think that was wise of me?"

" I guess so," Bonham said. " But, tell me, why do you
feel you want Ron to go into this thing with me? After
all, you hardly know me."

" For his health," Carol Abernathy said. " For his health,
and for his mental health. He works very hard at his plays,
you know. It's a very nervous-making, very wear-and-tearing
kind of work. Because of that he needs all the pure relaxa-
tion he can get. I think your boat, and diving with you like
that every so often, say three or four times a year, would
be the best thing in the world for him!"

They had reached the door to the big dining-room bar, and
the voices of the others came out faintly to them through
the screens where they stood among the mosquitoes. Suddenly the big generator began to chug and all the extra lights,
all those not in the main building, went on all over.

" So if I pretended to be your ' enemy ' now and again,
every now and then, you'll understand what my purpose is,
won't you?" Carol Abernathy said primly. " And you'll
know that I'm really on your side, and trying to help you
with your deal."

" I'll think about it," Bonham said, somehow perplexed.
" You want me to go ahead and try to sell him on it?"

"Of course I do! Didn't I just tell you! And now I'm going in and have a cocktail with that nice sweet Cathie." Bonham watched her walk away from him with that hunch-backed, very self-satisfied walk she sometimes got. Then he turned on his heel and went back to do his interrupted wash-ing up. Grant was asleep on one of the beds as he came in, with only a towel thrown across his crotch and under it what was very obviously an enormous hard-on. Grinning, Bonham did his washing up before he waked him for dinner. When he touched the playwright gently on the shoulder, Grant sat up like a flash, grabbed at the towel on his crotch and blushed. Bonham only laughed, roaring, "Don't worry, I won't tell anybody! Come on and get dressed and let's go eat."

ELEVEN

"Where is everybody?" Grant said as he came back out of the bathroom. He had grabbed up his shorts and slacks and taken them in there with him and put them on in the bathroom.

"They're all over at the bar. I been workin' on that damned camera with William and came back to wash up." Then Bonham grinned. "Did you have a good pee?"

Grant looked embarrassed, and Bonham roared again. Grant reached for his shirt. "I guess I better hurry up."

"It ain't nothin' to be ashamed of," Bonham said, and a sudden fleeting dark look which Grant did not understand crossed his face.

"Has Ca—— Has Mrs. Abernathy gone over yet?"

"Yeah. She's already there. She seems to have taken quite a shine to Cathie Finer."

Grant put on his shirt and a pair of rope-soled espadrilles. "I noticed that. Well, maybe it'll be good for her. Come on, let's go."

They walked down the hall as far as the door outside in a sort of cautious silence. "What's the matter with her?" Bonham said finally. "Is she some kind of nuts or some-thing?"

"Well," Grant said, "no. I mean, not the kind of nuts you'd have to lock up or anything. Or dangerous. She's highly neurotic though, I think."

"Where I come from somebody would up and knock her on her ass," Bonham said unequivocally.

"It might do her some good. Then again, it might not do her any good at all. At least with Cathie Finer here she'll have somebody to talk to. Wanda Lou's not much of a talker."

"The hell she's not!" Bonham said.

"I mean, she talks. But she doesn't say much of anything."

"That's fer damn sure," Bonham growled.

"You seem to be having your troubles with her husband, too," Grant said with a slight smile.

Bonham's face looked suddenly weary, stoically weary. "Well, he's got that cutter of his which we could sure use. And when he sells the building where he had his sports shop up in Jersey, he'll have some money to put in. I just hope we can get old Sam to go for the schooner deal. I think we can get her for seven or eight thousand. But she'll need a good bit of yard work."

"What does he say about it?" Grant said casually.

"I haven't had a chance to talk to him yet. We're going to talk to him to-night."

"But he knows about it?"

"Yeah, he knows about it. You wouldn't like to put some money in it yourself, would you?" Bonham asked, rather heavily Grant thought.

They had been walking along the walk-way, an uncovered one now, between the widely spaced lights and between them you could see the star-studded sky, each star gleaming like a lightbulb in the clear, absolutely cloudless tropic canopy. Mosquitoes didn't much bother Grant, and he had been enjoying it, the air smelling of sea, the insect noises in the slight breeze, the faint chugging of the electric generator off somewhere. Now he was suddenly startled, shocked even. He had been expecting this question to come some time, but now that it had he was still startled.

"Who, me? No, no; no, no. I haven't got that kind of money. Shit, I wish I had."

"As a part owner, you'd get all your diving cruises and trips free. Say three or four a year. Ten days. Or two weeks. We could cruise up here, cruise to Tortuga in Haiti, cruise to the Caymans, cruise to Cozumel and Yucatan even. Be a lot of fun. Lot of diving."

"I don't have that kind of money," Grant said quickly. "It sounds great, but I don't have that kind of money at all."

"Wouldn't have to put in as much as Finer. Say three thousand. Even two thousand. For starters. Well, think about it. We'll talk about it later."

They had reached the screen door to the main building's porch. Far inside, in the dim bar with its lights gleaming on local pine panelling, they could see the others, and a faint murmur of talk and laughter and glasses clinking came out to them. It sounded good, happy, as if they two were about to enter a group of people with no problems who had nothing to do but enjoy themselves and life. Bonham must have been trapped by the same illusion. He stopped with his big hand on the door handle and took a very deep breath, which he then let out in a long slow sigh. It seemed to take a full minute for him to complete his exhale. "Meantime," he said, his eyes taking on a really fierce, ferocious look, "I'm gonna *eat*! And *drink*!" He went in.

Grant followed. It was maybe another full hour before they sat down to dinner, and during that time they all except for Carol Abernathy put away an enormous amount of booze. The manager was entertaining, since it was the first night, and the drinks were all on the house. He was a heavy-drinking, half-English, half-white-Jamaican man with a penchant for telling very good, mildly dirty stories which no one had ever heard before, in a very King's English voice. He had known Bonham, Grointon and Raoul the pilot for years, and had built his hotel here all by himself and was in fact more than half owner of it. He liked to talk about diving and listen to diving stories but had never done any of it and did not, he said, ever intend to. Sam Finer on the other hand could not talk about anything else except diving, and his overwhelming passion for it earned him a good deal of razzing from the others. His admiration and hero-worship for Bonham was even greater than Grant's.

The drinks flowed freely, since the black barman had received instructions from the manager to keep all glasses filled, and when they went to dinner finally they were all except for Carol Abernathy more than a little pissed—as the British manager liked to say. " I'm pissed!" he said. The dinner was free too, anyway, since it was composed solely of sea-food which they had caught themselves, and the manager as host was serving a very good white wine, a Muscadet which he imported himself via Nassau from Europe for his guests, and which, being served freely also, did not allow the ingestion of food to sober anybody up. By the time dinner was over they were all except Carol Abernathy even more pissed than before it started. " More pissed!" the manager hollered. Finer and Orloffski had taken several big crawfish, or langouste as they were getting to be called more and more, which was served first in a Bahamian recipe with a very hot sauce. After that there were high-piled platters of batter-fried fish—grouper, snapper, hogfish, rockfish—enough to feed a small army. Finer and " Mo " Orloffski, as he liked to hear himself called, had taken it all that morning.

Grointon and Raoul the pilot had made a point of coming into the bar much later, only a few minutes before dinner was served, and would have sat at a table by themselves had not the manager and Bonham invited them to join the larger group.

Grant, who had already been drunk once to-day, as had Bonham, did not know just when Carol Abernathy went to bed. All he knew was that suddenly he looked up and found she had gone ; as had Orloffski and his loud-mouth girl-friend, not intending to waste any more goddam valuable sacktime, as Orloffski so handsomely put it ; he could imagine their stable-like sex life. Grointon and Raoul were just in the process of leaving. Bonham and Sam Finer were down at the far end of the room talking business in low voices, and he himself was sitting over coffee with Cathie Finer who was a little drunk too and the manager, who was very drunk. The manager was just on the point of excusing himself sleepily to go to bed, which he did, and then cautiously got up and stiff and erect as the Guards Officer he said he once was, marched carefully from the room. Grant and Cathie were left alone.

"Thanks for this afternoon," she said in a quiet voice with a small smile.

"Are you kidding?" Grant asked. "I wouldn't do anything to hurt you. Not if I could possibly help it."

"I know that. But when they told us you were coming, and I knew you didn't know I was here, I was afraid when you saw me that you might say something or let something out, just out of surprise."

Grant shook his head with stubborn drunken bonhomie. "Bonham told me that Finer had recently married a good-looking New York model. But of course I didn't connect it with you, or think I might have known you. It's weird, isn't it? I mean, it's funny. Meeting down here like this.

"I like your husband," he added gallantly, although the truth was he didn't know Sam Finer well enough yet to like him or not.

Cathie Finer looked straight at him soberly for a moment before she answered. "He's a nice man, Sam. And he's worth a *lot* of money. He's kind of crude maybe, by uh by New York standards; but underneath that he's a very nice man. And he needs me," she added simply.

"Well good for you," Grant said. For no reason he could feel a kind of twisting gripe inside himself. He had never really known her, just that one long week-end together. He had never tried to explore her. Of course, she had probably changed some too in the past two years.

"God only knows why he needs me," Cathie Finer said. "But he says he does. And after thirty-two, modelling gets to be slimmer and slimmer. And slimmer. Unless you're a Dorian Leigh or somebody and can open up your own business." She smiled. "He doesn't step out on me, and I don't step out on him. See, Sam's a very jealous man. Anyway I wanted to thank you."

"Hell." Grant flushed. "Forget it."

"And I also wanted to talk to you about your uh foster-mother there," Cathie Finer said, her voice getting a little straighter.

"Yeah?" Grant said. "What about?"

"Well, first place, she's not really your foster-mother, is she?" Cathie Finer said quietly. "She's your mistress, isn't she?"

Only a few people had ever asked him that question point-

G

blank. Lucky had been one. He had always denied it. "She was," he said, not really knowing why he was admitting it now.

"I like her," Cathie Finer said. "She's got a lot of marvellous qualities in her. She's a nice woman. And she's just about to crack up."

"You think so?"

"I sure do. And I'm guessing that it's all because of you, isn't it?"

Grant wanted to talk suddenly. "Well, it is and it isn't, you know? This thing you see in her's been going on a long time, growing a long time. I've been there and seen it grow. She used to be marvellous. When she was younger. Or else I was just too young and green to see that she wasn't." He stopped to collect his thoughts, which were in some confusion. He couldn't remember what he meant to say next. He found he was both shocked and surprised by Cathie Finer's sympathy for Carol, and a little angered. "Well, you see, I don't know what I can do about it. If she is beginning to crack up."

"She broke down and sort of cried three times this afternoon when she and I were talking."

"Did she talk about me to you, you mean?"

"No, no. Not at all. Except for that son shit, you know?"

"Well, she helped me a lot when I was younger and just starting out. She and her uh her husband, who is down here in Jamaica with us now, you know, practically supported me. But, hell, Cathie, she's old enough to be my mother. No, now! I mean it. Literally. She's eighteen years older than I am. And I've paid them both back pretty much, pretty well. Should I be expected to throw away the whole rest of my life for her?"

Cathie Finer shifted a little in her chair. "Well, it's not my problem, of course. I shouldn't butt my nose in. But I liked her. And I just wanted you to know how close to the edge she is."

"You really think so? But she's been more or less like that for three years now. Almost exactly the same. Listen, Cathie, do you know a girl named Lucky Videndi?"

"Lucky Videndi? Lucky Videndi? Why, yes! Yes, I do know her! Not very well. She never did very much modelling. But I used to see her at a few parties. She had some little bit of loot of her own, I think." She looked at Grant closely. "So that's how it is?"

Grant flushed for the second time. "That's how it is. Just like with you and Sam."

"She's a real beauty! . . . Well, that poor lady!" Cathie said, helplessly. Then, as his second phrase took effect, she turned and looked down at her husband sitting with Bonham, and smiled proudly. In Grant's mind a small rebellion took place, something he did not want, did not want his mind to think, but which his mind maliciously went ahead and thought anyway. He had known her quite intimately, that week-end, and his mind viciously began recalling her in full intimate detail. His mind was not as gallant or gentlemanly as he was. She had peculiarly shaped labia minora, for example. Nobody can take that away from us, his mind giggled.

At the same time from the other end of the room, as Cathie continued to smile fondly toward Finer, Grant overheard the words "stock," "loan," and "interest." ". . . don't want any stock . . . your baby . . . long term loan . . . low rate of interest . . . two per cent . . . even one and a half . . . just don't want to own stock in another man's . . ."

Cathie Finer turned back to him. "Wish you luck anyway, Ron," she said. Then she shook her head. "What I really mean is, I wish that poor lady, that poor Mrs. Abernathy luck. She's the one that's going to need it."

"Let's talk about something more pleasant," Grant said. "What about your husband? Do you think Sam will go in on Bonham's schooner deal?"

Cathie Finer's face got cautious. "I try not to know anything about Sam's businesses. But I know he loves diving with a real passion. And he has a great hero-worship for Al Bonham." She smiled brilliantly. "He's small, you know, smaller than you. He loves to have big men around him . . .

"Now let me ask you something.

"Why do you think it was that you and I never really made it together?"

"Ahhh," Grant said. "Who the hell knows? That was what, more than two years ago. I guess, just guessing you understand, neither one of us really wanted to make it with somebody then. We both have changed a lot since then."

"But you really have it solid and hard for Lucky Videndi, do you?" Cathie smiled.

"I sure do. At least, as far as I can tell now."

"Well, as you told me a while ago, good for you."

Down at the other end of the room the two talking men got up and came toward them. Sam Finer hardly came up to Bonham's armpit.

"What have you two been yakking so hard about?" Finer said in his high voice, his rock-hard eyes moving fast from one to the other and back. He was pretty drunk, too. And it was easy to see he was an intensely jealous man.

"Mostly talking about diving," Grant said easily, and then grinned. "And a little bit about whether you might be interested in going in on Bonham's schooner." I've had your broad, you dumbhead, his mind giggled suddenly. He hated his mind.

Finer grinned drunkenly. "If you were pumping my wife about any of my business affairs, I'm sure you didn't get very far."

"You're absolutely right."

"But," Finer said, "I think I can tell you, I guess it's safe enough to tell you, it looks like Bonham's goin' to get his fucking schooner."

From behind him Bonham nodded once, happily, as Grant stood up quickly. "Well! I think that calls for something! Jesus! I'm glad! A congratulations drink at the bar maybe? John!" he called.

The black barman, bored as only a black barman can be when he is amongst a bunch of happy white drunks and is wanting to close up and go home, began setting up four glasses. He couldn't have cared less about Bonham's schooner, or anything else, and almost certainly hadn't even been listening.

"What's the matter with you?" Sam Finer growled suddenly, and his eyes just as suddenly got dangerous. "Ain't you glad Mister Bonham's gonna get him a schooner?"

"Hey, hey," Bonham said quietly, and Grant watched Cathie get up quickly and go stand just a tiny bit in front of Sam's right shoulder.

"Oh, yes, sahr," the barman said. His face grinned. "I is veddy hoppy."

"Then set up a glass for yourself!" Finer ordered.

The barman did. And when they drank the toast, doing it very formally, holding their glasses high to each other while Grant pronounced it, he calmly drank it with them.

Sam Finer slammed his glass butt-down on the bar, and put his arm around his wife. "All I want is for us to be on that first cruise."

"That's for sure," Bonham said quickly, "and absolutely certain."

"Come on, old lady," Finer grinned, "let's go hit the sack. I'm drunk and lonesome and beat. I need me some loving."

When they had gone, Bonham let out a long, tension-relaxing "whew!"

"Will he remember in the morning?" Grant said.

"Oh, sure. I've seen him a lot drunker than that. I'm beat too as a matter of fact. But I ain't going to bed. John," he said to the barman, "give us one more and we'll let you close up and go home."

"Sure thing, Misteh Bonham," the barman grinned.

"He's not bad, you know. It's just he gits a little rambunctious sometimes when he's drunk."

"No need to tell me. I know the type." He filled their glasses.

"You're not going to sleep?" Grant said as they touched glasses.

"No," Bonham said very matter-of-factly.

"You think he'll really come through?"

"Yeah, he'll come through. He's like my grandfather used to say: 'My word is my bond.' But only as a loan. He won't take any stock. I don't know why. But 'Don't look a gift horse in the mouth'."

"How much is he letting you have?"

"Ten thousand."

Grant whistled ,and raised his eyebrows.

Bonham acknowledged this with a nod. "It's a real break. Of course, he'll get all his divin' and divin' trips free. In perpetuity. As they say."

"Diving vacations could cost him almost that much in five years," Grant said. Bonham nodded. "You're really not going to bed?" Grant asked.

"No, I'm going in to town," Bonham said matter-of-factly.

"Maybe get me some of that handsome black ass. You should pardon the expression, John."

"Harr, Misteh Bonham," John grinned.

"This is a day I don't want to forget. I never really thought he'd come through. You want to come along?"

Grant thought it over while he finished his drink. "Your pal Orloffski didn't help you a whole hell of a lot."

"No," Bonham said. "He didn't, did he? Well," he said and sighed, "I told you he was a clot."

The British word sounded strange in his American mouth, to Grant. Go to town? An explosive charge was working in him, probably from all the booze he'd put away to-day. Then there was this sort of raging disgust at himself over the way at least part of him had reacted to Cathie Finer. And he didn't want to have to see Carol Abernathy, should she still be up.

"Sure. I'll come. But we have to be up and ready to go divin' by eight."

Bonham grinned from behind his storm-cloud eyes. "The hell with it. We'll just stay up all night then."

"All right. Good!" Grant said just as toughly.

As it turned out, they didn't stay up all night. They were back by five-thirty. But in the light of what happened after that, it might have been better if they had stayed up. "But how're we gonna get there?" Grant asked as they left John in his bar cleaning up. "Oh, that's the easiest part," Bonham promised. It appeared that the hotel manager had three cars on the premises, and the oldest most beat-up one of the three, a tiny British-made station-wagon, was always kept reserved for Bonham when he was here. The keys were in it. Sometimes he took clients diving in it, in the daytime, on the other side of the island. "But won't somebody steal it? Like that?" Grant asked as he climbed in.—"What would they do with it?" Bonham said. "They couldn't drive it, or hide it, on the island. And they couldn't get it off. There's only about four hundred people live on this rock." He had thoughtfully brought along a bottle of Scotch whisky from the hotel bar, and they each had two slugs from it on the mile and a half trip in to the town.

In the pale light of the thin crescent moon the town itself, named—like so many other tiny Caribbean towns on tiny islands—simply Georgetown, had an eerie aspect. It consisted of maybe sixty ramshackle buildings made of coral rock and wood with tin roofs, and of these twelve were warehouses and six were bars. Not one wall could truly be said to be in plumb, and all in all it made the village of Ganado Bay look like a sleek great modern city. Like in any port town at two in the morning, whereas the respectable places such as warehouses and homes were shut up tight and darkened, all of Georgetown's six gin mills down by the wharves were wide awake and going full blast. And as long as any money was coming in they would stay that way.

One of the reasons they did not stay out all night was because on the way into town in the car Grant made it plain that he was not on the lookout for any fucking. "You ain't?" Bonham said, though he still did not use the word itself, and then he grinned. "From the way you looked under that towel back at the hotel when I woke you up, you looked about ready for *some*thing." So for the first time Grant confessed to him that he had himself a new girl in New York that he might marry and that he was uh—ludicrous phrase— keeping himself for. The big man's face changed instantly and got respectable and he nodded his great head ponderously with equally ludicrous understanding; but it put a sort of damper on things because he too then decided, with gentlemanly thoughtfulness, that he too should not try to get laid either. So they went from joint to joint, drinking more and more whisky and eating more and more hamburgers, watched the various crops of available girls, and talked about diving and courage. Bonham was not worried about Grant's courage; he had seen him in two fairly tight spots, the swim through the cleft into the big cave and the shooting of the ray, though neither was seriously dangerous, and he had functioned perfectly fine. He had also seen his springboard diving—which was why he let him do those things so fast, in the first place. Bonham would trust him anywhere completely, soon's he had little more experience. But even such talk could not keep two drunken men awake forever.

Being out all night with Bonham in a port town that Bonham knew was an experience. Two drunken seamen from a freighter that was in, who showed up and as quickly disappeared, were the only white people that they saw. Bonham knew maybe half of the people that they met, and some of them were always coming over to shake hands and offer to buy a drink. He had been to Grand Bank only four times with diving clients, but anybody who met him apparently did not forget him. Being with him was also comforting. Not since his youth in the Navy when he would go on pass with four or five buddies had Grant felt so secure among the pimps and whores, thieves and con-men, brawlers and drunks of a waterfront port town—coloured or white. Some of the stevedores who worked on the local docks were powerfully built, mean-looking men and all of them were drunk, but nobody bothered Bonham. And clearly nobody was about to. He sat like a solid small mountain at whichever table he happened to be eating more hamburgers and drinking more whisky, and his dark storm-cloud eyes got brighter and more stormy. He was perfectly polite to everyone, but everyone was perfectly polite to him. But even all of this could not keep Grant's head from dropping lower and lower toward the table as the time wore on. He had not been nearly so drunk either of the other two times he had been drunk to-day. He had not been nearly so drunk anywhere, for a long time. His nose was almost touching the beer-wet Formica tabletop when Bonham staggered over to him from somewhere and said thickly, " C'mon. Lesh get outta thish.

" The spark'sh gone out. There'sh no fire. Shit, it ain't worth it," he said when they were outside in the incredibly fresh air. " Whew! What a drunk!"

The moment he climbed into the little car, though he was drunk, Grant caught a strong whiff of sex in the air of the interior. Aha! so Bonham did get himself laid after all. But then he wondered. It could, in this joint, just as easy have been any other couple, staggering outside to find the first car they could to hump in. He said nothing.

Though he was staggering when on his feet, Bonham drove cautiously, very slowly and well. And of course there were absolutely no other vehicles on the long straight road from Georgetown to the hotel. And the marvellous air had sobered and wakened both of them a little bit.

" Why do we drink like this?" Grant croaked suddenly from his side as he dully watched the seaside hotel come into view in the headlights at the end of the straight, flat road.

Bonham didn't answer for a moment. " Oh, to stand ourselves; and other people," he said calmly, and turned the little car carefully into its parking space on the grass. By five-thirty they were in bed asleep.

The last thing Grant heard before he dropped off was Bonham saying from the other bed, "The hell with them. I'm gonna lock the door. Let 'em go out by themselves to-morrow morning. We'll go in the afternoon." As he fell bodily into peaceful drunken sleep, Grant thoroughly agreed.

But it was not to happen that way. At ten minutes off eight, they were awakened by an enormously loud pounding on the door of the room. It was Carol Abernathy, and she was cursing them and yelling at the top of her voice for them to get the fuck up in there.

Almost automatically, Grant was on his feet and stumbling toward the door in his shorts, his eyes still gummed almost shut and his head feeling like an over-ripe squash—anything to stop that crazy embarrassing screeching.

A muffled "What the hell?" came from Bonham's sheeted bulk, and he too sat up. "For God's sake, yes!" he declared in agreement. "Open the door and let her in and tell her to go and——"

He never finished, because Grant had already flipped the lock and flung open the door. There was Carol, in a bathing suit and terry-cloth robe, and in her right hand—rather awkwardly—she brandished the eight-inch blade of Grant's razor-sharp diving knife which Bonham had sold him in Ganado Bay. It was with the butt of this knife that she had been pounding so incredibly loudly on the door. She advanced with it, swinging it amateurishly before her, slicing widely with it back and forth, and Grant backed away. A glance at the bureau where he had put it last evening showed him the plastic scabbard was still there. She had sneaked in during the night and taken it while they were gone. From the other bed Bonham was staring at him with his eyebrows up and an astonished, disbelieving look on his face.

"You lazy no-good sons of bitches!" Carol Abernathy yelled at them, swinging the knife. Her face was tomato-red. "Drunken bums! Whoremongers! You're going diving whether you want to or not! And I hope it kills you! You think I'm going to let him do this to you?" she yelled at Grant. "Taking you out and getting you drunk and fucking nigger wenches! Just so he won't have to take you diving! How do you know what you could catch!

You're paying for this shitty trip, and I'm going to see you get your money's worth! You!" she screamed at Bonham, "get out of that goddam fucking bed! I mean it!" She advanced on him, still swinging Grant's knife.

Bonham had begun to come awake now. "Here, here, now," he said sitting with his back against the headboard and looking as if he didn't know whether to laugh or not. Carol Abernathy came right on toward his bed.

"You think I won't use it? I'll slice you to goddam shreds!"

Bonham stared at her. Then suddenly he threw back the sheet and, for a man of his bulk, skipped with incredible lightness out of the bed on the side away from her. From somewhere within him there emanated a peculiar sound which the still astonished Grant could only describe as a giggle, a bass giggle.

As if his retreat proved her moral rightness, Carol Abernathy grinned, a strange tomato-red rictus, and changed her line of advance to come around the bed end. She came on until she was only six feet away from them, and then stopped, still flourishing the knife at the two standing men, Grant in his shorts, Bonham in his pyjamas.

"Carol! Carol! Are you out of your mind? What the hell are you doing?" Grant was saying.

Either man was well enough trained, well enough experienced, in unarmed combat and brawling that he could have disarmed her with no more than a superficial cut, but neither made a move to do so. Grant had the feeling that it was all an act, a scene perhaps from one of his own plays, it would make a great second-act curtain. He made a mental note.

"What a pair!" Carol Abernathy screamed at them. "Men! Men! You, you nigger humper!" she yelled at Grant. "And you, you great lump of degenerate tissue!" she yelled at Bonham. She swung the big knife back and forth in front of her, without even keeping the point directed at them. "I say you're by God going diving! And you're by God going! If you stay out all night drinking and whoring with nigger cunts, then that's just the price you have to pay! But you!" she screamed at Grant, "you're going to get your money's worth out of this shitty trip if I have to slice you up!" She did not advance further, as if she knew—or so Grant thought—that to do so would imperil her up to now winning position.

Bonham turned his head completely away from her and looked over at Grant. "Well, shit. We're up. We might as well go, hunh?" he said. Grant nodded.

"Your fucking goddam well right you'll go!" Carol Abernathy yelled, and brandished Grant's knife.

"Mrs. Abernathy," Bonham said in his deepest voice, "if I'm goin' diving, I got to get dressed. Don't I?" He grinned at her with his storm-cloud eyes, and shucked out of his pyjama jacket which was already unbuttoned anyway, then untied the drawstring of the pants. Smiling at her, he let them drop.

Carol Abernathy was already almost outside the door. More swiftly than she entered, she retreated, yelling "I'll be right outside the door!" in a voice that now held a shrill note of peculiar terror. She shut the door after her.

It was something Grant wished he had thought of first. But then, being—having been—her lover, it wouldn't have made any difference if he had done it. Or would it?

"Fucking cunts! Goddam fucking cunts! I hate them all!" Bonham muttered to himself as he went about putting on his sloppy tent-sized swimming trunks. It was the first time Grant had ever heard him use the big bad word. His face resembled a long-suffering thunderstorm that was wanting to break out into lightning and hard hail but never could.

Outside the door, when they emerged, Carol Abernathy was still holding the knife. "Okay, march!" she said. She was no longer screaming. But the contemptuous tone of her voice made them both stop stock-still in their tracks, and she suddenly looked frightened, as if she knew she had gone too far.

"Carol, give me that knife," Grant said, putting into it all the force he had.

"Not on your life!" Carol Abernathy said. "You think I'm crazy? Not on your life!"

"I could take it away from you if I wanted," Grant said quietly. "So could he," he jerked his head at Bonham.

"But you'd get yourself cut bad doing it, wouldn't you?" Carol Abernathy said. "It's sharp." She put her thumbnail on the blade like the rank amateur that she was. "Move, I said!" but her tone had softened considerably.

" Mrs. Abernathy," Bonham said, using again his deepest voice. " After you."

" Ha!" Carol Abernathy said. " I'm not turning my back on you. Either one of you."

Bonham stared at her for a long contemptuous moment, then turned on his heel and started down the hallway. He did not speak to her again.

Grant hung back until Bonham was a ways ahead, and then started to follow, Carol right behind him. " What the hell are you doing?" he said in a low voice. " You're embarrassing the *shit* out of me. In front of all these people. They'll think you're crazy."

" They can think what they want," Carol Abernathy said reasonably. " But I'm not so crazy I'll let you spend a fortune on this trip and then not do any skindiving."

" We're going diving," Grant said. " Now give me my knife. And go take a nap or something."

" No, sir! Not on your life," Carol Abernathy smiled. " I'm going with you, and I'm staying right there with you all goddamned day.

" Fucking niggers! Fucking dirty niggers!" she said in a low, intense voice. " How do you know what you got? You could get the syph."

" I didn't fuck anybody," Grant said reasonably and then realised how totally unreasonable everything was.

" DON'T LIE!" Carol Abernathy thundered.

Still walking, half a step in front of her, Grant too looked at her for a long moment and then turned on his heel and walked away. But this deliberate action did not faze her either. She followed both of them, still carrying the knife.

When their little procession marched out on to the dock, the waiting Orloffskis and Finers had the same benumbed expression Bonham had worn earlier. Carol Abernathy marched right through them—and through Bonham and Grant—and climbed into the big sixteen-foot diving dinghy and stationed herself in the very forepeak of the bow, and there she stayed with Grant's knife.

" Well, come on!" she called raucously. " Let's get this show on the road!"

But it was at that exact moment when her self-appointed role began to fail. Whether it was the presence of Cathie Finer whom she had taken such a liking to, or whether it was something else, Grant did not know. Whatever it was, her emotional oneness began to shrink, visibly. And with it, she herself seemed to shrink physically, shrink up into herself as if she were putting her arms around herself and curling up into a foetal ball, a foetal self pity.

"Come on, get in!" Bonham said to the others shortly and savagely.

"Well, say, what the hell?" Orloffski said.

"Shut up!" Bonham said. "Just shut up, and get in, will you?"

The two women took the crossboard seat nearest Carol, Orloffski and Finer the middle one, and Grant and Bonham climbed into the stern.

"How are you to-day, Carol?" Cathie Finer said sweetly. Wanda Lou, for once, was saying nothing.

"Oh, I'm all right," Carol Abernathy said. "Only I didn't get much sleep last night with these two drunks coming in and hollering and yelling at all hours."

"It's a lovely day to-day, isn't it?" Cathie Finer said.

Carol Abernathy looked around. "Yes, it is," she said and suddenly looked as if she were going to weep. She smiled tremulously at Cathie.

They were about a mile out when she said she was deathly sick.

TWELVE

Bonham, whom everyone accepted tacitly should be Captain and take the tiller of the big Evinrude, was heading for the famous Grand Bank "Lagoon." Finer and Orloffski deliberately had not fished it yesterday, in order to save it for to-day. It was not really a lagoon at all but a long inlet protected on the seaward side by three small islets covered with pine and scrub. The long point where he would turn into the "Lagoon," off which these islets lay, was still half a mile ahead of them, and it had taken them almost an hour to cover the mile they had covered. Because of Carol Abernathy, the trip had been uncomfortable for everybody.

"Well, I don't see how I can take you back, Mrs. Abernathy," Bonham said. "It'll cost us another couple of hours." He looked questioningly at Grant, who shrugged.

"What do you think is wrong with you?" Grant said, and found himself wondering anxiously if she really was sick. How could you tell with a nut? He didn't want her to die or anything. And—as Bonham obviously felt too—he felt that injury or sickness, especially at sea, superseded all other wishes or plans automatically. But of course Carol Abernathy knew that. "What do you think it is?"

"I don't know," she said dully in a deathly sick voice. She was sitting all hunched up now in the forepeak, still clutching Grant's knife.

"Are you seasick?" Bonham asked.

"No, I never get seasick," Carol Abernathy said in a choked voice. "I don't know what's wrong with me. But I feel terrible."

"I tell you what," Bonham said, squinting into the sun "There's three little islands up there ahead. With trees on them. Good place to picnic. I'll put you off there, and you can lay down in the shade of the trees. Then we'll pick you up on our way back. How would that be?" he said gently.

"I don't know," Carol said dully. "I guess it would be all right. If I don't die."

Grant, who was fuming now, smothered a desire to laugh harshly out loud. He was convinced now that it was all some kind of an act, a warped sense of shame and depression coming out backwards in a crazy plea for some kind of pity. At the same time, he was still anxious. But he was so embarrassed he wanted to lie down and hide in the bottom of the boat.

"I'll come with you, Carol," Cathie Finer said kindly. She looked at the men. "And look after you. We can always signal the boat if you feel worse. They won't be far away."

"No, I don't want anybody to come with me," Carol Abernathy said.

"We'll leave you some food," Bonham said.

"I couldn't eat," Carol said.

When the boat grounded gently in the sand, she dropped Grant's knife in the bilge and stood up and leaped over the prow, staggered away a few steps in the ankle-deep water and then fell and lay still on her side in the shallows. Grant watched her with disgust and horror, and fascination. She did not move.

Bonham tossed a sack of sandwiches and a bottle of water up on to the dry sand above her.

"I'm going to stay with her," Cathie Finer said. "How do we know? Maybe she's really sick. I never dive anyway, just snorkel around."

"I'll stay with you," Wanda Lou said. "We never do no real divin' us girls anyway." She looked disturbed.

Grant knew that if anybody should stay with her it should be himself, but he wanted to make the dive, and selfishly, and furiously, he just didn't care. He retrieved his knife.

"Here, then," Bonham said. "Take some more sandwiches with you, and some beer." When they were safely ashore, he clapped his big hands together smartly. "Now, for God's sake, let's go!"—"Christ, yes!" Orloffski said, and he and Finer jumped over the sides to push the big boat off. When Grant looked back Carol Abernathy was still lying on her side in the water, the two girls were sitting quietly together up on the beach above her, and he didn't care. He just didn't give a damn.

When Bonham steered them across the point, the "Lagoon" suddenly opened up before them, a long sandy beach with the three islets sitting like guardians off shore, the sun glinting merrily off water in which there was almost no wash at all. On the shore tall pine trees soughed in a morning breeze that would soon begin to fall. Maybe half a mile from the islets and a quarter of a mile from shore Bonham heaved over the little patent anchor, warped the line around a cleat, and boomed, "Well, boys, here we are!" Everybody had a drink of gin. Then they were getting into their flippers.

The nearest of the little islands, where Carol and the girls were, looked calm and peaceful from here.

"I'll stick with you," Bonham told Grant as they donned their masks. "At least until you make your first dive or two and get to feelin' at home." Then they were all in the water.

Grant had thought for a moment—while they were dressing out—to, after yesterday, remind the big man that he was paying his expenses on this trip in order to be taught free-diving, but then had thought better of it. Now what he saw below through his mask was so eerily breathtakingly beautiful that it took all thought of that out of his mind as well as all thought about most everything else, including Carol Abernathy.

As far as the eye could see in every direction stretched a vast plain of pure yellow sand that was absolutely flat. For the most part the sand was totally bare, except for a single sea plume or purple gorgonia here and there swaying gently as the water moved it, but every thirty or forty yards in all directions were what appeared to be piles of carefully pre-arranged rocks. Closer inspection showed these to be coral hillocks, too young in creation to have grown together to make themselves into a reef. And two or three feet above each hillock as far as the eye could see hung one or two or three big grouper gently moving their fins to keep themselves exactly over the centre of their pile. It was like looking down on the domain of some primeval dukedom from the air, a land tranquil, peaceful, alien and dangerous, ready to explode into killing war, into flight and pursuit, at any second ; a land to—Grant couldn't really say what it made him feel— a land to conquer. Half drunk as he still was, with his terrible great hangover, floating face down on the surface, he could hear his breath coming slow and steady through his snorkel tube, and a tingle of a sense of danger, of a forever alien misunderstanding, slithered around through his viscera and groin and finally settled itself in his scrotum.

Beside him Bonham touched him on the arm and when he looked over, wiggled his eyebrows in his mask proudly like someone showing off a friend's art work to an interested collector, Grant nodded vigorously, and the big man rolled over easily till his mouth was out, plucked his snorkel, and said, "To the top of the rocks is thirty-six feet, to the sand itself forty-three."

Grant raised his own head, much more awkwardly, and treaded water. "But what are they doing?" he gasped.

Bonham rolled on his side again. "Doing! How do I know? Who the hell cares? These grouper here're almost always like that in the middle of the day." He took a breath. "Watch."

He lay on the surface taking several long deep breaths— "hyperventilating" ; he had already explained this to Grant —then surface-dived and swam down kicking rhythmically and easily, left arm back along his side palm up, right arm extended with the gun. At maybe twenty feet Grant watched him snake his left hand up to his mask and clear his ears. Six or eight feet from the two grouper resting stationary above the pile he stopped kicking and coasted down, waited two or three seconds, speared the biggest of the pair, rolled over and headed back up, his head back, sunlight glinting on his mask, his arms at his sides and the fish trailing along wildly below him at the end of the spear and line. His heart in his mouth from the eerie beauty of it, Grant thought he had never seen anything so beautiful. It was like a ballet conducted in non-gravity. It was twice as beautiful as when the bulky lung tanks were on the diver's back.

Just as Bonham started down Sam Finer had touched Grant on his other side and swept his arm with excited appreciation across the underwater scene. He was again wearing his Scott Hydro-Pak (he was still on his first set of tanks) and at the moment was breathing through the snorkel-like " air economiser " on the side of the full-face mask. He carried the little Minox Bonham and William had repaired for him last night in one hand and his speargun in the other.

Grant had spared him one quick glance, not wanting to miss any of Bonham's dive, but now as the big man surfaced still trailing his gyrating fish Finer touched Grant on the arm again. " Great, hunh?" he said in a faint, strangely squeaky voice from inside his full-face mask, and spread his arm again over the underwater scene. Grant nodded. " Ever see anything like this? What a life! Okay. See you later," Finer squeaked, and went swimming off.

" Okay, now you try it," Bonham said, coming back from boating his fish in the nearby boat. Grant looked down. The other grouper, which had disappeared when Bonham speared his companion, had now returned to his exact same position above the centre of the coral pile. He maintained himself there calmly with little movements of his pectorals, as if nothing had happened. Grant began to " hyperventilate," himself. " Not that one," Bonham said from beside him. " He's spooky now. We'll save him for later. Pick another pile."

Grant nodded and swam off toward another one, which had its own grouper floating serenely above it as though he was not aware human predators had invaded his land. Looking down at him, wanting more than anything in the world to get down there to him and put a vicious, triumphant spear into him, Grant lost all sense of time. It took him

at least four tries before he could finally get far enough
down even to shoot, and when he did he was so nervously
out of breath that he hurried his shot and missed by at least
two feet. Bonham waved him on to another pile patiently.

"Relax more," Bonham said, rolling over on his side
and floating easily while he made a lecture. "Don't kick so
hard. Don't try to go down fast. Take your time. You
got plenty of time. Believe me. Don't get scared down there.
Don't panic. It isn't lack of oxygen that makes you want to
breathe. It's excess carbon dioxide that makes your diaphragm
heave like that. Remember how I made you stay down in
the pool till you couldn't stay any more, and then made you
turn and swim underwater across the pool? Relax more when
you hyperventilate. Don't work so hard at it. Relax. It's
not dangerous. Relax more." It seemed to become a running
comment that never left his ears. They moved on to another
pile.

The very first time down the pressure on his ears had really
begun to hurt at twenty feet, and he had stopped to clear
them ; by the time he did, his momentum was lost ; he
had given a few frantic kicks and then had to come back up.

On the second try he had been prepared for the ear-
clearing problem, had kept on kicking as he cleared, gone
on down, but the moment he realised how deep he was
below the surface now his heart had begun to pound, he
was suddenly out of breath, and he had to come back up.

He did not know how many piles he spooked before he
finally shot a fish, two or three maybe. But when he did
succeed and hit one, and turned, elated, to come back up,
he thought for a moment the fish had anchored him to the
bottom. Frantically trying to swim the other way below him,
it effectively held him down. He considered letting go of
the gun, but the shame would be too great. Remembering
Bonham's advice, trying not to let himself get scared and
step up his carbon dioxide content, he worked his fins rhythmically and easily at the ends of his legs, and slowly he rose,
the fish below him dragging heavily at the gun in his hand.
Far above him, while his chest heaved uncontrollably, he
looked up at the undulating sun-glowing surface as a haven
the like of which he had never dreamed of before. When
his head burst through it, and he blew out his snorkel and
gasped, and then just lay floating and breathing, it was as

much of a return to the Promised Land as he ever expected to feel. Twelve feet below him his fish swam around in slow circles on its side at the end of his spear and line.

"That's the ticket," Bonham said from beside him. "That was a pretty good dive. He'll go twelve pounds."

"They sure put a drag on you, don't they?" Grant laughed, gasping. He looked down again at his trophy affectionately. The feeling that he had accomplished something, something that neither he nor his body had wanted to do, gave him a new elation.

"The really big ones really put a drag on you," Bonham said, and grinned at him. "Feels good, hunh?"

"Sure does." This time Grant raised his head completely out, and treaded water. "Where's the boat? I'll go and——"

Bonham cut him short. "Too far. Here, give him here." He pulled a cord fish stringer out of the crotch of his trunks. "If we swam back to the boat to boat every fish, we'd lose all our time. Look at it."

Raising his head, Grant at first couldn't see it. Finally he picked it out as it bobbed up on a wavelet. It was at least two hundred and fifty yards away. A kind of spear of loneliness pierced through him. He looked at his watch, and saw he had been in the water forty-five minutes!

The most he had ever swum before, swimming normally without flippers and snorkel, had been fifteen minutes when he had swum a hundred yards for a Red Cross life-saving test. And then he had been exhausted.

It was only the beginning. They moved on from pile to pile, Grant diving and diving. Bonham repeating over and over his lecture to relax.

"Okay," Bonham said finally, after a dive. "I'm gonna leave you on your own awhile." He now had three of Grant's fish on the stringer. He pulled another stringer from the crotch of his trunks and passed it over. "If you want more fish, use that. I have to spend some time with Sam and the camera. Besides, Sam isn't all that good to be off by himself like that, anyway. And we want some good pictures. We'll be over this way," he said, and pointed southwest and slightly out to sea. "Work your way over that way."

Grant felt a small chill at the thought of being alone. "Where's Orloffski?"

"He's over that way too, I think. Now, did you see how I handled them fish?"

Grant nodded. Bonham had taken both of the two which were not dead by the eyeball sockets exactly as if he were picking up a bowling ball. The pain made them stiffen and cease to move. Then he had cut through the head into the brain with his knife. He had pulled a gill open with his fingernail to show Grant the sharp gill rakers that made it impossible to hold these fish by the gills. And when he pushed the metal tip of the stringer in through a gill to come out the mouth, he did it gingerly.

It seemed to Grant that there was never a minute that passed when he was not learning something. Sometimes it was hard on the ego. He rolled his own head out now, plucked his snorkel, and suddenly realised that he was getting the hang of that much, anyway, "But isn't it dangerous? Carrying a fish stringer? Because of sharks?"

"Yeah, I guess it is," Bonham said, and shrugged irritably. "But don't worry about it. *I'm* carrying it. If you don't want to shoot any more fish, don't. We got more than we need to eat. Work your way on over toward us, we might see something interesting."

Then he was gone. It was all so matter-of-fact.

For a while Grant simply lay still in the water, looking down, moving his flippers idly only enough to keep him headed in the right direction. The blue and green world was eerie and beautiful. This way, floating with only the back of his neck out, breathing slowly and easily through the snorkel, he was totally and completely relaxed.

After a while, he began swimming leisurely from one coral pile to another, making a dive now and then, but not trying to spear anything. It was the first time he had ever been really alone in the sea, and it gave him a peculiarly satisfying feeling. He even began to feel a little bit at home in it. He tried to remember where he had had this feeling of odd satisfaction before, and then realised that it had been at home as a kid, when he was alone in the big old house, totally alone and with nobody else there. If anybody else was there, it spoiled it, his parents, his kid sister, his two older brothers. But sometimes, once in a great while, his mother would be out, at one of her countless ladies' club meetings, and everybody else would be off somewhere, and he would—age what? ten or twelve?—come home from school and know that he was going to be there alone for a certain number of hours. He would walk through the big old rooms in the stillness and quiet, the hallway, the kitchen, the dining-room with its big oval table, the middle parlour where they were allowed by his mother, the front parlour where they were not allowed by his mother (" Living-room Number One and Living-room Number Two," his father sarcastically called them), all the bedrooms upstairs, all the bathrooms ; and in the silence of aloneness everything, every object and every space, the air and light itself, would appear new and strange as though he had never seen it before. Knowing that eventually he would go up to his own attic rooms—attic apartment was more the word for it—and masturbate in tranquillity, he would touch this chair or that lamp with this odd satisfaction of entity. And that was the way Grant felt now in the sea.

But then honour came into it and disrupted all that. He had to spear a fish. He had to spear a fish, and he had to carry it on the stringer. If Bonham—and Mo Orloffski, and Finer—could swim around carrying bleeding fish on stringers, then he had to do it, too. Every book he had ever read about skindiving warned against this. It was dangerous. It was an open invitation to sharks. Some sharks were known to have come from down-tide as far as a mile or two miles after the scent of fish blood, the books said. Grant didn't even know whether the tide was coming in or going out at the moment. He had forgotten to ask. None of that mattered.

Picking the biggest grouper among all the " rockpile " grouper within his visibility, he swam over to above it, hyperventilated enormously, surface-dived, and started down, although he didn't want to.

It turned out the most beautiful dive he had ever made, with or without aqualung. It was very nearly perfect. Swimming down in the classic stance, clearing ear pressure as it built up, he could feel his legs beating easily and relaxed with their flippers against the water resistance, driving him, loose all over as goose grease. He watched the big fish come closer and felt he had all the time in the world. The grouper was resting two feet or so above his coral rockpile which meant he was diving, what? thirty-six feet? Stopping his kick, he waited just long enough, but not too long, calculating

the angle of entry of the spear for a brain shot from
behind and above, and shot the slowly moving fish exactly
through his brain. The grouper quivered and became still,
and Grant rolled over delighting in himself and his movements
and started back up slowly, watching the glistening, never-
quiet water-sky come down to meet him as he rose. He
was—at least for as long as he could hold his breath—a
free man, free of gravity, free of everything, and revelled
in it. With only a couple of heaves of his diaphragm, he
swam back up as slowly as he could, sorry that it was over.
When his head broke the surface, he felt—erroneously or
not—that he was a different man.

But then the anxiety returned. The fish was dead so there
was no need to cut him, and being hit well in the head there
was almost no blood. But he was anxious anyway. Constantly
looking to right and left and behind, he got him off the spear
and on to the stringer, tied it to the hip strap of his bikini
and went swimming off in the direction Bonham had taken,
looking all around and behind every few seconds. He wished
now that he had not had to do it, but it was equally
unthinkable to unstring the fish and drop him—an idea which
had entered his head—just leave him and swim away. He
swam on, alone and peering down into a world of water.

Before he had gone very far, he noticed that there were
no more grouper floating above any of the coral rockpiles
ahead of him. As if by some signal, they had all just disappeared. A shock tingle of alarm charged through him,
because he did not know the reason. Had maybe sharks
come into the area? Then ahead of him on the left, inshore,
at just the outer edge of visibility, he caught just a glimpse
of a faint blue shadow descending. Taking a good grip on
his speargun, which was practically worthless as any kind of
real defence anyway, he swam over that way, and saw that
it was Orloffski he had seen.

Orloffski had a stringer of fish—or two stringers, because
Grant didn't believe one stringer could hold so many—so
huge that he could hardly dive with it, and he was going after
another. Grant watched fascinated as he speared the fish,
surfaced, and set about adding it to the string like a man
in a field shucking ears of corn into a wagon. Such brutal
greed disgusted him. He was aware he was seeing in action
the quality in man which had destroyed the forests and the

plains buffalo of America. Orloffski had not seen him and
went swimming off looking for more fish, and Grant turned
back toward finding Bonham.

As he swam on alone, he kept peering behind him every
few seconds in the approved manner, to make sure no hungry
shark was bearing down on him. These goddamned fucking
masks, it was amazing how they cut down your side vision.
It was like wearing blinders.

On one of these sweeps of his head he happened to raise his
face far enough above the surface that he caught a glimpse of
the three little islets sitting there behind him in a string, and
on the nearest of which were Carol Abernathy and the two
girls. This made him think of her briefly for a moment,
but only for a moment and briefly.

THIRTEEN

Great rolling black thunders in clouds and vivid crashing
arrow-shots of blinding lightning roared and wrassled inside
her head, making her want to shout, as she leaped over the
end of the boat into the sand and staggered away to fall
in the ankle-deep water. That was the only way she could
describe it. But she did not shout. Bravely, she kept her
strong-willed, self-disciplined lips closed though no one knew
of her heroism.

Well, she would not tell them.

The strong are sometimes tested almost beyond their
capacity. Only the Strong are tested Strongly. And if they
cannot encompass it, rise above it, rise above the Dead
Ashes of their Selves, they only drop back down one level,
one material evolutionary level. And to shout with Spiritual
Rage before the ears of material men is to go unheard.

In the warm shallow water the bright sunlight turned her
closed eyelids a warm pulsating red. A million bright bees
buzzed in this red space, each with his tiny stinger glowing,
a red-hot wire ready to inflict upon the strong and magnificent,
the true sacrificers, a hundred million burning fiery stings.
It was not unjust. It was the Karma of all. The boat had
already left, she had heard it go. And now she could hear the

two women up on the sand beach behind her talking in the low tones people use in the presence of invalids. Carol Abernathy smiled to herself, but did not open her eyes. The warm sea water was vastly soothing, healing. The Sea as Great Mother. Slyly, she voided her bladder in her swimming suit, feeling in the warm water the greater warmth of her urine on her thighs and crotch, thinking how she had fooled them all. She had not really been sick at all. She had simply had to pee. But she could not come out and say that openly to a drowned boatload of men and women; crude men, and younger women.

Slowly she sat up, as though she was not quite sure where she was, looking all around.

"How are you feeling, Carol?" Cathie Finer called down to her. "Feeling better?"

"Oh!" she said. "Oh!" She put her hand to her head. "Yes. Yes, I am. The water is so soothing. The sea is healing. The Sea is the Great Mother. I think it's helped me."

"Would you like something to eat?"

"No. I couldn't eat anything. The very thought of eating . . ." She shuddered. Actually, she was ravenous. The sea air was certainly good for one, and for the appetite as well.

"What do you think it was?" Cathie Finer asked as she slowly climbed up the sand to them.

"I think it was some kind of intestinal *crise*. An acute colitis, perhaps. People with very sensitive nervous systems often get that, and I've had trouble with it before. But never anything like this." She smiled wanly at the two women, who appeared to look relieved, especially Wanda Lou Orloff-ski, and then looked beyond them. "What do you say we explore our island?"

"There isn't very much to explore," Cathie Finer smiled. "Just that clump of six pines there in the middle, and that heavy brush down at the end."

"I think I'll go over and lie down in the shade of the trees a while," Carol said.

"You go ahead," Cathie said. "We'll stay here and get some sun and maybe eat something after a while. Are you sure you're all right?"

"I'm a little shaky," Carol said and smiled at her, and suddenly felt tears well up in her eyes and turned away to hide them, but not before she was absolutely sure Cathie had seen them. One knew one's friends. No word need be spoken. That young woman had much good Karma.

It was lovely in the pines. A light little breeze played under them, moving their long leaves softly, and the floor of brown needles where she sat and then lay down smelled deliciously of pine. But then the rolling black thunders and slashing lightnings began to clash and smash and roil in her head, effectively cutting off all her exterior senses, as she thought again of Grant.

Who the *fuck* did he think he was? She had not come all this long way all these long years from the back hills of Tennessee, to see herself muzzled and her power cut off, just when it was just *beginning* to have some serious national voice. She had not disguised her Self and her Motives all these years—for *twenty years* before she even *met* Grant—to have him think he could divest her of all she meant to accomplish in the world with a flick of his little finger. Did they think, all those selfish fools, that she had married Hunt Abernathy because she loved him? or because she merely wanted to be number-one social arbiter in a hick town like Indianapolis? Ha! She had suffered almost twenty years with Hunt Abernathy, biding her time, playing her little role, waiting. Him, with his drinking to such excess and chasing piggish waitresses, the more piggish the better. She had saved his Mind and his Soul; she had made his career for him in brick manufacturing just in her spare time, while she was preparing herself and waiting.

Of course the producers and publishers all hated her. They were terrified of her and of her force. They lived dirty little status quo lives behind the façade of which was their true degeneracy which they didn't want exposed. They knew they could handle Grant. Because Grant was easy to handle.

But there were Forces on her side, Forces of Good and of Evolution in mankind, which were not to be toyed with. When she had deliberately burned all of her writing and play manuscripts that time years ago on that beach in Florida, accepting the role of Sacrifice of her talent and her selfish ambition, she had put into her own hands enormous power, psychic Power, which neither producers nor publishers, nor Grant, could even conceive the force of. And especially

Grant, the ungrateful Grant. She had made him into a man. She had saved his Talent and his Soul; she had even given him her body to use, suffering in silence all the unpleasant —things so that he might concentrate on his great work toward the purpose—her purpose—of changing mankind. He would turn against such psychic Power as that at his peril, if he did.

Suddenly the black roarings ceased and she began to cry. Oh, Ron, Ron. You were so beautiful then. I was so beautiful.

After a while the crying ceased, but it brought no relief. She got up nervously from the unenjoyed bed of pine needles, looking anxiously for the two women, deciding to go back to them.

Well, at least Bonham was on her side. That little trick of telling him she would get Grant to put in money. That had worked good. She would decide more about whether to go ahead with that after this horrible, stupid trip was over and she got back to Ganado Bay and looked the situation over. But it was not inconceivable that the more and more Grant gravitated to these men, the less and less he could care about *any* woman. She had noticed about adventurers that the more they got their kicks out of adventuring and danger, the more they tended to consider all females as less important except for a quick fuck.

And anyway, quite apart from all that, she had another quick little trick up her sleeve, for as soon as they got back to GaBay.

As she came out of the trees and down the path to the beach where the two girls were still sitting, now amongst the eggshells, sandwich wrappers and empty beer bottles of a picnic, she carefully put on her face her expression of fatigue and depression and low energy. She would dearly have loved to have eaten something.

They were, of course, when she came into earshot, talking about their husbands. Carol looked out to where they could just make out the boat in the distance on the sea. There they all were, playing, playing, playing, kids playing games.

FOURTEEN

It did not seem like kids playing games to Grant. Playing yes, maybe. But not kids' games. When he finally did find Bonham, Bonham was doing an—at least for Grant—unbelievable thing. Bonham and Sam Finer, with the camera and one speargun between them, were playing with a seven-foot nurse shark, trying to get close-up pictures of it.

After seeing Orloffski that one time, Grant had swum alone slightly out to sea roughly in the direction Bonham had indicated, over the long flat field of coral "rockpiles." The rockpiles here had no fish floating above them either. Bonham and Finer had scared them away, had both taken quite a few fish—though nothing like Orloffski. They had laid their fish and the other speargun, Finer's, on the forty-foot bottom for temporary safekeeping, much the same way a man might without worry leave a suitcase in a quarter locker at Grand Central, in order to deal with the nurse shark.

On his swim across the field of "rockpiles" Grant had found a small ravine which sank maybe fifteen feet below the sand plain, and deepened as it ran out to sea. The far bank of this ravine did not rise as high as the rockpile plain, and beyond it instead of the pure flat sand was a jumble of black rocks and dead coral heads that looked ugly and uninviting and deepened gradually as it ran on south parallel to the coast. This was apparently the end of the "Lagoon," and Grant had turned and swum along the near edge of the ravine directly out to sea.

For some ridiculous reason he was nervous about swimming in water that was deeper than where he had been, though this was patently silly. But as he swam along the edge of it and got more used to it, he experimented with a few dives to try and reach the bottom of it. If his guess of fifteen feet was right, it would be about fifty-five to fifty-eight feet deep. He never reached it. On one dive, his best, he was able to touch the tip of his speargun to the bottom, which meant with the length of his arm added to that of the speargun, he had done maybe forty-five feet; but swimming back up from that dive his diaphragm was heaving so much that with his nose he sucked all the air out of his mask and made his eyes bug out. It was depressing.

It was at the seaward corner of the field of rockpiles where it ended against the bank of the ravine that he found Bonham and Finer, and the nurse shark.

It was the first nurse shark Grant had ever seen. It was the first shark he had ever seen, close up. But there was no mistaking that it was a nurse, with the two barbels hanging from its small mouth and the long thick single-lobed tail. He had read about it of course, and without exception all the writers on diving he had read warned that the nurse had bitten more skindivers than any other shark, largely because people insisted on playing with it just like now, though the bites were never massively serious. But if Bonham and Finer had read the same books, they didn't show it.

What they appeared to be trying to do was to get a close-up of the nurse's face head-on. To achieve this Finer, swimming in his Scott lung at a depth of fifteen feet, level with the nurse, would advance on the shark until, just as he was about to snap the picture, the nurse, waving its tail and pectorals, would suddenly shoot straight backwards ten feet. And there it would wait. It showed no inclination to leave. And this was when Bonham entered the game. With Grant watching from a safe distance, ready to help if he was needed but afraid of disturbing the shark by getting into the act, Bonham, from the surface, swam down on the shark from behind, trying to scare him forward toward the would-be photographer, whom he had motioned to stay still. But instead of moving forward, the nurse shot off sideways, just exactly like a skittish horse, and then stopped again, looking at them. Bonham tried again and the same thing happened. He kept on trying, always with the same result, and every time he surfaced Grant could hear him roaring with maniacal laughter.

It was just then that Orloffski swam up from somewhere. Orloffski had none of Grant's scruples about a third person scaring off the shark. Diving to the bottom he left his two enormous strings of fish (which he appeared just barely able to tow) at the other speargun with those of Bonham and Finer, and in the same dive then swam up directly under the nurse shark apparently intending to spear it.

Bonham waved him away. The two of them held a hurried conference on the surface. Then, this time, they swam down on the fish together, from behind and on each side, still trying to scare it toward Sam Finer. The nurse made a little dive, then shot suddenly around in a turn so fast it was only a blur, to reappear again stock-still at its old depth of fifteen feet, facing them, exactly ten feet behind the two of them. Grant had read that sharks, having no air bladder, were heavier than water and therefore had to keep swimming or sink; but this nurse shark seemed able to sit still. The two frustrated free-divers, out of air, surfaced, and Finer crept toward the fish again.

Grant was beginning to laugh now too, and nearly choked from some water that got into his snorkel from a wavelet. He swam closer, intending to help with the herding process. But Bonham was not about to give up. Determination showing in the set of his shoulders, he got around behind the fish again, dove to fifteen feet and swam slowly up behind it and grabbed its tail with both hands. Kicking his flippers mightily (he had passed his speargun to Orloffski) he literally shoved the nurse shark right up into Finer's face. Apparently, Finer got his close-up.

The shark, startled apparently, or perhaps having seen enough to satisfy his curiosity, gave a light flick of his tail that knocked Bonham five yards off, and swam off slowly and disappeared into the water-fog that marked the limit of the visibility range.

The three of them, Bonham, Orloffski, and Grant, were roaring with laughter as they swam over to each other, directly over the stringers of fish down below on the bottom. Treading water to keep their heads up above the surface, they let their snorkels fall out of their mouths and shouted with laughter. Grant didn't really know why. Then Finer who had been below, swam up to them in his Hydro-Pak, scowling blackly through his full-face mask. He was swearing and cursing in a muffled voice from behind it. "Goddam it! Oh, Christ! Oh, goddam it! I didn't have the fucking thing cocked!" he complained. He had thought that it was cocked, but it hadn't been. This set them all off again. But

Grant wondered why had they been laughing in the first place?

It was a hard thing to try to describe to anyone. It was hard even to understand. The comedy of errors, sure. And then the nervous inoffensive shark, swimming off slowly like a person trying to keep his dignity. And then Finer missing his picture, after all. But Bonham had been laughing before any of all that even became apparent, and in the end so had he. And, after all, it was a somewhat dangerous situation they had been in. The nurse maybe couldn't have eaten one of them up or bit off a leg and killed one of them, but it could have given any one of them a bad nasty bite. Why so funny? Then he realised that that was just it, and that that was why they were laughing. They had gotten themselves into a potentially dangerous situation, and they deliberately had done it, deliberately. And now they were laughing about it. It made Grant think of certain things that had happened to him during the war. He didn't say it was smart, or intelligent. But he liked it. He treaded water to keep his open mouth from choking him with sea water, and roared helplessly with the others, and not since the old days in the Navy in the war had he felt so affectionately close to any group of men. He felt, and it was shared, a real warmth of really deep affection for all three of them. And he didn't need to be ashamed of it. It was something you could never explain to any woman and, he realised, something no woman would ever be able to understand.

"Well, come on," Bonham said finally. "Let's git our fish and haul ass. It's gittin' late, men."

Raising his head to look Grant realised he could no longer even *see* the boat. But it would be easy to find your way back to it by following the landmarks of the bottom. Looking at his watch suddenly he was astonished to see that he had now been in the water without ever touching land or boat or any other support, for more than three and a half hours. It was almost 3 p.m. And he must have swum at least three or three and a half miles in that time. Maybe more. Then he suddenly thought of Carol Abernathy back there on the little island waiting for them, with the other females. Well, he thought with deliberate care, *piss* on Carol Abernathy.

He watched the other three go down to get their fish, Finer switching off his " air economiser " and using lung air, the other two simply free-diving it. When Mo Orloffski picked up his two enormous stringers of big fish it looked like he would never make it back to the surface. But he did. Then they stared the long swim back to the boat.

She was waiting for them with the other two girls, all three of them sitting in a row on the beach, when Bonham gently grounded the boat's nose on the sand. She seemed okay and perfectly all right, as she helped the other girls pick up the picnic gear and their other things. But then when she came up close to the boat, a startling thing happened. Finer and Orloffski had leaped out to hold the boat steady, and when she saw the four happy, replete and self-satisfied men close up, something in her face changed. It was as though one light in her eyes came on and another light went out.

" I'm not getting in that boat unless I have the knife!" she cried out, suddenly, as Wanda Lou was just climbing over the side. But her tone was no longer commanding. It was self-pitying, almost whiny, and falsely fearful, as though with her manner she was letting them know she knew what thieves and dangerous unscrupulous types they were who might do anything to her.

For a moment Grant didn't say anything.

" Give it to her," Bonham said in a voice of long-suffering toleration. " You know she's not going to hurt anybody with it, anyway."

" Not unless somebody comes near me," Carol Abernathy said with the same fake fearfulness. " Keep away from me!" she cried as Cathie Finer turned to smile at her.

She didn't say another word, and it was the same uncomfortable, unpleasant ride back to the dock that the ride out had been, in which everybody else tried to talk as if everything were normal.

While the other men were taking care of the fish and the gear, Grant helped her out of the boat and repossessed his knife. He started immediately for the hotel, and she followed him looking curiously repentant.

" What are you going to do?" she asked nervously.

Grant didn't say. He didn't even know, yet. All he knew was that he didn't have to live this way. " I don't have to live this way," he said. "I don't have to. And I'm just not going to. I don't have to spend my life doing things and being reminded by you that I mustn't enjoy them because it might hurt my 'art.' If that's self-sacrifice, fuck it. If that's what you have to do to be a 'great artist,' fuck that too." He meant every word.

"What are you going to do, Ron?" she said again.

"I—First I'm going to take you back to Ganado Bay. Right now. To-night.—If I can—You go and pack your stuff. I'm going to find the pilot and——"

"You can't do that!" Carol Abernathy cried. "I won't let you ruin your trip you've spent so much on to have!" He was walking fast so that she had to half run to keep up, and when he stopped she almost ran into him.

"Then you can stay here by yourself with these people. I'm going. I've been embarrassed enough." He did not even feel like bothering to remind her that it was she who had spoiled the trip.

"You can't make me stay here! You can't force me to stay in this horrible place!" Carol Abernathy said.

"Then go and pack our stuff," Grant said sharply, and then immediately regretted the "our." "You don't really believe I mean it, do you?" he said more softly, dangerously soft. "I'm really through."

Carol looked at him a moment without saying anything, then hurried away toward the hotel, and she seemed to be almost scurrying.

Raoul and Jim Grointon had not yet returned from spearfishing, he found out when he went back to the dock. And in the end it was another hour before they did return. Grant stayed on the dock and did not leave it. He took Bonham off to one side and told him quietly what he had decided to do. It was a shame, but he had to do it. He did not intend to ruin everybody else's trip too because of his personal problems. Bonham nodded solemnly. He was sorry, but he guessed it was probably the best thing to do. Grant simply nodded. His face felt very bleak. The whole thing was terribly, painfully embarrassing to him, but it had to be done. He told the others. They were all sorry he was leaving, too, but he noted that none of them urged him seriously to stay. The only thing about it all that bothered him, when he went back to Bonham, was whether Raoul would be able to make the flight to-night, after it was dark, so they wouldn't have to stay till morning. He hoped to avoid that.

" I don't see why not," Bonham said. " They've got all the instruments on that plane, and good radio. And Raoul plays around but he's really a very good pilot. A night flight shouldn't bother him."

" Well—I hope not," Grant said. He stayed around on the dock, talking to the others, helping to gut out the mass of fish. Orloffski was for selling it to-night in the local market. " What the fuck," he said in his brutal way. " What's left that we don't eat's worthy forty fifty bucks. Pays some expenses." As the sun-heat left and the sky turned rosy the evening air came on fresh and cool. Grant breathed it with the feeling that he was drinking a delicious glass of cold water and regretted his decision. But not enough to change it.

There was a considerable bit of time lost when Grointon and Raoul came in with Grointon's ground shark prize, which had to be weighed, and measured, and talked about. He had found him in among some big coral heads they knew about, at a depth of about eighty-five feet, where he had run into a coral tunnel arching between two of the heads. Raoul couldn't go that deep but had managed to go deep enough to scare him back into the tunnel so Grointon could take him as he came back out the other end. He had missed a perfect brain shot, but had managed to hit enough of the spine to half-paralyse him so he could horse him up to the boat, gaff him and kill him there. For a while he'd thought he'd lost a spear, Grointon smiled modestly. There was some discussion as to just which species of ground shark it was. Grointon thought it was the Large Black-Tip, but Bonham and Orloffski thought it was a more than usually dark Dusky (or Shovelnose). Grant studied it and wondered if he would ever have the courage to attack such a creature with a puny speargun, then suddenly knew somewhere deep inside himself that some day he was certainly going to have to try. He would just simply have to. And he hated the thought. Carefully, he didn't mention this to anyone. Finally he was able to get the excited Raoul off to one side and ask him about the flight.

" Ho, shoora!" Raoul said. " Hot ass eassy."

"He says it's easy," Grointon said, coming up in his easy relaxed way. Grant nodded. He knew what he'd said.

"Bat, why you wan' a go?" Raoul said looking puzzled.

"Mrs. uh Abernathy isn't feeling good," Grant said stiffly, making his face flat. "And I want to get her back to Ganado Bay to her doctor."

"Hokay! Hwe go!" Raoul said cheerfully.

"But it'll cost you more than the regular trip, Ron," Grointon pointed out. "If you could wait——"

But Raoul held up a hand. "Hwe mak eet wan hondrad flat," he said. "Eet ees heemergency. Hwe com back tomorro' morning, Jeem. Hyou see," he said to Grant, "hwe got to com back far the hothers."

"That's okay with me," Grant said. "That's fine. That's more than fair." They all three shook hands.

Grant went to settle up with the hotel manager. Bonham followed him a ways, and shook hands too. "I'll give you a call as soon as I get back to GaBay." Grant thought he seemed sad, and felt good. When he got back to his and Bonham's room, Carol Abernathy was sitting on her suitcase in the middle of the floor of her own room, he saw through the open door. There was a black defiant look on her face which bespoke nothing of her former "repentance," and Grant's stuff in the other room had not been touched. But then he had anticipated as much. He threw everything into his suitcase hurriedly, not bothering with trying to fold and lay flat. The little duffel bag for his minimum of diving gear was no problem.

Jim Grointon rowed them out to the plane in silence. Raoul was already aboard, he said. In silence they climbed aboard and strapped themselves in. In silence they took off. Raoul circled the hotel once as he climbed, and in the deepening dusk the main building was aglow with lights and very cheerful looking. Grant looked down at it thoughtfully, feeling a sort of immutable sadness. They all would just be beginning to drink.

Almost the whole trip was passed in silence. Grant had seated himself up front without looking around, and Carol Abernathy had taken her old rear corner seat. Once Jim Grointon came back politely to talk, but sensing Grant's mood thoughtfully left after a little while. At one point Grant fell asleep for a while and had a nightmare. He had just speared a huge fish and it had gone under a deep coral ledge. And now he was trying to swim back up with it, but he was stuck and could not budge it. Pride would not let him let go of the speargun, the pistol-grip of which he could feel plainly in his hand as he pulled and worked his flippers and tried to swim, and so he knew he must stay here and drown. His lungs were bursting, and far above him through the green water the surface undulated and shimmered invitingly like quicksilver. He woke up in a cold sweat.

He did not know whether Carol Abernathy slept during the trip or not.

When Raoul revved up over the Yacht Club, which had been alerted via radio to the airport which in turn then telephoned them, they turned their two big searchlights on out over the bay. Raoul in his turn circled back, turned on his own powerful landing lights, and brought the little plane in neat as a pin. They were not unused to the night seaplane landings at the Yacht Club, but they were nevertheless rare enough to be considered occasions and the veranda was crowded.

As the Club's peon rowed them all in, Grant could see that Hunt Abernathy was waiting for them on the dock with another figure. When they got close enough, he was surprised to see that it was Doug Ismaileh, one of the few other successful playwrights to come out of the Hunt Hills Little Theatre Group and who, or at least the last time Grant had heard, was living in Coral Gables below Miami.

Carol Abernathy was waving and smiling at them as though nothing at all untoward or unpleasant had happened.

FIFTEEN

On the dock Carol kissed Hunt deeply on the mouth, a practice which always rather irritated Grant—or perhaps mildly shocked, would be a better term. It was not jealousy so much as that he was old-fashioned enough to believe a woman with a lover should be ashamed to kiss her husband

like that. Then she, too, kissed Ismaileh on the mouth,
and gave him a long hard bear-hug around his tall thick
frame. Doug was one of her living proofs that Grant's
talent had not made and sustained the Hunt Hills Little
Theatre Group totally alone.

Grant had always been of two minds about Doug Ismaileh.
Doug, like most of the others, had come to the Hunt Hills
Little Theatre Group on his own. But unlike the others he
had some money. He had driven down on a whim from
Detroit, where his father was a fairly wealthy hotelman whom
he worked for sketchily, when Grant's *Song of Israphael* was
still in its first year's run, with the idea that he wanted to
write and that maybe Grant could help him. He had not
heard of the Hunt Hills Little Theatre Group, but Grant
was in New York at the time, and Carol Abernathy had taken
him under her wing and started him on the self-disciplines
which she demanded of every member of the Group. However, since he had money, he did not have to live on the
premises in the " barracks," the living quarters which Grant
had built around the Theatre which he had built, like the
ones without money had to do. He had stayed there a couple
of times for a short while, in summer when it was nicer, but
after three weeks the restrictions on serious drinking and
going out had him champing at the bit. He and Grant had
become good friends, and he could have stayed in Grant's
house, but Carol thought this unfair to the other, broker
members. So he stayed mostly in Detroit where he had a
woman whom he subsequently married and divorced, writing
on his play, coming down only when he was in trouble
with it, and otherwise stayed away. One winter he rented
an apartment in Indianapolis to be near them and stayed
there five months with the woman while he was finishing up
his play.

He had had a fabulous career during the war in the OSS
in Greece, Yugoslavia and Persia, where his Greek-Turkish-
Armenian blood, knowledge of the language, and relatives
who had not emmigrated all helped him greatly, he said,
and where he had become the youngest Lieutenant Colonel
the Army ever made. He had once, after that, run an
illegal gambling establishment on the West Coast, and
apparently had all sorts of very interesting, and very helpful,
underworld contacts. His play, however—his first one—

Dawn's Left Hand, was about Persia, and drew heavily on his war experiences there for its material. He had obviously had them. And yet one afternoon, while he was still working on the play, he had come to Grant and asked him to tell him all he knew about hand grenades, how they felt, how they worked exactly, how they were operated, how they sounded exactly. Grant, who had only thrown three hand grenades in his life and those three in training, told him and wondered how a guerrilla fighter of his experience and repute could not know about hand grenades.

The play itself (*Dawn's Left Hand*, the title Grant had given him once in a moment of inspiration while thinking about Persia, from the second stanza of the *Rubaiyat of Omar Khayyam*) was in the end a love story—a love story intermingled with tough combat fighting and death—of an aristocratic Persian girl and an American colonel; and a love story curiously reminiscent of Grant's Sailor and Whore in *The Song of Israphael*, albeit a much more exotic one. It was a huge success (Grant had taken him to Gibson & Stein) though not quite as big as Grant's first one. But Grant felt he detected in it, and in Doug—had detected all along—elements of sentimentalities and gross romanticisms about life (as well as false toughness, which was only the other side of the same coin) which might make it hard for Ismaileh to carry any further into himself his study of himself. And then there was that curious echo of similarity to his own Sailor and Whore.

That didn't matter. Everybody imitated some when they started. But it was true that Doug loved him and his work doggedly, even slavishly—though the word would have angered him—to the point where it disturbed and embarrassed Grant. He was always trying to buy him rich presents, take him on trips, do things for him, help him with something, carry him places, all of which offers Grant kept declining with almost nervous severity, because some deep instinct he couldn't formulate into words warned him it would be dangerous to accept.

All of this had sorted itself out one night during the fall and winter Doug had spent in Indianapolis finishing up his play, when Doug had driven out to Grant's house in Hunt Hills with a truck-driver he had picked up in a bar downtown. Doug had two tricks when he was drunk, tricks he had picked up from a fakir in Persia, he said, of walking barefoot on broken glass and eating light bulbs. These had apparently intrigued his pal the truck-driver, who was also drunk. But when he mentioned that he knew Grant and that Grant had written *The Song of Israphael*, the truck-driver had become ecstatic. He had been in the Navy and had seen the film of the play (though, as he told Grant, he had never seen or read the play itself) and Grant was his sole literary hero.

This was at a time when all such uncritical adulation was beginning to wear very thin for Grant, though he had not long before (and occasionally would again) found it fun to get drunk in a bar and talk about the "Old Navy." Also he was working very hard trying to finish up his own new play and wanted to get up early, having had just the right amount of drinks to let him sleep. After two dull and very unproductive bottles of beer sitting around the kitchen table with them, he got angry, feeling he had been imposed upon. Doug had never really seen him angry before. Grant had called him into the bedroom for privacy (Carol had come over from across the street, and was sitting with the truck-driver) and told him.

"Listen. You get that fucking ape out of here. You brought him, now you get him out," he said, with a cold, half-drunken fury. He could feel from his heartbeats, that his face had gotten white all over. "I don't want to embarrass you. But either you get him out of here, or I'll ask him to leave in front of you. And you, too."

"Aw, c'mon. What the hell? The guy loves you. He thinks you're a king," had been Doug's somewhat drunken rejoinder.

"I don't give a *fuck*!" Grant said. "This is my house! This is where I live! And you are not welcome or free to come here drunk with strange drunks you picked up!"

Doug's face had suddenly contorted itself into a drunken, and strange, totally *mea culpa* expression. "Okay! I know I did wrong! Hit me! Go ahead! Hit me right in the mouth! I got it coming! Go ahead! I want you to!"

"Are you crazy?" Grant had said coldly. "I'm not about to hit you! I'm not about to have a fight with you, here. What, and tear up the insides of my own house?"

Doug had grinned, though there were still tears in the

eyes of his still-contorted face. "Okay, then! Let's go outside!" he raged. "Let's go outside and have a real fight! A real one! A real good one! A real, old-fashioned, knockdown, drag-out, no-hold-barred, good old fight! Like we all used to do! Back in the old days! A real friendly, smash em-up, break-their teeth, buddy-friendly fight! Like we did in the Army!"

Grant had simply stared at him. He was shocked to think that that was just exactly what he used to do.

"A real old-fashioned, buddy-buddy fight!" Doug raged on. "We'll beat each other's fucking brains in! And then put our arms around each other and come back in and have a drink! We'll come back in the bar and drink a toast! To *men*! Real *men*!"

It was just barely freezing outside and there was a thin skim of snow on the ground. And it was just then that Grant's revelation about Doug Ismaileh hit him. Grant had boxed a lot, back in the so-called "old days." He thought he could take him. Though Doug was a good bit bigger than he was, he was in better shape. None of that had anything to do with what he had suddenly understood.

"Listen," he said much more calmly. "I want to tell you something important. I'm not about to let you make some kind of a father figure out of me." Doug had always hated (and loved) and had trouble with his father. And now he stopped raging and leaning forward, peered at Grant, his eyes screwed up shrewdly almost shut. He didn't speak. "You know why? Because you don't want a father.

"You're always talking about a father. But you want one and you don't want one. You want to make a father out of somebody, anybody, simply so you can then set about destroying them, to prove to yourself that you're a man.

"Strong. Free. Horse shit!

"Well, you won't do it to me. Because I don't care about you that much. And I never will.

"I've got too many problems of my own to take on your love, just so you can start destroying me.

"And I'm not vulnerable, because I don't need the adulation.

"You want a hero to destroy, go and find somebody else. And get that drunken bum out of my house."

And that was the end of the story. Doug Ismaileh had said nothing. Either one way or the other. He had collected his truck-driver and left. The relationship between them went right on pretty much as it always had, except that maybe he left Grant alone a little more than before. But not much. Probably he couldn't help it. Probably it was a compulsion of some kind. But after that Grant was never able to feel much of anything about Doug Ismaileh except indifference, both to him and to his role he played.

And now here was Doug, three years later, after taking his new-gotten, author's wealth to Florida, and buying a house and becoming an ardent Everglades and backwater San Marco fisherman, standing in the dock of the Ganado Bay Yacht Club, in Ganado Bay on Jamaica. They shook hands quite warmly.

"Well, what the hell!" Grant grinned. "What a surprise! What brings you down here?"

Doug was grinning happily, too. "Well, when I got——"

But here Carol Abernathy intervened. "Yes, what a *lovely* surprise!" she said in the breathless rush of a self-confident conspirator. "Did you just decide to come down for some fishing? But *how* did you know we were here?"

Grant noticed that Hunt was looking at her with a peculiar look, his eyes all squinched up, his face expressionless, but as was usually his way he said nothing. Grant didn't say anything either.

"Well, Gibson and Stein always know where you are," Doug Ismaileh said in an oddly muffled voice, and grinned again. Later on, as soon as they were alone together, which was not until the next day, he told Grant the full story, the true one.

Grant had decided to go diving alone the next day, and Doug after hearing his glowing, impassioned descriptions wanted to go with him. Bonham had told him, on the dock at Grand Bank while they waited in the twilight for Raoul and Jim Grointon to return, that he could use Ali and the boat by himself if he wanted and go out alone, at the same normal regular price of course. "Ali will tend for you," the big man said. "Just remember he's no good in any emergency, that's all. So you'll have to look out for yourself." He had paused, thinking, looking out at sea from the dock. "If you're nervous about going out alone for the first time, just go out on the shallow reef and poke around. Don't go to the deep reef." Then he had slapped him heavily on the shoulder. " I ain't worried about *you*. *You'll* be all right. Hell, you could practically free-dive that, now." Grant seriously doubted that, but, cautiously, it was to the shallow reef that he decided to go, and he told this to Doug.

"Well," the big, swarthy "Turk" said enthusiastically, " I'll just snorkel around in a mask a bit on the surface and watch you down below. Okay?"

Grant agreed. Certainly he should not try the aqualung until he had at least had a pool check-out. They were just coming down into the town off the hill, Grant driving one of Evelyn de Blystein's several little British cars, and the humid heat of the island hit them just exactly as if they had driven into some low-lying invisible fog, popping the sweat out on them both. Down here the lush tropical island vegetation and palms, grey with the dusk of the town, looked peaked and straggly.

He had not wanted to lie last night, Doug said suddenly. But he figured it was the best way. The truth was that Carol had called him long distance in Coral Gables, apparently a couple of days before the Grand Bank Island trip, and had asked him to come down. Grant needed both their help, she said. " Apparently you got some little girl in trouble?" Doug grinned.

Grant smiled. " Well. Let's say some little girl's got *me* in trouble." Doug nodded, or rather ducked, his head vigorously ; he understood that very well. Grant went on and told him about the knife-wielding episode in Grand Bank.

Doug chuckled. " Well, she always was what you might call a forceful character. Remember the time she ran those three so-called intellectuals from the University of Arizona off the place with brickbats?" Both men laughed. One of the three had subsequently written a very disparaging article about the Hunt Hills Little Theatre Group in general, and about Grant's talent in particular, for a Chicago literary quarterly.

"Only this time it's different," Grant said. " It's me." He braked for a bandanna-headed woman with a great bundle of clothes on her head. " I think she's losing some of her marbles. Seriously."

They had never discussed, or even tacitly acknowledged, between them that Carol was Grant's mistress, and Doug did not bring this point up now. " Yes," he said, his face looking graven. " She seems different. More erratic."

" You've always liked her."

" Sure," Doug grinned, " and I'm payin' her ten per cent to prove it too, ain't I?" This was a fairly recent development in the Hunt Hills Little Theatre Group, and Grant had agreed to pay her ten per cent of this one, his newest play.

" I don't know what she wants me to do about helpin' to save you," Doug said. " She hasn't told me yet."

Somehow, Grant realised, suddenly, a sort of male conspiracy had developed between them. A male conspiracy against the females.

As if he too suddenly sensed this tacit feeling, Doug said, " Look. If anything happens, if it comes to some kind of a showdown, I want you to know I'm on your side. You've always helped me more than she has anyway, really."

Grant rather disliked him for saying it. " Well, thanks," he said.

They had come to the plane trees that stood alongside Bonham's shop, and Grant pulled the little car in under them into the welcome shade and parked it.

" Is she nice?" Doug grinned. It was, tentatively, one of those sort of evil grins males give each other over cunt. And Grant didn't like that either.

" She is," he said crisply. " If I told you how nice, you'd say I'd lost my power of judgment."

" Well, good for you. All I know is, a man's gotta live," Doug said gruffly. " If he can."

" He sure does," Grant said, and the sense of male conspiracy became stronger. He still didn't like it.

Ali was loafing around the shop, obviously quite happy to be doing nothing, and while he looked chagrined at the idea of doing some work said Shar in his curiously flattened East Indian accent, he would take them out, if they was sure Misteh Bonham said it are all right. Grant assured him that he had. Would they both be wanting lungs, he asked. No. Grant said, just one.

Doug talked more about Carol Abernathy on the way out. She seemed really different this time, he thought, much

more nervous and high-strung; but Grant was thinking about
the diving now and didn't say much in reply. When Ali
anchored the little boat off the airport over the shallow reef,
he went about dressing himself out nervously but quite
proud in front of Doug, and made a very professional back
entry, always an impressive sight. When he rolled over
and looked down, he recognised the area and realised that
Ali had anchored them above the big coral cave where
Bonham had taken him down that first day.

Behind him he heard Doug splash in his mask and snorkel
and motioned for him to come on over, and when he
did Grant who was showing off a little took off swimming
straight down for the green sand bottom, sixty, sixty-five
feet below. Now, it all felt so natural, comfortable. On
the bottom, lying just a few feet above it so as not to disturb
the sand into clouds, he rolled over on his back and waved
up at Doug who waved back, a tiny figure now on the
undulating silver of the surface. When he first had recognised
the coral hillock which contained within it the big cave,
the blood had risen in his ears with an odd excitement as
he remembered his dream—dream, and half-promise—of
coming back alone to this place some day and masturbating
in it. Swimming along the bottom on around the hillock,
he motioned Doug to follow him on the surface.

He did not intend to re-enter it by the narrow fissure
he and Bonham had gone in by, even though his sense of
honour made him feel he ought to try it, plus the fact that
it would be quite a spectacle for Doug on the surface;
but he knew pretty well where the other entrance was,
and as he swam on around to the other side of the coral
hill to where a narrowing sand-bottomed trench ran shoreward, Doug followed him on the surface, watching, obviously intrigued. The other entrance was only fifteen or
eighteen feet deep if he remembered right, and when he
thought he had positioned himself correctly, he started
swimming up the living coral cliff faces. At seventeen feet
of depth it appeared, only a few feet off to his left.

From the brightly sunlit water outside it was impossible
to make out anything within the black hole of the mouth,
but he remembered the interior exactly. Motioning to Doug
what he intended to do, then pointing at his watch and holding up first five, then six fingers with a shrug, Grant took

a full, deep breath, let out half of it, and swam inside.
From above him Doug had shrugged too and held his hands
out helplessly.

The alcove-tunnel was still there, and when he swam around
its corner into the main cavern, the shafts of sunlight from
the ceiling holes still slanted down through the water to
strike against the coral walls or sand floor. He remembered
that the coral toadstool where they had sat was invisible from
this high up, but after he had swum down ten or twelve feet
it became visible, far down, resting on the sand floor.
Breathing carefully and slowly from the lung Grant swam
down toward it, thirty-five, forty feet below him. So still,
so dim, so green and cool, so lonely. So uninhabited. All
the cathedrals, all the churches, all the empty school buildings
after five o'clock, all the childhood lonelinesses, came back
to him, and he could feel his penis hardening in the little
bikini. Not breaking his kick-rhythm or his quiet calm of
breathing, he swam on down what seemed endlessly then
rolled up and turned over just above the giant toadstool
and by exhaling to make himself heavier, let himself bump
to rest sitting on its scratchy surface. The cathedral-cave
was unchanged, looked exactly as it had the other time. But
now he was alone.

Liquidly and using no violent or wasted motion Grant
hooked his thumbs into his bikini straps and slipped it down
to his knees, then lightly took it off over his flippers, first
one leg then the other. Immediately everything felt different,
cleaner, more beautiful, as always in nude swimming. The
water now reached the angles of his crotch and anus as it
did the rest of him. As an afterthought he stuck the bikini
underneath his weight belt so as to be sure not to lose it.
Then he looked down at himself and was startled to see
that, due to the refraction of the light rays passing through
his mask, his hardened cock appeared to be sitting in the
middle of his chest! He fingered himself, lightly, and then
realised that he didn't really want to masturbate. Instead,
he took off and swam back and forth across the cavern
delighting in the movement of the water against his naked
crotch and organs. Then he came back and descending
on an impulse to the sand floor near the toadstool, rubbed
and flogged and ground his bare penis, testicles and crotch
against the sand, raising a small cloud. It was just then that

he looked up and saw a huge jewfish studying him quietly and curiously from twenty feet away.

It was enormous. As long as he was, it was more than twice as big around. It must easily have weighed at least 400, 450 pounds. It was the first one he had ever seen, and it looked like a grouper, which in fact it was, with the same big mouth. Only, this mouth was big enough to take in his head and shoulders with room to spare. And he had read that they occasionally attacked divers. All this had run through his mind in one flash and without even thinking he drew his knife from its sheath on his leg and swam up the few feet to put him on its level, ready to fight, but reasonably certain he would lose. He had not brought a speargun with him, not expecting to see fish, but even a speargun seemed a puny futile weapon against a creature such as this.

Fortunately he didn't have to fight. When he reached its level, the huge fish with its great goitrous-looking, perpetually startled eyes gave a flick of its body that was like a minor explosion and disappeared across the cavern into a dark area Grant had not explored. It had all happened so fast he had not even lost his hard-on.

Still fingering it, and feeling somehow quite pleased, he swam over to the area cautiously, to find that here was apparently still another exit. A long low tunnel seven or eight feet in diameter led away through the coral hillock over a rising, then falling, then rising again floor of rippled sand. No sunlight was visible at the other end of it, and Grant did not feel like exploring it. Swimming back, he sheathed his knife and put back on his bikini. He still had more than sixty feet of water and coral above him to get out of yet.

But if he worried about his erection remaining so that it might be noticed by Doug Ismaileh as he came back out of the cave, he needn't have. As he swam back up toward the entrance and the sunlight it went away as quietly and mysteriously as it had come. And as he swam back out of the cave mouth into sunbright water, he felt curiously fulfilled. He had been down in there just a little over nine and a half minutes. Above him still lying on the surface, Doug Ismaileh was gesticulating at him nervously with both hands.

" Jesus Christ! " he protested when they were both back

in the boat. "What the fuck were you doing in there all that time? I thought you'd gotten yourself killed!"

"Just exploring," Grant said. "I told you at least six minutes."

"You said *five*, or *six* minutes!"

"Well, I lost track of the time a little."

"You lost track! I was gettin' ready to swim back to the boat to get Ali."

"He wouldn't have helped any," Grant grinned. "He doesn't even dive." He described the big cave to Doug but he did not tell him about the jewfish, largely because he would have felt honour bound to go back after it with a speargun if he had. He had done two dishonourable things to-day, he calculated. He had not gone in through the fissure like he should have, and he had not gone back after the big jewfish.

But he did tell Bonham about it, later on. The big man only grinned. "You mean you went down there alone without a speargun on your first dive alone? I ain't worried about your guts!"—"I just didn't think there'd be any fish. But shouldn't I have gone back after it?" Grant insisted. "Wouldn't you have?"—Bonham rubbed his jaw. "Maybe. I'm not sure. He was probly long gone. I know that exit. Anyway spearin' big fish in caves is ticklish business. They can drag you into a narrow hole and knock your mouth-piece out of your mouth. Can be very dangerous. Always remember that in divin' the cautious decision is always the best one. It's your life you're playin' around with," he said with a solemn pious look—and Grant suddenly knew that that was not at all what Bonham really believed, or at least not all of the time, that Bonham was talking sop for customers. He had had to be content with that. He did not, of course, tell anybody about his erection.

"Well, what do you think of it?" he asked Doug as they towelled themselves off in the hot sun on the boat. Doug thought a great deal of it, he said, and would like to learn it. Especially he would like to see the inside of that cave.

"Well, I can teach you if you want," Grant said. "Now that I know his methods, I can give you a pool check-out about as good as Bonham."

Doug seemed to take quite a long time in answering.

They were sitting in the cabin cockpit in the shade now, near the wheel, and all the windows and windshields were wide open. A warm soft little breeze swept through it carrying the smell of the sea, and occasionally smelling of the hot muck of the mangrove swamps that formed the extreme right side of the harbour. The tropical skyline there was mysterious and dangerously inviting as though they might be the first non-native ever to make land fall here, and on the other side the skyline of sprawling hotels called luxuriously to modern pleasures of booze and broads, martinis and models. The noon jet from New York had just landed at the airport and was disgorging its vacationing passengers into the air terminal. The little boat rocked gently in the sea wash, and they could hear the hiss of water moving in the bilge. Grant was feeling the sense of vast relief he always got now, when the diving for the day was over and he did not have the prospect of it before him. Doug was looking out through the open windshield at the hotels and the high hill behind them with Evelyn de Blystein's villa on it. "Is it safe?" he said finally. "I mean, I don't mean safe. I mean is it easy to learn?"

"Well, it took me three days to learn all the techniques he wanted to teach me. Course I couldn't do them as well as him. And still can't," Grant said. "I think it's easy. Of course everyone is a little nervous at first, naturally."

"Well, might's well give it a try," Doug said turning back, "I guess. Since I'd down here, and everything's handy."

Ali who had been sitting in the tail stowing gear came forward. "Ahre you rahddy to go in, Meestahr Ghrant, Sahr?" he said.

"No," Grant said. "No, not yet. Let's just sit here a little while, okay? It's so pleasant."

"It is pleasant, ain't it?" Doug said with a sudden grin. He broke out a half bottle of scotch he had brought from the villa and they drank it together, mixing it with tepid water from the water jug without ice, sitting together in silence and just feeling—the movement of the boat, the shade and hot sun, the breeze on their faces, the smells of sea and mangrove swamp, the view of both banks of the harbour, the view of the airport, from which the big jets soon trundled out and took off going over their heads again with a whistling roar.

"Well, I guess we better be gettin' back, hunh?" Doug said reluctantly. "We got to sing for our supper to-night yet, don't we? Who's old Evelyn havin' for dinner?"

"Christ, I don't know," Grant said with a start. He got up and motioned to Ali to start the motor.

In the next two days Grant took him four times, twice mornings twice afternoons, to one of the hotel swimming pools and tried to teach him, suspending his own diving and taking him through the same training routines step by step that Bonham had put him through.

But Doug simply could not learn. Not from him, anyway. He advanced swiftly through all the mask techniques, breath-holding techniques and such-like, all of which he knew something about, but when it came to using the aqualung itself he simply could not do it. It was all right at the shallow end of the pool, but the moment he arrived at the deep end swimming along the bottom, he would be forced to rush coughing and spluttering to the surface. "I think it's the goddamned shape of my mouth!" he said with angry disgust, but with a peculiar veiled look on his face. "No matter what I do, water keeps leaking in around my lips!" On the third day, when Bonham got back from Grand Bank, Grant turned him over to Bonham.

But Bonham had no better luck, and could not teach him either.

The thing about the shape of his mouth being wrong was obviously an excuse. Hanging around with Bonham on his teaching rounds, Grant had by now heard four neophytes complain of the same thing, one of them being Carol Abernathy. None of them had ever succeeded in learning to dive. He had discussed with Carol her own feeling about being in the lung, and had about decided that the real trouble might be some kind of an underwater claustrophobia, perhaps augmented by the confinement of the face-mask. Aware that a certain volume of water existed above her, she simply had to come up. It might even be that this claustro-phobic fear, upon reaching near-panic proportions, caused them to relax their lips and let water get in. Or perhaps the water getting in the mouth thing was simply a face-saving lie. Tactfully he discussed this with Doug, and Doug admitted that on the bottom of the deep end of the pool he did get this panicky feeling of being closed in, pressed down. Grant himself had never had this feeling in a lung, though he had plenty of other fears, and on the contrary being in a lung underwater gave him a feeling of opening up panoramic vistas, as well as the delight in being gravityless. " It's stupid!" Doug said angrily. " Because I'm not afraid!"—— " Of course not. That's not what it is. But if that's it," Grant said, " a claustrophobia, there's not a damn thing you can do about it. Has nothing to do with being afraid." Doug shook his head stubbornly. He tried several more times, always with the same result, and finally had to give it up and quit. " It's the thought of never ever, never in my life, being able to see the inside of that damned cave of yours that bugs me," he said despairfully. " I'm cut off from it."

He continued to go out with them in the boat whenever Bonham took Grant out, which was almost every day, after he got back, snorkelling along over them when they were on deeper dives, free-diving down to them sometimes when they were on the shallow reef. He got so that finally—on the shallow reef—he could free-dive twenty, even twenty-five or thirty feet down to the corals. He was therefore able to free-dive to the cave entrance and peer in, but of course there was nothing to see until you swam far enough in to turn the corner, another twenty or twenty-five feet, and this he could not do. He tried the lung a couple of more times in a pool, but always with the same result, and Bonham advised him not to try it in the sea. He was very frustrated, especially whenever Bonham and Grant went back into the big cave, which they did from time to time.

Grant was fascinated by the cave, but it was more than that. Bonham, since getting back, had suddenly acquired quite a few new clients in the hotels from the big influx of tourists because of The Season, and the cave was one of his chef-d'œuvres. He took all of his neophytes there, as soon as he was sure they could handle the dive, and Grant and Doug usually went with him—paying much less for the trips when there were other clients, fortunately. Bonham's policy was always to help his more permanent clients financially when he could.

They had taken to hanging around with Bonham a great deal more since his return, Grant because he wanted desperately to stay away from Carol Abernathy as much as possible. But Doug Ismaileh had taken a great shine to the big diver with his, to them, marvellous accomplishments —as Grant had known he would. Bonham had a favourite bar in town called The Neptune, where he had once introduced Grant to the two Jamaican girls, and where he hung out with his local pals when he wasn't out diving, or giving lessons. Naturally, this place had no social connection at all with the de Blysteins and their high-class social friends, and Grant and Doug spent a great deal of time there with Bonham, drinking. Also they met his wife and he invited them to his home.

Bonham's home, which he had bought and like almost everybody in this age of credit and time payments apparently was having difficulty paying off, was a little clapboard house with two small bedrooms, kitchen, living-room and bath, set in a tiny yard on one of the side streets in the middle of the town. It was a somewhat impoverished-looking place, not at all like the houses most white people lived in in Ganado Bay but more like the home of a coloured bank clerk or assistant store manager, but Bonham's wife Letta had done a lot with the inside, and Bonham had built himself an American brick barbecue outside in the little yard. When he had returned from Grand Bank, the Finers and the Orloffskis had flown back with him and William, the Finers immediately catching the jet to New York, and now—as they found out when he invited them up the evening of the first day he was back—the Orloffskis, Mo and Wanda Lou, were staying with him.

His wife Letta was a small, superbly built, quiet-spoken, medium-dark Jamaican girl, who looked as much schoolteacher as she in fact was, and who apparently took a rather dim view of the Orloffskis in her house although she entertained them nicely. Not that the Orloffskis needed entertaining. They had already moved in and taken over, and appeared to be more the hosts than the guests. But, as Bonham told Grant, it wouldn't be for long. The plans, as he told them both—or rather Grant, since Doug knew nothing about Bonham's set-up except what little Grant had told him—were that Sam Finer after a few days' business in New York would be flying back out to Minnesota, where he would forward the money immediately. Then Bonham and Orloffski would go down to Kingston to look the schooner over once more (Orloffski had never seen it), buy it, and arrange to have it hauled. Orloffski would then fly to Jersey and bring the cutter down the inland waterway to Florida and sail it to GaBay. Meantime, the Orloffskis were house—or apartment—hunting. When they found a place Wanda Lou would move in there and Bonham and Letta would help her out and look after her. He told them all this as, with loving sausage fingers, he prepared his barbecue in the yard for steaks in the late evening light.

The steaks were excellent. So was the booze, though they all drank more of it than was probably good for them. Grant noticed that Letta was not above drinking a fair amount herself, which surprised him, even though it was apparently never enough to make her really drunk. William and his wife and four kids had come over too. so that with the Bonham's maid washing glasses and dishes there seemed to be almost more people ramming around the little house and yard than it could handle or contain.

And after that the two of them took dinner with the Bonham ménage every night, and were little seen at the villa. The second night they ate at Bonham's again with the mob—because even with the absence of William and family, who did not appear again, the six of them in that tiny house (especially with the two huge and hollering figures of Bonham and Orloffski) made it seem like a mob. The third night Letta was not with them, and they ate at The Neptune, Grant and Doug picking up the tab. It turned out Letta worked as a hostess in an Italian restaurant five nights a week (excepting Mondays and Tuesdays, when the place closed for its " week-end ") to augment their meagre income. It was run by an Italian (aided by his Jamaican wife) who had been maître d' at one of the big hotels, and Grant had eaten there with Evelyn and the Abernathys, but he did not remember Letta. The fourth night they again ate at Bonham's, again without Letta, when Bonham made them marvellous barbecued ribs. Every night everyone drank far more than was good for them, but it seemed to be the norm around Bonham—and Orloffski—and around Grant and Doug, for that matter.

It was surprising that Carol Abernathy (on behalf of Evelyn) left them alone that long without complaining. But the days were running down, and time was running out. On the morning of the fifth day after Bonham's return, Carol Abernathy caught the both of them at breakfast coffee (they weren't eating because they meant to dive that morning) and divulged her plan for the saving of Grant by Doug Ismaileh.

She started off by employing her role as den mother of the biggest cub scout pack in the county.

"You two guys have been pretty scarce around here the past few days." She had come down to the terrace where they were in her pyjamas and robe. It was not quite nine o'clock in the morning. "Here Evelyn's got two of America's biggest and handsomest playwrights staying in her place as house-guests and she can't even utilise them. When are you going to stay home an evening?"

Grant decided he would not answer that, and let Doug do it. Doug said, "To-night, I guess. We been seein' a lot of this guy Bonham."

"So I understand from Evelyn," Carol said, "who got it from her maid, who got it from the jungle telegraph." Having Doug around as a sort of third-party observer seemed to have straightened her out quite a bit, as though having an audience kept her remembering the right role. There had been no more crazy scenes like the knife-wielding episode in Grand Bank. "Also, you both look like you've been drinking a lot more than you should or is good for you." She peered at Grant keenly. Grant filmed his eyes over for her.

"That's usually the case, ain't it?" Doug grinned. "Especially when we get together."

"Anyway," Carol Abernathy said, and smiled, "this is what I wanted to talk to you about: It turns out Doug has got relatives in Montego Bay, did you know that?" she asked Grant. "And he wants to visit them while he's down here."

Grant deliberately did not answer her. He had known, everybody had known, for at least four years, that Doug had Greek-Armenian relatives who ran a restaurant and small hotel in Montego Bay. They had come down there from Florida and opened it up immediately after the war. Doug was forever talking about them, and meant to do a play about them.

"So," Carol went on cheerfully, "I thought it might be a good idea if the two of you went over there for a week or so. It'll save 'trouble' here at Evelyn's. And you can pick up some cunts and have yourselves a *good* bender. It might serve to take Ron's mind off all his New York pussy-cats."

"It's okay with me," Doug said and looked at Grant.

"I think it's a fine idea," Grant said with a chilled voice. "I'm ready to go right now, to-day. The sooner the better." He got up.

"Then maybe you'll feel more like yourself," Carol smiled at him. "You might even feel like getting down to work again."

This had been one of her techniques of "personality control" for years: the instillation of guilt about not working, not "creating": more, the idea that none of "her boys" had strength of character enough to get their work, their writing done, without her around to crack the whip over them. Grant did not intend to let her get by with that this time.

"I doubt that," he said coldly. "I haven't done as much of this skin-diving yet as I want to." He looked over at Doug. "I was thinking I might take along an aqualung from Bonham, and do a little diving over there."

"Good idea," Doug said.

"It's only seventy-five miles," Carol said. "You can do it in an afternoon."

"I'd rather go right now," Grant said. "This morning." And with that he put his napkin on the table and went to his room to pack a bag. As he climbed the big staircase he could hear Carol and Doug still talking, swiftly, then Doug followed him.

They rented a car in town. While Doug was doing that, Grant picked up a set of tanks and a regulator from Bonham's shop. "It's okay. I'll put it all on the tab," Bonham grinned. "There's a guy over there named Wilson who's got a compressor and can refill 'em for you if you need it." An hour and a half after Grant had deposited his napkin on the table they were on their way out of town along the north coast road.

SIXTEEN

The moment he woke in the hotel bed, with a terrible hangover, he knew he was going to call her and reached out blindly for the phone even before he opened his eyes or took his face out of the pillow. The phone in his hand, he opened his eyes and stared at the untouched, unperfumed, unlipsticked pillow beside his own. He had had it all up to here. It was what, now? three weeks! And he had had a bellyful of everything, of just about everything.

In one way he felt it was a weakness. To call her. He had wanted to do this diving thing all on his own, alone, and concentrate wholly on that. But he was too weak to do even that. Couldn't even be without a broad for three weeks or a month without sinking into a suicidal depression. But he didn't give a damn. He placed the call (there would be a delay of thirty to forty-five minutes the over-sweet voice said) and rolled over on his back staring at the ceiling and contemplating his weaknesses.

The false and professionally happy voice of the operator, demanded of her by her company's personnel training course, made him as lonely and nauseated him almost as much as the catalogue of his weaknesses. He ought to be used to them. He was not. He ran once more fruitlessly over all his problems: Carol Abernathy and responsibility: when did it stop; that goddamned white elephant of a house in Indianapolis that he no longer wanted and that was costing him a fortune; his financial problems (it was embarrassing to have made as much money as he had and not have one nickel invested; and he was already worried about Bonham's forthcoming bill); his other, essentially a drinking, problem with Doug Ismaileh (and other artists of that particular drinking type).

How to get out of Indiana? How to get money so he could afford to live somewhere else? How to get out of skindiving, now he had gotten into it? How to get *into* Lucky? *That* weakness? Well, he wasn't going to marry her. He'd take her to Kingston, for a while, and see what happened. How to get rid of Doug, whom he liked and didn't want to hurt—at least at certain times? Right now Doug was firmly and unequivocally shacked up with a gorgeous model in the next bedroom across the connecting bath, in which the rush of water had wakened him three times during the night—or rather, the morning—as she came in to douche. Grant looked at the snowy rounded untouched pillow beside him and longed for Lucky. He must really be in love. He had had his choice of three of them!

He had talked to Doug about Carol Abernathy on the drive over. Grant had never been to Montego Bay. Doug knew MoBay but had never been to Ganado Bay, and so neither knew the road. Grant had driven. And probably because of that, almost certainly because of that—because he was driving——he suddenly found himself talking and talking and talking about Carol Abernathy, about art and life, about his past, about Lucky. As can so often happen, he became hypnotised with the car and the road, the movement of the land backward, the movement of the windshield forward, and talked and talked.

The ride itself was beautiful. Almost all the way the road ran alongside the sea, glinting and sparkling cleanly in the bright tropic sunshine. Almost everywhere inland thick fields of green cane slanted slowly to the forested, jungled mountains sometimes several miles away, sometimes only a few hundred yards from the road. Only the villages and towns were ugly. Dusty, jerry-built and dilapidated except for one or two rich planters' town-houses with their gardens walled in so you couldn't see them, they appeared at regular intervals like misshapen pearls knotted into a string. Peeling ad signs and busted neon tubing along the main streets. Like the beat-up cars nobody knew how to drive or take care of. Parts of a blunted salient of the civilisation the tourist vacationers came here to flee but which itself must inevitably come too, brought by them or those who catered to them. All the tourist hotels along the sea were beautiful, they noted, and modern, and there were many of them. Between Ocho Rios and St. Ann's Bay they stopped at the Roaring River Falls for a beer at the falling-down garbagy beercan-strewn concession in the chill fern-laced clearing beside the giant's rock staircase over which the water never ceased its noisy pouring, and ate sandwiches. Evelyn had insisted on packing for them because the concession was notoriously foul and germy. Then Runaway Bay, Discovery Bay, Rio Bueno, Falmouth. Over all always there was a smell of an unusually pungent woodsmoke, the fuel the black peasant used for everything, from cooking to heating wash water.

When he told Doug that Carol Abernathy was his mistress and had been since they'd met him, Doug only grunted. When he added that her recent nervousness and neurotic actions and fits were almost certainly due at least in part to the fact that he wanted to break off with her—in fact, *had* broken off with her, Doug grunted again. Of course, Grant qualified, her dictatorialness and paranoid formulations had been increasingly discernibly the past few years, even in the time Doug had known her. Here Doug nodded. But of course, Grant added, trying hard to be honest, that could be due—or partly due—to the fact that for a long time she had felt Grant slipping slowly away from her, as she got older. Hell, he didn't care whether she was crazy or not. He wasn't going to try to commit her or anything. All he wanted was to get out of it. Whether he married Lucky or not, he knew now he had had it with Carol and was through with her. Lucky did want to marry him. The only trouble with her, at least as far as he could tell up to now, was that she was just too good to be true. Every quality he would want a woman he'd marry to have, she had. All of them! But when he tried to describe Lucky's qualities (other than her sensuality and beauty), he failed miserably and lamentably.

He was astonished to hear himself pouring his guts out like this, about all this. This made the third time he had told somebody about Carol. In as many weeks. Or was it . . . No. No, no. It was the *second* time. He had told Cathie Finer, and now Doug. But up to then he had never told anybody about it, had not even let on to anyone. Not even to one of his best friends. Although he had to admit he had had very few of these.

Doug said very little. In fact, in the end, he seemed much more interested—with an intense unwarrantable concentration—in how Hunt Abernathy felt about Grant's long-term affair with his wife.

"Christ, I don't know! How the hell would I know? We

never talked about it," Grant said. "But we've become pretty close friends, over the years," he said, "you know?"

But it was not strictly true, that first, he remembered suddenly. They had talked about it. Once. Sitting in a car, they had been, just like now. Hunt's car. Only that car hadn't been moving. It had been parked out in front of the Abernathy's house in Hunt Hills. They had either just been some place and returned, or else were going some place and Hunt had not yet started the motor. Or else they had gone out to the car for privacy, Grant couldn't remember. It had been very early on in the relationship, when Grant was still living with them, long before he ever had any success. Hunt's face had had a set stiff look, and his eyes if cold were very deep as he stared straight ahead out through the windshield. He sat quite a long time in the still, quiet, parked car before speaking.—"I guess you wonder why I'm doing all this," he said finally, referring to what he was doing, and had done, for Grant. Grant hadn't answered, largely because he didn't know what to say.—"You must be wondering why I tolerate this 'situation,' and what's going on." This time he didn't even wait for any answer. "Well, it's because I'm trying to help Carol. I don't give a damn about you. Or what happens to you. And you just remember that Carol is my wife. And remember that I'm her husband." —"Of course," Grant had said, delicately. He was terribly embarrassed. Hunt had sat on without saying more for a full minute, staring straight ahead out through the windshield.—"Just don't forget that," he said finally, and opened the door to get out and go inside, or was it that he had then started the motor? Grant for the life of him couldn't remember. His puzzlement at the time had been total. Anyway, they *had* talked about it. If you could call that talking about it. But he wasn't about to tell Doug Ismaileh any of that.

"I wonder why he stayed with her?" Doug said from beside him. "Why didn't he just throw her out?"

"Who knows," Grant said. "Habit?" He was beginning to sweat a little, and felt flushed and uncomfortable. He wished he hadn't brought the subject up. "I'll tell you why!" he said suddenly and violently. "Because she had him by the balls, that's why! Like she had me. But she won't have me that way any more."

"Maybe he liked it," Doug said. "Being cuckolded."
"That's kind of faggy, isn't it?"

"Not necessarily. Lots of guys are like that. I've known quite a few." Doug grinned, but his eyes had a peculiar hungry look. "Do you think she might have been fucking him too at the same time all those years?"

Grant was startled. "Well, no. I never thought so. I mean, I assumed she wasn't." He wasn't going to tell Doug that in his heart he had never been sure she wasn't.

"You're pretty sure then she wasn't fucking anybody else all that time."

"Well, no. I'm not," Grant said. "Since you bring it up. Now that I think about it. But I just don't give a shit, whether she was or not. That's the truth. If she was, that just makes me that much more of a sucker, that's all."

Doug didn't answer for a moment. "She probly wasn't."

There was something odd in his tone. From the wheel Grant gave him a sharp glance for a split second, then put his eyes back on the road. Doug was looking straight ahead out through the windshield, slumped down in his corner, his arms folded across his chest. "Well, if she wasn't," Grant said, "I guess that puts me in even a worse position."

"In any love affair he who quits first wins," Doug said. "Ismaileh's Law."

Grant was suddenly angry without knowing why. What the fuck did he think he was doing? Was he trying to imply he knew something he wasn't telling? It sounded like some kind of police interrogation. "I believe you, but I'd hate to live like that," he said. It was half a lie. There was a part of him that was both pleased and proud that it was him who was quitting, was him who was not feeling the pain. He was the superior. It was the old "Get the Upper-Hand" theory of personality development. But underneath that was the further knowledge that he probably couldn't have done it at all without the existence of Lucky. Where *was* the truth! God! "Funny, my new girl told me that same thing, in New York," he lied viciously. "Those exact same words."

"I thought I made it up," Doug said. It was his turn to be startled.

Grant relented. "Maybe you did. You could have both

made it up separately. I never heard it anywhere else before."

They were just pulling into the ugly little town of Falmouth, and Grant felt a vast wave of relief wash over him. Exaggeratedly, he leaned forward and craned his neck this way and that, pretending to look with interest at the surroundings, to cut off the conversation.

" What a hell-hole," he murmured.

" Yeah. Wouldn't like to be a field nigger and have to live here," Doug answered.

Where *was* the truth? the *true* truth? The true truth was that Decameron L. Grant, goy Anglo-Saxon white Protestant from the Middlewest (whose people both came over on the *Mayflower* and met the boat, as his grandfather who was a quarter Cherokee was fond of saying), wanted everybody in the world to love him. Or if not love, at least like him, and think he was an honourable fellow. Even Doug Ismaileh, whom he couldn't care less about. And everybody else. It could get to be pretty difficult when it was a Red Chinese on one side and a GM Executive on the other. Or two male humans after the same cunt. Phoo-ee. He continued to pretend to look.

After Falmouth there was five miles of marshy salt flats not unlike parts of Florida in the Keys, and they both remained silent through all of this too, Grant still biting his tongue for having talked as much as he had. Then, as though having tried it on for size and finding that it fitted, they continued to ride in silence the next twelve miles all the way to the outskirts of Montego Bay. Only when the luxury seaside hotels began to appear on the beach on their right, did Doug perk up and begin to give instructions.

" There's a short-cut over the shoulder of the hill called the Queen's Road. Saves goin' all the way around the airport on the beach road. It's at the—There it is! Just up ahead."

Grant braked and swung left on to the curvy road that led past the jet airport on the right, curved up over the flank of the high hill island, then dropped straight down into the hot dusty insufficiently shaded town. On the descent they passed the entrance to the Racquet Club, a steep side road leading straight uphill on the left, and Doug pointed it out.

" We'll have to go up there. They're a good bunch of

guys. Big drinkers and partyers, and they know where all the action is and what's going on."

They drove straight through the sudden heat to the hotel-restaurant of Doug's relatives. This was located on Union Street, one of the main east-west streets running from the harbour straight back into the hills. There, it became Something Drive (Doug said) and curved around amongst many trees to give entrance to some of the better white or near-white homes of the town. The Khanturian (that was the family name) Hotel, a four-storey modern-style brick building, was set in the midst of a bunch of Charles Addams houses made of wood with high mansard roofs of corrugated tin, and had a bar and dining-room on the ground floor and three floors of rooms above. The bar, dim and cosily lit, was more than twice the size of the dining-room, Grant noted, and was practically deserted. The dining-room was totally deserted. It was in this bar that they had almost immediately met Sir Gerald Kinton.

Doug of course had first to say hello to his relatives. There was much whooping and crotch-grabbing and back-slapping and goosing involved, since they had not seen each other for over two years. Although the family (father, mother and five unmarried sons) only two of the sons were present, working the bar and dining-room respectively, the noise was enough to startle the Negro hired help and bring them running to look, and to wake the few scattered drinkers out of their various reveries, as the brothers Khanturian hauled their guests to the bar to buy for Doug and his friend "Whoever you are!" It was at the bar that Gerry Kinton was standing, all alone.

Sir Gerald, as he pretended not to much like being called, but it turned out did not really mind being called at all, was on his third New York-sized martini before going off to lunch. Tall, horse-faced, with a receding chin and a whinny of a laugh, he was such a caricature of the upper-class Englishman that it would be impossible for him ever to be employed as an actor in anything but a vicious satire. But then Sir Gerald wasn't an actor. He was in import-export, he explained to them after offering to buy a drink, and (but only when asked point-blank) was the heritor of an hereditary baronetcy of a family that was in banking, hence the title. Later they found out—from his friends of course, and he had

many, all of whom hated him for his money, his good
nature and particularly for his title—that the import-export
he was in was the import-export of an exile, a firm bought
for him and kept running by the family to keep him out
of England, and at which in fact he did nothing, or almost
nothing, which did not matter—said his friends—since his
allowance was ample, which was also fortunate, because
he was stupid. Ron and Doug, naturally, both liked him
immediately. He spoke in a peculiar high voice with a
perfect King's English accent, but interlarded this with
oddly out-of-place words of Madison Avenue hip slang
pronounced with a strong American accent. This was because he made quite a few trips to New York every year
" during the season " he explained cheerfully, when Ron
asked him about it. " Is a bit odd, isn't it? " He had seen all of
Ron's plays and both of Doug's, and had loved them all,
indiscriminately. " Love to be able to write something. Like
that. You know. Cahn't even write m' own name what? "
He was about their own age and had been a Guards officer in
Italy during the infantry war. " Could write about that, eh?
No bloody red blouses there."

It was Sir Gerald who like a bloodhound led them straight
to the models: " I say! I say, if you two cats are really
on the loose for a day or two, I know just the thing. Buick
or GM or one of those American cars is doing a big
' romantic tropics ' ad layout here just now. *And they are
some chicks*. Their headqua'ters are out at the Half Moon
Hotel. What say we all three head out there for lunch,
what? "

They went in his car. After sauntering in (he was wearing
those obscenely loose-legged shorts the British affect in
the tropics, a Madras shirt, and a short-brimmed Madison
Avenue-style pork-pie straw) and blandly demanding an introduction from the manager, he invited the entire crew
to lunch—photographers, wardrobe supervisor and all—on
his tab. " No, no. I was going to do all this on my own
anyway," he giggled nervously when Ron and Doug offered
to split it. He guffawed. " Wait'll the local spies report *this*
back home to the family! " After further imperious inquiry
of the manager (" And I am quite sure he is one of them! "),
he returned to whisper, " I also now understand they'll be
wo'king at the Racquet Club this afternoon. We could

follow them up there, have a swim, cause general hell; and
take them out to-night. What?" He gazed fondly at the
girls and said in his American accent, "*Ain't they something?*"

They were indeed. Tall, slender, long-legged, with tight,
taut bellies, bellies so flat they were practically concave,
all of them had the hips of women and obviously were well
practised in using them, and they didn't care who knew
it. All in their teens or early twenties, they had the world
by the ass with two fingers as if it were their own personal
bowling ball and until they gave up the gay life and
became proper wives and mothers, nothing interested them
except parties, money, titles, travel and celebrities. That they
would ever later pay for the sins of their youth seemed highly
doubtful. They were all far too beautiful to ever pay for
anything, and what was more, they all knew it. If none
of them was especially bright, it was clear that none of them
would ever have to be. It was enough to make a reflective
man resentful, but neither Ron, Doug nor Sir Gerald were
worrying about any of this.

"Christ, you really have got it bad, haven't you?"
Doug whispered late in the night when Ron refused to pair
off with any of them. Grant could only nod miserably and
dumbly.

In the end, after the lesbian wardrobe supervisor had
quickly disappeared with the one that was her special friend,
and after a long lingering dinner by candlelight out under
the tropical moon in a restaurant on the shore, Sir Gerald
took the remaining five and the two playwrights off to his
place. This was a recently built, rambling villa beside the
sea constructed around a central pool brilliantly lit by underwater lights. With everyone still drunk from the bottles and
bottles of red wine Sir Gerald had been pushing at dinner,
it was only a short easy step from the scanty, already supremely revealing bikinis of the girls to out-and-out nude
swimming. Even Grant participated in this. But when it came
to the next stage, the groping and porpoise-diving down under
the shrilling girls, he retired to the pool-edge, put back on his
bikini, and found himself a bottle of Scotch to nurse his
misery. It seemed to be the history of his life. Everybody else
once again was having fun and once again, for whatever

the variety of reasons over the years, Ron Grant was unable
to take part, was on the outside looking in again.

The underwater light illuminated everything superbly.
After five minutes at the pool-edge, he knew all five of
their young bodies about as intimately as if he'd been
married to them all for five years. Their insolently carefree
beauty made his back teeth ache. Nipples, navels, haired and
vastly protruding Venus mounds, the delicious sag of breast
from corner or opened armpit, all ran disembodied around
in his head like a strip of experimental movie film, and the
hurt they brought him came from the certain knowledge that
never ever in his life could he ever possess one tiny smidgen
of all this teeth-aching beauty. He could hump them till he
was crosseyed, and it would do no good. He would remain
as far outside of them, and they outside of him, as ever. Hell,
they couldn't even possess it themselves. Age, withering,
death, yes, but not possession. He ached to have all of
them, all at the same time. Sir Gerald surfaced near him,
grinning cheerily with his huge teeth. " By Jove! We don't
get fucking windfalls like this down here very often. Once
or twice a year." He disappeared again beneath the waves the
cavorting bodies kept generating, and one of the girls
shrieked quite happily. When they were all towelling off,
modestly but quite certain of their nude loveliness, rosy
skinned from the chill water, Grant told Doug and Gerry
he was going back to the hotel.

" All right then, by God," Doug said with drunken staunch-
ness. " I'll go, too, Ron. Come on, honey. Let's get our
clothes on."

" What's the matter?" one of the girls, whom Doug had
singled out, or perhaps who had singled him out, said. She
had wrapped one of the terry-cloth robes Sir Gerald had
thoughtfully provided over her delicious body. " Are you
two guys queer or something?"

" Now, cut it out," Doug said patiently, and drunkenly.
" This poor slob's in love. Really in love. You may not
believe it. I can't let him go back to the hotel on his
lonesome all by himself like that. I'm his old buddy. You
and me'll go with him and keep him company in his misery."

" But I like it here!" the model protested.

" I don't want anybody to go with me," Ron said irritably.

" We got a great suite at the hotel, too," Doug went right

on nevertheless. "Anything you want. And a great view of the bay." This last was an outright lie. The Khanturian Hotel had no view at all, of anything.

Sir Gerald suggested they all have a drink first, out on the terrace, and discuss it. This was done. "Why don't you just sleep here, Ron?" he suggested when Doug refused to budge from his position. "I've plenty of bedrooms. Have one to yourself."

"Christ, are you crazy? It's bad enough at the hotel. Just let me go," he said to Doug, "and go on with your party." All he wanted was to be alone with his drunk ache. Doug shook his head. "Christ, I think you guys really are fags," the model said; "well, it might be interesting." And in the end it had been the three of them, himself, Doug, and the model, who drove back to town. Sitting in the car while Doug drove with the girl between them, Grant had felt very virtuous about himself, and quite self-admiring. When the tall, lovely model suggested matter-of-factly that he could come on in the bed with her and Doug as far as she was concerned, he had merely smiled.

(When they finally saw Gerry Kinton the next day the Englishman roared with laughter at himself. He had gotten so drunk after they left he hadn't been able to screw any of the four that remained and they had all gone innocently to sleep together on the big living-room floor in front of the fire.)

In the hotel bed, Grant shook his aching head in the horrible morning sun. He still felt supremely virtuous this morning, but sober, was a little more amused at himself for it. He looked again at the untouched, unperfumed, unlipsticked pillow beside him. Then, on the bed table the phone rang. Grant looked at his watch. Instead of the thirty to forty-five minutes he'd anticipated, the call had been one solid hour coming through.

Overseas calls from Jamaica were notoriously buzzy, but through all of that he could hear a faint squawk and then a thin wail. Immediately he had a throbbing, full-taut, blood-filled hard-on. "What are you doing?" he asked the mouth-piece huskily. "What are you doing on that great island of Manhattan?"

"What am I doing?" the lovely, sad, curiously little-girl voice came back faintly. "I'm getting dead drunk. That's what I'm doing. And I've *been* dead drunk for the whole three goddam weeks."

"Ahh," Grant said. It was all he could think of to say. Under the covers he fingered himself with his other hand. "Do you know what I've got in my hand?" he said suddenly, spur of the moment. He was suddenly completely happy, in a warm nest of feathered perfection.

"Yes. And I have, too," Lucky whispered. But then her voice raised to a wail again. "But I'm mad at you. I hate you. All my friends say you're a worthless prick and I should completely forget you."

"Fuck your friends," Grant said.

Just the same, she meant it. She went on to tell him how miserable she had been, nothing but drinking and drinking from morning to night, and lying in bed all the time crying, and not one word from him. He wasn't worth it. Nobody was worth it. Grant listened contentedly and happily. It seemed he was a lousy prick after all. How could he be contented and happy over making this girl so miserable? But he was. She had a girl-friend whose boy-friend owned a private airline, and they were flying down to Palm Beach in his private plane, and she was going with them. After that she was going to go and get herself a cabin somewhere in Key West and live by herself.

"How would you like to fly down to Montego Bay instead?" Grant said contentedly.

"Montego Bay! I thought you said you were going to Ganado Bay. To see your goddamned foster-mother. And then to Kingston."

"I am. I have. But a buddy of mine named Doug Ismaileh came down from Coral Gables for a visit, and he and I decided to drive to Montego for a few days. He wrote *Dawn's Left Hand*."

"I know who he is," Lucky said. "I didn't like his play. He hates women."

Grant was startled nearly out of his complacency. Another of those perceptions. "Well, for a guy who hates women, he sure fucks a lot of them"—("It figures," Lucky put in.) —"There's a bunch of fashion models down here on a job and we were out with them last night and a crazy English man we met."

There was silence at the other end. Something about her,

ɪ

something, could make him feel so manly. "But don't worry. I didn't take any of them on. I couldn't. I just couldn't. I wanted you. And that's why I called. I couldn't have gotten it up. Will you come?"

He could hear the silence on the other end change from fearful, suspicious silence to hopeful silence.

"Will you come?" he said again.

Her voice, when she spoke, had changed back to that plaintive wail. "Well, I don't have any money again. I spent it all on booze in fact—to try and forget you."

"Then how were you going to go to Key West? Look, I'll call my lawyer. You'll have it in time to make the one o'clock plane. You'll be here to-night."

The wail. "Well, you know I'm no good at doing things like that. You know I'm not."

"Call Leslie. Will you come?" There was silence in the earphone. "And we'll go on to Kingston."

"All right," she said with a soft sigh.

"And do you know what I've still got in my hand, here?" Grant said softly.

There was a pause in which he could hear her breathing. "Then go ahead and do with it what you know you want to do with it," she said. There was another pause. "And think about me all the time." A third pause. "And I will, too," she said breathlessly. There was an incredible, impossible, honey-rich sensuality in her voice.

"I love you," Grant said.

"Oh, yes," Lucky said. "Good-bye." The phone went dead.

After he hung up the instrument Grant followed her instructions exactly and consciously. Afterwards he lay sleepily in the bed. He felt totally replete, if only she were here to touch. Finally he got up and showered. Then he put the call in for his lawyer. By the time he was dressed the call came through and he told him what to do about the money. Then he went to wake Doug and the girl.

As he did so, he stopped frozen with his hand already on the doorknob of the door into the connecting bath. After his recent, self-induced orgasm a whole new attitude had come tinkling and tickling into his mind, and now it crystallised itself in a conscious question. Why had he not done it? Why had he not taken one of the models last night? He could have. Very easily. And just not have told Lucky. If he had, he probably would not have called her to come down.

He could almost kick himself. A simple, friendly fuck, with no commitments on either side and no desire for any. Nobody hurt, and nobody would be the wiser. Why hadn't he? Payment? Atonement? Some fuzzy superstitious spiritual disbursement, which he felt that if made, paid, would aid him in some unclear metaphysical way? Some private expiation for his guilt in treating Carol Abernathy as he was, and had been, treating her all these years? Or was it just that he enjoyed being frustrated, that it excited him to deliberately frustrate himself? And that he took dubious pleasure, painful pleasure from his own deliberate frustration?

There was certainly that in him.

There was also the question of monogamy. He was aware that over large areas of the world the Christian-oriented institution of monogamy was laughed at, and that large portions of those areas were among the Christian countries themselves. But none of this helped him because he had been raised, brought up, indoctrinated and oriented in the belief that the only sexual perfection lay in the one man—one woman monogamous love affair (never mind marriage). And he couldn't shake it. And his fourteen-year experience with Carol Abernathy, and all the infidelities he had been forced into by her coldness and perhaps by his own inordinate desires, as well as all the busted and unhappy love affairs and marriages he had observed around him over the years, had confirmed this. It had caused to grow in him a flat decision that—should he ever be so lucky as to find another love—he would be completely faithful to the covenant. The minute one party started stepping out something irreparable was lost which could never be got back. And the loneliness of the practiser of friendly fucking was at least as great as the loneliness of the long-distance runner. He didn't make the rules. But then neither did all those other people he had observed, who were also so constructed that they too, whether they willed or not, must live by them.

What he really wanted, he thought suddenly, the thought rising unbidden, coming up from some deep and completely disconnected area, an area totally separated from the logical progression of his previous conscious thought, *what he really wanted was to enslave himself to some woman, become her creature, her grovelling possession, contemptible, and contemptuously treated by her* . . .

And that was why, his conscious mind said, taking the thought over, that was why all these years he had had to be so careful in picking himself a wife. He must not pick himself a bad master. In his pants he felt his penis stretch itself toward hardening. It was, he was convinced, a typically American reaction. Convulsively, he tightened his grip painfully on the doorknob, which he had forgotten he was holding. But of course he would have to be the boss in the family, too.

When he opened the door on the other side of the bathroom, what he saw made him stop irresolutely. Doug and the model (she really was beautiful) lay curled up together cheek to cheek with their free arms around each other, cuddled in sleep, as if they really knew each other well and actually needed each other. Hunh, they were probably as scared, sick at heart, and lonely as him or anybody. And instinctively some sensibility made him sure they would both be embarrassed to be caught and wakened in such a position. Stepping back outside quietly, he shut the door and then pounded on it.

"Come on! Rout it out!" he bawled. "Come on, you guys! I got news! We gotta meet a plane to-night!"

The two of them met her on the evening plane. The model (whose name was Terry September) of course had to cut out and get back to her job of work, as she called it, before noon; but they would be seeing her to-night. They had lunch with Gerry Kinton who told them his story, guffawed at himself and promised that he would not get that drunk again to-night; he had already arranged everything for an even bigger party to-night. Ron had wanted to rent a small boat, maybe from Wilson, and make a dive on some local reef with the lung he had lugged along, but in the end he didn't. In the end he wound up sitting in the Khanturian Hotel bar with Doug and the rest of the Khanturian brothers who had gathered like some species of great clannish bird and immediately clustered around Doug, everybody drinking far more than he should as they all admitted, and talking about the old family, the old country, the old war. The eldest Khanturian brother had been a Sergeant of Infantry and had frozen his feet in the Hürtgen Forest and they still bothered him. Doug once again savagely bemoaned the loss of all of their fearless, violent youths. To Grant it seemed that the moment the diving and its impetus was removed—down here—everything went to hell, and everybody was drunk alla time. He had noticed it with Bonham, too. When they piled into the car to go to the airport, and were waved away by the cheering Khanturians, they were both pretty drunk; and although they were not anywhere near dead drunk, not anywhere near, it was still something Ron had not wanted to be.

It was just dark, and the big jet winged whistling insanely in over the bay with its landing lights on, screeched rubber as it touched down, roared as it immediately began braking, ran on to the end of the runway as if it might go right on off into the excavation they were making to lengthen it, then rolled like a fat awkward bird back to its disgorging station. The bureaucratic necessity of mid-Twentieth Century, the same old deathly impersonality of handling large groups of people which they both professed to hate, separated them from her just as surely as the electrified barbed-wire fences of a concentration camp, but they could stand out on the Visitors' Balcony and, leaning on the railing in the sultry sea-smelling air, watch for her as the jet spewed forth its full load of dressed-for-winter vacationers and business-trippers who trooped amiably down the mobile stairway and across the tarmac after the pretty airline hostess.

Grant saw her almost before she was out of the dark cave of the hatchway, the champagne hair, the small head, the wide long-waisted shoulders, the flair of female's hips above the long sleek legs, and began to holler and wave like a mad bull. The sight of her filled his chest cavity with such additional pressure that he wouldn't have been surprised later to find he had afflicted himself with an air embolism. He kept trying to point her out to Doug in the trooping crowd. She did not see them at first but when she did she waved only once. Smiling with embarrassment, she came toward them in that walk of hers and passed in below them to the customs desks. When Doug finally saw her, and was sure that it was she he saw, all he could say, in a voice of protest, was, " Jesus S. Christ! "

"You're so damned loud," were the first words she said.
"I'd forgotten how loud you are." She was smiling and,
for some unstated reason (Grant knew the reason but couldn't
state it either), she was blushing. The totally defenceless
love on her face was, at least for Grant, a joy to behold.
And his mood of this morning, when he wondered why he
hadn't taken on one of the models, seemed to him now to
have been totally insane.

"Now don't worry about a thing," he told her as soon
as the passport stamping, customs declarations, baggage
inspection and the rest—all the small but continuous pay-
ments-out of pieces of spirit to the organisational forces
which made such marvellous transportation possible—were
paid and finished and they were rolling back to town. "We're
having a ball. We've got everything laid on for a big fun
party to-night." Lucky, sitting between them, as he turned
his head from the road to look at her eagerly, looked a
little disappointed. But then she put her hand on his arm,
quietly and unobtrusively, on his biceps that was manipulat-
ing the wheel. "It'll be a ball," Grant reassured her. "You'll
have more fun than you've ever had in your life. On this
trip. I promise you."

Doug had obviously fallen madly in love with her from
his very first sight of her, not carnally but like a fellow
knight of the Round Table with another's lady, and he now
interrupted to take over and tell her about everything.
This included his relatives the Khanturians, father, mother,
and five unmarried sons, and their hotel, Sir Gerald Kinton
and the models, and the wacky party last night at which Sir
Gerald had so uproariously tripped himself up. Lucky kept
her hand on Grant's arm as she listened, and the light touch
of it there made Grant swell up with happiness, pride, and
that peculiar super-manliness she in some way always could
make him feel, although he noted nervously that she was
not roaring with laughter the way she should be.

As if by some unspoken understanding they had not kissed
at the airport, had in fact refrained from even touching
each other seriously, and they did not kiss until they were
alone together in Grant's bedroom of the hotel suite and
Doug had tactfully gone off somewhere—for a swim, he
said. Then, finally, Grant took her in his arms, in the
privacy both instinctively knew would be required for such

a kiss. It was a kiss of such thirst and depth and questing tongues that Grant imagined he felt his soul being sucked down from within his brainpan and out through his mouth into this girl by the force of it, and happily he let it go. At the airport, during all the time since, and again right now, he was surprised by the sense he had of some invisible and fatal Rubicon-crossing in his life in the bringing of Lucky down. Just last year he had had an affair, with some local wealthy girl back in Indianapolis this time, an affair of some emotional violence, but all during the months it lasted there had never been any question of fatality, he had known all along it would end as it did end, that he would wind up back in his old life with the Abernathys. The Indianapolis girl had been such an unmitigated bitch, really, was why. But not this one, not this one. Not this one, to whom he was going to enslave himself and all he had, his work, everything he stood for, and hoped to stand for. Nothing mattered. Nothing but that. And he didn't care.

Of course, he could not tell her all this, or even any of it. So as he shoved his nose between her ear and hair he said again what he had said several times before.

"Hansel and Gretel," Grant said huskily. "Hansel and Gretel to the road again. Hello, Gretel."

"Don't ever let them destroy us," Lucky whispered against his throat. "Promise me you won't ever let them."

"I promise," he said. "That I'll promise. They never will." He pushed his nose in further. "But maybe we're just being paranoic. They say all the world loves a lover."

"That's not true and you know it," she said against his neck. "There's nothing the world hates more than a lover."

"I guess so," Grant mumbled gently. "Because 'Duty' must come before everything, including love. Especially love."

"If they ever suspected what we have," Lucky said, "they'd have to dedicate themselves to destroying it."

"We won't let them," Grant said. "We'll hide it. And pretend we're just like any other ordinary couple full of hate."

They made love twice before Doug Ismaileh came rattling around and routed them out for Gerry Kinton's dinner, and both times Grant went down on her to bring her to orgasm.

SEVENTEEN

Lucky didn't want to go. And she said as much to Grant as they were getting back into their clothes. She would much rather have gone off somewhere for a quiet dinner alone with him where they could be together and talk and look at each other and enjoy each other, without a big gang of people around watching them.

"Aw, come on, honey. We'll have fun. Doug's an old friend. An old, old friend. Even Sir Gerald's practically an old friend by now. We'll have plenty of time together. I want to see what this town's like." There was no combating his nervous ebullience.

"All right," she said. "You know I like to go out. I always have." But she looked at him strangely.

And in truth he was in a strange mood. The magnificence of their love-making, which he had been without for so long, instead of relaxing and releasing him had heightened his excitement into hilarity. All the drinks he had had to-day didn't decrease it. The sense of having crossed some vague but dangerously final Rubicon had increased his adrenal output enormously. And the awareness of all the lies he had told both sides in this business made him more aware than ever that somewhere somehow, soon, some kind of a showdown with somebody was coming. He felt a lot like he used to feel during the war on the carrier just before a big fight.

"They got a couple pretty good night-clubs going here too, I hear," he said. From outside in the suite's living-room Doug Ismaileh pounded on the door again impatiently. "My God, what are you two doin' in there?" he roared in a voice of raucous laughter. "God, not again!" Beside Grant, Lucky blushed. Grant kissed her. "We're coming! We're coming, goddam it!" He opened the door.

Sir Gerald Kinton's second big evening started off auspiciously enough in spite of all. First they all had drinks up at the Racquet Club, sitting out on the cool terrace overlooking the harbour. A tourist cruise ship was in and gaily all lit up from stem to stern it added to the festivity. The town would be inundated with chubby tourists wearing peculiar-shaped native straw hats and floppy Hawaiian style shirts. " Fawtunately," Sir Gerald drawled, " they don't know the really good or right places to go."

With a sensitivity he was capable of displaying at almost all times when he wasn't absolutely dead drunk, he had thoughtfully rearranged the party for to-night. There were no extra girls. In deference to Lucky, who was there as the real girl-friend of one of them, there were only four models present and each of them had a bona fide date. Sir Gerald and Doug had two, the manager of the hotel (" the Spy from Home ") was there for the third, and (and apparently this was Doug's doing) the eldest Khanturian brother, the ex-Infantry Sergeant with the bad feet, who was really way in over his head and playing out of his league with this group, was dating the fourth. The fourth model's nose, because of this, was quite a bit out of joint. So it was not as if there were not troubles looming on the night horizon. In addition, Lucky was almost painfully shy.

Still, the drinks at the Racquet Club and the dinner at still another romantic seaside hotel went off nicely enough, especially since Sir Gerald took care to take them to a hotel a long way out of town where no boat tourists appeared. It was only when all the drinking finally took effect —martinis at the Racquet Club ; wine at dinner ; whisky at the night-club afterwards—and they arrived at that stage of " Being Totally Honest " in which drunks feel required to tell each other the Truth about each other, that the various predictables began to happen.

This was at the night-club, which was only a short distance from the hotel where they had eaten. The fourth model (who last night had been swimming nude and squealing with Doug and Sir Gerald) slapped the face of the eldest Khanturian brother for trying to feel her up under the table and called him a " fat, greasy pig." The eldest Khanturian brother called her a " lousy New York whore," and Doug, incensed at this treatment of his cousin, called her a " cunt," whereupon she fled weeping to a taxi. The eldest Khanturian brother did not bother to follow her and stayed on. Doug told Sir Gerald the story of his cousin's frozen feet in the Hürtgen campaign; but Sir Gerald, instead of being sympathetic, began to demand in a belligerent voice where the hell the " bloody fucking Americans " were in 1940 when the British really needed them and were fighting their bloody battles for them all alone. This led to several disagreements about the American Revolution, of which Sir Gerald maintained that " If Gentleman Johnny Burgoyne had been backed up by the Secretary for America Lord George Germain as he should have been, there never would have been any United States of America and damn their squirrel rifles." Nobody could refute this because nobody knew who Lord George Germain the Secretary for America was or had ever heard of him.

In the meantime Grant had got into a malicious-wit battle with the sharp-witted American comic who had recognised him and introduced him from the stand with a spot on the table. Grant, who resented this and who could be quite funny when he was drunk enough or flattered enough to let himself go, got the best of the exchange but was hampered by the fact that the comic had a loudspeaker microphone. But by then Lucky had fled outside to the car Fortunately there were not many people in the place, but the few boat tourists who had found it almost certainly disqualified Grant from the contest for his use of four-letter words.

When he finally noticed she was gone, Grant hurried outside after Lucky in a panic, and after a while the others came traipsing out after them. But before they did that he and Lucky had their own truth-telling session in the dark car in the irregular-shaped parking lot bordered by lush lovely bougainvillæa, under a gorgeous royal palm.

" What's happened to you?" Lucky demanded in a kind of furious half-wail, when he stuck his head in through the open car window. She had been crying. She was not sober, either.

Grant withdraw his head, almost as if he expected to be hit. " Who, me? What's happened to me?" Drunkenly he moved his head back and forth and then flapped his arms up and down in a gigantic shrug of miserable inexpressiveness.

" You're not the same man I knew in New York. You're not the same man I left in Miami."

Grant didn't know what to say. " I'm not?"

" I think Doug is bad for you," Lucky said. -" Whenever

you're around him, something in you changes, and you become a different person. Meaner and malicious and more cruel. It's as if——"

"Aw, that son of a bitching comic," Grant growled. "He had no right to pull shit like that. They think they can get by with anything."

"That's not what I mean——"

"They're all phonies. Their whole profession is phony. Show business is phony. *Everything* is phony. Everything in the whole world is phony. Everything and every*body* is phony. Nobody says what he means. Except me. Except me and thee, as the Quaker said, and I wonder about thee." He was suddenly raging, but he had to stop for breath.

"Maybe they are," Lucky said. "But it's not your job to go around correctioning everybody. Didn't it ever occur to you how you were embarrassing me?"

"What the hell?" Grant said. "What the hell?"

"What were you doing, showing off for Doug?" she said. "So he would admire you? That's what it looked like to me. Every time you get around him you change personalities. It's as if—It's as though he deliberately set out to change you into somebody else, handle you."

Suddenly amiable, Grant nodded his head up and down lugubriously. "That's the truth. He'd like to. He'd sure as hell like to. But he's not about to. He's not about to handle me. Not ever. I got him taped."

"I wouldn't be so sure," Lucky said.

"Well, you ain't no goddam plaster saint either."

She stared at him. "I don't understand you. I really don't. In New York you were gentle and tender, and kind. And understanding."

"Not all the time," Grant said, low.

"What is it that's eating you up?"

Grant was first astounded, then outraged. "What is it that's eating me up? You want to know what's eating me up? I'll tell you what's eating me up. I'm going to die. Some day. That's what's eating me up. I'm going to die. Me. And nobody in the whole fucking world is going to give a good goddam. That's what's eating me up. Not even you. I could marry you to-morrow and drop dead the day after and within a year you'd be married to somebody else and just as happy. Because you can't stand to be without a lover for more than fifteen minutes at a stretch. Any more than me. That's the truth. That's the truth about everything. About everybody. And all this love shit and caring and integrity is so much horse-shit. Only, people won't admit it. They pretend it isn't so so they can go on living with their terror. They make up stories. When they write them down, they call it History. You want to know what's eating me up? That's what's eating me up. And - all - I - want - is - just - once, just once to make them admit it for one half of one third act."

In the middle of this impassioned declamation Lucky had begun to sob quietly and when he stopped she said, " Oh, you're terrible. How do I know if I would ever fall in love with somebody else? I know I love you now. How do I know if I know if I would ever marry anybody else? I certainly wouldn't marry anybody else like you! And I'm not so goddamned sure I want to marry you, right now."

" Okay," Grant said, suddenly amiable again, like a man who has just been relieved of a serious case of constipation, " then let's just go to Kingston and have ourselves a good time and worry about everything else later." He heaved a great sigh, in which there was a certain amount of self-satisfaction for some reason or other, and leaned his head back and looked up at the sky.

" Come here," he said after a moment, in a totally new, tense voice. " Come on, get out here! Look at this. Come on, look!" She did and was standing beside him her shoulder just touching his, the small fine head just coming up to the tip-top of his ear, when he spoke again. Above them in the night sky from horizon to horizon literally billions of stars glittered and blinked at them. " Isn't that the most chilling, freezing, horrendous thing you ever saw? Do you think any of them ever give a fuck whether me and you ever lived or died?"

" I don't know," Lucky said in a subdued tone. " I suppose not. I'll tell you one thing. I certainly don't give a good goddam for them."

It was just then, when he was kissing her seriously, that the rest of the group came meandering out of the night-club looking for them.

Of course they all went to Sir Gerald's seaside villa from

there. And, of course, inevitably, unavoidably, it got around to the nude swimming party in the underwater-lit pool. Indeed, " the Spy from Home " who at his hotel to-day had heard all about the party of last night, was panting like an aroused bull for them to get on with the show. Of course it did not start all at once, cold turkey, and everybody decorously got into trunks or bikini in the two dressing-rooms for the first act, but finally the moment came when one of the models complained about the restrictiveness of all bathing suits even bikinis and shucking out of her two bandannas tossed them from the water up on to the pool-edge. This was the signal. And this was when Lucky rebelled.

She wasn't wearing a bikini, in the first place, but one of those Olympic-style black one-piece suits of thin double-layer nylon. Her figure was a little bit too lush to look good in a bikini, she said. In this suit she had swum by herself four or five slow lazy laps which showed she had done quite a bit of swimming, and then had climbed out on to the pool-edge and sat, cheek resting on the knee of one leg which she had drawn up and clasped against her and looking apprehensively (and not a tall happily) as though she knew beforehand exactly what was going to happen. Grant had swum around near her porpoising and spouting, enjoying the now strangely amateurish feel of swimming without mask or flippers, and occasionally kissing her other foot that still dangled in the water. But when the first model threw up the first bikini, she pulled her foot out and got up and walked up to the shallow end nearest the house and sat down in one of the beach chairs in the dark out of the light. Grant followed her.

" Hey! What's the matter?"

In the slung-canvas chair she had curled herself up into the smallest ball possible, like a foetus.

" Maybe I don't know what all your tastes are," she said in a small low voice, " maybe we haven't known each other that long after all, but I don't go in for orgies."

" Hey! Hey! Wait a minute."

" When I told you I'd slept with four hundred men, it was a good round figure give or take a few, and probably accurate. But I never slept with them in tandem, or in groups. No orgies."

" Oh, come on," Grant protested. " This is no orgy. Everybody's got his own date. Except Khanturian, and he's s. o. l. But I don't care if you don't take——"

"Do you *want* me to take my suit off and let those men see me naked?"

"Well, no," Grant said promptly. "Of course not." This was not strictly the truth, he realised immediately; but it was only half a lie. There was a kind of breathless anticipation to have her do just that but the thought of her doing it, at the same time, caused an acutely painful cramp in his innards. Even more painfully, he thought of all her "Four Hundred Men." She could be a little more circumspect about talking about it. He'd like to beat the shit out of all of them.

"But you knew all along this was going to happen, didn't you?"

"I didn't think about it," Grant said, lamely, although this was the exact truth.

"But you heard Doug tell me in the car that that was what you all did last night," Lucky insisted.

"I just didn't think about it," he insisted back. But in spite of that he knew enough to know, and was honest enough with himself to admit, that he *should* have thought about it. If only to consider whether his preference was in having her participate, or in having her not. There was some kind of self-subterfuge there, all right. "Look, what the hell?" he said.

Lucky's eyes flashed at him dangerously. "Listen. And believe me! If you want me to, I will. Just say the word! And if I *do*, you'll be the most jealous little gentleman that ever lived. I can promise you that!"

"Certainly not," Grant said calmly. It was a false calm, and his ears were ringing. "Absolutely not. Of course not. Look, we don't *have* to do anything. We can just sit right here. Or if you want I'll take you——"

But it was just then that Doug's girl, Terry September, walked by still in her bikini on her way back from the Little Girls Room and interrupted him.

"Hey! Aren't you two joining the fun?"

"Thank you, no," Lucky said coldly.

"Aw, come off it," Terry said irritably. "I knew you in New York, sweetie. You've been around plenty. Why don't you just relax and loosen up a little bit." Then smiling, she sat down on the edge of the beach chair and put her arm around the other girl friendlily. As if she were being physically burned by her touch, Lucky leaped up from the chair and ran weeping into the house.

"I'm not a whore! I'm not a whore!"

Grant heard her say that much. Nobody else noticed a thing, it was all done so quietly. Except of course Terry.

"Hey! What did *I* say?" she complained.

"Nothing. It's okay," Grant said. "Forget it. I'll go and get her. She's tired from the trip." And he hurried off.

He found her in one of the bedrooms. She had run into the walk-in clothes closet and shut the door and was huddled on the floor in a corner, back among some hanging coats. She was weeping like a busted child, newly orphaned. "Honey, honey! Come on, come on. Don't cry like that, don't cry." The words didn't matter, as long as he said them as softly as he could. She acted like a wounded animal. Finally he got her to stand up and got her out of the closet into the bedroom, where they sat down on the bed and he held her and finally she stopped crying.

"You're a son of a bitch," she said finally, wiping her red eyes and still snuffling. Grant got her some tissues from beside the bed. "You've got no right to treat me like that. I've never done anything to you to give you the right to treat me like that. Like I was one of those girls."

"Certainly not," Grant said. "Of course not. But they're not whores, Lucky. They're just young girls living it up while they can. Like everybody."

"I know that," Lucky said. She was pulling herself together. "No, that's not true. They're sick. I was never sick. Not like that."

Grant stared at her, listening. It was as close as she had ever come to talking about herself. But she didn't go on. He himself was feeling that—in his own eyes at least—he had lost considerable face, displayed considerable lack of courage by backing down out there on the nude bathing business. Almost automatically, he had been positively cowardly in front of her challenge. But he had sensed also very strongly, with a powerful, alert, slow-breathing sense of impending danger, that if he had not, if he had let her go ahead and go through with it, had with her joined the naked swimmers, they would have destroyed something between them that could never

be got back. But would she realise that? know what he had
done? And was he *right*? Silently, he continued to pat her
on the back as she dried her face and stopped her sniffling.
And it was just then that the eldest Khanturian brother wandered in upon them.

For some reason known only to himself he had put back
on his gartered socks and his shoes, so that he looked rather
strange since the only other thing he was wearing was
his baggy wet swimming trunks. He peered at them as if he
didn't know them for a moment or two and then groaned
somewhat drunkenly. " Jeeze, my poor old feet are killin'
me," he announced mournfully. " I wish I just had somebody to rub them for me for a minute." It was ridiculous.
Of course he had no girl, she had left him weeping, and
she almost certainly would not have done it for him even
had she been there. It was clear he was pretty tired of watching the other men playing with their girls in the pool.

" Would you rub my feet?" he asked Lucky.

" Here sit down," Grant said with a grin at her. " Sure.
I will." And when Khanturian flopped back on the bed
he knelt and taking off his shoes with a wink at Lucky
rubbed the bony feet in the silk socks for a minute. Khanturian sighed blissfully. " I hope I ain't disturbin' you
guys any," he said.

" No," Grant said. " No, no. Why don't you take yourself
a nap?" he felt very sorry for him; for everybody. Getting
Lucky's arm, he led her out.

" He really is a fat greasy pig," Lucky whispered dis-
tastefully when they were outside the bedroom in the big
beamed living-room. " She was right."—" Well," Grant said.
He had to admit he was pretty greasy.

" And I'm an Italian," Lucky said.

" Come on," he said. " I'll take you home to the hotel.
I'll just tell Doug and Sir Gerald we're leaving."

On the long dark drive back to town she held on to his
arm with both hands, close up against him, her head pressed
against his shoulder as he drove. She felt like a scared little
girl holding on to her daddy. At the airport, as they went
up over the hill, only a very few lights were still burning.

" I guess I've got a thing about old vets," Grant said
finally, after a long silence that had extended from the
moment they got into the car in Sir Gerald's long curving

driveway outside the villa in the dark. They had sat a long moment, listening to and looking at the laughter and the lights inside. " Old sailors *and* old soldiers. I know what they went through. And I know what it's like to be a nobody. To be manipulated, statistics moved around like chess pieces on the board to gain some overall strategic goal.

" And when it's all over the Players line you up and thank you in bulk, statistics to the end. Nobody important ever knows your face or name. You're just there, a pyramid of faces to be stood on. And the oldest Khanturian is like that in peace the same as in war. A nobody. He's even a nobody with that gang of ours to-night."

" The oldest Khanturian and all the other Khanturians," Lucky said. They had all three of them amongst themselves, after Doug started it, taken to referring to the five Khanturian brothers by their numerical position of birth: the eldest Khanturian, the second oldest Khanturian, etc. ",I didn't like to see you rubbing his feet."

" Well, I didn't want you to do it. And somebody ought to be willing to rub his feet. All old vets deserve more than that, but *I* don't know how to give it to them."

" Sure. They deserve the right to go down to the American Legion and become reactionaries."

" I know, I know," Grant said, moving slightly to take a curve, " I know it's sentimental. But I can't help it. It scares me. I don't like to see it."

" See what?"

" See the helplessness of the enormous bulk of humanity, supporting on its pyramid of faces the ambitious, the intelligent, and the talented (who all love it, naturally——in bulk) and who, simply because we all believe with a deep animal instinct in the pecking order, will go down in ' History.' They deserve better."

" Rousseau's Fallacy! You mean you still believe in ' the noble savage '?"

" Not at all, not at all. I know they're bastards, animals. But so are the ambitious, intelligent and talented. It's their *helplessness* that scares me. They have nothing to say about what happens to them. And it's going to get worse. It's the Age of the Future, I'm afraid, and it'll be just as much in peace-time as in war-time."

" But it's always been like that."

"But not the same. If Augustus Caesar could get away with being more cruel than Harry Truman or General Eisenhower would be allowed to by the people, he still did not have their modern means of imposing and making stick with the people a loving picture of himself."

"I like beautiful people," Lucky murmured into his sleeve.

"Unfortunately, there just ain't very many of them in the world."

"You're one," Lucky said.

"Me? Sure. I'm famous. And if you get to be famous like me it's almost as good as being a politician. You don't have that problem. Of being a nobody any more. The people whose lawns you used to mow and battles you used to fight invite you to dinner to show you off to the people whose lawns you didn't use to mow. They elect you to the Club. Hell, I even played poker with a general once, after I got to be famous."

Lucky snorted against his sleeve. She was still the helpless, scared and embarrassed little girl again. "What's so wrong with all that?"

Such a strange one. "Nothing at all. I'm in favour. I deserve it!"

"You're not like the oldest Khanturian, anyway. You never were a nobody."

"Oh yes I was! I remember well."

"Why do you think he never married?"

Grant felt a prick of start, of caution. He steeled his voice to a tone of analysis. "That's easy. Did you ever see the mom? She believes in 'Family.' Meaning, *her*. She's not about to ever let one of those boys get out from under her thumb. And if she tells him to, even though he might not want to, the Old Man will cut their money off. They haven't got a chance." He waited, but Lucky did not make the obvious comparison.

"I hate my mother," she whispered against his sleeve, instead. "And she hates me. We understand each other, only I admit it and she smiles with her hard stupid selfish eyes and claims she loves me. How can I prove to anyone she doesn't? Everything she's ever done to hurt me, she's done 'for my own good.' People believe it. The only thing she really loves is her own ignorant greedy stupidity. But that won't be provable."

"She doesn't sound much like the kind of lady who'll give us ten thousand dollars as a wedding present," Grant said, suddenly remembering old Frank Aldane's nod of drunken approval when told that very thing.

There was a small silence. "That was a lie," Lucky said against his sleeve. "She's more likely to give us one or two small pieces of the silver my daddy collected." Another small silence. "I lied to you and told you that because I thought it might make you more inclined to marry me."

The car had dropped down past the Racquet Club into the edge of the town. Grant didn't answer for a moment. Then he laughed. "Well, don't worry about that."

"I'm not worried about it," Lucky said. "But I am worried about us."

At the hotel, after they were in the suite, she clung to him bodily, even more so than she had done in the car. "We mustn't let them destroy us. They would, all of them, if we gave them half a chance. I can't protect myself against 'Them.' But maybe together we can. I'm a little drunk. I don't like it here. Please, let's get out of here. Please!"

"Them," Grant understood, was just about everybody, everybody who had ever made a dollar off another person, everybody who had ever put a bayonet in another, everybody who had ever demanded allegiance from another, everybody who had ever sustained life or limb or bank account or ego at the expense of another, just about everybody in other words, beginning with her mother, her playmates, her teachers and schoolmasters, her university professors, and carrying on to the US House of Representatives, the United States Senate, the voters, especially the voters, who knew? even the President himself—if he knew about her. But then he didn't have to know about her, did he? Nor did any of the others. They all knew she existed somewhere. And you could go on and include the Bankers of England, the Communist Presidium, every Army in Europe, all churches, the Arab League, the Israeli Army, the Red Chinese social structure, and every howling tribe in Africa. Plus the NAACP, Black Muslims, Klan, and John Wayne and the Birch Society. Grant understood, because it was a feeling he had had himself most of his life. And more than five years in the US Navy fighting for Democracy had not helped alleviate it.

Paranoia, Mr. Analyst? You bet your life. You bet your sweet ass. The Condition of Modern Man. And you show me, Mr. Analyst, the humanity you talk about that doesn't have the need or the necessity to destroy, even down to the tiniest word and never mind the atom bombs.

" We'll go," he said. " We'll go to-morrow. First thing in the morning. I promise you. Come to bed and let me hold you."

They did not leave the next day, however. And it was strictly Grant's fault. When they got up in the middle of the morning it was to find that Doug and Terry September had come back to the hotel and were there in the living-room of the suite already having their own breakfast. The eldest Khanturian had gotten bored hanging around Sir Gerald's private paradise without a girl and had asked to be taken back to town and they had driven him. Then instead of going back they had come on here, where they could be by themselves. " A little bit of that shit goes a long way," Terry said with a raucous laugh. " I'm more like you, Lucky. I'd rather make it with just one guy at a time who I enjoyed." Doug beamed at her. They were both still half drunk and had slept practically none at all.—" Did you ever see anybody more in love than these two?" Doug asked her.—" Well, not since I got out of high school anyway," Terry laughed. It was from them that Grant and Lucky learned about the picnic which Sir Gerald planned for to-day.

" Got this place over on the west end of the island he goes to, y'know," Doug said with a quite accurate imitation of Sir Gerald's King's English. He had always had a great ear. " Place called Negril Bay. Doesn't own it. Place owned by a little sod of a farmer. Chap raises a few papaya and lives off his coconuts. Pays him a few quid a year to use the beach. Lovely beach. Great marvellous reef right off it. Takes along a special rum punch he makes, and cold cuts, cooks hamburgers on the little brick barbecue. Great fun. Swim all you want. Lie in the sun."

Terry of course had to put in an appearance on the job, she and the other girls. " But we're through after twelve o'clock noon. And we finish up to-morrow and leave the day after. I thought it would be a sort of nice you know finale." There would just be the four couples of them, with Doug, Sir Gerald, Ron and " the Spy from Home."

Grant immediately wanted to go. Partly he wanted to get a chance to try out on the " great marvellous reef " the rented aqualung he'd brought which had been mouldering in the trunk of the car ever since they'd gotten here. And partly, he suddenly discovered in him a great reluctance to do anything that would hurry up his departure and force him to get on with it, go on back to Ganado Bay and have his showdown with Carol Abernathy about going on to Kingston " alone." He had told her once that he was taking his " new girl " down there with him, but he hadn't really meant it, then, and he was pretty sure she hadn't believed it. To avoid trouble, and yelling and screaming, he was going to tell her he was going down to Kingston alone but he knew it would still cause a lot of upset. God; in spite of all she had done to him so callously and selfishly, evilly, over the years (and to just about everybody else, including Hunt), he still acted as guiltily around her as if he were a god-damned weak little philandering husband. A regular unmanly little Rotarian. The image again: dark, mantillaed, and still standing on the church steps pointing, pointing at the great nail-studded, dark evil doors. It was that feeling that he'd started this whole damned diving junket to try and get over.

He told Lucky about wanting to go on the picnic as soon as Terry had left and they were alone together in the bedroom to dress for the day. " I'd like to see this Negril place. I've read about it. And I'd like to get one chance to try out this damned aqualung, which is really why I came in the first place." She agreed to go without much argument, but again she looked at him strangely. " I really don't like it here," she said after agreeing. " And I don't really know why. It's just a feeling. Of something terrible hanging over us. Something horrible that's liable to happen to us any moment."

" Is it that you don't like Sir Gerald?" Grant said, guiltily.

" No. No, not really. I like him. I like him a lot——"

" A lot? You mean like that? Really a lot?" Grant said jealously.

" Don't be silly. And I like Doug, too. I like him a lot.

And those girls are really okay. Like you said, last night."
She paused, inconclusively. " I just don't know what it is.
But something's wrong. And I'm scared."

Grant decided not to answer this, and when they finished
dressing and came out into the living-room of the suite
again, they found Doug waiting for them.

" Jesus, if you two aren't a rosy-looking pair," he said.
" You look like an ad for the Great American Lovesong
Industry. Right out of *McColl's*. Christ, I swear, when I look
at you two I think I oughta fall in love again myself. And
I thought I was through with that kind of shit-thinking for-
ever."

He put up his big arm and scratched his curly hair and
strode with explosive energy back and forth across the
room. " What do you think of that Terry girl? Underneath
that façade of hers, she's really quite a nice girl. And as
shitless-scared as the rest of us, I guess." He looked up
at them. " Hunh?"

" I think she's a great girl," Grant said.

"Well. Anyway, we're meeting them all at Doctor's Cave
for a beer at twelve-fifteen and taking off from there." He
grinned at them with explosive delight.

It was, all told, forty-eight miles to Negril Bay. But it
took an hour and a half to make the trip because the road,
none too good anyway, ran alongside the sea and curved
in and out of every little cove. Doug and Terry rode with
Grant and Lucky, and " the Spy from Home " and his
model with Sir Gerald. Doug and Terry did little but neck
and feel each other up in the back seat, and drink some
of the beer Grant was carrying for the picnic. When they
pulled off the road beside Sir Gerald's car, and then followed
him in through the sand under the half-jungly growth of
papaya trees and coconut palms, Grant could see through
their back window that " the Spy from Home " and his
girl had been doing pretty much the same.

When they drove past the tiny house, set charmingly on
its stilts in the shade of the sandy grove, the " farmer "
came out. Sir Gerald stopped his car, got out, and towering
over the diminutive Negro man so that he had to bend
almost double, walked off with him, listened for at least
five minutes to whatever it was the " farmer " was saying so
smilingly, at one point put his arm over the small man's

shoulder, and then slipped him what could only be a bank-note. Grant, sitting impatiently behind the wheel of the second car, wished he wouldn't take so damned long and wondered how much hatred there might be under the small Negro man's smiling exterior. If there wasn't any (and Grant could not be at all sure of that), some organisation like CORE or the NAACP or some Jamaican equivalent would be damned sure to agitate to create some, and rightly so, probably. One Negro could not be happy until all were happy. One human could not be happy until all were happy. Maybe. But for a brief moment he felt a keenly cutting envy for the diminutive Negro, with his grove of breadfruit, papaya and coconuts, his ramshackle house on stilts that needed no stove in winter, only protection from the rain, and his front yard of blindingly brilliant sea which from the car Grant could hear rubbing itself softly against his deep sand beach. What more could anybody want out of life? And for that moment Grant would gladly have traded places with him, colour and all—provided, of course, he could have Lucky here with him, he added, some-what surprising himself. But then that Other Part of his mind said Sure, and if the two of you lived here you'd both drink yourselves to death in a year. Grant had once made liquor in the far Pacific by putting sugar in coconuts and fermenting them in the sun. Sir Gerald came back after taking his own sweet time, and as they drove on in Grant saw in rising echelon four pairs of large white eyes staring at him over the rim of a windowsill from inside the house, and in that dark interior they appeared to have no faces.

"What the hell were you doing all that time?" he asked Kinton when they stopped and got out.

"Ahh," Sir Gerald said, grinning with his horse-face. "Have to butter them up a bit, you know. Time to time."

"But what was he talking to you about all that time?"

"Ah. About some life insurance he wants to buy."

Grant had never seen such brilliant sunshine in his life, not even in the tropical Pacific. It seemed at least double that of Ganado Bay or Montego Bay, and was so bright, so hot, so white that it turned everything that was out in it no matter how dark or bright the colour into a shade of off-white, and at the same time caused everything that was in shadow no matter what colour to become dead black.

After a while one's dazzled and sun-scorched eyes ceased to
see colour at all. This extra-brilliant sunshine was due,
or so Sir Gerald Kinton maintained, to the fact that this
westernmost tip of the island was not, like the rest, on
any of the what he called " cloud flyways," and was never
therefore shaded or soothed by them. He was able to point
this out by showing them out at sea a long straight line
of large white clouds sailing serenely along to the northwest
in the general direction of the Cayman Islands like a flotilla
of great white sailing ships in line. Grant found this hard
to believe but visually, in the sky, it seemed to bear out Sir
Gerald's contention: every cloud over the island seemed to
channel itself into this long line moving northwest while
on either side of this markedly noticeable line there was not
a cloud in the sky as far as the eye could see.

Under this burning white-hot sunshine was a little four-
sided unroofed room made of woven palm fronds and here
the girls, murmuring among themselves, changed to their suits.
On the beach in the blaze it was as still as death, and Grant
with the hot sand burning the bottoms of his bare feet was
suddenly made to think of summer Sundays back home in
the Midwest and the special feel they seemed to have, in the
very air itself, different from other days. The sea lapped
at the sand with the tiniest of sounds. By the time the men
had changed to their suits Sir Gerald had his rum punch
and the beer set up for utilisation on a car hood.

Whether it was the sun, the water, the rum punch itself,
or a combination of all three, they were all of them practically
falling-down drunk in twenty minutes. The punch, Sir
Gerald bragged proudly, steadying himself with a hand on the
car door and smiling with slightly glassy eyes at his motley
crew, had five kinds of rum in it, some lemon juice and
a little molasses syrup. It was even good warm, he maintained, though he had brought plenty of ice. In any
case its effect, in this still hot sun, was somewhat like being
rapped at the base of the skull with a white-hot sledge-
hammer. From this state it was only a short step again to
nude swimming and sunbathing.

There was something curiously innocent and childlike
about it this time. It was exactly as though a group of children became engaged in doing something bad and giggling
about it, something which wasn't really bad at all, and which

they instinctively knew was not bad, but which they also knew their elders would think was bad and would be shocked at. Doug and Terry were the lead-off pair this time, and after they had left their suits on the edge of the sand and swum out a ways " the Spy from Home " and his girl joined them laughing. When Sir Gerald and his model joined the rest, Grant looked over at Lucky.

They were sitting with their drinks at the round picnic table in the shade of the one big tree where the barbecue had been built. Lucky, who was quite drunk and had already fallen down once in the edge of the water to prove it, stood up and started to take her one-piece suit off.

" No! " Grant whispered painfully. " No! Don't! "

She grinned at him fuzzily, a little red-faced. " You want me to do it," she chided. " I know you do. I can tell. I can smell it. It shows on your face."

" It's true," Grant said. " I do." He felt breathless. " But don't. It would hurt too much."

" You're chicken," Lucky said. " And I want to do it," she added stoutly. " I *really* want to. Matter fact, I'd *love* to do it."

" Okay, then. I'm chicken. But I'm asking you not to."

Without a word Lucky put the strap back on over her arm and back over the white mark on her shoulder, and sat down and picked up her drink.

The group of temporary nudists, laughing and splashing, had swum back inshore a ways and were now standing not quite waist-deep in the water, having a water-fight. A group of Jamaican natives in swimsuits with three naked children among them walked past on the beach smiling at the nude water-fighters.

" They're only playing," Grant said. " Having fun. Did you see that?" he nodded at the smiling Jamaicans.

" I know," Lucky said. " I know that. You're funny. You're very funny. It would hurt too much, you said. But you still wanted me to do it. Still do."

Grant didn't answer this. The water-fight in the shallows had broken up, and Doug and Terry came ashore. Facing it, Doug stood and squinted at the small Negro man's house twenty yards back in off the beach, then turned around and lay down and stretched out on a blanket with Terry stretched out beside him. The other four came

splashing in and sat down with them. From the lack of
conspicuous difference between the models' bottoms and
the rest of them it was plain that they all were used to a lot
of nude sunbathing. None of the men sported erections,
Grant noted. Nor did he. Curiously enough it was just
the reverse, actually.

Beside him Lucky suddenly got up and walked down into
the water. She lay down and half-crawled, half-paddled out
a short distance, all of her under but her head. She seemed
to wriggle around a little bit, Grant watching her, and
then suddenly stood up, her arms over her head in a classic
ballet pose. She had taken off her suit and was completely
nude. The water seemed to pour off her in slow motion
as it were, and then there she was in all her glorious sensuality, the lovely white breasts and lean, rounded hip making
the other, skinnier girls look mechanical and asexual. Her
arms still up and not quite knee-deep in the water, she
did a series of classic *ballonné fouetté*, a real *pas de bourrée*
directly toward them, all beautifully done. It was a movement which, forcing the raised leg out at a complete right
angle to the standing leg as it did, before the little leap,
gave the impression of opening up the crotch completely, and
she must have chosen it deliberately. There was a hush
of stillness from the shore as she did the *pas de bourrée*. The
champagne-coloured hair had not gotten wet and it flashed
about her as she moved like white gold. Then she turned
and dived under back to where her suit was and with only
her head above water put it back on.

From the shore there came a burst of applause and yells.

When she got back to Grant she was both laughing and
blushing. Taking his arm in one hand she kissed him on the
mouth. " Are you mad at me?"

" Mad at you! God you're beautiful! God I love you!
It was beautiful!"

" Make you a little hot?"

" Hot! Wait'll I get you home."

And yet, somewhere way down underneath, he *was* angry
at her. At the same time he had never been so sexually
excited in his life; the heat of it was so great he was
afraid it would melt his ears, ignite his hair, and burn the
top of his head off. Sometimes she seemed to understand
him better than he understood himself.

At the blanket Sir Gerald Kinton uncoiled his long lank nude frame and stood up, and smiling a little ruefully said, " Well, I don't think I really ought to go about my cooking chores dressed like this," and went over and put his trunks back on before going to the barbecue. Slowly the others casually redonned their suits, and that was the end of it.

It was not however the end of the picnic, or the end of the drinking. Even the delicious hamburgers and steaks Sir Gerald cooked over the driftwood-smoky fire could not sober them up from Sir Gerald's punch. With a great, hectic, self-destructive but unbrookable drive that Grant for one could not understand or calculate the cause of, Sir Gerald ladled out more and more rum punch from what appeared to be an inexhaustible supply.

The " great marvellous reef " turned out to be a bust. When Grant swam out to it with his mask and snorkel, he found it consisted of little coral heads about three feet high and only six feet below the surface. Only a few sergeant-majors and a few tiny butterfly fish inhabited it. As a diver, even as a snorkeller, Sir Gerald was obviously below the level of even the rankest amateur. So the aqualung stayed in the car trunk again. Anyway, he was too drunk to try to dive seriously. He was too drunk to do just about anything. Then when he thought about Carol Abernathy he reached for another drink.

The sun was so strong and dried them out so much that after a couple of hours of it they actually felt toasted— not sunburnt, but toasted, like dry toasted bread. Once during the long hot afternoon Grant fell asleep on the blanket with his arm around Lucky in the shade of the tree, and had again the nightmare he had had before. Once again he had speared the same big fish and it had gone under the same big ledge. Once again pride would not let him let go of the gun, the pistol-grip of which he could feel so plainly in his hand. The surface beckoned. Then his last air burst out of him and he watched the last big bubbles of it rising toward the shimmering, quicksilver, undulating water-sky. His last breath. He woke with a strangled cry.

" What was that? " Lucky asked.

" I had a bad dream. That's all."

" What kind of a bad dream?"

" Oh, nothing much. I dreamed I shot a big fish and

can't get him up but I won't let go of the gun. I drown." He laughed suddenly. "I've had it before."

"God!" Lucky said, looking at him strangely. "If it makes you have dreams like that, why do you do it?"

"Why," Grant said tonelessly, like an echo. Then he felt irritated. "I'm not makin' it my profession. It's not something I'm gonna do all my life. It's just something I want to learn about, that's all."

Then thinking about Carol Abernathy he reached for another glass of punch.

It showed up on the way home. All of them feeling crisp all over, they left just before sundown, and in the first little town they passed through Grant ran into a street island. The left front wheel bounced up over the curbing, jolting them all but causing no damage. The jolt was enough to wake up Doug and Terry who were asleep with their arms around each other in the back seat. When he saw what it was, Doug laughed raucously.

Lucky waited to speak until she was sure they were asleep again. "I really don't know what's wrong with you, but something is. All of you. Something terrible is hanging over all of us, and I'm scared. You've got to get me out of here and away from these people. We've just got to get out of here, Ron!"

"You're right," he said. "You're absolutely right. And we will. On the other hand, that could have happened to anybody. What the hell do they want to put a goddamned street island in a place like that for anyway in this little burg?"

But he slowed down. Sir Gerald, at least as drunk as he was, was miles away in front ahead of them. He didn't care. By the time they reached Montego Bay he had driven himself sober with the aid of a bottle of beer Lucky opened for him. "Jesus God, that punch!" he said as they pulled into town. And with only a quick sandwich to sustain them they packed what little they had left for Ganado Bay that same evening.

Doug did not go with them. Smiling at Terry September, he said he had decided to stay on until the girls left when their job was over. Maybe Terry would stay down another day or two.

So the two of them made the night trip alone.

EIGHTEEN

She couldn't remember ever having made such a wild insane night ride before. The car winged along between the sea and the mountains almost as if they were actually airborne in bumpy air. Everything was flavoured with a weird hangover quality. The only thing remotely like it in her experience was that crazy night out in California years ago when she almost ran down Buddy Landsbaum with his own limousine. They were all drunk that time too. Course she and Ron were sober now. But they were sobered up into that dehydrated, over-nervous fatigue and interior jiggling, from Sir Gerald's rum punch, which gave the same distorted grotesque scary effect as if you were still overdrunk.

She spent most of the trip huddled up and half-lying down in the front seat, pretending to be asleep. So she wouldn't have to talk to Grant.

She knew something about him now that she hadn't known before. She didn't know what it was exactly that she knew, but she knew she knew it. And knew she knew how to use it. He wasn't invulnerable, after all. And she had made up her mind that some day she would make him pay.

Pay for everything. For leaving her in New York like that, for making her pull that silly nude bathing stunt and embarrassing her this afternoon, for bringing her down here into this stupid drunken week-end with that bunch of creepy sick drunks. Make him pay, most of all, for having made her fall in love with him. That most of all she would make him pay for. For the first time since she had met him Lucky again felt strong, self-sustaining. And she knew she could make him marry her. Too. No question about it. Easy as pie. She could make him do anything.

At the same time she felt more in love with him than ever, with a greater depth of tenderness. The poor slob. The poor *slave*. She had always wanted her very own slave. She felt tough and hard, even conquering, after this afternoon, and at the same time she felt a great pity for him. How could you respect your slave?

There he sat beside her behind the wheel, as solid as any rock, as dependable as any Gibraltar insurance company, his face lit dimly by the dashboard, no idea in his mind at all of what she had in store for him. She loved him more. He believed in things. The idiot. Or thought he did. Even though he professed to be cynical. Oh, would she hurt him.

He was probably the best road driver she had ever ridden with, except maybe for her daddy. She had learned that on the trip to Florida. And now he herded the big rented convertible along the winding, bumpy roads like some master rider totally in control of his mount, pushing hard, but never pushing beyond capacity or safety point. Yes, she'd make him pay all right.

Then slowly the mood washed itself away. He had insisted on leaving the top down, to keep himself awake he said, although it was cold. She huddled down into her coat. Under the thin fingernail moon, which seemed to darken things rather than lighten them, the ocean loomed on their left, a flat black expanse of potential danger, while on their right the black humps of jungled hills and whispering black fields of cane twelve feet high threatened them also. From time to time they passed clusters of shacks along the road where the field hands lived, almost always unlighted, and heard guitar chords; were taunted by murmuring voices, rich black laughter. Once or twice black men jumped out into the light of the headlights brandishing machetes and shouted at them. It was as if the night, falling, had released the primitive, the jungle, the Africa from what in day-time were only politely murmuring stock figures. While along the way the towns slept, deadly. It seemed to Lucky that only the bright double beam of the headlights, running on before them, kept back total primitivity, primevalism, from engulfing them; kept civilisation alive. She felt terror at the thought of them suddenly extinguished. At least out there in Hollywood that time what happened, happened in *civilised* surroundings. Not drowsy at all, huddled in her warm camel's-hair coat, she peeked up once at Grant and her mind settled itself into a spicy luxury of secret remembering.

Buddy had invited her and Leslie to fly out to the Coast with him, his expense, where he had to meet with Don Celt

about a film they were going to do together in Canada. Yes,
Don Celt! He who was directing Ron's new play! She
had only been fucking Buddy about two weeks then. Yes,
fucking him, she repeated to herself deliciously, aware that
Grant thought she was asleep, could not know what she was
thinking. It had seemed a lark to both of them, both girls,
at the time. But when they got out there it had gone to
hell, fast. She had known Buddy was tight. But, only
having gone with him for two weeks, just how tight she
hadn't realised. This showed up immediately on the Coast.
If there was anything she couldn't stand it was somebody
who was tight with money.

First he had stashed them in some cheap little motel way
out in nowhere on one of the freeways. The spending money
that he gave her for them was barely enough for hamburger-
shack lunches, not even enough to get them into town unless
they rode the bus. Then he had rented himself a big limousine
and chauffeur and disappeared. That, the big car, was necessary for business he had explained. And after that they
saw him only at night. All the dinners, of course, were invitational. Whether at someone's home or not. Buddy had
many many friends out there. And, of course, so were
all the after-dinner parties that he took them to, invitational.
Don Celt was always with them of course, trying in a rather
lukewarm and lackadaisical way to make Leslie, who on her
side wasn't having any. Both girls knew it was Lucky that
Don Celt really had the hots for, and talked about it between
themselves and laughed.

Then one night Buddy took them all to Clinton Upton's
house, after a very heavy-drinking dinner. Clint Upton had
been as big a playwright in his generation as Ron Grant
was in his. In later years he had done few plays, always flops,
but had done an enormous amount of movie work, largely
as a trouble-shooter on scripts that were in big trouble,
for which he was paid fantastic sums. He had an enormous,
incredibly expensive house, a fantastic collection of records
for one of the world's most fantastic hi-fi sets, an invalu-
able collection of Klees and Kandinskys and the like, had
decorated everything in original Restoration antiques. And
he showed the two girls, especially Lucky, all of it. Right
down to the tiniest item. And it soon became clear that
Buddy, in the nicest politest way possible of course, was

offering Lucky to Clint Upton—who, for his part, was taking.
It turned out later that Buddy and Don Celt were in trouble
with their Canadian script. They wanted Upton to work on
it.

She couldn't believe it at first. Not her. Maybe Hopie
York, or other girls like that that she knew. But not *her*.
So she laughed, and joked, and flirted, on and on, getting
more embarrassed, making it look worse. When she finally did
believe it was when she left. And she did not leave quietly.
Of course she was very drunk by that time. They all were.
She threw her drink at Upton, who ducked, so that the glass
smashed on the big stone fireplace behind him, and then ran
outside to the car. Fortunately the chauffeur was loafing
somewhere in the servants' quarters, as she had been pretty
sure he would be. But by the time she got the unfamiliar
controls of the car working, the men had run out after her.
They had tried to stop her, Buddy and Don stepping out in
front of the car in the light of the headlights. She had
rammed the car right at them in the long expensive flowering-
bush-bordered driveway and Celt, not quite as close as
Buddy, had been able to step back. But Buddy had only
saved himself by putting both hands on the headlight and
fender and vaulting himself off head-first into the flowering
bushes. God, he had looked funny, the last part of him
to disappear into the bushes being his two worn shoe-soles
glaring whitely at them all in the light from the headlights.
She wouldn't have cared at the time if she had killed
him. Later of course she was glad he wasn't. But her pride
was hurt. And nobody got the chance to hurt her pride
twice.

She had driven the big car back to the motel and parked
it. They had arrived soon after, as she had known they
would, in Upton's big car, though Upton was not with
them. Buddy, Don, the chauffeur, and with them Leslie
who could not keep from bursting out into laughter every
so often. Buddy's white dinner jacket was all covered with
loamy soil, and he kept mopping with a no-longer-clean
white handkerchief at the blood oozing from several deep
scratches on his face.

She never knew whether what she did then was simply
for Leslie's benefit or not. She didn't think it was. But
in another, more hollow way, she hoped that it was.

In any case when Buddy had begun—somewhat sheepishly —to remonstrate with her, she had simply stared at him contemptuously and turned to Don. " How would you like to take me out to-night?" she had asked.—" Where?" Don had said, in a low voice.—" Where do you think? There's nothing open this late. To your place," she had answered. After a moment, Buddy made a half-strangled sound of protest. " Well——" Don said, and glanced at Buddy.— " Well, what is it?" she said. " Come on! Yes or no?" —" Well, it's yes," Don had said, in that low voice. Without a word she had walked around and gotten into his car, which he had left there earlier when they had started for Clint Upton's. It had taken Don quite a bit longer to get in, and she had stared at Buddy from the window. Buddy did not say anything, he was taking it quite well, except that under everything else on his face—chagrin, shame, unmanliness even—there was a distinct look of painful, anguished pleasure, perverse enjoyment of what she was doing to him. They were all enjoying it. She was enjoying it herself. Only Leslie really looked shocked.—" Bye!" she had called sweetly as Don turned the car. " See you!"

Men! she had thought contemptuously, then, looking at Don behind the wheel, as *Men!* she thought contemptuously now again, cracking her lids just enough to peek up at Grant's face lit by the dashlight.

He had not really been a bad lay. Once nature had time to get him over the initial awkwardness. She had helped time by being calm and amenable, sitting down in a chair and making herself at home. The only cruel thing she did was to refuse a drink when he offered it. But he had had that coming, and he seemed to sense that as he coughed and fidgeted around. When he finally sidled over and sat down by her and kissed her, she kissed him back. But in the morning she was up and gone before Celt, who had to be up quite early to get to the studio, had even begun to start waking up. *Men!*

Men, she remembered having thought oh so many times really, *God how I detest them all.* A pair of tits and a cunt, and that was all they wanted. The only really honourable man with real honour she had ever met was her daddy, really.

But it was after that incident that she first really began

K

to worry about herself. She couldn't really be a whore, could she? God, what if it turned out she was? Back at the motel she had found Leslie waiting with, " God! You really made him pay, honey!" in a half-scared awed admiring voice. Buddy it turned out had cried a couple of times between drinks, and then tried to climb into the sack with Leslie, unsuccessfully of course. Lucky listened. Trying to save his pride and get even. Still freezing cold emotionally, she had called up Clint Upton on an impulse.

" Sure, you can both come on out for a few days if you want," he had said in his amused, still-Jewish, still very-Bronx accent. " What? You haven't got . . .? God, those boys sure treat you right, don't they? Okay, I'll send the car for you." He had regaled them with stories of stars and gossip of people in high places, they swam in his pool, he played them his records, his Mexican maid cooked them excellent dinners for three days. " What do you want me to do about their job?" he asked her finally, smiling. " Do you want me to take it or not? I'll leave it up to you."—" I refuse to even answer such a thing," she had said coldly.— " No, come on. It's your right. You say the word, I'll turn it down. Or take it, if you say so."—" I absolutely refuse to make such a decision!" she answered coldly, and would not budge. In the end, she learned later, he had taken the job; but the Canadian picture was a flop anyway. On the fourth day he said, " I think it's about time Leslie got back to New York, don't you?" In all that time he had not touched, or tried to touch, either of them. " Leslie?" she had said.—" Oh, and you too, if you want to go. I had thought maybe you'd like to stay on a while longer. But you have a ticket to New York any time you want it. After all, somebody has to uphold the reputation of the brethren of this trade." Sweet man.

She had stayed. What the hell? And Clint Upton turned out to be really an endearing man. Though quite a lot older. As she was to say over and over in the years after and had been saying for at least two years before, the only way to really get to know somebody was to fuck them. Then one day he got carried away and chased her (Lucky) around the swimming pool with a Gillette razor wanting to shave her pussy. " Come on! You'll like it! I know you will! Just try it once!" Fortunately he was older and hadn't much wind and finally ran himself down. The next day she had invoked his offer of a plane ticket back home to New York—on the grounds that because after all she had to get back to her real life some day didn't she, so that they would part friends, and which was a good part of the truth anyway, more than the thing about him wanting to shave her pussy. The thing had just run itself out. Because if it hadn't, she would have let him shave it. Clint of course had learned a lot about her too and one day only a couple of years later she was to see herself turn up as a character in a play of his, vastly distorted of course. It was a flop too. *Men!*

Men!, and Lucky peeked up at Grant again from under her silvered lids. *Well, there's three of the Four Hundred Men you will never know about, My husband. How about that?* Except that that wasn't really true, either, was it? He already knew about Buddy.

She did not really know why she was so angry at him and as she paused to wonder why, the anger itself sieved away. Partly because the black night and the black night-time Negroes scared her. And then besides, that kind of life was nowhere, out there, on the Coast. That wasn't the way she wanted to live. And besides twenty-seven going on twenty-eight is not twenty-three going on twenty-four, either. The changed mood made her remember her so-oft-repeated promise to herself, and, silently, to him. To Ron. She *would* make him a good wife. She would. Sliding down a little, she reached out one hand and let it rest on his hard thigh. His broad ugly tough-looking face was strong and almost good-looking in the dim dashlight.

Suddenly she choked back tears. Oh, Daddy, Daddy! Why did you have to go and die so suddenly like that and leave your Little Girl?

Grant continued to herd the car. She continued to pretend to sleep.

She was depressed again. Like in New York, though not as bad. The superstitious feeling that she would be punished came back over her. Doom-gloom. The fucking Catholics. She understood it all. All that, plus the Electra complex bit. Understanding did not make it cease, or go away. Pride: Anger: Silence: Guilt: They always took the same course with her predictably, and now she was in the Guilt phase.

She loved "Authority," but at the same time hated it. She knew she had a too strong penchant for contempt for men. (If she didn't like cocks so well, she might have been lesbian. Except she could never put her face down there, like men did. Ugh!) But fear of Grant offset that somewhat: her man-contempt: she never knew what he was going to do or say. His honesty about himself was almost too much. He would say anything about himself, confess anything about himself, totally shamelessly. He didn't seem to have any repressions like other people. Just the opposite, he seemed to have a compulsion to tell everybody everything about himself, and this embarrassed her. Psychologically, he was not hygienic, not—sanitary and she hated that. *Damn him!* she thought, and then realised she had come clear around the circle back to Anger. Pride and Anger. When she realised this, her depression doubled.

The thing about Grant was, he was real. She had never felt real, herself. So, whatever she said or did didn't really count. She wasn't real, it wasn't real, and so it didn't mean anything. Take her feeling about telling him about the $10,000 wedding present her mother was going to give them. The only way she could describe it was that a sort of "evil spirit" of "Charm," a naughty devil of charm, had possessed her. It was a mistake. She was being charming, and he was being charming, and they were kidding and laughing about their marriage (which neither one of them believed in, then), and it had just popped out. And when she said it she knew it wasn't true, but that didn't matter because she wasn't real, and none of this was real, and so it didn't count. And anyway when she said it it *was* true because she said it. She still didn't know what his reaction to the real truth had been when she told him. He hadn't reacted. But, what had he thought?

And furthermore, how could she go about explaining to him that it wasn't really a " *lie* " at all? She couldn't. It would simply sound like an excuse.

Okay. But that wasn't what was really disturbing her. Go further. All right. The thing that really disturbed her was that on that first night of nude swimming in Sir Gerald's brightly lit pool, way down deep inside of her she had secretly wished that Ron had said, had ordered her, " Take off your suit," had demanded that she expose herself naked to all of them. That was what had scared her, and looking into it even deeper—as she had done then sitting there in the deck chair just as Terry September came walking back from the Little Girls Room in her bikini—she had found way down there in some very deep bottom of her mind one of those sexual fantasy pictures that one cannot tell to anyone, not even to an analyst, a played-out-in-full imaginative sexual fantasy of her screwing another man in front of Ron, of making him stand there and watch her screw another man in front of him and maybe, say, play with himself while he watches. That was what had terrified her, and the weeping fit came from the terror and from the idea that she could even in her imagination imagine such a thing. Hide in a closet!

She still felt, even now, that she had lost considerable face with him, had shown a big lack of courage. But she had also felt, very strongly, with a powerful feeling of impending danger, that if she had taken off her suit that night they two would have lost something between them that they could never have gotten back. But how could Ron be expected to understand that? Especially since it was exactly that that she was making him pay for the next day, when she did take off her suit and show herself nude at the picnic?

God, those people! And especially his " old buddy " Doug Ismaileh! They were not the kind of people that they—she and Ron—ought to be hanging around with. God, was everybody in the world sick? She huddled down further into her coat, as if that would save her, and well, it would all sort itself out, she had to believe that, now that they were away from them, were on their way to GaBay and going to Kingston. René and Lisa would be so glad to see her. René and Lisa and their funny Grand Hotel Crount. She had stayed with them so many times and so long during her long affair with Raoul. Lightly, lovingly, scared and panicky, she dug her fingernails gently into the hard meat of Grant's thigh as he drove on.

Thinking of Raoul so soon after thinking of her mother's " $10,000 Wedding Present " made her couple the two and suddenly remember the time Raoul had given her $10,000 in cash that time. She hadn't thought of that in ages. Another example of how she was not really real.

Usually Raoul gave her jewellery, most of which she subsequently sold or pawned, after his death. God, they were all so rich those South Americans, what with their great estates and peon peasants and no taxes at all, hardly even any law. An ordinary American couldn't believe it. This time he had simply given her this money at the airport when she had ridden out with him to see him off. She had come home with a purse so jammed with bills she couldn't completely close it. The very sight of it had panicked her. "What am I supposed to do with this?" she'd cried.—"I don't care," he'd said. "It's a present. Buy yourself something with it." When counted it had turned out to be $10,000. And it had lasted like a week. She had given hundred-dollar bills to all her friends. She had loaned hundreds and hundreds of dollars to people she knew damn well would never pay her back. She threw big parties. Once she had scattered twenty-dollar bills all around the apartment to her girl-friends like it was ticker-tape confetti. It just wasn't real, and she couldn't make it seem real. She herself wasn't real holding it. Then it was gone. But she was still proud of herself for it. Of course, she didn't know then he was going to get himself killed down there.

She must have dozed because the sound of the car's motor getting lower and lower until it was idling seemed a dream, and then the car itself rolling gently to a stop, and then it brought her back with a start. Grant leaned over her and said gently, "Well, sweetie, we're here." Sitting up, she saw a decrepit-looking kind of Charlie Addams house with high steep mansard roofs of corrugated tin.

Although it was after midnight, the little house was ablaze with lights. Rock 'n' roll music poured from its windows. When Ron called, an enormous figure appeared in the screen door literally filling it, and stood there silhouetted against the light like some huge terrible gorilla from the forests of Africa, bellowing.

"That's Al Bonham," she heard Grant say from behind her with almost boyish hero-worship. "The best damn aqualung diver in the Caribbean."

"Haw! You son of a bitch! I thought you'd gone to China or someplace!" Bonham was roaring.

Once inside, the two men began beating each other on the back. A third man, naked to the waist and heavily muscled with that thin layer of protective lard just under the skin that she had seen professional football players have, came over from the table and gave Grant a punch on the arm that sounded like a butcher hitting a side of meat with a flathead hammer. She watched Grant wince, suddenly feeling a little sick in her stomach. But he came back with a punch to the belly swift and hard enough to make the other man whoof. "And this is Mo Orloffski," he said with an apologetic grin, "sailor, diver, and owner of the biggest sporting goods store on the South Jersey Shore." Orloffski roared with laughter. "Used to be, honey. But I'm sellin' it. You want to buy one?" Two women, one of them a light-skinned Jamaican coloured girl, sat by the trumpeting record-player holding cans of beer. One of them, the Jamaican girl, was knitting. Everything, every flat surface in the room except the floor, was crowded with empty beer-cans and beer bottles. Around the edges of the floor and crowding the corners of the room were duffel bags packed with gear, rubber-hosed aqualung regulators and sets of tanks. On the table, crowding the beer-cans outward to the corners, was an aqualung regulator all opened up with its innards showing that the two men must have just been working on. On the floor beside the table was a haphazard pile of marine charts upon which several stuffed-out cigarette butts had fallen. Lucky felt a horribly strong distaste rising in her.

"You were right, old buddy," Bonham grinned after all the introductions had been made. When he grinned, it was as if some huge black ominous cloud of foreboding covered his forehead, eyes and eyebrows. "Your new girl sure is a looker."

"You ain't just shittin'!" Orloffski bellowed.

Lucky looked again at all of it, everything, and at the people. So; such was her introduction to her man's diving world. And she'd probably see a lot more of it. She pulled up the waist of her tight-fitting slacks cockily, stuck out her breasts in the sweater, and grinned. "Me? He's been telling you about me? Well, how about a beer for the looker?"

"Hot damn! Comin' up!" shouted Orloffski.

"You'll have to excuse the way things are," Bonham told her very gently as he led her across toward the kitchen. "We just got back from a trip a few days ago. Did Ron tell you? And they're," he nodded at Orloffski, " they're staying with us a few days till they can get settled. Don't usually look like this."

Grant had come back to GaBay at just the right time, he said after things had settled down and he had gotten them beers, because to-morrow they were going out on the deep reef for a dive. He had three new customers at one of the hotels. And not only that, they'd be good for at least three or four more days after that. Lucky sat silent and listened. Bonham had swept the regulator and its pieces into a bowl and set it on the beer-can-crowded bureau, freeing the table.

" Fine. We'd like to go," she with partial disbelief heard Ron saying. She had been under the impression that they were leaving for Kingston to-morrow. But first, he went on, they were going to have to do something to see about some place to stay.

" Why don't we just go down and register in at one of the big hotels on the beach?" Lucky asked. All three men turned to stare at her.

" They're terribly expensive," Bonham said.

" Yeah, well. Yeah, mainly it's because I'm tryin' to save money," Ron said, and then grinned. " Largely because I owe this big son of a bitch so much already."

" That's true, he does," Bonham said with a smile. " What happened to Doug? Anyway."

Grant explained about Terry September. " He'll be along in a couple of days. Maybe he'll bring her with him." Anyway, the first thing, the main thing, he went on, was to see about some place for them to stay to-night. He certainly didn't want to go down to the rich hotels on the beach, and them probably booked up anyway.

Bonham was looking at Grant with some kind of a private, knowledgeable look that Lucky could not read. She watched him immediately sort of take over: He would have loved to put them up himself, he said, but they only had one guest room and the Orloffskis were in it. However, there was a friend of his—only just a few doors down the street —little Jamaican guy—who sometimes took in roomers (couples, he corrected himself), in his extra bedroom during the season.

"It's close to here?" Ron said, a little nervously she thought.

"Right down the street."

"That sounds fine then. We'll be close to here." He sounded curiously guilty, Lucky thought.

"Come on," Bonham said. "Get yourself another beer, and you and me'll walk down there right now."

"Won't they be in bed already?"

"Naw. Hell, no. They never go to bed this early."

Lucky watched them leave. With the two of them gone, the air of conspiracy she had felt before, disappeared. The two women got up from the bawling record-player and brought their beer over to the table. Orloffski helped her to another beer and said cheerfully in his brutal voice. "They'll be back in a few minutes." She noticed that whenever he sat down he acquired a considerable paunch on his totally hairless torso that he did not have when he was standing up.

"So you come from New York, hunh?" Wanda Lou Orloffski said. "Me and Mo used to go up there to New York quite a few times when we lived in Jersey."

"Yeah, but we never seen the New York Lucky knows, I'm sure," Orloffski grinned, and belched.

Lucky smiled. You bet your sweet ass you didn't, baby, she was thinking.

Letta Bonham, who had never been off the island of Jamaica, let alone to New York, kept looking with a bright, childlike, very female attention from one to the other and said almost nothing. She was the only one of them all that Lucky decided she might be able to like.

They had a very difficult time making a conversation until the two men returned.

And Lucky found her distaste for the whole scene, the whole operation, growing even greater. She realised these three were only trying to make her feel at ease, as much at home as possible, but they were doing a very bad job of it. Something about her—she hated to use the word, but there was no other word for it, and maybe she didn't hate it so much after all—something about her "class" put them off balance and made them nervous. She could not make *them* feel at ease, either. She already actively detested Orloffski and "his" Wanda Lou. And there was something in her—especially toward the man—that kept them at a great distance, and she couldn't help it, and she was glad she couldn't. What in the name of God could Ron be doing with people like this? When you haven't been around insensitive members of the lower classes for such a long time, you tend to forget how crude and brutal and insensitive they and their lives are.

She was immensely relieved when the two men came back from their room-hunting. Bonham slammed the screen door behind them with a curiously exuberant finality. And conspiracy came back into the room again.

"Well, it's all set!" Grant said cheerily. "We can have the room for a week if we want it."

"A *week*!" Lucky was unable not to exclaim.

"Well, we won't stay that long of course," he said. "What I meant to say was we can have it for as many days as we want to stay." He laughed suddenly. "Ha! We had to rout them out of bed after all! I figured we would." His face was flushed, and he looked to Lucky as if he might have had a couple more drinks, maybe down there, and he sounded as if he enjoyed having waked the people up. Her own two beers had relieved the last remnants of her hangover considerably.

"Well! Now that that's all settled, what do you say we all wrap it up here and adjourn to the good old Neptune Bar to hoist a few?" This was Bonham.

"Haw! Great idea!" the almost equally massive Orloffski shouted.

"I don't really think I can," Lucky said. "We've had a pretty hectic day of it. I'm just beat." She looked at Grant. "But Ron can go if he wants to."

"No, no! No, no! I'll go with you," he said hastily. "She's right," he said to Bonham. "We've both had it We need some sleep." He looked disappointed though, she thought.

"Okay." Bonham said. "Well, all you have to do is back your car up back down the street. It's only three doors down. Then pull it right up into the yard." He had sat back down at the table. Apparently if Grant was not going, none of them was going either. Because of the tab, no doubt. Lucky thought icily.

The little homemade-looking house, almost a replica of

Bonham's, was completely darkened when Ron backed the big car past it. There was no kerbing, no street gutters, as he pulled the car up into the grassless, bare dirt yard. Above their heads palm fronds clattered softly in a breeze, and some straggly flowered bushes gave off tropic scents to them in the warm humid tropic night Everything felt strangely quiet. Ron had been given a key and he let them in, showing her the way and carrying her bag, and with dutiful meticulousness turning off all the lights behind them as they went.

The little room was horrible. A three-quarter bed (that, she didn't mind), an ugly badly de-silvering mirror, two flamboyant chipping plaster-of-paris statues from Woolworth's or some local festival, a Woolworth rickety floorlamp, an armoire whose plywood doors would no longer come near to closing, an uncomfortable modern chair, that was all. What a place for a honeymoon. As she climbed into the bed beside him, she heard someone turn peevishly in bed just beyond the thin wall. Instinctively, they talked in whispered tones.

" Take that damned thing off, goddam it."

" I can't, Ron. Not here. Didn't you hear?"

" Take it off anyway. You got to." She did.

" What in the name of *God* are you doing with people like that, Ron?"

" They're the people I have to go to to learn what I want to learn. I didn't *pick* them. I told you this wasn't going to be an *easy* thing. I probly shouldn't have brought you down, my first idea to leave you in New York was probly right. But I missed you so. And I got scared. I got scared I might be untrue to you. You wouldn't want that, would you? So soon?

" Look, I know it's horrible here. But it's only a place to sleep. We won't spend any time here. And we'll only be here a few days."

" A few *days*!"

" I want to make a few more dives with Bonham before I go. He's really good. You just have to believe me. And I want to wait for Doug to come back. Look, I've got to go and tell my idiot ' foster-mother ' that we're going off to Kingston. And I want Doug to go with me. The old cunt is going to kick up an awful fuss. She thinks every young woman in the world is out after my ha-ha money. If Doug is with me, she won't raise such a scene."

" Are you scared of her?"

" *No*, I'm not scared of her!——"

" —Shhh."

" You know how you felt with your mother."

" I left."

" Well, I'm leaving too. But I want to do it as nice as possible. Don't you see?"

" All right."

" But don't you?"

" All *right*."

" I probably shouldn't have brought you down. But I - just - couldn't help it . . ."

She had curled up against him, her left leg over his left leg, and was rubbing her left breast into the angle of his half-open armpit. His kiss now was as deep as sanity. Maybe deeper, she thought as he shoved her back and scrambled over her.

After they had made love she lay awake a long time thinking.

What was it Ron and Bonham could have been conspiring about? And what was all this coy tickly business about renting a cheap room? She knew better than that. Something cold suddenly ran all over her.

Could it be that Ron wasn't straight with her after all? That he was holding something back from her all this time after all, like so many of the others, like *all* the others?

A secret wife hidden away some place? An alimony wife and alimony kids he couldn't afford to give up to marry again? A lover or mistress he hadn't told about, and didn't *want* to give up? Was it this foster-mother who ran his life and wouldn't let him?

Jesus, a lone woman was so vulnerable.

It was like an old bad dream coming back. How many possible situations were there? In her time she had been just about through the entire lot. He didn't *act* like the kind of man who was dominated by his mother, his foster-mother. She had known one like that, too. Did this mother, this foster-mother hold that much power over him?

Could it be, even, one of the other possibilities?

One third sleeping, Lucky looked bleakly back over the

whole long long list of them in her life, suddenly half-smoth-
ered in a real fright and jerked back awake. It stretched
all the way back to the age of twenty-two when she had
first come on to New York and the handsome society gynæco-
logist—who wouldn't even help her out with her first abortion after causing its necessity. Not one of them but who
had lied to her about something.

Even Raoul, who had *told* her he had a wife down there,
and who was *trying* to get a divorce, had not told her the
real dangerousness of his revolution activities. He had told
her how they sat him naked on cakes of ice for hours,
and how they had wired his teeth with electricity, but he
had laughed about all that. And even under her questioning he would never admit that it could go so far that anybody would actually kill him. God! And all of them. *All*
the others.

No. It couldn't be. It just couldn't. Not after the way he
had been to her, the way they had been to each other all
that time in New York. That had to be real. There couldn't
be any lie behind, underneath that. She had to believe in
him. She just had to.

So she did.

She just would.

Seeking warmth, she cuddled up and curled herself against
him in the bed. In his sleep Grant moved away, and again
she followed, curling up like a baby kitten blindly curling
up against any warmth. Warmth. Warmth.

She felt loose, at loose ends and out of place here with
these people like Bonham. She had nothing really, no past
experience of it, to judge by. She had always disliked sports.
And " sportsmen." And kept as far away from them as possible. There was something funny, sick about them, as if they
did all these things because they didn't like women.

That Orloffski, for instance. Orloffski had made her
think of somebody. In her senior year at Cornell she had
gone with, been the girl-friend of, the Captain of the Football Team. For campus fame. For campus glory. And in
that year, after losing her virginity—losing it? giving it
away gladly!—the year before to a hometown non-college
boy, she had had an affair with her football captain. Afterward he had gone on to play pro ball, and she had dropped
him. For a year or two after that he had used to call her

up in New York whenever his team was in town. He apparently couldn't get her out of his mind, some kind of a challenge, although he was married by that time. But she had never gone out with him again, because he was a man who preferred the company of men to being with a woman. Being with a woman to him was essentially only something to talk about later with the fellows. You could even sense that in him, when he was with you. Like Orloffski. A Cornell graduate, he was still very much like Orloffski. He had been built exactly like Orloffski, in fact—except that he wasn't hairless. He had, in fact, been very hairy. Her fingers remembered that. But that other, odd quality was there.

What was it? It was not so much pro-male as it was anti-female. Or rather, it *was* pro-male. Super pro-male. Super-duper pro-male. But it wasn't homosexual. Or not usually homosexual. Just the reverse, the type usually hated homosexuality with a fearful passion. But it was male. Male-to-male. Males together against the world. Shoulder-to-shoulder. Soldier-to-soldier. Male, male, male. Every-thing male. Every-where male. Maybe it was only anti-female insofar as femininity encroached upon maleness. It fairly oozed out of Orloffski. It had oozed out of Tad. Tad Falker. God, she hadn't thought of that name in so long. And Bonham had it too for that matter, as far as she could tell. The trouble with that was . . .

Thick on the edge of sleep, an image kicked its way up into her head, squalling loudly. She tried to refine it and make it sayable, as she pressed her face against Grant's armpit.

It was like the Circle of Politique, she had learned so well during all the dreary, boring years of Political Science at Cornell. You could only go so far Right without becoming Left; and you could only go so far Left without becoming Right. The rabid extreme Right became Leftist; and the rabid extreme Left became Rightist. The Clock Face of Politics. If 12 o'clock was extreme Right and 6 o'clock extreme Left, you could not pass above or below 9 or 3 without moving toward becoming your own opposite, what you hated, your enemy. And this pro-male, Masculinity thing was like that. The Circle of the Sexes. When you became more Masculine than Masculine, you could only become, move toward Feminine. You simply couldn't go on becoming more and more Masculine than before. When you became more Masculine than normal, than 9 o'clock, you automatically came closer and closer to the Feminine. There just wasn't anywhere else to go. Whether you liked it or not. So they *were* all fags together, in a totally non-fag non-sexual physical way. With this clarified in her mind, when she thought of Orloffski it stuck out all over him. His physical vanity, his preoccupation with his own beauty (beauty?), his posing, his preening, his instinctive dislike of women. But my God, did Ron have that problem too? And if he did, what could she do about it? Delicately, she slipped out the tip of her tongue, touched it lightly to the tips of the long hairs of his armpit, tucked it back in, and slept. Grant had borrowed an alarm clock from Bonham, and when he woke her at seven-thirty it was as if she had been used to getting up that early all her adult life.

It was a beautiful day. With the flat, glinting, silent sea stretching hotly away and away like a table, the hot, beating tropic sun in the small breeze, the little boat's ice-chest full of beer and scotch, the multiple picnic lunch the hotel had prepared, it couldn't have been a more beautiful day. The wives of Bonham's three new clients were all hip, chic New Yorker types Lucky could talk to and be at ease with, and with the six of them plus herself and Ron, the two Orloffskis, Bonham and Ali, the little boat was crowded with gaiety and laughter.

But by ten-thirty in the morning she had seen something that was to ruin the day for her, and begin to ruin skindiving for her forever. Swimming around on the surface in the mask, snorkel and flipper Bonham had provided her with and watching the lung-packing spearfishermen down below, she saw Ron—her Ron; her lover—spear a nice-sized fish, and then nearly have it taken from him by a shark before he could get it back to the boat. She could hardly believe her eyes. The fish looked like some kind of a snapper, though she couldn't be sure, and no sooner had Ron speared it than this shark appeared from nowhere and made a grab for it with all his rows and rows of teeth. It wasn't a very big shark, not as long as Ron himself, and it was black and swam with an ugly awkward undulating motion not at all like the fabled lethal torpedo, but still it was enough for her. Putting her head up to yell once, she started swimming toward the boat with her head down so she could watch Grant and the shark. Bonham, who was lying on the surface in a lung not far away looking after his charges, swam over to her, but did not offer to help Grant. With Bonham between her and the shark, she felt safe enough to stop and watch. What she saw astonished her even more, and then made her furious.

Ron was playing with the shark! Looking for all the world like a guilty sheep-killing dog, the shark would dart up and make a grab for the fish, and Ron, holding the spear-gun at arm's length, would give it a little jerk. At the other end of the double length of line and spear, when the dead fish moved, the shark would veer off and flee, only to come back again a moment later. Once when he circled up and in between Ron and the fish, Ron, hauling in on his gun and line, turned back and swam directly at him—whereupon the shark turned and fled ignominiously in panic, only to reappear again in a few seconds. Then as Ron swam on up and closer to them near the boat, the shark, apparently seeing reinforcements, turned away and swam off and disappeared.

When Grant boated the fish ("Mangrove snapper," Bonham said) in the dinghy, unscrewing his spearhead, he was laughing in a bright-eyed, almost drunken way (though he hadn't had a drink) that she had never seen him laugh before. And her fury turned into a kind of superstitious awe and fear. They were both crazy, he and Bonham.

"I was a little nervous," Ron laughed. "Especially when he circled up to me that time."

"You sure didn't show it the way you handled him," Bonham grinned, obviously proud of him. "Was real professional."

"Do you think we can still find him?" He was reloading his gun.

"I seriously doubt it. If we do, we'll never catch him now. He's too spooked. But we can give it a try. Come on."

From beside the boat's ladder, where she kept one hand reassuringly, Lucky watched them until they faded out beyond the circle of visibility. When they came back, they were empty-handed. They hadn't found him.

She did not spend much time thinking about it. She ate the delicious picnic lunch, had some drinks, sunbathed on the cabin roof, swam a little more, joked with the New Yorkers

who were enjoying their vacation. By three o'clock they
had used up all the air bottles Bonham had brought with
them anyway, and so decided to go back in. But whenever
she did remember it, accidentally, then and later, a heart
palpitation of fear would run over her, to be followed
by a fury of shock and outrage.

When she talked about it to him, on the boat's long run
back in to port, he only looked irritated. " He was more
scared of me than I was of him. Hell, even I could see
that."—" But you *liked* it! "—" Yes. Yes, I did like it. That
part. I can't help it."—" But a big one could come along
at any moment."—" I suppose one could. But it doesn't
happen very often. Obviously." She did not tell him what
she was also thinking, which was that a man who may go
down in history as one of the greatest (if not *the* greatest)
playwrights of his generation had no right to go taking
chances with his life like that.

That night they all got drunk together at Bonham's hangout The Neptune Bar with Grant and the New Yorkers
picking up the tab, and Grant insisted on singing *Summertime*
over the bar's entertainment speaker system, embarrassing
her intensely. She did not know what it was, but around
Bonham, as around Doug, he seemed to become an entirely
different personality.

The next day it was the same thing all over again, only
this time without any sharks. Lucky, however, could not
forget that one.

But that evening Doug Ismaileh came back from Montego
Bay. Lucky had not thought she would ever be that glad
to see him again. But she was.

NINETEEN

Grant too was glad to see Doug back again. It was true that
he really wanted to make more dives with Bonham before
going off to dive alone in Kingston, but he didn't want to
have to go on diving with Bonham for ever. And while
his little ruse with Lucky about the cheap room (mainly to
avoid running into the de Blysteins or the Abernathys at

one of the hotels) had worked well enough, he was bright
enough to know in spite of his violent state, that it could
not go on like that forever.

He really was in a violent state. He seemed to have
lost all power to act or think ahead. Something about
that mantillaed she-witch who had been taking over small
pieces of his soul bit by bit for so many years, or so he
believed, had taken all moral force, all will out of him.
It was ridiculous that he should be so concerned over his
moral responsibility to her, when she so obviously didn't
give a damn about any moral responsibility she might owe
to him. But there it was. He could no more go over there
alone and beard her in her villa-den than he could take off and
fly by flapping his arms. So he simply marked time, some
mindless will-less chicken, waiting for Doug to come back.
Any gratification he might have got out of his first shark
encounter was more than ruined by this knowledge.

It was strange. Bonham seemed to have divined—and fallen
in with—his " cheap room " ruse almost as if he had been
briefed on it beforehand. But he had never told Bonham
about Carol Abernathy. Had Bonham, then, guessed it?
Doug could not have told him, because Doug had not seen
Bonham since Grant himself had told Doug the story. Certainly Cathie Finer would not have told him. Yet Bonham
had gone right along, conspiratorially conspiring, helping
more than he had been asked to, just as if he knew exactly
what was going on and what needed to be done about it.
Grant was grateful to him, but at the same time it oddly
irritated him.

When Doug pulled into the front yard in his own rented
car that evening, they were all sitting out in the back yard
around the barbecue where Bonham was making ribs again,
his contribution to Grant and the three New Yorker fellas
(as he said) for the dough they laid out on the party at The
Neptune last night. It must have cost him a buck-seventy-five,
five bucks if you counted the beer. Of course, they all knew
he didn't have much money. Grant and one of the New
Yorkers had brought whisky. Grant was grateful for the
New Yorkers. Lucky liked them, and they helped to keep
her occupied. Slyly, he had noted that the three New York
males had taken a great shine to Bonham, with the same
almost boyish hero-worship he and Doug sometimes showed

for the big, tough diver. For no good reason, Grant made a mental note and filed it away in the grab-bag part of his mind where he kept his future material.

There was more of the Haw!-ing and hooting and back-pounding and arm-punching from Bonham and Orloffski, under which Doug who was almost as big as they stood up at least as well as Grant. Lucky's face showed her disdain for this physical-pounding kind of greeting, Grant noted. Then Lucky, who was sitting on an old hewn-log bench with the three New Yorker women, leaped up and ran over and gave Doug her own kind of greeting, which was to throw her arms around him and give him a big kiss as if he were her long-lost brother. Grant felt an irritational but none-theless powerful twinge of jealousy move slowly all through him and then run on out of the ends of his fingers and toes. By the time he grasped Doug's hand in his own all vestiges of the twinge had departed.

Later on in the evening, in the night rather, as they all sat around with cigarettes butts glowing like echoes of the glowing, dying fire in the barbecue, when they had drunk sufficiently, Doug joined Grant in some close-harmony sing-ing of old cowboy songs like *The Streets of Laredo*, com-moner folk ballads like *Down in the Valley*, and songs they had marched to in the war like *I've Been Working on the Railroad* and *For Me and My Gal*. To Grant's surprise this time instead of being angry Lucky joined in. She knew all the songs. And she had a clear, perfectly pitched, not very strong soprano which was somehow very moving because of some oddly defenceless little-girl quality in it. But before any of this pleasant, illusory immortality got started Grant had already discussed with Doug and decided what he was going to do to-morrow about Carol Abernathy.

He approached Doug while Doug was talking to Lucky. Lucky had left the three New Yorker women and gone off with Doug to sit on an old beat-up wrought-iron loveseat, and as he came up to them he overheard Doug wryly and ruefully talking to her about Terry September. When he stopped in front of them they both looked up and smiled.

"What the fuck's going on here?" he growled with a lot of mock anger. But underneath that, he was childishly jealous.

Doug looked up at him, shrewdly. "I was just tellin'

your Old Lady here that I think I'm fallin' for Old Aunt
Terry September. I'm gonna look her up when I go up to
New York."

"If it's private I'll leave, if you want," Grant offered, but
suddenly felt melancholy.

"Horse shit!" Doug said.

"Are you kidding?" Lucky said.

"What I really came over for was to ask you what you
think I ought to do about old Mom. Our 'Mom'." He
twisted the word. "Would you be willing to go over there
with me to-morrow while I tell her I'm going off to Kingston
with my sweetheart here?"

"Why, sure," Doug said after a moment. "Sure I would.
I reckon. I guess my heart can stand the strain. And two
targets is always better than one. If your side's the side
gettin' shot at. *One* may survive."

"What is it about this weird woman?" Lucky said. "Are
both of you so terrified-scared of her?"

Doug grinned. "No, we ain't scared of her."

"Well, what is it then?" Lucky said. "What's the hold
she's got over both of you? What's her power?"

"There's no denyin' she's got somethin'," Doug said. "I
wisht I knew what it was." He grinned cheerfully, with
his large, mug's face. He was playing up heavy the lousy
English to-night, whatever it was his mood was. "I guess
it's because she believes—*believed*, in you when everybody
else didn't and thought you were fucking nuts to ever want
to be a playwright." He shrugged.

"What do you say?" Lucky turned to Grant.

"You know about me," he said. "They practically supported me. Did support me. I feel like I'm adopted by
them."

Doug grinned. "Unfortunately, she's got this thing about
her boys. This fixation. She believes that every female in
the world is out to marry them for their money—after she
helped make them successful."

"Well, maybe they are," Lucky said. "So nu? What's
wrong with that? Men shouldn't get married?"

The *So nu* brought back to Grant suddenly New York,
Leslie, the little apartment, all the days he had spent there
so happily, with a painful, pleasant rush.

"It certainly is strange," Lucky said. "Two grown men

running around like a couple of dogs with their tails between their legs, whenever they have to think of going to talk to this weird woman." She sniffed.

Doug grinned at her and shrugged, and Grant broke in on her. "You'll go with me then?"

"Sure." Doug looked up at him with all the innocence on his face of a totally naïve man who has never told even half a lie in his life. "I'll help you tackle old 'Mom'." He too twisted the word.

So it was decided. They would go to-morrow. "Come hell or high water," Doug grinned. And Lucky was apparently none the wiser, was completely taken in, accepted totally their untrue evaluation. She would wait for them at Bonham's. But first they made the next day's morning dive with Bonham. It was the last day for the three New York couples, they were leaving on the evening plane, and meeting and diving with Grant and Doug had been the big "Extra" of their whole vacation and they wanted them to come. Also, Doug wanted to go out with Bonham one more time, because after Grant and Lucky left for Kingston he was heading back for Coral Gables and then on to New York. For business. But also to see Terry. "What the hell? If you two can be that fucking lucky, why the fuck can't I?" He grinned at them.

The dive that last day, as so often happens on last days of anything, was singularly unexciting. A few fish were taken, they explored around down on the deep reef, the three New Yorkers picked themselves some choice specimens of elkhorn and staghorn corals that Bonham had promised to dry and clean and send on to them, but nothing very unusual or exciting happened and Grant for the first time found himself bored with a dive. He would never be bored with the first part, the dressing out, the anticipation of—what? danger? miracle? something? the splashing back entry, the first singing breaths from the regulator in the sudden stillness, the first look down through the slanting sun rays as the bubbles cleared. But once on the bottom he found there was little to do that he hadn't done to death, there were no big fish to-day, and so he occupied himself with knocking down with his heavy diving knife Bonham had sold him the long wavy rows of fire coral which grew profusely on the reef and could give a diver a seriously pain-

ful sting. And when he finally surfaced and poked his head
out into the bright, hot, penetrating Caribbean sunshine he
could not help wondering for a moment what the hell he was
doing here? Then he ducked back under and with a now
smooth expertise unstrapped and shucked the bottles off over
his head while still breathing from the regulator, took one
last look down into the mysterious realm which was no
longer so mysterious when you were down there, and handed
the rig up to Ali.

He would have been surprised, as he climbed the little sea
ladder to where the New Yorkers had already congregated
sadly after their last dive, to know that Lucky and Doug
while he was futzing around unhappily down below had had
a long, very serious conversation about him. He would
probably not have been so surprised to learn that Lucky
had in doing it, as she had with the Aldanes, and most of
the rest of his friends, acquired another ardent partisan in
Doug.

Lucky was a little surprised by it herself. She did not
believe in having heart-to-heart talks about people with their
intimates. It always made for bloodshed, and it was indeli-
cately unprivate. So she was surprised to be doing it. Looking back later, she was able to understand that it was Doug
who broached the whole thing, and to place exactly the point
of conversation where he had done so.

The two of them, not diving, had snorkelled around on top
for a while close to the boat, like the New Yorkers' wives.
Having seen what she had seen down below Lucky had no
desire at all any more even to swim in the sea, and had to
force herself to it. With Doug or Bonham or someone like
that with her she was willing to snorkel around a little bit
as long as she stayed close to the boat, but Doug wanted
to follow the divers so she climbed back on board and
stretched out on the blinding white cabin roof to sun.
Sometime later with her eyes shut against the sun she felt
someone come forward and sit down beside her on the edge
of the towel she had spread on the hot cabin roof. It
was Doug.

" Got tired of following after them," he said in a somewhat
dejected voice.

Lucky moved over to make more room for him. She always

felt ticklish and uncomfortable about her boy-friend's friends possibly touching her. " I wouldn't do it for anything."

" I just wish I could do it," Doug said morosely.

" Oh, I don't mean diving," she said. " I mean just snorkelling along after them. Away from the boat."

Doug laughed. " You're a girl."

" Well, I hope so! Built like I am. I'd sure make a funny boy."

Doug laughed again, more so, this time throwing back his head. " You sure as hell would." For several moments he plucked at the towel edge irresolutely. " But I didn't come up forward to bother you with chit-chat. There's something I wanted to talk to you about, and tell you."

Lucky turned her head to look at him in the bright sun but didn't answer, squinting her eyes behind the dark glasses against the light. Doug's mug's face stared back at her with great seriousness from the towel's edge. But when he began to talk, he looked away and down. " See, I've known Ron quite a while now. Almost four years. I think I've formed a pretty accurate impression of him by now." There was none of his deliberately lousy English now. " I think he needs a woman. His own woman. A wife. He's not like me: I'm the kind of guy, I'm fairly certain, who'll never find that; and I've accepted it." He looked sad, but Lucky for some reason could not believe in it. " I'm uh I'm trying to say I think you ought to marry him."

" What do you think I'm down here trying to do?" Lucky said, a little too thinly she thought.

But Doug nodded. " He's really quite a guy, Ron is. He takes to this diving stuff like a duck to water. As they say. He's as brave as a lion I guess he's probably the best man I've ever met. Physically, mentally, and uh and morally: spiritually. The best."

" Well, don't expect me to disagree with you." she said. " I'm in love with him." Big compliments to anyone always made her slightly uneasy and embarrassed.

" So it's a shame. If he had only been bigger," Doug concluded, " he could have been a great athlete "

Lucky could hardly believe she'd heard right. " A great athlete! My God! Who in hell wants to be a great athlete?" Tad Falker. My God; Tad Falker.

" Just about every American—every *man*—who ever lived,"
Doug said.

" More than being a great writer?"

" Well, of course, there's that. But of course it's possible
to be both."

" Like who?"

" Oh, I don't know. Like Byron, maybe. Even Hemingway maybe, in a small way."

" Well, I think the two are basically incompatible. In-
trinsically," Lucky said flatly.

" Maybe you're right. Of course that could be called a
typical woman's viewpoint." It was a sort of polite sop, with
a back-handed slap tacked on. He plucked at the towel
edge again for a little while. " Anyway, I know that knowing
him the few short years I have has completely and totally
changed my whole life."

Something about the way he said that, that last, sounded
stilted and false and irritated Lucky. " What about this weird
woman? This Mrs. Abernathy?" she said thinly. " I thought
it was her who changed your life."

Doug plucked at the towel. " Well, she's helped me some
of course." He paused. " But she's not really very intelligent, you know. And Ron says she's gotten worse and worse
over the years. I've seen it myself, a little. She uh she sort
of makes me think of all those old cunts. Susan B. Anthony,
Elizabeth Stanton, old Mary Walker, Lucy Stone."

" All the old lesbians."

" Well if *you* want to put it that way, yes I guess. She
certainly hasn't got much sex in her, I don't think. And
she doesn't much like men."

" And yet all you fellows buzz around her like flies
around some goddamned honeypot."

" No, and that's what I wanted to tell you," Doug said.
" Don't think that about Ron. Because it won't be true.
He's his own man, believe me."

" I hope so. I hope I wouldn't fall in love with anybody
who wasn't," Lucky said.

Doug was staring at her, and suddenly he gave a twisted
lopsided grin. " You're quite a gal.

" Look. The old gal—Carol—' Mom '—is hipped on all
this mystical and metaphysical stuff. That's been going on
for eight years. She stumbled on to some book called

Hermes Trismegatus in some New York occult bookshop and that started her off. And now she's developed this theory, which is not original, that any artist or creative genius diminishes his vital energy, his force, his genius whenever he marries and takes on a wife and family."

"It's not hard to see why she chose to believe that," Lucky said.

"Sure. She even goes so far as to say that every time you get laid, have an orgasm, and use your sexuality, don't sublimate entirely, you're diminishing your creative power. And maybe there's some truth in it. I don't know. How do I know? Hell, Gandhi believed it. But Ron's not like that. And neither am I."

"My God!" Lucky said. "I should hope not."

Doug grinned a crooked grin. "Just the reverse, we're probably the two most oversexed guys anybody'll ever meet. Anyway, Ron's at the stage of his career and life right now where he needs to get away from her, break her influence. He's *broken* her influence; but he's very loyal. The only thing that can break his loyalty to Carol and Hunt is a greater loyalty. And only love can give him that."

"Well, that's exactly what I'd like to give him."

Doug nodded crisply. "Right. And between us, you and me, we can probably make him the greatest playwright America's ever seen."

Lucky was first astonished, then shocked. "Yes? What would *you* do?" she said faintly.

"Oh, be there when he needed me."

She felt this to be incredibly presumptuous. For several moments she didn't answer. The white-hot sun beat down on both of them pulsatingly. She felt completely at sea, caught and pulled by currents and counter currents she couldn't understand.

"Well look, Doug," she said finally, and somewhat faintly, she noted. "I don't give a good goddam about any of all this stuff. All I know is I'm in love with Ron. I like him. I respect him. I admire him and what he wants to do. And what's more, I trust him. And so, I'm going to fight for him. Any goddam way at all that I can. I'll fight Mrs. Abernathy, and her husband, and you too, and anybody else that'll try to keep me from marrying him, if they do try. Anybody.

If you're on my side in that, okay. If you're not, that's okay too."

Doug was grinning at her with his twisted lopsided grin. It made his eyes appear smaller than usual. " You're the kind of a girl any man in his right mind would give his right arm for," he said huskily.

" I don't want any right arms. And I don't want to make a ball collection. I've only been in love twice in my life before now. And both times I was so young and so green, and so cocky, that I couldn't *be* in love. So in effect this is the first time I've ever *really* been in love. Nobody's going to make me give that up if I can possibly help it."

Doug got up. " Anything I can do to help. And now I better be getting back aft. They'll be coming up pretty quick. And I don't want Ron to see me up here talking to you."

" Why not?"

He paused at the edge of the cockpit roof and windshield, which came up just to his chest, and looked back at her over it. He was grinning again his lopsided strangely twisted grin that made his eyes look smaller. " Didn't you know? Ron's a very jealous man."

For several seconds in a kind of continuing silence which she could not bring herself up out of to speak, like a sudden lull after a heavy wind, Lucky watched him walk away from her without her answering his parting shot, though she was trying to. Then it was too late and he was gone. What did he mean? And what was he trying to imply? Her mind was an utter blank and she realised her mouth had fallen open.

Later on she watched Doug go up to Grant after he had handed up his aqualung and climbed in over the side. Doug began to talk to him smiling and laughing, patting him on the back. There was this strange feeling that in some odd way Doug was trying to usurp, or had usurped, her man. Then she looked at Ron. Jealous? Could he really mean he believed Ron could be *that* jealous? To suspect something between his girl and his best friend, if he just saw them talking alone together? And if he didn't mean that, what the fuck did he mean? She was suddenly angry.

She would have been more angry if she had known the import of the so laughing and smiling conversation Doug was having with Grant. The gist of this was that he, Doug, had just spent a long time up forward talking to Lucky and that as a result he had fallen in love with her all over again.

Grant, on the other hand, didn't think anything about it one way or the other, and merely grinned and went on with whatever he was doing, which at the moment was getting himself a cold beer out of the ice-chest. He was now so much in love with Lucky himself that he actively expected all his friends to fall madly in love with her, except possibly, perhaps, the two Abernathys! So when he brought the subject of Doug up to her later in the afternoon when they were shopping for hamburger meat, it was because of something entirely different Doug had said.

Standing beside him at the ice-chest, getting a beer for himself, Doug said, grinning: "And I don't think she tumbled to our little routine about Carol at all. Not even a little bit."

·That angered Grant. He didn't want a conspiracy between himself and Doug against Lucky. He wanted help, he needed it, temporarily. But that wasn't anything you talked about. Straightening up, putting on his face a narrow-eyed squinting stare as if against the sun, he fixed Doug with it. "I'm glad. But I don't think you and me ought to talk about it."

"Of course, you'll have to tell her eventually, some time."

"I intend to tell her about it eventually, some time. But I intend to tell her in my own time. When *I'm* ready," he said flatly.

Doug had ducked his head and nodded. "Of course."

"And whether you go over with me to see Carol or not, that part of it isn't any of your business, I don't think."

Doug said: "Of course it's not."

"Then just don't forget it."

Throwing his head back, he had taken a long-swallowing, silent, pregnant-with-meaning drink from the neck of his open beer bottle. Curiously, almost ludicrously, Doug had done exactly the same. And it was this little exchange which later prompted him to say to Lucky what he said about Doug, later when they were shopping for hamburger meat.

They were shopping for hamburger meat because, partly to avoid spending money sillily, partly because she had

come to dislike intensely Bonham's hangout The Neptune
Bar, Lucky had suggested she make her spaghetti bolognese
for them all to-night at Bonham's house. The New Yorkers
were leaving too soon to take part, but the suggestion was
met with enthusiastic approval on board on the run back
in, approval almost bordering on the wild in the case of
the almost-idiot Orloffski who whooped joyously and almost
jumped overboard to show his pleasure. Bonham was
pleased too, but pointed out that almost certainly none
of the ingredients including the canned Italian tomatoes
Lucky wanted would be available at his house, and this was
not one of his wife's days off. So Grant and Lucky were
shopping.

Grant could not have *not* gone with her. She didn't know
her way around, she was not used to driving on the left side,
a whole bunch of things. But the thought *of* going made him
exceedingly nervous as he drove them down. It was, in fact,
the first time they had been into the town together, except for
The Neptune Bar at night, which was on the other, inland
side of town and on the outskirts, anyway. And sure
enough, after he had parked, and just as they were approaching the " New " Chinese Supermarket, " New " meaning it had been started six years ago, the first in Ganado Bay,
they ran head-on into Evelyn de Blystein and her fat Jamaican maid coming out of it, shopping also.

Grant introduced them.

" Well," the Countess Evelyn said in her gravel voice,
studying Lucky with her sharp, perpetually squinted eyes
and all of the great, dedicated gossip's relish, " So this is
Ron's new Girl Friend I've been hearing so much about.
Hello, my dear."

Insanely for a moment Lucky felt like curtsying. Instead
she stuck out her hand. Evelyn took it and then patted it
with her other seamed, veined, immaculately turned-out hand.
" My dear, you *are* Lucky, you've picked yourself a guy
who obviously has great taste in girls."

Grant could almost hear her smacking her lips. But in spite
of that he somehow knew she was on his side. Something
dirty in her eyes made him know he had an ally here. He
took the bull by the horns and told her they were leaving
to-night for Kingston for two weeks.

The Countess smiled narrowly and with pleasure with her

eyes. " I suggest you stay at the Sheraton," she said. " *All*
the bedrooms *there* are air-conditioned. And please think once
or twice of dear old Auntie Evelyn while you're having uh
fun.

" Bye-bye, children."

" That's the Countess where your Mrs. Abernathy's staying?" Lucky said, unable to resist looking back at her. Evelyn
was looking back at them. She waved. Lucky waved back.

" Yes," Grant mumbled.

" I would certainly say that you have an ally there,"
Lucky said. Then she laughed. " Or rather, I would say
that certainly *I* have an ally there!"

" If you mean," Grant grinned, " that she would recom-
mend to you that you marry me, I'm not so sure."

" I think she would," Lucky said and impulsively took his
arm, at which gesture he was unable not to glance nervously
around. In spite of that he was proud, idiotically, insanely
proud, at having had the chance to show her off to Evelyn.

Evelyn had mentioned Doug, how was he, and it was this,
as they walked on toward the " New " Chinese Supermarket,
that reminded him to tell her about Doug what the little
incident at the ice-chest had made him decide he wanted
to tell her about him.

" Incidentally, since she mentioned Doug, it reminded me
there was something I wanted to tell you, straighten you out
on about him."

Lucky's ears got alert. She was remembering Doug's
jealousy speech. Was this it, now? " Yes?" she said.

" It's true he's a friend of mine. A good friend. But he's
very strange in a lot of ways. He loves to put his nose in
everybody's everything. He likes to manipulate people, be
a Svengali. He thinks he's a great behind-the-scenes manager. There's a lot of things about him I don't trust, and
I don't want you to trust him completely. Don't think
that I do."

Lucky waited. And as she did she felt anger growing
in her head making her ears hot. What kind of cheap
cowardly beating-around-the-bush was this? " Yes?" she
said again finally when he didn't go on, but this time with
more tension.

" That's all. I wanted to warn you. There's a lot of things
about him that just aren't straight."

" Like what?"

"I can't go into it all right here, now. But for one thing, he's got a real thing about me, fixation, in some strange way."

" Are you trying to tell me—in some roundabout way—that he might try to make me?" Luck said flatly.

"What?" Grant said. "No." He paused. "Well, yes. Maybe he might, at that." He paused again. "No. No, I don't think he'd do that. But he——"

" Because you certainly picked a hell of a fine time to tell me after leaving me around in his company so much for the past five days."

"Whaf?" Grant said. "What do you mean?"

" Also, I find it somewhat peculiar, this way you have of picking for your ' best' friends people whom you can't trust not to try to make your girl the moment you turn your back." She was furious and her ears were burning.

"Hey, now just wait a minute! *That* wasn't what I was——"

" In addition," she went on, interrupting again, "I must tell you I find myself considerably insulted that you feel you need to explain this to me and warn me, that you do not trust me enough to know beforehand I would take care of such a thing automatically."

Grant stopped in the middle of the street, for all the world like some goddamned mule. " Aw, come *on!* I don't need that kind of shit about *that!* I didn't say one damn thing about——"

" Whether you know it or not," she said, but feeling foolish now, which only made her more furious, " and whatever you may think you know about me, I am not the kind of girl who generally makes a practice of going out with more than one man at a time." This was not strictly the entire truth, she reflected, but it was near enough to it to be *truthful*.

Grant was still standing in the middle of the street. " Now just *shut up* a minute!" he commanded, and he didn't say it quietly. Several incurious Jamaican folk glanced at them briefly. "I don't know what got you off on *this*. But you misunderstood me. Anyway, this is not the time or place for this kind of a discussion. If you want, I'll take *that* up with you later. Right now we're supposed to be shopping. There are people all around looking at us."

" Largely because you don't know how to talk quietly!"

Lucky said furiously. He had planted himself solidly in the street, and his irises were blazing behind narrowed lids. " Just shut *up*!" he hissed, and grabbed her arm and hustled her inside the supermarket. God, he was really beautiful when he was angry! she thought as he pulled on her arm.

The icy cold stiffness between them that resulted from this last move, his dragging of her into the supermarket, lasted all through the rest of the shopping expedition ; and it continued in the car all the way home to Bonham's house. Grant could not understand what had gotten into her, and obviously in her present state of anger she was not about to tell him. God, one really knew so little about anyone else, he thought glancing at her. She had really gotten really mad, over something. At the house he helped her carry all the groceries into the kitchen, where she set about beginning to make her spaghetti sauce without another single word to him. Doug was waiting for him in the living-room with Bonham and Orloffski.

" Well, what do you say we get this fucking show on the road?" he growled as he came up to them, and selected one of the several full, open bottles of beer on the table. He drained off two-thirds of it without a breath. He felt better.

" Whatever you say, boss," Doug said easily. Bonham, Grant noted, was grinning at him—at himself, at Grant— a grin marked by a great deal of relish, and by much more of the voyeur's simply " scientific " interest than of sympathy. Well, normal enough, he thought sourly, but could not be just sure whether it was over his fight with Lucky or over his proposed visit to Carol Abernathy. Clearly, they had been talking about him. Orloffski, of course, was as usual not aware of anything but his own beery self.

" We should be back in an hour," Grant said to Bonham, and grinned himself. A look of something passed between them. He turned on his heel. Then he went back to the kitchen doorway. " I'll see you in a while," he said to Lucky. He did not get an answer.

They took Grant's car. On the way across the bright, sun-hot, dusty, always insufficiently shaded town he thought about that strange look that had passed between him and Bonham, a look which Bonham had flashed him and which he had unconsciously, automatically reciprocated. What did it mean? As he crossed the little viaduct (it could hardly be called a bridge) across the broad flat bed of the town's river, only a trickle now but which could become a torrent whenever a tropical rainstorm hit the hills behind, he felt he was moving into enemy territory.

"I'm going to tell Carol I'm going down to Kingston alone," he said finally as they started up the hill. "She doesn't know Lucky's here. We ran into Evelyn in town this afternoon. But I'm sure, somehow, she's not going to mention it to Carol."

"She's going to mention it to everybody else though," Doug said. "Eventually."

"I don't care about that. I'll be long gone. That I can take care of later. But I think it's better all around to say I'm going by myself. It'll cause less misery and unhappiness."

Doug said: "Okay by me. It's your play." Then suddenly he turned and smiled at Grant warmly. Underneath his smile there was a giggly look in his eyes of excitement over the prospect of the "action" before them. "I'll back your play, Ron. Whatever way you want to carry it."

Grant could feel the adrenalin working in himself now, too. The excitement itself was actually pleasant. "Well, I think that's the way to do it," he concluded. They were almost at the villa.

That was not the way it worked out, however. The way it worked out could hardly have been worse.

They found almost nobody in evidence at the villa, and wandered in and through the great salon and then out on to the terrace, then back in and up the grand staircase toward the bedrooms. They could have been robbers or kidnappers. Evelyn was not around, Hunt and the Count Paul were out, none of the hired help appeared to ask who they were. The place appeared deserted. Carol they found in her bedroom, working. She was editing a play by some member of the Hunt Hills Little Theatre Group which had been mailed on to her, using a red pencil with huge bold strokes which stood out from the page like a series of slaps in the face. She was cutting and slashing and scribbling all over it, as had increasingly become her way since Grant had built the theatre for her. The table where she was working was set against the double french windows, so that all they could really see of her was a silhouette in which the whites of her two large dark eyes showed dimly.

"Well," she said, and white teeth appeared dimly in the silhouette also as she smiled. "The two prodigals are home. Did you have a good time in MoBay? and get laid and all?"

"He did," Grant said stolidly. "Myself, I didn't feel much like it. For some reason. So I didn't."

"Oh, la! My, my!" Carol Abernathy said sarcastically. "Really! Really?"

"I just came back to pick up a few things I left," Grant said. "I'm off to Kingston to-night on the evening plane."

"Alone?" Carol said.

"Alone," he said. "Villalonga is no longer even there, I gather, as I guess you know. But Jim Grointon is, and others are. I understand the reefs are much more versatile there, and there's a lot more of them to choose from. And," he heard himself saying, the first time he had ever mentioned this secret to anyone at all, "I want to try to shoot a shark or two."

"Shooting sharks!" Carol Abernathy exclaimed. "Quite the adventurer you've become already, isn't it?"

"Sure have," Grant said. "I plan to stay there two or three weeks, then I'm off back to New York." He shouldn"t have said that, he knew, why wave a red flag at a bull, but he couldn't help it.

Carol Abernathy laughed. "Oh, so that's the way it is, is it? You're off back to New York, are you?"

"I sure am," Grant said. He wondered suddenly why he had thought he needed Doug to come with him at all anyway.

As if stung by some insect, Carol had jumped up from her chair. Now she seized a blank sheet of paper from the table and advanced on him with it, waving it. "Then there's one thing you can do for me, if you will. Since you owe it to me. I want you to write out an acknowledgement, a dedication, to this new play telling just how much I helped you with it. Since I may never see you again, I better get it now. With you, out of sight is out of mind. And don't say you don't owe it to me."

Grant could hardly believe he was hearing right. His latest play, the one called *I'll Never Leave Her*, she had "worked" on not at all; hardly even read in its entirety; and openly detested—and rightly so, since it was pretty clear it was herself and himself, and Hunt, he was writing about. Even if she had "worked" on it, to openly ask for a . . .

L

"That's what you want, is it?" he said thinly. "That's all you want?" He took the paper and walked with it to the typewriter sitting on the desk at the other end of the room. Standing, bending over without even sitting down, he ran two sheets and a carbon in and tapped out a dedication which was substantially exactly the same words as the one he had written, years ago, when he had dedicated his first play to her and to Hunt sincerely. It took maybe thirty seconds.

"Hell, that's easy," he said bringing it back and thrusting the carbon at her where she had sat back down again in her chair by the window. Then, folding the original and putting it in his shirt pocket, he turned to Doug. "Well, Doug." Doug got up out of the chair where he had placed himself when they first entered. "Come on," Grant said. "Let's go."

"Why, that's nice!" Carol said in a surprised voice from behind him. "That's *very* nice!" There were tears in her eyes when he turned back to her. "I didn't know you really felt that way about us any more! That's sweet! Look, Doug!" Grant could hardly believe she was not being sarcastic, but she wasn't. She really meant it. She couldn't tell the difference.

Doug scanned it and handed it back. "Yeah," he said shortly. "Nice."

"I'll mail it to Paul Gibson on my way out of town," Grant said thinly.

"Listen, I just had an idea," Carol said with an eager smile, "while you were doing that. A great idea! Why don't we all *three* go to Kingston *together*. Hunt has to get back to the business in a few days anyway, and Doug hasn't got anything to do at the moment. Doug and I will go with you to Kingston and we'll make it a real vacation. Just the three of us. The three musketeers of the Hunt Hills Little Theatre Group. I think it's a great idea!"

"I want to go by myself," Grant said.

"Why? We'll go out with you in the boat afternoons, and you can dive. At night we'll eat, and go around, and we'll go out to Port Royal and those other places and see all the historical stuff. It will be fun!"

"You won't understand, will you?" Grant said.

"I could really use a real vacation myself," Carol Abernathy said.

Grant could feel his breath get fast and light in his chest and there was a dull roaring in his ears. " Well, it's impossible, you see," he said stolidly. " My new girl is down here with me. My girl from New York is here, and I'm taking her with me."

There was a continuing silence after this remark. It seemed to go on a long time. Then everything began happening so fast that it was hard to follow it all. Carol Abernathy was staring at him. " Your ' *girl* '!" she screamed at him, twisting the word contemptuously. " Your ' *girl* '! You're thirty-six years old! You sound like a . . ." Then she screamed " Oh!" and jumped up, knocking the frail Empire chair over backwards.

She continued to scream that same sound, that short sharp " Oh!", over and over again at almost exactly regular intervals, say, roughly, three or four seconds apart. It sounded more like " Oh!", or " Ow-w!". It was a very animal sound. She would stop one, apparently just have time enough to think, then just when you thought she might be desisting, do another. Or maybe it had to do with her rhythm of breathing. After several of these, standing half bent over from the waist like a downfield blocker, she charged past Grant toward the door. Her shoulder hit the door-jamb exactly as if she could not see it, but Grant thought that she could. Then, straightening up in the doorway, her eyes wide and starting like a mad person's, she placed her hand under her left breast and screamed at them: " My heart! My heart!" Then she disappeared. They could hear her caroming off first one wall then the other down the corridor toward the stairs, continuing to scream that " Oh!" or " Ow-w!" sound at the same three or four second intervals.

" Come on!" Doug said in a clipped voice, and made an imperative follow-me gesture with his arm. He ran out the door. Grant followed more slowly, listening to her ricocheting down the grand staircase from rail to rail. He arrived at the top just as she reached the bottom, still, he noted, on her feet. Doug was right behind her. She darted left, still running half bent over in that downfield guard position, still screaming " oh!" or " ow!", Evelyn de Blystein had appeared from nowhere and caught her as she rounded the corner of the dining-room. As Evelyn seized her, Carol Abernathy allowed herself to fall heavily to the floor, Evelyn half-breaking the fall. Grant didn't care. He didn't care even if it was a real heart attack. Something cold and calm, cruel even, had descended over his mind. He walked on out of the big front door and got into his car and drove away, feeling rather pleased with himself.

Probably he had been too cruel to her, he was to think later. At the time he had been uncertain of his toughness, so that maybe he leaned over backwards in cruelty. But the truth was it had been easy, the cruelty, easier than he could ever have imagined.

He got the rest of the story from Doug, when Doug came back to Bonham's house an hour after him. He had told them at Bonham's, including Lucky, only that she had thrown a sort of a fit, as he had thought she would. But Doug was under no such obligation to reticence. He told all in full detail, half-laughing and in a kind of giggling, breathless, excited way of a harbinger of truly malicious tale-telling. Real gooey gossip makes bed-fellows of even the most anti-pathetical persons, and soon the whole household was giggling and laughing as breathlessly as he and the feeling that somehow a marvellous triumph had been achieved welded them all solidly together into a band, a group. Beers were passed around. Even Grant joined in, accepting a cele-bratory beer and laughing some himself, though he knew that this was really *truly* cruel. She had lain on the floor groan-ing and moaning and hollering about her heart, and yelling that " Oh!" or " Ow!" every now and then, until she realised that Grant was actually gone, whereupon she got to her feet as calm as anyone present, calmer than the rest of them by this time as a matter of fact, and went upstairs to her room saying she thought she would be all right, it was just some kind of an attack, an indigestion maybe. In her room she had sat down on her bed quite calmly, and then had seized a large bottle of Miltown on the bed-table and taken a handful of them before anyone could stop her. In the fact, as Doug who was almost near enough to stop her saw, there were only seven of the pills in her hand though she tried to make it look like more. A call to a doctor reassured them that only seven Miltown would not really hurt anybody. She was now sleeping the sleep of the dead, the deserving dead, Doug grinned.

" My God!" Lucky said grinning a little shamefacedly. She had forgotten her anger. " To do all that for just . . . And you're not even her real son. Only a foster-son. If that, really. She really must be . . . A little . . ." Her finger went up to tap her temple.

" She is," Doug said fervently.

There was a midnight plane out to Kingston, the last of the day, and after Lucky's big spaghetti dinner that was the one they were taking. Her sauce was made, and while Grant was at the villa she had carefully packed them all up. This had been her peace offering. The bags now rested by the screen-door, ready to be hustled out to Bonham's car in which Bonham would take them to the airport after Grant turned his in. Also by the door was a small, worn, green duffel bag of Bonham's into which Bonham had packed all of Grant's incidental diving gear, and beside it stood a two-tank rig with, unattached, a superior regulator hanging from it, which Bonham had put together and rigged up for Grant in exchange for his cheap equipment he had brought down from Indiana. The tanks had been filled (free) to maximum pressure, and though this was against airline regulations, Bonham had carried full tanks on planes many times and there was nothing to worry about. Down there in Kingston he could get them refilled at one place which handled filtered air for hospitals. Jim Grointon would know about that if Grant wanted to look him up. But Bonham would give him the address anyway. Jim, he smiled, didn't do much lungdiving any more. His bill, which when Bonham presented it to him came to something over $1,000, was for everything: all the equipment he had bought, the trip to Grand Bank, all the trips out on Bonham's boat, all the training and pool checkouts. It was itemised. It was also big enough to give Grant a moment of perturbation.

" You can give me half now," Bonham smiled, " and the rest in two weeks when you get back from Kingston. If you want."

" Well," Grant said. " Of course we may not come back here from Kingston. I rather think we'll go right on up to New York from there. I'm pretty sure."

" Well," Bonham smiled. A kind of hard steely look came into his eyes under the smile. " You can always send me the other half down from up there, if you do it right after you get back."

"No," Grant said, reluctantly. "No. That doesn't make any difference to me. I only get paid on a quarterly basis anyway. Might as well give it all to you right now." He wrote out a cheque on his New York bank. He didn't mind paying for what he got, but he hated to see it go out like that, so fast. The steely look in Bonham's eyes relaxed.

Grant had noted again, in his little talk with Bonham, that more and more lately—he didn't know just when it had started—his mind had come to accept the unspoken, but tacit, position that he would stay with Lucky after Kingston, would wind up with her, possibly, probably, married. This, though his conscious mind balked and backed off from that idea whenever it came up. He picked up his camera, the expensive Exacta V William had not had time to make a case for, and put it with the bags by the door. He was to remember later that he did that. Then he looked over at her standing in the kitchen doorway, and went over to kiss her. From behind her the spaghetti sauce smelled delicious.

"When do we eat?" he asked.

"Whenever you want," she smiled and tucked a hand into his armpit. "It's ready now. All I have to do is cook the spaghetti itself. For seven minutes."

A guy could do a lot worse, his mind was telling him. It was eight o'clock and still light. "What do you say we wait a while and do some serious drinking first?" There was general agreement to this from almost all quarters. It was strange how everyone present now felt themselves to be, and enjoyed feeling, part of a lovers' conspiracy. "Shall we figure around nine?"

So she served at nine. That would still give them two hours to eat leisurely and still easily make the plane. Grant had bought two big bottles of Chianti to go with the spaghetti. Bonham had gone ahead and built a fire in the barbecue anyway, because it looked so pretty after dark. They served themselves from the kitchen doorway and ate out in the yard, most of them coming back a second and even a third time. The spaghetti was delicious. Orloffski came back a fourth time. If they could leave by 11.15 they'd have plenty of time to make the airport.

They did not, however, because exactly at 11.10 the phone

rang. They had all long since finished eating, and were now sitting around inside still drinking the red wine. When the phone rang Bonham looked around and then got up and walked over and picked it up, with his slow drunken movements.

"Who the hell could that be?" he said. "At this hour? Yes?"

He listened a long time and though pretty drunk his face got long and solemn. After a while he asked some short questions, like: "Where?" "What time was it?" "How many people?" "What make of car was it?" Then finally he said: "I don't know. Sure. I'll try. But I can't do anything about it now, to-night, for God's sake!" After saying good-bye he hung up and came back to them. "There's been a bad accident," he said, and rubbed his sausage-fingered hand over his great face.

It was Saturday night and a local Jamaican businessman, apparently on his way back to Ganado Bay from a wild party in Ocho Rios with a local Jamaican girl, had gone through the bridge out east of town and into the river with his Chevrolet. Another car following along behind them had seen the whole thing. They had stopped, but no trace of the car showed on the placid surface of the river, and nobody swam up from it. They had driven on in and called the police. That was the police who had just called. They wanted Bonham to dive to-morrow to recover the car and the bodies.

Bonham rubbed his big hand over his still-drunken face again. "We all know the girl. She was a great sport. She was a receptionist at a local doctor's. But always laughing. Alway out on some party. The trouble is the guy is married —was married—with a wife and four kids at home."

He paused. "It's worth a couple hundred bucks. The County pays." He picked up his glass of red wine, looked at it, and then with a twisted mouth put it back down. His wife Letta, who had only just got home from her restaurant job a few minutes before, came over and put her small arm around him.

"Who was it?"

"Anna Rachel. Anna Rachel Bottomley."

"Oh, no. I thought maybe. It's so sad."

"I've got a lot to do in the morning. We'll have to get the big mobile derrick. They'll have to weight it. It's a hard

dive. The river's about sixty, sixty-five feet deep there,
and muddy. There'll be current. Fortunately there haven't
been much rains lately."

He looked over at Grant, as if just remembering he
was there. " If you want to go along on a real, serious
working dive, here's your chance. I don't know yet whether
I'll have to use a torch on it or not. I'll have to look first.
You want to come along?"

" Not me," Orloffski said. " I'll stick to spearfishin'."

Grant looked over at Lucky.

" You're insane," she whispered, her eyes widening.

" I wouldn't take him any place where he could get hurt,"
Bonham said stolidly. " I like him, and his talent, too much
to do anything like that. I'll be doing all the work. He'll
just be observing."

" You can see I have to go," Grant said to Lucky. " It's
something like this I've been wanting to do since I started.
I may never get another chance like this."

Somewhat numbly, she thought, Lucky got up and went
over to the bags to get one to unpack. Bonham would go
with them down the street to his " friend's " house to wake
them up and ask them to let them stay another night, he
said.

Doug, who did not want to go back to the villa and those
women to-night since the lovers were not leaving, decided
he would sleep on Bonham's living-room floor. That way
he would be right here for the dive to-morrow, too.

TWENTY

The silence was enormous. Only by taking a breath from
his regulator could Grant reassure himself he still could hear.
He had expected that; but only by thinking about it most
seriously could he be sure which way was up and which way
down. His only contact with the entire world really, was the
thick chain to which he clung thirty feet down. It disappeared ten feet below him, and ten feet above him. And
from it some gentle—terrifyingly gentle—omnipotent, ubiquitous force tried perpetually to pull him.

Looking around itself, his mind tried desperately to relate this to some experience he and it might have had together in the past, and failed. Physically, it was a little like being blind, or half-blind. Or, because of the " No Up and No Down," like being an eyeless embryo floating in the womb maybe. Once as a child, to test his eyes, the doctor had put drops in them which dilated the pupils and when he tried to see with them everything was hazy and blurry and would not focus. This was like that. When he put his depth gauge against his face-mask, he could by straining his eyes just barely read the luminous numbers. When he moved one hand away to full arm's length, it all but disappeared into invisibility as a shadow. When he wiggled his fingers his eyes could not be sure they moved.

But emotionally, it made him think of something quite else. When he was five years old his father had tried to teach him to swim in a swimming pool by putting a float on his back and pulling him out into the water. He was all right as long as he could stand on the steps, or hold on to the ledge on the side, but the moment that his arms and legs, moving in the water, seeking, could find no solid material to support him he began to scream, literally scream, with rage and fear. It was sheer blind animal cowardice and panic. No amount of explanation or aid by his father could change it. That was the way he felt now, and he tried hard to swallow it, put it down, down there somewhere in the region of his belly, of his trained abdominal muscles, where he might possibly control it. What in the name of God, really, was he doing here? Lucky was right.

It had all begun auspiciously enough, Heroically, even picturesquely. The bridge here crossed a complex of shallow mangrove swamps, then just as it hit the deeper river channel bent left in a long sweeping curve inland and along the shore to cross the river—a curve the car had failed to make. The big mobile crane, with its huge additional truck of extra equipment and weights, could only be utilised by positioning it on the bridge itself, and it took up a good three feet more than half the roadway. This automatically required a cordon of local police constables to stop highway traffic a good distance off from the work area and then filter the cars one at a time through the narrow space remaining. That already made the whole affair something of an occasion, a lark. Many of the cars preferred to pull off the long bridge, park, walk back and watch. Many other cars, knowing beforehand of the b g flap coming, had driven out from town to watch. So there was quite a considerable crowd hanging over the bridge balustrade or milling around.

Before this audience Bonham directed the positioning of the big crane, after calculating as best he could from the hole in the balustrade the arc of fall the car had taken. A diving dinghy for them to dress out in and dive from was stationed out in the stream, attached by two hawsers to bridge supports to keep it in position. From it a heavy anchorline would be dropped to where Bonham thought the car was. A Jamaican boatman tended the boat. Orloffski would tend for the divers. Bonham's authority in all of this was immense, formidable. Even police inspectors took orders from him. Then they two were dressing out in rubber wet suits because of the chill river water, and then the rest of the gear, under the eyes of the goggling crowd up above.

They had ridden out with their gear in the constabulary's largest police van with the Chief Inspector in charge of the job. The five of them: himself, Bonham, Orloffski, Doug and Wanda Lou. Lucky and Letta Bonham had chosen to stay at home. On the way Bonham had hauled out a bottle of gin under the eyes of the Chief Inspector, helped himself to a large belt of it, and handed it to Grant. " And we're gonna need at least one more of these snorts before we're done with *this*," he said grimly with his storm-cloud smile; " make sure it's in the boat." Everybody drank, including Wanda Lou who was giggling and grinning like a kid on a picnic, the only one abstaining being the coloured rather prim Chief Inspector. But he made no comment. And it was like that with all the rest of it. Whatever they might all think of Bonham, publicly or privately, they needed him now. And he knew it. He was the only one who could do the work that must be done. And he could do it cheaper than any old-fashioned hardhat diver from Kingston that they would have to fly up with his air hoses and compressors and special tender.

In the boat, after the anchorline had been placed to his satisfaction and they were dressed out, Bonham told Grant to go first. In the bow, pointed upstream, the water made a smooth heavy little curl against the forepeak, Grant noted. Bonham handed him a coil of light manila line with a heavy metal clip spliced expertly into one end, a loop of the rope spliced into itself at the other. "The water will be moving you. Look for the anchorline. If you miss it, don't worry. Swim up to the surface to orient yourself in this muck, and swim back upstream to the stern to catch it. Go down it thirty feet and wait for me. I'll be right behind you."

Grant nodded. (He was afraid to speak.) He made a back entry and rolled over to look down, exhaling to make himself sink a little, and saw what he could only describe as a sea of grey skim milk, in which he appeared to be immersed. Then almost immediately on his right, so fast it surprised him, the anchorchain moved slowly past him in a stately way, a shadow-line which he grabbed for and caught. The catch brought him up short, like a running man grabbing a tree branch overhead. The line descended below him into nothingness, and when he looked up it ascended above him into nothingness. There was some light in the skim milk, but it did not seem to come from any particular direction and instead was omnipresent. That was when he first got scared. Only his bubbles mounting gave him a sense of direction. It took every ounce of will he possessed, each time, to haul himself another arm's length down the chain in this cold soup. At thirty feet he stopped and waited, and that was where he still was. Where the hell was Bonham? Peering at the luminous bezel on his diving watch, he read that he had been down here a minute and twenty seconds. The luminosity of his watch bezel was as warm to him and as sane and as safe as a roaring fire in a fireplace. Where the *fuck* was Bonham?! What the *fuck* was he doing here?!

He remembered Lucky had told him practically the same thing about herself, last night as they were getting ready for bed, after they had gone to bed. They had both by now learned automatically to speak in whispers before the thin walls of the miserable little room. "I don't know what the hell I'm doing here! I really don't! You don't want me! You don't want a woman! You want some kind of a movable beast, that you can hop on and fuck, after you've spent the day killing fish, and playing with sharks, and the nights getting drunk with your boy-friends! Then you

want to come home and get laid! I don't like killing, and
I don't like dangerous games, or men who like danger, or
sportsmen! And I don't like you! I like people who are
sensitive, and intelligent, and—and *sensitive*! . . . And *you*
don't want *me*! You want a Wanda Lou! That's what
you need!" He had lain, cold and silent, and heard her out.
He wasn't angry. He was miserable. *Already* miserable,
before she started. Talk about sensitivity! How insensitive
did she have to be not to know he was miserable, already
as miserable as he could get? He hated the thought of the
dive to-morrow. He didn't want to make it. He would give
anything *not* to make it. And it terrified him that he would
have to force himself to go ahead and do it anyway. Of
course he understood her tirade was only an attempt to
relieve herself. After a while, after she quieted down finally,
he tried to explain to her this thing about himself and idiot
courage, lying with his hands clasped behind his head, his
face white and cold, talking in the automatic whisper, staring
at the idiot ceiling miserably.

All his life he had been a coward. And just because of
that, all his life he had had to force himself to do these
things just to prove to himself that he wasn't as much of
a coward as he already knew he was. A ridiculous proposition. And it never worked. So that day after day it was
to do over again   Pride, yes! Proud, he was. But not
brave. Not courageous. That had been his life, day after
day after day, all during the war. Could she imagine living
like that day after day for four and a half years, except
for one or two or three times when the bloodlust got up
in him—what the scientists called " mob feeding pattern "
when they referred to sharks, but preferred to label " heroism " when they talked of humans—could she imagine that?
Some men were brave, and some just were not. He was
one of the ones who weren't. And he had to learn it. If
he could, he had somehow to learn it.—" If you were a
Cro-Magnon man, maybe!" Lucky cried out in the automatic whisper, " back then! But even they had their artists
and their cave-painters, and their shamans!" And they
killed their cripples. Warriors! Hunters! Warriors, warriors!
in the war there were so many who had done so much
more than he had. So *many* many. That was *his* memory
of the war: so many who had done so much more than he

had.—"Every man I ever heard talk about the war said exactly the same thing!" Lucky yelled, still in the automatic whisper. "I knew a boy at school—a man—who had the DSC, and he said the same damned thing! And with that same damned lugubrious look!" Did she think he wanted to make this dive? Finally she had said dully: "All right, you go! Go ahead! But I don't have to! And I'm not going to! I'm not going out there and sit on some boat and suffer agonies! I'm going to stay at Bonham's!—I'm going to stay at Bonham's, and get drunk, by myself!" In the morning she had found she had an ally in Letta Bonham, who didn't want to go either. For the same reasons. So the two of them, since it was Sunday and Letta Bonham's day off from teaching school, stayed at the house, well fortified with a supply of beer.

Beside him a shadow appeared in the skim milk soup, and as it came closer—to half an arm's length—he recognised it as Bonham. The big man came close to him, putting his mask almost against Grant's, and studied his face. Grant pointed to his watch and grimaced inside his mask, and made a questioning gesture with his head toward the surface. Bonham frowned inside his own and made an irritable shrug. Some or other damn' thing had detained him. Then motioning Grant to follow, he passed him, his coil of manila line over one arm, and started on down hand over hand on the chain. Grant followed, keeping him in sight just inside the circle of visibility, which here seemed to diminish to six or eight feet. It seemed to shrink some as they descended. From below Bonham stopped and glanced up at him once questioningly, a dim apparition, the mask appearing to be one huge Cyclopean eye in the middle of his great head. Grant had seen blind newts, eyeless, in caves in Kentucky. It must have been like this for their remote ancestors, when they began to lose their un-needed sight. The pervasive current had by now become such a part of his existence that his body automatically allowed for it in its movements, a sort of horizontal gravity along which at any moment he could fall.

Bonham wasted no time at all. On the bottom where the heavy anchor rested on what appeared to be mud-silted rock, he clipped his manila line on to a link of the anchorchain ten feet up, motioning Grant to watch. The other end with the loop he made a slipknot out of by pulling the rope back through the loop, and snugged this up tight over his right armpit. Then motioning Grant to stay where he was, he took the coil of line in his left hand, let go of the chain and began paying the coil out with his right. Motionless except for his hands, his head toward Grant, he began to move away from Grant backwards, carried downstream by the current. Once, at just about the outer limit of Grant's visibility, he stopped and swam off to his left, then back and off to his right, for all the world like the huge pendulum of some strange horizontal clock swinging in a horizontal gravity. Then he disappeared into the world of skim milk.

Grant watched the rope, hanging on to the chain with one arm, feeling very helpless, very much the neophyte. Twice more it did its pendulous arcing search, then Bonham reappeared in the murk, calmly recoiling the rope as he pulled himself back to the chain. By his gestures he communicated that the car was too far away to work on, that they would have to move the dinghy and anchorchain. Then, almost as an afterthought, he tapped Grant and motioned a question: did Grant want to go and do what he had done. Numbly, Grant nodded.

It was ridiculously easy. Lying relaxed in the water, he paid out on his line and watched Bonham and the anchorline fade from sight. He did not have to arc-search, since Bonham had indicated the wrecked car was at the very end of the manila line, and off to the left toward the bridge supports. When he reached the end of his line, with the slipknot tugging securely at his right armpit he swam thirty, thirty-five feet off to his left, and sure enough there it was, about six feet below him. It seemed sort of unbelievable. It had nosed down some into the layer of silt, but otherwise was sitting upright on its wheels on the slight slope. Two bright spiderwebs on the safety glass of the windshield showed where the people's heads had struck. Staring at it, Grant stopped swimming; and immediately the current began to carry him away from it back to the centre of his arc. When he swam a little, he stayed stationary; when he swam a lot, he moved back toward it. He could see what Bonham had meant about the impossibility of working from here. He stopped swimming and let himself be carried. Then he started coiling his line into his left hand. Soon Bonham and the anchorline appeared in the murk. When he was back on to the chain, Bonham motioned that they should go up. Using Bonham's knowledge and techniques he had moved, blind, sixty feet downstream and back, thirty-five feet sideways and back, seen the car, and had expended very little energy. He was beginning to get cold.

Back on top in the boat Bonham gave instructions and then sat and relaxed, breathing deeply, while the boatman and two men on the bridge supports set about moving the boat to where he wanted it. Orloffski changed their tanks for them. They were using the large-size single tanks for this operation, because it was so shallow, but Bonham had brought along a lot of them. " No use having to worry about air too, while you're working."

In the sun-heated air and sunshine the wet suits very soon began to get uncomfortably warm. After splashing over the side to cool off and opening the zippers of the shirts, they climbed back into the boat and Bonham hauled out his gin bottle. "Well, what do you think of it? The dive?" he grinned. " Like it?"

" I can't say I really like it," Grant said cautiously, " with those people in there. Or even without them. But it seems ridiculously easy, the way you do it."

" Experience, kid," Bonham said and winked. He seemed very pleased with himself, very satisfied with his work, despite the tragic reason for it. " We're in luck, actually," he said. " The way it's sitting I don't think I'll have to use a cutting torch on it. Some get so smashed up they look like accordions." He paused and frowned strangely. " But I haven't decided whether we ought to get the bodies out first, or not. Well, we'll have a look first. Hey!" he called to the boatman. " That's about it! Right there! Let off easy now with that anchor!"

Up on the bridge the crowd appeared to have grown, when Grant looked. He waved up at Doug and Wanda Lou, who waggled a bottle back at him. " She set, boss," the boatman said.—" Well?" Bonham said. " Shall we go?"

It would have been possible to say with some truthfulness that it was easier for Ron going down the second time, but it would not have been all the truth. He was prepared for certain things. He knew more about, and how to mani-

pulate, the clip-on lines. He was prepared for the limited
skim-milk visibility, ready to grab for the slow, stately
moving anchorchain as it passed him. But the truth was,
when Bonham said " Well? Shall we go?" like that, he
didn't want to go down again. He had been down there, he
had done it, he had seen the car. He wanted to rest on his
laurels, and stay up here and not go back. But he could
find no unabject way of stating this to Bonham, so silently and
idiotically, he went.

This time the heavy anchor rested about twelve or fifteen
feet from the car. They could just make out its bulk dimly
through the murk as they hung on the chain. Bonham had
judged well in his moving of the anchor. Also, it was almost
directly upstream from the car now, thus reducing enormously the swimming arc necessary to move around at
the ends of the clip lines. Side by side they calmly and
easily drifted down on the car as they paid out on the lines.
This time Bonham had clipped his line on much closer to
the actual bottom, so that as they came alongside one on
either side, drifting backward and peering over their shoulders,
they were just level with the windows of the car.

The window on Grant's side was closed. Peering in, he
could see quite clearly the man and the girl, both black
Jamaicans. Both had their heads thrown back and their
mouths open with a look of sort of wondering stupefaction
on their faces, but the man had slipped and slid down a
little toward the girl while the girl had slid closer to her
window. Grant could look straight down into her face. Her
eyes were wide open ; but he could not tell, further away,
about the man. The girl's long hair drifted slowly to and fro
around her head as the water within the car moved to some
rhythm of its own. And drifting in unison with it about a foot
above the man's head was an object which after several
seconds Grant was able to make out as a pair of women's
panties. This struck him, in the words of some asshole poet
or other, as " passing strange." It was the only phrase for
it. It was also somehow very sad. Looking down, he saw
that the woman's dress was clear up around her waist, and
that from the waist down she was nude. He could see her
navel and the black spiky hair on her vagina. Whether
she had been like that before, or whether the crash and

then the water rushing in had hiked it up, was impossible to tell.

It could not have been more than a few seconds that he stared at her through his face-mask, breathing slowly to the sing of his regulator, but it seemed a long time. She certainly was dead. So was the man. A little fish of some kind darted out from somewhere as if anticipating an easy meal here, then as if sensing the presence of larger life than himself close by, darted away. Then Bonham, who had taken all this in from the other side, came swimming up over the top of the car on the end of his clip line. He had decided, he gestured, to take the bodies out of the car first, and he motioned Grant to go and get the hoisting-and signal-line which they had brought down with them this time and Bonham had clipped to the chain. Grant made a motion as of breaking the window on his side with something, but Bonham shook his head and held up a finger. The window on his side was already open, he informed Grant by pointing and making a cranking motion. And again he motioned for Grant to go get the line.

Grant swam away, pulling himself in on his line and coiling it as he moved upcurrent. He unclipped the extra line at the anchor. From here in this grey gloomy water the car was almost invisible. Bonham was completely so. Grant felt a pang of loneliness, and suddenly realised he was cold. He recalled that, had he not come along, Bonham would have done this job alone, had done others like it alone. Tugging three times which was the signal for more slack, he took a turn of the line over his arm and let himself drift back down, his admiration for Bonham growing.

Bonham had managed to get the door open on the driver's side and to insert himself far enough to get his hands on the body of the man. But he was having trouble with the door. Grant watched fascinated for a moment, then hurried to help. Just as would a high strong wind, or gravity if the car were hanging by its front bumper on a chain, the current kept gently but persistently pushing the door shut against Bonham. In order to back out with the man he had to keep patiently pushing the door part-way open again, then inch himself backward a bit before it pressed him again. Why hadn't he waited on Grant? Grant didn't know. In any case, with him to help it was easier. Paying out a few feet of his line till he could grasp the door, he hauled back in on the line until he held the door standing wide open in the current. Nodding vigorously at him, and holding up one hand in the thumb and forefinger circle salute for: Good! Okay! Bonham went on back out with the man.

Once outside, holding the body firmly in a sort of life-guard's cross-chest carry so as not to lose it to the current, he motioned for the extra line, wrapped it around him under the arms and knotted it in a perfect bowline. Then he tugged four times, and the dead Jamaican, his arms splayed outward from the rope and looking ridiculously helpless, went sailing off upward at a flat angle into the current, for all the world like some dead soul rising to some skim-milk heaven. Ten feet above them he grew dim, then disappeared in the murk.

One down, Grant thought. He was glad he had not had to touch him. And one to go. But then Bonham did an incomprehensible thing. Worming his way back into the front seat of the car—which was certainly dangerous enough in any case, pressed against the wheel like that—instead of trying to get hold of her and work his way back out, he began meticulously and carefully with his sausage fingers to put the panties back on the body of the dead Jamaican girl. All of him now, except from his heels to the tips of his long professional flippers, which projected beyond the nearly closed car door, was cramped longitudinally into the car's front seat.

Grant had noted, while holding the door for him to get the man out, that the panties had disappeared from the former position where they floated a foot or so above the man's head. And later, when he let go the door to pass Bonham the hauling-line, he had noticed that they were stuck into Bonham's weight belt. They were white and showed up notice-ably. But in the stress of working and of even being down there, he had not thought anything of that one way or the other. Probably Bonham was going to keep them as some kind of gruesome souvenir of the job? But now he could hardly believe what his eyes were showing him, so he peered in through the door. Hauling in a little on his line, he swam around to the front and peered in through the wind-shield between the spider-webby cracked spots. What in the name of God could he be doing it for?

Bonham was not having any easy time of it, either. His big behind was jammed in between the wheel and the seat, and his great shoulders pressed down between the dashboard and the belly of the girl. His chin and face-mask pushed practically right down into her spiky crotch. He could not move anything at all except his arms. And with these he was doggedly trying to get her slippery right foot that was down on the floor through the right leg-hole of the panties.

Grant watched from outside as success kept eluding him. Finally Bonham shrugged his whole tightly pressed body to try and get into a better position. Grant felt a suffocating faintness of terror at the thought of being in that position himself, of what would happen if the big diver should bump his mouthpiece against something and lose it. He would never get out. He would simply have to lay squeezed in there and drown. Even with Grant's help he could not get out fast enough to do any good.

What in the name of *God* was he *doing* it for!

Again the big man shrugged his entire body irritably, and Grant could feel the car shake a little under his hand. Bonham had apparently succeeded with the right foot and was now turning his attention to the left.

But this proved to be an even more obstinate obstacle than the right. Partially this was because his weight pressed down on her in this position he was in and would not allow her legs to come together. To Grant's eye beyond the windshield it appeared grotesquely that even in death this girl was determined to keep her legs apart, a defiant unruly gesture to the, perhaps, whole of humanity.

Suddenly, furiously. as 'f driven beyond normal expectation, Bonham shook his whole body from top to foot rather the way a dog will shake himself from head to tail in separate sections. The result of that was to pop his body up out of the combined pressures squeezing it, and his tank rang alarmingly against the car roof. From outside Grant could only float at the end of his clip-line helplessly and watch. The girl had now slipped down in the seat, her two legs in the air in a position of copulation. From above her, floating against the car roof, Bonham, bending the left leg in from the knee, could slip the left foot through its panty-hole. But more than that he could not do. Carefully he worked the panties up her legs to above her knees, but having no leverage with which to lift her body, he could get them no further. He had made a herculean effort. Looking up furiously and ferociously at the windshield, he motioned Grant violently to get the door open.

Grant, who had just looked at his watch wondering about air, nodded vigorously and then just as he turned to swim back to the door saw Bonham reach back with his left hand and pull his reserve wire! Grant felt no need to pull his own. But Bonham, having expended a great deal more energy, especially in this latest effort with the panties, had also used a great deal more air.

So time was getting important. In spite of that, once he had her outside, which took at least a minute and a half of worming and snaking backward while pulling her, Bonham handed her to Grant.

Grant, hanging in the water at the end of his own rope in the current, and now holding the girl too under the arms so that his two hands pressed her lush firm breasts in their bra, felt distinctly peculiar. He had seen her around town a few times, he remembered now, usually in bars. She had been peculiarly attractive sexually. The bare skin of her arms was very slippery when the backs of his hands touched it, and being so limp she was hard to hold. He did not get any sensation of corpse-coldness from her in the chill water.

The current of course had immediately carried her dress down to its full length at her knees. Bonham was forced to push it irritably back up. He motioned for Grant to hold it. Then slowly and carefully he went about putting her panties properly back in place. He was breathing very slowly now, holding each breath a long time, to conserve his air.

During Bonham's struggle in the car the extra hauling-line had drifted back down toward them in the current, and Grant had swum up for it and attached it to the car bumper. Now Bonham got it and tied the girl to it, tugged four times, and they watched her ascend into skim-milk heaven as the man had done. Bonham immediately tapped his mouthpiece and heaved his shoulders in the signal that he was almost out of air. He took off swimming on a rising angle toward the anchorline. His air of course would come easier as they rose and as it expanded in the tank under the lessening pressure. Then slowly they came up the anchor-line side by side, Bonham shaking his head disgustedly. When their heads popped out into that always-surprising, always-strange-looking world of sun and free air, he dropped his mouthpiece and pushed his mask up on his forehead, and the first thing he said was: "If I'd known it was gonna be that hard, I wouldn'a done it."

"But why . . ." Grant began, dropping his own mouthpiece and pushing up his own mask. He got no further because Bonham motioned him to silence, jerking his head toward Orloffski and the boatman in the boat above them.

Another small boat was just taking off the girl's body, as they climbed in. Up above on the bridge the crowd watched in silence. The men in the other boat had immediately wrapped the body in a blanket as if they didn't want to look at it, as if to do so would be obscene. Their gesture made Grant immediately think of his own act of holding the dead girl, her two breasts in his hands, the feel of her slippery wet skin. What would those guys have done in his position? "I'd tell you all about it later," Bonham said shortly, and stretched his arms out along the gunwale.

"Tell who about what?" Orloffski demanded bluntly, as he went to work changing their regulators to new tanks.

"None of your goddamned business," Bonham said. "How do you like them apples?"

Orloffski, unpredictably, suddenly grinned. "I like it well enough, I guess," was all he said. "Can't stand to be around dead people, hunh?"

Bonham, leaning back against the gunwale and relaxing, grinned at Grant and then winked openly at him so that Orloffski could see it. "We're down there doin' the dirty work, ain't we, Ron? You want to come down and do the dirty work with us, we'll take you in on our secrets. Okay?"

"I got your message, I got your message," Orloffski said with a half mock scowl.

"Okay," Bonham said. Grant felt ridiculously pleased, and flattered. But then his naturally suspicious mind wondered if this might not all be a put-on act on the part of the two divers, for his benefit. It turned out, when they did talk about it later, the great panty-replacing episode, that Bonham—quite erroneously, obviously—had hoped to do it quickly enough and unobtrusively enough that Grant simply would not notice it. " Besides, I was afraid of losing them in the current, if I took her outside."—" Them? The panties?" Grant asked.—" *Yeah,* damn it! *And her! And/or* her!" Bonham said irritably, and then added: "But I didn't know it was going to be that hard to do!" But basically, he would have preferred that nobody know anything about it except for himself. And the main reason he had decided to do it: and here a simple-minded fatuous look of smug sexual propriety came over his big face: was because of the guy's poor wife and four kids back home in GaBay, who would have to live all this down. It was true that: and here a schoolboy leer fleeted across his face, shredding momentarily the look of sexual decorum: he had taken Anna Rachel out a few times himself, sneaked her out on the sly so to speak, and she was a good kid. But mainly: and here the sweet decorum settled back in place heavily, and stayed: he was thinking of the guy's poor wife and four kids. No gossipy scandal like that ever helped anybody.

All of this conversation took place some time later of course, at The Neptune Bar in fact, that evening, where the whole gang of them sat drinking innumerable gin-tonics and waiting for Grant's and Lucky's late plane to come in. Bonham had taken Grant to another, empty table to make his explanation privately. But by that time Grant had already learned something else about Bonham that forced him to re-evaluate his conception of the man, something Lucky had found out during her long day of beer-drinking with Letta Bonham.

But they had finished the dive first. The last part was pretty anticlimax, after the removal of the bodies, but Grant would not have missed it now for anything.

It was strange, he thought as they zipped shut their wet suit jackets and donned their tanks, but he was at home now with this kind of diving as he was before with the other, clear-water kind; and his fears of last night and this morning seemed ridiculous now. If Bonham had only explained everything to him beforehand, instead of taking him into it totally cold turkey and ignorant, he might never have been afraid at all, he realised, and suddenly shot a glance over at the big man. Bonham winked. And after it was all over and the dive completed, he had quite a bit to say on that same subject of Grant's fears himself.

There was very little to the dive itself. Except hard work. Bonham took with him a light line attached to the big crane's heavy hawser which, when he tugged on the line down on the bottom, was lowered to them. While working on the girl he had thoughtfully opened the other car door window, and now with Grant helping with the awkward, heavy hawser, he simply passed the big metal rope under the frame just in front of the rear wheels and hooked its heavy hook balk on to the line. When he tugged on his signal line, the crane began slowly, very slowly, to take up the slack and lift the car. Bonham had violently motioned Grant away, and Grant knew enough about heavy construction work to know that danger—except for falling objects, or falling people— usually comes when a taut chain or cable parts, or slips. Here nothing slipped and the hawser didn't part. Slowly the car disappeared above them. Bonham, keeping down low at the front where if the cable did part it would probably miss him, rose with it guiding it with one hand until he reached the limit of his clip-line. Then he reeled himself back in to the anchorline and they came up. Back on the surface, they looked at the car hanging in mid-air, water streaming from it with its mashed front end in a long cascade. Slowly the big crane lifted it on up and deposited it on the roadway where the wrecker's haul truck could take it over. The unpleasant job was over.

It was while they were stripping off their wet suits, towelling themselves and putting on their clothes alone together on the riverbank, that Bonham spoke about Grant's fear.

"You're a strange guy," was his preamble. He looked off thoughtfully and then brought his candid storm-cloud eyes back to Grant. "I never saw anybody as scared and nervous as you were this morning, and yet the minute we got underwater you were as cool as a cucumber. With most people it's just the opposite: they're cool and collected in the boat but the minute they get under they start to panic. Especially in a place like this. Yeah, I got to admit you're a pretty rare type. What is it you think makes you so scared beforehand?" he asked bluntly. "Just imagination, hunh?"

"I guess so," Grant said. This was both a rare and rich fare of praise he was receiving, and he felt shy and embarrassed. Besides, his hero-worship of Bonham had gone up another large number of points on the graph to-day.

"That's why I didn't tell you more about what to expect before we went," Bonham said, "in case you wondered. I figured it would be better to show you right there, on the scene."

"It might have helped me if I'd known," Grant said mildly.

"I don't think so," Bonham said shortly. "Anyway, you're a pretty goddamned good man, *I* think," Bonham went on placidly. "Over-rich imagination or no. When you're down there, you put out when it counts. Just between you and me I wouldn't have trusted Orloffski not to get panicky on that job."

Grant coughed in his embarrassment and lit a cigarette. He was already dressed and standing waiting for Bonham to don his tent-sized shirt. "I didn't really do anything though," he said.

"Oh yes you did. And you did exactly what we needed just exactly when it was needed. If you weren't already rich, and didn't have a compulsion to go on writing them damned lousy plays," Bonham grinned, "I'd offer you a job to work for me——"

"—and I'd have taken it," Grant put in.

Bonham jutted his chin. "Come on, let's get back up to that fat old Chief Inspector's paddy wagon."

Grant followed him up the long steep bank toward the road. In spite of his embarrassment, he was feeling pretty expansive, pretty cocky. He was, in fact, exactly like a kid whom the coach had bragged on in front of the rest of the squad. And in fact Bonham had no shyness about making his feelings known to the rest of the gang. He told them substantially what he had told Grant about Grant, except that of course he did not repeat what he had said about Orloffski. Grant tried not to bask. Doug's reaction was to grumble again about how he wished he could do the stuff, and then slap Grant on the back. Doug and Wanda Lou were both a little loaded from the bottle they had had on the bridge. "What was it like?" he asked.— "Eerie," was all Grant would say. "But Bonham was marvellous," he added; "I'll tell you about it later"; and both of them looked over at their occasionally mutual hero.

Bonham obviously enjoyed that role. And why not? Grant thought to himself; to-day he had certainly earned it. And that mood, of hero-worship, stayed with him, stayed with all of them, all the way back into town and through the quick lunch of sandwiches they ate at The Neptune before Bonham went off with the Chief Inspector to get paid. As a result, when Grant did get back to the house, and Lucky did impart to him the new information she had learned about Bonham from Letta, it was more of a surprise, more of a shock, more difficult to accept, understand and evaluate, than it might otherwise have been. It was always harder to come down from a high mood of admiration for somebody, and get back into the normal prosaic every-day feet-of-clay way of looking at everybody that one employed usually in one's world.

The upshot of it was that Bonham could not get it up with his wife.

Letta Bonham had told this to Lucky. The two girls on their beer were at least as high as Doug and Wanda Lou had gotten with their bottle on the bridge. They had made themselves sandwiches, but neither had been able to eat more than a bite. So they had played gin rummy and gone on drinking beer. They discovered they had a mutual dislike, fear and hatred of skindiving. All this Lucky told Grant while they were alone in their ugly little room down the street packing their toilet articles and the one little bag she had reopened last night. And as she told him, she gazed level-eyed straight into his face.

There was more than a little triumph in Lucky's telling of it. She tried to hide that, but it probably showed. She had debated a long time whether to tell Grant at all or not. But since he was so obviously, and Doug along with him, getting himself personally involved with the man, she thought it was her duty to tell him. To her, it could only mean that there was something seriously wrong with Bonham. She never had liked him. She had felt vaguely that he was somehow trying to come between herself and Ron. But more than that there was the feeling that he was—how to say it?—that he was "accident-prone," in his personal life if not in his work. Witness his taking up with the Orloffskis like he had. And how could you know that that accident-proneness mightn't lap over, crop up, at any time into the work, his dangerous work? She didn't think that was an unreasonable supposition on her part. And after all, why hadn't he been more successful in his life?

In one way, despite the small malicious triumph, she was sorry Letta had told her. It was better not to know that kind of thing about your friends and acquaintances. She had liked Letta Bonham from the start: an innocent, not very hip, sweet-natured girl. And when Letta started offering confidences, she hadn't known how to stop her. Finally the Jamaican girl had broken down and cried. Of course being loaded on all that beer had had a lot to do with all of it.

"You're a pretty sophisticated girl, Lucky," was how she began. It was between hands in the gin game and Lucky was shuffling. Letta had just gotten them beer. "You—you know a lot about men. More than I do."

"Well," Lucky smiled. "Maybe. Maybe and maybe not. Sometimes I wonder if any woman ever knows anything about any man." She yawned nervously "What time is it?"

"Ten after twelve," Letta said. "They should be finished and home before very long."

"God, this waiting drives me crazy. Do you have to wait like this for Al all the time?"

"All the time," Letta said. "But some jobs like this one are worse. I didn't know it would be like that when I started. But now I love him. But there's more. Let me ask you. My husband won't sleep with me."

"Well——" Lucky said, completely at a loss. She felt logy and half-drunk from all the beer. "What do you mean, he won't sleep with you?"

"He won't make love to me," Letta said anxiously. "He won't—He *can't* make love to me. He can't—get it up, have an erection, you know? I think."

"Does he try?"

"Well, no. He doesn't. As if he's afraid. Ashamed. But sometimes when we're in the bed I touch him. You know? It's always soft. He just turns over away on his side. And yet I'm sure he loves me."

"Well, was he hurt in the war? Or anything like that?" Lucky said, feeling foolish.

"No, no. Nothing like that. He used to make love to me when we were first married and before. But now for two years he hasn't touched me at all. And I don't know what I'm going to do. I thought maybe you could tell me what to do—to make him excited."

Jesus, Lucky thought. There was a problem for you. A real one, this one had.

"You see," Letta Bonham said, falling a little bit into the Jamaican lilt in her anxiety, " I only have one boy before Al, and I didn't like it. But with Al, I like it with heem. I discover I am very passionate girl. And now I just don't know what I'm going to do. I can't talk to him about it. He won't talk about it."

" Did you ever try getting him drunk?"

" Drunk. Sober. Makes no difference. And I don't know what is wrong with me. What I'm doing wrong. I thought maybe you could tell me."

Despite the girl's heartache Lucky suddenly wanted to laugh, thinking of the huge Bonham and the tiny light-boned Letta. Maybe he's afraid of mashing you, she wanted to say, but bit her tongue.

" I probably shouldn't tell you all this," Letta Bonham said. " But you're a very sophisticated girl. And I had to talk to somebody. I can only assume that I'm not just exciting to him any more. But I don't know what to do to make myself more exciting."

" It's hard to tell what excites everybody," Lucky said. " But you look exciting enough to me." And she did, with her full breasts, slim legs and lovely hips. " Perfume?" Lucky said. " No cold cream at night? Don't put your hair up in curlers?" It all sounded ridiculous.

" I've tried all that," Letta Bonham said.

" You've got yourself a problem," Lucky said. " And I don't know what to tell you that could help you."

Letta Bonham was looking down at her hands clasped in her lap. " You don't think it could maybe be because I'm coloured? Part Negro?"

Lucky was brought back, shocked now—really deeply— and angry. " Of course not!" Then she asked herself *why* not? " He would never have married you in the first place if it was that, would he?"

" I don't know," Letta Bonham said. " We Jamaicans don't think much about that down here where almost every-body has some coloured blood except a few English people.

A touch of the tar brush, was what my father used to say and laugh. But Al's American. I don't know."

"Certainly not!" Lucky said furiously. "And Al's not from the South. He's from New York State somewhere, isn't he?"

"New Jersey," Letta Bonham said.

"And I've watched him," Lucky said. "He doesn't have any sense of discrimination toward coloured people. I'm sure it can't be that." She had to believe that.

"Then I don't know what it is," Letta Benham said. "I'm sure he doesn't go out with other women. That I couldn't stand. Under the circumstances." It was just at this point that she broke down. "And I want to have *babies*!" she wept suddenly. "I want children."

"Every woman has a right to have children," Lucky said with as much dignity as she could muster. She didn't know anything else to do but put her arms around the sobbing girl and pat her head. Finally, not knowing what more to do, she went and got them two more beers. And after a few minutes just exactly as if nothing at all had happened or been said, they returned to their gin game.

All of this, more or less in detail, she told to Grant in their grubby little room after she had finished packing for them, watching his face for reaction. She could pretty well guess now, knowing Grant as well as she knew him (but did she really know him?), what kind of a reaction to expect from him: one of embarrassment, and an attempt to minimise or ignore. And that was exactly what she got.

An embarrassed, strangely closed look on his face, he apparently didn't want to look her in the eye. "Well, they've got themselves a piece of bad luck, it sounds like. But I don't see what that has to do with us. We're leaving here to-night. Anyway, we both know lots of people all over who've got that problem. It's not all that horrible, or new."

"It has to do with us in that you're putting your life in this man's hands every day, and at the same time making for yourself a hero out of him. It has to do with us in that Al Bonham dislikes me intensely for some reason, and I'm your girl. He's—He's—It's actually true—He's *jealous* of me with you."

"Aw, come on," Grant said. He was obviously talking

about all this unwillingly. " I do know he's not impotent with other women, anyway."

" You actually saw him screw a woman!" Lucky said.

"Certainly not. Of course not. But I did see him go out with not one, but two hot-looking coloured gals from The Neptune Bar in his car one night when I was first down here. He wanted me to go with them. And he sure wasn't going out to just ride them around in his car."

"God! You better never tell Letta that."

" I don't intend to tell anybody anything," Grant said. " It's none of my business. And I don't intend to get mixed up in it. He wanted me to go out with them that night; but I didn't because of you." He plainly hoped that that would maybe soften her up a little, at least momentarily. But it didn't. Lucky had one further trump card up her sleeve.

" Are you thinking of putting money into this schooner deal he's fixed up with Orloffski and this other man, Finer?"

Grant was completely surprised. "Well, yes. I have been thinking a little bit about it," he admitted reluctantly. " Not much money. It would be nice to own a part of a boat that you could come down here to take free diving vacations on."

" Then don't you think that what I just told you is important information you should have before you make that final decision?"

"Yes, I guess it is," he said unwillingly. " But I don't really see what it has to do with it. And it's embarrassing.— And anyway," he suddenly burst out angrily, " we're not married yet, goddamn it!"

Lucky was smart enough to recognise his angry outburst for just what it was: an angry outburst, and to ignore the implied insult that might have been in it but in fact was not because Grant, stung, had just simply hollered out. She remained silent in front of him.

" I'm sorry I said that," he said after a moment. " But you——" He paused. " How did you know I was thinking of buying in a bit on the schooner? How *could* you know?"

" One of my little intuitions," Lucky said. She grinned and came and put her arms around him. " I love you. You may be a drunk, and a complete jerk about half the time, but I don't even care about that." She rubbed her head against

him, feeling him. "Anyway, that's one problem you certainly don't have, isn't it?"

Grant, holding her and feeling that lush body against him
and sensing again that peculiar and nourishing electrical
contact their two skins had whenever they touched bare, and
which she had told him she felt also, wondered with mild
surprise again at just how much the past few days he had
come to accept the fact that their marriage would take
place. Proximity. Proximity, *and* that electric nourishment.
Was that all it was after all, in the end? Love? "Come
on," he said; "let's get back up there to the house before
they miss us."

As they went out, him carrying the bag, and he paid the
Jamaican woman for the extra night, he could not resist
adding: "But you should really have seen Bonham on that
dive to-day. He was really marvellous."

"And you went off to eat lunch with him without even
telephoning me that you were safe," Lucky countered mildly.

"Ah, honey. It was only another ten or fifteen minutes.
And they all wanted to stop."

"It wasn't a very thoughtful thing to do," Lucky said.
Then she hugged his arm. "Anyway, we're leaving. We're
leaving this awful place and these awful people. That's
all I care about."

But later on, when they had all congregated back at The
Neptune Bar. Grant thought about it. It would have been
such an easy thing to telephone her and just let her know
it was over and they were all right. Why hadn't he?
Partly he was embarrassed to, after how easy the dive
had been. But mainly it was because they were all so excited
over the dive and wanted to talk about it. And he and Doug
were excited over Bonham and Bonham's part in it. He
had spent that fifteen or twenty minutes' time talking to Doug
about Bonham, he remembered. And it had been thought-
less.

But now as they all sat in The Neptune again still one
more time, laughing and drinking and toasting each other
because now the finality of leave-taking was really on them,
they were really leaving, Grant could not keep from watching
Bonham. There really was a difference in his attitude toward
Lucky, though it was so tiny a difference that it was almost
not noticeable unless you were looking expressly for it. His

smiles toward her were always a bit more bitter, a bit
more cynical than his other smiles, and any remarks he
addressed to her more wry, more knowing in some odd tiny
way. It was as if he were saying to himself: this gal is
going to try to take my new friend away from me; and
what's more she's going to succeed; because it's sex. He
seemed to have adopted a slightly more long-suffering air.
It was as if he wanted to say to Grant " Why can't these
goddamned women leave us men alone just once in a while,
with our own interests they don't understand?", but was
being too polite to do it. And whenever Grant did look
at him, he could not get out of the forefront of his mind
what Lucky had told him his wife had said about the big
man.

It was ridiculous and silly that it should colour the way
he saw the big diver and his feats, colour what he felt about
him, he had been around long enough and was sophisticated
enough to take such things in stride, but colour it it did.
Being unable to make it with his wife didn't necessarily
make him more unmanly, but it did make him more neurotic.
Grant had always thought of him as essentially an uncomplicated totally straightforward type of man, unlike himself,
and that had been one of his main hopes in him, one of his
main admirations. And now it appeared that he was as
nutty as the rest, and worse off than some. As Lucky was
so fond of saying: " Sometimes I think the whole of the
United States is totally and completely sexually sick, sick
to danger point." Well, it had been one of Grant's main
themes all his life, in all his work. And now here was good
old simple, uncomplicated Al Bonham in it too, up to his
balls.

It was just about at this point that Bonham, with his
dumb look of curiously smug sexual propriety, took Grant
off by himself to give him his rendition of why he placed the
panties back on Anna Rachel: the wife and four kids
back home. They had all had quite a bit to drink by this
time, and Grant didn't know what to say.

" I suppose there'll be a lot of gossip about it anyway,
hunh?" he said finally after they had discussed it all.

" Sure, but at least this way they won't know, will they?"
Bonham said.

"Well, I guess from all I've heard about Anna Rachel, they'll still be able to guess pretty close. Won't they?"

"But they won't have *proof*," Bonham said. "Anyway I think I did the right thing, don't you?"

"Even at the risk of your life?"

Bonham made a throw-away gesture. "It wasn't that dangerous."

"It could have been."

"Well, it wasn't. And I figure I owed her that. Don't you think I did the right thing?" he said again.

"I guess you did, Al," Grant said, and then saw that that was simply not enough for Bonham. He pretended to think. "Yes. Yes, I'm sure you did the right thing, Al," he added.

Back at the big table, while they were settling up the bill (which Grant and Doug paid), Big Al proposed the last toast: "To your trip, both of you! May it be as much fun for you both as this part of it has been for us!", Then he smiled that curious smile at Lucky. "I got to admit I hate to see you go. This guy's been the best customer I've had in a long, long time."

It was almost as if the big man seemed to have sensed something about what they knew about him. Could he have guessed that Letta might have told Lucky what she in fact had told her about him? Surely not, Grant thought. But he seemed to have on his face that look Grant had seen there before when bad things happened, the set pained look of a man walking down a long, long street in a driving rainstorm and knowing there was nothing for it but to go on, go on and get wet.

It was at the airport that Grant missed his camera, his expensive Exacta V that he had not felt quite rich enough to have William make a case for.

He had gone around to the back where Orloffski was unloading all their gear from Bonham's car, thinking it might be there though he always carried it with him. But it wasn't there either.

"You haven't seen my camera by any chance, have you?" he asked the bullet-headed Pole.

"Yeah. It was on top of the pile of stuff at the house, wasn't it?" Orloffski answered blandly. He turned away to pick up the set of double tanks. From something about the set of his back Grant suddenly knew he had stolen it.

Bonham had a funny look on his face when he mentioned it to the rest of them. Without much hope Grant made another search of the entire car. It wasn't there. They had begun to call the plane. Bonham had once told him Orloffski had curiously sticky fingers, " taking ways," he'd said.

" Well, maybe I left it at the house by mistake," he said finally, lamely. " Will you look for it for me, Al?"

" I certainly will. If I find it, I'll send it on to you in Kingston," Bonham nodded. He looked a little shamefaced. It was a fine note to leave on.

Doug slapped Grant on the back and kissed Lucky. " I'm sure going to miss you both. Maybe after a week or so I'll come on down and stay a couple of days with you. If you want me, send a wire."

Then the commotion took them over. The noises, the pushings, the shoving-alongs, the no-turnings-back-without-dire-consequences, the whisper of shoe-soles and the sighs of the passengers.

When they were finally airborne Grant felt both angered and relieved. He told Lucky what he suspected about the camera, and then kissed her in their dim back seat.

TWENTY-ONE

His big hands palming the wheel of the old Buick, his big feet moving delicately on to and off the three pedals in various combinations as he herded the old car up and over the hill-road from the airport, Bonham concentrated on feeling and enjoying what his body was doing and tried to ignore his mind, which was in a fury.

He was as convinced as Grant that Orloffski had stolen the Exacta. Probably it had shown on his face, damn it. And Grant had seen it. He had no proof but he had seen him do things like that before, up in Jersey. But even if he had proof he couldn't bring it up here in the car with Doug here. And even if he did have proof what could he do with it. Without Orloffski there wasn't any schooner deal, any corporation. Because without Orloffski's cutter and money from his shop,

M

Finer wouldn't go. So his hands were tied. He had to protect Orloffski.

So he sat and drove the car in silence, seething. Beside him Letta his wife sat in silence also, sensing his mood. In the back the other three talked quietly and the gurgle of a bottle was heard now and then. Letta knew exactly what was happening, she hadn't missed a trick. And she was backing him up in her way. Instead of pleasing him this irritated him. *Goddamn it!* he thought, why couldn't women leave a goddam man alone once in a while, why did they always have to try to be inside you, part of you, why couldn't they understand there were things a man wanted to be himself with, handle!

It was such a stupid idiotic thing to do. A stupid $200 camera, not very new. It might very easily alienate Grant from them for good. Stop him from being any use to them at all, with the schooner or anything else. All for a dumb camera. Once up in Cape May at a ships' store house Orloffski had stolen a twenty-dollar brass door-knob when they had gone there to see about appointments for the cutter. Orloffski had shown it to him after they got outside, jogging it in his hand and laughing. That had been like this. For some bit of an object, some cheap next to nothing, he took a chance on getting caught, with the resulting public embarrassment, the subsequent loss of credit, the loss of his local reputation. Bonham wasn't against stealing so much, if you could steal something important and of real value to you, like a schooner, and be sure you got away with it. Only, you never could. But to risk so much for a lousy camera or brass door-knob, it didn't make any sense. When he got him home after they got rid of Doug he was going to read him out good, and if he had the camera make him turn it over. If he shipped it to Grant, it might still save the situation.

But he was saved from this chore by Orloffski himself. Leaning forward blandly with his elbows on the seat back, Orloffski said blatantly from behind Bonham's right ear, " I think your pal Grant thinks I stole his lousy camera."

Bonham glanced back over his shoulder, then back straight in front. " Well?" he said. " Did you?"

" Are you kiddin'?" Orloffski said belligerently. " How could I have? I was right there with you all the time. Hell's bells, you want to search me? I'll stand search."

Bonham was very aware of Doug in the back seat. "Oh, come off it. You know as well as I do that anybody who stole that camera could have stolen it at the house and just hid it away, in the confusion. But I'm hoping it will turn up when we get back to the house. I'm sure nobody we know would steal it."

In the back seat Doug was saying nothing.

"You want to help us look, Doug?" Bonham said, "when we get back to the house?"

"Sure," Doug said.

"You know what I think?" Orloffski said. He leaned forward again, but spoke loudly. "I think it was one of them damned nigger porters who snitched it. I'm sure I saw it with the stuff in the back seat when we unloaded it. Then when I looked around a minute later it wasn't there. But I know damn' well I saw it. Did you see it, Al?"

"No," Bonham said honestly, "but then I wasn't lookin' for it."

"Did you see it, Doug?" Orloffski asked.

"No," Doug said. "No, I didn't."

"How about you, Wanda Lou?"

"No, I didn't see it out there," Wanda Lou said. "But I'm sure I saw somebody stick it in somewhere when we were packing at the house."

"Well, I think that's what happened," Orloffski said. "I'm sure I saw it, and I'm just as sure one of them lousy black field nigger porters swiped it. They're terrible thieves, these field niggers. Ain't that so, Letta?"

"Yes," Letta said. "A lot of the field niggers are bad thieves." It was a great hit, Bonham thought, for him to ask Letta, who cared so much for her bourgeois background. And it was true that a great many of the lower-class field workers, ignorant, uneducated, were notorious thieves and proud of it.

"I don't think we'll find the camera at the house," Orloffski said.

Bonham tried to keep his despairfulness out of his voice. So that was the line he was going to take. "Well, we'll have a damned good look when we get home to make sure." But of course they'd never find it. "And give me a slug out of that bottle you got back there whatever it is," he added despairfully and put back his hand.

"This is vodka," Orloffski said and handed it to him.

A stiff hot snort of the vodka that brought tears to his eyes and warmed his belly, nevertheless did not make him feel any better. Everything was going wrong. Everything was pressing in on him, squeezing him in from all sides until he couldn't move a muscle. Timing was all off. With complete success just ahead of his nose like some damned carrot, he couldn't reach out and grab it. And now this!

About the only thing that wasn't going wrong was Sam Finer and the money. The money had come in two days ago. He had not told anybody about it. He had taken the cheque to the Royal Canadian manager, who put it through for collection and would hold the ten thousand for him without putting it in any account. When they had formed the corporation, here in town, after the Grand Bank trip, the three of them electing him president, it had given him that right. And he wasn't taking any chances on anything happening to *this* money.

At the meeting Sam Finer, who had wanted no stock but only a long-term loan at low interest, was finally persuaded to take two per cent of the stock, as a plain gift, not as any kind of repayment. That had been Bonham's idea. Orloffski had gone along. It left Bonham with forty-nine per cent and Orloffski with forty-nine per cent, and Finer with the deciding two per cent. Bonham preferred it that way because he was pretty sure he could count on Finer to go along with him on any decision against Orloffski, rather than have him and Orloffski with fifty per cent each and bucking heads.

When the money had come in, he had called the marine agent who was handling the schooner for the owners and by stressing that he would pay cash managed to Jew them down from $11,500 to $10,200. On the strength of the cheque the bank manager had given him a thousand to send to the marine agent as earnest money.

Bonham had looked up the owners. They were a small American oil corporation, who wanted badly for some reason to get rid of all their real property quickly so that they could liquidate their corporation. And the schooner, used only for deductible pleasure trips, was about the last of their real property. In spite of that the $10,200 was all he could get them down to. But he did get them to agree to put the boat up for him, their expense. As soon as Orloffski went north to bring the cutter down, he was going to take the money down to Kingston to settle up, and by showing them the cash try to get them to come down another thousand.

But outside of that nothing else was going good. The yard in Kingston had called him to say that the dry rot damage in the starboard bow was much more extensive than anticipated and had even got into the deck planking; that they were going to have to pull a whole flock of hull planking they had not expected. Two thousand bucks wouldn't anywhere near cover it. It would be more like six thousand. And Orloffski showed no signs of coughing up any of the dough he had promised. He was becoming increasingly vague about money, and about the sale of his sports shop. Where was that money going to come from? Bonham had been hoping Grant. He had told the yard to go ahead.

Bonham was pretty sure that some " earnest money " had been paid Orloffski, say three or four thousand, and that that was what the Orloffskis had made their trip down on. Orloffski had as much as told him so. And from the way they were living at Bonham's, and paying so little on the food, there must be a good deal of it left. But now Orloffski denied any such deal had happened or that any such money had been paid, and claimed he would have to find a buyer, find him and sell him, when he went back north for the cutter. And now he had to pull this silly damn'-fool thing about Grant's asshole camera. Just when Bonham was beginning to consider Grant as a serious contender for taking up the slack on the cash lag. The whole thing was damned insane!

Bonham clamped his big palms down on the wheel, and eased the old car around a steeper curve on the dark hill road so easily that his passengers hardly felt the change of direction. His jaws clamped together with frustration.

The truth was, he thought, Grant was an enigma, now. An unknown quantity. Apparently, just now, while diving and vacationing in Jamaica, Grant had chosen that moment to make a major policy decision about his personal life. Bonham was pretty sure he could have handled the old broad, crazy as she was. But this new girl was something else again.

What a hell of a lousy damned place to make that kind of a decision! On vacation!

Despite all her silly kooky politicking he could have handled the old one. No matter what she might say from one minute to the next she was basically in favour of Grant coming in.

All you had to do with her was use flattery and keep larding it on. But the new one was a "diff'rent cup o' tea" as his British pals would say. She was like a she-bear with cubs when it came to her man or, he thought, to her man's money.

Bonham had no qualms of conscience when it came to Grant and his money. The guy had come to him to learn to dive. He hadn't even looked the guy up. It was true Grant was a fast, good learner. But he was teaching him as well and as fast and as safely and probably as cheaply as probably any diving teacher could teach anybody. Probably a lot more cheaply. This girl didn't know that. She should meet some of the other professionals he knew.

But apart from that Bonham simply did not like women like this girl. Too demanding, in the first place. She simply couldn't let Grant out of her sight. Too beautiful, in the second place. Women that are beautiful never had any character. They always expected to have everything handed to them, on a silver platter. Going around showing off those tits of hers and that gorgeous ass so cocky as if she expected every man who looked at her to fall down on his knees and worship her hairy shrine. It damn' infuriated him. Men, at least sometimes, had other things to do.

And he didn't like her language, or the way she went around laughing about all the men she'd had in her life. He didn't mind men cussing and using bad language if they wanted. The only reason he didn't say fuck himself was because he didn't like the way it came out of his mouth. But women who went around saying fuck and using four-letter words like men, and talked about their sex lives as if they were trying to be one of the boys, only made themselves look like whores instead of ladies, whether they were whores or not. Usually they were. He wasn't surprised if this one had been a lez at some point in her hot career. Next to fairies, whom he detested completely, Bonham hated lesbians more than anything, kissing each others' pussies, and all the other things they did. He knew all about it all; that you were supposed to be sophisticated and laugh about it; but he couldn't. Involuntarily, Bonham cast a quick glance over at his wife as if she might be reading his mind.

Living in mid-Jersey, with his old man in his law practice travelling to New York to Baltimore to Washington so much, Bonham going to school up in Montclair had seen a lot of that type of city broad in his time, enough to know them well. How any man could marry one of them was beyond him. And how Grant could marry this one he could not fathom. But he was willing to bet his bottom dollar Grant was going to. And that meant automatically that any friendship Grant and Bonham might probably have had, was out.

They just couldn't leave you alone. None of them could stand to see two men alone together liking each other and happy and having fun.

The first time one of those so-called sophisticated city broads had hinted to him she would like for him to kiss her pussy, he had got dressed and left and never come back. And every one thereafter.

Ah, Christ! It was all going to hell. He had about as much chance of getting any money out of Grant now as of getting blood out of a turnip. He was going to have to really bump Orloffski for some dough now, two thousand at the very least. Well, Orloffski deserved it. He sure did. More than. He had only himself to blame.

In his agitation, in the *sum* of all his various agitations, a sudden deeply peaceful-making thought and picture came to Bonham. He saw the green-blue undersea out on the deep reef, reef coming perceptibly closer to him as he glided down, heard the calming eerie sing of his regulator in the all but silence. Alone. Alone and safe. Because safety was action. It was having to think all the goddamned time that ruined you, hamstrung you. Everybody in the world to bug you with their goddamned personalities or problems, your wife to pick and devil at you with her damned complaints. Complaints about nothing. Well, he knew what he was going to do. To-morrow he was going out to his old shark hole out on the deep reef and kill himself a goddamned shark He'd take the boat, all by himself (except for Ali), out through the harbour and down west to the deep reef, and it would all be there, and everything he saw would be his.

Surreptitiously, he glanced over at Letta. She always seemed to divine when he was going to go shark-shooting. He hadn't told her now for a long time when he went. But she always seemed to know and always kicked up a fuss.

She was a problem, his wife. She had seemed so pure and so fine when he first met her. That was what had made him love her so. Jamaican or not, " touched by the brush " or not, her upbringing had been of the strictest and most Christian kind, the upbringing a girl should have to become a lady. That she was not a virgin when he met her didn't matter; nobody was. What mattered was that she had given herself to him without liking it, because she loved him. He had understood that and appreciated it. Properly brought-up ladies just were like that. Then along about a couple of years ago or so something had happened, she had changed.

A sort of deep unplumbed, unacknowledged gloom settled over Bonham in the car and he glanced over at her secretly. Had she found another boy-friend along the line somewhere that he didn't know about, was that it? *Boy-friend!* he thought contemptuously, *a lover!* Was that what had happened? He could still remember the first time she had reached over in the bed and put her hand on his leg and run it back and forth. Who had taught her that? Where had she learned that? It had worked, of course, that first time. And a few times after. He could still remember it with horror. He couldn't really believe she had a lover. He had checked, in his own quiet way, very carefully. Well, they said tropical peoples, people who lived a long time in the tropics, were more carnal.

But it was just all too goddamned dirty. And it was a terrible shock to find your own beloved wife reacting like the black pigs you ran into at The Neptune Bar like Anna Rachel and sometimes, drunk, took out. If she liked it with you, why not with others? Aha, why not! He simply couldn't help thinking like that. No man could. And that was enough to throw any man off his feed and keep his pecker down. The truth was he simply couldn't stand that rapturous look she got on her face now. With her eyes shut like that it could be any man. "You *like* to make love! You *like* to make love!" he had wanted to shout at her accusingly. Just like the whores at The Neptune Bar. But of course he never had.

Once right after the war, when he had come home still a young guy and unmarried, an old high school ping-pong buddy —who was married—had offered him the opportunity to go ahead and make his, the buddy's, wife. The offer was in private, of course; not in front of her. He never had understood what crazy psychological depths might have prompted such an offer! But him! *him!* he had gone ahead and *done* it! It was horrible. And, more horrible, the wife liked it!

For no reason a picture of Cathie Finer in her swimsuit,

her bikini she had worn in Grand Bank, came into his mind and he felt his pecker begin to swell between his legs as he sat in the car seat. Now there was really a sexy broad, and she wasn't foul-mouthed like this Lucky. And she didn't brag about her hundreds of lovers.

Sometimes he positively hated Letta. How dare she be like all the others? He also hated her because he needed her. And because she didn't realise it, this, and took it all for granted.

In our generation—To-day—we need women and hate them for it. But we *do* need them. Otherwise we'd destroy everything. The world. Women are nest-builders and so they love property and protect it. Meanwhile they use us to satisfy their carnal desires—quite happily and selfishly—while attacking us for being dirty-minded. Well, it wasn't like that in his mother's generation.

Ah, he hated all of it. Everything in life was so dirty. Why couldn't anything be pure? The only pure thing by God he ever knew was his mother by God, that he ever knew. They, her generation, they had been different.

What was she doing right now, Letta? Was she out fucking some guy maybe? While he was out here on the boat working? He got again suddenly that belly-pit excited feeling of inviting cuckoldry by leaving his wife at home alone. It both excited and infuriated him. Then he suddenly realised, of course, that she was sitting right here beside him on the car-seat.

Pleasurably, relievingly, to stop the savage tooth-edge see-sawing of his mind back and forth, Bonham in the car watching carefully out at the fifty-yard cone of light the headlights made, thought about and went back over vividly the last time he had gone shark-shooting.

It had been one of the better days, not one likely to be equalled soon. Bonham had no idea why the sharks preferred to hang around this spot he called his old shark hole. Certainly it didn't have sufficient fish to be called a feeding ground. It was down near the far, western end of the deep reef, about seventy-five feet deep. It did have a natural bridge of coral over a deep sand trough running out to sea through the reef and about ten feet wide. Over the centuries the corals growing out in overhangs on both sides of it had finally met and fused and gone on growing until now there was an arching solid rock bridge six feet wide across the ten-foot trough. Possibly the sharks felt safer resting under this natural bridge between feeding forays, though Bonham had only seen one or two ever actually lying under it. But no matter what time of day or night he went there, there were one or two or more sharks lying up under the various coral overhangs or swimming lazily around the area.

The last time he had been out there, which had been just a day or so after he first met Grant, he had gone over the side with his triple-rubber gun for a look around, leaving Ali in the boat to tend it and cursing his boss for a crazy fool like always.

At first there had appeared to be nothing at all down there. Then he had spotted a small four, four and a half foot ground shark cruising along the trough near the coral bridge. It hardly seemed worth the effort but he cocked two rubbers of the gun.

Then he saw what he had missed before: a Great Blue about twelve or thirteen feet long. It had been swimming slowly over a large mass of dark reef and he had missed it. Almost at the same moment he saw another good-sized shark (he couldn't tell how big) swimming at mid-depth out at the edge of his visibility range. He had been trying to decide whether to go for the Blue with the triple-rubber gun, and this decided him. If the other was swimming at mid-depth he might be hungry. And they might have some fun. Swimming back to the boat he handed up the loaded speargun carefully and hollered to Ali for the Brazilian rig and his Hawaiian sling and free spears.

The Brazilian rig (which was no more than a spear with its free line attached to an inner-tube on the surface instead of to the spear-gun) was always kept ready in a double-rubber Arbalete on these trips. Ali handed it down to him. The Brazilian rig was great for situations like this, or for any big fish you weren't sure you could handle by yourself with one spear. Then Ali handed him down the Hawaiian sling and its three free spears. The sling Bonham slid up over his left forearm and tucked the free spears into his weight belt. If the others didn't want him, he'd get him with those. Then hurriedly he started loading the two rubbers of the Arbalete. Emotion and excitement boiled all through him so that his hands shook a little. Oh the fuckers, oh the cocksuckers! If only they don't get away! But when he looked down, the loaded gun in his right hand, the coil of long line in his left, they were all still there, swimming back and forth and having moved hardly any at all.

Swimming on the surface and towing the inner-tube, Bonham had got above the Great Blue and dove almost straight down on him, the heavy line uncoiling smoothly from his left hand. He held his breath so that the regulator would not sing. But when he was within fifteen feet of him the shark turned and started swimming a little faster, out toward deep water. Immediately Bonham turned and swam away from him, to the shark's left, as if frightened. And the shark turned back, to look at him, but swimming at his own depth without rising. Bonham swam along parallel to him. He was only ten feet from him now. With a sudden twist he turned back and swam out over the shark, diving as he did. The shark turned and darted again toward the deeper water but Bonham was already above him. As he darted by underneath Bonham put the spear in him just where he wanted it: alongside the spine over the gills, about half-way between the brain and the dorsal fin.

Immediately the shark bucked in the water, bending almost double, then took off to run out toward sea. Above him the inner-tube on the surface was pulled under about six feet, but as soon as its drag slowed the shark it bobbed back up again, totally indifferent. Nothing could fight that. Down below a small green cloud of blood had begun to pour from the Blue shark's right gill openings like smoke. Green smoke. Bonham had backed off. Letting the Arbalete hang from its wrist thong on his right wrist, he got the Hawaiian sling off his left and loaded it with one of the spears from his belt. Then swimming back away from the struggling shark and slightly upward toward the boat, he watched.

The bigger of the other two sharks was swimming in from his incessant cruising out at the edge of invisibility. He turned out to be about a seven and a half or eight foot mako. He swam in a cautious circle around the struggling Blue. Then, apparently deciding the fortuitous gift was on the up and up, he darted in, the great grim mouth opening for a bite. Don't ever let anybody tell you sharks have to turn on their side to bite, Bonham thought. He was still swimming slowly and easily toward the boat. Down below the mako shook its head and body like a dog worrying a bone. When it came away a great empty black crescent gaped in the side of the Blue where there had been flesh and hide. From behind him the little ground shark darted in for a bite near the tail. Then the mako, having swallowed, returned. Bonham wanted to laugh so hard he was afraid of losing his mouthpiece and grasped it with his left hand. Go, you mothers! go, you cannibal bastards! Cannibals! Eat, cannibals! Eat, eat! He was almost to the boat now and when he reached it he shucked out of the aqualung and Arbalete and passed them to Ali, put on his snorkel and with one hand resting on the boat ladder so he could get out quick, he put his head under to watch the carnage, holding the Hawaiian sling ready.

Down below the cannibal banquet went on. Another, a third, shark had joined the two at their feast, swimming up the current. The three of them tore at the Great Blue in a kind of ecstatic frenzy. The mako went up and down one side of him like a man chomping corn on the cob. The Blue, still alive but dying now, only struggled feebly. But the driving attacks of the other three as they fed were enough to bobble and sink the inner-tube three feet under.

Bonham was almost as frenziedly ecstatic as the sharks. Hatred seemed almost to boil from his every pore, making gooseflesh rise on his skin. Evil bastards! Evil, horrible, worthless bastards! Cowards! Scavengers! Sneak attackers in the night! Cannibals! He knew they were only mindless instinctive animals but it didn't make any difference. There was life for you! Look at that! There is what life on this planet consists of, all you preachers, all you affirmative yea-sayers! Look at it! And you think humanity is exempt? Ha! They're the worse, I say! Or at least as bad. Trembling from his ecstasy of hate, excitement, revulsion and rage, Bonham let go of the boat ladder and swam out over the struggling fish. He knew it was a foolish thing to do but he didn't care. God, how he hated them. Them and everything they stood for on this earth.

Down below the mindless fish snapped on. The Great Blue was by now reduced to a mere lump of flesh and gristle, cartilage. Only the spear in the back of his head held him there and kept his dead carcass from sinking. From above them Bonham hyperventilated, took an enormous breath then dove down toward them where they were fifty feet down, the Hawaiian sling with its free spear extended out in front of him.

The three of them were so insane they didn't even see his approach. But he didn't get too close. From about twelve feet above, which meant that his spearhead was seven and a half feet from the shark, he put a spear squarely into the head of the mako, then turned and streaked for the surface watching the action from between his feet. The mako jerked as if hit with an electric current, then started swimming all around in wild circles. In seconds the other two were on him. And the same process occurred that had occurred before. Bonham, back at the boat and breathing quickly over his own recklessness, kept his hand on the boat ladder and stayed in the water to watch. Because the mako was not attached to any line to the surface like the Blue he began drifting away down-current, the other two sharks darting in to strike at him again and again. At the rim of visibility Bonham saw the shadow of another shark join the mêlée. Then they all passed from sight.

Exhausted beyond saying, emotionally exhausted, he climbed back into the boat and they went to pick up the Brazilian rig and its line and spear.

"You got one, hunh, Boss?"

"Yeah, yeah. Yeah, I got one." How could he tell him any more than that?

"You crazy. You really crazy. You know that?"

Bonham got out the gin bottle. What would he say if he knew about the second one? He drank. He really shouldn't have done that. Well, he had lost a free spear, that was all, and he had expected that. But he really shouldn't have done that second thing. That was really foolish. He was glad he'd done it, anyway.

Back in the car, thinking it all over again and remembering it all with painstaking detailed relish, Bonham was still glad. Out of all the many sharks he had killed over the years that was the only time he had ever instigated, or even seen, a mob-feeding. The same situation had been there often enough, true. But sharks were really much more cautious cowardly creatures than most people believed. God! he wanted to laugh out loud when he saw in his mind that mako swimming wildly around, and the other two turning and going for him. I bet he wondered what the hell had hit him. Suddenly he became aware that his wife was watching him.

He looked over at her and smiled. "We're almost there."

"Is it as bad as all that?" Letta said quietly.

"Is what what?" he said.

"I say, is it that bad? The camera and Grant? All that?"

"I don't know what you mean," he said sullenly.

"Your eyes very bright, my love," Letta said.

"Oh, come on," he said. "Cut it out."

"Hokay," Letta said. She turned her pokerface toward the window and looked out.

She knew, goddamn it. Now how could she know? God damn. Ahead of them the town appeared. Its high street-lamps hung above the dusty grubby streets, each one an apex of a cone of dust. Then their own dusty little street with all its high mansard-roof homes of corrguated tin. Their own was still brightly lit up. Could she have told that Lucky anything about their own uh their own private problems to-day? When they were alone together all that time? He remembered the funny feeling he had had about that at The Neptune, from Lucky and Grant both. Well, screw them all. They didn't know anything. About anything. So what if she did? Bonham clamped his big jaws together in their storm-weathering position and the dark storm-cloud look came back over his eyes and forehead. What the hell did any of them know about ladies? The main thing now was that he had to get that goddamned Orloffski out of here and on his way back north, so he himself could get on down to Kingston.

At the house, after they had searched hard and thoroughly for the camera and not found it and had had a couple of drinks, as a gesture he offered Doug his car to go home in.

"Well, thanks, Al," Doug said. "I uh—Okay, I'll take it."

"I'd just like to have it by ten-thirty or eleven," Bonham said. "Because I'm going out. Maybe it would be better if I drove you."

"Maybe that would be better," Doug said. "I probly wouldn't get up that early."

They did not talk on the way, but when he let Doug out at the big iron gates of the villa he said again how sorry he was about the loss of the camera. "I expect Orloffski's right and one of them damn' porters stole it."

"I expect so," Doug said. "Anyway it's a little thing, really."

"What'll you be doing now? With Grant and his girl gone?" Bonham asked.

"I don't know. Probly mosey on back to Coral Gables and get back to my snook fishin', I guess," Doug said. He turned toward the villa. As he went up the curving walk Bonham heard him start to whistle. The song was a popular song that had been a big hit, called *The Party's Over*.

Bonham waited till he had gone in before he drove off. The dew was finally beginning to settle the dust, and the air was cool on his flushed, embarrassed, angry face. God, it was good to be alone. God damn all of them.

TWENTY-TWO

After he shut the big glass and iron front door behind him, Doug Ismaileh stopped and stood in the villa foyer several moments. He listened to Bonham's old car chuff and chug away. Its sound faded and silence settled around him. The villa was totally silent, appeared to be totally deserted to-night. Only one night light burned in the foyer. Everything else was dark.

After hesitating several seconds more in the deep silence, Doug snapped on the lights in the grand salon where the bar was—where *a* bar was; there were bars everywhere here—and went in there and made himself a very stiff scotch and soda. Then, holding the glass, he looked at all the empty chairs and love-seats and divans under the bright lights in the great room. The sight increased his depression. Bonham probably thought his reserve to-night was due to the stealing of the camera (and Doug very deliberately had not straightened him out) but the truth was that he had been reticent and distant because he was having a real put-down. Again, something had changed, a period was over, an adventure had ended in his life. When Grant and Lucky became airborne in the Kingston plane, a serious melancholy settled over him. Now there was nothing for it but to head back home and back to work on the new play. No more excuses. If he went to Kingston it wouldn't be the same; down there they would be a couple, a sealed-shut couple. And his former heated ideas about going to New York for a while, and looking up Terry September, made him grin ruefully now.

God *damn* that fucking Grant! He was shot in the ass with luck. Everything came to him on a platter. With no more talent, brains or hard work than a thousand other guys, everything he did turned to gold and fame and happiness. Look at how he had found this goddam Lucky, for instance. He hadn't even found her! She had found him.

Holding the drink up to the light, Doug admired it; self-consciously admired himself admiring it. The giant-killer, old Hemingway used to call booze. He was sure right. The old man always was. Still, he couldn't drink it in here under all these bright lights and only himself among all these empty chairs. Turning on his heel he took the big drink out on to the terrace where only small reflected light from the salon penetrated. It felt much better out there.

Pulling up one of the big high-backed wicker chairs, he sat down and cocked his feet up on the terrace balustrade. Below him lights in the town showed where a number of tourist honkey-tonks and local shag bars for locals were still open. He felt like going down to one of the local joints and getting into some kind of a fight with some ape. Or hit a tourist trap and pick up some tourist for a nice drunken poker game, or maybe get him dead drunk and fuck his wife. But, no. Anyway, he certainly wouldn't run into Bonham and Orloff-ski down there, he thought wryly, now that their two chief sources of drinking money (himself and Grant) were no longer with them. They'd be home. He sure would not like to have to tangle with Bonham. Nor that Orloffski, he wouldn't like to tangle with him either.

Doug was as sure as everybody else that Orloffski had stolen the camera. But in a way it tickled him. It made him want to chuckle instead of making him angry. It was good once in a while to see something that wasn't quite perfect for fucking Ron Grant!

Of course, why Orloffski would do such a thing when he knew Bonham was trying hard to sell Grant on going into their schooner and diving business, was something else again. As Doug saw it he just had to be some kind of a klepto.

So, let him be a klepto.

No, what had made him distant to them to-night was something entirely else.

His whole life seemed to be going past him fast, and faster, like an express passenger train picking up speed until the windows blurred into one, and all without leaving any residue or marks on him. And to see Grant and Lucky together made him intensely aware of it. What did *he* have? Ha! His first wife out in L.A. with that dumb kid of theirs they'd had ; who needed it? His second wife in Detroit, the fat pig, with her dopey teenage son ; he never should have signed all the income of the first play over to her, now she had that *and* his house in Detroit ; he had sure had bad advice on that one from all his Greek cousins in New York in their try to save taxes ; still, he had all the second-play income himself although it wasn't as big a hit. He had his house in Coral Gables, and his little boat, and a bunch of fishing experiences and opportunities—which, unless there was an audience to see them or somebody to tell them to afterwards, didn't mean all that much anyway. And he had his third play, which although he was half-way through the second act, he still couldn't get the first-act curtain for. Which meant it wasn't even off the ground. That was what he had.

And that fucking Grant! That son of a bitch! How dare he come up with such a great broad as old Lucky? He had no more right to her than anybody. She was as loyal to him as a tigress. She *loved* him. And why? She had met him. A mutual friend had introduced them. A mutual friend had introduced them, and she had been ready to fall in love with *somebody*, so fucking Grant fell into the gravy. Why had he met her? Why hadn't Doug met her? It could just as easy happened. What was so great about Grant? His Moral Integrity? Ha! Here he lived with this older broad for fourteen years, screwing her in her own house, in her husband's house, letting her husband support him—until his work started making money. Hell, he wouldn't even have to pay her alimony now when he left her! What kind of luck was that? But moral integrity! Did Lucky think he had moral integrity?

His next thought caused a kind of astonished stillness in Doug.

What if somebody told Lucky all about Carol, what would she say about moral integrity then?—was the thought.

Why hadn't he? Why the hell hadn't he? He could have slipped it to her so easy she probably wouldn't even have known where it came from. And Grant the fucker deserved it. Why, by God, he hadn't even *thought* of it! What kind of a brain-thinker did that make Ismaileh? No. No you couldn't go doing things like that to your best friends. Even if they deserved them.

Sitting in the high-backed wicker chair Doug sensed rather than heard someone come up behind him out on to the terrace. Silently he tensed his body in the chair and grasped the heavy crystal ashtray that had been sitting in his lap and grinned, somehow feeling vastly relieved suddenly. Okay, come on, you!

"Doug?" the soft voice of Carol Abernathy said from behind him. "Is that you, Doug?"

He relaxed and got to his feet. "Yes. Hi, Carol! God, did I wake you up? I'm sorry."

"No, you didn't wake me. I woke on my own, and then saw the lights on down here and thought it might be you."

"I'm just havin' a nightcap before goin' off to bed." He turned to look out over the town again, his jaws tightening for some unaccountable reason. A few of the lights had gone out. She came and stood by him, looking out too. She was wearing one of her better-looking robes, tied in with a wide Japanese-style sash, and mules with long-haired pompons on them. Above the sash her heavy breasts, even though they sagged a good bit, didn't look bad.

"Did you finally get the pair of young lovers off for Kingston?" she said in a mild voice.

"Yeh," Doug said lightly. "Yeh, I did. And everybody was as happy as clams."

"Where were you all day to-day? I thought they were leaving last night."

"Well, Bonham had this dive to make to-day. Couple crashed through the bridge in a car. And he wanted Ron to make it with him. So they stayed over a day So—I stayed with 'em."

"Yes, I heard about the accident. Some poor married man and his girl. Did they seem happy to you?"

"Yes," Doug said, not without a certain twinge of particular pleasure. "Yes, they seemed very happy to me."

Rather sadly Carol pulled a big wicker chair over by his and sat down on it, putting her heels up on the balustrade.

"Do you think he'll marry her?" she asked.

"Yeah, I pretty much think he will. He was sort of of two minds about it in the beginning, but he's come around to accepting it as sort of his Fate. And she'll do just about anything to marry him."

Carol was silent for a long moment, looking out over the town. "Of course she will," she finally said, sadly.

There was a cool, sane mildness about her to-night, an acceptant melancholy that answered his own. This was the way Doug remembered her that first night he had met her, when Grant was in New York, after he had driven down from Detroit to Indianapolis.

"Do you think she would go out to Indianapolis to live with him?" Carol said.

"Why?" Then he spoke with a relish he could not avoid but hoped was concealed. "Yes, I think she'd go out to Indianapolis to live with him. I think she'd do anything, absolutely anything she had to do to marry him and be his wife. She's crazy in love with him." How did he get into all this? But he was enjoying it. He didn't really believe that all that strongly, himself. But he almost did. "But why do you ask that?"

"Why?" She turned her head to look up at him where he stood against the balustrade, and it was as if her eyes had gone totally blind, become sightless. A tear welled up in each but didn't drop. "I guess you never realised, nor noticed. But I was his lover. All those years. You never guessed that?"

"No!" he lied. "No, I didn't. I guess I thought about it once or twice, but it seemed too——" he had meant to say *incongruous* but choked it off. Instead he shrugged and spread his hands and flattered. "I guess it was just too well covered up."

Carol was looking back out over the town now. "Well, I guess it was a dirty trick on my part, but I got him to buy that house and tie up all that money in it just to keep him away from New York and that kind of girls. Now, he doesn't have all that much money, to try and move away."

"What about the new play?"

"Well, of course if the new play is a success it won't make any difference."

Doug chuckled. "Yeah, that was kind of a dirty trick. How is the new play?"

"I don't know. I'm not qualified to judge it. I'm in it," Carol said thinly. "As to whether it'll make money or not, I couldn't say. It ought to."

" And if it makes money he can move away from Indianapolis with his new bride, is that it?"

" That's right. I'm assuming she won't like me, naturally."

" On the other hand, if it doesn't, he'll have to bring his
bride out there to live, yes?"

" Yes."

" Across the street from you?"

Carol glanced up at him then, then looked back out across
the town. " Yes."

Doug bit his lower lip. He had to admire it. But what a
broomstick up old Grant's ass! Screw him, he had it comin'
to him! Something in Doug's nature, something feminine, or
maybe it's just something conspiratorial, responded deeply
to what Carol Abernathy's feminine wiles had cooked up. He
had played some pretty dirty pool in his time, some of which
he was proud of, some not, but this beat him hands down.
What an underhanded handicap to pin secretly on to a new
marriage! Suddenly angry at all women for a moment, he
thought of telling her that Grant had already told him about
them. Instead he said: " She'll have *some* mother-in-law
troubles, hunh?"

" I'm just interested in his work. Now. That's all I have
the right to be interested in, now," Carol said.

" Well, you knew it was goin' to happen to you some day,
didn't you, I guess?"

Carol's mild face continued to brood sadly out over the
darkened town. " I guess I did," she said. " But I thought I'd
have more say-so in the choice he made."

Jesus! Doug thought admiringly. He was envious. Pick her
own successor; who she wanted him to have. And she would
really go that far, too! Had it planned that far! Christ, it's
like some kind of a fucking Greek play. No wonder she's
crazy! The wonder is that Grant ain't. Or maybe he was too.
What a thing to saddle a young bride with! What a *play* it
would make! All natural-born writers had to be born gossips
too. Where else would they get their material? You couldn't
make something like this up!

" Solely because I'm interested in his work," Carol said.

" That's all we're all interested in, ain't it?" Doug said
harshly. " Well look," he said, more harshly than he meant
now. Because he wanted to be honest. But maybe there was a
bit of malicious pleasure in it too maybe, hunh? Probly there

was. "I'll tell you what I think. I think this girl is probly the best for him that he could find. In the whole goddam fucking world! And I mean it! And *she* cares about his work, too. If anybody would be good for him to marry, it's this girl."

"You really think so?" Carol murmured.

"I do. I sure do," Doug said, watching her face. He *was* enjoying it. "And I think you've got to realise that. Hell, I'd marry her myself, if she was in love with me instead of him."

"You would?"

"I sure would."

"And then you'd have three," Carol smiled, "you'd be paying alimony to. Instead of two."

Doug grunted, then grinned. "Okay. Touché. It's true you did save him from payin' any alimony all those susceptible years. But I mean what I say about this one. And you better take that into account." God, now why had he said that? So strongly? He didn't really believe that. Not that strongly. Like any other relationship it would be a toss-up. Who knew?

"And she's very bright," he added. "She's got a brain on her."

"I always thought he should marry a good-natured stupid woman," Carol murmured. "Like Joyce." But it had not really been an answer to Doug, and she was still staring moodily out over the town. "It's a hard role I've got picked out for myself, Doug," she finally said, broodingly. "Sometimes I wonder if I can hack it."

Doug pushed himself up and away from the balustrade. "Well, I'm goin' to make myself another stiff drink. And go to bed."

"I'll come along," Carol said, and got up. But at the door she stopped. "I've got to get away from here, Doug," she said suddenly. "Will you take me away from here? Somewhere? Anywhere? I can't take it here any more. I can't stand their faces. I don't want to look at them. Especially Hunt I can't stand looking at."

Doug chewed his upper lip. "You mean you want to go now? To-night?"

"No. I would. But I don't want to take one of Evelyn's cars, because I don't know where I'll go or for how long." She sighed and rubbed her forehead. "Let's go to-morrow.

Let's go to Montego Bay. To your friends. Relatives. Just for a week. A week away. Then I'd be all right. Maybe we'll go right on. Right on around the island. They say it's a lovely drive."

"Okay," Doug heard himself say. "I'll pick up a Hertz car to-morrow. But I wouldn't advise trying to look *them* up in Kingston."

"Oh, no. Oh, no," Carol said. "Nothing like that."

When he turned back from the bar with his refilled glass, she had gone.

His mouth pursed in a thoughtful whistle that made no noise, Doug took his big belt of scotch with its little splash of soda back out to the terrace. But first he took the precaution of turning out the lights. His room was down at the other end of the long gallery so she wouldn't know if he came up or not, if the lights were out.

Back in the wicker chair, his feet back on the railing, he thought about Grant's new play, and about his own. Carol—despite all her present upset and anguish—appeared to be awfully cool about talking about Grant's play with him. Grant had been reticent too, when he had pumped him about it on the way to Montego Bay and after. So she was in it? As a character. That might explain why both of them were unwilling to talk about it. Or, it might be because neither of them trusted Doug Ismaileh not to steal it. Or a part of it.

Goddamn that Grant, he thought with a kind of admiring irritation. How *anybody* could have made that third play of his work, and not only work, be a success, was beyond Doug Ismaileh. He had read it in its entirety long before it ever came out and was produced, and he would have bet his last nickel it had to fail. He had not of course told Grant or Carol that. Why make waves? But—five sailors trapped in an engine-room in a destroyer sitting on the bottom of Pearl Harbour the day after Pearl Harbour. That was all it was. One set. One set almost in darkness. And five guys sitting waiting for their air to run out, waiting to die. Five guys who talk about death and about life and about their own lives. Once in a while somebody off-stage raps on a piece of steel plate for purposes of suspense to indicate the divers are still trying to get to them. It should have bombed. And did it? No, siree. No, siree-*bob* it didn't. It was almost as big a hit as his first one.

Doug had to admit in all honesty that the good thing, the great thing about it was how all these guys sitting there faced with certain death tried to pretend they were tough, honest and brave, that they were men, and how each man slowly, as he talked, proved conclusively by what he said and told about his past that he was none of these things. Proved it conclusively for the audience, if not for his fellow prisoners who, being in the same boat (literally), were forced to accept his fictions if they wanted their own roles respected. Talk about irony. And so they just all died dumb, learning nothing from the experience.

But that was no reason for it to be such a hit. Rather just the reverse. And yet it was. People flocked to it. *The Whites of Their Eyes*. It was a good title, but it wasn't that good. But they went.

Doug knew he would never have tried such a thing himself. Even if he had thought of it, which he hadn't. But he would never have thought of it. It wasn't his kind of thing. A kind of deep, miasmic, bottomless hollow opened up in him at the thought of his own new play. He didn't want to think about it.

He had based the hero on himself, plus a guy he had known in the war in Persia. The situation was a love affair he himself had had a couple of years after he got married. That, and some violent events that had occurred in Persia during the war. Not to him but to the other guys. He had known all along that the biggest danger in the idea was in the possibility of making the hero *too* heroic. And yet he couldn't seem to help it. He just couldn't seem to make the guy do bad things. And any way besides, he had to be *somewhat* heroic. He had tried to prepare for and cover this by making the guy tougher and more cruel than he probably normally would have been. But then Paul Gibson who had read it all all along wrote back that he thought the hero was too mean and cold-blooded, that he needed some kindness and compassion in him. But whenever he wrote anything kind or compassionate about him, Paul would write back that that wasn't compassion, that was sentimentality. What the fuck did they want from him. Aw, fuck it he thought and finished his glass and got up to go to bed.

Up on his feet, he discovered that he was pretty drunk. Well good. Then maybe he'd be able to sleep. So to-morrow he'd be taking old Carol off to MoBay. Well, a week or so more away from work, what the hell? He almost welcomed it.

He had a copy of the new play with him. He would show it to Carol and have her read it. Maybe she might come up with something. Possibly she wouldn't. Probably she wouldn't even get what he was driving at. She'd been getting more and more like that the last couple of years. But it was worth a shot.

The last thing he thought as he settled into the bed and let the peaceful buzz of drunkenness engulf him into sleep was that if she stayed as calm and as sane as she seemed to-night it might even be a pleasant, fun trip.

Unfortunately, as he could see immediately as soon as he saw her the next morning, that was not the way it was going to be.

He did not know what was bugging her now. But whatever it was that had made her mild and rational last night, it was no longer with her She was roundly insulting and unpleasant to just about everyone. Evelyn of course she almost never criticised, or the old Count Paul there. Doug cynically believed that this was because she knew damn' well what side her visitor's card was buttered on. But with everybody else she was horrible. And as always, it was *moral issues* that she bugged everyone about. At breakfast on the terrace in the bright hot lovely sun she launched into a tirade against some hapless junior member of the Hunt Hills Little Theatre Group whose inept second act had just been delivered to her in the morning mail. The causes of this ineptitude were always *moral* lapses on the part of the individual who had written the material, as far as she was concerned: laziness, sloth, gluttony, greed, drinking, sex, etc. She had just finished reading it before Doug came down, and she knew. Then it was Doug's turn. She upbraided him because he was down here in Jamaica loafing in the sun when he should be up at Coral Gables working, even though it was she who had called him down here in the first place and who was taking him off to MoBay for a week to-day. She castigated him for the late hour at which he had risen to-day. She herself had been up since six.

As he had learned to do long ago, Doug simply pulled down and snapped shut the fasteners on his earflaps. He answered in monosyllables, affirmative or negative, and then only when addressed directly with a question. Why did he sit around and take it? He knew why. Because, in spite of these kooky crazy moods, she had helped him in the past and might still help him again. He would take help wherever he could get it, and sticks and stones.

Then it was Hunt's turn, as he came out in his robe for breakfast looking a little bleary-eyed. What in the living hell was he doing down here in Jamaica when he ought to be up home in Indianapolis taking care of his business. Mark her word, those goddamned slippery partners of his were going to slip his business right out from under his feet if he wasn't careful. It went on and on. Drink, sex, that lousy fucking escapism golf. Wasted lives. As Doug watched, a curious transformation slowly took place in Hunt. Instead of getting angry, he got guiltier and guiltier—with a sort of self-castigating, self-loathing, total culpability on his face. Christ, Doug thought looking at his face, he's going to come in a minute if she don't let up.

Purely academically, Doug wondered what would happen if somebody was really cruel to Carol. Really mean. She would probably become their slave. Out on the West Coast after his discharge and before he got married he had worked for the rackets a while running a gambling and call-girl place, a hotel, and had gotten to know some really superior professional pimps. And under their tutelage had done some serious pimping himself. It was amazing what you could get a woman to do if you were just cruel enough to her. They loved it. But you had to make them love you first, then be mean to them. It was all amazing and Doug looked at Carol Abernathy shrewdly as she went on throwing her weight around, and grinned suddenly to himself.

Actually it was clear that she was about on her last legs as far as nerves went. Probably, Doug supposed, she had been waiting and waiting around for him to come back, hoping that in the end something would change and Grant would not go. When Doug didn't come back and she heard from other sources that Grant had stayed over a day, she probably had taken that as a sign, one in her favour. And now, of course, it was all over. The birds had flown.

Fortunately, when he returned with the hired car later and loaded their bags in the back, she appeared to have about hollered herself out. She was practically silent. Unhealthily silent.

While she was still upstairs, Hunt had taken him aside to talk about her. In that authoritative, command-giving, I-expect-to-be-obeyed businessman's voice he had normally and which was so different from the abject way he presented himself to his wife, Hunt asked him to take care of her. " She's had a pretty rough time these past few weeks, Doug. She really needs to get her mind off all this business and get some rest. I can't give it to her. But maybe you can."

" Sure," Doug said, and patted the diminutive Hunt on the back. " That's what I'm doin' this for, old buddy. I know what she's been through. Ron was her first boy, and her favourite, as well as her most famous one too. I understand."

Hunt Abernathy nodded. " I myself think he'll come back. Even if he does marry this girl. Why shouldn't he?" he said and gave a sad tired smile.

When Carol did appear she went straight to the car and got in in silence. Hunt came to the window to kiss her good-bye. After that, she waved and smiled to Evelyn up on the porch. Hunt stepped back. "For God's sake, let's get the fuck out of here!" she said under her breath to Doug. Her voice sounded desperate. It was the last word she spoke for about an hour.

Doug was grateful. He had hoped that while he was gone for the car she might run herself worn or wear herself out. Now she tucked herself up in the car-robe-blanket she had brought along and turning her head toward the window she slept. Or pretended to. Doug couldn't be sure. He sensed somehow in some animal way that she was awake and not asleep. But to find out he was not going to ask any questions that might turn into another conversational tirade like this morning. Silence was fine with him.

He had run into Orloffski in town this morning while getting the car, just long enough to have a quick beer. Bonham had already gone out—Orloffski told him—in the boat, early, by himself. Orloffski was downtown to see about his plane ticket to Baltimore, to go back north and bring down the cutter. It had started Doug off to thinking about Bonham and Grant and himself, all of them, and the diving. Now he resumed it. Waiting for all the rigmarole and paperwork that had to be done to get the car, and thinking about all of that, he had in the office of Hertz Company about convinced himself that when it came to diving in the aqualung he was nothing but a lousy ratfink coward. He simply could not make himself breathe through those fucking tubes down there on the bottom of the pool. His throat would choke up, his nerves would get all jumpy and tricky, gallons of water would seem to be leaking into his mouth, he would have to claw for the surface, it would always astonish and embarrass him to find that there was hardly any water in his mouth at all. Now in the car he went back to contemplating this. He had made a big fuss and to-do about burbling and spitting, but about the only water in his mouth was water he had let in there himself after getting back to the surface. He wasn't a coward about anything else. And anyway he didn't have any big grand passion for it like Grant did. He didn't even care that much about it. So what the hell?

That goddamned Grant! With all that polite kindly shit of his about some kind of claustrophobia! Who the fuck did he think he was? And who did he think he was being kind *to*? Fuck him and his kindness. If you don't like a goddamned sport, what's the point of forcing yourself to do it?

Doug looked at his watch and saw he had been driving almost an hour. Looking out he saw they were almost to Dunn's River. And just then, whether it was because he had been thinking irritably of his friend Grant, or whether because his eyes in looking out fell on the rigidly still form of Carol Abernathy—or whether, even, in the end, from some other and unnameable source he would never isolate—the soft, big thought like the tone of a bell vibrating on in the air after the strike, the thought came into his mind that he wanted to fuck this woman in the car here, that for a long time he would have liked to fuck her.

He couldn't really believe it was him who was thinking it. He had had no preparation for such a thought. Never in all the years had he ever thought of Carol in that way, or if he had, it had certainly never reached his consciousness. She was like a second-string mother to him. Why now? Why suddenly now?

Could it be because of Grant? But that didn't make sense. She wasn't Grant's any more. He had thrown her over, tossed her out. Was Doug Ismaileh the kind of guy to go around picking up on Grant's leftovers?

Maybe it was just because she had never been available before? That he had known instinctively she was committed to somebody and so never allowed the thought to reach his conscious mind?

Later on, when he had time to think about it and try to analyse it, he became convinced that it was Carol herself lying there so rigidly and wide awake who somehow put the thought in his mind. In some one of her occult, mystical tricks of thought concentration she concentrated so hard she made him think the thought she had picked out for him to think. In the light of what she did about it all and of what happened after, he couldn't see how it could be any other way.

None of this, however, was in his mind at the moment. He drove on through Dunn's River. He continued on, slowly. The desire, hot and liquid, was there in him, existing, powerful, to be dealt with. It would be a " delightful escapade ", as they liked to say in some quarters, a " delightful escapade ". But how to go about it? He decided the best thing to do was wait until Montego Bay. But no sooner had he decided this than the whole thing was taken out of his hands by Carol.

Somewhere beyond Dunn's River the road moved inland and lost sight of the sea. Just here on their right, on the sea side, was a broad flat spit about a mile wide covered by a wood of big pine trees and choked with undergrowth below. It was here that Carol suddenly sat up in her car-robe blanket and cried out, " Stop! Stop! I want to go in there!"

Doug had seen the side road himself. He hadn't been driving particularly fast. It was easy to back up to it. The sandy side road dipped down off the road grade and slid in under the pines amongst the undergrowth and disappeared. Once inside and further out toward the sea where the pine trees thickened the underbrush thinned out. He followed it maybe half a mile until it came to and mounted a little knoll where a group of pines growing closely enough together to make a canopy formed a sort of grove with no underbrush at all. From it you could look out under and see the sea blue and glinting. Without the undergrowth a soft sea breeze blew across it.

" Stop here!" Carol commanded.

He did. She got out with her car-robe and walked out on to the little knoll. It was covered with pine needles and it looked as if nobody had been here for at least fifty years. Doug got out and followed her.

By the time he got to her she had spread the car-robe out on the pine needles and stretched her arms out sideways and was breathing deeply of the pine- and sea-scented air. When he stopped beside her, she turned to him, backed off three paces and said, " I want you to make love to me, love to me, I want you to make love to me."

" Okay," Doug said. He grinned.

" Here," Carol said. " Now." Without another word she lay down on the robe, closed her eyes, and pulled her skirt up to her waist exposing the fact that she had no panties on. Nor did she open her eyes when Doug took his time.

Doug was embarrassed. He had no erection nor the imme- diate prospect of one. It was such short notice. And it also had the emotional climate about it like some sort of Com- mand Performance almost. He stepped out of his pants (which necessitated taking off his shoes too because of the narrow legs) and took off the sweater he was wearing in the car, but he kept his Hawaiian shirt and his shorts on as he lay down beside her. That lack of an erection bothered him. Well that would be coming along. When he kissed her on the mouth she returned it, but when he tried to put his tongue in her mouth she tightened her lips together. Well, hell, he thought, okay, and put one hand down to tickle her crotch.

" Don't do that! " she said sharply, without opening her eyes.

" Don't do what?"

" Don't play with it! "

Christ! she sure puts up the handicap; like a regular obstacle course, Doug thought grimly. Poor old Grant! Hell, poor Hunt! But he took his hand away, and tucked it up inside the sweater above the skirt against her belly. He felt her breasts through their brassière. But he was all right now, he was coming along, and he slipped out of his shorts.

But when he went to mount her he found he had another problem. She was lying there with her legs together and her arms straight down at her sides like so much dead weight. He had to pull her legs apart with his hands before he could get his knees between them. She did not aid him. Not even one of the fingers on her limp relaxed hands so much as twitched.

But finally, simple male sexual brutality came to his aid.

With his two hands under her two knees he pushed her legs apart where they ought to be, where she should have put them herself. What the hell? After that, it was better. He looked off at the sea for a while through the trees and across the brown floor of pine needle. Christ the scenery was like something out of Hemingway. But he wasn't Robert Jordan. And this certainly wasn't any Maria. Then he felt it coming up, rushing up through his chest, up along his spine and across his shoulders and down his arms. When that hit you, it didn't make any difference any more who they were, they were all the same. That was the God's truth. *And balls to you, Grant!*

He lay down beside her for a while, but she did not touch him. So he did not touch her. Screw it! In a while she got up and walked off and stood looking off through the trees at the sea. Then she came back and completely blank-faced got in the car. "We'd better be getting on," she called.

Back out on the road it was just exactly as if nothing had happened. They drove clean on through St. Ann's Bay, then Priory, then Laughlands, without one word being spoken.

Doug was just as glad. He didn't have anything to say to her really. He was in a strange state of high teeth-clenching euphoria, so strong that he gripped the wheel tight with both hands to keep from laughing out loud. *I've had your broad, Grant! I've had your broad!* was what he was feeling, though his mind did not present it to him in exactly those words. It didn't present it in words at all, but that was what it was. *I've had your broad, Grant!* And what a lousy lay. He was just as happy not to talk. And it was Carol who finally spoke first.

"Was it good?" she asked faintly.

"Of course it was good!" he said. "It was marvellous!"

"No, it wasn't. I know it wasn't. I'm just an old-dry-bag." She said it as one word. "That's what we used to say in school."

"Come on now," Doug said. "That's not true."

"Yes, it is. I have always felt that sex just was not very important. I know some people don't believe that."

"Oh, come on, now. Sex is important only when you don't have it," Doug said profoundly. "When you have it it's the most unimportant thing in the world."

"I did like it when you pushed my legs up like that," Carol said.

Doug glanced at her. " Didn't anybody ever show you that?"

Carol's eyes narrowed suddenly as she looked back at him, as if she was savouring the import of her words. " No. Nobody. Never."

Doug found this impossible to believe, especially of Grant, but he certainly wasn't going to pursue it. He grinned. " Well, hell. All you need is a little experience and practice, honey."

But if that was all she really needed, and Doug didn't believe that, it became quickly clear that it was not going to be him who was going to give it to her. During the rest of the trip she did not ask him for any more, did not even mention the subject. And Doug did not offer to give her some. The hell with it. They registered at one of the better beach hotels, in separate rooms, instead of going to the Khanturian Hotel and his relatives, and she sat in the sun on the sand all day for six days and then suddenly said she was ready to go home. Or, back to Evelyn's, rather.

In fact, Doug saw very little of her during the six days. The first evening he introduced her to Sir Gerald and they all had dinner together. But she could not stand Sir Gerald. And Sir Gerald automatically disliked her intensely. After that they had dinner alone together every night, in the hotel dining-room, and after dinner when she went to her room Doug would go out with Sir Gerald scouring the town for ass. Unfortunately, after the great magazine modelling bonanza, the town was as bare as a bone of unattached females. Except for the shag joint whores.

He did spend some time with her during the days, on the beach. But he spent more time in the cool, dim bar of the Khanturian Hotel with the five Khanturian brothers and usually Sir Gerald, drinking. Carol didn't seem to need anything from him at all really.

She did read the play. But, as he had suspected she might, she came up with no criticism that was helpful. She talked a little wildly, and pointlessly, about changing this and that in it. But she did not even note the basic and valid criticism that Paul Gibson had pointed out about the too great heroism.

As far as he was concerned the trip was about as much a total loss as anything could be, and in Coral Gables the fucking play was still waiting.

"Who is this strange woman you've got travellin' with you?" Sir Gerald asked him once when they were drinking and hunting unsuccessfully for pussy. "What's wrong with her?"

"She's bereaved. She just lost a boy-friend to another gal," Doug said.

"Who?"

"The guy? Nobody you'd know," Doug said.

Sir Gerald sniffed with his long English nose. "I should think she'd be too old really to have any kind of a 'boy-friend'."

Doug had laughed. "Come on, Gerry. You know damn' well women aren't like men. Women never get too old to have an erection."

Sir Gerald nodded gravely. "Quite true, I must say. They do have it on us there, don't they?"

On the trip back to Ganado he slowed up as they passed the side-road entrance into the pine-grown spit, and Carol leaned across him to look at it. She then gave him a strange conspiratorial look that left him wondering if, in the end, he had had her, or the other way round, she had had him. She said nothing.

He didn't care. When he got back to GaBay he was going to pack up and get out the very next day. And he wasn't going back to Coral Gables either. Except to get some clothes. The truth was he was sick of all this shit, he was sick of Jamaica, sick of Florida, sick of this "country living", and all the rest of that shit. And fuck fishing. He was going back to New York. And if he couldn't get this play going there, he was going to throw it away. Throw it away and take that fucking film job his agent had been bugging him to take. God damn plays anyway; he *preferred* films. At least there you had somebody else, a director or producer or another writer, to throw your ideas at. It wasn't so fucking lonely.

That was not however the way it worked out, because the day after they got back, while Doug was preparing to pack up his one bag, an accredited visitor presented himself at the villa. This was the local Jamaican *Time*-correspondent flown up specially from Kingston, a black man but with the same sneaky mean face most of the white Time-men had. He was here, he said, to find out what Mrs. Abernathy thought about the marriage of her number-one protégé Ron Grant to a New

York show-girl. Ron and Lucky had been married two days before at the Grand Hotel Crount in Kingston. He was prepared to stay around several days and talk to her, and his face wore a look as if he had been briefed on at least several things he was not telling. He was curious to know, he said, why she and her husband had not been invited to the wedding, particularly since they were in Jamaica themselves at the time. Had there been trouble between them and Ron Grant over the marriage perhaps? He'd be glad to talk to her about it, and make notes on anything she wished to get off her chest about it

After he left Carol was almost beside herself with fury, and Hunt's face was set and hard and white. Doug who had been introduced to the *Time*-man was along with Evelyn called into the war council that proceeded.

It was almost unbelievable to see Carol's immediate bald-faced assumption, her taking up of her old foster-mother role again. Doug watched with amusement and admiration. And occasionally with envy. It was next to impossible to believe that she had ever fucked Grant, to look at her. Or that she had ever fucked Doug. Maybe she had never fucked Doug? he wondered.

"They want to cause trouble between us—Hunt and me—and Ron," she said. "Well, I'm not going to let them. We didn't raise that boy for fourteen years, I didn't teach him all I knew, support him, make him into America's number-one playwright, for these people to try and make a family scandal out of the fact that he got married. What the hell? Sons always get married. Finally."

"Maybe he ought to come back here for a week or two with uh with his wife?" Doug said quietly.

"He's simply got to come back here with her," Carol said in a cold bright voice. "That's the only way out. For a week or two. To show no hard feelings. I'm going to call him down there in Kingston. But I'm not even sure he'll speak to me. That's where you come in, Doug. Is your bag packed?"

"Yes," he said. "It is, Mom." He had already made up his mind to go even before she went on. He wouldn't miss this for anything. Evelyn he noted was smoking from her long holder, and had on her face that deep, gimlet-pointed look of deeply hidden cynical amusement she very often wore. She obviously felt the same.

"Well, you're not flying to Miami," Carol said. "You're flying to Kingston. You've got to explain it to him. How much we need him. He'll always talk with you. And you're an old pal from The Group, so it won't look funny for you to go down there like it would if Hunt went."

"That's all true enough. Okay. I'll go," Doug grinned, making it sound as if he had just decided. And what the hell? He'd like to see how they were doing now down there, now that they were hitched. And to watch the rest of the developments, back here, ought to be more fun than a barrel of monkeys.

"Otherwise," Carol said, "they can ruin, destroy all my work, all my plans, everything I've worked for all these years for my Hunt Hills Little Theatre, by making me a laughing-stock. Well, Ron was my first protégé. He helped me found that group."

"He sure did," Doug said, staunchly. He looked over at Hunt. But Hunt wasn't seeing any humour in it. His face was perfectly serious, perfectly righteous, perfectly middleclass. Christ, didn't he know he was a cuckold? how much he had been cuckolded? was being cuckolded? Or did he perhaps know? And if so, what kind of odd ball did that make Hunt? Doug wanted desperately to laugh. "Of course, I may not be able to get right on the plane to-day," he said, instead.

"You won't mind if they stay here a week or two, will you, Evelyn?" Carol was saying. "To help me out?"

"Nothing I'd like better, darling," Evelyn de Blystein grinned with her gravelly voice, and took a puff on her cigarette.

"Ron will be glad to help out with the food and liquor bills and such-like."

"Never give it a thought, my dear," said Evelyn.

At the door as he prepared to go out to Hunt and the waiting car with his suitcase Carol said to him alone: "Tell him I really need him. It'll only be for a little while."

Doug nodded, patted her on the shoulder, and kissed her on the cheek.

TWENTY-THREE

Ron Grant had been in Kingston Jamaica nine days, nine very much hectic days, when his old fishin'-and-playwritin'-buddy Doug Ismaileh hove half-drunkenly into view on the porch of the Grand Hotel Crount. And for four of those days he had been married to Lucky Grant.

Lucky Grant.

God. Or, to Lucia Videndi Grant, if you wanted to be more formal. Or, if you wanted to go all the way with the formality, to Lucia Angelina Elena Videndi Grant. That was the name on the Licence. He didn't believe it would ever happen to him. And Lucky, when it came right down to the last final and hysterical sticking-point moment, clearly hadn't believed it would ever happen to her. Lucky Grant. Lucky Grant. It didn't even sound right, or natural, let alone make any sense, and he couldn't get used to it, and she couldn't get used to it, and they both of them loved it, and both didn't love it. He jumped up to run and greet Doug when he saw him, leaving his 10 a.m. in the morning Bloody Mary on the table with Lucky's and the others.

It seemed to him now when he looked back over the nine days that he had been drunk every single moment of that time. But that couldn't be strictly true because he had been out diving every day but one, and with no less a personage than Mr. Jim Grointon whom he had met on the plane to Grand Bank Island with Al Bonham. He had also slept a lot.

The Grand Hotel Crount at the time he and Lucky arrived to stay in it was probably the choicest hotel in the whole of the Caribbean. Grant of course, the Indianapolis hick, had never heard of it but Lucky had stayed there quite a lot with Raoul, her rich South American. The day before they arrived John Gielgud had departed for New York after a two-week stay, and Charlie Addams the cartoonist was due to arrive in a week for an even longer stay. Residing in one of the hotel's suites at the moment was a famous Broadway musical comedy writer with her husband, and in another a very famous conductor with his wife. Peter Lawford the actor and his wife had wired for reservations in April. Travel writers for just about every publication that hired travel writers had been writing it up for a couple of years as *the* choicest and *the* hippiest place to go in the Caribbean. All of this fame, fortune, publicity, income and happiness was due to the shrewd ministrations of one man, Lucky's old friend and the Crount's owner and manager, René Halder, and his wife whose name was Lisa and who was herself Jamaican.

Halder, a French Jew who had been one of the top American movie-cameramen overseas during the war, and whose name everybody automatically pronounced " 'Al-*dare* ", was an ebullient fizzing bubbling little man who had met his wife in New York where she was studying dance and after encountering colour discrimination there because of their marriage, had removed with her to Jamaica and bought the Crount from the heirs of an old British Navy sea captain. And that had been the sea captain's name: Crount.

When asked by Grant—as he admitted he usually was asked by almost everybody—why he had not changed the name, he grinned his tubby little smile and shrugged. " W'y shange heem, Ronnie? 'Ees got mahzel. 'Ee ees so 'orrible I tink I like it. And he canfuse ever'body so much when 'e try to say *Crownt*, instead of *Croont*. So I leave him."

Old Captain Crount had apparently built his small hotel both to take care of him and support him in his old age, and to at the same time allow him to be close to the sea. Apparently he had been given some kind of grant of government land for services rendered the Navy, and he had chosen to take his land out along the seaward side of the long sand spit known as the Palisadoes which encloses Kingston Harbour and terminates in the old pirate town of Port Royal. Here he built his small place, low and heavy and of stone on the ground floor because of storms, cheap and of wood and corrugated tin on the second floor so it would be easy to replace if blown away, all of it together constituting just enough rooms to let him live out his life and keep him in whisky. Situated a mile and a quarter east of Port Royal village and three miles west of Kingston's International Airport on the Palisadoes spit, it perched or rather squatted on the sandy beach staring out south over the sparkling sea with nothing around it except sand, scrub, a few brackish ponds, and the black-top road. And mosquitoes.

But René and his personality and his ideas made up for all of that that might have looked so unprepossessing. By some dubious and marvellous chicanery which he never explained, René was able to take over the old Captain's grant, which should normally have reverted to the government which had given it to him, and by buying out—or paying off—the heirs, take over these rights himself. He had added on to the small place, keeping the same outlandish architecture as being too beautifully ugly to change or demolish, building along the sea-front and in an L back toward the road enough new rooms and suites to make him capable of taking care of thirty clients, or couples. Getting his money whenever and wherever he could, usually from acquaintances in the swiftly widening circle of friends among his clients, he did all this, planted more palm trees all around, built a small swimming pool in the angle of the L, added three small cottages, and managed to pay the whole thing off in the six years he had had it, especially in the last two years of its new notoriety. Now just about all the young executives and editors along Madison Avenue were clamouring for winter, and even summer, reservations, and most of them were getting turned down for simple lack of space. The main lot of these he did accept René relegated to the long L back toward the road which he had added, and which he called " Purgatory ", saving his suites and rooms along the sea-front for his more celebrated clients. This was not so much because he catered to celebrities, he explained to Grant in his strange Jewish-French accent on the first day he met him, as that generally he found celebrities or people who had made their mark on the world more interesting and amusing and more fun for him to be around. And that was all he cared about. This was not to say that an occasional celebrity of unpleasant personality (such as the famous conductor who with his wife was at this moment staying in the hotel, for example) did not find himself relegated to " Purgatory ", as indeed Grant found the conductor was (" I 'ate ze pederasts," René grinned), but in general the celebrities were better to talk to. And René loved to talk. More than that, he could on occasion even listen.

René had met them at the airport in the hotel's pink and white striped jeep with the fringed top. He took to Grant immediately. He had read all of his plays and stories and had even seen two of the plays, whilst on trips to New York.

And he had always loved Lucky, from the very first time she had stayed in his place three years ago. He was, clearly, just the man to further, to throw himself into furthering, Lucky's underhanded and chicanerous plans for marriage. And with his quiet but immensely efficacious wife Lisa on her side too, Grant really had no chance from the start. But then, as he had been telling himself for about two weeks now, he was not so sure he wanted a chance. If he had really wanted a chance, if he had really fought it, not even René and Lisa running in tandem alongside of Lucky could have cornered him.

Lisa, who though quiet could also be a hell of a talker every now and then when she got started, and who apparently loved Lucky as much as René did, occupied herself with arranging and organising the marriage, which was why it was accomplished in five days. And she as much as told Grant, half-laughing, that she was going to do so. And yet Grant did nothing. He certainly would not have organised it himself, the marriage (and probably Lucky wouldn't have either), but he did nothing to stop Lisa doing it. He did protest a little, and looked shamefaced, as becomes a male, as males are expected to do, but that was all. He guessed half of him didn't believe she could really accomplish it.

Lisa, who was half Haitian, had a friend, a long-lined, long-necked, small-headed, beautifully curved, coal-black African beauty of a Haitian girl named Paule Gordon, who had left Haiti when the troubles started and now lived with them in the hotel, and she turned all of the leg-work duty of arranging the marriage over to Paule since she herself could not be absent from running the hotel now during the height of their season. Every evening just before cocktail hour descended on them, in the dim cool uninhabited bar the three women would hold a progress-report conference huddled at a corner table (while René engaged Grant in conversation and bought him drinks at the bar itself) discussing such interesting items as the fact that yes, they *could* get a civil servant to come to the hotel to perform the ceremony or the fact that yes the American consul *would* validate the marriage for American law with an official paper from his office. The date for the ceremony was set for Wednesday next, at five o'clock at the hotel. And still Grant did nothing.

It was all half a joke, of course, and all not half a joke. Everybody laughed and kidded about the forthcoming tying of

Grant's knot, including Grant. But at the same time he was in a strange benumbed half-functioning state during those five days. And only a small part of it was due to drinking. He did not know if Lucky sensed this. If she did she did not say so. It was easy enough for all of them, and easy enough for her too. She had damn' little to lose when you looked right at it, only Leslie and half a tiny rented apartment, and a life of doing TV and movie jobs she hated. Whereas he would be changing his whole life. His whole life pattern he had set up over a number of years. He didn't even know if he had enough money *to* do it, thanks to goddamned Carol Abernathy. For example, should he take her back out to Indianapolis to live? Or should he not? (She had said she was willing to go. But wouldn't it be an awful dirty trick to take her out there to live across the street from Carol Abernathy?) And if he *shouldn't*, where the hell was he going to take her to live, and where get the money to do it on? Maybe he should tell her the truth, all of it, right now before the marriage. That would be the *honourable* thing to do. But he was sure, in his guilt, that if he did tell her now, she wouldn't marry him at all. And he needed her. In fact, now, after that time away from her, then getting her back so marvellously, he felt that he literally could not live without her, and at the same time he hated himself for feeling that way because he felt it was unmanly. A man should be able to live without any damned woman. So he vacillated. And the three inexorable women moved on like the three inexorable Fates. Christ, even René, a man, wasn't on his side.

Christ, if only they could wait till the fall, see how the new play made out, or at least give him time to settle up out there, sell the house maybe, he wanted to tell her that, but he couldn't tell her that, because she didn't care, she was willing to go out there, Oh Christ.

And all this time, every day, except the actual day of the marriage itself, he had been diving with Jim Grointon.

Jim Grointon it turned out, Jim Grointon with whom he had flown to Grand Bank and whose six-foot ten-inch ground shark he had envied, was as much a fixture at the Grand Hotel Crount as the Negro doorman René kept standing by the main entrance stairs in a Haitian general's uniform. He spent about half his spare time there, and drew about a third of his business from René's clients. His steel and glass catamaran was docked at an anchorage around on the other side of the spit near the garrison wharf not far from Port Royal village, and he could have it around to the Crount on call in less than an hour. And in fact, during good weather, he half the time left it anchored right out in front of the hotel just off the beach. Grant learned all this the very first day when, after he inquired about diving facilities, and while the women were already huddled together in their first marriage consultation, René called up Grointon to come over and meet him.

" Usu-al*ly*," René said, " Jeem leave zat boat right out een frawnt 'ere," and swept an arm toward the empty beach beyond the veranda where some paying guests swam in the heavy quiet noonday sun. " W'enhever zay clients want to go div*ing* I call Jeem. " Ee ees a real ganzer macher. 'Ee make plenty beesness off me."

Grant explained how he had already met Jim Grointon. Five minutes later the stocky sandy-haired Irish-cop-looking diver pulled in in his battered old jeep.

" Bes' diver een Kingstone," René grinned after the other two had shaken hands. " But you got to watch heem, Ronnie. Rarly does 'ee teach a man how to dive without 'ee teach ze man's wife someting to! Eet's a shande. 'Ee ees ze biggest Don Huan between 'ere and ze Windward Road. Eef not een ze 'ole Kingstone."

" He's flatterin' me," Jim Grointon grinned with his pale strange lashes, and slapped René on the back with the familiarity of a comrade. " I'm not quite that good. So! I'm glad you finally got down. When do you want to go out?"

" Anytime."

" Then we'll go right now. This afternoon."

" Fine. Come on over and I'll introduce you to my uh——"

" Hees wife," René said.

For just a second Grointon gave Grant a look from behind his pale lashes. " Sure. Glad to meet her."

" She wasn't with me when I went to Grand Bank," Grant felt called upon to explain. " She came down after. And she's not my wife, she's my girl."

" She weel be," René grinned. " Do not to worry. She weel be. When zos t'ree get ze 'eads together." And he bobbed his head toward the table.

" Will she be going out with us?"

" I don't know. We'll ask her. She doesn't dive but maybe she'll want to go along."

She did. " I'm not letting this guy out of my sight for the next two weeks or whatever it takes if I can possibly help it," she grinned. And thus began their daily, day-by-day exodus and return out to the reefs. There were quite a number of them within a radius of four miles from the hotel. The nearest of these, Gun Cay and Lime Cay, which were about a mile away and a mile from each other, they visited first and then slowly branched out day by day among the others: Rackhams Cay, Maiden Cay, Drunkenmans Cay, West Middle Rock, West Middle Shoal, East Middle Ground, Turtle Head Shoal, South Cay, South East Cay. Only a few were actually visible from the surface, so that if you did not know where they were you would not have found them. They averaged in depth from two or three fathoms shading off down to ten or twelve. They were not very interesting diving really, but in spite of that they managed to keep themselves in enough fish for eating. A couple of days the musical comedy writer and her husband went out with them. One day the famous fag conductor and his wife went out, but they did not go again. This was just as well. Grant did not like the conductor, and the conductor equally disliked him. Jim Grointon had a small air compressor at his anchorage with which he could refill Grant's tanks and he was willing as he was with any other client to do all the dirty work, but Grant did not like this. He was a do-it-yourself-and-learn man. So he spent a good deal of time over at the anchorage with Jim, cleaning and filling and repairing, and even helping with the chores of the boat.

The weather held fine. Each day they went out shortly before noon, taking sandwiches and beer, baking in the heavy sun on the near-windless sparkling sea until with the tans they already had Lucky and Grant were soon almost black, darker than the freckled Grointon. The catamaran was perfect for this kind of sailing. With its twin steel hulls, airtight and sealed, its big retractable water-glassbox, powered by two enormous outboard motors, it was comfortable and about impossible to scuttle, turn over or sink. On a framework of pipes a tarpaulin was stretched overhead to make shade, running between the two masts fore and aft, because not even Lucky with her ivory, easy-tanning Italian skin could stand all that sun all day long. The two men were in the water most of the time, and Grant discovered he got sunburned only on the back of his neck and his shoulders which floated free, and on the backs of his knees even though they remained a foot or so under. He was using the aqualung less and less, though they always carried a couple, and was free-diving more and more. Jim Grointon never used one, since a man who could free-dive a hundred and ten, hundred and twenty feet had no trouble free-diving ten or twelve fathoms. Lucky had taken to him in a way she had never taken to Big Al Bonham so that there were no currents of antagonism on the boat, and the long days out on the water were great fun and marvellous even though she still refused to try to dive. She soon discovered that Jim despite his surname was Irish after all, and that however much the " Don Juan " he was and however brave and tough he was underwater, he was still easily shocked and considerably embarrassed by her New York female's outspokenness. A number of native fishermen worked the cays and shoals during the good weather, poling in shallow water or rowing in deep water with their little home-made boats. Invariably they worked totally naked, standing tall and lean in their skiffs, and almost invariably there dangled from their groins the longest and largest penises Grant anyway had ever seen. Only when the catamaran came close enough for them to see there was a woman aboard would they duck down and come up wearing a garment looking like a cross between a priest's cassock and a woman's pullover cotton dress, smiling in terrible embarrassment. So Lucky took to carrying a pair of high-powered binoculars borrowed from René. With these she was able to study their unbelievably large penises from afar without embarrassing them, and this became (she claimed) her " pastime " and her " hobby ", while the two men were out in the water, diving, and when they would return to the boat after a dive she would hold up her hands grinning and measuring what she had seen, or thought she had seen, this time: ten inches, a foot, a foot and a half ; with some such comment as : " Oh, those beautiful big long chocolate things ! Yum !" at which Jim Grointon would retire to the stern with a strained grin to start the motors, his freckled ears red under his tan. Invariably when they returned to the hotel where Jim left the boat now every night, René would chortle and holler, " Et alors ! What you 'ave seen how big to-day ?" Grant knew that at least two-thirds of her little routine was done to shock

Grointon (and any other prudes who might be around the hotel), while almost all of the other third was simply pure iconoclasm, and he would catch Jim looking at her with confused and embarrassed wonderment, and perhaps admiration, whenever he thought no one was watching. And so the marvellous, laughter-making fun days passed. The only day that they did not go out was the Wednesday, the day that they were married.

But in spite of the fun and laughter, the further laughter and drinking and repartee in the bar and on the big porch at night, in all of which Grant joined lustily enough, the only times Grant felt himself to be fully functioning and not numb were those times when he was actually in the water diving. Only then could he completely forget his problem, his marriage problem about which he was doing nothing. Even out in the catamaran, out on the sparkling, always-heaving, never-quiet, sunburnt splendour of the sea, when he would climb back in and strip off his gear, sometimes the lung but more usually now only snorkel, mask, flippers and gun, it was as if some switch would click off, some curtain would fall, in his mind and he would again be facing his problem that he knew he had to solve but which he could not begin the solving of. Should he? Shouldn't he? He preferred to stay in the water. And as a result his diving, which he hated to leave even for a moment now, progressed enormously and by the day of his wedding he was free-diving fifty feet quite easily. But all the rest of this two-some vacation was all truly only half alive, benumbed.

Then too, as if the rest were not enough, his jealousy had come back, and come back with an incredible vengeance, an unbelievable force. He had had it for her all that time in New York, and strongly. But he hadn't had it since she came down to meet him in Montego Bay. Now he had it again. This had happened on the third day when Lucky introduced him to her old, two-year-old, two-and-a-*half*-year-old (time, distance in time, became very important now) Jamaican lover.

He knew the story well enough. She had not been averse to telling it to him. Actually, she had told it to him on that long ride, that long lovely ride down to Florida. How on one trip, one particularly long trip back into his South American country where he insisted on playing his idiot's game of politics, Raoul had left her stashed a particularly long time

at the Grand Hotel Crount. How this guy Jacques, who used
to hang around the Crount and dine there like so many of the
hipper young people of Kingston, had made a big play for her,
and how she figured what the hell, Raoul had it coming to him,
she'd give it a go. They had had a two weeks' affair, going
around everywhere together, and then Raoul had come back
and had hustled her out of there and back to New York so
fast she didn't know what hit her. Yes, he knew the story
well enough. He had even laughed about it on the way down
to Florida (though it hurt him too), largely because he liked to
think of that goddamned Raoul getting one put over on him,
but when he had to shake hands with Jacques Edgar, who was
a handsome pleasant well-off importer son of a well-off
importer father, and feel the heavy warm clean friendly pressure of Edgar's hand in his own, he didn't know if he could do
it, or stand it. All sorts of sick, painful pictures and imagina-
tions ran through his mind, of them together, of her lying back
and opening her legs to him, of her kissing him as he entered
her. What he wanted to do was hit him in the belly as hard
as he could. Instead, he smiled and said hello and pretended
he was civilised.

He should have known he would have to meet him down
here, in Kingston, at the hotel, sometime or other. But that
thought, that possibility, had never entered his head apparently. He would have expected a black man, not that that
mattered, coal-black as Paule Gordon was coal-black. Lucky's
delighted iconoclasm about her Negro lover had made him
sound at least that black. Instead the truth was, with Grant's
dark sea-burnt tan, the pleasant civilised Edgar, who worked
in an office all day, was at least as light as Grant was. And
he was obviously a very nice fellow.

The whole thing was silly, really. Especially was it silly
when he thought of all the women he had slept with himself,
before meeting Lucky. But it didn't matter. It was so painful
that he could hardly keep from flinching and yelling out loud.
This was the first of Lucky's ex-boy-friends he had ever met
face-to-face, and whole new chasms of gloom and doubt
opened up under his already benumbed near-nonfunctioning
state. Was he marrying himself to some kind of a damned
little hustler? Was he letting himself be caught by some kind
of goddamned two-bit whore of a nymphomaniac? But he
loved her. And of course the old clincher: if she liked sex

that well with him, with Grant, why wouldn't she like it just as well with somebody else, with anybody?

Hansel and Gretel, my ass.

And as if all this were not enough to unnerve and unman him in his state of total indecision, a new torment had to be added as if by some cynically laughing fate. The day after they arrived a pretty big *Time*-man, a Contributing Editor, had flown in with his wife from New York for a three-week vacation at the Crount. He had even been given one of René's more exclusive suites fronting on the water. ("I make ze mistake, Ronnie, I'm ze schnuk," René groaned later. "Even I am not ze totalment parfait.") He turned out to be a man Grant had met a couple of times in New York. He had the same sly, half-queasy, overly boyish face so many of his breed had, and he began almost immediately to live up to his looks. When he learned that Grant and Lucky were very likely to be in the process of getting married, he immediately began to insert himself (and his physically attractive, sexless, mentally arrested wife) in with them and their group of friends. Grant stayed away from him most of the time, or managed always to be with somebody when he came around, but finally the Contributing Editor trapped him alone at the dim cool bar on the hot afternoon of the fourth day.

"Hello, Grant," he said with his too easy smile, which crinkled and overly warmed his eyes. "Buy you a drink?"

"Thanks. I've got one."

The Contributing Editor, whose name was Bradford Heath, leaned his arm on the bar in a sort of intimate way. "So you're really gonna hitch it up to-morrow, are you, eh? She's a real beauty. Ron Grant, the last of the bachelor writers. That's news."

"I don't know," Grant said evasively. "They're split into two parties about that. One party says yes, to-morrow. The other says no, not to-morrow."

Heath hitched himself a little closer, boyish cheek resting on his knuckles. "Well, if not to-morrow, within the next couple of weeks."

"I'm not so sure," Grant said.

"Well, anyway, you two are gettin' hitched? Eventually?" Heath smiled.

"Maybe not."

" I wouldn't tell Lucky that," Heath smiled. " That won't be so nice for her. She's crazy in love yith you."

" Well, I'm crazy in love with her."

Heath bobbed his head up on his knuckles, appreciation of the admission. " Anyway, if you do get hitched I'm gonna have to send a release home about it, probably a squib for the *People* page. I hope you won't mind."

" Don't see how I can," Grant said. " Like you said, it's news. Though I seriously doubt if very many people care that much about what's happening to me."

" Oh, people always want to read about celebrities," Heath said, almost bitterly.

" I can never quite think of myself as that much of a celebrity," Grant said.

" Oh, you are," Heath smiled. " You are." There was almost a nasty edge to his smile now.

" Tell me," Grant said without any expression on his face. " What year did you graduate from Harvard, Heath?" He was beginning to get fed up with him.

" Me? Oh, 1950. Why?"

Deliberately Grant did not answer him, and continued to look at him expressionlessly.

Heath's reaction was to hitch himself a little closer, and put back into his smile that over-warmth. " What really interests me, and the reason I'm bothering you," he smiled, " is I'd like to know what your uh foster-mother thinks: about you marryin' a uh showgirl." The way he said " showgirl " was not especially nice either.

Grant could feel his face stiffen a little, but on the other hand he did not feel like he ought to cut and run either. Any reaction but a calm happy one, that would also keep him talking, would look bad, the way Bradford Heath had so sharply and so shrewdly set it up. " Mrs. Abernathy? She's got nothing to say about it. It's me that's getting married. But if you're really interested, she thinks it's probably a very good thing for me."

" She gave you her permission then?"

" Permission?" Grant said sharply.

Heath bobbed his head on his knuckles. " I mean well let's say her blessings."

" Oh, sure. But I don't need anybody's *permission*. Except, of course, yours."

Bradford Heath bobbed his head and grinned. Suddenly he raised his head from his knuckles long enough to look all around cautiously, over-cautiously. " You know there were a lot of us at *Time-Life*," he smiled confidentially, " what never really swallowed that foster-mother story that young kid wrote when he came out to Indianapolis. But he was one of our sharpest young reporters, so we all accepted it. And printed it. But a lot of us still didn't believe it, privately. Incidentally, how does your ' intended ' feel about all that?"

Grant could hardly believe he had heard right. " My ' intended ' feels exactly like I tell her to feel," he said coldly.

Nobody but a fool, an utter complete fool, would have approached him like that. He was being invited to admit to this queasy sneaky tall Ivy League fucker that he had had an affair with Carol Abernathy, after having gone out of his way for fourteen years to conceal it.

" Then you're a lucky young fellow," Bradford Heath said, and smiled.

" I make my luck," Grant said.

" Do you, now?"

Grant nodded solemnly. Then after a moment he said, with a perfectly straight face, " Well, of course you're quite right. And it's quite true. She couldn't possibly be my foster-mother because I was already twenty-one when I met her and Hunt. You can't adopt somebody once they're of age."

There was a little silence in which Bradford Heath's eyes studied Grant above Bradford Heath's knuckles. Then he remembered to smile. He was backing down, Grant could sense, or at least backing off. Perhaps he thought he had gone too far. " Uh, yes of course that's all quite true," the Contributing Editor said in a serious resonant tone.

Grant thought it was a good time to get out. " Well, see you around. Got to go and find out what my uh showgirl future wife is up to."

" Didn't she used to be Buddy Landsbaum's girl-friend, some time back?" Bradford Heath asked after him.

" Yes," Grant said over his shoulder without stopping. " As a matter of fact it was Buddy who introduced us."

Even the greasy sea-slime of a coral reef was bracing and clean alongside of this, Grant thought as he went to find Lucky, and all he could think about—underneath all his other problems to which this problem was now being added—was

to get back out to them as quickly as he could in Jim's boat.
But they did not go out on the next day, on the Wednesday,
because in the end that was the day they were really, finally,
and irrevocably married after all.

Actually they could have gone out on the Wednesday too if
it had not been for Lucky. The wedding ceremony was set for
5.30 in the afternoon, after the heat of the day, in the big
hotel bar (the Crount had no " Lobby " or " Reception " and
the master received his clients in the bar). So there was no
reason that they could not have packed their usual sandwiches
and beer and gone out to the reefs except for one and the
one was Lucky.

From the moment she got out of bed on the Wednesday she
seemed a totally different girl than any of her myriad personalities Grant had seen. She giggled, she flirted (but then she
always flirted), she laughed at everything like a flitter-brain,
she acted extravagantly at the pool pouring champagne
down the bosom of her swimsuit, she acted like an idiot school-
girl about to go out on her first date and too unsure of herself to know whether she liked it or not. In short, from the
moment she got up, had her shower, dressed and went down to
the veranda for breakfast she was totally hysterical and as the
day wore on she got more hysterical than totally. And Lisa
Halder was her accomplice.

For Grant, to lie or sit on the bed in the morning after
having made love and watched that long, deliciously curved,
rich, warm, heavy-breasted, round-hipped, lean-legged body
come out of the shower to dry itself and then finally begin to
dress itself, was one of the greatest pleasures of his day, every
day. It was quite clear to him on this particular day that
neither had Lucky any more than he ever thought that it, It,
wedding someone, Marriage, would ever happen to her specifically. Perhaps she had sometimes thought that at some
indefinite time in some indefinite future she would some day
marry some indefinite man, but not specifically and not here
and not now and not *him*. When he suggested later after
watching her that they go out with Jim in the boat anyway
like on any other day, thinking this might calm her, she said
she did not want to go, but that she *would* go if he said so
because he was going to be her Lord and Master to Obey and
she better be getting used to it. Then she giggled. Grant said
no. Thinking twice, he decided he would not like to have her

out in any boat in this condition, especially with him off in the water diving.

So they did not go. They played at the pool with their new friends they had made, the musical comedy writer and her husband, and a wealthy young psychoanalyst and his wife who was a designer of children's clothes. But finally, after nearly everybody had gotten three-quarters drunk at lunch and her idiotic shenanigans with Lisa got worse and worse, he took her off to their suite and made her a speech, a lecture, a serious down-to-earth let's-face-our-facts talking-to. He probably sounded pompous as hell he thought, listening to his own voice, but he meant every word of it. The upshot of it was that getting married was a serious business and not a joke and you didn't do it as if you were playing games, and that was the way he was taking it: seriously, and that was the way she had better take it too. He was marrying her for good and always and for keeps and that was the way she better think of it. He was astonished to hear the grandfatherly responsible tone of his voice, amazed at the responsibility in him. " If there's anything I've learned by watching people, married people, at all," he said, and he was thinking mainly of Hunt and Carol Abernathy at that moment, " it's that the minute one of them ever steps out on the other side, the whole fucking thing is blown to hell, over, and the pieces just never fit back. That's the way I'm marrying you, and that's the way you better be marrying me, the way you *are* marrying me, whether you know it or not, and you better remember that." She sat on the edge of the bed like a little girl with her two hands in her lap and listened to him quietly without smiling and two big tears rolled from her eyes down her face. " I know it," she said, " and I am."

But at the ceremony itself the shenanigans started up again. She and Lisa. And Lisa was at least sixty per cent the instigator. Lisa who had been married twenty-three years. Well, maybe every woman resented it a certain amount, and maybe not a one of them ever entirely got over it entirely. So they giggled and made fun. He had to admit it was ludicrous-enough-looking: the tall solemn black civil servant who was to perform it for them wore as his badge of office a long black frock coat and a very wide-brimmed black hat which he never took off, so that he looked like he had just stepped out of a Western film where he had been portraying Sam Grant,

and appeared to be at least as likely to shoot them down as to
wed them. Of their four witnesses, who all had to be locals,
three were black: Lisa, her friend Paule, and Sam the bartender; and the fourth, René, as he himself said later, probably could not count as white either since he was a fat French
Jew who could hardly speak English. They all laughed like
hell over that later. An auspicious beginning, Grant said,
later. But then, at the moment, when the two women started
their infernal indecent hysterical giggling again as they all
sat facing the black civil servant, he bent such a ferocious
frown on them and hushed them so viciously that they both
said later he scared them three-fourths to death. He at least
scared them to silence. Long enough anyway for the ceremony
to get over.

But afterwards, during the required celebrations, she and
Lisa started up again, giggling hysterically together and,
together with Paule who also had some resentment against
males apparently, the three of them had great sport at his
expense about how they had concocted the snare and trapped
him in it. And even that did not quite end it. Because that
evening, when it was all over, and they were hitched, " Itched
tighter zan two Jamaican mules " as René had guffawed, and
everybody had celebrated and all drunk a great deal, but not
eaten, because it was not even yet dinner-time, they two went
off together to their suite and a-little-more-than-half drunkenly
went to bed. And after making love for the second time that
day, Lucky, lying in his arms with her eyes shut while he
leaned looking down at her on his elbow, said in a low but
quite clear voice, " Some day I'm going to cuckold you."

It did not sound so much like a simple statement as like
some oracular prophecy that had come out of her and for
which she was not responsible. He understood that she
resented somewhat having given up her " freedom " to him,
but he did not know what to say in response to that remark.
The silence seemed to go on and on and Lucky seemed to
show no signs that she was going to break it. " Then I'll just
cuckold you, too," he said huskily.

" No, no. No, you must never do that," she said, her eyes
still closed. " It would hurt me too much."

Grant didn't answer. Suddenly he thought of the day she
had done the nude dance in the water at Montego Bay. Inside
himself he seemed to get more and more and more breathless.

"Well, then if you ever do cuckold me, you'll have to let me watch it," he said, even more huskily.

For response, Lucky opened her eyes and smiled up at him. She didn't say anything. She didn't say a single word. She simply lay with her eyes open smiling up at him. After a moment Grant got up and reached for his underpants. "Come on, let's go down and eat dinner," he said gruffly.

He was suddenly dangerously angry. She should at least have said something. About how she knew it wasn't true. On the stairs going down, after they had dressed, he leaned forward and tapped her roughly on the shoulder and said roughly, "Just remember that fantasy isn't reality." Again she looked up at him, over her shoulder, and smiled in silence. What he wanted to do was hit her. Then she reached back up the stairs and took his hand in one of the most loving gestures Grant had ever seen. He shrugged her hand away. You should never say things like that to anybody. Especially when they were things you didn't mean at all. If he could have seen Jacques Edgar in front of him, or Forbes Morgan, or even Buddy Landsbaum, he would have punched any one of them, or all of them, in the face.

And who should he see standing in front of them, as they rounded the turn of the stairs and debouched down into the narrow foyer? Bradford Heath! Standing by the potted papaya! Fortunately, because of the turn of the stairs, Heath had not seen his brusque gesture.

"My congratulations, Grant!" the Contributing Editor said with his alert queasy smile. "And to Madame all my best wishes!" He shook hands with both of them. "I watched it all from the periphery. Oh, uh, can I see you for a moment, Grant?" he added as they made to pass on.

"No, you can't," Grant said roughly and shouldered past, but Heath put a restraining hand on his arm. Lucky had by now already gone on ahead.

"I just wanted to tell you that I sent in my little story," Heath said, as Grant jerked his arm loose.

"I don't give a fuck what you do, Heath," Grant said roughly. "You just do whatever the fucking hell you like."

"My, my! Don't get angry!" Heath smiled.

"I'm not angry, Heath," Grant said and started on.

"And I just wanted also to tell you," Heath called after

him, "that I just learned that Mrs. Abernathy is staying
with the Countess de Blystein in Ganado Bay."

Grant stopped and swung round.

"In case you didn't know," Heath smiled.

"So?"

"Naturally, it made me wonder why you didn't invite her
and her husband down for the wedding?" the Contributing
Editor said softly, still smiling.

"You figure it out," Grant said. "You're so fucking smart,
you figure it out for your fucking self. And now for Christ's
sake, *leave me alone!*" He turned on his heel.

Shit on them, he thought as he followed Lucky's deliciously
swinging bottom and long straight back into the candle-lit
bar where everybody was getting up from the set-up dining
tables to applaud the newlyweds, fuck them all. All of them.

When the phone call came in from Ganado Bay three days
later, he was not so surprised and it was as if he had been
anticipating it. And when Doug came up the steps and across
the porch the day after, he was reasonably sure what he had
come for. He was glad Lucia Angelina Elena Videndi Grant
knew all about the phone call.

Then, as he charged across the porch to say hello to Doug,
he saw the big lumbering bear-like figure of Al Bonham, who
had been discussing something with the cab driver, start up
the steep angled steps a few yards behind Doug.

TWENTY-FOUR

Because of the flattening of the angle of sight across the porch
from where she was sitting back against the house wall with
their new friends, Lucky did not see Bonham until she had
already waved and smiled and yelled at Doug. She was always
glad to see Doug, for some reason that she could never quite
define, but she remembered she was always just as glad to see
him go away. This was not the case with Bonham. When his
huge head appeared over the edge of the porch, and then was
followed on up by his great Kodiak-bear-like body (that was
the only way you could really describe him), she thought *Oh
no!* and the intermittent kind of half-despair she had been

feeling off and on since the day of the wedding came back over her, more strongly. Now they would have that big oaf hanging around, drinking up Ron's money, trying to sell Ron something, taking him out diving or some damned thing, like that goddamned yacht of his, sporting his only too open dislike of her, which she returned. She and Ron had little enough time together now as it was.

Grant, she noted, was shaking Bonham's hand just as happily and with just as much pleasure as he had shaken Doug's.

Lucky could not say what it was that caused her to feel this half-despair and depression every now and then. Usually there wasn't even a reason, such as the presence of Bonham now gave her. It would just come over her, perhaps out on the boat, or at dinner, or at the pool, anywhere, anytime, and while she continued to laugh, or pretend to do whatever it was she had been doing, some other part of her would go on wondering with a gritty taste for minutes if it all wasn't some huge ghastly joke of a terrible mistake. Christ, how long had they known each other, after all? Two months? Six weeks? What could she possibly know about him in that length of time? Or he of her? All of this would taper off, down into a pungent melancholy in her that would last a long time, and wherever she was she would look for him quickly, and go and take his hand, or perhaps just touch him, the Hansel-and-Gretel babes-in-the-woods feeling coming over her again. The melancholy would linger on, like an echo.

It all had to do, of course, with whether she had misplaced her love. By placing it all on him. And how could she be sure she hadn't? Only when she read, or re-read, the work he had done. But he hadn't done any new work now since they had met. And didn't show any signs of being about to do any. Maybe she should have waited, damn him.

It was essentially this feeling of terrible double-mindedness that had caused her to get so kooky hysterical the day of the wedding. She had at the eleventh hour—eleventh hour? twelfth hour?—suddenly discovered that she did not want to get married, not married at all. And if it had been anybody but Ron, she by God wouldn't have. And yet she did. Did want to. The condemned girl ate a hearty lover. And when Lisa, who when she egged her on in her rebellious kid's play also taught her conclusively that *she* had not been all that happy all these years either, got her to giggling and sniggering, she couldn't stop, or help herself, even though she knew what she was doing. And that was why she loved him so for his serious pompous, Boy Scout's lecture.

The strange thing was, and they had both discussed it—both before and after—they were fooling the whole world by getting married. Because getting married could not—and did not—legalise their sex life. That would—and it did—remain just as dirty and good as before. Neither did getting married give them any more social responsibility. They would pretend all that—and they did—when they went demurely before the US consul, and why not? If anybody found out, they might very well be fined and imprisoned. And they laughed a lot over their hoax. But at the same time she was terrified of and resented marrying any goddamned man. Of course, she was no spring chicken at twenty-seven-nearly-twenty-eight either, and she had to remember that.

And it was these same incongruous unmatchable feelings that had been in her that afternoon after the ceremony when she had told him that someday she was going to cuckold him. She was angry at him for his having let her marry him so easily. It was right and proper for men not to want to get married, and for women to want to marry them, that was life, women *were* nest-builders, men *were* rovers, and Ron *hadn't* wanted to get married; but he hadn't done enough about it, damn him. After the ceremony, she had been appalled by the enormity, the irrevocability, of what she had done to herself. Putting herself in some man's hands forever, in some man's power. And lying there in the bed with her eyes shut but aware of him leaning over her, after they had made love, their first married one, and looking ahead down the long long stretch of years, ten years, twenty years, thirty years, crystal anniversary, silver anniversary, golden anniversary, how could *any* two people stay faithful to each other all that time, she had never seen it. So it just slipped out. She knew the minute she said it she shouldn't have. And she didn't even mean it. But she was so angry.

The unexpectedness of his answers interested and amused her. She understood that he didn't mean it, that it was fantasy. She understood about fantasy, she had played fantasy games before, and would again—and had—with Ron: the cold princess ordering her slave to go down on her, the slave girl being ordered to go down on the prince, the audience game. There was nothing wrong with playing fantasy. The only thing wrong with fantasy was when you actually tried to indulge your fantasies and really do them, make them real. But then coming down the stairs he had acted as though he thought she didn't understand. The poor dear was suddenly angry because he was ashamed of what he'd said. That was when she had reached back to take his hand. She just as suddenly wasn't angry any more.

The whole thing was over before it started anyway, with that goddamned *Time*-man standing there at the foot of the stairs. As she walked on ahead of them, she could hear Ron's voice telling him off loudly. He told her about the whole thing at dinner. So neither was she surprised when the phone call came from Carol Abernathy three days later. And she, like Grant, was pretty sure, when she saw Doug, of what at least part of his mission was going to be. But not with Bonham.

The phone call itself was a strange and pathetic thing, really. It had come directly in to the suite, and she had been in the room with Ron when he took it. Here was this poor woman, ousted from his life, and after throwing that terrible fit they had all of them laughed about so at Bonham's, calling up to ask for help. Ron had been very noncommittal.—" Yes a True—guy? A *local*!" He listened. " Well, there's nothing to worry about . . . No, I don't know him. But I know the guy who started it. Yes. Bradford Heath. No, you don't know him. I met him in New York. . . . I'm not sure we *can* come up there. And I don't think it's necessary. . . . All right, I'll think about it. But I don't think it's necessary. What? . . . Yes, I *know* Evelyn is inviting us. You must remember that my main responsibility right now is my wife, Carol. And what's good for *her*. . . . Well, that's just the way it is. You what?" He had taken the phone down from his ear and looked at her, Lucky. " She wants to talk to *you*."

"All right," she said calmly, " I'll talk to her." But she noticed as she took the phone that her stomach was suddenly fluttering. " Hello?"

The sweet, utterly charming voice came back with its distinctive Middle-western nasal twang, urging her to come back up to GaBay and make the visit. " I don't see why not," she said. " Of course, it's all up to Ron really. I'll do whatever he says."

" Well, you talk to him," Carol Abernathy said charmingly.

There was a smile in her voice as if they two, being women, understood. "He's peculiar sometimes." . . . "No, I have nothing more to say to him. Good-bye, dear."

Lucky hung up. She stood silent for several moments. "I don't see why we shouldn't go up there, really," she said finally.

"I don't know," Ron had said, with a hollow look. "I just don't know. I'll think about it. Maybe we could. But she's a nut, you know."

"She sounded perfectly charming."

"Oh, sure. She could *charm* a wooden dog."

"What can she do to hurt us?"

"Nothing," he exploded. "Not a fucking damn' thing!" He took her in his arms. That was the way it stayed.

Lucky got up. "Please excuse me," she said now to the musical comedy writer and her husband, and the young analyst and his designer wife. "Surely you know Doug Ismaileh? Or know of him? I'll introduce him to you. The other one, the big one, is Ron's first diving teacher and Ron has a special soft spot for him which I for one think entirely undeserved." My God, she thought. She was beginning to act like a real wife and hostess. With good grammar, even yet.

At the table, after the introductions and after the two new-comers had sat down, it came out soon enough what Bonham was doing down in Kingston, but Doug hung back and appar-ently didn't want to talk in front of the others—which was perfectly correct, Lucky thought. He had just wanted to come down and spend a few days with them, see how they were doing, he said, before going on back to Coral Gables.

But later, after all the others including Bonham had gone off, Doug still hung back. He continued to hang back until Ron told him forcefully that she, Lucky, his wife, knew all about that goddamned phone call. That puzzled her.

But in the meantime, while they were all still there, Bon-ham had taken over the floor, rather expertly, and he held it expertly, with a persuasive wit and charm Lucky had never seen in him before, once he had been introduced to the famous musical comedy writer and her husband and to the analyst and his wife. When he first came up, he had looked at her with those strange storm-cloud eyes of his and that knowing grin, and had said, expansively, "Well, Mrs. Grant! Please accept all of my very best wishes." You couldn't fault that. But behind that it seemed to Lucky he was saying to her privately with the eyes and the grin *Well, baby, you finally made it, hunh? and I just wish to hell you weren't here*. But Ron of course did not notice that.

The upshot of all that Bonham had to say, and he seemed to assume that the four new acquaintances would be as interested in it all as Ron, Lucky and Doug, was that he had already been in Kingston two days finalising the purchase of the schooner, that he had arranged to meet Doug at the airport and come see them when he learned from Doug in GaBay that they were married and Doug was coming down to see them, and that he would like for them all to come down to the yard and have a look at the ship. He had managed to make them come down a thousand dollars on the price after he had seen her (he very carefully did not say " Jew them down " since it was clear the four new acquaintances were all Jewish). This was largely because the extent of the dry rot damage in the bow was worse than had been anticipated.

" So-o-o, it looks like instead of two thousand or fifteen hundred," he said with a wry smile, " our yard bill is gonna run five thousand or six. Anyway, I'd like foi all of you to come down and look her over up on the cradle if you'd like to. You folks too," he added politely to the four New Yorkers.

It didn't take much for Lucky to see through that. It was Ron he wanted to get down to the harbour to look that boat over, and he didn't give a good goddamn if anybody else went or not.

" Well, I'd love to go," she smiled. " I'd love to see it." Doug and Ron, of course, were both enthusiastic. The other four wanted to go too, but it turned out they had made an appointment to drive up into the hills and have lunch at the Blue Mountain Inn to-day, a beautiful hidden-away retreat-like place where she and Ron had had dinner once. It was decided to do it to-morrow, to-morrow during the morning, but it seemed to Lucky that Bonham's nose seemed a little out of joint. She was glad.

" What are *you* doin' this afternoon?" he asked Ron.

" Well, we'll probly go out again with old Jim Grointon," Ron said. " We've been out with him every day except our wedding day. Whyn't you come and go along?"

Bonham grinned a wolfish grin. " I'm not so sure it's the

proper thing to do. Since we're sort of competitors, you know."

"You're not competitors in Kingston. What the hell, I'm payin' for the goddam boat. I can ask anybody I like along as a guest."

"Okay, I'll go. If it's okay with Grointon. Look, I've got a few things to do over at that yard on the other side of the spit. I'll go there and do that and meet you back here—when?"

"Oh, twelve-thirty?"

"Fine."

Then just the three of them, herself, Doug and Ron, were alone together. And still Doug went on with his holding back and hedging, which surprised her.

He talked about nothing for fifteen minutes, until Ron insisted he get to his point. "Look, we know who sent you down here. Come on."

"Well, I——" He stopped and looked at Ron.

"Well, come on," Ron urged fiercely, his eyes squinting. "What is it? Lucky knows all about that phone call. She even talked to her. Didn't you know that? Shit, you must have been standing right there."

Doug seemed to blink without blinking. "Oh, it wasn't that. I just wasn't going to tell you I'd been 'sent', as you say. Because I wasn't really. I was going to come around to it gradual-like, and tell you what I thought.

"Anyway, all of them up there including Carol think you and Lucky ought to come back and stay there a week or two. Just to show there's no hard feelings between you and them. And I sort of think so too. This local *Time*-guy's been bugging Carol every day for a statement about your marriage, and he's getting very pushy. She gave him a statement saying she thought it was a fine thing, but that's not what he wants, says he could have anticipated that. He's convinced there *is* hard feelings, and he wants to get a statement out of her to that effect, which would make more interesting news than what she said. Meantime, he spends his spare time marlin-fishing. He's havin' a ball."

"Well, there *were* hard feelings," Lucky put in. "My God!"

"Yes, but there's no point in lettin' these people publicise it in their fucking rag," Doug said.

"He's right there," Ron said, "damn it." But he looked doubtful. "I know who's behind all this," he said to Doug. "I'll point him out to you. Name is Heath. He's a Contributing Editor or some damn' thing. He's the one who sent that local guy up there."

"Well, I think you ought to do it," Doug said. "If Lucky doesn't mind." He swung his strange, enigmatic, Turk's eyes on to her.

"I told him I was willing to go," Lucky said. "It probably won't be pleasant. But it can't do anybody any harm for a week or so."

"Oh, I don't know," Ron said thoughtfully. "But I s'pose we ought to do it." He looked at Doug.

Lucky found herself angry at Doug. "Well, I said I'd go!" she said hotly. Then she straightened up and smiled. Jim Grointon was coming up the steps. "Oh, hello, Jim! Here we are." Then when she saw he was empty-handed, she made a face. She had been teasing him for two days to borrow an even larger pair of Navy binoculars from some English lord friend of his who ran the anchorage on the other side of the spit, and which he had inadvertently told her about. She loved to tease his prudery. "You didn't bring my Navy binoculars?"

Grointon reddened, and grinned. Ron laughed and told Doug about her anatomical study of chocolate penises. When the two were introduced, Lucky watched them shake hands sombrely, taking each other in, studying each other. Men always did that. Like two strange dogs in the street. It both irritated her and made her want to laugh.

There was something very physically attractive about Jim Grointon that Lucky couldn't quite put her finger on. And in spite of all his prudery there was a cold, bitchy quality, an egocentric indifference about him that back in the old days with Raoul—or, back any time before Ron Grant—would have made her want to take him and deliberately cold-bloodedly fuck him once or twice, make real love to him a couple of times, then cast him aside like a tattered used old flour sack just to see how he would react. It was pretty clear he was the one who was used to doing the casting aside. And she was completely confident he had never laid a woman as good-looking and beautiful as herself, or who was as accomplished in bed as she was. How would that affect his cold bitchiness? In the old days she might have done it. Once driving in Jersey on a summer Sunday with some musician friends, professional classical musicians—violinists, harpists, cellists who all made a good living for themselves in New York playing all the concerts and classical record dates, and with whom she had run around for a year or so—she had seen standing in front of a rag-tag motordrome a cocky, dirty, arrogant young fellow wearing sideburns and levis, black jacket and boots, clearly a low-class cat of some totally uneducated kind, who obviously thought he was a ladies' man, and maybe was even hung well (certainly he was muscular enough), and she had had somewhat the same feeling about him as she had about Jim Grointon. He had obviously never screwed any kind of a lady before, and she had wanted to cold-bloodedly take him on as a one-or-two-night-stand stud and then gently but firmly throw him away. She had told her musician friends her fantasy. Her friends had urged her to do it, saying they would all go back to the motordrome and, while pretending to watch the motorcycle performance, really watch her. But she had not done it that time, either. Sticking to her theory that fantasy indulged is not only fantasy lost but might also be actively dangerous, she had declined. But Jim Grointon made her feel somewhat that same way, and so she didn't really like Jim that much better than Bonham after all. Except that she did.

"Are you married, Jim?" she asked him pleasantly later on that same day, when they were finally all out together on the boat.

She was sitting back in the stern on the starboard side near the motors, which Grointon steered with his bare foot on their coupling bar while standing in his characteristic position leaning on the tarpaulin's pipe frame to look ahead. Ron was almost across from her, talking to Bonham on Ron's left and to Doug on Bonham's left. When Jim had learned that Bonham was coming with them, he had immediately suggested that they go some place other than their usual stamping ground, and Lucky thought she knew why. Ron had complained to her mildly that these near reefs they had been going to were not really very good diving since the reefs were too small for big fish and the banks were almost all pure sand. She did not know why Grointon had kept taking them there unless it was pure laziness or the desire to save money on fuel. In any case, almost certainly because of Bonham, Jim had suggested that to-day they go down the coast to Morant Bay where he knew some better reefs. His excuse for not taking them before was that it was a much longer trip and anyway Ron hadn't been ready to free-dive that deep yet, which was between fifty and sixty feet. Now he could—though they would take along a couple of lungs anyway just in case.

It was on this first leg, the long trip down, that she asked her question about his being married.

"Yes," he said, without taking his eyes off the horizon. Quite a large number of ships traced their way among these reefs and shoals into and out of Kingston harbour. Then he looked down at her with his blue cop's eyes behind their pale lashes. "Yes, I am. To a local Jamaican girl. Got two kids by her. But we're separated." He looked back out at sea.

"Is that because, as René says, you're such a 'Don Huan' around the Grand Hotel Crount?" she smiled.

Again Grointon looked down at her, and then grinned. "No. No, it isn't. It's because I just simply can't stand to live with her any more. She's stupid, and ignorant, and she won't learn—won't try to better herself. She's a hick. I like it at the hotel, like to spend time there, but I could never take her there. She wouldn't fit in." He looked back up again out over the sea. "And on top of that's she's almost totally neurotic. A nut."

"But you must have known all that when you married her, hunh?" Lucky said.

Grointon made an embarrassed grin. Without looking down he said, "She was young. I thought I could teach her."

Lucky made a provocative, provoking laugh. "When are you going to learn you can't teach women anything?" she teased.

Again Jim looked down at her, penetratingly, with those strange eyes lined with blond fur. "I guess that's right," he said noncommittally, and looked back out to sea.

Across the way Ron, who apparently could listen to her conversation while engaging in another one with Bonham, suddenly looked back at her, slightly over his shoulder because of the way he was sitting, and jerked his chin at her pugnaciously, and flashed for one second at her such a deep stare of ferocious fury that it almost seriously scared her.

Grointon was looking out at sea. Bonham and Doug were talking. So for answer she arched her back, threw back her shoulders and grinning, shook, wiggled her breasts at him, all in a second's time, so fast none of the others saw. But it did not make him smile as she had hoped it would. God, she loved him so much more than all the rest of their weird, screwed-up types put together.

Apparently she was not alone in this. For after they had been anchored for about twenty minutes somewhere off Morant Bay (she couldn't see any *bay* anywhere, only straight shoreline), Big Al Bonham came swimming back to the catamaran with several fish and climbed into the boat grinning and singing Ron's praises to the point where it almost became embarrassing.

Before that Doug had come back even earlier. They were swimming in water too deep for him to even get anywhere near the bottom. And he and Lucky had sat for almost ten minutes in silence. At first he had seemed as if he wanted to talk, but she had discouraged him. He said, " I hope you don't mind my sayin' what I say, but I do really think Ron ought to go back up to GaBay." She said, " Of course not. And we'll go. If Ron decides that that's what he ought to do," and then went rather pointedly back to the book she was reading. So Doug was there too when Bonham came lumbering in over the side bragging about Ron.

" That's really some guy, your new husband," he said, shaking his head. " I never would've believed it. The son of a bitch is free-divin' deeper than I can go already."

" Aw, come on," Doug said.

" I crap you not. He's doin' fifty-five and sixty feet out there to-day. Sixty feet is about all I can do on my best days. I never saw anybody pick it up so fast. He's a goddam genius or something."

" Then it ought to make him feel good," Lucky said.

" That's the funny thing," Bonham said quizzically. " It doesn't. He goes right on worrying and stewing and being gloomy. What is it with him, anyway? I can't understand. Now he's worrying because he can't keep his diaphragm from heaving for air on the way back up. Says Grointon doesn't do it."

" Then he's probably going too deep," Lucky said, " for his experience." She was suddenly nervous and felt a panic start to flutter in her stomach. "Doug, hand me a beer, will you?"

"No, he's not," Bonham said. "That's not what I meant. That happens to just about everybody. What I meant was, I just can't figure him out. Every time he gets ready to do something, he's nervous, and moody, and high-strung, and scared. Then when he——"

"I think it's just because he doesn't happen to be an aggressive type," Lucky said. She drank the beer down fast.

"Haw!" Doug called from where he was getting himself a beer. "The fuck he's not!"

"Well, anyway," Bonham said, "I think he deserves everything he's got, and everything he can get. I never met anybody who ever deserved their success as much as him. He's what I'd almost call the perfect human man—mentally, physically, every way. Well, anyway," he said, and then slapped his big hand down hard on his thigh with happy satisfaction. "You know," he said, "I've got a theory. Would you like to hear my theory?"

"Sure. Why not?" Doug said.

"About Ron?" Lucky said, more cautiously. She didn't want to have to hear any Bonham theories about Ron.

"No, not about him. Though he comes into it too. All of you do. I graduated from the University of Pennsylvania after the war," he said directly to Lucky. "You didn't know that, did you?" With his storm-cloud eyes he was looking at her with that enigmatic, mocking look again that he turned on her so often. He didn't wait for an answer.

"My theory is about what I call the Chosen Ones or the New Aristocracy. The Chosen Ones simply mean celebrity-hood. If you're worried, both of you qualify. So does Ron. Lucky qualifies because she's married to Ron. In our own time this celebrity-hood jazz has become world wide due to technological advances begun in World War II and expanded enormously since then. Lumped together these advances are called Mass Communications. Whatever the process, a Chosen One, once arrived, once 'chosen', becomes different from other people, actually lives by different laws almost. They are protected by everybody, they get better service, are treated with deference, are given better deals on everything, live off the fat of the land. All for the publicity. They become protected symbols of what everybody would like to be.

"Now the other phenomenon that has grown out of the technological advances begun in World War II is Mass Cheap Travel. In this age of 'You-must-work-forty-hours-a-week-government-required', the carrot under the nose of a 'Citizen' or a 'Comrade' is that for two weeks every year (or a month, if you're an executive) he can live like a Chosen One lives all the time. Not really, of course, but enough to make the pretence digestible. If he saves his money the other forty-eight or fifty weeks of the year, he can go just about anywhere in the world, be catered to, be treated as if he really were a Chosen One. This is known as the Tourist Industry. All the exotic places, the faraway romantic names, he can now visit and pretend (for a while) he is one of the New Aristocracy he has helped to choose, and preserve. The whole world is opening up due to Mass Cheap Travel egged on by Mass Communications—in the East as well as in the West. It's an entirely new field, the Tourist Trade, a real 'Frontier' (probably the only one left), being 'Pioneered' by people who want to live like the Chosen Ones live all the time. And the Chosen Ones, the real Chosen Ones, are the kings of and key to it all.

"Take the Grand Hotel Crount, for example. It's a Chosen Ones' hotel. Hell, if you're not a Chosen One it's hard as hell to even get in there. But where the Chosen Ones go, the unchosen ones want to go. Did you know that when Kingston became popular with the Chosen Ones because of the Crount, the tourist business and the hotel business boomed all over the area?

"No, it's all coming on fast. All over. Everywhere. And for the U.S., at least for the next twenty years, it's going to be the Caribbean. It's all being prepared for. Soon the big advertising will start.

"And that's where guys like me and Jim come in. We cater to the tourists—with our 'special skills'—mainly the unchosen ones, but preferably the Chosen Ones. Because that's where the loot is. Look at René. What can an unchosen one do with his lousy little two-week vacation? You think he can really learn skindiving in two weeks? Of course you don't tell him that. But the Chosen Ones have *time, and* the money. Jim's got himself a booming business in Kingston, not only at the Crount but all over the town. Yet he makes most of his real money at the Crount.

" And that's what I hope to do in GaBay, once I get my schooner out and to going." He slapped his leg again, hungrily. " I want to live, with and like, the Chosen Ones."

He had seemed to get carried away as he talked, and both of them had listened, fascinated by the businessman inside Bonham the adventurer.

" But," Doug said now, " you haven't got any Grand Hotel Crount in GaBay."

" Sure we have. We've got *one*," Bonham said. " The West Moon Over Hotel. They get lots of celebrities there, and it's still coming up. Some of the Kennedy family stayed there last year." Again he slapped his leg, a sound like a hungry pistol shot. " But don't you see, with my schooner I'm not committed to any one town or one hotel. I can make the entire Carribbean my ' work area '."

" And what's gonna happen to your lovely primitive seas and pristine unfished reefs after several thousand other guys like you do the same thing?" Doug grinned. " You're contributing to the desecration and destruction of the very thing you love."

Bonham grinned back. " I don't care. I'll be dead when that happens. Meanwhile *I* can escape ' Civilisation '." Then suddenly he sat back and relaxed. " But you people, you're already members of the New Aristocracy, you're already Chosen Ones. All you got to do is sit back and enjoy the gravy. Enjoy our, *my*, services."

Lucky had been wondering all this time what this big spiel was all about, and she suspected that it was directed directly at her. " Yes," she said with asperity. " Yes, all *we* have to do is maintain that high level of success. Did you ever try it? If Ron Grant has one big flop, he won't have enough money left to be one of your Chosen Ones. And I imagine that's true of Doug, too."

" Haw!" Doug said. " It sure as shit is. But he's right about most of those film people, though. Liz Taylor. Burton. John Wayne. Kirk Douglas. Mr. Zanuck."

" Well, maybe it's not true all the way of Doug and Ron," Bonham said. " But I think Ron really is one of the Chosen Ones, and of all the people I've ever met he is the one who deserves it the most." Then he grinned. " But for my purposes it's true enough, anyway. Besides this guy Sam Finer, Ron is the only one of the Chosen Ones, or nearest to being one,

that I've ever had as a client." He grinned again, winningly.
"If he likes me, maybe he'll tell other Chosen Ones among
his friends."

"Then why do you try to antagonise and alienate his
woman?" Lucky said. "I'd think you'd be smart enough to
know that's not the way to handle any man—even if he's *not*
in love with his wife. And Ron is."

Doug laughed suddenly, as Bonham stared at Lucky. Then
the big man smiled his most winning smile. "But, honey, I'm
not! I've been trying ever since I met you to find the key to
you that would make you like me." Behind his smile his
storm-cloud stare at her belied everything he said.

Lucky's Italian anger was rising. She found she had gotten
the bit in her teeth and couldn't stop, though she wanted to.
"You know what I think about you? I think you're accident
prone in your social relations. Not in your work, obviously.
But in everything else I think you're a loser. Because like all
losers psychologically you want to punish yourself. As for
finding the key to me, it's easy enough. All you have to do
is——"

They were interrupted by a shout from the water.

"Hey! Help!"

For a man of his enormous bulk Bonham could move
incredibly fast. He was off his seat, back to the stern and had
the huge long pole gaff over the side struggling with something, before Lucky, moving as fast as she ever had moved,
had barely stood up. Her heart beating in her ears, the only
thing she could think of at all was *shark*. God, how she hated
this fucking damned sport! For a moment she thought she
was going to faint, the way she had used to do as a child
whenever anything horrified her. Then Doug had his arm
around her and was shouting in her ear: "It's all right! It's
all right! Nothing's wrong! I can see!" Then in a calmer
voice, "Here. Come over here. It's all all right. You can
see. They've just got a big fish, that's all. A *huge* fish!"

By leaning over the port-side seat she could see that Bonham
had got the big gaff hook into an enormous fish. Grointon
and Ron, their masks still covering their faces, their snorkels
dangling by their straps, were shouting at Bonham and
laughing with triumph, swimming in opposite directions to
hold the big fish steady between them on their two spearlines.
Seeing her, Ron yelled at her: "It's a jewfish!"

"Hey, Doug!" Bonham gasped. "Come back here. I can't get enough leverage. There's another gaff under the starboard seat. Gimme a hand."

Doug looked into her eyes clinically, like a doctor, then let her go and grabbed the other gaff. Between them, straining, their faces red, the two of them got, hoisted, the monstrous flapping organism up on to the floorspace of the catamaran, the deck. While they held it with the gaffs Bonham reached under the port-side seat and got a short stout club and whacked it soundly on the spine, on the "neck", just behind the head. The great fish's entire body, its fins and its tail quivered and stiffened and it lay still. A strange purplish iridescence shot out from the spot where it had been hit and spread all over its body which was unpleasantly coloured in many shades of off-red, red-brown. It lay still now but rolled its eyes all around and kept opening its mouth and gaping its gills trying to breathe. Lucky stared at it fascinated, horrified. It was beautiful. And its mouth was big enough to almost take in a man's head and one shoulder. It must have been all of five feet long and twice that around. Behind her Ron and Jim climbed in over the bow end laughing and slapping each other on the back.

"Boy, you should have seen Ron!" Jim Grointon told them laughing. "He came down and in there like a real old pro, Al!" He slapped Ron on the back again. "Buddy, if you can make a dive like that and hold your breath that long you can dive eighty feet right now, and there's no reason you can't do a hundred feet. I made a miscalculation about you. I didn't know you've got all you've got."

Lucky watched her lover and husband blush shyly. "Aw, shit. It was the excitement of the moment," he grinned. "I couldn't do it again."

"If you could do it once, you can do it again," Jim said. Still half breathless, he told them the story. And as she listened, Lucky watched the reddish colours of the fish slowly fade away until its eyes were dull and its colour a dun brown. That hurt her the most, the eyes going as it died. That and the vicious clubbing. They had been swimming maybe two hundred yards off the boat, Jim said. He had seen this big jewfish come out of a cave, and he had gone right for it without thinking about anything else except getting him. There never would have been time to get out a Brazilian rig

anyway, and they would have lost it. They almost lost it
anyway. He had speared it from in front in the head, maybe
forty yards out from the coral overhang, but had not made a
killing brain shot. After a monstrous flip like an explosion (Al
had seen them kick), which would have broken a man's back
if it hit him, it started for the cave. The depth was probably
sixty feet to the bottom, and the fish was maybe eight or nine
feet up from that. Of course he couldn't hold it. That was
when Grant came down. Diving what must have been a full
fifty feet from the surface, he put his spear into the fish's
head from the other side, he even had the presence of mind to
think of that. He didn't make a killing shot either. But
between them they were able, by both swimming as hard as
they could backwards and to each side, to halt the fish's
progress toward the cave where he could have cut the lines on
the coral. Finally, they had been able to horse him up near
enough to the surface where they could get their heads out and
breathe.

"Man, I was never so glad to get a fresh breath of air,"
Jim laughed.

"Me either," Ron said. "But you were down about twice
as long as I was. I never could have stayed down that long."

"Buddy, you stayed down long enough," Jim said. By the
time they had got air, the jewfish had pretty much given up
the fight. "One of the good things about them is they poop
out fast."

Beside them Lucky had begun to cry. As the life had faded
from the big fish so had all its colours faded too, as if the life
itself were actually the colour, and now it was only a piece of
dead brown meat that stank of fish slime. "You're bastards!"
she cried suddenly. "All of you, bastards! What did you
have to kill it for? It wasn't bothering you! It was trying to
get *away*! Bastards!"

"Honey, honey," Ron said soothingly. He put his arms
around her. "It's only a fish."

"Don't think he don't kill," Grointon said mildly. "How
do you think he eats?"

"She almost fainted, when you guys hollered," she heard
Doug explaining to Ron. "She was scared. She thought
there'd been an accident."

"That's got nothing to do with it!" she cried. "And as for
you," she said to Grointon, "what do I care whether he kills

or not? You're supposed to be men! Civilised men! Human beings! You're not fish! Or are you?" But she was beginning to get herself stopped from the crying. "You might have gotten yourself killed," she said to her husband. It was funny. Normally she didn't think of him as "husband".

"Impossible," Ron said, still holding her. "Honestly, I couldn't possibly have. And look at all the fish we got. We got enough to feed the whole hotel for two or three days."

She was wiping her eyes on his bare shoulder now. "Let the fishermen get the fish," she said, in a more subdued voice. "And buy them at the market. That's what they're for. They make their living that way. But no, you have to kill. It was beautiful, that fish. It was alive."

Jim Grointon was staring at her. "Men like to kill fish and game," he said, and there was a strange, profoundly deep, totally icy quality in his voice. From Ron's shoulder Lucky looked up at him fascinated. "They always have liked to kill fish and game. And I guess they always will. And women usually like them for it."

"And, sometimes, they like to kill each other," Ron said in an odd little voice. He, at least, understood what she meant, Lucky thought.

"Yes, I guess," Jim said. "But that's what makes men. That's what it is to be a man. That's what a man needs to feel he is a man. I didn't make the rules. I didn't create this world. If I had, I'd probly have changed a lot of the things."

He seemed coldly furious. Lucky allowed Ron to sit her down on the port-side seat and accepted a beer. "Of course you're absolutely right," she said. "I was just upset. I thought somebody'd gotten hurt. Uh, incidentally, what would you have done if there hadn't been anybody else on board but me?"

Ron and Jim both stopped and looked at each other for a moment. They both grinned. "I guess we'd have gone ahead and shot him anyway," Ron said.

"Oh, we could have got him killed some way or other," Jim said. "In the water." Then he smiled. "You don't realise that you don't get a chance at a fish that big every day."

"I guess that's what upset me," Lucky said. "He looked as big as a human being. And then I watched him trying so hard to breathe. And he rolled his eyes around at me as if

asking me to help him." She smiled at Grointon, why tell
the oaf the truth? "That didn't bother you," she smiled, half
asking.

" No," Grointon said.

" Fish don't feel," Bonham said. She smiled at him too. She
did not tell him what she wanted to say, *That fish felt*, why
tell any of them the truth? Except Ron she'd tell. But nobody
else: Their hunting was perverted. A fisherman's wasn't.

"What do you think he'll go?" Bonham said to Grointon.

Grointon squinted at the jewfish. " I think he'll go three
hundred at least."

After that, she mainly watched them all, in silence on the
trip back home. It was soon clear why Bonham had pulled
the fish up on the catamaran's deck. Grointon towed a little
plastic dinghy behind the boat and usually the fish they
caught were kept in there, where the three fish Bonham had
brought back earlier now were. But the enormous jewfish
would have swamped the dinghy. So now it rode on the deck
between them, and the four men kept looking at it from time
to time. From time to time they talked about it affectionately,
as if it were some kind of a goddamned friend, and they kept
rehashing the story of the kill. She seemed, and felt, totally
excluded.

She felt the same way that night at dinner. Bonham ate
with them at the hotel, and somehow amongst the four men
she was a complete outsider. They talked, they laughed, they
joked, but they left her out of everything, seemed almost to
forget she was there. It was not that they were not polite, or
that they actually turned their backs on her. And it was not
that Bonham himself caused it, or even that Bonham's advent
caused it. But it was as if the four of them, being together,
and being men, more: being spearfishermen (because even
Doug was one in a small way), and having been on a successful hunt to-day, had developed instinctively some kind of a
common feeling, a common personality, of which they believed that she could not be a part, or even understand. She
did not mind it much, because she had had her evening nap
and tender, deep, love-making session with Ron before cocktails. But it was hard to believe, sitting back and watching
him with these other three men now, that this Ron was the
same Ron who had loved her so well upstairs. He roared with
the others, telling horribly terrifying stories about the war

which they all laughed at. They guffawed, they slapped each other resoundingly on the back between drinks, they gave each other great rib-cracking nudges with their elbows standing at the bar after dinner. The big fish had of course made a great to-do at the hotel and they kept congratulating each other on the taking of it, while expansively receiving the congratulations of the other clients. Of them all Jim Grointon was perhaps the quietest, but it was quite clear he was very definitely of the same persuasion. She suddenly remembered having been in London once with another lover, on a short trip, and he had taken her for a walk down Jermyn Street where he wanted to go to his shirt-makers and pick up some pipe tobacco. Jermyn Street, the " men's street " of London : shirt-makers, tailors, tobacconists, men's hairdressers, men's shoe-makers, and of course the pubs. Everything for men. She saw one other woman, also looking very out of place, guilty almost like herself, in all the time she was there. She had felt the same way there in London, then, as she felt now, here, to-night. She had hated men.

She told him about it all afterwards, after they were alone and had gone up to their suite. But of course they were both quite a bit drunk by then, so probably she shouldn't have.

It was hard to explain to him, in the first place. Hard to explain to anybody. What did she really want to say? Brutality and insensitivity, was the upshot of it. Did men, when they got together in groups, have to become brutal and insensitive, to prove to each other they were manly? Did manliness and insensitivity have to go hand in hand? If so, it boded no good for the race or anybody. What kind of manliness was that? Not any kind she wanted.

But it was more than that even. All this contemptuousness toward women, all this standing together in a block against the suffocating inroads of womenkind, this *need* to have a world apart that women could not enter, were incapable of understanding, all this had to come from a deep-seated dislike of women, a misogyny, that could only be the result of insecurity and lack of confidence.

She didn't like the way Bonham loved him so much. Was it only because she was jealous? Was it only that? She didn't think so. But there was something strange and violent about Bonham. He was a violent man, even though he was an adept at covering it up. And only violence, something bad, a losing situation, could come from associating with him. And the same was probably true of Doug.

When she had said it all and finished, she found she still hadn't said what she'd wanted to say.

Her husband was looking at her with eyes that were having difficulty focusing, though he didn't stagger at all. " Well, gee, honey, if I'd known you felt outside of everything, I'd have . . ." He made as if to put his arms around her.

" No!" she said. " Don't do that! That doesn't help anything! I'm trying to talk to you seriously. It's not just Bonham. It's you. I'm worried about you."

He had turned on his heel and sat down on the bed-edge after she backed away from him. He sat there totally nude, his hands dangling between his knees, while she talked on. When she stopped he looked up at her, his eyes bright, his face an animal snarl almost, and his voice was the voice of a different person. What could have happened to him? In so short a time?

" Okay. I'll take it under advisement. I'll think about it. But it's my fuckin' money. And if I want to put some of it into Bonham's fuckin' boat I'm fuckin' damn' well goin' to. You fuckin' *got it*?"

Lucky had recoiled and was staring at him. She had never seen him like this. He was positively almost ravening like an animal.

" And while we're on the subject of complaints, I've got a couple of complaints of my fuckin' own. I'm the boss of this fuckin' household, and I'm layin' down a couple of rules. You stop flirting with that goddam fuckin' Grointon—or I'll punch your goddam head in and his too. An' the other one is that I'm not meetin' any more of your goddam ex-boy-friends. Period. Jesus! I can't stand shakin' hands with the sons of bitches. I want to go wash my fuckin' hands. It makes me sick in my stomach. I am a very jealous man."

Lucky felt exactly as if she'd been slapped in the face, it even hurt up there, on her cheek, and her mind went totally blank. It was as if a block of hot, burning ice had formed all round her. She said, " You knew damned well you'd almost certainly meet Jacques here, when you came here. And as far as that goes you'll probably meet a lot of others before your life is done. So you better get used to it," she said coldly.

"What would you have had me do, not even say hello to him?"

Her husband grinned. "Sure," he said. "Why not?" Then he laughed. "I want you to give me a list of every man you fucked. I want it to-morrow. That's an order." He giggled. "Then I'll know who not to shake hands with. Christ, there may be another fuckin' dozen of 'em around here for all I know."

"Sweat it out," Lucky heard herself say coldly. "You'll never get it out of *me*, you son of a bitch."

"Aw, shut up and go to bed. Leave me alone." And he stretched out on the bed and pulled the sheet up over him. Stiffly, like a person walking amongst unbroken eggs, she went around to her own side of the pushed-together double beds and got in and lay there, a stiff frozen block.

"Shit, it's like being married to a goddam whore," his pillow-muffled, stranger's voice said, "for Christ's sake."

"I never took any money," she said coldly. Then she heard him move and added, before he could, "except for Raoul, and you know he was going to marry me."

"Aw, shut up and leave me alone."

"Gladly," Lucky said. She had never felt so totally frozen up inside. He had deliberately hurt her in her most sensitive place. Deliberately. Or had it been deliberate? She lay in the bed thinking of what she could do to him. As she went off to sleep, finally, she remembered thinking it was the first real fight. As far as she cared, it could be the last, too.

He woke her at four-thirty. He himself was still asleep, but he was moaning and gritting his teeth. He was rigid. His face was covered with sweat and his hands kept clenching and unclenching at his sides, while his feet jerked and made little fluttery motions every now and then.

"Ron!" she said. "Ron!" and touched his shoulder. He sat bolt-upright in the bed, his eyes wild.

"What is it? What is it?" she said.

"Oh, that damned nightmare again," he said in a muffled voice after a moment.

"About the fish?"

"Yeah."

"I think you're crazy," she whispered. Ron didn't answer. "But you weren't scared to-day. Were you?"

" No. No," he admitted. " No, I wasn't scared to-day."

" Then what is it you're brooding about so now?"

" I guess it's because I'm scared now," he said. After a moment he lay back down, and then turning toward her put his hand lightly on her shoulder. After a moment, she covered his hand with hers. And after a while they made love and then lay clinging to each other in the darkness.

TWENTY-FIVE

Day the next morning came grey and damp, and the good weather had broken. The wind had shifted to south-southeast. Looking due south from the now cool porch of the Grand Hotel Crount, clouds—a heavy seldom-broken cloud layer with the slanting falling blue streaks of rain squalls scattered all along its length—stretched all the way to, stretched right on around, the sea's horizon to the south and east. It darkened the high hills in the west. If the wind should freshen —and it did—Jim Grointon had already decided at eight o'clock to run his catamaran back around inside to the anchorage and not dive to-day. When the Grants came down for breakfast on the covered terrace at ten-thirty, the wind was already whipping the red and white checkered tablecloths and driving the less adventurous like Bradford Heath back inside, and Grointon and his boat had disappeared.

At eleven it began to rain. Bonham appeared in a borrowed car soon after. He did not appear inclined to put the visit to the schooner off for a prettier, sunnier day so, piling in hastily to avoid the rain, into Bonham's borrowed car and a hotel car which René loaned to Grant, the large, already slightly damp party pulled away from the hotel. No one of them seemed to have quite enough courage to tell Bonham they did not want to go.

In one way only (because there was no diving) was it a good day to visit Bonham's new pride and joy. In every other way it was not. But this did not seem to bother Bonham.

The boat—the ship—had been hauled at a small yard not far from the Royal Yacht Club around on the inland side of the harbour. Bonham led them there in the cars, and then they all ran for the shelter of the boathouse—all, that is, except Bonham. He walked, slowly. The musical comedy writer and her husband, and the young analyst and his designer wife, all close good friends of the Grants by now, were not sailors and therefore were not used to walking around fully clothed and drenched, even in a moderate rain. They spent the entire visit in the big, musty old shed and only looked out at the schooner, upright in its cradle in the rain, through the big open doors. Only Grant and Bonham seemed impervious to the rain. Grant seemed even to enjoy it, as if climbing the ladder to the slippery deck and getting soaking wet put him in some closer communication with spray-drenched sailors. Doug went with them on board, and tramped all around with them, but both his face and figure had the look of a wet angry cat. He had by now found himself a blonde good-looking middle-aged Frenchwoman, a refugee from Haiti staying at the hotel, whom he had brought along. This lady stayed in the shed with the New Yorkers, not looking happy at all. But Lucky Grant went with the sailors. Wearing sneakers without socks, shorts and a sleeveless jersey, with an old yellow sou'wester hat of Bonham's pulled down on her head to protect her hair, she climbed around the boat with the others, inspecting the foremast, looking at the enormous mainmast and its rigging, inspecting the interior, and got as wet as they did, clearly determined not to be called anything but a good sport.

Grant could read it in her. It was strange but in these few days since they'd gotten married, caused by some occult alchemy of close warm wet sexuality, it was as if the two of them had actually become one personality, the two separate eyes in one head as it were, so that each knew at any given second exactly what the other felt or was thinking. Grant grinned his appreciation at her and she smiled back.

The old ship—for it was a ship, once you got up on its deck and looked at the size of the main boom; it was not a " boat "—was not very much to look at, except maybe to the eye of an expert. Sixty-eight feet long overall, it was not beamy enough to be really comfortable, and this fact immediately became apparent once they got below and looked at the accommodations. From the cockpit a five-step ladder descended through a sliding hatch into the main saloon and the four of them in it all together crowded it. The big main-

mast came right down through the centre of it, and the table
was built around it, with a dropleaf on either side. With
the leaves up there was no room to pass, or even to get up or
down, and the whole thing turned itself into a sort of dinette.
On the port side forward of the saloon separated off by a
bulkhead, was an open single bunk which could be extended
into the central alleyway to make a double, and on the starboard side, extending into the middle so that the central alleyway ran forward a little bit to port, was the "main cabin".
In this, which had its own door, was a three-quarter bed with
barely enough room between it and the bulkhead to walk,
provided you turned sideways. And while it had its own
door—for "privacy"—the bulkhead, to provide aeration,
only ran two-thirds of the way to the ceiling. Standing in
the "main cabin" you could look right down on the portside
bunk across the alleyway.

"This is certainly not a boat built for lovers, is it?" Lucky
said cheerily, after peering into this compartment. Bonham
merely glared at her.

Forward of the sleeping quarters the rest was conventional:
galley on the port side, the smaller head on the starboard to
take less room from the "main cabin", and in the forepeak
two crew's bunks and an open toilet. When Bonham said it
slept eight he was correct technically, but they had better be
a very tiny eight. Everywhere, as on the topside, paint was
peeling and the old dark varnish cracked and flaking. Gear
and mouldy-looking sails were piled in the portside bunk and
all around the saloon. A heavy musty odour of old canvas
and long-since-dried sweaty socks pervaded everything, and
was not lessened by the heaviness in the air caused by the rain
outside. Indeed, the very rain itself seemed appropriate,
seemed to lend itself to the gloomy smelliness of the entire
inspection. All in all, at least to the neophytes, it was not
very prepossessing looking.

As if he sensed this in them, Bonham said, " Of course, we'll
fix all this interior stuff up eventually before we *really* start
chartering her out. Anyway the insides don't matter much.
She sails like a son of a bitch. I've been out on her. I think
what we'll probly do, once we get the money, is rebuild
the whole interior by another plan. I'm workin' on a plan for
it now."

"Will that be soon?" Lucky said pleasantly. Bonham

stared at her with his cold eyes before he grinned. "Not bloody likely," he said in an English accent, then reverted: "We can't even pay for the real structural, necessary repairs yet, right now." It was a war to the finish with them, she could see that, and had been ever since she had been so bold as to tell him what she thought was wrong with him. "That's a shame," she said pleasantly.—"Yeah," Bonham smiled, "ain't it? It sure is." Both of them watched Grant moving around touching things with a rapt, gone expression on his face.

He really had it bad. The bad smell, the cracking varnish, the peeling paint, the mouldy gear, none of that had any effect on him at all. He seemed instead even to like it. More, he somehow seemed to feel curiously at home in it. He did not know whether he had gotten it before, up in Ganado Bay before he had even seen the boat, maybe he had. Maybe he had come all prepared to fall, already brainwashed. In any case he had it now. He would give anything in his life except his wife—and the success of his next play—to be the owner of this boat. This ship. And failing that, to be a part-owner, even a tiny, piece-owner, of it. He crawled and scrambled over the whole interior of it again, his third complete tour. And Bonham watched him happily. Triumphantly.

Bonham took him outside in the still-falling rain, though falling less heavily now, to show him the dry rot area starboard forward, and pulled aside the tarp that had been hung over the hole to keep out the weather. Lucky, peering out through a saloon port, watched them and thought later that it must have been then that Bonham talked to him about the loan. In fact it was not. Bonham talked to him back at the hotel, after they returned when, having showered hurriedly, he went down to the bar ahead while she was making up and dressing. Bonham had, without ever having said he was going to, waited on him all that time down there in the bar, and Bonham was not about to miss his chance now, and both he and Grant knew it. But of course she was not there for that.

"Well," the big man grinned from the bar, and raised his glass of whisky and bottled soda. His wet clothes had practically dried on him by now. "So you liked her, hunh?"

"Christ!" Grant said huskily. "She's a real beauty." And to him she was, though he knew nothing about boats. "All that inside stuff can be fixed up and redone any time."

" Sure," nodded Bonham. " Though once she's all cleaned up and you throw a little paint and varnish on her, you'd be surprised how nice and comfortable she'll be below. Without *changing anything*."

" Yeah," Grant said. They two were alone at the bar, except for Sam, René's Jamaican barman and one of the witnesses at the wedding. " Gimme a double scotch with a splash of soda, Sam," Grant ordered and then turned back to the big diver who was leaning on his forearm on the bar and smiling. It had been a big day for Grant. Since coming down in the morning and finding the bad weather, he had had a sense of vast relief that to-day he would not have to go out, not have to dive, not have to swallow down all his fears still another time. It was like having a day off from school. And as always, around sea ports and sea resorts, the advent of bad weather had brought with it a sort of gala feeling of vacation and vacation-excitement. Perhaps that influenced his feeling about the schooner also. But he would have loved it any way. It was the first time he had ever been this close to somebody who could and would own a boat like that. And more, who would put his whole everyday professional life on the line for it. Looking at him he wished he had ever wanted anything in his life as much as Bonham wanted that schooner. The only thing he had ever wanted that badly was to be a great writer, a great playwright. But that was not a concrete object like the schooner. That was something he would never know about, in his own lifetime. But Bonham, with his concrete, wood-and-rope-and-canvas schooner, had a dream to live on that any man could envy.

" 'Course," Bonham smiled, " I can't do that work now. Shit, I can't even pay for the repairs, like I said." He paused and sighed, still smiling. " They stopped work on her yesterday, you know."

" No!" Grant said. " I didn't! Why?"

Bonham shrugged. " No money. They want at least a thousand bucks right now, to-morrow, to continue work. I haven't got it. So, no work. She sits there till I get it. And after a week they'll start chargin' me rent." He had timed it beautifully, and had read the lines just about perfectly. " I shot off a wire to Orloffski this morning. But I'm worried about him. I got a hunch he won't come through with anything."

"Yeah." Grant nursed his drink a moment, then finished it off and motioned to Sam for another. "I'm convinced that he stole my camera up there in GaBay, you know that?"

Bonham's face was bland. "Well," he said. "I don't think he did." He paused again. "We searched the whole damn' house when we got home, you know. Doug was with us."

"Hell, he wouldn't hide it in the house if he stole it."

"No," Bonham said. He took a drink. "But what would he want to do a damned thing like that for? Christ, he knew I was tryin' to interest you in our operation. It's crazy."

"Maybe he can't help it. Maybe he's a klepto."

"Naw," Bonham said, and grinned. "I don't hardly think that."

"I'd be damned careful with him as my partner, I'll tell you that."

"I told you before," Bonham said. "I need him. I got to have him. To swing this deal. Without his cutter Finer would back out." Then, suddenly, he was silent. He studied his drink.

Grant nursed his own drink, jiggling it and watching the ice swirl.

"A thousand dollars," he said finally.

"Yeah," Bonham said. He did not look up.

"Just to get them *started* back to work."

"Yeah."

"Well, look," Grant started, then stopped, and rubbed his jaw vigorously.

"Yeah?" Bonham said.

"Look. How much do you think you could get by with—the absolute minimum—to get her fixed up and back into the water? I mean, the *abso*lute *mini*mum!"

"I don't know," Bonham said. "Like I said. I figured five to six thousand, probably six. But certain things ain't absolute necessities. I mean, they don't have to be done to make her *run*. Oh, I guess. Say four thousand, maybe. Say forty five hundred. To be sure."

Grant took a deep breath, and blew it out in a sigh. "All right. I'm going to loan it to you. You got to get that boat in the water."

Bonham's face and eyes lit up like a Christmas tree. "You wouldn't! You really would?"

"You got to get that boat in the water," Grant said again.

It was more as if he were explaining his decision to himself than to Bonham or somebody else.

"But you don't hardly even know me. How do you know I'm—How do you know I'm good for it?"

"Oh, I guess you're good for it. But look. This isn't anything easy for me. I don't have that kind of loot just layin' around. It's gonna put a big hole in me to loan it to you. So be sure. Be sure you can do it on that."

"Oh, sure," Bonham said. "I can do it. She won't be pretty maybe. But she'll *run* just as good. She'll *run* anywhere in the world."

"All right," Grant said. He looked as if he was not sure he was not crazy, as if he were still surprised to have heard what his mouth had just said. "We'll fix it up to-morrow. I'll cable my lawyer in New York."

Bonham drew himself up to his full height, with his face delighted. "But that's not enough! You got more than that coming to you! To do a thing like that! Look. I want you to know first, right now, that when we take our maiden cruise you and Lucky are invited to go. As my guests. You don't pay a nickel." He held up his hand for Grant not to interrupt him. "More. I want you to accept ten per cent of the company. I'm sure I can get Orloffski to give you five of his forty-nine per cent, and I'll give you five of mine. But if Orloffski *doesn't*, I'll give you the whole ten out of mine. I've only got twenty-nine per cent right now because I signed twenty per cent. of mine over to my wife. To Letta."

"Why did you do that?" Grant asked curiously.

"Oh, taxes. And some stuff like that. But I also wanted her to feel part of it, feel like she was in on it." Grant could not help remembering what Lucky had told him Letta had told her about their sex life. Very carefully he made himself not lower his eyes, or look away. "But aside from all that I want you to accept ten per cent."

Grant held up his hand, and found he was grinning foolishly, was embarrassed. He looked for a long moment out through the big french doors at the sea, where the rain had stopped now and some sun was showing through, enhancing the dim dark and shade of the bar. Tropical Jamaica, and the Caribbean Sea, and a strange old chic hotel bar, and he was lending a professional diver and ex-professional sailor almost five thousand dollars. To save a ship. "I don't care about that. I'd love to accept the invitation to go on that maiden cruise, though, on behalf of Lucky and myself."

"But you got to accept the ten per cent," Bonham insisted. "This ain't gonna be any bum deal, you know. We'll make money." Then he paused and looked all around the empty bar suspiciously, then moved closer to Grant. "Look. I'll also let you in on something else." Again he looked around. There was no one there but Sam up at the other end of the bar, studiously polishing glasses. But Bonham was talking almost in a whisper. "How would you like to go in on a salvage operation with me? Half and half."

"Where?" Grant said.

"Off Ganado Bay. I discovered a wreck. Just a few days ago. Right after you left. Day I was out by myself."

"You mean, like, treasure?"

"Naw," Bonham said scornfully. "Nobody ever found any 'treasure', except Teddy Tucker. These are brass cannon. Bronze cannon. Twelve of them. All stretched out and layin' there on the sand in the same oval shape the ship that carried them had. I seen them."

"Where?"

"Off the western end of my deep reef, where you've dived, outside of GaBay. I've swum over them a thousand times. The only thing I've figured out is that currents must have just lately swept the sand away that covered them. Mid-Eighteenth Century bronze cannon."

"But what if they get covered back up again?"

"So much the better," Bonham grinned. "Then nobody else will find them. But anyway it's deep. Nobody ever dives out there except me."

"Are they worth anything?"

"Hell, the bronze alone must be worth six, eight thousand bucks. As relics they might even be worth more. We'll split it. Half and half. Just you and me."

Grant found himself beginning to feel a little leery. It sounded too good. "How much will it cost me?"

"Not a dime. Oh, we may have to rent a boat with a winch heavy enough to haul them up, but that's peanuts. And they're just layin' out there right on the sand. If currents cover them up we'll just dig 'em out. I know where they are now."

"When would we do all this?"

"Any time you say. I got nothin' to do now until that schooner gets out of the yard. We could do it now, this week. Next week."

"How long will it take?"

"Oh, a week. Maybe two. Not more. You see, salvage law most every place is, now, that the government whose coast the salvage is found on gets a cut. Half. Usually. But we might be able to hide these and wait till the schooner's out, and take them to Mexico or the States and sell them black market. Shit, museums buy that stuff black market all the time."

"I don't want to get caught breaking any laws," Grant said.

Bonham shrugged. "Then we'll declare them. I don't give a damn."

Grant was thinking. "Well, it might fit in with our plans," he said finally. "We were thinking of spending a week or so at Evelyn de Blystein's before going on back home."

"You were?" Bonham said. He looked surprised.

"Yeah. Why not?" Grant demanded.

Bonham moved his head, guiltily. "No reason. Is Mrs. Abernathy still there?" he added.

"Yeah, that's the point. Listen," Grant said, to change the subject. "Why didn't you pull up these cannon to pay out your schooner?"

"That's what I was going to try to do," Bonham said, "until you came up with the money for me. Hell, you might even make back what you're loaning me. But I doubt it if we have to declare them to the government."

"I'd like to do it," Grant said thoughtfully.

"Okay, we'll do 'er."

"It's an idea. Just for the diving experience, if for nothing else." Then his heart skipped a beat, and sank. Shit, here he was getting himself back into more goddam fucking diving again.

"It'll be diving experience all right," Bonham grinned.

"And you'd really do that for me? Just give me half like that?"

"Why not? You'll be doin' the work. Half of it. And it's hard work. And you're puttin' up the money to get the schooner out, aren't you?" Bonham had straightened up again. Lucky was just coming through the french doors. "But don't tell anybody about the salvage. Don't even tell

Lucky. Not yet." They had had two more drinks apiece while they were talking and Bonham looked at the bar. " Uh have you got enough cash to take care of these drinks for me?"

" Sure. I'll just sign for them," Grant said.

" Then I'll see you to-morrow. Hello, Mrs. Grant," Bonham said politely, and tipped his white captain's cap to her.

" What was he up to?" Lucky said after he left. " Up to no good, I bet."

" Nothing," Grant said. " Nothing much, anyway." But it gave him a bad taste in his mouth to lie to her. So later, over dinner, he told her all about it all, all except for the salvage job. Certainly he told her about the loan. And she listened quietly. They were dining alone that night. Alone? With Doug, and with René and Lisa, and with Doug's French-woman But at least Bonham was not there, and that made it seem alone to Lucky.

But René picked up on the loan business even before Lucky had a chance to say anything. " You just geev eet to heem? Like zat? No security nor not'ing?"

" Well, no. I don't know. Maybe. I mean, he don't know anything about banking and interest and all that crap."

" Mais, no-o, leeson! Ronnie, my friend, eet eez crazee, no?" René said. Then he shrugged. " Enough from ziz mishugas. Zat eez not zee beezness. You must not to worry. I weel taking care of 'eem to-morrow. You go for meeting him to-morrow, no? Zis Bonham?"

" Well, sure. I have to wire New York for the money."

" Hokay. 'E come weeth you. We talk to heem."

" Okay, René. But he wants me to take ten per cent of the company, you know."

" Zat is different. Zat is okay. Fine. But zat eez not zee security. We talk to heem."

Grant had not expected such a swift and belligerent—or if not belligerent, aggressive—he had not expected such a swift and aggressive response from René. And he had expected Lucky to be angry. She was not. She had always had the feeling that once a thing was done it was done, like it or lump it good or bad it was done, a fact, and that was the way she felt about this. Besides, it was his money, he had a right to spend it how he wanted. " Maybe I was wrong about Bon-ham," she said. " I don't *know*. All I have to go on is my instinct. And the fact that he doesn't like me. Any way I'm sure he's *honest*."

"Eez not ze question of hon-est," René said. "Eez ze question of security."

"Why doesn't he like you?" Lisa asked.

Lucky shrugged. René answered. "Perhaps eet eez because 'ee eez afraid you go to steal Ronnie from heem?" he grinned.

"Steal him!" Lucky said. "How can I do that? I've already got him. I'm his wife!"

René shrugged. "Eez just ze idea."

Lucky grinned impishly. "Well, I've got something Ron wants. Something that he *needs*. And I know for goddam certain sure that Bonham hasn't got one of those!"

They all laughed. Doug's blonde Frenchwoman despite her native coldness had begun to take to Lucky too, by now. No, it was not the loan that caused any trouble between them (even though he didn't have that much money really to spare), the trouble was caused the next night, and it was caused by such a ridiculous thing, when he thought back about it, and when she did too, that the whole scene was completely stupid.

But before that happened in the evening, Grant and René had had their session with Bonham in the morning.

Grant's' telegram had gone off, in response to which the money should be arriving by cable the next day, by the time Bonham showed up at the hotel. There was still a good bit of sea running, though the storm had begun to fade, so they were not diving this day either. René came right to the point as soon as he had had Sam serve them drinks in the bar.

"'Ow eez 'ee set up, zees compagnie of you?"

Bonham explained it.

"Zees Fin-ér, 'ee 'as zee two per cent, hein? An' 'eez loan, eet eez hagainst ze compagnie? or against ze schooner 'eemself?"

"Against the company. But of course the schooner's owned by the company."

"Ah, mais oui, chéri. But ze schooner 'ee eez clear, non? Bon! I not weesh make kibbitz. But I am ze lawyer—ze guard'*ouse* lawyer—for Ronnie 'ere, hein? Hokay? Hokay! W'at 'ee want eez thees: 'Ee want a first mort-gage on ze schooner 'eemself. Not ze compagnie, hein? Eez hokay?"

Bonham rubbed his chin for a moment and scratched his

cheek. Yeah. Yeah, it's okay. If that's what you want. But I don't see what——"

René threw up a hand. "H-i *hex*-plain. Eef ze compagnie 'ee go broke, ze schooner 'ee eez to going sold, right? And w'en ze schooner 'ee eez sold, ze money 'ee go be assets for compagnie, hein? An' ze compagnie, broke, 'ee use 'eem money to pay off debts, right?"

All through this Bonham had been nodding. "Right."

"Hokay, w'at Ronnie——"

"But we're not expecting the company to go broke," Bonham grinned.

"Mais non, of course not. Still, eez possibility. 'E mus' be kosher. Hokay? Hokay, w'at Ronnie want ze first mortgage of schooner, *not* compagnie, an' ze sale of schooner pay Ronnie forty-five 'undred dollair *before* ze assets go to pay compagnie indebtedness."

"Oh, I see!" Bonham said finally. He looked a little surprised. "Sure. Okay. That's fine with me. That's the way we'll do it then."

René moved his head. "Wait un moment. 'Ee must vote zee partnairs for zees decision, non? Za ozzers, 'ee weel vote like you?"

"No," Bonham said right away. "No, that ain't necessary. As president and captain I got power-of-attorney for the company, all signed."

René nodded crisply. "Hokay. H'l 'ave my lawyer—" he chuckled—"my *real* lawyer, draw heem up like zat. You hunderstand me? Zees way eez zee real security for Ronnie make ze loan."

"Sure, I understand it now," Bonham said. "And that's fine by me. I wouldn't want it any other way. And you tell him, too," he said to René, jerking his head at Grant, "that he still has ten per cent of the company. Yesterday he didn't know if he wanted to take it."

René moved his head. "Zat eez between you two. Zat eez autre chose."

Bonham nodded and turned to Grant. "Like I told you before when we were in Grand Bank, as a member of the firm you get your divin' vacations free once or twice a year, or almost free."

"Oh, I'll take it, I'll take it," Grant said looking suddenly embarrassed. "It was just that I didn't want to push you.

On that." He mutely admired René's business precision and dispatch, but it embarrassed him to talk about the other fellow as though he didn't want to, or couldn't, pay.

" Well, you can start considerin' yourself a ten percenter, partner," Bonham said. He got up grinning and shook both their hands. Then he stopped. " Say, listen, Ron. I worked myself a little job while I'm down here. Pay expenses. One of the oil companies's got an underwater oil and gasoline unloading pipeline here in the harbour. I inspected it for them yesterday, like I always do when I'm down here. Well, one of the gas line pipe sections is about to go so I'm going to replace it for them to-morrow. Would you like to come along? I'm renting a little boat. We could pack everybody up with food and booze and have ourselves a picnic in the harbour. You could bring Lucky, and Doug and his girl," he nodded downward, " René and Lisa too. And Grointon if he wants."

" Yes, I'd like to very much," Grant heard himself saying. " I'll talk to the others."

" It's a real working diver's working dive," Bonham grinned.

" Sure," Grant said. " Fine." Now why had he said all that? He wanted to take himself by the arm and shut his mouth. He didn't want to make a working dive with Bonham. He didn't care if he never did any diving again at all, of any kind, at the moment. What he wanted was a break from diving right now. Except for that brass cannon job, he'd like to do that. He thought of his nightmare. And he thought of the other working dive they had done together, retrieving those bodies and the wrecked car. But he had had to make himself go ahead and say yes. " But what about the weather?" he hedged.

"Weather never bothers you in this harbour," Bonham smiled. He looked out across the porch at the sea. " And it'll be too rough to go out with Jim to-morrow. And there's going to be sun to-morrow."

" How deep will it be?" Grant asked.

" Oh, only ten feet or twelve, maybe fifteen. Nothing exciting. But it's interesting to see the layout they got. And you've never seen any underwater torch work. I helped put those pipelines in."

" Well, sure, I'll come along," Grant said. What the hell, he couldn't very well get into any kind of danger or trouble at only fifteen feet, could he? But as it turned out, he did get into trouble, anyway, and it was the worst trouble he had ever been in in diving up to then. But before that happened he was already in other trouble, domestic trouble, that took place that night. One might know. Or have known.

His thought, the next day, as he lay on the bottom trapped in an old abandoned fishing net, was that it—trouble— always seemed to come in bunches.

The night before had seen the worst fight, the bitterest *feeling*, he and Lucky had ever had. And it had all been his fault, really. Why couldn't he control his damned jealousy? At the same time he realised very soon after it happened that he had triggered some kind of response, reaction, in Lucky that was all out of proportion to the cause. That would take some evaluating.

He did not think about this too much while he was caught in the net, he had too much else to think about. But he did think about it before that, all the time they were getting ready for the picnic, all the time they were out on Bonham's little rented boat. It was after two o'clock in the afternoon by the time they finally made the dive, and all that time Lucky would still hardly speak to him at all any more than was needed to maintain formal politeness in front of the others.

It had all happened, once again, because of that fucking son-of-a-bitching Jacques Edgar, her ex-boy-friend. Ex-*lover*.

They had all been sitting down at dinner, for the second night in a row without Bonham—René and Lisa, Doug and Françoise, Grant and Lucky—when Jacques the ex-boy-friend had arrived at the hotel with a party. He had stopped at the doorway much further down the huge half-open porch-terrace where they were eating, and smiled and waved. He took two steps toward them, smiling, said "Hello, all!" politely, then raised his hand, shook his head and backed off to rejoin his party in the manner of the European politesse which never never interrupts anyone while dining. It had infuriated Grant, the very mannerly suaveness of it outraged him, and that magnanimous "*All!*", snobbish and fake-high-class, aping the fucking British, and seeming directed straight at him, had angered him most of all. He had gone into a slow burn. Lucky had done nothing, had simply waved and smiled and called hello back like the others, but Grant's slow burn smouldered on anyway, getting hotter. Finally, over coffee, he had retaliated.

It was a joke he made, not a particularly insulting one, not insulting at all, if perhaps a little crude. Half-drunkenly, they were all talking about how drunk they had been the night of the wedding. "Christ, yes!" he said, leaning forward with his eyes squinting and his eyebrows arching wickedly, and told them how he had waked up in the morning half-lying between the pushed-together double beds, in up to his shoulders. "We keep them pushed together, see. And there I was, in up to my shoulders and I couldn't get out. For a minute I thought what the hell have I got myself married to? The Grand Canyon?" The others all laughed, a little nervously.

It was directed straight at Lucky of course, and while maybe it was mean, the reaction it triggered in Lucky was enormously out of all proportion and totally unexpected. She looked at him for a moment, then leaped to her feet and all in the same motion struck him across the face with her handled purse. For a second he was blinded. The clasp of the purse had cut the bridge of his nose and he could feel the blood trickling down the side of it. He caught it with his finger and said with a whining falsetto, trying to make a joke out of it. "Hey, look what you done! You *hurt* me!"

Her eyes had widened at the sight of the blood, but they narrowed again. "You no-good son of a bitch," she said and walked off the porch without another word. Stemming the flow with his napkin, there wasn't much, Grant had laughed and shrugged, but deep in his mind in the midst of his still stunned surprise he was already at work trying to figure out and analyse what there was in what he could have said to create such an astounding reaction. What had made her change so suddenly, flip out like that? At the same time he was angry, embarrassed. He had stayed at the table. Later when he went over to their suite she was not there.

Earlier in the day Lucky had received at the hotel a local telegram from an older couple she had known in Syracuse, friends of her mother, who happened to be in the harbour for overnight on one of the Caribbean cruise ships. Word of her marriage had filtered back home through *Time* and the news services, and the older couple would very much like to see her and her new husband. When she showed it to Grant, he had grimaced, and she had agreed with him and decided not to go in to see them. Grant was sure now that that was where she had gone, and in fact it was where she had gone. She had walked out through the inner court of the hotel to the outer court near the road where two or three beat-up local taxis were always waiting, loafing around and gossiping as if they actively hoped they never would get a fare, and had taken one of them around into town to the pier where the big ship had docked for the night so that its ticket purchasers might see Kingston, Jamaica, to see her mother's friends. Cold fury and a kind of hollow ache of fear possessed her. There he was calling her a whore again, or practically doing so, and in front of people. In front of her *friends*. What did the son of a bitch expect her to do? She couldn't do over again all the things in her life she had done, could she? Maybe there were some things in her life she didn't enjoy so much, now. But that miserable pipsqueak son of a bitch. Fuck him. But when she met and talked with the middle-aged couple from home, the hollow ache opened up even deeper in her, became almost bottomless. Their accents, the way they thought, their stupidity, their *kindly* stupidity, and insensitivity, overwhelmed her with sense and picture memories of that place and her life there. Who could go back there and live that kind of life? It was condemning yourself to deliberate slow death. She had left them earlier than she'd expected to, at eleven-thirty, and caught a cab back to the hotel, but of course by that time Grant was no longer there in the suite. He had sat a while, and then gone back over to the bar to get drunk with his friend Doug, and fuck her. Well, fuck him; she didn't know he was in the bar; she had gone to bed. Gone to bed feeling once again as if encased in an inch-thick layer of hot, cold ice all over her body.

It was one of those nights. Grant had noted, even before going up to the suite, that Jacques Edgar and his party had already left the Crount, and a kind of fearful terror swept all over him. If she did that, he'd beat her up within an inch of her life. Beat her up and throw her damned ass out. She was so goddamned fucking beautiful. How dare she be so beautiful! Doug was right there in the bar almost as if waiting, expecting him to come. His Frenchwoman had gone to bed. She only used Doug, with the same cold-blooded carnality that he used her. Furious, hurt, as miserable and unhappy as he had ever been in his life, Grant had, with

Doug's expert connivance, taken to kidding, teasing René and Lisa about his injured nose. With a wink at Doug, he had begun by talking to them about how sorry Lucky would feel if she came back and realised that she had really seriously hurt him. From there it was just one logical step further to get out his little penknife and suggest to Doug in front of them that they two cut his nose—just a little bit—to make it worse for Lucky to see when she came back. It was crap but somehow in some strange way it made him feel better just the same. And all this time she was of course up there sleeping, and having bad disturbing dreams about him, but of course he didn't know that. Doug of course complied, taking the knife and ostentatiously testing its sharpness. "You ought to see how this bum can sharpen knives!" he crowed. René of course knew how well Grant could sharpen knives, ever since Grant had gone through his kitchen honing up every knife until two of the Jamaican cooks cut themselves and he had to stop. "He can sharpen knives till you can shave with them! Come on! Come on over here, Ron! To the light! I don't want to make any mistakes!" It was a shitting thing to do to them, because they really were both so sweet, and they believed he really meant it, really would do it, so that they both became near-hysterical in the almost empty bar. But he was drunk. And Doug was drunk. And he, for one, was teeth-grindingly miserable. Finally of course he let them talk him out of doing any such horrible thing to himself.

Some time later, just how much later he did not know, he and Doug had gone out to piss among the palms in the moonlight and the now soft breeze from the sea. Leaning against a palm afterwards Doug had slipped slowly to his left and then fallen flat on his back. For several moments he lay still, and then as if the fall released some switch or opened some floodgate in him he suddenly jumped to his feet and began to caper madly like an idiot. "I've had your broad, Grant!" he bellowed in a high voice. "I've had your broad! I fucked your broad! I fucked your broad, Grant, I did!" Grant almost went for him. For a moment in his confused drunken mind he thought Doug was referring to Lucky. But of course it wasn't Lucky. It was Carol Abernathy. And Grant found he didn't give a good goddam about that one way or the other. What did Doug expect? that he would care? be mad? It had obviously happened after he and Lucky had left GaBay and it was a pitiful little jealousy to expose. He found he was embarrassed that Doug would even bring such a thing up. Not knowing what to do, he had simply stood and stared at him. After a while Doug stopped, and they stood and stared at each other. Then as if by a common consent they turned and walked back inside together and neither mentioned it again. Next day Grant did not even know if Doug remembered it.

It was already getting late, and Sam was clearly getting anxious to close the bar. So they only had one more drink apiece. Back over at the suite he found Lucky was back and in bed asleep.

If she woke, she said nothing. Neither did he. And that was just about the way it stayed—except for the necessary polite conversation they made in front of other people—all the next morning, and all through noon, and all through the picnic on board during the early afternoon, right up to the very moment he dropped over the side with Bonham to make the dive.

And now here he was, though he wasn't thinking about any of that, fifteen feet deep and trussed up in this fucking goddamned seine net thirty feet away from Bonham's barely visible, winking Airco oxy-hydrogen torch. How in the name of God could he get himself into such fucking messes?

In the murky debris-filled harbour water he couldn't even see Bonham, only the torch, and that was partly the reason he had got himself trapped. Bad visibility. But the truth was he had been peering behind him to see there were no sharks or anything on his tail, when he swam into it. Maybe he would have seen it otherwise. He had felt just the lightest touch on his ear, and then on his shoulders, and then he was into it all wrapped up and his arms trapped at his sides. It was unbelievable how fast it had happened. One end trapped among some rocks on the bottom, its lead sinkers and cork floats removed, it had been floating three or four feet off the bottom where some idiot had thrown it overboard and abandoned it. It was strictly a dangerous and illegal thing they had done, but that did not help him any now. He had tried swimming away with it, only to be brought up short and have his feet and flippers trapped too. He had tried to cut himself out of it by working his right hand down carefully to get the knife out of the sheath on his leg, only to have it catch by the guard in the mesh, pull from his hand and sink away into the silt on the bottom. And that was when he really got scared. Because now there was nothing to do but lay here and wait for Bonham to see him.

But what if Bonham didn't see him? What if Bonham went right on working till he ran out of air and went up topside for another bottle? How in the name of fucking Christ could he get himself into those things? Who the *hell* wanted to be a diver anyway? God *damn*!

There was no real reason why Bonham should try to look for him. Who could get in trouble over a flat sand and rock bottom in fifteen feet of water? Only Ron Grant, that's who! He had started out by looking over the pipeline installation, had watched Bonham start the torch with the lighter, had studied how he went about making his first cut, then had motioned he was going to go off and explore around. There was no reason for Bonham to think he wasn't perfectly safe around here.

Carefully, trying to keep his breathing from getting faster, he worked his right hand which was still trapped along his thigh around to the back and rapped on his tank with his knuckles. The sound was so feeble he could hardly hear it himself, and a tendril of panic crept through him accelerating amazingly his need to breathe faster. He concentrated on his breathing, trying to slow it down, stop gulping air. He had nothing else of metal to tap with, and no way of getting hold of it if he had. There was nothing else but to lay there, trussed up like a beef for the slaughter-house, and hope that Bonham would think to look for him. From time to time he could see the light of the torch reflected on Bonham's mask as the big man turned his head, but he could not see Bonham himself at all and so was sure the big diver could not see him. Christ! He could see the New York *Daily News* headlines now. BEAUTIFUL YOUNG ACTRESS WIFE MARRIED AND WIDOWED IN SAME WEEK BY DIVING ACCIDENT TO PLAYBOY PLAYWRIGHT!

He knew he had enough air for about fifteen minutes. And Bonham, working, would almost certainly need air before he did—unless of course Grant himself panicked. And Bonham might then go back to the boat and find he had not returned and come look for him. But, by then, how the hell would he know where to look? And Grant wasn't even sure how much time he had left since his watch was on his left wrist, trapped against his leg.

A sort of marvellous stillness came over him as the idea came to him. He thought about it for maybe twenty full seconds. Watch. Aha! *And what would you do, Mr. Interlocutor, in my situation?* Then carefully he began working his hand back around his thigh picking carefully with his fingers under the mesh. When he had it beside the tank and could feel the tank with his fingers, he made a cone with all his fingers in the little free angle between the tank and his back until he could twist his arm and turn his wrist over, and then he rapped with his metal watch against the tank.

Almost immediately he saw the head turn, changing the reflection on the mask. He rapped again. The torch went out. Grant rapped and kept rapping, and in a moment Bonham appeared in front of him like some huge cyclopean walrus and he was never so glad to see anyone in his life. Shaking his head, the diver looked him over. It was only a matter of a couple minutes to cut him loose, then Bonham motioned toward his empty leg scabbard. Grant pointed down. The diver descended, looked around, apparently saw a glint of it, retrieved it and handed it to him. Then he motioned upwards with his thumb: did Grant want to go up?

That was exactly what Grant was thinking, but after a moment he shook his head. Together they gathered up the dangerous net, hacked it into small pieces and stuffed it into the silt under the pipeline. Later Bonham explained why he did that instead of taking it up: he hadn't wanted those in the boat to know about it. It was only a matter of five minutes to finish up his job and then when they went up he motioned Grant to the anchorline, instead of swimming to the stern like normal. As soon as their heads were out, he dropped his mouthpiece and said in a low voice, "I wouldn't say anything about that to Lucky. Or anybody. What they don't know won't hurt them, and it would only make them nervous —mistakenly, and for no good reason."

Grant nodded, and they swam to the stern.

Once back in the boat Bonham began to eat, since the two of them had not taken any food before the dive. But Grant didn't feel much like eating. Instead he sat in the stern by himself. He wasn't scared any more, but the sombre thought of what actually *could* have happened was a little sobering.

He could really have got deaded, as the kids used to say.
Then he felt a hand on his shoulder and looked up and saw it
was Lucky. She did not take the hand away.

"What happened?"

"What do you mean what happened?" he said.

"Something happened. I don't know what. I can just tell."

"Oh, I just got caught in an old net some idiot threw
overboard."

"Was it dangerous?"

"No. It could have been. But Bonham was right there,"
he lied.

"Did he ask you not to tell me?"

"No," he lied again. "Why should he? Christ, it wasn't
anything."

"Then why didn't you tell me?"

"Why should I? Anyway I was going to," he lied a third
time. "Later."

She looked deep into his eyes, and there was no more anger
in her blue ones. "Oh, Ron, we've got to stop this."

"I know," he said. "I told you, it wasn't anything."

"The babes in the woods," she said. She looked out across
the harbour at the Palisadoes. "If we lose each other, we'll
both have lost just about everything."

"I know that, too," he said. Doug and Françoise, and René
and Lisa, were all talking to Bonham in the tiny cabin. Since
Jim Grointon had declined to come, Bonham had to do it all
himself, and he had started the motor, steering with one hand
while he ate a huge ham sandwich with the other. Lucky
turned from the Palisadoes and looked up that way. "Even
diving, and Bonham, aren't worth that," she said.

Grant took her hand. "Of course they're not. Nothing is."

"I can't be responsible now for everything I did before I
met you," Lucky said conversationally.

"I know that, too," he said.

"Don't you want to eat?" she said conversationally.

"I will in a minute. I'm a little tired."

"I'll get you a sandwich and a beer," she said.

"Okay."

Back at the hotel he told her about the salvage job as he
should have done before, the twelve brass cannon, and that he
wanted to do it. "Then we'll be through. We'll go back north,
to New York. Until they're ready to make the maiden cruise

on the schooner." They had just finished making love and he had gone down on her to give her an orgasm in perhaps the best performance he had ever achieved. They were lying side by side across the sheeted, unblanketed, pushed-together twin beds.

" And we can stay at Evelyn de Blystein's and kill two birds with one stone," he said.

" But this uh this ' salvage operation ' is the main reason we're going back there, is it?" she asked.

" Let's say it's one of the main reasons. That guy Heath stopped me—*accosted* me—again to-day."

And Bradford Heath had. He had stopped him on the porch after they had come home from the combination picnic-dive, and he had been particularly nasty, even for Heath.

" Oh, hello there, Grant," was the opener. And he placed himself squarely in front of Grant so that he had had to stop. " Well, I guess it looks like your older lady friend ain't gonna talk. And I guess I can't get the truth out of you, can I?" He smiled his sick smile.

It was more than Grant could stomach. " Mr. Heath, why should I tell you the truth?" he smiled. " Why should I tell you the truth about anything? If you want to know about my life, read my plays. It's all in there. Now if you'll excuse me." He had stepped around him. " As a matter of fact," he said as a parting shot, " my wife and I are going up there to visit the Countess and Mrs. Abernathy in a few days when we leave here."

" It certainly won't hurt us to make a little show of friend-ship," he said now to Lucky after explaining. " And I think she'll probly be all right. It's to her benefit to be." Then he wondered. Was Bradford Heath really the motive? Did they really have to go because of Bradford Heath? Or was there some other, deeper motive pulling him back up there? Subconsciously maybe? Subconsciously for a showdown. Maybe. " Don't you think?" he said.

" All right," she said calmly. " If that's what you think. I know I can handle that mother shit all right." She paused. " All I really want is a chance to love you." She smiled, and then actually blushed a little. " You really did me beautifully to-day," she smiled. " To love you, and to help you do the work you want to do. Have to do, maybe."

Grant had cupped a hand over her nearest breast. " As a

matter of fact," he said slowly, " I have got a new idea for
a play. But it's only a dim idea. I don't really fully understand it yet."

" What's it about?"

" Diving, *Skin,* not muff." Then he shrugged. " I'll tell you
more about it when I know more.

" Of course," he added, " I got a dozen others too. This is
just one more to the pile."

TWENTY-SIX

It was amazing how much time was required just to go
through the mechanical processes of loaning a man forty-five
hundred dollars. The whole next day was spent on business.
Grant and Bonham spent most of the morning at the Royal
Bank of Canada in Kingston, proving Grant was Grant,
proving Bonham was Bonham, getting the money transferred
from Grant's name on the cable draft to Bonham's Kingston
account. And as soon as this was done, Bonham had to go
round to the boatyard's little business office in town and turn
over a cheque for a thousand dollars to get them back to work
on the schooner. The afternoon was spent drafting and
signing with René's lawyer a First Mortgage agreement for
forty-five hundred dollars on the schooner. René signed as
witness.

The storm had completely gone (though the last seas from
its winds were still slowly running down) and the heat in the
sun-drenched, dusty, unkempt streets of the town was fierce.
There was one rather elegant air-conditioned bar on Tower
Street (or was it Barry Street?), and Grant and Bonham (and
in the afternoon, René) routed themselves on their journeys
afoot about the business section so that they passed it every
time, both coming and going. The popular drink of the
moment was something called a Bullshot—vodka in a small
glass of ice-cold consommé—and long before lunch-time
Bonham and Grant had already more than consumed their
lunches in the form of cold bouillon soup.

And while they (and later René) were ramming around the
town in the heat, Lucky played by the pool and held small

court for Doug and all her new-found friends, which by now included Jim Grointon. It was becoming increasingly clear that Grointon was fascinated by Lucky in a way he had never been fascinated by a woman before—at least, not at the Grand Hotel Crount, so Lisa said. He was known to have had (or rather, was *suspected* of having had) several affairs among René's clients, so Lisa said, and had certainly had one they knew about because the irate husband (fortunately a client of another hotel) had threatened to shoot him (again fortunately, the husband had hustled his wife back to New York instead). But none of these ladies had ever so much as ruffled one feather of Jim's, and certainly none had ever affected him as Lucky did, so Lisa said, with a sly grin, and she thought it was about time he got some of his own back. He simply could not stay away from Lucky, it appeared. Wherever she went he appeared or followed, and sat around her with his slow smile, blushing, while she teased him with her outspokenness about sex and men and herself. Anyway he certainly wasn't like Bonham, was he? Lisa giggled to Lucky.

Bonham wanted to buy them all dinner that night when with Grant he returned from town a now affluent man. But Lucky begged off on the grounds that she had drunk too much champagne at the pool, was sick, and did not want any dinner. She would take to her room. Bonham affluent to her came on even worse than Bonham broke. " But Ron can if he wants to," she said holding her head with more tenderness than was strictly necessary.

But Grant did not want to either. " I'd better stay with her if she feels that bad," he said dutifully. He was wise to the fact that she had had about as much of Bonham as she could stomach, at least for a while. And he was counting on her to make the maiden cruise of the *Naiad* with him. On the other hand he did not want to become categorised as a " dutiful husband ", either: the kind he detested back home in Indianapolis. In front of Bonham or anyone else. To-day when Bonham had told him he was heading back to Ganado Bay to-morrow and would they like to take the same flight with him, then they could get started on the salvage job, he had answered that they wanted to stay on down here for three or four days more of honeymoon before coming up, because he knew Lucky would have detested making the flight up

P

with Bonham. Probably his discomfort had showed on his face then, this morning. Probably it showed now, as he turned down the dinner. Anyway, Bonham did not press. Well the hell with it! he never had been a good liar. Bonham had received no answer from his wire to Orloffski in New Jersey, but he had had a wire from the new proprietor of Orloffski's sporting goods shop that Orloffski was already en route down the inland waterway with the cutter.

On their way to their suite Lucky squeezed his hand. "We'll phone René on the sly and have him send us up a sumptuous spread and stay in!" she whispered, and Grant reflected that if he had appeared too "dutiful" just now, it was well worth it.

"Stay in and play?" he whispered back.

"Stay in and play *dirty*!" Lucky whispered.

It was just then that they ran into Mr. Bradford Heath, coming down the big, long porch.

Only this time Mr. Heath turned away, to make it appear he had not seen them. With Lucky on his arm, Grant hailed him. "Oh, Mr. Heath," he smiled.

"Oh, uh yes. Hello there, Grant," Bradford Heath replied, turning round. "Beautiful sea to-night, eh?"

Grant halted. "I just wanted to ask you how long you intended to stay down here now?"

"Oh, a week or ten days, I guess," Heath smiled. "If they can spare me Up There. Why?"

Grant smiled back. "Because my wife and I are going up to GaBay for a week or so, and we wanted to be sure and leave for there before you left. On the other hand, we wanted to put in three or four more days of honeymoon here before we left."

"Oh, I think you can feel safe in stayin' that much longer," Heath smiled. "I can guarantee you we won't leave for a week."

Grant grinned. "Fine. Good. See you, then."

"I don't think you ought to go out of your way to antagonise Heath like that," Lucky said after they had walked away. "It only means that he and his pals will lay for you and knock you and your new play when it opens."

"They would anyway," Grant said. "Whether I'm nice or not. So I might as well enjoy myself."

The dinner in the suite was exquisite. After they closed all the venetian blinds, no one could see in to tell whether they were eating or just sitting and reading. The old-fashioned circular fan on the ceiling turned slowly and silently, and they were served by one of René's oldest and most trusted waiters. They ate in their robes, and after they had eaten stripped off the robes and fell upon each other in the pushed-together twin beds.

"Let's do something special," Lucky said.

"What?"

"Let's play with ourselves. You play with yourself and I'll play with myself and I'll watch you and you watch me. Didn't you ever do that with some little girl when you were little?"

"No," Grant said, feeling breathless and tensely excited. "But I always wanted to." It seemed to him there were so many things he had always wanted to do but never done, until he met her, met Lucky. Like walking into a joint knowing you had the best-looking girl in the place on your arm, for example. Like making love and knowing at the same time there was always more love-making there, still waiting for you, and you didn't have to make excuses or explanations about it. Whenever he looked at her he felt like a miser in his bank vault counting his gold. It was like, after a long drought, long dearth in his life, a landslide gold rush had happened.

They did not see Bonham again the next day before he left. He had come by early in the morning, René said, but had left to catch his plane before they came down. Later on, with a not very decent grin, Jim Grointon told them Bonham had been sleeping on board the schooner while he was here, to save money. When she heard this Lucky looked at Grant with a sad smile he completely understood. But, "Oh, the poor man," was all she said.

With Bonham gone it was as if an irritant had been removed. It was as if the old group closed ranks over the empty space and came back into their former closeness. Every day they went out with Grointon, with Doug, and with the musical comedy writer and her husband, or with the young analyst and his designer wife. The analyst, though not his wife (who could not swim) had become a fair diver now under Jim's tutelage and could do twenty or twenty-five feet like Doug.

Those few last long sun-bright, sun-hot afternoons diving in the glassy, tranquil-coloured green sea gave Grant such a sense of security and pleasure in and under the water that several times he almost entirely forgot to be afraid. He loved the going down especially, hyperventilating then rolling over and heading straight down, kicking slow and easy, effortlessly, totally without gravity sucking at him, sure and confident that he had enough air in holding his breath to take him just about as deep as he would want to go, then drifting back up slowly, almost reluctantly, with a struggling fish on the end of his line, toward the dappled moving never-quiet surface to breathe. He had become an expert with the speargun now. But Lucky steadfastly refused to put on a mask and look below. She would swim around the boat without a mask, practising her sidestroke and her crawl, but she absolutely would not put on a mask and look down and see what was below her. Grant, and just about everybody else, tried to explain that this was absolutely silly. It made no difference.

On the last day, their last day out, something happened which gave to their leavetaking the next morning a marvellous flavour, a marvellous after-taste. They had already come in, from the last dive, and were all sitting around the bar in their swimsuits having a drink with Jim Grointon, when a sudden squall had come in from the west, leap-frogging the green western hills. Sentiment was high in all of them because it was Last Day, and Jim had anchored the catamaran off the beach and brought the fish in in the dinghy, while the rest of them had swum in. One of his constant chores when parking the boat off the hotel was to keep always one eye out for the first signs of weather and be prepared to rush over to the Crount at any time of day or night to sail it around into the harbour anchorage if some weather came up. Now, in what seemed like only seconds, rain was lashing the porch and the big glass doors along the covered terrace, and in the sudden wind the sea was building up three to four to five-foot waves and sending them smashing against the beach and the catamaran anchored off it. The patent anchor couldn't possibly hold it in the sand, and in mid-drink, in mid-swallow almost, Jim was off trudging, half-running, down through the sand to swim out, board the little boat and sail it around.

"Do you want me to come along and help you?" Grant called after him.

Jim stopped and turned. He looked both tired and disgusted. Then he shrugged. "No. No, it's my job. And my boat. I can manage it all right. I've done it often enough." Then he turned back and trudged on. The cold rain was already making him shiver, and he looked so forlorn half-running down the beach that Grant on the porch suddenly stripped off the sweater and dungarees he had put on because he was cold and took off running after him. "Get René's car and come around and meet us on the other side!" he yelled back at Lucky.

The worst thing about it was the cold, but it could have been dangerous, as Jim pointed out. From the hotel's beach on down to the harbour entrance at Port Royal the shore was mostly sharp volcanic rock which could have cut them to ribbons had they capsized and been forced to swim ashore in these waves and with that wind behind them. Out further, where Jim immediately ran them and where the four-foot waves were not yet breaking over into five-foot surf, the little catamaran still had to take quite a jostling and knocking about from the waves which it had to take broadside on, and they both had to hold on every moment. At one point Jim (who was really doing all the work anyway) suddenly put on a mask with a snorkel attached, pushing it up on his forehead in the heavy rain and pulled a pair of flippers near and advised Grant to do the same. It seemed a bit histrionic to Grant at the time, and proved to be an unnecesary precaution, but later when they were around the bend and in calm water the diver explained: "I know what I did seems silly," he said with a shy, Irish cop's smile, "but I just suddenly remembered that I had one of America's best writers—best playwrights—with me, and realised I had no business letting you come. It would have been very hard to swim in over that rock, even with a mask, and while if anything happened to me it wouldn't matter, it would certainly have mattered about you. And I would have been responsible." Grant, embarrassed, could only grin and shrug; it still seemed a bit theatrical to him, but he thought it sweet. And it wasn't any easy trip. Though the Point Royal spit was less than two miles from the hotel it took them over an hour and a half to make the entire voyage. When they arrived at the anchorage around inside, the entire gang from the hotel led by Lucky was standing under a lean-to shed roof in the rain waving at them happily, and they all had a hot toddy together at the anchorage bar because they were almost as frozen as Jim and Grant. It was then that Jim Grointon clasped Grant with his arm across his back and squeezed his bare shoulder and said: " You're a hell of a guy, Ron. And you're one of the very best free-divers I know. *And that's no bull!*" He said exactly the same thing and clasped him the same way again the next day at the airport, where he had come with René and Lisa to say good-bye, though now Grant was wearing his white linen summer suit, and grinned his white-eyelashed, Irish smile. Then he kissed Lucky gently on the cheek. Grant found this thought-ful, and even sweet. Lucky, on the other hand, was not so sure.

Nobody met them at the Ganado Bay airport. Doug had wired ahead that they were coming, but no car from Evelyn's estate was there to meet them. Looking at her husband's face to see if this was the sign of some bad omen, and finding nothing there at all, Lucky felt the butterflies start up in her stomach again, the way they had when she had spoken to Carol Abernathy on the phone. *Mothers!* she was thinking *God damn all mothers!* She had had enough trouble with her own. And now she had his. And a foster-mother yet, at that! And a powerful one. Grant on the other hand, though he showed nothing on his face, was convinced the absence of a car was a deliberate ploy on the part of Carol Abernathy. So was Doug, from the look on his face. And so it proved to be—or so Grant believed. It was so well handled that he never could be sure.

" Well!" Doug said, as they stood in the heat amongst the surly, pushy Negro porters who served to make nervous every liberal who arrived at GaBay. " Ain't no point in us rentin' a car. There'll be half a dozen layin' around loose at Green Hall. So we might as well rent us a one-shot chauffeur job."

This they did. The coloured chauffeur was quite impressed to be driving somebody to Green Hall. He had driven past it for many years, he said, but only once had he ever carried someone inside. " It ve-ry pret-ty, Mom," he smiled. And Lucky was impressed too. Ron showed her where the estate began, then showed her the beach house and beach on the sea side of the road as they slowed and then turned in, up the hill, away from the sea, on the long winding drive that finally ended in a great loop at the manor-house. Green Hall certainly lived up to its name. Grant tried as best he could to point out to his wife the various lush rare tropical trees and plants whose names he remembered being told by the Count Paul who had collected them, as they wound up the black-top drive. " She must be very rich, the Countess Evelyn," Lucky said.—" Rich?" Grant said. " She owns just about all the coal in Indiana."—" But for God sake don't call her that: Countess," Doug said from the front seat. " It ain't chic."—" Oh, for God's sake shut up, Doug!" Grant said viciously from beside her. When the butler opened the great wrought iron and glass doors for them, they found the whole gang already all drawn up to meet them.

Evelyn took the ball right away. " I'm terribly sorry! We did want to have someone there to meet you. But Doug neglected to tell us just which flight you were on!" Grant, who had not actually seen the wire, could not tell if this was the truth or not; and Doug, later, said he could not remember. " Come!" she said with all her cynical charm, " let me introduce you, Lucia! Lucky, is it? May I? Charming nickname!"

They were: the Count Paul (simply called Paul), Evelyn herself, Hunt Abernathy, Carol Abernathy, and a girl named Patricia Wright who worked for an aviation magazine who was staying with them and had come down to do an article on Paul de Blystein's amateur seaplane flying. Bloody Marys were served immediately. A cold buffet of mainly ham and chicken was already out, on the terrace.

" Hello! Hello!" Carol Abernathy said to her when it came her turn. " But it isn't really an introduction, is it? Ron has told us so much about you that I feel I know you already, Lucky!" The coloured Time guy it turned out had flown back to Kingston, apparently on orders from Heath, just the day before. He had had one last try at Carol before leaving.

Evelyn put them half-way down the hill in " The Cottage ". " After all, you are still honeymooning, aren't you? even though officially you're not now! And I thought you'd much prefer to be alone!" " The Cottage " turned out to be no cottage at all but a marvellous, very modernistic small house built in such a way that the free-form out-door swimming pool actually entered into the building in the place of one wall on its ground floor. Formerly it, or at least the ground floor, had been used for the big poker games Evelyn de Blystein loved so much. "Of course now while you're here we'll play up in the salon! or on the terrace! Doug of course can have his old room back, up in the great house! And if you want to take any of your meals, luncheon and dinner, down here alone, which I'm sure you will! all you have to do is telephone up to Greg the butler!" There was one telephone in each of the four small rooms. "We almost never use the pool except at around five o'clock," Evelyn said. "And seldom then."

"I like her," Lucky said when they were finally alone. "I liked her when I first met her, that time in the supermarket, and I still like her."

"Oh, she's all right," Grant said cautiously. He was still trying to feel his way around, get the lay of the land, because, in the overall, he had not wanted to do this—and would not have done it except for that son of a bitch Bradford Heath. Or would he? Anyway, he did not feel at all smug, or manly, super-manly, or proud of himself, at having introduced his wife to an old lover.

"She's mean, probably," Lucky said, answering him, "but in the end it's all only for kicks. To get her kicks. And that's not bad."

"She loves gossip," Grant said. "And poker."

"She's having an affair with that girl Pat Wright from that aviation magazine," Lucky stated calmly.

Grant was flabbergasted. "She is? Is she!"

Lucky nodded calmly. "Normally I don't like lesbians. But I like her."

"But, Christ! She must be sixty-five, anyway."

"So?" Lucky said.

"Look," he said. "What did you think of Carol?"

"I didn't really have a chance to form an opinion."

"Well, look. If any of these people start bugging you, like especially Carol, you just let me know." He felt he really had to say that. "I really want to do this diving salvage job with Bonham. But I can scrap it. We don't really have to stay here more than just a few days."

"Wouldn't it look funny if we moved out and still stayed in Ganado Bay?"

"Maybe, but to hell with it. Anyway, I don't think Bradford Heath would hear of it."

"He might. If that guy of his left word with somebody in town to call him."

"Well, screw him."

"I'll stay," she said. "I can handle mothers. I've had experience."

It hurt Grant deeply to hear her say that, in just that way, and made him feel even more of a criminal. "Doug," he said to change the subject, "Doug asked me at lunch to-day if I thought he could make out with that Pat Wright."

"That's funny!" Lucky said. "What did you tell him?"

"I said why not? Maybe I'd better warn him."

"Tell him nothing," Lucky advised. "If they're really smart, he'll make a good front for them."

"You're really sure?" he said.

Lucky nodded, "You watch. I do wish we could take most of our meals down here by ourselves, though."

"Certainly," Grant said. "We certainly will. Except that to-night we'll almost certainly have to make a command performance at the great house."

The trouble started the next day. Grant and Doug had telephoned Bonham the afternoon before, after the lunch, and to-day were going out with him to make an exploratory dive on the salvage site. All of Bonham's great need for secrecy seemed to have disappeared once they had arrived in GaBay, and he did not even mind Doug going along for the dive. It was a great site. On smooth almost level sand stretching several hundred yards out toward the beginning of the deep water drop-off, and only about twenty yards from the deep reef itself, there they lay, green with verdigris, most of them much more than half buried in the yellow sand, at a depth of exactly one hundred and twenty feet. Grant was almost positive he once had swum over this same spot with Bonham on a deep dive and had seen nothing but sand. Bonham's craving for secrecy in Kingston seemed a little theatrical now, here, since Doug, on the surface, could not even see the cannon from up there. To-morrow they were going to rent the boat with the biggest winch in Ganado Bay harbour. The next day they would try to start diving. It was all very exciting. Lucky had decided to stay at home on the estate that day, largely because of her dislike of Bonham, and when her husband finally got back home to the Cottage, she told him what had happened to her.

It wasn't really trouble really, so much, but it was certainly nervous-making. "You know, I think she's really crazy," she said.—"I told you," he said.—"No, but I mean really crazy." she said.—"That's what I meant," he said. Well, Evelyn had called her after he and Doug had left, saying she knew she was alone and would she like to have lunch with them on the terrace. Paul was off with Pat Wright to make a preliminary flight in his seaplane, Hunt had gone off as usual to the golf club, so there were just the three of them. It was all very decent, all very charming. Carol couldn't have been more charming. And Evelyn was her same normal, witty, cynical, helpful self. "I think she's on our side, rather than the side of your foster-mother, if she's on any side," she said. —"She almost certainly isn't on any side," Grant said. "She just wants to see what's going to happen. That's how she gets her vicarious living." Lucky had changed from a tight jersey and crotch-tight shorts to a prim cotton print before going up because she wanted to look proper, but the two of them were just sitting around in old beat-up shorts and sleeveless men's shirts. She grinned at Grant. "Of course I never could disguise my tits." Anyway, all that part of it, the lunch, had gone off fine. She had come back down and changed to a swimsuit and hauled a chair out beside the pool and into the sun to read. After three Bloody Marys and almost half a bottle of Bordeaux with the lunch, she had fallen asleep. Something had wakened her, she didn't know after how long a time. When she opened her eyes, she was looking straight at a group of the Count Paul's tropical shrubs about twenty yards away. As she watched, they moved, then moved again a little further on, as though something or somebody was moving stealthily through them. Scared, not even knowing whether it might be some kind of damned wild local animal, she had jumped up dropping the book and yelled for their maid Evelyn had given them, Mary-Martha. At that, even still further along the group of shrubs, Carol Abernathy had come swinging around the end of them as if out for a health stroll. "I know she was watching me," Lucky said, "but I don't know for how long." Beside her when she said this Grant cursed. "Would she be likely to ever do anyone physical harm?" she asked.

"No. No, no. Nothing like that. I'm sure."

"Well, I'm sure she was watching me from behind those bushes. She wanted to know if she had startled me, and I was angry and I said yes, if that was her rattling around in those bushes, and she said no, looking surprised, that wasn't her. It must have been a mongoose. There were lots of mongooses around, did I know that?"

"Maybe it was," Grant said hopefully.

"No, it wasn't. I know. Well, I asked her in and offered her a drink, which she refused, then, changing her mind, said she'd have a little mineral water."

"She doesn't drink," Grant said.

"I know," Lucky said. "Then she marched all around the place as if it were hers, looked in the bedroom, looked in the bathroom, then, seeing a pair of shoes of yours on the floor picked them up and said to me, ' My God! does he still have those?' Then she excused herself and left. Later I saw her driving out in one of Evelyn's little cars without even a glance over in my direction, though she must have seen me standing by the pool. Now if that's not crazy-acting, I don't know what is."

"Well, I told you she was crazy," Grant said. "She didn't used to be, when I first knew them. It's happened over the years. I really do owe them a lot. Look, if I can make this damned ' visit thing ' work, if only because of the publicity, I'd like to do it. Don't forget, we're liable to be living across the street from them back in Indianapolis."

"I know," Lucky said.

"It all depends on this new play. Maybe you would like to come out with us on the boat to-morrow, instead of staying here?"

Lucky thought this over. "No. No, I don't think so. I don't want to spend any more time around Bonham than I absolutely have to. It only makes for bloodshed."

"That's something else I wish you'd think over," Grant said. "This about Bonham. I don't agree with you at all. I like him. I really do."

"Oh! That was something else! Just before she left Mrs. Abernathy asked me if I wasn't worried about Bonham's influence on you? wasn't I afraid you were too dependent on him, listened to him too much?"

"Why, God damn her!" Grant exclaimed.

Lucky held up a hand. "I didn't tell her you loaned him the money for the schooner. No. No, I think I'd rather stay here to-morrow, just the same." She paused. "But I do wish we could have our dinner down here alone. Do you think we could?"

"Sure we could," Grant said getting up. "I'll go and call Greg about it. To-night anyway. But to-morrow night Evelyn's got a huge party laid on, to introduce us—you—to all her rich social local friends and acquaintances. We'll have to go to that."

Behind him Lucky sighed. "I suppose we will. Since we're her guests. Well, let's wait and see how to-morrow goes."

Curiously enough, to-morrow went fine. And so did all the succeeding days, until finally the storm front came in, down from the north and the States, which caused Bonham and Grant to suspend their diving operations. But during all those days Carol Abernathy left Lucky alone, did not come near the Cottage, and indeed—on the night of the party—(at which Lucky was an unqualified, enormous, scintillating success, captivating everybody) went to bed early. It must have been pretty hard on her, Grant thought thinking about it, but on the other hand it was she who had asked for it herself. Anyway, as the fair-weather days full of sun passed, more than a week of them, Lucky stayed by herself, usually lunched by herself, swam in the pool, read all the new books Evelyn had had sent down from the States, and only appeared at the great house at cocktail time with Grant after he had come back from his diving. Then they would have their dinner alone, served by Greg's number-one male helper Beverly, in the Cottage, and their evening in bed together. Neither of them could seem to get enough of the other. Several times late at night they swam nude together in the pool. Ron could now do two to two-and-a-half lengths of the fifteen-yard-long pool underwater just holding his breath, wearing flippers but without a mask. A couple of times, because Lucky had been such a success at the first one, they had to appear at Evelyn's big parties but these hardly counted. Lucky became more and more happy, more and more contented with her, perhaps unfortunately, temporary lot. Only once she went out on the winch boat with Grant and Doug and Bonham on their salvage diving, and what she saw so frightened her that she refused to go again.

There was no real reason for this. She had long ago tried mask and flippers, looked at the underwater-world reef life, and refused ever to look again. Ostrich-like, she would swim on the surface of the sea without mask (and without flippers) as long as she didn't have to look. This meant that, in the unlikely possibility a shark or a 'cuda did make a pass at her, she would be unable to help or defend herself, and was totally silly. This made no difference to Lucky and nobody could convince her otherwise. This one time, after much argument on the part of Doug and Ron (Bonham stayed totally out of it), she was persuaded to don a mask and go out with Doug holding her hand and watch Ron and Bonham working on the bottom. She lasted exactly a minute and a half of it, and immediately decided both were insane. All she could see when she finally did see them was two tiny figures far, far below her, head-down and kicking around while sand boiled up around them, and a little off to one side the long, long chain of the anchorline descending, and beyond that the long, long line of the winchline descending, and somewhere between her and them a few fish swimming around. It was like leaning out and looking down on the street from the roof of, say, about a nine-storey building. She ran for the boat. And yet in spite of that, as she swam in the tropical pool of the Cottage or lay in the tropical sun beside it with the tropical herbage of the Count Paul all around her, she never doubted for one second that her husband would come home every night safe and sound from his adventures. Somehow, though she didn't like him, she trusted Bonham completely underwater, and knew that nothing could happen as long as he was there, though this might not apply above the surface on land. After all, he had been doing this shit for years, hadn't he? It was just one of those things. She just didn't want to have to look.

It was Grant's first experience with decompression. While he had made lung dives to a hundred and twenty feet before, and even below, he had never stayed at such a depth long enough to need to decompress. Now there was no choice, and Bonham explained it all to him very carefully, although he knew it (that is, had *read* it). But even Bonham had no idea in the beginning how much or how often they were going to have to decompress on this job. This was due to the fact that more than half of their brass cannon, bronze cannon—eight, to be exact, of the total number of twelve—were not lying free in the sand at all but were really attached to ancient, now-dead coral growths underneath the surface layer of sand. Apparently, back at the time the now-non-existent ship carrying their cannon had for some reason or other sunk, what was now a flat sand bottom on the ocean floor had been part of a living coral reef, probably part of the one twenty yards behind them which Bonham called his " deep reef ". Unpredictable, whimsical ocean currents had apparently carried sand slowly in over this one, or this part, since the shipwreck sometime in the mid- and late 1700s, choking off the life of the coral, a great deal of which nevertheless had lived long enough to attach itself solidly and infuriatingly to the ship's indestructible cannon as the ship itself disintegrated. (*Christ, nothing is stable*, Grant thought, *nothing in this world, not even the ocean bottom*.) Now it lay, this dead coral, only a short distance below the sand, a dead grey mass but nevertheless firmly glued to two-thirds of their cannon, and the difference it made was enormous.

For example. on the first day of real work-diving they took out two of the four free cannon and in doing so spent slightly under half an hour on the bottom, decompressing for fifteen minutes. The second day they took out the other two with only slightly more bottom-time. The next cannon, the first of their eight coral-attached ones, required three entire days making multiple dives, two dives a day for a total of one hour and twenty-five minutes total bottom-time per day, plus ninety-six minutes decompression time per day. This meant roughly three hours a day in the water, half of it decompressing. It seemed to Grant they spent most of their time hanging on the anchor line staring at each other and breathing.

It was not an easy dive programme to plan, once it was established that eight of the cannon were grown to coral, and it had to be planned exactly. Hauling out his grubby, well-thumbed NAVSHIPS 250-538 U.S. Navy Diving Manual, Bonham calculated that exactly 50 minutes bottom-time (which included the descent) would require exactly 47.7 minutes decompression time: 15 minutes at 20 feet, 31 minutes at 10 feet, plus 1.7 minutes ascent time to first stop. Sixty minutes bottom-time at 120 feet, however, would require 70.5 minutes total decompression time, a considerable difference. He decided 50 minutes would be the maximum they could stay down.

There was still a problem with air, however. The U.S. Divers large-size tank, with a capacity of 72 cubic feet, was about the largest commercial tank around and the one Bonham preferred to use. One of these would give 20 minutes of air at 4 atmospheres or 130 feet. Two, rigged together in what the manufacturers liked to call their " TWIN 72," would give 40 minutes. Bonham had a number of both rigs. But the Twin 72 wouldn't by any possible stretch give him 50 minutes bottom-time at 120 feet and still allow for adequate decompression, and if they used it, and made shorter dives of twenty or twenty-five minutes, they would more than cut in half their working time on the bottom ; they would be months getting their cannon up.

There were only two answers to this problem. One was to hang an extra tank for each of them on the anchorline at twenty feet to decompress on, where they would have to take out their own mouthpiece when its tank ran out and turn on and insert the new one. The other was to use triple-tank rigs, and Bonham didn't have any triple-tank rigs. They were normally too heavy and cumbersome. But he could make some up in the shop, and after deciding this would be an easier method for Grant than changing mouthpieces at twenty feet, he made up four of them the morning of the second diving day, after spending the afternoon of the first day making his calculations, while both times Grant hung around watching and learning. " You probly won't hardly be able to stand up in the boat with this on," Bonham grinned ; " but once you're underwater you'll never notice it."

Still this did not solve everything. There still remained the second or " multiple " dive problem. To get the maximum amount of working time on the bottom to finish the job in two or even three weeks, they would have to dive more than once a day. And this presented all sorts of other problems. Breathing compressed air under pressure as a diver did caused him to absorb nitrogen into his bloodstream and tissues to equalise his body's normal nitrogen pressure. The deeper the dive and the pressure, the longer the dive, the more nitrogen he absorbed. That was the reason for decompression: that excess nitrogen had to be got rid of by exhaling it slowly or it would form bubbles in his tissues and bloodstream at surface pressure. *But* when the diver surfaced safely *after* decompression, it did not mean the nitrogen in his blood and tissues had returned to normal for sea level as it was before the dive. Twelve hours was required for that, and for him to slowly exhale all the excess nitrogen he had absorbed on the dive. And if he entered the water for another dive before that twelve-hour period passed he would still be carrying with him a certain percentage of the nitrogen he had absorbed on the first dive, making his second-dive compression correspondingly greater. The Navy had worked out a descending scale for this twelve-hour period, and checking the NAVSHIPS Manual Repetitive Dive Charts, Bonham calculated that after a 50-minute dive at 120 feet they would be in NAVSHIPS Manual Group " N ", that after 4 hour 4 minutes on the surface they would have descended to NAVSHIPS Manual Group " E ", that Group " E " making a second or " multiple " dive to 120 feet must consider itself to have already spent 15 minutes on the bottom before beginning the dive. In other words, they could only spend 35 minutes on the bottom during the second dive if they wanted to come up in the same decompression time of 47.7 minutes as the first dive—always provided they had remained on the surface 4 hours 4 minutes between dives and descended from Manual Group " N " to Manual Group " E ". Had they dived immediately after coming up while still in Group " N ", they would have to consider that they had already spent 46 of their 50 minutes on the bottom already. And, if they stayed two or three minutes over that second-dive 35-minute limit, they would be forced to come up in the next greater decompression time, that for 60 minutes bottom-time of 70.5 minutes—which, of course, especially if they had seriously exerted themselves working below, would seriously stretch their air, and perhaps even force them to come up too soon.

" And there ain't no decompression chamber on this boat for us, either," Bonham grinned. " As far as that goes, there ain't even one on this *island*. The nearest one—old buddy— is Key West," he grinned, " and there isn't anything worse for a man who comes up with the bends than to be put in an airplane and flown somewhere, at an even lower pressure than sea level."

Bonham went over his calculations four or five times that first afternoon. Any slightest miscalculation in them could cause one or both to get decompression sickness, or "the bends", with effects running all the way from a slight headache, to permanent crippling, to total paralysis, to death. Grant felt a slight chill run over the back of his shoulders as he stood looking down over Bonham's shoulder.

"I want you to know exactly what you're getting into," Bonham said soberly. "This kind of stuff is always dangerous, now that we got to *work* on those cannon to dig them loose. This is real pro-specialist, trained-frog and stuff. And there's no real guarantee that even if every precaution's taken, somebody won't get a case of the bends, largely due to the big variations in individual tolerance. I just want you to know before you go."

"Okay, I still want to go," Grant heard himself say. "I just hate to quit, now that we've gotten started."

"That's the way I feel," Bonham said. "The main thing is to just not ever over-exert yourself down there, or get nervous and try to come up too fast. If you'll just follow me, and do everything I tell you to do, and do everything I do when we're down there, there's no reason to worry.

"I've worked this deep before, and I know what my tolerances are. But I'll not be using them as any kind of criterion for you. We'll go much lighter. Just remember that the danger is always once removed from the present. It's what happens after you come up that hurts you."

Once again the chill passed across Grant's shoulders as he nodded.

In the actual practice, of course, both men would be wearing D.C.P. Automatic Decompression Meters, one of which Bonham had already sold to Grant who had never yet needed it, though he had worn it a few times on deep dives just to see how it worked. Bonham's own, which when he first found the wreck he had sent in to Miami to be checked, was a battered old one, but when they dived with them and checked them both showed almost identically the same markings. Because it worked on an ascending curve of decompression as its indicator needle descended, rather than on the ten-foot and five-foot step stages of the Navy charts, it provided an additional slight safety factor; and it came equipped with a "Memory Zone" at the bottom of its scale to allow for the twelve-hour Surface Interval period.

All this business was something he had hoped to avoid,

Bonham told him with a wry grin. If all the cannon had been loose like the four, they could have breezed through this like a snap, but now they were going to have to work. With crowbars. Chipping the damned things loose. If they wanted to get the job done in any two or three weeks.

It all sorted itself out into a system quite quickly. Grant would set his alarm for seven, allow himself only one cup of coffee for his breakfast because he was diving, which he made in the Cottage for himself while Lucky still slept, and then met Bonham on the dock at eight. In the bright sun on the slower moving winch boat they usually got to the site around nine. Suiting up, dressing out (Bonham too wore a wet suit shirt now, and Grant wore shirt, pants and hood), checking gear all took about twenty minutes to half an hour. Bonham believed in doing everything slowly and never rushing whenever it had anything to do with diving. Especially deep diving. And he never stopped preaching it. Then the First Dive, from 9.20 to 11.00? to 10.58 to be exact, if the First Dive began exactly at 9.20. But Bonham never stayed the exact full 50 minutes down below. 48.5, 49 was usually the limit, a slight added safety factor, then he would be tapping Grant on the arm to rise for the long decompression. Usually they were back in the boat by 11.00 or 11.05, and then the long wait began.

Bonham never timed the "Surface Interval Time", as the NAVSHIPS Manual called it, to the exact 4 hours 4 minutes the Manual recommended, always allowing five or ten minutes over, so it was usually 3.20 or 3.25 before they were back in the water and heading down the long line of the anchorline for the Second Dive. By 4.43 or 4.48 they were back, and it was time to haul in the winchline and the anchorline and head in. By 5.40 or 5.45 they were back at the dock, and by 5.50 or 6 o'clock Grant was back at the Cottage just in time to dress for cocktails up at the great house.

It was impossible to understand how Bonham had ever thought he could hide the raising of these cannon from the authorities and spirit them away to sell black market in Mexico or the States. Perhaps if he had had the schooner, and had equipped it with as big a winch, but certainly not by using the port winch boat and the harbour dock facilities. Every night when they came in there was always a crowd waiting on the dock to see how they'd made out, and the operation itself had become one of the main subjects of gossip in the little town, with even Evelyn and her rich social friends asking Grant all about it. On the second day when they came in with the second two free cannon, the harbour government man and the local chief customs officer were both already waiting on them. The cannon as they brought them in were kept in a harbour warehouse building the customs man loaned to Bonham, and since they didn't need Ali, Bonham had him in there all day working at cleaning them with acid. It was soon established that they were French by the historian who came up from Kingston, probably from the late eighteenth-century fleet of de Grasse when he was manœuvring against the English in the Caribbean around the time of Yorktown, but nobody could find in the archives any mention of any ship French or otherwise which had sunk or been sunk anywhere near this position. All the local papers from the nearby towns wrote it up, and the *Gleaner* sent a photographer and reporter up from Kingston to take pictures and do a story. And of course they all made a big thing of Ron Grant, the famous American playwright, who was Bonham's partner and fellow diver in the project. Bonham of course gloated over the publicity. Bonham was even in favour of getting in touch with *Time* and *Life*, and over Grant's feebly expressed protest telephoned both offices in Kingston, but neither wanted to do anything with it.

The work itself was not so terribly hard, and indeed Bonham insisted that it not be made so. In this kind of deep multiple diving, nothing was more dangerous or could bring on the bends quicker than over-exertion deep underwater. He kept insisting and warning Grant every day about this, until Grant who was already scared became every day more scared.

In spite of that, the actual work down below was almost boring. In addition to the large and small crowbars he also had brought along short-handled sledge-hammers and cold chisels. These were good for working close against the cannon's cascabels or trunnions, but they took much longer, and mainly they worked with the large crowbars, beating them with the sledges and hacking away, then trying to prise. More than anything it made Grant think of how he had once helped his father break up part of their old concrete driveway. The difference here was that when you tried to prise, without any gravity to give you leverage, you often moved yourself more than the dead coral. It was often ludicrous.

Perhaps the worst thing was the sand. They dismounted and carefully cleaned their four regulators every night on the way in because of the sand. On some of the attached cannon the sand was very shallow but on others it was deeper and on these it gave a lot of trouble. Even kicking it with your flippers while on the bottom could raise a cloud of it. Every movement had to be delicate and very slow. Sometimes when too great a cloud of it got raised they had to wait a few minutes for it to settle to see anything at all. It settled very slowly. Usually, after the first few minutes of the First Dive, there was always a cloud of sand to work in. About the only way to move the deeper sand was to carefully scoop it away with both hands, piling it up a few inches from the cannon. Whenever this was done it was necessary to go away to another one for twenty minutes and come back, or else wait till the next dive. It could be infuriating, a great cloud of it could suddenly raise at any moment for no apparent reason.

But the thing that disturbed Grant the most was the long wait between the two dives. In the water, and on the bottom, he was calm and collected, though alert and somewhat nervous. But once back in the boat after the longer morning dive, with nothing to do except wait four hours, his nervousness and imagination afflicted him with all sorts of horrible propositions. And it got so, as the days passed, that he came to dread that 4-hour 4-minute wait much more than the diving itself. At least on the dives themselves he had something to do which occupied his mind. The truth was, once he was in the water he was no longer afraid; it was just all the rest of the time. And on the boat, during the long mid-day wait, there was nothing, nothing except to lay around and try to read.

Part of the trouble was that raising the anchor and winchline and the relowering and replacing of them properly, was such a job and required so much time that it precluded them from moving the boat during the wait. Otherwise they could have gone in to shore in the four hours. Or they could even have gone fishing. Out farther, in the deep water, they could see sport-fishing boats trolling for marlin and kingfish about two-thirds of the time. Unfortunately, they were attached to their cannon like an old-fashioned criminal attached to a ball by a chain. They would come up from the last long minutes of decompression of the first dive, get out of their gear in the water and climb aboard, and it would begin. They each ate one small ham sandwich and drank one bottle of beer immediately, and that was all since they wanted their stomachs to be empty by the time they went back down. So they were hungry most of that time, too. But Bonham was very strict about this. A man who over-exerted and vomited into his mouthpiece 120 feet down was in serious trouble, especially if he needed decompression. In addition, there were always some little dribbles of sea water getting inside your mouth and mouthpiece down there, a certain percentage of which you could not avoid swallowing, so that Grant's stomach, anyway, was always sour from salt water.

After the first day of "multiple" dives, when he realised what it was going to be like, Grant had brought with him a good number of the new books Evelyn de Blystein had had sent down to her from home and none of which he had much chance to look at during the past three months. But he found it hard, and increasingly harder, to concentrate on them. His mind would continually snatch him away from some book with a thought of some little mistake he had made that might have been serious if, say, he had panicked; or, of some thing that *might* just have happened, though it hadn't, and hadn't even been near. Every little headache, every little ache or pain, every little bit of gas in his gut (of which there was a lot because of the salt water he swallowed) would send him into heart-shivering spasms of panic terror, of physically debilitating fear that he had gotten the dreaded "bends". How did he know? He had never had them. How did he know what they felt like coming on? Slowly, as the days passed one by one, he watched the level of his stock of courage descend almost imperceptibly, as the level of water in a bottle with a tiny hole in its bottom will descend imperceptibly, invisibly, until finally the bottle is empty.

None of any of this seemed to be the effect created upon Bonham, however. The placid big man with the storm-cloud eyes seemed to be more at ease and more restful than Grant had ever seen him. He did not once, to Grant's knowledge, crack the cover of a book—or even a magazine—the whole time they were out there. Not even when Grant offered them to him. He slept a good bit. And the rest of the time he just

sat. He tried fishing a few times, with a handline, and caught
nothing, as they both (who knew the terrain below them like
the palms of their hands, knew he would not. But the rest
of the time he just sat, while Grant read, or pretended to read.
Sat, and looked off at the misty green, jungly mounds and
hills rising to form the Jamaican skyline in the steamy heat
and which must not have changed much since the first eyes
of white men in Columbus's crews first saw them, or at the
brightly coloured hotels along the beach beside the airport
fading off into the harbour whose interior was invisible from
here. What in the name of God did he think about? Or did
he think at all? He seemed totally contented.

At least a million times Grant asked himself why in the
name of God he was doing this, when he didn't have to. The
only answer he could find was that, afterwards, he would be
able to say with petty ego-pride that he had. Brag to people
that he had done it.

Sometimes Bonham talked. But not much. He told Grant
about his ol' shark hole, and how sometimes in certain moods
he liked to go out there and shoot a shark or two, and asked
if Grant would like to go with him one day and shoot one
himself. Grant said that he would, but he had no intention of
doing so. Not this trip. Perhaps on some future trip. Or
when they made the maiden voyage of the *Naiad*. But not this
time. Grant's nerve was completely gone.

It wasn't far from here actually, Bonham added, and in fact
had been responsible for his having found the wreck, one day
when he was out around here alone looking for shark. Grant
had not seen a single shark since they began the salvage
operation, and thought unhappily: So now he tells me!

He never did see one. In all they worked nine full days on
the operation, before a cold front from Florida and the Gulf
Coast came down bringing weather with it forcing them to
quit. They had brought up two cannon the first day, two the
second, taken three days for the fifth, three days for the
sixth, and on the ninth day, after getting lucky, brought up
a seventh cannon which, tipped steeply downward so that only
its cascabel and part of its breech showed above the sand and
which they thought would be difficult, proved to be attached
to coral only by its mouth, and was easy to break loose once
they got down to it. Then, on the morning of the tenth day,

after they had made the First Dive and begun work on another, difficult cannon and were resting and waiting out the
Surface Interval Time, a handsome-looking Bermuda-rigged
sailing vessel hove into view in the northwest and ran down
on them sailing close hauled into the freshening breeze, quite
far ahead of the weather whose head was just beginning to
show on the far horizon and heading for GaBay harbour.
"By God!" Bonham exclaimed when it got a little closer,
and jumped up excitedly. "That's Orloffski and his cutter!
But what the hell's he doin' comin' in from the west?"

It was indeed Orloffski. The vessel came on, heeling well
over, until they could make out the two men on board,
Orloffski at the wheel and another man forward holding on to
and leaning on the mast. Orloffski gave them a happy grin
and a wave. But then Bonham leaped up on the winch head
and spread out his huge arms and bellowed. Recognising him
Orloffski, surprised, jumped up behind the wheel and gave
him another, now delighted, more intimate wave, then
motioned vigorously with his free hand and pointed in
toward the port. Then the sleek cutter was gone, on past them,
running on in.

"Come on!" Bonham said, jumping down and coming forward. "Let's wrap this up, here. This is a big day!"

They did not dive that afternoon, and it was the last time
Grant was ever to see the wreck site. If he had known that,
he might have looked it all over a little more carefully for
memories and suitable sentiments before leaving it. He had
become very close to Bonham the past ten days, as men
almost must who have worked together on a potentially dangerous project amicably, and like almost all pupils whose
teachers take an interest in them and in teaching them well, his
respect, love and hero-worship had increased. He wished
Lucky didn't dislike him so much.

Back in the harbour the cutter had dropped sail and
anchored in a protected spot in the bay instead of pulling into
the Yacht Club. Orloffski and his friend (who had come
down just expressly for the sail and the chance to look around
Jamaica for a few days) were busy battening everything down
and cleaning up when they came on board from a skiff. Both
were anxious to get on shore and away from the little ship.
It was indeed Orloffski, and for the first time since he had

met him Grant felt some liking for him. He was still excited by his trip, and by the prospect of making final landfall, and was talkative and high.

He had had to decide in Miami, when news of impending weather came, whether to go down through the Bahamas, or to sit the weather out in Miami. If he did that, he would almost certainly have to hang around Miami for at least two weeks, maybe more. The new front forming over the Aleutians should take three to five days to work down to the Gulf Coast and the Mexican mainland, so that gave him about a week's head start. He had crossed The Stream that night and then followed the classic route: through the Providence Channels, headed southeast, passing Eleuthera and Cat Island to starboard, farther south to thread the Crooked Island Passage, then southeast again to Matthewtown in Great Inagua, where they stopped just long enough to take on stores, and from there on out into the Windward Passage and the strongest Trades. They had pulled out of Matthewtown at 3.30 in the morning and, he calculated, made just about 180 sea miles in the first twenty-four hours' run. When he took his morning sight at 10 a.m. he figured they were only sixty miles or so from Ganado Bay. That was the mistake. When he brought her in to sight Jamaica, they had run west as far as Discovery Bay. That was why when they sighted Bonham and the winch boat they were beating back in from the west. "Those fucking Trades, man! They really move you along! But except for that it worked out perfect! That weather won't get here till to-morrow or the day after!"

"To-morrow," Bonham said.

"Yeah? Well, I tell you this," Orloffski said, "I hope I don't have to look at the *Lazy Jane* for a couple of weeks."

He was understandably proud of himself. Later Bonham explained to Grant that he was not really that adequate a sailor for a trip like that, not ahead of that weather. And as a navigator, he didn't know his ass from third base; witness that screwed-up morning sight! But it had worked. "Well it's good to see you you son of a bitch!" Orloffski said again and punched Bonham on the arm. "It's good to see you you bastard!" Bonham said and caught him in the belly. "You never will learn to keep that guard up, will you?" They all rowed in together, and Bonham explained about Grant putting up the money and coming into the company. "Yeah?

That's great," Orloffski said. " Sure, I'll give 'im five per cent a my share. How's my old lady?"

" Just fine," Bonham said. " Why?"

" Because she better prepare for some heavy fucking, that's why," Orloffski said. " I ain't even seen a cunt since I left Miami. How long does this weather usually last down here like that?"

Bonham squinted at the sky in the west. " Five days."

A cold front coming down from the north usually caused from five to seven days of weather, he explained, bringing with it lots of cold rain, squalls and sufficiently high winds to cause seas high enough to stop all sport fishing, and certainly it would not allow any diving. All of them looked at the west for a moment, with that awe and dignity and respect for the sea all men acquire who have ever seen the sea angry.

This particular cold front lasted exactly six days, but when it ended and passed on south and east so the diving could resume, Grant was not there to see it clear, nor was Lucky.

TWENTY-SEVEN

When he thought it all over later on, as he did and was to do many many times, he came finally to the conclusion that it was his proximity, his actual physical presence around the villa during the spell of weather when they could not dive, that caused the breaking down of everything and Carol Abernathy's final blow-up. Which of course, in turn, necessitated his telling Lucky, finally, about his old (old)? affair with Carol. One could—it would certainly be easy to—declare that it had all been inevitable from the beginning, that this particular development of all their mutual histories had been included and totally contained in all courses of future action from the moment that he called Lucky up the day after their first disastrous date. Especially if you were a fatalist.

Yet Grant tended to think that if the storm, the south-ward-moving cold front, had not come along to disrupt their diving leaving him free to hang around the place and be under foot and visible, it might not have happened. Certainly after that first afternoon Carol Abernathy had not caused any more trouble all those days that he was out with Bonham. But probably that was wishful thinking. He did not know what Lucky thought. Since It happened, he had not felt with her that sense of being one personality, the two separate eyes of one head, and no longer exactly knew what she felt and thought. But he could see no innate necessity, no absolute logic, which inevitably demanded such a total confrontation.

But if not, what kind of sense did that make? Just that a storm came, and at a certain time, was all. Or, in other words, no sense at all.

They had not even seen much of Carol or the rest, really. More than when he was diving, certainly; but not all that much more. The first two days of the storm after they suspended diving he had been content just to lie around the Cottage and loaf, swim a little bit in the safe pool, and try at least partially to refill the receptacle of his courage which had been flat empty now so long. Evelyn had one of those quick-drying tennis courts, and in the afternoons between the driving rain squalls that lashed the tropical foliage he and Lucky essayed a few sets of tennis—rather comically, since neither was anywhere near a good player. Once Carol came down with Hunt and Evelyn to watch them. She and Hunt had never played, and Evelyn hadn't played for years. Everything had been perfectly charming then. On both of those nights they had taken dinner up at the great house at Evelyn's invitation. Lucky was so glad to have him back from the diving that it lent everything a festive air. There was no reason to think everything would not go on being all right until they finished bringing up the cannon and then left for New York. The cold front storm would only push it back a week or so, that was all. And Grant had a private reason for thinking everything would be all right.

On one of the mornings when they were still diving, as he left the Cottage about seven-thirty, he had found Carol waiting for him on the end of the terrace at the point where he had to cross it to get to the garages. He had tried very carefully to avoid seeing her alone, and now she had gotten up early to confront him at a point she knew he would have to pass. He waved at her and grinned and went on, deliberately not slackening his pace.

"Ron!" she had called. "I want to talk to you."

"Yeah? What about?" He let his reluctance show as he

stopped and turned, and made his face and eyes very cold. He *felt* cold.

"About several things," Carol Abernathy said. "Have you five minutes? One thing is I want to talk to you about this girl."

"You haven't got anything to say to me about Lucky that would interest me."

"Oh, but I have. I've been checking up on her. I've got some friends who live in Syracuse, and when you left with her for Kingston, I wrote to them about her. That was before you were married," she added, as if explaining she would not have done it afterwards. "They know her and her family very well and for a long time, and they wrote me some pretty terrible things. I think you ought to know about them. For one thing that Italian family of hers are all hoodlums and gangsters and have been since the days of Prohibition."

"I know about all that," he said grimly, "and it's not like you say." If he had been cold, he was now furious.

"Another thing they wrote me is that all those years she lived in New York she was little better than a whore."

"Well?" Grant said. "So what?"

"Well don't you see what all this means?" Carol said. She smiled and stepped back. "How can she have any integrity? I think you ought to know about these things."

"I do. I know all about that too. Now let me tell you something. You don't seem to understand that Lucky and I are married. Man and wife, like you and Hunt are man and wife. I love her and she's madly in love with me. I haven't loved you for a long time, for years and years. But apart from all that we are married, legally and everything. And there's nothing you or anybody can do about it. *I* can't do anything about it. And you better get used to that."

"Another thing I wanted to talk to you about was your work," Coral Abernathy said. "All this other, all the rest, all this diving, even your getting married, is all unimportant alongside of your work. When are you going to get back to work?"

"When I feel like it. And that's not now. Another thing you should understand is that now that I'm married you no longer even have any right to ask me about my work. That's my wife's job. From now on I'm going to run my own career." It was cruel, but he had to do it. More, he wanted to do it. Because she had had no business starting this. Strangely enough, she did not answer this either, any more than she had his first rebuttal.

"The other thing is Bonham. He's just taking you for every nickel he can get out of you, selling you things you don't need, not even teaching you well. I made a mistake when I first introduced you to him."

"I'll take care of that, too," he said flatly. "It's no longer any of your business. Now let me explain something else. The only reason I came up here with Lucky is because I'm trying to protect your reputation, yours and Hunt's. That *Time*-guy I met down in Kingston, and apparently a lot of others, about two-thirds of New York to be exact, seem to believe that you and I were lovers. So you only have two choices. You can be a nice girl and shut up and protect yourself, or you can keep on doing things like this. Don't forget we may very well have to be living across the street from you in Indianapolis. How do you think it would look if we moved out of here right now? And went and stayed with Bonham? Or better yet moved into the West Moon Over?"

"Not very good," Carol said, "of course."

"Especially if that local Kingston *Time*-guy you saw left some local paid spies to keep an eye on all of us. They'd all love to do something with this story. Well, these are your two choices."

She did not answer him and only stood, leaning forward from her lower back in that peculiar prissy way she had, her eyes wide and listening, a little sad half-smile playing about her face.

"Have you told Lucky about us?" she asked.

"That's none of your business. But, no. I haven't. Not yet."

"I hope you won't," Carol said.

"That's for me to decide."

"Because the less people who know about it, the less——"

"I said that's for *me* to decide," he said.

Carol Abernathy said nothing.

"Well, see you later on," Grant said, offhand, and walked away. It was the last conversation he had with her.

So he had been reasonably sure that everything would go all right, at least until they left here anyway. Then on the third day of the storm he had gone to town to see Bonham, about the weather and the job.

It didn't rain all the time during the week of cold-front storm, and that particular day at that particular moment was beautifully fair. The rains had cooled everything off and laid the dust in the town although they made the air humid and very muggy, and from up on the hill you could look out to sea and see groups of large dark clouds marching south-eastward in stately anger, and the slanting blue lines of rain squalls dotted the ocean's surface. Bonham loafing in his shop with Orloffski (Orloffski's sailing buddy had taken the bus down to Kingston) said it would take three days after the front moved on for the seas to calm sufficiently to hope to dive. When Grant got back to the villa and walked down to the Cottage, Lucky told him what had happened.

It had rained up on the hill while he was in town although it hadn't rained in town, and in the midst of the slashing rain-storm Carol Abernathy had appeared at the door of the Cottage wearing Hunt's trenchcoat which was almost too small for her and a pair of ravelled old sneakers without socks. Her close-cropped hair with its not unbecoming streaks of grey was plastered to her skull, and she was in a fury. She had come for her suitcases, she said. If Ron Grant was big enough, old enough and mature enough to get married and assume the responsibility of a wife and family, he was also big enough, old enough and mature enough to buy and use his own goddamned suitcases instead of hers, and she wanted them, she raged, and she wanted them right here and now. Lucky, who was all alone with Mary-Martha (who was ter-rified) had no idea of what could have set her off. " Are they her suitcases?" she asked.

Grant thought about this and then had to go and look. " As a matter of fact they are," he said, coming back. " I bought them for her. They're the same two I had in New York. But I don't know what she's hollering about, nobody in our—nobody in our family ever paid any attention to what suitcases he grabbed when he went on a trip." Obviously, he added, Lucky had not given them to her.

No, she said, she hadn't. She had told her they were not hers to give and she would have to wait until Grant came back and talk to him, whereupon Carol had said she would take them by force, then. " No, you won't," Lucky had said.

She had treated her like a disobedient child " Look, Carol,
you don't want to fight me over a couple of suitcases. Ron
will be back in an hour or so. If they're yours, he'll give them
to you. Come and sit down and have a drink with me and
wait for him." At this Carol Abernathy had sat down on the
nearest couch and begun to cry.

Lucky had been scared to death, her belly was full of
flutterings, but she did not intend to be intimidated either.
But when the older woman began to weep she had gone over
and put her arms around her, remembering always to treat
her like a child. She had read that somewhere. And at this
Carol Abernathy had begun to talk. Incoherently and in
broken phrases she said that she had always tried to help Ron,
that she had always believed he had a great talent, but now
that was Lucky's job. She was passing her the torch. It was
a tremendous responsibility.

" She actually said torch?" Grant asked.

" Yes," Lucky said.

" Jesus!" Grant said. " I'm a torch."

" Wait. You haven't heard it all yet." Carol had gone on
to say that he was a strange wild boy when she first met him,
probably half crazy from the war, but she had tried her best,
and had kept him going until he became a success, for which
he had thanked her little. Lucky should note that last.
Then, wiping her eyes and lifting her face from her cupped
hands with a strange sly little smile, she said that she thought
Lucky ought to know that she, Carol, had always suspected
he was a queer. A homosexual. She had never told anybody
this before, but she thought Lucky ought to know. And now
that she had told it, she said, she might as well go on and say
that she thought he and Al Bonham were having an affair.
A regular affair.—" I always thought that perhaps he and
Hunt, my husband, were having an affair," Carol said. " I
know they used to go off together and get terribly drunk. And
I know that Ron used to go off and stay for days and days. I
know for a fact that he used to go to whorehouses in Indianapolis and over in Terre Haute. And sometimes Hunt went
with him. What they actually did there I have no idea." She
had gone on, elaborating on this theme for quite a while, and
then apologised for having told Lucky all this but she thought
she ought to know, and then she left.

" Jesus!" Grant said.

Lucky had been so stunned she had simply listened and hardly said anything in reply.

Grant was stunned too. "Jesus!" he said again, hopelessly. "What the hell could you have said?" He stopped and thought. "I guess a couple of years ago that would have made me so furious I'd have flipped my lid. Well, what do you think we ought to do? Do you think we should leave?"

"I don't know," Lucky said. "I do know I'm not terribly happy around here."

"And I've about had it with this salvage diving routine. I've done it, I know what it's like, and I'm ready to move on. I don't really give a damn about the money from it anyway. Orloffski can finish it up with him."

"By the way," Lucky said, "none of that stuff is true, is it?"

Grant stared at her. "Well, yes. I mean, no. I mean, *some* of it's true. I mean, I used to go to whorehouses a lot in Indianapolis, and Terre Haute. Yes. And why not? I wasn't getting laid good at—I wasn't getting laid good anywhere else. But I never went with Hunt. I thought of asking him a couple of times. But he was always so sealed-off and distant. And I didn't feel that, you know, in my place, I ought to.

"And as far as my having an affair with Bonham, that part's absolutely true. You ought to know that. Can't you tell from the way I treat you?"

Lucky began to grin, then threw back her champagne-coloured head of hair and laughed. Grant went over and put his arms around her. "Maybe we should leave."

"On the other hand," Lucky said, "maybe she's straightened herself out for a while, blown off enough of her internal steam that her pressure is relieved and she won't bother us for a while. They say they do that. Boy, you sure picked yourself some foster-mother! But maybe she'll let us be now. For a while."

"Maybe," Grant said dubiously.

But they were disabused of this illusion about an hour later.

Grant happened to be in the shower at the time. Suddenly over the rush of the water he heard voices from the vicinity of the kitchen, and then the word "cocksucker" repeated over and over several times in Carol Abernathy's hysterical shout. When he shut off the shower, and the water noise ceased to act like the filter screen that it was, it all came in clear. Too clear. "I don't give a damn! You'll not lock me out! I have as much right here as you have! More! Don't you *ever* try to lock me out! What did you ever do for him? Fuck him, that's all. He only married you because you were a good easy lay! The best cocksucker in New York! That's what he told me, yes! The best cocksucker in New York! The best . . ."

Calmness spread over Grant in a slow quiet flow. Curiously enough he felt exactly the same way he had felt that time when he watched the big jewfish dragging Grointon off towards its cave and knew that he was going down there, the same way he felt each time on the bottom during the salvage diving. Methodically and carefully he wrapped one of the big lush towels around his waist and tucked it in and, still wet, went out toward the kitchen. It didn't matter. Nothing mattered. If he was dead five minutes from now, it wouldn't matter. Carol Abernathy was standing just inside the splintered remnants of the screen-door, bent forward tautly from the waist, her eyes hysterical, her mouth shouting as if it were a separate creature. Lucky was standing in the centre of the room eight feet away, small and brave, and saying in a quietly nervous voice between Carol's shouts, " Carol Carol. This is my house. This is my house. You can't come in here and do this. You can't come in here and do this." She obviously had not backed off, and Carol obviously had not come any closer. And by the sink Mary-Martha the maid was standing utterly terrified.

Grant moved in like a slow-moving but inexorable avalanche, using his chest and belly like a snow-plough blade. Carol did not allow him to come near enough to touch her and backed off still shouting. If she had had a gun or a knife in her hand it would not have mattered and he would not have cared. Slowly but swiftly he bellied her toward the door. Unfortunately the shattered screen-door was still locked and after fumbling with it once he did not bother and stiff-armed it with the heel of his palm as if stiff-arming a tackler. It popped open, its latch broken (what the hell it was already smashed anyhow), and Carol backed out past it, still shouting. Grant followed her, his face feeling like a plaster-of-paris mask. "Out! Out! Get out!" was all he said. He continued to follow her down the walk like some pacific but nonetheless inexorable Nemesis until she turned and fled. Then he came back to the hysterical kitchen and broken screen-door.

Lucky was white. Reconstructing it all it appeared that Carol had come up the walk, whether to reclaim her suitcases from Grant or for some other reason, and at just that moment Mary-Martha had—as she was wont to do—reached over and pulled shut and locked the screen-door which because it was warped had a habit of standing open slightly. Coral had interpreted this to be the result of an order from Lucky who was sitting in the little dinette, a deliberate hint, snub or insult to herself to show her she wasn't wanted. She had then kicked in the door, smashing the thin lathing that held it together, and come in through it actually lacerating one arm.

"I don't know," Lucky said half-hysterically, "I don't know. I never saw anything like that." She stood breathing in a shaky way for a moment and smiling a shaky smile. "I have to pee," she said.

Grant followed her out of the kitchen into the little corridor, down which she disappeared. At that moment, for no especial reasons, he decided that he had to tell her the truth about himself and Carol. And now he thought about it. It was not at all unpleasant. He was sure she would understand. And what if she didn't? He didn't care. That great calmness of non-caring came over him again. By the time he heard the water flushing and she reappeared at the other end of the corridor he had prepared himself.

"There's something I have to tell you, Lucky," he said, making his voice grave so she would catch the great import of what he had to say. "I was Carol Abernathy's lover when I met you."

There was a pause as she continued to walk toward him along the corridor. "You weren't," she said finally. "Really? Not really!"

"Yeh," Grant said. "Really. That explains a lot of the things that have been happening around here."

"It sure does," Lucky said. She suddenly let out a high-pitched peal of nervous laughter that rather than running its course and tapering off seemed to be cut off in the middle deliberately so that it left a shocking echo of itself in the air. Then she stepped into the kitchen. "Mary-Martha, go up to the great house and get us two bottles of gin, will you please? We've run out down here." Grant realised he never would have thought of that.

"Yem," Mary-Martha said, and left, but it was clear that she didn't want to.

Lucky stood in the little bay-window of the dinette looking after her until she disappeared. "How long?" she said finally, without moving.

"Ever since I first met them," Grant said. "Fourteen years ago. But for the past ten years——"

"And you *lived* with them!" Lucky said, cutting him off.

"I sure did."

"And Hunt *paid* for you! Everything! He *supported* you!"

"He sure did."

"Why?"

"I don't know why," Grant said truthfully.

"Because *she* dominates him," Lucky said, still standing there, still looking out. "Like she dominates you."

"Maybe. But not any more," Grant said. "If she ever did. I——"

"She did," Lucky said, still looking out. "And did you fuck her again down here? After you sent me back to New York from Miami?"

"No," Grant said, then bit his tongue. "Well, yes. Once. No, twice. I'm trying not to lie. But the only reason I did was because I felt so sorry for her I couldn't hurt her that much to turn her down. She came to me asking. Can you understand that?"

"Sure," Lucky said. "Sure. I can understand everything. That's my job. That's what you pay me for. Isn't it? You actually put your thing in me again after sticking it in that dirty old hole!"

"Oh, Lucky, come on," he said desperately.

"And you had the temerity, the *gall* to accuse me about my old boy-friend from three years ago, who wasn't even a love affair!" she said. "And so all our love affair, everything that happened to us in New York, was all a lie," she said. That was when she turned to him and Grant saw he had totally miscalculated. Her eyes were two bright, bright buttons, glinty, impossibly concentrated to two tiny points like some addict's. They did not at all match the horribly wide, stiff smile of her mouth below them. Grant suddenly remembered that time in Kingston when she had slapped him across the face with her purse, and how he had promised himself to try to analyse her unexpected reaction, and hadn't. " I *was* a whore. I really *was* a hooker, a New York lay, a two-week party-girl whore. And you were the businessman from out of town in for a fling who wanted to get his ashes hauled. Only it all turned out different, and I married you. Only because you just didn't happen to be married. Only you didn't even have guts enough to tell me——"

" Lucky! Don't say that! You know that isn't true!" Grant said.

" Only you didn't even have guts enough to tell me how much you loved the little wife. Back home. You didn't even have that much courage."

" Lucky, please."

Unaware of what she was doing, still with those bright bright, starry, almost pointed eyes and the horrible smile below them, she put her right hand under her left breast and hefted it, hoisted it, as if weighing something " Men. Goddamned miserable asshole-licking men. Self-pitying sons of bitches. Ass-lickers. I might have known. I *should* have known. Nobody's ever *really* free, without some kind of a Stud or a free lay around somewhere. But I'm just stupid. Some stupid whore. So! Another Buddy Landsbaum I get."

Grant felt something click in him and the strange calmness he had felt in the shower stall swept over him even stronger. After all, what could happen? They could shoot each other, at the very worst. Otherwise she could divorce him and take half his loot in alimony, if she wanted. Fine. Good. What the fuck did it matter? " Well, what do you want to do?" he said.

Lucky Grant didn't answer that and went on absently hoisting her left breast, and her face became normal. " It's not such a bad deal at that, I suppose," she said. " All I have to do is fuck you every now and then, whenever you want to get laid, and maybe blow you once in a while. And I'll have my charge at Saks and my charge at Bonwit's. I love Mancini shoes. They're hard to find in New York, did you know that? There're only two places that I know of. I guess it's not such a bad deal really. I'll be just like everybody else. Did you really say that?" she asked. " What she said you said about me?"

" Lucky!" Grant said, stung. Then he pulled himself back down. "Of course not. You're not."

"I know," she said. "I'm fair. But you couldn't really call me the best cocksucker in New York. That was what surprised me."

Grant wanted to scream at her from pain. Instead he pulled himself back down, and made himself listen for that click into the calmness that didn't care. "Well, let's stop, hunh? It's the second act curtain. What do you want to do?"

"I certainly don't want to stay around here any longer," Lucky said. "That's for sure." She seemed as far away from him as he felt from her. It was horrible. But he didn't care, did he?

"We'll leave for New York as soon as I can get tickets."

She turned to look at him then, her eyes wide and hardly seeing but not that horrible brilliance any more, and took her hand away from her breast. "New York? New York? I don't want to go back to New York. Not now. All my friends would know right away. All they'd have to do would be to look at us. I'm proud."

An ironical defence seemed the only thing left to avoid this kind of pain, he thought. "Okay. Well, where do you want to go?"

"I don't know. I really don't know. I have to think. This is all a bit of a shock, you know. I have to think. I don't know where I want to go. I don't want to stay here, I know that." She gave him a glacial smile that was light-years away. "It's really not such a bad deal at that, you know. It's just that it's not a love affair. But businesswise it's okay." The horribly glacial smile disappeared. "But how could you have brought me *here*? Really! How could you have?"

"It was easy," Grant said. "You think it over and you let me know where you want to go, will you? We'll go there."

"Are you going to take me back to your ' house ' in Indianapolis?" Lucky said.

"No," Grant said. "I guess that's out."

"Yes, I think it ought to be out," Lucky said. "I want to go back to Kingston," she said. "That's where I want to go. I want to go back to René and Lisa. For a while anyway, at least."

"Okay. I'll go to town and get the plane tickets. But I would like to suggest," he added, leaning heavy on the irony,

" that Lisa of all people is about the worst choice you can pick at the present moment. She hates men about as much as you do at this moment. She can't be very good for you right now."

"Yes," Lucky said and gave him that light-years smile again, a smile totally different in kind from that first horrible one. "Yes, she hates men. All *but* René. You really are a cheap gutless no-good prick, you know that? How *could* you have brought me here back to *her*? That horrible old bag. How *could* you have been her *lover*?"

"I'll go and get the tickets," Grant said in a stony voice. "For as soon as we can get out."

She didn't answer. He went and dressed. He was exhausted, he discovered, when he got out of the house, the Cottage. When he put his hands and feet on the steering wheel and pedals of one of Evelyn's cars they were all four shaking. No hour and a half of bottom-time with a crowbar had ever exhausted him half as much. He forced the car to move anyway, by sheer force of willpower. It had happened. His estrangement with Lucky over Carol had happened. And it had happened just exactly like he had dreamed it so many times in his horrible wide-awake daytime day-dreaming nightmares. Just exactly.

In town, after seeing to the plane tickets (they would be flying out once again on the midnight flight), he went to the Ganado Beach Hotel and called René in Kingston. The Ganado Beach had a dim quiet bar with fishnets on the ceiling and those green glass balls for floats. It was soothing, and he needed soothing. He ordered a double martini. When things are so bad that nothing else bad can happen to you, it's sometimes almost pleasant, almost peaceful. The end of the line. But of course he'd find room for them René had said.—"You want ze same suite? We'ave now ze John Gielgud suite, ze Sharlie Addams suite, and now we 'ave ze Ron Grant Honeymoon Suite. I move somebody. Wa ze matter, my Ronnie? Eez somesing bad happen you?"—"No, nothing's happened," Grant said, "why?"—"You soun' fonny," René said.—"No. I've caught a small cold is all," Grant said.—"I 'ave everysing ready for you. I meet you at ze airport. Kees ze Lucky pour me."—"Sure," Grant said. Ha ha. Hansel and Gretel and the Babes in the Wood. After he finished his drink he went around to Bonham's.

The big diver was sitting in his swivel chair with his feet up on his desk, and Orloffski was loafing lazily in a chair on the other side of it. "There's nothing like some weather to give a guy a rest," Bonham grinned, and took his feet down.

There seemed to be no way to tell him except just come out with it. "We're leaving, Al. Lucky and me. We're going back to Kingston for a few days."

"Kingston's got the same weather," Bonham said. "You won't be able to dive there either."

"I know. But that's not why we're going. Lucky wants to see René and Lisa again before we head out for New York. So it looks like the salvage operation's over for me."

"There's still five cannon to get out," Bonham said. "We ought to be able to dive in five six days."

"Not me. I got to be getting back to New York. See about my new play. Starting rehearsals." It was strange when you felt like this how hard it was just to talk. It was all dull, nothing mattered.

"What's the matter with you, pal? You look like you lost your best friend," Orloffski said bluffly.

"I don't have any best friends," Grant said, making it crisp. "I thought you knew that." He was back to not liking Orloffski again, now that the first flush of the Pole's successful voyage had worn off. He was still convinced Orloffski had stolen his Exacta camera. "You can help Al finish the salvage job," he added, as an afterthought.

"Are you kiddin'?" Orloffski bellowed. "Multiple dives at 120 feet with 47 minutes' decompression time? I ain't about to. I ain't no chance-taker. I ain't no workin' diver. I'm a simple spearfisherman."

Grant looked at him with amusement. "Was it all that dangerous, Orloffski?"

"You knew how dangerous it was," Bonham put in quickly from behind the desk. "It's all right. I'll do it myself. It'll take longer that's all. Or maybe you and me'll do it when you come back down for the *Naiad*'s first trip. But what about your share of the seven that we've got?"

"I don't care," Grant said. "Put it in on the schooner. Send me a statement, but put the money all on the schooner." He got up. He found he was having trouble sitting still, now. "But there was something else I——" he mumbled, embarrassed. He discovered he hadn't known what he meant to say.

Or cared. He thought a moment. "Oh, yeah. What about —— What about the possibility of silver and gold ; you know, other stuff, artifacts, that might have been on that ship?"

"No chance," Bonham said. He shrugged. "It would take equipment like Ed Link had on the *Sea Diver* to find anything under that sand. Now that it's located somebody like Ed Link might do it someday, but we couldn't. Anyway it might even be too deep for Link." He got up from behind the desk and followed Grant outside. "Listen, I just got word that the *Naiad* may be finished soon. In a couple of weeks maybe. That means that once I get hold of Sam Finer we may be pullin' out on our cruise in less than a month. If that's true, it would be silly for you to go back to America and then come right back. Why don't you just stay? You could just about live on the extra plane fares."

"I can't," Grant said. "I've got to be getting back to New York for my play. And Lucky wants to go back to Kingston before we leave. Anyway, you've got my New York address. Send me a wire. Anyway uh Lucky might not be going with us on the cruise."

"Is something the matter?" Bonham said.

"No. Why?"

"You seem so strange," Bonham said. "I thought maybe something bad might have happened up at the villa."

"No," Grant said. "Nothing." He found he could hardly think, actually, and he wanted to get done and be gone. "Look, send me that wire. I figure we'll stay in Kingston a week or so. Okay?"

"Okay," Bonham said. They shook hands, rather sadly, Grant thought. But then he found he couldn't really think about much of anything. He couldn't think consecutively. His mind just jumped around. All he seemed really able to think about was just that Lucky was mad at him, more than mad at him—totally and glacially separated from him. Light-years. Wherever he turned he came up against that like against that same brick wall. On the other side of which was all the sunshine. And there was nothing to do.

Back at the villa he went to see Evelyn. "Lucky and I are leaving."

"I rather thought you might be." Evelyn came out on to the veranda with him.

"I wanted to tell you myself. And thank you for everything

you've done for us. We're taking the midnight plane to Kingston."

"Carol is shut up in her room," Evelyn said. "She would like to know if there's anything she can do to rectify what she's done. And she asked me to help any way I can."

"There's nothing to be done. We couldn't possibly stay here now. I wouldn't want Lucky to. And she certainly doesn't want to."

"I suppose not," Evelyn said. "Carol said some pretty insulting things."

"Insulting! Did you hear it?"

"How could I help it?" Evelyn smiled. "Still . . ."

Grant looked at her, their hostess, this tall statuesque woman with her cynical face, whom he had known off and on for years now. Just two nights ago, when he had walked out into the grounds well after midnight, he had seen her and the girl Pat Wright sitting side by side with their heads together on a set of old stone steps that led nowhere on the hillside. As he watched Pat Wright had begun to comb Evelyn's long grey hair on her thrownback head in the moonlight. He had tiptoed away so they didn't see him.

"Your screen-door is all busted up down there," he said.

"That's of little importance," Evelyn de Blystein said. "It's been awf'ly hard on Carol having you here with your new bride."

"It was her idea," Grant said. "It wasn't me who asked for it."

"It's pretty easy to see that she's madly in love with you," Evelyn said.

Grant did not know how much to say, how far to go. "She told you that!"

"No, but . . ."

"I don't think she's capable of loving anybody. Or any thing. Except maybe herself, a little bit."

"She thinks she loves you," Evelyn said.

"Foster-mothers often fall in love with their sons," Grant said. "Especially if they haven't any children of their own."

"Yes," Evelyn said. "Have you seen Hunt?"

"No. I haven't."

"Don't you think you ought to say good-bye to him?"

"I suppose so," Grant said. "Where is he?"

"Paul and he went down to the gardener's greenhouse to

look at some new plants. They're both trying to pretend nothing has happened, the asses."

"They would be," Grant said. "Well, thanks. I'll go down and see him."

Hunt Abernathy saw him coming from inside as he approached the greenhouse, and came out to meet him rather than let him come in. Quietly he took Grant by the arm and led him away, off across the lawn. His grey eyes were anxious, enhancing the deep crowsfeet wrinkles around them. "What are you going to do?"

"Go back to Kingston, Hunt. We leave on the midnight plane."

"Oh, maybe it won't be necessary to do anything as drastic as that," Hunt said. "Perhaps if——"

"No, Hunt. Lucky doesn't want to stay here after that. And I can't very well ask her to." Grant didn't want to say anything about his and her own troubles now.

"I suppose you can't," Hunt said thoughtfully.

"We've done what we came to do anyway," Grant said, "which was hush up any rumours that ass Heath might have wanted to start." Suddenly he put his hand warmly on Hunt Abernathy's shoulder. "You know, this probly means the end of the house in Indianapolis for us, too, you know that, don't you?"

Hunt stopped. "Really?"

"I can't expect Lucky to go back there and live now, across the street from you and Carol, in a house that Carol practically decorated."

Hunt had already stopped, and now he turned and focussed on Grant his tough grey eyes, cool and all screwed up behind their heavy crows-feet. In the last four years he had had three drunken driving accidents. "Then this is really goodbye, then, almost, isn't it?"

"I guess it is," Grant said. He took his hand off the other's shoulder. It was strange that he should feel so terrible about leaving him, after cuckolding him and screwing his wife all those years, but he did. "We'll go on to New York from Kingston. I don't know when I'll ever get back out there to Indiana. Probably I'll turn the house over to somebody and let them sell it contents and all. I'm going to be in a terrible way for money now. Thanks to Carol."

"She only got you to buy that place to protect you," Hunt said. "She only wanted to help you."

"I'm not sure of that," Grant said.

"Well, I'm her husband," Hunt Abernathy said.

"And I'm Lucky's husband," Grant said.

Hunt nodded and looked at the ground thoughtfully. Funny, Grant thought, it was really where the screwing was that mattered in the end. It was where you were getting laid, and who was laying whom. People Who Fuck Together Stay Together.

"Well, I can drive you to the airport, anyway," Hunt said after a moment. "How soon do you want to go?"

"Any time," Grant said. "Right now. It's almost eight now. We can have dinner out there at the airport, and then wait in the bar."

"All right," Hunt said. "I'll meet you out front. Are you packed?"

"Should be by now. Where's Doug?"

"I don't know," Hunt Abernathy said gloomily. "I haven't seen him since—I haven't seen him since this morning."

Doug it turned out was at the Cottage with Lucky, when Grant got back to it. Grant was glad that he was. He had handled all this other, the farewells etc., the plane tickets, Hunt, and René, but now when it came to talking to his own wife again after that scene they had had, he found he couldn't think of one single thing to say. And more, he found that he didn't want to. His fury and anger with her increased in direct ratio to his swiftly approaching nearness to her, and by the time he stood before the two of them he was almost trembling with it, and not sad, guilty or miserable at all any more.

She and Doug were sitting in two deep chairs talking calmly out on the green-and-brown-tile floor of the room the pool entered, and which seemed, and felt, like a patio though actually in fact it was not. "Well, it's all set," he said. "We have reservations on the midnight plane. The good-byes are all said. We can leave here any time we like. Are the bags packed?" And screw you, he thought.

"Yes, all set," Lucky said politely, almost sweetly, even. "I did them while you were in town." But her eyes were as distant as they could get. She was as far away as the moon.

A hell of a lot farther. Hansel and Gretel Light-Years, that happy Navaho Indian couple.

"We can leave right now, then," Lucky said. She got up, and Doug got up with her.

"I think that's a good idea," Grant said crisply. "Hunt wants to drive us to the airport."

"Hunt?" Lucky said, looking at him with surprise.— Hard to believe eh? he wanted to say, but didn't.

"Yes. Hunt. Carol's husband," he said instead. "He said he hated to say good-bye to me, and he would like to drive us." It was only a *little* poetic licence. If Hunt hadn't actually said that, he had certainly meant it, felt it. "He's already waiting for us out front."

"I suppose it was self-contained, all in the cards, that something like this had to happen," Doug said, "but I'm sorry that it did." Nobody said anything. Looking at him, Grant could not really believe him, somehow. But what did that matter? "I don't think I'll come out to the airport with you this trip. But I might drop down to Kingston for a day or two, before I take the straight flight there back to Miami, when I leave. If you want me, that is."

"We'd be very glad to see you, Doug," Lucky said politely before Grant could answer. "You've been very nice to both of us and have been a great help to us actually."

"Come on, I'll help with the bags," Doug said.

Hunt was waiting for them out on the great loop of drive-way as they came out around through the side gate of the villa. In the car Lucky sat between them in the front seat with the bags in the back seat and in the trunk. They were waved away by Doug, Pat Wright and Evelyn standing on the steps. But the Count Paul for whatever private reasons of his own had preferred to stay in his tropical greenhouse even though by now it was almost full dark. After he got them started down the winding hill, Hunt turned his grave eyes on to Lucky briefly for a moment and said, "I want to apologise for what Carol did, and said, Lucky. But," he said, "she's been having a pretty hard time lately."

"I guess she has," Lucky said simply.

"Well, enough of that," Hunt Abernathy said. That was about all that was said. Grant, sitting with his arm out the open window up to his shoulder to give Lucky more room in the middle, didn't feel like talking either. It was strange to be sealed off back into his old Single Viewpoint of Life again, after getting so used to their Double, Composite Viewpoint as he had. Absently his mind turned back to one of those nights when they had been still diving on the wreck, and late at night after everybody else had all gone to bed he and Lucky had swum nude again in the pool. They had swum nude other nights, but this night they had made love there, in the water. Proud and confident now of his ability to hold his breath, he had swum down along the bottom from the other end and come up under her in the deep end and buried his face in her crotch. When she made it to the side of the pool, he came up and trapped her against the side of the pool between his arms. Then he had put it in her and holding her with her back against the side of the pool with one arm on either side fucked her invisibly down there in the water while the cool ripples laved her breasts and his shoulders. He had thought then about the incredible suppleness of her body and how she could actually put both feet behind her head and had done it for him once, in the bed. No woman could get physically closer to a man.

At the airport Hunt did not get out. " I won't get out," he said. He had pulled up alongside the long brightly lighted open-sided building with the airline companies' desks strung out all along its back wall. He shook hands with each of them through the open window, Grant lastly. Tears had come into his eyes and were running quietly down his cheeks. Grant saw the look of shock and surprise come into Lucky's eyes. But when she saw him look at her, she filmed her eyes over for him coldly. They stood like that and watched Hunt Abernathy drive away.

TWENTY-EIGHT

The tears in Hunt Abernathy's eyes glinted, splintered and shivered his eyesight as he pulled the car away from Grant and his new bride, but he waited until he had turned the corner around the parking lot buildings into the exit avenue before slowing down and wiping them out with his thumb because he did not want the two of them to see him do it. But as he did this a sudden breath spurted from his nose in an uncontrollable snort of weeping and new tears spurted into his eyes. He was forced to pull the car off on to the shoulder and stop.

After a moment or two it stopped but this time when he wiped his eyes out he did not go on but simply sat in the car with the motor running, rubbing the centre hollow of his palm around and around on the gear-shift knob. He was reasonably certain that Grant meant every word of it about this being the end of the house in Indianapolis, the end of his tenancy in Indiana. On the other hand, he was sure Carol could not have avoided or altered her outspoken little blow-up at the Cottage. Patience, suppression had never been Carol's strong point ; her power came from flamboyance, total openness, lack of inhibition ; whereas his, Hunt's greatest weakness had always been his tendency to almost total inhibition. As she was so fond of telling him. Slowly, with the clutch pedal depressed, he ran the gear lever up through the four forward gear changes and then back down again through all four, 4 to 3 to 2 to 1, while the car remained motionless, its motor still running.

It had been him, Hunt, who had taught Grant to drive. As he had taught Carol. Day after day, year after year even, he had sat beside him (" Riding shotgun!" they had called it) with the then-much-younger Grant at the wheel, drilling and drilling him in every tiniest little thing, on every little or large trip they took. (Such as never taking a curve too fast, so fast that you had to cross over the centre line to flatten your arc.) Until finally Grant had become at least as expert a road driver as himself, and perhaps even better. The miles they had put in. And that had been thirteen and fourteen years ago. Slowly Hunt put the car in low and pulled it back out on to the roadway. You didn't just throw away fourteen years of experiences and memories like that without also uprooting and throwing with it some part of yourself.

The by-now-familiar Jamaican countryside slid past him and his headlights, and Hunt hardly saw it. He was filled up with a totally complete and terrible sadness over the way the world just moved on so inexplicably, and just *kept* moving on. When this sadness hit him was when he needed a drink bad. There was a flask in the dashboard and he reached for it, gulping down a swallow of raw straight scotch. If asked, he couldn't have put it into words. He had never had many words. Technical words yes, as an engineering graduate for his work, but not literary words. Like Grant. It was this same attribute of sadness that had first attracted him to Grant. Not so Carol. She was always sanguine; always had to be optimistic. Not Hunt. The Abernathys were an old, old family of means and position, and decadent because of it. Carol was fresh blood to the likes of the Hunts and the Abernathys.

Grant came of an old, old family too, and maybe that was it. Anyway when he first came out to their house with all those other wounded vets who hung around Hunt and Carol to drink (after all, that was about all they could do for them, wasn't it? feed them booze?), he had been different. He brooded about it. Those others, they all only wanted to forget it as fast as they could. That had been back before the war was even quite finally over.

Hunt didn't remember quite when he first began to suspect Grant was sleeping with his wife. It was sometime around the time she started taking her car to go up and see him in Chicago, probably. Ron was still in Great Lakes Station in the hospital then, and could only get one week-end pass a month. Letters came in from him for Carol quite often, but then she was always getting letters from lots of the other kids, too. Hunt of course would never allow himself to look at *any* of them. And she was always taking her car and going off on trips, to visit a sister, or go see one of her brothers stationed somewhere in the Army. How could he know? Then somebody said they had seen her in Chicago. But he still didn't know. She had used to go to Chicago shopping every now and then. And he could hardly suspect her of it. She had never been what *anybody* could call oversexed. Though, of course, he knew she was interested in literature and the theatre like Grant. But he didn't really know. And if he did anything about it, and it *was* so, other people would know.

Then Grant had come home to Indianapolis to stay with them after his discharge. He stayed a month or six weeks, Hunt thought, and during that time he wrote three one-act plays. Then he went off to New York for his final years of school. He had brought enormous energy into the house. And he was more uninhibited than Carol even. Hunt had never seen anyone with so much energy. And he was funny. He had them both laughing out loud a good deal of the time. His parents were dead and the rest of his family scattered, the only relation he had in Indianapolis now was a first cousin and his wife, and they were now poor after the '29 Crash as were all of the others. It was rather like having a son in the house. Of course there were looks and little gestures that passed between them. Some of the time. Once in a while. Hunt could not fail to notice those. But if they were sleeping together they kept it very private and were very discreet about it. There was no gossip. All that would come much later. And he didn't really *know*. And then of course Grant left for New York. Maybe the truth was that he didn't really want to know.

Hunt reached for the dashboard and the flask and gulped down another hot snort of the raw scotch as the headlights swept past two shaggy goats standing on some roadside rocks. Then just beyond them were three more. All of the natives down here seemed to keep them. He took another quick little, smaller drink before putting back the flask.

If they had brought it out in the open or said something to him about it, he would have done something about it. But as long as they didn't . . .

When, three months later, a letter had come from Grant (another, one more letter) asking Carol to come to New York for a visit, he had decided then, Hunt remembered, to do something about it and had forbidden her to go. And Carol had said she was going to go anyway. She had shown him the letter. There was certainly nothing about a love affair in it, but of course they could have prepared this letter especially to show to him. But he began to wonder if maybe he hadn't been wrong all along with his suspicions and his suspicious imagination. He didn't really *know*. Carol said Grant was working on his first full-length three-acter along with carrying his studies and he was about to crack up and needed her help. And of course, Carol could go on her own if she wanted. She had some money of her own (though nothing like he, Hunt, had)—in spite of the fact that she had started neglecting her own real estate business since starting to write plays. Hunt had always taken a dim view of and had never paid much attention to this playwriting business. He knew nothing about plays and didn't want to, but he was pretty certain no neurotic

Indiana housewife or small-town-boy ex-Navy enlisted man were ever going to become bigtime playwrights

In the end, he gave her the money to go, though he never did know quite why. Probably because of that very thing: that she had enough money of her own to go anyway. If he was labouring under the illusion that it would be good to have her gone, he was soon straightened out on that. It was very lonesome not to have anyone, someone in the house when he came home at night and the first couple of broads he brought home to the house after she left immediately began working on him as soon as they found out that his wife had gone away.

She stayed away three months. Then she came home full of bitterness toward New York and carrying the first large group of books that would go into what would eventually become her really extensive occult library. During the last two months of Grant's final year she made two quick flying trips to New York and after the second one came back with the information that Grant was totally disillusioned with school and with New York also. Neither had anything to teach him about playwriting and after his graduation he wanted only to go someplace off somewhere and work. So she had invited him to come back to Indianapolis and live with them. There was plenty of room in the house, and Grant's tiny Navy pension was not enough for him to live on and work unless he held down some kind of full-time job.

And thus began what Hunt was later to think of—and indeed thought now, driving back to the villa—as the best three years of his life. He still did think that now, though perhaps it was hard to understand just why. He reached into the glove compartment for the flask and another snort.

Grant turned out to be the companion he had never had in his life. They made all the football games both local and collegiate together, the hockey matches, the fights, the baseball games, the Indianapolis 500 and the lesser races, the Indiana U basketball schedule. They also did a lot of serious drinking together, because Grant too liked the serious kind of low-bar-crawling Hunt enjoyed. Grant was full of strange and wonderful ideas about life, or so it seemed to Hunt. Ideas Hunt would never have thought about. He had finished his three-acter and it had been turned down by every producer in New York. He had then rewritten it while still in New York, with exactly the same results, except that a firm called Gibson & Stein had shown enough interest to ask him to rewrite it again along slightly different lines they themselves suggested which they thought might help it. This Grant engaged himself in when he came back from New York, using one of their upstairs bedrooms, and he worked like a demon at it, six, eight or even ten hours a day four or five days a week. But the rest of the time, the nights and the week-ends, he was free and ready for whatever " action " happened to be going on. Weekends the two of them would drive to South Bend, or over to Champaign in Illinois, or down to Bloomington depending upon which team was playing where. Only in the matter of women was there any reserve between them, but on that subject they both for some reason remained reticent with each other. Hunt did not know if Grant was still having—or had ever actually had—an affair with his wife, but he did know— because he got it from the women themselves—that he and Grant were often screwing, or had been screwing, the same broads. It was the kind of friend Hunt had always wanted to have.

Sometimes they would visit the two country farms Hunt had inherited but which never paid well, just to inspect and see how the tenants were doing, and during those times Hunt would show him some of all the many things of his childhood.

Somehow it all went back to his own father and his own mother, the great huge roaring moustachioed figure that was his father and the tiny whining mealy-mouthed social snob that was his mother, and to the woodshed where—back even before the '20s and college when their big place was not even yet part of a suburb and was practically a country farm itself —the woodshed where the huge powerful vague figure of his father would take him and make him drop his pants and underpants and bend over a barrel and strap him unmercifully on his bare bottom with his big leather belt to teach him discipline and the importance of being serious. Somehow, though Hunt did not quite know how, it was all tied in with that. His father. And his mother. Both of whom he hated, and feared, unmercifully. His father and his mother and the son he had never had, but had promised himself he would never treat as his father had treated him. Those unmerciful beatings. Why Grant evoked all that Hunt could not say, except of course that he fulfilled the image of the unhad son.

His father, whom he had wanted so much to love but had never been allowed to, had made him into a solitary, a virtual recluse, and a loner. And the coming of Grant had alleviated all that so very much.

If it had not been for that first goddamned damnable abortion, they might have had children. Or so Carol always told him. But, back then, Hunt hadn't even wanted them, to tell the truth. Neither had Carol.

Hunt Abernathy leaned over toward the glove compartment for the flask and took another, tiny drink.

Of course, with the success of the first play and the resulting fame for its author, all that fun and happiness of those first three years had changed. Trips to Europe for Grant. Longer and longer trips to New York. Only when Grant was back in Indianapolis actually working did they see each other much at all. Grant had rewritten the first play as Gibson & Stein had suggested, only to have it rejected still again. Then he had worked two, two and a half years on still another play which he had had the idea for and which G & S had suggested he do in lieu of the first one. That was the play that became *The Song of Israphael* and a success. By this time Hunt, who had watched how hard he worked and seen what a strange novel inquiring mind he had, had come to believe in his eventual success and so was not surprised.

But even when Grant was back in Indianapolis after that it was not the same. The available Midwestern sports and athletic contests no longer interested him so much. And his nights of low-bar-crawling that Hunt liked so much got fewer and fewer. Grant preferred to do his drinking in hotel cocktail lounges and more sophisticated bars. It just wasn't any longer the same.

Ahead of him Hunt saw the beach-house loom up on the right and turned into the villa driveway. Once inside and off the highway he had himself a real drink from the flask, then pulled away on up the drive.

He did not really know whether Grant had ever had an affair with his wife or not, that was the truth. He just didn't know. And, really, he didn't want to know. He would never know, now, and he did not want to think about it. Suddenly he giggled to himself. He had suddenly remembered something that had happened in some dive in Indianapolis years ago where he had been out drinking. A big truck-driver standing at his end of the bar, a guy he had known around the lower quarter of Indianapolis for a long time, had been talking and at the same time watching at the other end of the bar a huge, rather mean, forceful man they both knew who was a big drinker, big liver, life-of-the-party, and powerful man around the dives. The huge, dominating " big liver ", drunk now, was roaring out some story to the group at his end of the bar, forcing them by the sheer weight of his personality to listen, and to laugh, and Hunt's truckdriver had been extolling his virtues and bragging him up. Smiling, he had turned to Hunt. " He had my broad," he said admiringly.

This was something like that. Hunt had understood what he meant. Well, if he had had her, and he didn't think he had, was reasonably sure he hadn't, he hoped he had turned her over on her hands and knees and spread her wide open and slipped it into that big wet wide-open gash all the way, driving it in as hard as he could drive. The bitch deserved it.

In front of him the villa now loomed up on the driveway loop, all its downstairs lights blazing and several of its upstairs bedroom lights still on also. As he stopped the car and got out and looked at it, one of the upstairs lights winked out. The image struck him. Grant's leaving was like the flipping out of one more window light in the building, the mansion of his life. There wouldn't be too many more. And soon the house would be all dark. Hunt looked at the luminous dial of his watch. It was eight-thirty, and with a sigh of relief and pleasurable anticipation he realized it was Time. He could go in and have a serious before-dinner drink or two.

He hoped Grant was happy with his new cunt anyway.

TWENTY-NINE

Grant was thinking about Hunt too. And also about Carol. There was little else for him to do. Though the food was good the airport dinner was a catastrophe, he and Lucky hardly spoke five words to each other, and by a quarter of nine they were finished eating with three more hours still to wait for the plane. There was nothing to do but go in the bar and drink.

The old cunt had really done him in, finally. And the depression he felt at leaving Hunt for what was probably the last time, on top of the depression he was already carrying, bowed him down. He was much much more sad at the prospect of never seeing Hunt again than he was over never again seeing Carol. He brooded on it. Once, one time, in the bar over their scotches he hunched up his shoulders and started out with, " Look! All I was trying to do was protect their reputations. I'd been doing it for years when I met you. How was I——?"—" I don't want to talk about it!" Lucky interrupted in a cold, icy, but almost half-wailing voice. " I really and truly don't!" She was all cold and ice. She was a one-woman ski resort by God practically. He didn't try again. Fortunately a stranger standing at the bar, an American from New York naturally, recognised him and came over and introduced himself, offering to buy a drink because he wanted to ask Grant about an obscure philosophical symbolism about modern man in a technocracy which he thought he had detected (and which he in fact had) in one of Grant's earlier plays. Grant asked him to sit down, and this kept them going until plane-time.

But once in the long darkened tube of the tourist section of the big jet, all of whose remaining passengers except himself and Lucky had boarded in New York for MoBay or Kingston and none of whom bothered to wake up enough to deplane for the twelve-minute stop at Ganado Bay, there was nothing left to do but think. He got himself a stiff drink from the slightly, cutely dishevelled stewardess and sat back down. Lucky in the seat next the window had looked out her port all during take-off and once airborne continued to look out of it though there was nothing to see now but stars. He would be damned if he would try to strike up a conversation with her. He was sick to death of swallowing *his* pride and kissing ass with proud women. He had had enough of that to last him all his life, and he damn' well wasn't going to do it. He was furious with her. How dare she? How dare she, who loved to brag so to almost anybody about her 400 men she had had in her life, take such exception to something like that? Were the sins of the fathers forever to descend to the sons? The sins of the mothers descend to the daughters? Well, he wasn't going to play that game, that stupid, superstitious, Old Testament game. He still could not understand how he had so grossly miscalculated her reaction to his confession of having been Carol's lover. Anger, yes ; but this kind of near-psychotic despair that had descended over her, no. Certainly there was something there that he had not seen, or if he had seen it, had not understood.

But underneath his anger, there was still this massive depression. And underneath the depression, like a dark sand cloud lying ominously below a layer of relatively clear water, was a terrible gloomy melancholy. Perhaps for this very reason his mind fell (in the susurrous quietly humming plane ramming and roaring its swift way through the night sky) back into recalling that horrible gloomy melancholy year of school in New York, and those first months and years he had spent with the Abernathys. Certainly his leave taking of Hunt had helped thrust his thought in that direction also.

It was Carol who first suggested he come stay with them after his discharge. He had been fucking her off and on for about five months then. And until then he had never given a single thought to its becoming anything like a permanent affair.—" What will Hunt say to that?" he had wanted to know.—" He won't say anything," Carol said. " He likes you."—" Doesn't he know we're sleeping together?" he had asked. He remembered Carol had rubbed the corner of her lip with her curled forefinger.—" I don't think he really does," she said finally. " Or if he does, he won't let himself believe it, or at least not think about it."—" But me live with you? It's a pretty dirty trick to pull on *him*," he had said.—" Not when you consider all the things he's done to me in my life," Carol said. " And what else would you do? Go and get a job in some factory? And then try to write plays at night after you come home dog-tired from work?"

The war was not even yet over then, and Great Lakes Station was like some great huge railroad yard, only this was a railroad yard for men. Hundreds of thousands of men in blue uniforms and white caps, coming in, going out, or stationed permanently. Not a face recognisable as a face among them. *Echoes of the World of the Future*, Grant thought with a shudder and went to get another stiff drink from the stewardess. You couldn't even pretend you were a soul there, to them. Souls were suspended for the duration.

Those of them in the hospital had had a ball. There was not a one of them but who expected to get discharged. The war

was over for them. They had all received months and months
of back pay in one lump. Five of them kept a two-room suite
at the Drake at daily rates for five months. In all he himself
had spent almost eleven months in Great Lakes Station, and
in all the myriads of female faces that had passed into and
out of the Drake Hotel suite or some other suite carrying
bottles or carrying glasses he had enjoyed quite a large
number and had finally seriously almost settled on one. So he
had had another girl there in Chicago when Carol finally
made her offer.

The other girl's name was Billie Wrights, and she had been
through at least three of his friends. He didn't mind that and
when they came together they hit it off, mainly because they
both were so highly sexed. Billie had come up to Chicago
from Memphis, Tennessee meaning to make a killing as a
lady welder before the war ended, and like so many other
people do had wound up in the same profession she had left
in Memphis, which was couture and ladies' dresses. She was
assistant manager at one of the larger independent ladies'-
wear shops in Chicago. At another hotel. where he took her
for privacy and to make sure that no more of his friends
latched on to her, he taught her to go down on him and she
liked it. He went down on her and she liked that. She liked
everything, but being from Memphis was naïve and had
never done those other things. "But isn't it perverted?" she
asked him innocently one time, "doing those things? All I
know is that I like it."—"No, it's not perverted," he laughed.
"It's perfectly normal. Men and women. It's only Bible
Belt preachers who think it's perverted." Finally she took him
home to her nice little apartment and it was an "affair". The
only times he did not see her were when Carol was in
Chicago, or when he got his monthly week-end pass and went
home to Indianapolis.

They talked a great deal, he and Billie, about him coming
to live with her permanently in her apartment after his discharge. He could live with her and work on his playwriting,
and she would keep her job, which she liked, and support him.
Neither of them said anything about marriage. Then one day
about a month before he was due to be discharged Billie took
off her rose-coloured glasses. "I just don't see how we can
do it, Ron," she said, looking at him anxiously. "I want to.
But I just don't make that much money. You see, I make out

with my salary and this apartment mainly because a lot of my meals and entertainment come from dates I have with men. I've noticed the difference since you've been coming here. And we won't have your Navy salary after you're discharged. Do you understand? You won't be mad? I know you wouldn't want me to be having dates with men."—" I'm not mad," he had said, with a strange kind of sad but pleasant melancholy, and patted the inside of her nude thigh, " and you're quite right. We've been kidding ourselves. Come here. Bring it here." Life. Life moves on, inexplicably. Carol Abernathy had made him her offer about six weeks before.

He had stayed with them in Indianapolis, he remembered, just a little over two months. Two months and two weeks, to be exact, before he knew he was going to have to leave. He had waked up suddenly in the night knowing that he had to get out, had to leave. There was a powerful feeling in him that his manhood was being affected by living in Hunt Abernathy's house while having an affair with Hunt Abernathy's wife; but he did not tell this to Carol when he told her he had to leave. He said it was to finish school. He had enough separation pay left to keep him going in New York until he could register and start collecting from the government under the Public Law 16 for disabled veterans. Grant, in the plane, suddenly remembered that it had been Hunt who had driven him to the station that time also.

There had been enough precedent for him to stay, actually. And Hunt himself had actually asked him to stay, or at least had indicated in that tightly inhibited way of his that he would like for him to stay on. Grant knew there were two other childless couples in town—or in that part of town, that set, in which the Abernathys moved—who had young men living with them who wanted to be artists or writers and who were pretty obviously the lovers of the mistresses of the homes they stayed in. So that part of it was all right. But Grant still felt he had to leave.

He had lasted three months in New York before he had had to send up the call for help, and it was the worst period of his life. Worse than the war even. And he knew also when he did send out his call for help that he was licked, that if ever the opportunity to live with the Abernathys cropped up again, he would take it and be glad of the chance.

After registering at the University and getting himself into the Public Law 16 programme with the Veterans Administration, he had taken a tiny room in a sixth-floor walk-up cold-water flat on West 63rd just off Columbus Circle. This belonged to a Swedish immigrant woman who could hardly speak any English, a widow, who sat up all night sewing piecework to make her own ends meet before going off to her regular job in the morning. The poor, miserable, totally hopeless conditions of this poor woman's life seemed to reflect in and colour his own in the mean, cold, hate-filled, muddy streets of the city. And it was here Carol Abernathy found him, without a doctor and sick in bed with the flu compounded by a return of the malaria he had contracted in the Pacific, two weeks after a healthy Grant had sent off his letter appeal.

He supposed he was in love with her, at the time. It was as if after giving up Billie Wrights, with whom he had been so completely and sexually compatible, he had, all totally unwittingly at the time, put all of his eggs in the one basket of Carol Abernathy. With whom, he rediscovered very quickly, he was not sexually compatible at all. And never mind the age discrepancy. She had nursed him, got him back on his feet and back to school, had with the fifteen hundred dollars Hunt had given her plus a little of her own found a nice little two-room apartment farther uptown, and stayed with him there for three months until he had a short-lived (week-end) affair with a young unmarried woman from the floor above, whereupon she had taken her group of occult books she had been buying up down on Fourth Avenue and returned to Hunt in Indianapolis, causing Grant to have to give up the apartment for a tiny room again.

And it wasn't only all of that. There were other things bugging him. He was not at all sure for quite a long while whether he might not be losing his mind. At the University, where when they saw his work they had immediately shot him up to their most advanced workshop in writing and playwriting, he found nobody could help him with his playwriting, teach him anything about playwriting that he did not already know; and all that he did know was still not enough. More, none of the professors or students he talked to seemed real. None of the women he slept with seemed real. It was as if, terrified, he was afraid he might push his finger or his hand clean through one of them. He made the Dean's List both semesters, and was graduated with honours at the end of the year, and he couldn't have cared less. About the only good thing to come out of the whole year was his meeting Gibson & Stein. He had been more than glad to return to the safety of the Abernathy ménage after that, though by now there was really no question at all of his being in love with Carol Abernathy.

God!

The lights in the plane went up, and Grant left off thinking of all that stuff. He had not thought so honestly or deeply of that horrible year in New York for a very long time, or of the fact that it was at that time, while she was living with him in New York, that Carol Abernathy first began to get messages by opening at random a book called *Hermes Trismegatus* which was some 19th-Century occult lady's journal. Had he caused her to go nutty? That was one of those things he hated even to think about and tried to avoid. But now he had to face up to it that he might have. Well, if he had, he had. Even though, if he had, he didn't care. It all still seemed so unreal. He had not been able to stomach New York since then, despite all the success, until he had met Lucky. Beside him, he noted, she seemed to be asleep. They were coming into Montego Bay where just about a month ago he had met her down here with Doug. Since they were going to be on the ground only ten minutes, he did not touch her or try to wake her, but he was not absolutely sure she was asleep.

He managed to doze a little bit himself on the longer flight to Kingston. Then René was meeting them with the Crount's fringed, pink and white striped jeep, and driving them back along the flat, scrubby, sea-smelly spit in the deep-night dark. Lucky's eyes did not appear to be at all sleep-swollen, like his own felt, Grant noticed.

"Hokay," René said from the wheel. "W'at eez all zees trouble now, hein? Tell me."

Grant was sitting in the back with the bags. He decided not to say anything at all. Lucky apparently decided the same thing. The silence ran on.

"W'at 'ave 'appen up zere in GaBay weez zees Messus Aber-nathy to make you change all zee trip an' all zee plan?" René persisted. "Some'sing 'appen. Il faut tell Papa René, babies."

"This son of a bitch took me up there to be friends with—

to *live* with—his mistress," Lucky said in an icily bitter voice. "That's what happened. Without even telling me one word. When everybody else around the place knew all about it, and were laughing at me behind my back. *That's* what happened."

"Ah, ho!" René exclaimed, and chuckled. "Ronnie eez zee foxy grandpaw, hein? Just like all zee men."

"Just like all the men," Lucky said flatly. "Exactly. Just like all the men. Except for you, René."

"Ahhh, chérie," René said with a deep Gallic sadness. He drove with both hands high on the skinny jeep wheel, hunched forward at the shoulders, and now between the hunched shoulders he shook his crinkly Jewish head with a great sorrowfulness, making it look as though he were repeatedly peering at first one hand then the other. But he did not elaborate. "Een any case, you two mus' not let go of to t'row away w'at you 'ave foun' just when it is beginning starting."

"That's just it," Lucky said coldly. "It never did start. It never got started. Because it was all a big lie from the very beginning."

"Zee life eez not for long," René said, "an' most of time 'ee's hard. Eet is maybe better in zee long run 'ave a marriage who eez zee frien' instead of who eez zee lovair."

"How can you be a friend to somebody who lies to you?" Lucky said. "I've never been so humiliated in my life before."

"Ronnie 'ave zee problems, chérie," René said softly, "weez zees *Time*-man give 'eem 'ard time down 'ere. You know zat."

Lucky did not answer this.

"We 'ave know you for long time 'ere, chérie, non? 'Ow long? Plenty years. We 'ave always love you. But you remember zee time Raoul leave you 'ere, go back to Sout' Amerique, and you start running h'around weez zat other fellow? You 'ember 'ow queeck Raoul snap you out h'of 'ere back to New York?"

Lucky's voice got sullen, very sullen, and from behind her Grant could see the sullenness in the stiffness of her neck and head. "That's not the same. Not at all the same. I wasn't married. And Raoul was going off leaving me all the time. I haven't left Ron since I very first met him—except when he kept sending me away. Because he didn't know what to do with his goddamned *mistress*!"

Grant leaned forward, stung, with a contorted face. He spoke to René, but what he said was for Lucky to hear. "That's not the truth. That's not even anywhere near the truth. The truth is I wanted to come on this diving junket alone because I knew if I brought any other extraneous element into it, a girl, it would all blow up. And that's just what it's doing: blowing itself right up in my face. I'd been protecting those people for years. I had to. How did I know when I met her and fell—— How did I know when I met her what kind of—— Or how to——"

"What kind of New York broad!" Lucky interposed bitterly, "you mean. What kind of easy lay New York hooker!"

"We not talk more," René said softly. "Lisa wait at zee 'otel for 'ave a drink wiz us. Lucky, w'en we 'ave your marri-age 'ere weez us in zee 'otel, we sink eez best t'ing ever 'appen for you and are verry 'appy. For you and Ronnie both tous les deux. Lisa say zees eez zee marri-age made in 'eaven." His voice was low and sad.

"Sure," Lucky said in a stony voice entirely different from her near-shouting voice of a moment or two before, and bobbed her small blonde head sharply, cynically, several times, making the champagne-coloured hair swing, and from behind her Grant watched it swing. He was furious with her, and at the same time deeply hurt, more hurt he thought than he had perhaps ever felt about anything, and he watched the blonde hair swing, sadly and unhappily.

At the hotel Lisa was waiting for them in the bar. The oldest of her three sons was sitting with her, and except for two small parties of three most all of the clients had already gone off to bed. Lisa had had quite a few drinks waiting and her lovely dark eyes were hazy, but not so hazy that she couldn't tell immediately when she saw them that something was seriously wrong.

"We don't talk about heem now," René warned her. "Is too late. Everybody tired. We 'ave zee one drink."

It was a pretty gloomy drink. And neither Grant nor Lucky did much to alleviate its gloom. Lucky tried several times to talk normally to Lisa, but it was not a very good effort, and anyway Lisa was more than a little loaded. Grant

caught her eyes glinting angrily several times when she looked
at him. Upstairs, the houseboys had put their bags into their
old suite and laid out their things. Somebody had even taken
out the centre bedside table and pushed the two double beds
back together for them the way they had liked them. A nice
ironic gesture, Grant thought, under the circumstances.—
" I'm going right to sleep," Lucky said in a very distant,
explanatory voice. " I'm terribly beat and worn out."—
" You do that," he said. He had carted a bottle up from the
bar by its neck for just such a contingency, and he sat on
the bed edge drinking from it in one of the toothbrush glasses,
mixing it with the French-style bottled water, and trying to
read. In GaBay he had picked up a new travel book on the
Caribbean Islands called *The Traveller's Tree* by an Englishman named Fermor, a good finely written book but he found
it exceedingly hard to concentrate on it. That beautiful body
had begun to taunt him already. Well what the hell, he could
take it for longer than that. After a while he switched off the
light and just lay waiting to sleep, trying to sleep, which was
always the worst way. Finally he dropped off.

The next day they found, as soon as they came down, that
even in just the short time they had been gone the social
façade of the hotel had changed considerably. The famous
musical comedy writer and her husband had gone back to New
York. The famous fag conductor and his wife had departed
also a few days later. A famous, fairly young, male movie
star and his actress wife had arrived from the West Coast for
a three weeks' stay between shootings, and both were the
main centre of attention in the bar evenings, where both
played the hearty, hale-fellow-well-met role to perfection.
René was running around trying to find a suitable suite to
name after them, since the one they were in was already
named the Charlie Addams suite. Bradford Heath the *Time*-
man and his wife had left for New York only two days before.
The Grants—as even Lucky apparently now thought of them,
despite everything—were glad of this. Only the young analyst
and his designer wife were still there from the " old days " of
before.

Perhaps that was all it was, really ; that they were, now,
" The Grants ". Just the simple inertia of life worked at
keeping them married now that they were married, as that
same inertia worked at keeping them unmarried as long as

they were unmarried. In any case, they had decided to have breakfast out on the big living-room porch of the suite that first day rather than have to go down and have to face a lot of new people, and it was while they were doing this that Lucky made the speech she had so obviously been thinking about and preparing.

"We'll keep up appearances," she said from across the snowy tablecloth while dawdling with half a grapefruit. "That's very important to me. I don't like acting out scenes of my private life in front of other people, or having them know all about what my private life is like. There's no reason to let all those goddamned people down there know what's going on between us. Is that all right with you? And you can fuck me whenever you want to. Since you're paying the bills. That's only fair. When you want to, you tell me."

"Okay," Grant said dryly. "But you don't mind if I don't do it now, do you? Since I'm all dressed and all?"

His irony did not apparently reach her, and she stared back at him across the table wide-eyed and sombre. "I don't know how to explain it to you, or even if you're interested enough to want to know. But when I found out you lied to me like that—and about a thing like that—something just happened to me."

"I didn't *have* to tell you," Grant interjected quietly.

"I know. Probably you shouldn't have. I might have gotten along all right if you hadn't. Anyway, now it's something I can't help. I don't have any control over it. I thought it was all pure, pure and straight. But if you can lie to me like that, about that, you can lie to me about anything any time. You'll always be able to lie to me, any time it suits your needs. I don't think I love you any more. I'm going to ask Ben and Irma to lunch with us, if that's all right with you."

"All right," Grant said. "But I've got a couple of things I'd like to say. I think this is a very adolescent way of looking at it all. You're not taking into account any of the pressures that were working on me, or any of the past I had been through before I even met you. And not only that, for some time after I met you, because there was no way of my knowing then even after I fell in love with you that I was ever going to love you enough to marry you. Also, there's no reason to suppose that you, who love to flirt over and brag about all your four hundred love affairs——"

"Four hundred men," Lucky interjected. "Not four hundred love affairs."

"Excuse me," Grant said politely. "Four hundred men. No reason to suppose that, with that, you would think this thing of mine so horrible. You *should* be more sophisticated than that. There's something about your reaction to what I told you that just doesn't have any handle I can grasp or get hold of. Hell, I thought you'd laugh about it. It just doesn't make sense, and I can't understand it." He stopped. "Them's my comments," he said.

Lucky was sitting quietly, as if waiting politely for him to finish. "I can't help the way I am," she said, now that he had. "And I'm not a bum. My family had more money, and lived richer and higher and with more culture, than yours ever did even before your old, Old-American grandfather lost all his money in the Crash. Don't you ever forget that. Is it all right about Ben and Irma for lunch?"

"It is," Grant said, getting up. "Is one o'clock all right? And now I'm going to go for a long walk along the beach."

"I'll see you down on the terrace by the pool then," Lucky said with complete calm. "Please do try and get back by one."

Ben the analyst spoke to him as he made his way out through the hotel, and even offered to go along as if he too knew there was something wrong (had he been talking to René?), but Grant put him off. The sea was as flat as a pancake and the sun was heavy and hot, but with a mid-, mid-late-morning freshness that was exceedingly pleasant to the body's senses. If not the mind's. Ha. The water made tiny rushing, then receding noises, then interspersed these with tinier, very small sucking hissing sounds, forming a three-beat definite, predictable rhythm in the sun-quiet. He walked barefoot along the more packed, still moist sand the tide had levelled and compacted, walking eastward toward the airport and the mainland rather than westward toward Port Royal. Eastward, there was absolutely nothing for miles and miles. This was serious. This wasn't any of their quick hot violent fights and quarrels they'd had before. Finally he sat a while in the shade of a single royal palm with his back against the rough trunk, looking out to sea. To the south and eastward it ran on forever, calm as a pasture under the sun. In the slightly cooler shade the skin under his eyes and on his cheekbones felt hot and pink as if he'd been eating Mexican tamales. After a while he got up and started back. He had come to no decision. What decision was there to come to? If any decision had come at all, it was that he would wait it out a while. If he had learned anything at all from his fourteen years with Carol Abernathy, and sundry other temporaries, it was that no matter how bitter the fight or how long, it was only when one or the other of the parties started stepping out, having affairs and actual sex contact outside, that it was all really finished. That was what broke the contact. And the contract. He had force-trained his mind that he would never again be the first to do that. When he got back to the hotel and made his way to the pool, he found them all sitting there laughing and drinking Campari-soda, and Jim Grointon he noted was with them, sitting at the pool-edge with his knees pulled up and smiling his slow smile. They shook hands warmly, but Grant was not at all glad to see him there at the moment.

It was inevitable that a serious confrontation should take place between Grant and the famous, newly arrived male movie star. The famous Playwright and the famous Star could not just put up at the same chic little resort hotel and ignore each other. On the other hand, neither could one of them just go up and say hello to the other, and have it appear that he instead of the other was soliciting acquaintance Protocol was involved. It had to be arranged. Grant, over lunch with his little band of partisans, which now only included Ben the analyst and his wife Irma, Lucky, Jim Grointon, and Lisa (René was off working), decided that for him cocktail time would be the best, preferably twenty minutes before dinner time, so that the two protagonists would not have to confront each other too long. Word of this, via Lisa, whose invitation it would be, was sent off to the Star, who obligingly sent back word via Lisa that he and his wife would be glad to accept the host's (René's) invitation to meet the Playwright and his wife at that time, but could they possibly make it twenty minutes earlier as the Star and his wife unfortunately had another cocktail date just before dinner. To this Grant obligingly sent back word, via Lisa, that that would be just fine. And so it was arranged. And so it was that at exactly 8.10 p.m. the Playwright and four friends and the Star and four friends met at the stand-up bar, three-fourths of which had been reserved and somewhat blocked off unobtrusively by tables and provided by Lisa with canapés, and (while René took pictures) were introduced, smiled at each other, shook hands in a friendly way, complimented each other upon each's various works, kidded each other a little to show that while famous they were still regular fellows, talking cautiously a little about Art, Artistry and future prospects, drank two cautious drinks apiece, and then went severally their several ways to eat and drink privately in relief. If the Star had another cocktail date, he forgot it. On the terrace-dining-room both remembered to smile and nod at the other in thanks for an encounter which had meant exactly nothing.

The Star, who had beautiful and marvellously corded abdominal muscles, largely because he carried a bongo board with him and did one hundred to one hundred and fifty sit-ups on it every day, had been, Grant learned the next day from Jim Grointon, going out with Jim diving just about every day since he had been here. He had done some diving on the West Coast apparently, both with lung and without, and could do about forty or forty-five feet free-diving, but he was not anywhere near the diver Grant was—Jim said. "He just ain't got the real passion for it like you have," Jim grinned, "and what he does he does about two-third of for show." An irritating egotism made Grant, though vastly irritated by the egotism, vastly pleased by this. Especially since he knew the Star was at least four years his junior. But it was hard for anything to please Grant for more than a few seconds just now. It was unbelievable how much misery he, one, could go through in just a few minutes, while sitting and talking, or eating, or having a drink, while—in short—pretending to be normal. But he was not going to give in.

"I'd ask you to come along with us in the afternoon," Jim said. "But I'm pretty sure he wouldn't want to come if he knew you were coming. And especially after he saw you dive. And I'd uh just hate to lose the business. And he's gonna be here three more weeks. I could take you out mornings though." He was charging the Star more than twice as much as he had charged Grant. "That's the racket," he shrugged with a grin.

"It's all right," Grant said. "I don't really feel much like diving now anyway. This trip." And he didn't. He didn't feel like doing anything, much. And not even the thought of diving carried any savour. Irritation. Anger. Fury. Depression. Misery. Gloom. These he had, especially the anger. But not pleasure. But he was not going to give in. And he was not going to let it show. He was not going to let his lack of pleasure show. He made trips with Ben and Irma and Lucky to Blue Mountain Inn, to Stony Hill, to Strawberry Hill, to the Pine Grove Hotel. They borrowed a car from René and drove up the hot, dry valley to Spanishtown and beyond it to Bog Walk, the land here so dry and deserty compared to the lush vegetation of the windward side which got the rain. Another time they took a car and drove clear across the central mountains to the Fern Gully and Ocho Rios and stayed the night in Ocho Rios, coming back the next day. They took lunch here, had dinner there. They drove in to the Sheraton Hotel in town where Grant and Ben could dive off the three-metre board. Usually the four of them dined at the hotel, and went afterwards to the tiny clandestine little (and strictly illegal) " Casino " gambling joint where René had got them cards. Lucky, it turned out, was an excellent crapshooter. Ben was a good chemin de fer player.

Ben Spicehandler (which name being an Americanisation of his Jewish grandfather's original Polish name) and his wife had been in Jamaica at the Crount for over a month, and planned to stay at least another month. So they would certainly be there at least as long as Lucky and Grant chose to stay, and this was probably a good thing Grant thought. They made the perfect, and always ready, buffer for the Grants at this particular stage of the game. Ben made so much money as an analyst in New York that he only needed to work nine months a year, so the other three months of each year he and Irma took off and travelled. " After all," as he himself lugubriously said with his broad-faced, narrow-eyed grin that made a washboard of his forehead, " we ain't none of us gittin' any younger." This year, having heard so much about it for the past two years in New York, they had decided on the Crount and Jamaica, and as Grant had already thought, it was probably a good thing for the Grants. Ben and Irma were always ready to go anywhere and do anything that any one of the four of them thought up. A compulsive humanist who had once studied to be a rabbi, Ben was a tall hulking fellow of Grant's age, thirty-five, an excellent swimmer and fair springboard diver, who could never think about anything seriously except helping people. That he made so much money at it was due to another, economically thoughtful side of his nature, which came from his paternal grandmother, he said. And, at the moment, he had made it his vacation project to help the Grants.

" Look," he said to Grant, on the first occasion of his offer to help, and as he was to say again many times later. " Look, buddy. I know you guys're havin' some kind o' trouble." (He came originally from Indiana.) " It don't take much to see that." He bent down from his greater height and narrowed his eyes slyly and grinned and bobbed his head seriously several times. " Now any time you want, anything I can do to help you and Lucky or both of you, you just tell me. Me and Irma like both of you a lot, see? Anything you want to talk about, you just tell me."

Grant had thanked him and said there wasn't anything wrong.

" Okay. Okay. Well now you just remember see?" Ben said, and narrowed his eyes and grinned and thrust forward his head.

" What the fuck?" Grant said irritably. " Do you carry a portable analyst's couch with you wherever you go? I can't afford your price anyway."

" Never min'," the analyst grinned. " If you need us, you just tell us. Me an' Irma'll be there."

And they were. Ready to do whatever and whenever anything Grant or Lucky thought up to do. They even came up with a wealth of ideas of their own, in order to keep the Grants occupied. And the tiny Irma, dark and almost Oriental-looking with her black bangs, huge bun of hair on the top of her head, and her crazy witch's cackle of a laugh coming out of her bunched-up mobile face, was at least as loyal to this vacation project as was Ben. They would cancel or postpone any dates or plans of their own, make enemies even, at a moment's notice, whenever the Grants had anything or any place they wanted to do or go.

It was after six full days of this kind of perpetual preoccupation that Lucky loosened up a little, or so Grant thought at the time. But it turned out that she hadn't. They had gone up to the suite for a siesta after a long and fairly heavy-drinking lunch, preparatory to going off to play tennis with Ben and Irma in town. Grant had been seven days now without getting laid and he was getting a bit horny. He had even taken to looking covetously at Lisa's beautiful unattached Haitian friend Paule Gordon (known everywhere locally around the hotel as the " Black Swan "), and maybe that had something to do with it, maybe Lucky had seen him eyeing her. She was lying on the bed and called to him.

" What?" he said.

" I said you may make love to me, if you like."

" Ha," Grant said. " Thanks a lot. Thanks but I've never got heated up over that kind of an invitation."

" Oh, for God's sake, shut up and come on and fuck me," Lucky said.

" I don't know if I can," Grant said honestly.

" Here," she said. " Try."

He found that he could.

" You may be my husband, and I may not love you, but I still like to fuck," Lucky said. " Ah. Ah. That's it. Ah."

" Go to hell," Grant said in a pillow-muffled voice. His orgasm was an explosion. Explosion was the only word for it. Like bomb-bursts he had seen at sea that you could feel coming toward you, then they hit you, and if you turned around, if you had the time, you could see them going away, disappearing over the water.

" Now get off of me, you mean no-good son of a bitch," Lucky said. It was not exactly the thing to say if she wanted a reconciliation, but apparently she really didn't want one.— " Just call me Rhett Butler," Grant said and rolled away.— " I really do hate your guts, you know," Lucky said. " I really do." Grant slept peacefully.

But none of this " renewed sex play " made them come any closer together. One would have thought it would. But It, the thing, was still there. The kernel, the nut, the rock, the hard core. Of whatever it was. Between them. They were actually not in love. Grant did not know what it was with Lucky—any more—but for himself he was too angry to love anything. And he was not getting any nearer to New York and the rehearsals of his play. Actually, they would not begin for another month at least. But he still wasn't getting any nearer them. And he was not getting any nearer to writing on another, newer play.

The showdown fight with René and Lisa came three days after. Grant had been expecting it for five.

It was a curious scene. There were just the four of them, it was late and the bar was empty, even the faithful Ben and Irma had ambled (in the case of Ben) and flittered (in the case of Irma) away to bed. It was Lisa who started it. She had had quite a few drinks. And suddenly all the flashing anger that had been in her eyes so many times when she looked at Grant escaped the cage—herself—in which she had so obviously tried so hard to contain it.

"You're a no-good son of a bitch!" she said suddenly and unequivocally to Grant, leaning across the table on her elbow and pointing with her other arm. "No man has the right to do what you did to Lucky. To any woman."

"Go and fuck yourself," Grant said bluffly. He had had quite a few drinks himself. "It's none of your fucking business."

"'Ere now. 'Ere now," René said. He had had quite a few drinks too.

"Tell 'im!" Lucky said. She was drunk. "Tell 'im, Lisa! Tell 'im what it's like to be a goddamned woman!"

"I'll tell 'im!" Lisa said. "I'm *making* it my business!" she said to Grant. Suddenly, all in one gesture, she raised her elbows and flapped her arms hiking her brightly coloured blouse up her back so she could lean across the table even further and at the same time stuck out her lower lip and blew a loose strand of her long black hair back out of her eyes. "Do you know who you're messing around with when you mess around with this girl? This girl is a lady. You don't take a lady to meet your ex-mistress without telling her about it beforehand! You don't! And let her think it's your goddamned mother!"

"Foster-mother," Grant said. "Now shut the fuck up."

"I'll not shut up!" Lisa cried. "I'm defending this girl. Nobody else will."

"She's no goddam plaster saint," Grant grunted.

"That's neither here nor there, you bastard," Lisa said. "You men. You goddam men. You goddam *fucking* men!" Even loaded, it was clear it cost her a considerable effort to get that word out. "You all want *us* to be so goddam pure! You *demand* that all of *us* be pure! And you! All you wan then is some skinny hipbone-sticking hot-assed twenty-year old torso to rub yourselves against. But let that torso get a little old, put on a little fat around the hipbones, have three o four kids and break down those tight vaginal walls! and you don't mellow with it. Oh, no! You're right back out looking for another hipbone torso! Men, shit," Lisa cried, and sat back triumphantly.

Somewhat loaded though he was, Grant did not fail to notice this sudden switch in emphasis. Whether she realised it or not, she had moved on from Lucky's complaints to what were so obviously her own. Remembering René's sad " Ahhh, chérie!" in the jeep when Lucky had told him he was different from other men, Grant thought that for the sake of his friend René he ought not to make any comment at this point, and so he kept his mouth shut.

René, however, was there to fill the breach. He too clearly had caught the switch in emphasis. " Eez all verry well for you holler," he said hotly. " You an' Lucky. Ronnie 'ave zee problems you don' 'ave. You don't want 'ave, eezair! Mais 'ee 'ave zee problem of zee responsability and of zee loyalty. Zee women, zay never compren zat." He had drawn himself up in his chair to his full height of five-three, and his hard tight round little belly was pressed against the table edge. " Because zee women are toujours zay animal. W'at you want her?" he cried with Gallic passion. " 'Ee marry 'er! 'Ee take over, take on, 'er responsability! W'at you want of 'eem? But w'en 'ee try be hon-or-able avec zee ozzer woman, 'oo 'ee owe somet'ing, hein, you say he dirty bum. Merde! To me fais chier! You make me shit!"

." He should have told her!" Lisa cried. " He married her under false pretences!"

" Wot you care, false pre-tences? Zee marri-age eez zee marri-age," René shouted back.

" You don't take a young girl's heart and play with it!" Lisa cried.

" You don' take zee man's cock an' play weez heem eezair!" René hollered. " Malheureusement!"

" I don't care!" Lisa shouted at him. " If I was her, and he did to me what he did to her, I would feel like a whore!"

" You are whore!" René shouted furiously. " All women are zee whore! Because zay are zee women! Eez zee nature! An' w'y not?"

The word *whore* struck a serious chord in Grant, but he couldn't place it in the right connection, or connect it. He filed it away to think about. Then he gave himself up pleasantly to listening to the big fight being conducted on his (and from the other side, on Lucky's) behalf. It was sort of like a sort of verbal mixed doubles tennis match with the males on one side and the females on the other. Lucky sitting across the table from him, at the side of Lisa, listened with a fixed bright-eyed drunken attention, turning her head from one shouting friend to the other as if listening with interest and curiosity to the life story of two strangers.

It didn't go on very much longer. Three or four more shouted exchanges between the ex-Frenchman and his wife, and then René stood up. "Eez enough! We finish nossing. Eez zee time to zee bed."

"You're damn' right you finish nothing," Grant put in, gathering himself to get up. "And in any case it's none of your goddamned business anyway, either one of you." He never did make it to his feet, and in what followed relapsed back into his chair in a slack-muscled disbelief and astonishment.

"You! You!" Lisa howled suddenly, and jumping up held out her arm, index finger extended like the parent in the melodrama when the daughter comes home with a baby. "You! You no-good son of a bitch! You bastard! You get out of my hotel! You do not spend another night under my roof! Get out! I mean it! Get out of my hotel!"

Grant was too flabbergasted even to react. "Are you kidding?" he said.

"'Ere now! 'Ere now!" René said, putting out his hand.

"You just get him out of here!" Lisa yelled. She had dropped her arm, now she raised it again, stiff as a board right out to the index fingertip. "Out! Get out! Out! Get out!"

And it was just here, precisely as if she were waking up from a nap, that Lucky got into the act. Blinking, she turned on Lisa slowly, at first echoing Grant: "Are you kidding? Listen, do you know who you're talking to? You're talking to the best playwright in America of his generation. You're talking to the best playwright America has had since O'Neill probably! Who are you telling to get out?"

"You can stay," Lisa said. "I want you to stay. You stay with us."

"Are you nuts?" Lucky said disbelievingly. "He's my husband! I'm his wife! You're crazy!"

"He's hurt you terribly," Lisa said. "And he had no right." Then she began to shout again. "And I don't give a goddam how good a goddam playwright he is! Out! Get out!"

"Please, please, 'ere, 'ere," René was pleading.

"He can——" Lisa was shouting.

"Come on," Lucky said grimly. Grant was still sitting dumbly in his chair, and she grabbed him by the arm and pulled him to his feet. "We're getting out of this, I don't have to take that kind of shit from anybody." Forcefully she propelled him toward the stairway still holding him by the arm. "We're leaving."

"Oh, come on," Grant protested feebly. "Are you goofy? It'll all be over by the morning. Let's go to bed." All he could think about at the moment was sweet sweet sleep.

"I will not!" Lucky said. "Nobody talks to me like that." And in the suite she dragged a suitcase out of the closet and threw it on the bed and began dumping clothes in it. Grant lay down on the other bed.—"Cut it out, Lucky." he said tiredly. "Nobody means it. To-morrow it'll all be a joke to laugh over."—"I certainly will not," she said, and went on packing. "Nobody talks to my husband like that. Whether I love him or not." And she did not desist until there was a tap on the door and René sneaked in quietly, all apologies.

"You know, she is, 'ow they use to say, a leetle zigzag, hein?" he said. "It mean nossing."

"Are you apologising?" Lucky said, still packing.

"I am," René said with great Gallic dignity. "I am apologise for Lisa, and for me, and for zee Grand 'Otel Crount, and for zee en-tire staff of zee Grand 'Otel Crount. I beg you. Please to not to leave."

"All right," Lucky said as evenly as she had been talking just before. "I'll stay." She began unpacking.

"I see you in zee morning," René said mournfully. "If all zee 'ead are not too large to get s'rough zee door."

"You leave me alone now," Lucky said after René left. "I mean it. You stay away from me. I mean it seriously. It's not that I'm mad at you. I'm not mad at you. But I'm not in love with you. It's something else. I mean it. I don't want you and you just leave me alone."

"Oh, sweet Jesus!" Grant said.

And on that note they went to bed on the extreme opposite sides of the pushed-together double beds.

THIRTY

So everything was just the same. And appeared that it would go right on being just the same. If Grant had expected some sort of reconciliation to be effected by Lucky's sudden and fierce upholding of the family unit " Grant ", he was mistaken. As a matter of fact, Grant wasn't even thinking that. He was thinking something entirely different, and the next day when he had sobered up and they had come down to be greeted by a smiling Lisa who did not even bother to apologise, he went on thinking about it. It was something that had come up midway in the argument between René and Lisa over how well or badly Grant had treated Lucky. It had to do with the word " whore ".

Lisa had said something about that if Grant had treated her like he had Lucky, she would feel like a whore. René had countered with Gallic passion saying that she in fact was, that all women were, that that was nature, and what of it? A succinct and reasonable Gallic attitude. But Lisa's use of that word had struck some particular thought chord in Grant, as if it were something that he ought to recognise and remember but could not quite. He had stuck it away, though, and held on to it, and the next day—next morning—when he was sober, while Ben and Irma and Lucky cavorted in the pool with Jim Grointon and some other guests, had tried with it again.

Last night when Lisa made her comment about " feeling like a whore " Lucky had simply sat, in her bright-eyed drunkenness, and had not reacted. But at least several of their biggest and most desperate fights had had something to do with that word " whore ". He remembered that it was that word—" whore "—uttered by Lucky, and only by Lucky— that had been the key to the scene the night of the nude swimming party at Sir Gerald Kinton's villa, when Lucky had run weeping and crying: *"I'm not a whore! I'm not a whore!"* into the big stand-up closet and hidden herself. He remembered that it was that same word " whore " another time which had caused a terrible fight one night late in bed when, drunk, he had been jealous over her ex-"Jamaican-lover", Jacques. He had said it was like being married to a whore, to have all her ex-lovers running around. She had been furious. More, she had frozen—absolutely frozen. He remembered she had said in a strained, frozen voice: "*But I never took money*," except from Raoul, she had added, who was rich and whom she intended to marry. It was all so ridiculous. And he remembered too the worst fight; the night she socked him in the nose with her purse and walked out of the hotel. He had been seriously wrong that time. But had the word "whore" come up then too? No? He couldn't remember. Anyway the reference was there, when he told about waking up stuck in up to his shoulders between the beds, and wondering what he had married. And he remembered now, too, that that was the first time he had noted, and been struck by, the total lack of proportion in her reaction, response. And now of course, since telling her about Carol, it was she who was constantly making the reference: "whore"; "hooker"; "New York lay"; "party girl"; "easy lay." Guilt-complex? Self-hatred? Was it something about his having been Carol's lover when he met her that made her feel he had thought of her as a whore? But it didn't make sense. And he hadn't. Christ, he'd loved her. It didn't make sense. And it was about to wreck their marriage before it even got started, even got off the ground.

Grant knew himself well enough, had studied himself well enough over the years, though he had never gone in for "Analysis", to know that he himself had a sort of "rejection syndrome" built into his psyche that could be triggered by the slightest and often most inoffensive thing. Knowing it, he had gradually trained himself to control it but once in a while, usually when he was drunk and therefore less in control, some real or imagined "rejection" could turn him into a snarling, near-murderous animal. That was what had happened to him that night he had turned on Lucky over Jacques Edgar. (He had remembered how smug and self-congratulatory he had felt about fucking—about having fucked—Cathie Finer when he met Sam Finer; and he could reasonably assume Jacques Edgar felt equally as smug.) And at such times—if drunk—he was powerless to do anything about himself. Did Lucky have some uncontrollable thing like that about whores or being thought of as a "whore"?

But nobody, *but no*body, even possibly, ever thought of her as a whore.

Grant cogitated, while watching Lucky have a laughing swimming-race with Grointon. If he didn't trust her so much, the way she flirted with Jim—with damn' near everybody—would rankle him. Had rankled him, in fact, a couple of times when he was half-loaded and less in control. Then suddenly the lightbulb in his head lit up and the bell rang. She was *ashamed!* She was *ashamed* of the life she'd led in New York. She was *really* ashamed! Ashamed like any little hick from anywhere who had been brought up on all the old bullshit morals. She was ashamed of " her past ", and all her lighthearted comments about all the men she'd had was a defence. She laughed to avoid admitting she was ashamed. *She* thought of *herself* as a whore secretly, apparently, but could not face or bear admitting that about herself to herself. So she turned it around and made it look as though Grant (or someone) thought of her that way—and then hated him (them) for it. What was more natural? And it was probably all as automatic and uncontrollable as Grant's own " rejection syndrome ".

Well. Well, but now that he knew it, what could he do about it? Not a damned thing, as far as he could see. He certainly couldn't talk to her about it. Christ, it would take her at least two years of goddamned " Analysis " to reach that point. Christ, a wife in analysis, like half the sons of bitches he knew. For Grant analysis, like religion, was simply self-indulgence for over seventy per cent of the people who engaged in it. And he found he absolutely hated the thought of any wife of his lying on some damned couch telling some ape of a shrink all of the sexual things about herself that she couldn't tell him. Then there would be the damned Transference. Maybe he ought to talk to Ben about it? On the other hand, if she was so damned sure she was a " whore ", maybe she was one! And if she was, what could he do about that? The other half of the sons of bitches he knew were in that position. And now (one way or the other) he would be like all the other damned married novelists and playwrights and poets that he knew! The very damned thing he had been trying so hard all his life to avoid!

Grant quit thinking about it and got up and ran across and dived in the pool. When he had swum the length of it underwater, he came up in the deep end and hung on the edge. Jim Grointon immediately came swimming over to him.

" I got some good news for you!" the diver grinned.

" What the hell kind of good news could you possibly have for me?" Grant said irritably.

" Hey, hey! Does it bite?" Jim smiled softly.

" I'm sorry, Jim," Grant said, and grinned. " I've got a lot of heavy weights on my mind right now."

" Anything I could possibly help you with?"

Grant stared at him. " Ha!" he exploded with a vicious snort. " I wouldn't hardly think so! What's your good news?"

" Well, my client and our mutual friend the Star quit me to-day," Jim smiled. " So the boat'll be free afternoons now."

" What happened?"

Jim smiled his slow smile that sometimes could seem to be very superior. " Well, I took him to a new place yesterday, place I know down toward Morant Bay. And we saw some sharks."

" You did! How many?"

" Only two or three. And they stayed out at the edge of visibility. You had to look sideways to be sure you saw them. There's always a few hanging around that spot. Anyway, our friend pointed them out to me after a dive. I guess he thought I hadn't seen them. I thought he wanted to shoot one, so I asked him if he'd like to try for one, though I couldn't promise we'd be able to get close enough. He said absolutely not. Then after a couple more dives he said he was tired. To-day he told me he'd decided not to go out again for a while, his wife was complaining because she wanted to do some touring. This morning they took a car and drove to Ocho Rios." Jim opened his mouth and laughed silently behind narrowed blond lashes, and Grant suddenly liked him less for a moment or two. " I think I've lost him, what do you think?"

" Well, I'll be damned," Grant said. " Were they big ones?" He turned himself so his back was against the pool wall and let his feet float up and hung on to the pool-edge above his head with both hands.

" I couldn't tell. They were always too far away to see them clearly Usually down around there they'll run from five to ten feet."

" Was that the place where you took us?" Grant asked.

" No, not as far. And shallower. Bottom's forty to maybe fifty-five in the corals. So that he could make it if he stretched himself." He laughed silently again. " So old Jim and his catamaran are free again."

" Let me think about it," Grant said. " Come have a drink with us before lunch and we'll talk about it with Lucky."

" Okay," Jim said affably.

Grant continued to hang on to the pool-edge for several silent moments, and Jim did not swim away. " I don't understand you," Grant said finally.

" What?" Jim said. " Why?"

" Surely you must have known beforehand that he would do just what he did. Given his personality, and his rather mediocre diving ability, used mostly ' for show ' as you yourself said, he couldn't very well have reacted about sharks in any other way. And yet you took him into a place where you knew sharks hang out."

Jim grinned. " You're pretty damned smart, ain't you?"

" I don't know. Maybe. I just don't understand. Not only all of that, when he pointed them out to you you asked him if he wanted to try and shoot one. You must have known that that was not the case, not the truth. So—you cost yourself about two weeks' work, and two weeks' income, at about twice the prices you were charging me you said, and for what? What did you gain?"

Jim's grin seemed to have stiffened, but only the tiniest bit. He looked more like an Irish cop than ever. " You *are* smart," he grinned.

" No, I just don't understand what you *gained*. You're also supposed to be a professional. That means taking care of your clients—any clients—and not letting anything happen to them, not letting them get into dangerous situations."

" He wasn't in a dangerous situation. I knew those sharks wouldn't come in."

" But *he* didn't. Part of your code as a pro is also to make your clients feel safe and at ease. You're supposed to teach them when they don't know, not scare them off. I don't understand what you gained that was so important to you that it was worth both losing the income and going back on what should be your ' code '."

" I didn't like him," Jim said.

"Then why didn't you tell him so? And stop all that pussy-footing around and that bullshit?"

"You can't tell a customer you don't like him. It's bad for business. What if it got told around?"

"It wouldn't do you any more harm than what you did. You think he's going to go around recommending you? Now? He'll hate your guts from now on."

"I'm a brave man," Jim Grointon said.

"I guess you are," Grant said thoughtfully. He kicked his feet a little against the surface. "But I don't see what that's got to do with it."

"And he's a fink."

"I don't like him, either," Grant said. "But that's not the point. He's a male movie star. You're a professional diver. He isn't. I think you did it because he's such a famous star. It pissed you off. You wanted what he had and knew you'd never get it."

Jim laughed again, this time out loud. "You're probably right. I've got one customer who doesn't want to do anything *but* shoot sharks. Now. He comes down every year just for that. That's where I take him. He loves it now since I've taught him. He's got a shark's mouth twice as big as your head that he keeps on his office desk in New York."

"Good for him," Grant said. "But I don't see what that's got to do with our friend."

"It made a man out of him," Jim said.

"Our friend?"

"No, my New York executive."

"Okay. Like I said, good for him."

"Did you ever shoot a shark?" Jim asked softly.

Grant thought this over, and kicked his feet against the water surface. "No," he said finally. "I played tag with a little one once that tried to steal my fish." After a moment he added, "But I've always wanted to. Ever since I saw that one you took up in Grand Bank."

"Would you like to try for one?" Jim asked, in the same soft tone. He was grinning again now. "We could go down to that same place. There's a coral bridge there, that they like to lay up under."

"Bonham told me that same thing," Grant said. He kicked his feet a little more in the safe pool. "Why is that, any-way?"

"Sharks can't float," Grointon said promptly. "They got no air-bladder like an ordinary fish. They have to keep swimmin' or they sink. So if they want to rest they have to lie on the bottom. I think they prefer coral overhangs and bridges because it makes them feel safer.

"Listen, it's not all that difficult or dangerous. That's all in your head, and you can overcome it. The truth is, it's hard to get close enough to one to get a spear in him. Sharks are cowards. And if they're hit and not killed, they always run. The only thing in the sea that will attack you after it's hit that I know of is a moray eel. Of course, there's always the off chance of one coming after you—usually after you've speared a fish. But it's really damned rare. And even if one does come after you, it doesn't mean that you can't handle it if you keep your head. It doesn't mean you're dead."

"It's the word," Grant said. "*Shark.* 'The truth is' as you said—The truth is, I'm scared shitless of the idea."

"Then don't go," Jim said softly.

"Let me think about it," Grant said. "We'll talk to Lucky about it.—But for God's sake don't mention the shark-shooting to her!"

"I wouldn't dream of it," Jim grinned.

"Let me think about it," Grant said.

There was a strange obscure, sexual (sexual in the sense that one's manhood, balls, were involved) challenge in it somehow the way Jim had handled it, but Grant was not about to let himself be influenced by that. Childish dares ("I dare you! I dare you!") had gone out of his life as far back as the war. But he found, when he did think about it, after Jim had swum away in the quiet, agitated pool, that he didn't have to think about it at all. He wanted to go, was *going* to go, and at least half of the reason was because he was pissed off at, and out of love with, his wife Lucky. Besides, as far back as Grand Bank and Jim's shark there he had promised himself that someday he was going to have to at least try for one, before he quit. The opportunity was here. So why not now? It made nervous tricklets of excitement and anticipation run up and down his legs and his back. He wasn't even afraid. Apparently his anger and perpetual furious outrage over Lucky was every day pumping a great deal of aggressive adrenalin into his blood.

So, he was back to the diving. Over lunch, which Jim took

with them along with Ben and Irma, Lucky said she didn't mind. And when Jim, laughing, said he had finally secured for her his English lord friend's pair of big British Navy binoculars, she came out positively in favour of resuming the daily diving trips. Jim promised there should be a great many native fishermen where they were going. Lucky giggled, grinned, and flirted outrageously with every male present, then stared coldly at her husband. When Ben said he would like to go too, Grant stared significantly at Jim. Jim blinked to acknowledge he had caught the look, but only nodded affirmatively to Ben. It was perfectly all right with him if Ben came along as long as he paid the regular (non-star) price. Later, he told Grant privately that there was absolutely no danger involved for Ben, he would guarantee it. Irma on the other hand cackled her crazy witch's laugh and said she was not going to spend all her afternoons out on some damned boat since she couldn't even swim. She would stay at the hotel by the shallow end of the pool and read, where she could dip when she got hot.

Grant went over to the inside anchorage to help Jim bring the boat around that first afternoon, and it was on the way back around Port Royal that he asked about Ben. " Are you absolutely sure it's okay for Ben to go? I wouldn't want to put anybody else in a dangerous spot simply because of my own silly bullshit stunts."—" I absolutely guarantee it," Jim said. " Look. The very worst that could happen would be that one shark down there might come in to try and steal somebody's fish. As for attacking a person, all you have to do is charge at them as if *you* were going to bite *them* and they'll run. And we'll all three be together, with guns. A spear in the gills will turn any damned shark away from Ben. Don't worry. Ben's a pretty cool cat. And you're cool."— " I'm not so sure I'm cool," Grant said.—" Well, we'll find out if you are, won't we?" Jim grinned.—" But don't you think we ought to tell Ben all this, too? Brief him?" Grant persisted.—" No. Don't tell Ben anything," Jim said. " He's liable to tell his wife. And she would tell your wife. Ben's going to be perfectly safe. I promise you." Ahead of them the white beach loomed up, with the white bulk of the hotel behind it in the sun.

It was all as if it had been actively, physically ordained beforehand somewhere, in some administrative Heaven. The

catamaran with its stretched tarp for shade, the hot afternoons, the cool green sea, dangerous but not seeming dangerous except as some quiet spiritual echo that kept warning
you. Grant had an enormously strong feeling that not one of
them could *not* have been here. Ben did not know about the
sharp-shooting objective of the trips, but then Grant and Jim
hardly knew it either since they didn't see a single shark. They
did not, in fact, see one for the first three days. They free-
dived on and swam under at sixty feet the coral arch where
the sharks were reputed to hang out. There were plenty of
other fish to take. Lucky kept busy with her binoculars.
Then, to keep Grant occupied since no sharks appeared, Jim
introduced them to a series of coral caves he knew about
nearby at thirty-five feet. It was during these three days that
Jim brought up again a subject he had mentioned many times
before during their first stay in Kingston: a four- or five-
day trip to the Morant Cays just about fifty-five nautical miles
south of Jamaica; and it was also during these three days—
on the third, to be exact—that Evelyn de Brystein called from
Ganado Bay. Evelyn and Doug Ismaileh.

She called just at noon, hoping she would catch them in at
lunchtime. Fortunately they were still up in the " Ron Grant
Honeymoon Suite ", as it was now officially designated by
René, so that Grant did not have to call or search out Lucky
to come and listen. He was not about to receive any call
from GaBay, especially from Evelyn's villa, that Lucky was
not there to listen in on.

" How are you both?" the calm wry gravelly voice said,
coming clearly and unmistakably over the instrument.

He had been sitting in the chair beside the bed just putting
on his white ducks and espadrilles. Quickly he motioned for
Lucky to come over and listen too.

" I don't need to listen in on your phone calls," she told
him coldly.

" Hello, hello! Just fine," he said, then covered up the
mouthpiece. " I don't give a damn whether you need or
not!" he said. " You come here and listen!"

She shrugged, but she came. Grant held the receiver slightly
away from his ear and Lucky bent her head alongside of his
until her hair touched his cheek and listened with her ear
half against the earpiece like his own. As the talk went on,
she placed one hand lightly on his shoulder for support, as

though, Grant thought, she had forgotten momentarily in the interest of the information coming over the phone that she was supposed to hate him.

"I was hoping I'd be able to catch you just before lunch, dear boy," Evelyn drawled. "Doug is here with me. I'll put him on in a moment. But we were talking about you, and we wondered if you both wouldn't like to come up and spend a week or two here with us now."

"Are you kidding?" Grant growled.

"But no, dear boy! The Abernathys are gone. They've gone back to Indianapolis. Left on the noon flight yesterday for Miami. I wouldn't have called you if they were still here. Heavens! But I did feel badly, we all did, about what happened. And we all wanted to invite you back for a pleasanter stay. It would be nice to see you again with the air clearer."

"I don't see how we can," Grant said cautiously. "So they've left, have they?" He felt curiously relieved.

"And not in very good shape, I'm afraid," Evelyn said in her gravelly way.

"What do you mean?"

"I mean that Hunt's in trouble with his business affairs, I'm afraid, that's what I mean. Carol and I both warned him, you know. Even before he came down he was in danger of losing managerial control of his lumber and brick business. And now it looks like the *fait* is *accompli*. I have lots of business contacts up there myself you know. It looks like there is no doubt he'll lose his managerial control, if indeed he doesn't lose it all."

"But surely his stock——" Grant said.

"Yes, he still has that. But they can probably force him out, if they want to. And I suspect, my information is, that they want to."

"He'll have to retire," Grant said.

"It would kill him," Evelyn said calmly, like some gravelly oracle. "Especially the way he drinks. I wouldn't give him two years. Well, I warned him."

"Yes, I know," Grant said. "So did Carol, except that Carol——"

"You're quite right!" Evelyn said. "Curiously enough, while Carol warned him, warned him a lot of times, it was really she who *brought* him down here when they came, and it was she who *kept* him down here all the time when you—when you *and* Lucky—were here. Well, it's a curious, sad tale. I don't know what I can do about it. Or anyone. What about your coming up for a week or two?"

"I don't see how we can, Evelyn," Grant said. Lucky was nodding vigorously in approval of his answer beside him. "I've made some serious diving commitments for the next week or two. And then I'll have to be getting back to New York for rehearsals. Is Doug there?"

"Yes. He's right beside me trying to take my own phone away from me! Wait, I'll put him on. Maybe he can make you change your mind."

Again Lucky moved, this time to shake her head not just as vigorously. "Hello. Hello?" he said.

"Ron? Ron?" Doug's voice came on. "Is that you, Ron? . . . Okay. Listen. Why don't you two come on up here for a week or so? You know, the weather cleared as soon as you left, and Bonham's got a lot of new customers now. We're having fun parties on the boat every day now. And he wants to get back to work on those cannon, now the weather's good."

"How would you like to make a trip to the Morant Cays instead?" Grant said.

"Those islands down south of Jamaica?" Doug said. "Sounds like a good idea."

"We may do that with Grointon. Take sleeping bags and camp out down there for four or five days. The spearfishing is practically untouched."

"That sounds great!" Doug said enthusiastically. "Listen, I've got a new girl. Can I bring her along?"

"Sure. We'll hire a small sailing boat to take us down. The girls can sleep on the boat if they prefer."

"You're sure you won't come up here?" Doug asked again. "Evelyn'd love to have you. And we've been having great fun."

"Can I talk?" Grant said in a low voice. "Is Evelyn near?"

"No, not too. What?" Doug said conversationally.

"Well, I've just got too many bad memories of up there. And so has Lucky. I really don't feel like coming back there," Grant said.

"All right. Okay. I dig. Then I'll come," Doug said. "With my girl. Don't leave without me, now!"

"I promise. We won't."

"I don't want to take the midnight flight, and the next thing available is the three o'clock from New York tomorrow. Okay?"

"Okay," Grant said. After a few farewells from and to both of them, shouted on both sides with that false heartiness that pretends noise can make up for triteness, he hung up. Lucky had already moved away from him to sit down on the bed.

"You really want to go on that trip? With Jim; and them?" she asked him in a strange voice.

"Sure. Why not?" he said lightly. "It'll be pretty close quarters, probably. Not much privacy. But that won't make any difference to me and you," he said with a bitter smile. "Will it?"

On the bed Lucky straightened herself and raised her head high. From this position she looked at him strangely. "All right then, we'll go," she said, in a rather hollow, strange voice. "I've never been much of a camper. But I might enjoy it."

Doug would not be coming until sometime in the afternoon to-morrow, so that left them two days more to go out in the catamaran and they went both days, with Ben. The Star and his wife were back now from Ocho Rios, and much in evidence around the hotel, and while they all spoke whenever they met and occasionally had a drink together, the Star did not offer to go out with them. He did not know, as far as Grant was aware, that they were going out to the last place he had dived. But before they went out that afternoon of the day of the phone call, they discussed with Jim over lunch the Morant Cays trip.

Jim had been there once himself, and he was very enthusiastic over the idea of going back. He had in fact talked up this same trip a great deal during their first stay at the Crount, but they had not wanted to go then simply because they were very close and did not want to be that long without the privacy of their own bed. Now, the way they were together, that part didn't matter, and Grant for one found himself highly enthusiastic, strangely enough. The three little islands lay just about fifty-five sea miles south-southeast of

Morant Point, about a seven-hour trip by sail from Kingston, and were used principally only as guano islands. In May they were visited to collect the "booby" eggs of the sea birds, mainly terns, which nested there every year in great numbers. But the rest of the time except for a guano boat now and then, they were totally deserted. "Don't worry about the guano," Jim said cheerfully, "that's only in a few separate places." All of them were flat and covered with scrub like the wild mimosa. The northernmost two had good beaches for landing, although the third was rocky and difficult, and the most northerly of the group, called with typical British imagination "North-East Cay", had tall coco palms growing on it also, supposedly planted there around 1825 by some thoughtful Jamaican planters for the benefit of shipwrecked sailors. They had coral heads and good reefs all around and in between them, the best of these being in a northeasterly direction from the same North-East Cay, which was to the windward of the island. But to leeward there were good reefs too. There were no mosquitoes and, when Jim had been to them two years before, no buildings except one beat-up old wooden shack, and he assumed there still weren't any. They could charter for four or five days the same boat he had used when he had first gone there—with another "skindiving couple" he had guided. ("This couple is no 'skindiving couple'," Lucky put in succinctly.) And if Ben and Irma wanted to go along, they could hire a bigger boat Jim knew about in the harbour that was available.

But Ben opted out from the start. He would have liked to go, but he didn't want to leave Irma for that long, and Irma the non-swimmer did not want to go and spend five days hanging around some essentially uninteresting, uninhabited islets. So that left the five of them, Doug and his girl, Grant, Lucky, Jim; and of course the captain. They could take sleeping bags and sleep on shore, or sleep on the boat if they preferred. The spearfishing was excellent because the area was practically untouched and the fish had not been shot at and spooked. They could take along some canned food, for variety, but plan mainly to live off the fish they caught, which —Jim said—they could cook on shore by a fire on the beach in the evening. The sunsets were delicious. What more could you ask?

"You don't care?" Grant asked later, as they got themselves ready to go out in the catamaran, "you're willing to go?"

Again Lucky gave him that strange enigmatic look he had noticed before. "Not if you don't care," she said shortly, "not if you're willing to have me go." Grant could not figure out what that meant.

"What would you do if I said I wouldn't go?" Lucky said in an odd voice.

"Then I wouldn't go myself," Grant said promptly. "You don't think I'd go and leave you here, do you? With that goddamned Jacques hanging around?"

"Ha!" Lucky said thinly. "You'd do better to leave me here than take me," she said enigmatically.

"Now just what the hell does that mean?" Grant demanded.

"Oh, nothing," she said, and suddenly smiled at him.

He had, the night before, availed himself of his "fucking privileges" with her, as he now called it to himself. It had not been too terribly satisfactory.

They had had dinner with Jim, and Ben and Irma, at the hotel and then had driven into town to the private gambling club. For the first time Jim went with them, though he made few bets and did it very carefully. Everybody won a little bit, except Grant who lost a little bit. Nobody got hurt. Then they had several drinks at the air-conditioned bar on Barry Street (or was it Tower Street?) and talked about the Morant Cays trip and about the day's spearfishing. Then they left Jim and went home. Grant waited, picking his time when she was completely nude between stepping out of her bra and panties and putting on the shorty nightgown she liked to wear, to put forth his demand—"I'd like to invoke my fucking privileges," he said politely. "You remember? I've been getting pretty horny, I've got an enormous hard-on, and I'd like to get laid."—"Sure," Lucky said immediately. "Okay. Come on." And she lay down on the bed and spread her legs ready to receive him, a tight little smile on her face, looking for all the world suddenly like one of the so many girls he had screwed in so many whorehouses across the world during his youth in the Navy. When he mounted her—and that was the only, and the exact, word for it—she worked her legs and pelvis and belly expertly, milking him as he moved in and out of her like any fist or any well-trained professional, until he achieved his orgasm. It was all pretty grim. Still, on the other hand it was a hell of a lot better than nothing.—"Was it good?" Lucky asked after he moved off of her.—"Well, yes," he said. "But not as good as it has been."—"Can I go to sleep now?" she asked.—"Yes," he had said. "You can go to sleep now."

In the catamaran running out he looked at her laughing and joking with Jim and Ben and was suddenly totally, absolutely furious with her. He was not going to give in. It burned all through his body like a white-hot flame. Then just as suddenly this was replaced by a depression so deep, so numbing that it almost made him physically, vocally inarticulate. There was his old "rejection syndrome" acting up on him again! Fortunately he was sober and so could swallow it all. This he did. And down inside him he could feel it begin to creep all throughout his system like some kind of poisonous acid, irritating tissue, burning cells and arteries and veins, and incidentally giving to the total organism that was Ron Grant a great deal of heroic belligerence. A half hour later he had shot—and killed—his first shark.

It very nearly got away from him. The creature measured eight feet nine inches when they got it into the boat and was, so Jim said, the large black-tipped shark but he wouldn't be able to be sure until he checked the teeth with one of his books. Its fins certainly did not appear to have black tips to them.

They had only been in the water a few minutes and had been swimming near the set of caves Jim knew about but in water sixty, sixty-five feet deep when Grant had seen the shark swimming along the bottom over the sand between two coral cliffs. He motioned to Jim and pointed and took off after it, but as he closed the shark appeared to speed up just a little so that it kept the same distance. In front of it the coral appeared to close over making a cul-de-sac so that the shark would either have to swim up over the coral, allowing Grant to catch up, or else reverse himself and come back toward Grant. Unfortunately, invisible to Grant, there was a tunnel under the coral for perhaps twenty feet before sand appeared again, and the shark swam into it and disappeared. That was when he thought he had lost him. But Jim had turned immediately at the first signal and started swimming fast out to sea, and as the shark emerged from the other end of the tunnel, Jim was able to dive on him and scare him back through the tunnel toward Grant. It was almost exactly the same way Jim and Raoul the pilot had trapped the shark in Grand Bank, Grant seemed to recall. At any rate, he was ready for him when he came back through the tunnel. He dove straight for him down into the trough between the cliffs to maybe fifty-five or sixty feet, remarking that the shark now appeared huge as he got up close to him, and speared him exactly through the brain—or at least through the spinal column. The shark stopped swimming as if hit in the head with a club. And that was all there was to it. Grant swam upward for what seemed eternally, dragging the heavy animal up with him while his lungs beseeched him for air, and was reminded of his old nightmare. Triumphantly, he didn't care. All he could think about was getting the thing back to the boat where he could show it off to his damned snotty wife.

"That's the same kind you shot in Grand Bank that time, ain't it?" he said in the boat, pleased with his catch, after Jim declared it to be a black-tip.

Jim grinned. "I don't know. I don't remember. I've shot so many."

"Oho! you snooty son of a bitch!" Grant roared, and slapped him on the bare back. "You don't remember because you've shot so many, eh? Well, fuck you, buddy!"

"Hey, wife?" he called. Lucky was standing at the other end of the catamaran as far from the shark as she could get; she looked as if she would have liked to jump into the water but was scared to. "Hey, wife! Aren't you impressed, wife?"

"Yes, I'm impressed," Lucky said. "I'm not sure whether the impression is a good impression or a bad impression, but I'm impressed."

Jim Grointon gave Grant a very openly private look. "There are some things about men women just don't understand, and never will," he said with a grin.

"That's probably true," Lucky said. "But then there are some things about women that men will never understand, too, so it's even."

"Don't be too sure about that," Jim said in a veiled voice, and looked at her quizzically. Grant watching them didn't get it. He remembered only the time she had blown her stack over the killing of the big jewfish.

But Lucky did not do anything like that this time. After a while, and a number of reassurances that the shark was absolutely dead, she came aft to inspect the gruesome creature closely with a kind of awed, superstitious interest which was exactly the way Grant himself felt.

" Well, I'm impressed," Ben Spicehandler said quietly. " I'm damned impressed. I would never have gone after him— even if he'd been in water shallow enough for my meagre talent. Are there many of them like that around here?"

" Not so many that you need to worry any about it, Ben," Jim said.

" Okay," Ben said, " I'll take your word for it," and picked up his flippers to go back into the water.

" I'll cut his mouth out for you, and you can keep it for a souvenir," Jim said getting out his knife.

" No, wait a minute," Grant said. " I want to take *him* back to the hotel and hang *him* up on the thing on the beach where the richies hang their marlin and have my picture atken with him first."

Jim was sharpening his knife on an oilstone. " It won't make any difference. It won't show in the photo." He grabbed the shark's snout and raised it. " Okay?"

" Okay," Grant said, fascinated by the opened mouth. " I ought to be able to get my head in that one, hunh?"

" Not quite without getting scratched," Jim said, going to work with his knife. " But damn' near." He seemed to take some great, very deep, personal pleasure in the mutilation he was doing. He was gingerly about handling the teeth. There were about five rows of them, getting smaller and less distinct the farther back in the mouth they were. " Sharks have no bones," he said, lecturing as he cut. " They're all cartilage. It'll take about a week or ten days for the mouth to dry out stiff. Then it'll get like tough thick leather. You'll have yourself a nice ornament for your desk." With his hands he worked the cut-out mouth, opening and closing it to mesh the fairly well interlocking teeth. When it was full opened, a grown man could just about get his head through it. Jim left it that way, full open, and laid it up safely on the transom in the sun. Then he looked at it with a peculiar kind of blood-thirsty satisfaction.

Grant kicked lightly the inert meat of the shark's corpse with his bare foot. " How long will he last? I mean, before he begins to rot? I mean, I'd like to leave him hang long enough for Doug to see him to-morrow."

" Oh, he'll last longer than that," Jim said. " We can leave him hang four or five days. We'll leave him hang long enough for all the customers of the hotel to see him, anyway. It's good advertisement."

" I wonder what our friend the Star will think?" Grant said.

" I don't know," Jim said shortly and crisply. " And I couldn't care less. I'm going to make it a point to tell him where we got him, though."

Jim was correct that the cut-out mouth did not show once the shark was hung by his tail from the hotel's fish rack out on the beach by the water, and the almost nine-foot shark made quite a sight when the five-foot-nine-inch Grant stood beside it for his photograph. René proudly took the shark's mouth and posed it on the end of the back-bar where it was shown by him to everyone, tourist or local, who came into the bar. But if Grant thought his manly feat would impress his wife enough to bring her back around to her duties of loving and obeying him, he was mistaken. She obeyed him well enough—and had done that even before the shark—if a little grudgingly. But love him she did not, she said. In the fact, Grant did not think about bringing his wife around to heel one way or the other much. His main reason for wanting to show the shark off to her after he had caught it was more to show her he didn't give a damn what she thought than anything else. He had made up his mind ; and he did not intend to give in. He was quite sure she would not like the idea of him shooting sharks, and he was quite right. And of course he and Jim did not tell her that that was what they had deliberately come out to this spot to do. But he had discovered a new mean, tough, almost reckless quality in himself since their trouble, probably because of it. He was not nearly as cautious, or overcautious, as he had been before. He was tougher, and he was more dangerous, because he just didn't give a damn.

" Makes you feel like a man, don't it?" Jim Grointon said, as they stood looking at the hanging shark. " You know, you're the best free-diving pupil I've ever had. *Ever.*"

" Well, let's say it makes me feel like a large boy," Grant said cautiously. " I am, hunh?"

This new quality showed up in other ways too besides the shark. That same day after shooting the shark, that same afternoon, when nothing else of much interest showed up in the area where they were, Jim upped his anchor and took them out into deeper water. He acted as if he had suddenly made a vast and important decision.

"I want to show Ron something I don't show to many people," he explained to Ben and Lucky. "It's kind of like a sort of special superstition, or a special possession, of mine. You can come along and look too from the surface, Ben, if you want. I don't care. But Ron's ready. I just hope the old bastard's around to-day, that's all," he said, and swung the rudder bar to port with his foot to run south down along parallel with the coast. Watching a prominent headland as a measuring guide, he finally cut off the outboards and threw over the anchor.

"The water we're in here now is about seventy-five to eighty-five feet deep. There are quite a lot of good big mangrove snapper out here, and you and me are going to shoot a couple. On the bottom."

"You're kidding me," Grant said, but he could feel his face looked pleased. And he thought, why not?

"No I'm not kidding," Jim said. "You're ready to do eighty feet. As ready as you'll ever be. You actually could do a hundred feet, if you wanted, just as easy. Once you get down to seventy feet, twenty or thirty feet more isn't all that much difference. You'll see."

"Okay, I'll have a go," Grant said and grinned.

"But there's also something else I want to show you," Jim grinned back. "If he's around to-day. Just so you'll know, I make it a point never to bring anybody out here unless I know he can—and will—go the distance, and I've only brought four of my people out here since I've been in Kingston. One was the guy from New York I told you about who shoots the sharks. Another was the guy who I took, him and his wife, down to the Morant Cays. She wasn't quite good enough, but I brought her too—like Ben here—because *he* was good enough. But there's only been four. Just so's you'll know."

"I take it this is a considerable compliment," Grant said thinly.

"It is," Jim said. "Come on, let's get in the water."

Lucky, who had listened to all of this, was saying nothing.

"What is this thing we're going to see?" Grant asked.

"You wait," Jim said. "If we don't see him I'll tell you all about it. If we do, I won't have to tell you."

The coral looked very far down, at least to Grant. The make-up of the bottom was considerably changed this far out, too, was the first thing that he noticed. Instead of the lush coral reef growths in the shallower water that he was used to seeing closer to shore, the coral here was all stunted, the rock on which it grew showing plainly beneath the various small growths. Instead of narrow sand channels running out between hills and cliffs of coral there were much larger patches of bare sand stretching away in all directions. Here and there on it a single seafan or black organ-pipe or basket sponge swayed softly with the movement of the bottom water. The effect was one of intense bone-cold loneliness. Green, *pale*-green, loneliness. Only a few fish nosed around the low rock outcrops which supported the meagre coral.

Jim motioned to them, and they started off swimming away from the boat south parallel to the distant shore. In less than five minutes they had spotted a large-looking mangrove snapper on the bottom. Grant could not tell just how large since he had lost his ability to judge sizes in this deeper water. In any case, Jim pointed to it and motioned for Grant to go for it. Grant nodded and adjusted his snorkel with his left hand and clamped his teeth around it tighter and began to hyperventilate. He was quite convinced he would never reach this bottom, but he was going to get as near to it as he absolutely could. The trouble was you always had to swim all that way back up.

But just then out at the very limit of his visibility range Grant saw something move. Peering closely he could just make out—as though whatever it was passing into and out of invisible transparence—the largest fish he had ever seen in his life. It was easily half again as big as the jewfish he and Jim had taken. When he blinked once, he lost it in the green fog of the visibility range. But in the meantime he was already pointing at it and motioning to Jim and Ben. Jim nodded back at him solemnly and slowly, pointed at it and motioned him to come on. After they swam a few yards slowly, his eyes picked the great fish up again. The high rounded head and the black spot on the tail as large as a man's head were clearly visible. As if watching them from off there, the huge fish swam slowly away from them at just about their own speed, so that it remained just at the edge of their visibility. After a couple of minutes of this, Jim motioned

to Grant and took off on a long slanting dive, kicking hard
and his gun trailing behind him as he put both arms back to
streamline himself. Grant and Ben followed suit. In this
way they crept up on him and Grant got a good look at him,
but then the fish, perking up, speeded up his own swimming
and put himself back out at the edge of visibility, and there
resumed his former pace. After surfacing they followed him
for maybe four minutes more, then Jim motioned them over
to him and raised his head out.

" You see him?" he called, plucking his snorkel.

"Hell, yes!" Grant said. " I've never seen anything so
big!"

"You know what it is?" Jim said.

"It looks like a snapper. A red snapper. But——"

" It is a red snapper," Jim grinned and nodded.

" But snapper don't get that big."

"You're wrong," Jim said. " This one did. You see him,
Ben?"

"Yeah," Ben said. " I couldn't hardly believe it."

" Well, let's go get him," Grant called.

" You'll never get any closer to him than you are right
now," Jim said. " See how he's stopped to wait for us?
Start swimming for him. He'll move right on, always at that
same distance. Unless he gets bored and decides to go away.
I've tried to spear him for over three years. Probably that's
one of the reasons he's lived long enough to get that big."

"Snappers don't get that big," Grant said again.

" *He* did," Jim said. " You guys are two of probably only
six people who have ever seen him. Nobody else ever dives
here."

"Did you ever try to get him with regular tackle?" Grant
asked. " Chum him up?"

" I wouldn't," Jim said. " Several of the locals have tried,
but nobody's ever got a hook into him. But if I can't spear
him, I won't take him." He rolled over in the water twice as
if loosening himself up. " Well, come on. Let's get on to
something we *can* take. Now you got to sing for your supper,
Ron!" he grinned.

"Well, has he grown since you first saw him?" Grant
asked.

" Not appreciably. Hell, how can you tell with a fish *that*
big?"

The dive, when it came, was a strange experience. There were a number of scattered fairly large mangrove and mutton snappers nosing around the corals on the bottom. Grant chose the largest one of three that were fairly close. Then he commenced his hyperventilation. When he dove, it seemed that he was on his way down for an eternity, but somehow he didn't mind and felt a curious and belligerent exhilaration instead of nervousness. He noted that his diaphragm heaved on him once uncontrollably even before he reached the bottom. And of course the fish kept getting larger and larger as he came closer. For some curious reason Grant had never felt freer, and physically freer, in his life. It seemed, whether true or not, that he had all the time in the world. He was suffused with a feeling of total well-being, and revelled in the slow lazy movements of his legs in their flippers. At some point he passed quite distinctly from a layer of warmer water into a layer of colder. Then he was down. The fish had been eyeing him, and finally he turned—too late—to run. Grant turned the angle with him, led him half a length and shot him squarely in the back behind the gills.

The fish was really huge, or would have been if he had not seen the really big one. Grant calculated he would go forty-five pounds. Even so, he nearly lost him by underestimating his size and thus underestimating the distance the fish was from him. Because of this the spear did not go all the way through him before it was pulled up short by the length of its cord. Taking his time, Grant paused to ram the spear into the sand once, pushing the spearhead and its flanges on through the flapping fish. Then he looked up and started the long trip back up there. Jim and Ben appeared incredibly tiny up there on the surface.

Slowly, he swam up. By the time he reached twenty feet his diaphragm was heaving uncontrollably every three or four seconds, but he had not let out any air and he knew he had it made. He even slowed down his kick the last twenty feet because he hated for it to end. Then he reached the surface and blew his snorkel so he could breathe again.

Not far away, after watching him, Jim himself took off down on a dive. It was an eerie and beautiful sight to watch the stocky diver leisurely kick his way down, down, down. It was as if Grant was seeing himself make his own dive from the viewpoint of Jim and Ben. Ben was grinning at him and shaking his head admiringly. Breathing on the surface, Grant watched Jim spear his fish and start back up. On the bottom, naturally, he looked as tiny as he had on the top from the bottom.

"You know what you did?" Jim shouted laughing after he was back up. "You did eighty, eighty-five feet there, man! That's easily eighty or eighty-five feet down. And you stopped to push the spear through him! That was cool! Hell, you could do a hundred feet, man, any time you want! You're a real pro!" He stopped his hysterically happy laughing. "Come on, let's get on back to the boat. It's late."

Back in the boat Grant showed Lucky his big fish, and sat quietly, smoking, while Jim lauded his eighty-five foot dive.

"I'll have a lot of things to tell and show to Doug to-morrow when he gets here to-morrow, won't I?" he asked Lucky.

"You sure will," Lucky said thinly. "I'm very proud of you."

Grant threw his cigarette end over the side, thin-lipped, and felt his eyes flatten in his face like the real tough man he seemed to have become. "Thanks," he said.

THIRTY-ONE

Doug's arrival did nothing to heal the split between them. Rather it worked just in the reverse, since he brought with him, not the new girl-friend he had talked so excitedly about over the phone, but Al Bonham. It was almost exactly like the first time they two had appeared here at the Crount, enough so that Grant had that eerie feeling of having done something before and that something was happening in time for the second time. The two got out of what could have been the same taxi, and came up the same steep set of steps, in what was almost exactly the same way and order. Only the late lunchtime cast on the veranda was different. Ben and Irma were still there, but the lady musical comedy writer and her husband who had become such good friends were missing. Instead, the male movie star and his actress wife were there. And Jim Grointon. Jim Grointon was always with them now, whenever, and just about wherever they were, excepting only at night when they actually went to bed.

Lucky conducted herself with complete decorum toward Doug and Bonham—as she had with Jim, Ben and Irma, the Star and his wife, and the others. Whenever any other people were around, she was the perfect wife and companion, even pal; it was only when they were alone together that she wasn't. It was beginning to look like Grant was going to pass the entire rest of his married life like this, just like almost every other son of a bitch he knew, and he was beginning to get damned tired of it. But there seemed to be no way to approach her, at all, to talk about it.

Bonham, it turned out, had considerable news for them— once Doug finished telling them about his new girl and why she was not with him. The first thing Doug said when he had arrived up the steps and been introduced to the Star and his wife was, " Say, did you guys *know* that that Pat Wright was a lez?" He washboarded his forehead at them and wiggled his eyebrows above his grin.

Lucky's eyes got brilliant and she made a small knowing grin at Grant. " Well, let's say that we *suspected* that she might be," she said.

" *She* was havin' a goddam *affair* with *Evelyn*, for Christ's sake!" Doug said. " I almost got my head in a real noose there!"

" How are you?" he said with his most charming smile, which was a considerably charming one, and went around the table to shake hands with the Star. " I've admired your work for a very long time."

Pat Wright, however, had nothing to do with his new girl, or why she had not come. The new girl was a wealthy married girl from Connecticut whose father was a bigwheel Supreme Court lawyer in Washington, and who was travelling with another married girl without any husbands along. Neither one was planning to get divorced, they just wanted to get away from their husbands for a while, and had come down to spend a few weeks in GaBay at the West Moon Over. She and Doug had made out from the very first moment they had met. The reason that, in the end, she had backed out and decided not to come down with him was that she did not want to—was sort of scared to—leave her married girl-friend she was travelling with. " It's a shame," Doug said, grinning at the

Star and his wife, " because she was a great lay, a great—and very sophisticated—lay." He turned to Lucky. " However ..." He shrugged.

Bonham's news, which he had politely remained silent about until Doug had finished, was—of course ; naturally—about the schooner *Naiad*. She was going to be finished much sooner than expected, was in fact almost finished now. That was one of the reasons he was down here: to look at her. The other reason was to see Grant. About the cruise. Because of the early date of finishing her, plus the fact that Grant was in Kingston, he had been in touch with Sam Finer in New York about the maiden cruise. Both Grant and Sam were invited guests, with their ladies, on the maiden cruise of *Naiad*. And because of this it was Bonham's idea, if it suited everybody, to just commence the cruise right here—in Kingston—once the ship was in the water, rather than sailing her up to GaBay first.

It had been, they should understand, his intention all along, for this maiden cruise, to take *Naiad* to the Nelson Islands, a small British-controlled group not quite half-way between the Pedro Bank and the Rosalind Bank over toward the Honduras mainland. This was about 92 nautical miles from Ganado Bay, and about 165 nautical miles from Kingston, via the Pedro Cays. Why sail the ship all the way to GaBay and then have to come back that extra distance? The Nelsons, where Bonham had been once several years ago, were great spear-fishing—and great living, because a number of wealthy Bahamians (as well as rich Americans) had winter houses there—and would be the perfect place for their initial cruise. He had spoken about all this to Sam Finer in New York yes-terday by phone and Finer was in agreement with all of it. Assuming Grant had no complaints about it (Bonham had told Sam about Grant's loan to the corporation), Finer and Cathie would fly down to Kingston, stay a couple of days at the Crount, and they would all start their voyage from Kingston Harbour. They would then be six: Bonham and Orloffski as crew, Finer, Cathie, Grant and Lucky.

Now, *Naiad* would sleep eight comfortably, if they used the saloon as a double cabin, and Bonham and Orloffski bunked in the crew quarters forward. Bonham had therefore taken the liberty of asking along two paying guests. What the hell, why waste the space when you could pick up some money on it? Finer had agreed. These paying guests were a Baltimore brain surgeon and his girl-friend, both of whom Bonham had taught to dive two years ago and who had happened to be in Ganado Bay on a vacation. The brain surgeon had to be back in Baltimore for a big operation on the twelfth of next month; they could therefore leave here in around two weeks, cruise to the Nelsons, spend a week or even ten days spearfishing and exploring the little island group, be back in GaBay on the tenth or eleventh for the surgeon to catch the plane. Assuming always, of course, that all this fitted in with Grant's own plans. Grant and Lucky could then stay on here at the Crount and save themselves all that plane fare to New York and back. If that was okay with Grant. It would even fit in with this Morant Cays trip, Bonham carefully pointed out with a look at Jim. But any way they did it, Bonham intended to see that Grant, as well as Sam Finer, was on that maiden cruise—to the Nelson Islands. It would be one hell of a great trip.

"Boy, you're *right* it would be one hell of a great trip!" Ben Spicehandler said enthusiastically. "I just wish me and Irma could go along that trip! I've read about the Nelsons."

There slowly descended over Bonham's eyes his normal and customary " commercial film " which Grant had seen so many times before. It was exactly like watching a veil being drawn across a window. ' As a matter of fact," Bonham said, "we could actually take along another couple. Only trouble is, you would have to sleep forward in the crew's quarters, which is a little bit more cramped than the other berths. Would that bother you?" He grinned with his storm-cloud eyes and inflated his great chest and gut slowly: "On the other hand, *I* can sleep there and get rest."

Ben's eyes were already bright. Now they got brighter. He looked over at Irma. Irma grinned, ducked, shrugged, and cackled. "How about it, Irm?" Ben said. "Okay? Okay, we'll go!"

"But what about you and uh what's his name? Orloffski, Ben added.

"We'll sleep on deck," Bonham said, the commercial film across his eyes once more.

"What if it rains?"

"We'll sleep on deck."

"Okay, then!" Ben said in a warning voice. "We'll sure go!"

"Done," Bonham said. "It's a deal." The really best news, though, he had to give, he said, was that Sam Finer had said he was willing to *think* about maybe putting another $10,000 into the corporation.

"But that's really *great* news!" Grant put in excitedly. "I mean *really* great! That means you'll be all set up! You'll have working capital and everything!"

Bonham nodded. "We'll be able to pay you back your loan. We'll even be able to insure the ship. And I think a lot of his willingness is due to the fact that you made us that loan."

"You mean the ship isn't insured?" Lucky asked.

"They looked her over in the yard," Bonham said. "She's not a young ship, you know. The premiums they're asking are too high. I wouldn't pay them. I *couldn't* pay them! Not now. Not then. Not yet."

"You mean we'll be sailing two hundred miles and back for a week on a ship that can't get insured?" Lucky asked.

"They'll insure her," Bonham corrected her. "They just want too much. Anyway, don't worry about that."

"But what's wrong with her, if they want such high premiums?" Lucky said.

"There's nothing wrong with her," Bonham said evenly, and patiently. "It's just that she's not a new ship, like I told you. But she's as sound as any ship of her size anywhere in the whole damned world. Take my word for it."

"I'll take your word for it!" Ben said enthusiastically.

Lucky said nothing. And she did not bring the subject up again, then. But later on in the suite she talked to Grant about it. "You expect me to go off with you on a beat-up old ship that can't even get insured?" she said when they were alone in the suite.—"I do," Grant said. "Hell, even Ben and Irma are going, for Christ's sake."—"Well, they're crazy to do it," Lucky said. "And I'm not going. I'll stay here at the Crount and wait for you."

Grant waited a few moments before he went on. "Look, you're willing to go off on a crapped-up, camping-out, stuck-together-with-chewing-gum cruise with Jim and Doug to the Morant Cays. With a captain we don't even know."

" I am ; but I'd rather not," Lucky said. Her face took on that veiled look Grant had not yet been able to read.

" I just don't understand. Bonham is a man we know. We know he's reputable. If he says the ship's all right, it is."

" I don't trust him," Lucky said, with a sudden strange irritability. " I never did. He's accident-prone."

" You trusted me to do serious diving on those cannon with him."

" That was diving. This is something else. I'm just not going."

" We'll talk about it later," Grant said, and stretched out, without being kissed, without offering to kiss.

It did not take Doug long to catch on to how things were between them. Grant could tell by the closed look on his face. But Doug said absolutely nothing about this, this time, as if their being married changed everything, including his right and/or his ability to give advice. But if he said nothing about them, he was enormously enthusiastic, and talkative, about the Morant Cays trip. So was Grant, and strangely enough, apparently, so was Lucky. They all talked about it with everybody for the two days it took Jim to set it up.

In the end, though, after they had gone and come back and seen and done it all, it was not really all that different from any of the other diving trips they had made.

In the end it was difficult, after a while, to see a reef or a beach or a coco palm that did not resemble generally the remembered aggregate of all the other reefs and beaches and coco palms one had seen. It was difficult, after a while, to see one mangrove snapper that looked any different from all the other mangrove snapper. The word about the Morant Cays was that there were lots of sharks of all varieties large and small in the waters around them, but then that was the " Word " about just about every place where someone else was going and oneself was not. It was said about the Caymans, the Nelsons, the Pedro Cays, it was even said by Montego Bay about Ganado Bay, and vice versa. Actually they saw only a few more sharks in their six-day trip than they would have seen in six days' fishing at the place near Morant Bay, say twenty-five or thirty, and almost always out at the outer edge of visibility where they sort of just cruised around. There was only one potentially dangerous shark incident on the whole trip, although no one was seriously hurt by it. It would, of course, have to happen to Grant.

There were all sorts and varieties of reefs available, all charged with fish, from six and ten-foot reefs even Doug could fish easily, on down to eighty-foot ones that Grant now fished fairly easily with Jim. After the pleasant, short, fifty-five-mile sail, all sail was taken in and the captain moved them about from island to island and spot to spot by motor. The weather stayed fine, and the sea was flat and tranquil. Even Lucky was finally persuaded, under Jim's expert tutelage, to go over the side and snorkel around exploring the very shallow reefs while Grant and Doug with spearguns " guarded " her from nearby like the outriders of a cavalry column, as Jim would take her by the hand and dive her down four feet or six feet to look closely at staghorn, elkhorn, brain or fire coral. She had to admit to them it was beautiful.

Jim, it seemed, was just about everywhere on this trip, and Grant dubbed him to himself rather sourly: " Ubiquitous Jim." And his ubiquity seemed always to place him in proximity to Lucky. He took her off to the other side of the cay to hunt for " booby " eggs, which he cooked for breakfast. During the hours on the ship, he continually took her off forward or aft or below to show her something, explaining to her the intricacies of sailing and the intricacies of its gear, something which hitherto (to Grant's knowledge) Lucky had shown no interest in at all. On shore in the evenings he cooked her fish especially for her, since she preferred her fish poached to fried, not an easy trick to do over an open fire with no grill. He seemed to know at least as much about sailing as he knew about diving and flying, and he seemed to know at least as much about camping as he knew about sailing. And all of this was made personally available to Lucky, and, of course, to the others, if they wanted to come along and listen.

Jim's command of sailing lingo and camping lingo was formidable, as was his command of the flying lingo. (He was, for example, in the habit of always saying " Affirmative " for " Yes " and " Negative " for " No " like a pilot.) All of this knowledge was put at Lucky's disposal. Even Grant, who had done a bit of sailing and had read lots more about it, and who had done quite a lot of camping and backpacking in the Michigan woods and in California, was often unable to understand Jim's lingoes and had to ask for explanations.

Through all of this Lucky flirted with him. But then she flirted with the captain, flirted with Doug, and even, on occasion when she forgot herself, flirted with Grant. Grant might have been jealous had he not noted that she flirted with Jim only moderately—not half as outrageously as he had seen her flirt with other guys, or with Jim himself for that matter, back in the very first days in Kingston. Neither did it occur to him to think she might be deliberately moderating her flirting with Jim, curtailing it for his, Grant's benefit, or perhaps for nervous reasons of her own. He was incapable congenitally of thinking in such a way.

Jim was obviously captivated by her. But Grant could not blame him for that. And Grant could not bring himself to believe that, even in her present state of fury, resentment and disillusion with himself, she would ever do anything like that to him. He had given her no cause, unless you wanted to count Carol as a cause, and he did not count Carol as a cause. Even if she did, she would not do that to him. (He found that the vague generality of " That " was as far as his mind would go; it balked at anything more specific.) And anyway, he thought rather biliously, she was certainly smart enough to know which side her future was buttered on when that future came to being with him or Jim Grointon. He was determined not to mention it to her. Especially in the light of what he now thought of as her " Fear-of-Whoredom Syndrome " it would be bad, and he was not even going to let on he noticed it. That carefully-studied-out and well-thought-over thing about her morbid over-preoccupation with anything having to do with Whore or Whores had changed a lot of things in his overall outlook.

Besides, he had his own honour to think of. Grant believed that any man who was capable of falling in love with and marrying a woman who was capable of cuckolding him (when thinking generally rather than specifically of himself, the word came easily enough) was a man either guilty of gross misjudgment or indifference, or else very very sick; and in either case deserved what he got. He, Grant, was not any type like that of Raoul-the-South-American to yank his girl, or his wife, out from under a lover and pack her up and whisk her back to New York. He would just simply be long-gone. And he was not the kind of man to hang around and ride herd on his wife to make sure she didn't do something to him. He would not undignify himself like that.

On the other hand, while he would not undignify himself, the shark incident that he had came very close to undignify-ing him all by itself. This happened on the fifth or next to last day, when the breeze having fallen, they were diving on the windward reefs to the north and east of North-East Cay. The captain had anchored them over a likely spot, and being already still dressed out from the last dive while the others were not, Grant had gone over the side alone, feet first and holding his mask against his face in the approved manner with his left hand, his double-rubber Arbalete in his right hand. When the bubbles of his entry cleared, he saw below him in water about forty-five feet deep a " rockfish " (that was the only name he had ever heard them called) nosing around some sparse coral growth. He had hyperventilated and gone for him, spearing him with a head shot which while not a killing shot left the fish flapping his tail only very feebly. He remembered noting at the time that because of the head shot there was no blood spoor in the water. Then something shot past him on his right, heading for the fish. Through his mask he could tell that it was a shark even before its hide began to sandpaper his right side along the ribcage, although he was so close he could not even see the dorsal fin. The only way to describe it was that a totally silent express train was passing him inches away at speed. It was at least half as big again as the one he had taken, up above Morant Bay. The curved, muscled, faintly, muscle-pulsating sandpaper sheet of its flank continued on past him, on, and on, and on. It was abrading his side. For one insane moment he thought it might just not ever stop, as though its length was in fact endless. Then the gun was jerked from his hand with numb-ing force. Instinctively he moved both hands, the good one and the numbed one to push the thing away from him where it was hurting him ; but by then the shark was gone. So were his fish, spear and line. He watched the shark plane slightly left, then pass out of sight in the green fog beyond visibility range. The shock of the force was so great it had snapped the stout line, and his gun—which was supposed to float but which was waterlogged from so much use—was sinking slowly to the bottom below him. Grant was astonished, amazed, disbelieving, and somewhat in a state of physical shock. He hit for the surface as hard as he could swim.

It seemed to him afterward that he swam up so hard that he literally swam himself right up out of the water until he was only knee-deep. Whether this was true or not, he was hollering " Shark! Shark!" as loud as he could as soon as his head was out. Then he started to swim for the boat, only a few yards away, looking behind him between his feet every few strokes. When he reached the ladder and grabbed it, he looked up and saw that Doug, Lucky and Jim were all looking over the side and laughing at him, laughing uproariously. Automatically he stopped himself from climbing up.

" What the fuck are you laughing at?" he said. " The biggest shark I ever saw just stole my fish, and damn' near rubbed off my whole right side doing it."

" You came up out of that water all the way to your waist before you fell back," Jim said. Grant saw him glance with amusement at Lucky. " Where's your gun?"

" He yanked it out of my hand," Grant said. " As a matter of fact my hand's still numb from it. It's on the bottom. The line snapped."

" Well, climb on in," Jim said with amusement. " I'll go and get it for you." Then they all three began laughing again.

" I can get it myself," Grant said stiffly. " Thanks."

" Well, here. Take my gun," Jim grinned. He handed his loaded but uncocked triple-rubber gun over the side butt first.

" I don't need a gun for that," Grant said. " There's no more fish down there now anyway." He swam away from the boat, hyperventilating, looked once all around the wide circle of his visibility range, then dove for the gun lying openly and bright blue on the bottom, and looking strangely incongruous among the coral and sparse gorgonias. When he climbed into the boat, he became aware that his knees were shaking violently and tried to hide this as they all started laughing again. He turned away to get a beer out of the ice-chest, aware that his back and neck were stiff with hurt pride which he could not relax.

He was aware that Jim thought he had panicked. He himself did not think he had. On the other hand he had certainly been shocked by the suddenness and unexpectedness of what had happened. He sat down with the beer, so that the shaking in his knees would not show, and tried to grin at them, and at least partially succeeded.

"You certainly looked funny," Lucky said and there was a malicious glint in her laugh. (Later, when they were alone, she would tell him coldly: "Well, if you're going to do these stupid silly things, you've got to expect things like that and take your chances."—"You don't exactly seem to feel that way about Jim," Grant would counter guardedly. And she would come back with, "That's his profession. You, you're supposed to be a playwright.")

"I guess I did," he said, answering her now, in the boat. "But you should have seen that shark." He raised his arm to show them his side. It was exactly as if someone had taken a metal comb with filed teeth and raked several series of parallel lines horizontally across the tender skin of his side below his armpit. Jim Grointon grinned at him amusedly and said, "I'll get some merthiolate for that." Then all three of them looked at each other and burst into laughter again. "It's only because you looked so funny," Jim grinned apologetically. Grant found he was able to laugh a little with them. But it hurt.

That night around the campfire they discussed the whole thing again. There certainly *had* been some danger involved for Grant, especially if the shark had hit him by mistake, and even Jim admitted this. And, Lucky put in, she had been well aware of this. Very well aware. And it was that very awareness that had made her, after her first quick fright, so furiously angry at him, at Grant.

"But you notice he didn't go for you," Jim pointed out. "He went for your fish. The fact that he bumped you and scraped you up was not deliberate, it was a pure accident." Jim had had a number of such encounters himself, though never, it was true, close enough for the shark to actually scrape him. "Probably because I've made it such a habit to keep looking behind me. I've always seen them coming in. We humans are naturally hampered by our particular kind of eyesight. Most fish can see forward with one eye and backward with the other, and register both impressions. Then we hamper ourselves further by our masks, which is exactly like putting blinders on a horse. And there's no sound, no footsteps or crackling twigs in the sea to warn you. So you have to keep looking back." Jim had had a number of fish stolen from him by sharks at close range. Never once had the shark tried to go for him too. Only twice had sharks ever come straight after him, and both times he had been down-current from wounded, bleeding fish so that the shark might well have mistaken him for the source of fish blood. Both times he had swum straight for the shark as if to attack him, once with a movie camera, once with an unloaded speargun, and both times the shark had veered off and started to circle. The moment he placed himself up-current from the bleeding fish, he was ignored. "Guys have tried all sorts of experiments with all sorts of blood, beef blood, hog blood, even human blood. None of them ever seemed to attract shark much. Only fish blood seems to do that. I'm not talking about the mob feedings that happened to guys off sunk ships durin' the war, naturally, but about normal circumstances."

Grant, lying on the warm sand before the red coals and flickering flames of the fire, could remember one of these, and for the first time in a long time thought of his old aircraft carrier, now lying rusting away somewhere on the bottom of the Pacific Ocean. He also thought of Jim facing down the two sharks with nothing but a camera or unloaded speargun to bump them in the nose if they came on in. He was not sure he would ever have the courage to do that.

"I'm convinced of two things," Jim went on, "about shark. One, they're total cowards and scavengers. And two," he paused here and let the dramatic pause build up, "I'm convinced they know who we are."

"We? You mean humans? Sharks know?" Grant said.

"Maybe not consciously. But I'm convinced that the word's gone out in the sea, however consciously or unconsciously, in whatever manner fish communicate, and amongst the regular fish as well as shark, that there is a new predator loose in the sea. A predator which is a direct competitor to shark, and which has even been known to attack and kill shark themselves. And I think that's why, divers at least, they're very leary of."

"That's hard to believe," Grant said.

"Not so hard. I'm damn' sure they communicate in some

fashion or other." Jim rolled over and up to sit on his knees. "Well, shall we go out to-morrow?"

"Of course," Grant heard himself say, and felt his neck and upper back becoming stiff again. "Why not?"

"No reasons," Jim said lightly. "Anyway, we'll have to make some provisions to look after you better, so this pretty wife of yours won't worry." He smiled a sort of private smile over at Lucky.

"I'd worry anyway," Lucky said in a thin short voice.

"Just the same, you let me get in the water first after this, okay?" Jim smiled at Grant.

"Of course, if you say so," Grant said evenly. "You're the white hunter on this expedition."

He had done other things like this before, Jim, made small dramatic appearances, usurped a sort of parental superiority —generally for Lucky's benefit; had acted out small dramatic roles, almost always for her benefit too; and Grant had never called him on any of them. And there was still all that other business, the sailing lectures, the camping lectures, the tern egg hunts, the elaborately laid-on process of poaching her fish for her instead of frying it. And yet in spite of all this, or perhaps even because of it, a curious closeness had been growing up, had grown up, among the five of them on this trip. Perhaps it was simply that there were no other humans anywhere around, nobody else at all to share or participate in any of it, and that this drew them together so closely and gave them the sense of sharing something nobody else would ever have a part of. In any case the close warmth among the five of them seemed to add to and en-hance everything that happened. Doug noted it, and com-mented on it to Grant. And after the first couple of days even the crusty old captain was pulled into it and drawn out to talk, telling long-winded Conrad-like tales of his gun-running days in Cuba and South America as they sat around the camp-fire in the night. It appeared quite probable that he might once have worked for Lucky's ex-fiancé Raoul. He would not, he was moved to confess to them finally, the very last night they were there, be caught dead skindiving, and could not understand anybody who would. Then the next day they packed up everything, boarded the little ship, spent a last two hours spearfishing without spectacular adventure, and set sail for home, their cruise completed.

There were supremely rememberable moments. A sunset one particular evening with weatherheads and squalls of falling rain far to the southwest of them moving north and west and backlit by the reddening sun. The sound of the dawn breeze in the fronds of the tall coco palms on North-East Cay as they rolled out at daybreak in the bright dawn light to wash in salt water and eat and row out to the little ship. The first true coral " heads " Grant and Doug had ever seen, rising before their masks from the bottom anywhere from thirty to sixty feet high and looking like nothing so much as the mushroom clouds of atomic bombs solidified in stone. A huge four-foot kingfish, silvery and torpedo-like, which Grant had found calmly tail-beating his way about for no good reason among the deeper reefs and speared, and from which Jim—in a dirty black greasy old skillet—made them the best kingfish steaks any of them had ever eaten. There was the particular evening, when after a hard day's spearfishing they had rowed ashore from the anchored little ship and set about the evening chores in the late-afternoon light: Grant and Jim cleaning the fish: Doug and the captain kicking up dried brushwood and driftwood for the fire: Lucky sitting on the sand furiously brushing and combing out her wet hair from the day's swimming. It was that particular evening that they all stopped what they were doing almost simultaneously and looked around at each other with a sudden acute awareness of the passing moment and of how pleasurable it was, and also of how inevitably, inexorably passing it also was, and then with ironic snorts of self-derisive anti-sentiment to hide all that and one wild whoop from Doug, returned without speaking to what they had been doing. Moments like this engendered the feeling they had for each other, or perhaps it was the feeling they had for each other that engendered the moments.

It was on the seven-hour sail back to Kingston that Jim came forward with his near-ecstatic eulogy of Grant. They were all sitting around in the cockpit around the captain at the wheel, drinking beer. Jim had gotten up and come around from the portside to where Grant was standing leaning against the starboard rail watching the bellying sails, a thing Grant never tired of. Once again, as he had done before that time in the Kingston airport, he clasped the slightly taller Grant around his now sweatshirt-covered shoulders, Roman-style.

" I just want to say, and I want you all to hear me say, that I have never had a diving client who was as good, or who was as much fun to dive with, or who learned as fast and as much—as this one! I think I can also say without embarrassing anybody that I have never had a diving client that I liked as much, or felt as much friendship for, or that I've formed as lasting a friendship with. I know. I *know* we all haven't seen the last of each other. In the meantime this trip is over, you all will be going off with Bonham in a few days, and anyway if we do go out together again now it won't be the same, not after this. I just want to say that this is the best trip I've ever made, bar none, and that includes that other trip I made to the Morants with that other diving couple I told you about. And as far as I'm concerned I want to say that this guy right here, this guy, is responsible for more than at least fifty per cent of the fun and success this trip has been. I'll never forget it, and I want him to know I'll never forget him!"

It was a rather long speech to keep your arm clasped around another's shoulders all the time, and it made Grant uncomfortable, and a little embarrassed, having to stand still under the embrace. He had an innate dislike of having most people touch him intimately. At the same time he was deeply moved because he had come to feel the same kind of friendship for Jim. Then Jim gave him a mighty clap across the shoulders, for all the world like one Roman soldier saying hello or good-bye to another Roman soldier, and said, " And that's my speech! If this guy ever needs or wants anything that I can do or give or get for him, all he's got to do is ask!"

He crossed back over to his portside seat and sat, resoundingly, grinning and his face deeply flushed. Perhaps he was a little high on the three or four beers he had had since they had gotten under way. In any case it was a positive enough endorsement.

" Well, thanks," Grant said shyly and feeling kind of silly. "And I want you to know the same thing goes for me, and that I feel the same way about you." And it was true. Because in addition to the depth of his feeling of friendship toward Jim, as with Bonham he had an enormous, profound, near-boyish hero-worship for the things Jim could do in or

on or above the sea, diving, sailing, flying, even the camping, all the romantic, and *real*, things that the bourgeois, small
town, and now pseudo-intellectual, types like himself could
not do and only dreamed about and sometimes, if they became pseudo-intellectual, wrote about. A really sweet smile
passed over his face and goosebumps arose on his bare thighs,
his arms and back, and when he realised suddenly that he
might quite quickly be caught with tears in his eyes, he sat
down quickly and preoccupied himself with getting another
beer from the ice-chest.

It was a rather deep and touching final act curtain to Kingston, Grant thought, or at least it would have been had not
Doug Ismaileh a little while later chosen to stir his own
particular oar into the general stew.

This happened maybe half an hour after Jim had made his
eulogy. Lucky had gone below to use the head. Jim had
gone forward to trim sail for the captain. So they two were
alone with the captain. Grant had gone forward to sit on the
coachroof and lean his arm on the main boom. Doug came
up and squatted beside him.

" That was a hell of a speech old Jim made you there,
wasn't it? I guess I was a little jealous," he said with a sly
Greek-Persian grin on his broad, sly-eyed Greek-Persian
face. " Ask anything and he'll do it for you. It's a good thing
you don't have to ask him to take care of your wife for you,
ain't it?"

Grant was startled. He hadn't thought Jim's crush on
Lucky had been *that* apparent. On the other hand he was
certain Doug had tumbled to exactly what the actual situation was between them, himself and Lucky, though Doug had
never once said a word about it, or asked a question. So
what kind of a remark was that, then? He did not answer
for a moment, and when he did, he grinned. " Yeah, it is,
ain't it? But I don't think that's likely to happen for some
very good long time in the future." He added, " Poor guy, he
does seem to be pretty stuck on her, don't he?"

Doug did not answer this. Whether this was the reaction
he had expected from Grant, or whether he had hoped for
some totally opposite reaction, Grant could not tell. After
a few minutes Doug got up and went aft and occupied himself with getting a beer from the ice-chest. Grant thought
Grant had won that exchange. But the theme was to be

repeated with variation, like some piece of 19th Century music, almost as soon as they got back to Kingston. This time it was Lisa.

Lisa had not changed much—externally—since the night of her big blow-up at Grant, either in her ideas of her application of them. She still obviously felt, like some clucking mother hen, that her Lucky had been treated badly and that Grant was responsible, but now she kept it to herself. She did not keep it to herself so much that Lucky did not know it though, and what the two girls—two women— talked about alone together he had no idea of. Lisa had never once said a word about her drunken blow-up, treating it exactly as though it had never happened (René had apparently talked to her), and everybody else had treated it the same way, choosing to let well enough alone. Whether she had changed internally was another thing, but her own worries and her troubles that she had brought out and displayed so openly that night now remained clearly in the open and visible to anybody who had been concerned that night. René spent an awful lot of afternoons in town, doing work for the hotel, when Grant was absolutely sure there was no work for the hotel that needed to be done, though he did not mention this to Lucky.

In any case it was Lisa who variated on the theme of Lucky and Jim Grointon. And she did it—so much more subtly than Doug—almost entirely by indirection. She did it by talking about Jim's other " skindiving couple " that he had taken to the Morant Cays.

She of course would not have done it had not just the three of them been alone, but the three of them were alone. Jim had gone on off with the captain to berth and batten down the little ship after the finish of the trip. René was in town. Doug had gone off to town too, to the Myrtle Beach Hotel where some guest staying at the Crount had told him a girl that he knew had checked in while he was away. So, after all the hellos and kisses and hugs and how-was-its had been given and accepted, the three of them *were* alone in the bar, the dim, cool, remembered bar with the remembered sea glinting susurrously outside beyond the white-hot beach.

Lisa's story differed from Jim's own only in one major stated point, and one unstated point. The wife of the " skindiving couple," Lisa maintained, was by far the better diver

of the two and was Jim's main pupil of the couple, while Jim
had stated plainly to them that it was the husband who was
the better diver. No, Lisa said; the wife was an excellent
skindiver, the husband a good bit less so. Lisa believed that
Jim had told this lie deliberately for protective coloration because of the unstated point. And, the unstated point, Lisa
said, because naturally Don Juan-Gentleman Jim would
never say so (though he might, and did, imply it), was that
Jim was screwing the wife all that time. Both before the trip
and after it, and apparently even during it. Here Lisa looked
at Lucky with a sly look, and both women laughed, a sort of
private but strangely obscene and raucous, special, women's
laugh. The story was, Lisa went on, that he took her off
" booby " egg hunting, that this was how he accomplished
it on the trip.

Grant very carefully forced himself not to look at Lucky,
who (he nevertheless felt) was looking closely and hard at
him. Didn't he trust her? Sure he did. Well then?

In any case, Lisa wound her story up, the husband and wife
had gone off happily back to New York or wherever the
hell it was they lived, and nobody was the wiser.

Grant found himself growing flamingly, dangerously furious. This story had all of the worst element of cuckoldry,
which was that the husband had been duped, had been so
stupid or insensitive that his wife could horn him and he still
went right on happily loving her. That was the worst nightmare of all. " But how do you know what kind of big fights
they had when they got home?" he finally said. " And anyway how do you *know* he was screwing her?" he demanded,
feeling somewhat *see* them screwing? Did anybody?"

No, Lisa said, but she would be willing to bet her bottom
ten-shilling note that she had. In any case, he got the credit
for it everywhere around, which was just about as good.
Again she looked at Lucky, and again she and Lucky laughed.

" Sure, and good for him," Grant said brutally, " except
that then he *didn't* get the fucking."

" Sometimes," Lucky said in a veiled voice, with that same
veiled look Grant had learned to recognise now but still
could not interpret, " sometimes I think Ron loves Jim better
than he loves me."

"Now what the hell kind of a remark is that?" Grant demanded, furiously:

"It's not a remark," Lucky smiled at him. "It's a statement."

Grant knew only that he had been 100 per cent right up in GaBay, when he had suggested that to come down here to Lisa was the worst thing Lucky could do under the present circumstances. That night he availed himself of his " fucking privileges " again.

Jim had been present for dinner that night at the hotel (on Grant's check of course) and so had Doug, but Al Bonham had not shown up. Bonham had apparently flown back to further prepare for the *Naiad*'s maiden trip. René and Lisa ate with them too. But in spite of that they were neither one very loaded when they finally went off to bed.

"I'm pretty hard up after that trip and not getting laid at all for a week," Grant said, "I'd like to invoke my ' privileges '."

"Okay. Fine," Lucky said. "I'm pretty hot myself."

"Ooo," she said after they had been at it for a while. "I do like it. I really like it." In one way this made Grant feel good and in another it did not.

"I would like to point out to you," he said afterwards, resting his forehead lightly on hers while he remained inside her, "that I love you very much."

"Sure," Lucky said, quickly and shortly, "me too. Now get off of me, will you?"

Grant, who had always been a counter-puncher, whose very nature it was to be a counter-puncher, said as he rolled away, "Maybe we could figure out some system of payment."

"What?"

"I mean, like so much for an ordinary lay, so much for a blow job, so much if I blow you. Then you could have your own cash, your own allowance." He had had about all of this that he wanted to take.

Lucky was eyeing him coolly with cold eyes. "That's not a bad idea," she said, thoughtfully.

"Oh, come off it!" Grant suddenly found himself levelling, something he had carefully promised himself he would not do. "Look, how long is this going to go on? I told you the truth. Because I thought I owed it to you. And because I thought it would help you. Help you understand something. Now how long is this going to go on?"

"You didn't tell me the truth very damn' quickly, though, did you?" Lucky said. "Oh, I'd like to forget it," she said, in that kind of child's wail he had often heard her speak in in earlier, happier days. "I'd like to. I want to. I really do. But I can't. Maybe there's something wrong with me?"

Without answering this Grant got out of bed. There was a bottle and soda on the table across the room. "Maybe we better have a nightcap drink," he said. Pride. Oh, damn pride, *fuck* pride! Lucky accepted the remark, and the drink, in cold silence.

It all came to a head the next night. This was the eve of Doug's departure on the noon flight the next day, and somehow or other it all caught up with Grant that evening. He would never be sure just how much of it Doug was responsible for. But in the end that didn't really matter. In the end everybody had to account for what he did and said himself. Jim Grointon had had dinner with them again, of course, and then stayed on to drink with them because it was Doug's last night and he wanted to make a good good-bye for him and because he really, as he said, hated to see old Dug go. They had all been out together on the catamaran that afternoon. In the end they four outstayed everybody so that finally there were only the four of them around a table and Sam the bartender left in the bar.

Lucky had been unusually scintillating even for her, keeping them all laughing with her wit and off-beat, iconoclastic (and generally sexual) humour and remarks. When she was like that, laughing openly and throwing back her head to shake that champagne-coloured hair, almost nothing could be as beautiful and as desirable. Finally she had told again the story that Grant had heard only once before (on their long drive down to Florida), and to which he could only give the Thurberesque title *The Night Somebody Peed or Peed Not in the Holy Water*. They were shooting one of those saccharine nun's pictures in the Fifth Avenue cathedral for some big-time Hollywood producer or other, and they had to shoot in the wee hours of the morning so they could have the cathedral empty. They had this horrible sickly-sweet lady star, one of those like Loretta Young had been for the last

generation, playing the nun. Lucky and all the other young
bit players had had to stand around in the cold while they
shot the star over and over to be sure they had all her
profiles right. All of them were sickened by it and stood
around making cracks about the church and Madison Avenue,
and somebody had a flask to warm them up, and at one point
Lucky said she wished she was a boy, and had a thing, she'd
pee in the holy water. Some Italian boy who also had had a
lousy Catholic background piped up and said he would do it,
but he would have to get paid in case he got caught and got
fired off the picture. So Lucky had bet him her night's pay
(and they were getting double-time because of the hour!)
that he wouldn't do it. He had done it (it was dark right
then at the back of the church), and she had had to pay him
her double-time night's wages. But it had been worth it when
later they shot (over and over, of course, to get her profiles
right) the sweet sweet star blessing herself in that same font
of holy water with pee in it. They almost all got fired for
giggling. Grant seemed to remember that the first time he
had heard the story the Italian boy had chickened out and
had *not* peed in the holy water, and she had not lost but had
won a night's pay of double-time. And he remembered nothing about the star blessing herself. But it didn't matter. Even
Sam the bartender at the bar was laughing to himself behind
his subterfuge of the glass polishing. And Grant remarked
the looks of total admiration—and sort of awed disbelief that
anything as outrageous and lovely as she could actually exist
—on the faces of Doug and Jim. It was those looks that
prompted him to say what he said.

"It's too bad," he said with his nose in his glass. "Too
bad old Doug has to be leavin' to-morrow. Now you'll only
have two of us in love with you."

It wasn't just only the looks. It was also everything that had
happened to them, so suddenly and so strangely, since he had
told her about Carol Abernathy. It was a whole host of
things, resentments including Lisa's cackling story about Jim
and the "diving couple", and Doug's comment the day before
on the homebound ship. She could be so damned infuriatingly
attractive. And of course he was drunk.

"What?" Lucky had flushed crimson. "What? *Two*
lovers?"

" O' course there's always old Ben," Grant said maliciously. " And René."

Lucky was blushing. " I only told the truth. A true story."

" Hell's bells, that's all right!" Grant said. " I only told the truth too. Well, look at them! They'd both give anything they got to screw you!" He *had* told the truth.

Slowly Lucky looked at the other two men.

" Isn't it?" Grant said.

Doug came up with a half-guilty smile and washboarded his forehead at her. " He's right. At least he's right as far as I'm concerned."

Jim Grointon said nothing, and only smiled his slow Irish-cop's smile.

" 'Course, unluckily for us, he got you first, honey," Doug grinned. Jim Grointon still said nothing, and only smiled, that same slow smile, as if he had the situation well under control.

" What the hell?" Grant growled.

" I guess it's time to knock it off," Doug said lightly. " I got to be out of this stinkin' joint by about eleven." He got up.

Lucky got up too. She shook back her pale-blonde hair and laughed. " Well, see you all to-morrow. We'll all see you off, Doug."

Then Grant and Jim got up. Grant watched the diver closely, all ready to really swing hard on his smug cop's smile if he made one wrong move, but Jim seemed to sense this and backed off easily, and confidently. " Good night," was all he said.

When they were in the suite and she had gotten into her robe, Lucky sat down at the dressing table and began to brush her hair furiously. Grant got out of his clothes and got himself a drink and sat down on the bed and stared back at her in the mirror. Okay, so she was pissed off at him. He still had told the truth. Always tell the truth.

In the mirror Lucky took her eyes off him and focussed them on her hair. She had on her face that same strange veiled look he had been seeing there so many times lately and had never been able to plumb or understand. " Would you like for me to have an affair with Jim?" she said.

The words seemed to hang on in the air after themselves, like the ends of the stanzas in Yeats's *Innisfree*, going on and on in silence after the words themselves have been said and have faded away. Grant felt almost exactly as he had felt when he watched the shark's flank going on and on and on past him and then the numbing jerk on his hand. Shock? *And live alone in the bee-loud glade*. Bing. Bing. Bing. He took a very deep breath, and let it out slowly. " Are you kidding?"

" No, I'm not kidding at all," Lucky said, her voice as veiled as her face. " I never kid about things like that."

" You mean you've got the hots for him?" Grant said.

" Well, a little. In a way. Let me just say that he's the first man I've met since I met you that I'd like to go to bed with."

" Well!" Grant said, and took another deep breath. His body started walking back and forth across the room with him. " Well. Let me just say this. You just go ahead and do whatever the fucking hell your little heart desires, sweetie. And then we'll just see what transpires." He thought that sounded threatening enough, but apparently it didn't.

" Is that all you care for me, then?" Lucky said in a sour voice.

" Look," he said. " I'm not about to ride herd on my own wife. I'm not about to yank you away from here and take you back to New York, either. You just go ahead and do whatever you want to do. Then I'll make up *my* mind about what *I* want to do. Okay?" He thought that *that* was plain enough, but later on he was to wonder if he had perhaps been ambiguous and not made himself fully clear. It *was* true, as Lucky would eventually point out to him, that he had not *actually* said that he would leave her.

" Okay," Lucky said. " Good night."

THIRTY-TWO

She lay awake a long time, staring up straight above her in the darkness at where the ceiling ought to be, at the blackness that had been the ceiling before the lights had been put out. She could focus her eyes exactly on the height of the invisible ceiling even though she could no longer see it. Funny how you got used to things. Physical things. She wondered, was deeply curious about, what kind of and how big a thing Jim Grointon had. From the bed beside her there was no sound. She almost wished he'd have another of those night-mares.

They had made up before over one of those.

But this time was not the same. This time was really serious. She realised he had put up with a lot of shit from her the past two weeks. She also realised that, in his own way, whatever that was, he really loved her too. The question was, was that love (whatever the *hell* that love was), was it worth it? That was the damned question.

The thing that destroyed her the most was that he had actually screwed that old cunt after knowing her—twice, he had—after sending her, Lucky, back to New York. How *could* he have? And if twice, why not more? If *once*, why not *five* times? *Fifty* times? In any case once was enough. That implied that everything that had happened between them in New York had been simply a lark, a joke, a lie, a short—if intense—fling with a New York " cutie ". In other words, her. That was all she meant to him: he was like all the other cheap pricks she had known, like Buddy, Clint Upton, Peter Raven, that Englishman, the Hollywood pro-ducer: an easy-lay beautiful New York " hot number ". And if that was true, he was only weak, like all the rest of *them*. Or just cheap inside.

She remembered how the marriage had been brought about mainly by Lisa, Lisa and her black swan friend Paule Gordon. *They* had done it all. Grant had done nothing. He had merely drifted with the current. So had she herself. If Lisa and Paule had not done all the hard and dirty work, there wouldn't have been any damned marriage. And she couldn't stand the thought of a *weak* man. A cheap-inside man.

Jim Grointon might not be very bright. But he certainly wasn't weak. She couldn't stand being married to a *weak* man. God! When she suggested to him having an affair with Jim, he hadn't even hit her!

Maybe she ought to do it to him. God knew he deserved it. He was really weak, a baby-boy who had got himself attached to that powerful Carol and could never leave her. Until somebody—and not herself, but Lisa and Paule Gordon—

had forced him, weakly, like some rudderless boat, to marriage.

Christ!

On the other hand, if she did do it to him, she knew that it was all finished. Even if she did it so secretly that he never found out, how could she respect a man who didn't even know when his wife was cuckolding him? And if he knew, he'd kick her out. She was sure of that.

God, but she was mad at him! *Sick* of him. It burned all through her, through all her arteries and veins and nerves like dry ice, searing everything.

Maybe that was the best way, really. She could always go back to the old Park Avenue tenement and Leslie and start waiting again. Waiting again for—how many years?

It would be hard on the pride. Her friends could all laugh at her. Lucky Videndi and her two-months' marriage to Ron Grant the playwright. But that would die down eventually. And he would have to pay her something, some kind of money, except that screw him she didn't want any of his damned money. She would have gotten even with him with Jim Grointon, anyway. Maybe after all that was the best way. How *could* he have done to her what he'd done?

He shouldn't have told her. In the first place. He should either have told her in the very beginning, or else not told her at all. She hadn't asked him. She hadn't even wanted to know. But above all he should not have carried her along all this time, and lied to her, *lied* to her!—and then try to niggle out by telling her "the truth" after the big climax had happened. That was just cheap. Cheap, chickenshit and cowardly. Why, that was just exactly what that old woman had been pushing him to do! And him! he had played right into her hand and done it, done just exactly what she had planned for him to do! If she herself, Lucky, had not packed up and left for New York right then and there, it was through no fault of Carol Abernathy!

And all that bullshit about how he wanted to protect Carol's and Hunt's reputations, how he wanted to save Carol's *literary* reputation for her, because he didn't want to destroy her totally—even though it *was* false, the reputation. Again a shudder of disgust ran all through her turning her stomach over sickly, only this time it was disgust with herself. To let herself get trapped like this.

But then the thought of going back, back to all that of before, that year and a half that she had spent after Raoul had been killed, the very thought of going back to that life was almost more than she could bear. The old Doom-Gloom feeling came up in her that was always there, lurking around somewhere in the bottom of her. The old superstitious goddamned Catholic that told her she must be punished. She was being punished now. The superstition had told her all along she would be punished by not being allowed to have Ron Grant, but she did not know then the manner of the method. Now, it was turning out, she would not be allowed to have Ron Grant because the Ron Grant she wanted did not exist. Never had existed. She had made him up. That was the worst of all.

She was not a whore! She was not a whore, and she never had been one, and she didn't care what any of them said! They were all lucky to have had her, by Christ! And she had never hurt a single one of them! Instead she had helped them all, or almost all.

As far as Jim Grointon went, she *was* attracted to him physically. She had always liked that kind of stocky wide-shouldered husky man best. Ron was one himself. And Ron *had* acted as though he wanted her to have an affair with him: telling her right in front of him that he, Grointon, was in love with her! What kind of half-fag stuff was that? She was getting sick and tired of these half-fag outdoor types that loved each other better than they any of them loved their women. They all treated women as if they were some kind of bottle which held their dope or booze and after they emptied the bottle of whatever necessary contents it contained threw it away, or better yet took it back to the grocery store and turned it in for a discount on a new one.

All these goddam men in love with each other. She had about had a bellyful of it. She had never seen so much of it. Bonham in love with Grant, and Grant in love with Bonham. Grointon in love with Grant, and Grant in love with Grointon. *Hunt* in love with Grant, and Grant in love with Hunt. Doug Ismaileh in love with Bonham *and* Grant. There didn't seem to be any place left for a simple ordinary female woman.

There was some quality about her husband that seemed to attract certain types of men to falling in love with him. For starters she didn't like *that* ; but further, she could tell, sense, smell that all these types in some perverse way ached to fall in love with her too. Have her, to use grandmother's phrase. Was it only to get that much closer to him, to Ron? Or was it just the reverse. Anyway, they all had it. Even Bonham had it, in the sort of reverse upside down way of a high schoolboy who insults and teases the young girl of his choice in order to attract her attention. And certainly Doug and Jim Grointon had it. Of them all only Hunt could she sense not to have it, and Hunt was . . . God, what was he?

She remembered that she could hardly believe it when she saw Hunt crying. It was sickening ; enough to make you vomit. Here was a guy who had been screwing his wife, practically right in front of him all these fourteen years- and when the guy leaves—finally, and for good and all—this sick creep starts to weep over his departure. How sick could you get? Pure disgust seasoned with a peppery sauce of strong dislike—even hatred—for most all men made her stomach turn over and caused her to shudder involuntarily. And as far as Ron went that made *him* little better than a paid professional gigolo.

Did he suspect that Jim had already told her *himself* that he was in love with her? Was that it? Could he have guessed? He was shrewd. It had happened the second time Jim had taken her booby-egg hunting, over on the far side of the island. She hadn't even told this to Lisa. Although Lisa apparently suspected it. The ugly birds had all flown off screaming (she *hated* birds, anyway) and hovered off in the air squawking and protesting from a distance. Jim had squatted by the first nest, and then had suddenly looked up at her with that dirty-Irish-cop squint in his eye. Really dirty. That was kind of intriguing too, in its way. " I guess you know I've fallen in love with you," he said.—" No, I didn't," she had answered immediately. "And I certainly never intended that." Jim had grinned that slow exasperating smile of his. "Well, I have," he said. "And I am. I want you."—" I think I prefer not to have heard what you said," she said. " I should also warn you that Ron while not a *professional* outdoorsman like yourself was a very good boxer in the Navy."—" Oh, I'm not really worried about that part," Jim had smiled. Then he got up. " Come on, we'll find a couple more nests." For a moment she thought of asking him what he would do if she told Ron what he'd said. How could he be so sure she wouldn't?

When she did ask him later on, he only grinned and said, " Oh, wives never do. They don't want to make trouble. In the family."

But then how could he, on the trip back to Kingston, and right in front of her, make such a really flattering eulogy of Ron? There *were* certain types of men who liked to screw another man's woman just in order to get that much closer to the man. The only other answer was that his eulogy of Ron was the most totally cynical thing she had ever seen, or heard, done. She was not about to let herself be made some cheap pawn in a half-fag love affair between outdoorsmen, but the cost was high: she could feel all over her again the hard, tough cynical self-preservation sense she had worn, posed in, for so many years in New York, and that she had thought with Ron she would be able to lose, abandon. Now, apparently, she couldn't. That was high cost indeed.

She just didn't know. She just didn't really know, that was the truth. There was about Jim, in addition to the physical, she had to admit, that attraction of the dirty-cop, the " devil " thing. It was somewhat the same feeling she had had about the black-jacketed motorcycle rider on that long-ago Sunday over in Jersey. This was certainly nothing to " build a life on ", obviously. It was true that Jim was also the only man she had been the slightest bit attracted to since she had met Ron. But she was also smart enough to know that had it not been for the entire Carol Abernathy thing, there would not have been the slightest incentive in her to be the slightest bit attracted to anybody.

Oh, that miserable *son* of a bitch! How dare he do something like that to her? To take her up there, to *live* with that old woman when *all* of them *knew* she had been his mistress all those years. How could *anybody* ever forgive *anybody* for doing a thing like that?

She didn't know. She just didn't know. She would have to wait and see.

It would be such a relief to run off and screw another guy. She was tired, already tired, of complex responsibilities of trying to cope with Ron Grant's complex nature. A simple fuck with a simple man would be such a relief. Especially if the other guy adored her, and was therefore easy to handle.

She knew Grant would throw her out if she did it, and she didn't want to lie to him ever (would not respect him if he believed her in her lie). So it would really be the end. The real end. And yet underneath all that she was sorely tempted. He deserved it. Being the wife of a Kingston diver was no great point in favour, certainly. Of course she could change *him*. But she didn't really *love* him. Finally she slept.

In the morning, while they got up and dressed to go down for coffee, he said hardly a word to her, one icily polite " Good morning," and looked at her with such chilling, such astral distance that she was at first disbelieving and then infuriated. Was that all he was going to do then? Was he just going to go right ahead and *let her do it*? Then by God maybe she would do it!

If he could have just once apologised, said he was sorry, admitted he was wrong about taking her up there to Ganado Bay to live with his damned ex-mistress. Ex? Ex-, my ass! She was hardly even ex-.

Doug was already down and packed, his two bags sitting there and heating up on the sun-drenched porch, and was having himself—apparently—the second of a series of celebratory Bloody Marys. Jim Grointon was having one with him and smiling and laughing, but he was really only sipping at his. Jim had never really been a drinker, not in the class with Doug and Grant. And that was as well. Neither had she been for that matter, until she met Grant.

René and Lisa were both there, Doug had paid his bill already, and was humorously—though clearly with a certain amount of serious concern—complaining about how high it was. After they had joined the group and sat down, Lucky secretly but seriously looked at Jim appraisingly, coldbloodedly, the way she had used to look at men back before she fell in love and became a married lady. She could break him all up into tiny shattered pieces and throw him away, she was convinced. He deserved it *too*. She remembered Bonham holding forth on him once in Ganado Bay, telling about him and some other diver's wife in Yucatan, another friend's wife he had done. The two men had finally had a big fist fight about it, which neither of them had won, and the other guy had left his wife. How any man could stand up as he had and openly brag upon another man as his friend when he was trying all the time behind his back to hurt him by cuckolding him with his wife, Lucky simply could not understand. It was truly awful. And it made some answering "devil" in her herself giggle secretly.

And Ron—Ron Grant—her husband!—was acting exactly as if he didn't care. He was treating Jim exactly the same way he had treated him yesterday, before her speech of last night. And when they left for the airport, and Jim asked if he might have lunch with them, Grant agreed and said of course he could. Ben and Irma would be there too of course, but even so! He had to be doing it deliberately.

Ben and Irma had wanted to go in too and see Doug off, so there had been quite a crowd since both René and Lisa were coming, plus their oldest son Ti-René (for Petit René) who had become quite a fan of Doug's, and wanted to come too. René drove the hotel's bigger car, not the jeep, with Lisa and Ti-René beside him in the front, and Doug sat in the back with Ben and Irma. Lucky and Ron rode with Jim, in his older much more beat-up jeep. Jim had asked Ron if they'd like to ride with him, and Ron had said of course they would. For clearly sentimental reasons of his own Jim had insisted on carrying Doug's bags in the back of his own jeep, so Lucky rode between them in the front on the little jump-seat cushion Jim had had installed. It seemed that the three of them were going everywhere together now, and had been for quite a number of days now. Sitting between them with one arm along the back of each of their seats to hold on in the jouncing jeep, while trying to keep her bare legs in their shorts out of the way of Jim's hand and the gearshift, Lucky suddenly remembered the time right after their marriage when she had told Ron that someday she would cuckold him, and that he had answered that "if she did, then she would have to let him watch." Ugh. Jesus! Was he actually trying to push her into something like that now? Her own fantasy, of screwing another man in front of him while he watched, made her blush now in the breezy wind-blown jeep, but that was only a fantasy. But what else could he be doing, the way he was acting? And she still was not *un*attracted to Jim? Didn't he know that?

At the airport, while the rest of them stood or sat around the air-conditioned bar as they waited for the jet to come in, Doug had gotten her off to herself to talk to her. Doug's really enormous personal charm could captivate, and capture, just about anybody, whenever he wanted to turn it on and use it—witness the way he had captured the love of little Ti-René, and after spending almost no time with him at all, and René and Lisa too, and even Jim. Now he was using it on her, and it was working on her too. He gave her his biggest most understanding Greek-Turkish smile, complete with the sensitively, seriously wash-boarded forehead, and put his big hand on her shoulder.

" Don't think I don't know what's goin' on," he said, " and don't think I don't appreciate you."

She had recoiled—inwardly. Not outwardly. " You do?"

" And I know you're goin' to work it out."

" You do." This time it was a distant, noncommittal statement, not a question.

" I know you've had a lot of shocks. And a lot to digest. The meal is almost bigger than the stomach, as the old poet says. But I want you to know *I'm* givin' you old Papa Doug Ismaileh's vote of confidence."

" Oh, Doug." She found herself somehow trapped into honesty, almost against her will. " I don't even know if he loves me. I don't honestly think he does."

" Sure he loves you," Doug smiled. " *In his way*. Don't you know nobody ever loves anybody in exactly the same way?"—there was no pause for an answer—" and nobody knows better than me how hard, how tough he is to get along with. It would take a saint to live with him for more than a week. But I also know you can handle it."

" You think so," Lucky said faintly.

" I know so. Remember I know him longer than you. You can, you know how (no matter whatever, what-*ever-ever* could or might have happened to you in your life up to now; maybe even *because* of that!), you have the ability to handle this, him, in just about any way you choose." He paused, perhaps significantly. " Did you hear me? *Any way you choose*. And let me tell you, whatever happens—whatever you do see fit to do—I'm convinced, I'm absolutely certain, that I'll be seein' you two—together—in New York in . . . six weeks or a couple of months."

Faintly, and for some unexplained reason half-disgustedly trying to unravel the somehow unstated meaning of all this, Lucky said nothing. If he was saying what she thought he was saying—She couldn't even think it. Or that he could be saying it.

"Don't forget what I told you," Doug smiled at her warmly and gently, kissed her on the ear, then took his big hand off her shoulder and as gently led her back to the others clustered noisily at the bar. As she walked with him, Lucky felt she ought to feel uplifted but instead she had the feeling of a real, an enormous, and an honestly acquired depression and put-down. Revulsion. Both for herself and for Ron and for just about everything. And when the big Greek kissed her gently again and winked sweetly, then went through the customs departure gate and out on to the sidewalk and across the apron to the big jet and then stopped in the black cave of the hatchway to wave once at all of them, she had the same feeling, even more strongly.

They went out in the catamaran that afternoon, after the lunch both Ron and Jim himself had invited Jim to. Ben and Irma went with them, because as Ben said he wanted Irma to get accustomed at least a little to what it would be like on the *Naiad*'s cruise. ('Course, Ben told her, she'd probly be able to spend at least some of the days ashore probly, in the Nelsons, studyin' the island and all that stuff.) Lucky was glad that Ben and Irma had come along. She simply could not stand Ron, or Ron's attitude. He was completely polite to her; he had helped her into and out of the jeep on the airport trip, had opened every door for her, and now he was just as considerate and solicitous of her getting into and out of the boat. But all the time there was this astral—*astral* was the only word she could give for it, it was so far away—distance about him. He even went so far as to go off spearfishing alone after a couple of snapper he had seen (bringing back three of them on a fish stringer, which she knew was not right, not safe, to do), leaving her alone on the boat with Jim. Of course Ben and Irma were there on the boat too, at least Irma was. But even in spite of that she noted (without understanding) that he treated Jim just exactly the same as he had always treated him. He did it almost scrupulously. That night just before dusk when they returned, they found that Bonham and Orloffski had arrived.

The arrival of Bonham and Orloffski took a great deal of the pressure off her. Much as she disliked the both of them, she was grateful for that. All of the talk all evening was of course of the *Naiad*, since they had come down this time to see her actually put in the water and take her over, and even Jim Grointon's talk was all about the ship and the proposed trip. Ron was so excited by all of it that he once so forgot himself he put his arm around her and gave her a big grin. He could be really lovable. He got so excited and enthusiastic over everything. He insisted they must go down to-morrow and watch her be put afloat.

Lucky went. But Jim Grointon (who was as high over it all as the rest of the men) also went too. Once again Lucky rode in the front seat of the jeep between the two of them, one arm along the back of each of their seats to hold on. Ben and Irma rode in the back. They rode back the same way. She had to admit it was a beautiful sight to watch the big wheeled carriage lowered down the gently sloping ramp by the big winch until she, *Naiad*, was actually on her own floating and rocking in the harbour water. Naturally they all went on board her, afterwards. And while nothing at all had been done about the sleazy, dirty, completely unprivate quarters and accommodations, Lucky could feel and had to admit also that the way the deck felt under your feet, more alive, when she was afloat, was different and more exciting, much more exciting.

The night before Bonham had briefed them on everything except the actual trip itself. Naturally, he and Orloffski had eaten dinner with them, naturally on Ron's check—although Bonham said (with his usual look at her) that this would be the last time, it was just too damned expensive for Ron, and he and Mo would catch their meals in town somewhere after this. And he and Mo would sleep on board, while they worked on her sails and gear and on getting her ready below-decks. He had made reservations with René already for Sam Finer and his wife, and they would be arriving in four or five days. The brain surgeon and his girl-friend would be arriving about the same time, but they would sleep on board too, to save money. The surgeon wanted to help with the work anyway. Bonham figured that after seven or eight days' sailwork, ropework, rigging, and some minimal paintwork and cleaning-up below—they would be ready to go.

The second night, the night after they had visited the ship and watched the " launching ", true to his word Bonham did not appear for dinner. But they came afterward, bringing with them all the necessary charts and maps and a pair of marine dividers and parallel rulers to lay out and brief them on the trip itself, those who were interested. Lucky wasn't. When they came to the charts of the Nelson Islands themselves, she took one look and retired to the bar for a drink without understanding these any more than she had ever understood any maps, including highway road-maps. Irma, who wasn't interested either and who understood maps no better, joined her almost immediately. So the two of them sat at the bar, drinking, and watched the five men, Bonham, Orloffski, Ben, Ron and Jim, huddling excitedly over the great mass of charts and maps on the largest of the bar's tables. Lucky could see that the other hotel guests scattered around, including the movie star and his wife, were all quite impressed. She herself wasn't.

" You're really going?" she asked Irma finally.

" Sure, why the hell not?" Irma said. Then she cackled her weird laugh. " I might even learn to swim. From those fucking boy scouts. Bonham's promised he'd teach me."

" Well, I don't think I am," Lucky said after a moment.

Irma leaned closer suddenly and glanced at the table of men. " I don't think you have much choice," she said softly. " Listen, Lucky. Ben and I've been talking. About you and Ron. We don't really know what the trouble is. Except what you told me about that ex-mistress-' foster-mother ' of Ron's. But we've decided, and I've been delegated by Ben to tell you, that you damn' well better go. If you want to save your marriage. Christ, you've only been married what? not even two months yet already." For Irma it was a long speech. " We think you *want* to save it," she added. " And we want you *to*."

" I'm not at all sure I want to save it," Lucky said thinly.

" Well, that's something else again," Irma said. She was not cackling now.

Lucky didn't answer, and instead turned to look at the men. She shouldn't have said that. It was her instinct not to talk at all about things like that, not to outsiders, even Irma. She studied the men at the table pointedly, and Irma followed suit.

They were really something. Bonham, who could—when he had to—be reasonably polite and civilised, was nevertheless completely out of place here in this chic international bar and set. But Orloffski was a horror. His crude, loud, brutal, totally insensitive voice and manner in that great beefy body made him seem doubly like an ape here in this place. A hairless ape. Unfortunately. And apparently even he sensed it this time. He kept looking around the place at the various men as if measuring them all to see if there was one man here that he could *not* whip. A sort of belligerent self-defence, which seemed to be felt uncomfortably all over the bar. A week or ten days on a ship with that oaf seemed to Lucky to be beyond the call of duty even for a wife. And Ron seemed to be liking it all so much! So did Jim Grointon, who wasn't even going along! Neither one of them had hardly spoken a word to her since Bonham and Orloffski arrived yesterday. She ordered another drink.

"Come on," Irma said. "Let's us wives get back over there."

The upshot of all this furious map-reading, discussion and measuring appeared to be that the Nelson Islands, situated in their position half-way between the Pedro Bank and the Rosalind Bank, and too small to be shown on any map except possibly those of the very greatest scale, consisted of four major islands and twelve tiny uninhabited islets strung out along and between them. The two northern ones, named appropriately North Nelson and South Nelson, which were the largest, were only about seven miles long altogether with a half-mile pass between them, and were shaped like a crazy drunken U lying on its side with the pass running through the exact bottom of the U. Because of this there was good anchorage anywhere inside the U. The two southern main islands, called Dog Cay and Green's Cay, lay sixteen miles to the south and were much smaller with a pass of only a hundred yards between them. One of these, Dog Cay, had been bought up in its entirety by a group of wealthy Bahamians, Englishmen and Americans and was in effect a private club, run English-style, with a full-time British resident manager even yet. They were notoriously hospitable to private yachts putting into their small anchorage during the off season. Three of the tiny islets lay between these and the north islands, with the other nine islets strung out in a roughly straight line south of Dog Cay for another twelve or thirteen miles. Reefs abounded everywhere along the entire group. It was Bonham's plan to head straight for North

Nelson where the capital, named Georgetown naturally, was situated, spend a couple of days spearfishing and exploring there, then head on down the rest of the group, stopping off a day or so at Dog Cay, then sail straight for home— Ganado Bay—from the small islet end of the chain. Lucky couldn't have cared less.

By the time all the chart-reading, calculation, discussion and measuring was over everybody had put away quite a large quantity of booze, including herself and Irma, who spent more of their time at the bar talking to Sam than at the table, and they all were ready to call it a day and go to bed. In a way Lucky was sorry, in spite of all the nautical shit. Going up to the suite every night now was the hardest thing she had to do in every day. She and Ron hardly spoke to each other again to-night. She herself was thinking about what Irma had said at the bar, and of the message Ben had had Irma relay. It was all getting to be that obvious, then. What must Jim think? She had a small instinct not to show herself nude in front of Ron, to do her undressing in the tiny bathroom where he could not see her, but it was only a tiny instinct and she didn't bother to indulge it. It would almost certainly only infuriate him and cause another fight and she didn't feel like fighting.

" Do you intend to go right on going out with Jim in the afternoons then?" she asked finally, after she had gotten un-abashed into her shorty nightie. She deliberately veiled her voice, so as not to make the question sound too important. Grant of course always slept nude.

" Certainly," he said from the table where he was pouring himself a last drink. " Why not?"

" What I said to you about Jim the other night didn't change the way you treat him much," she said.

" You think I intend to let Grointon know how he's managed to fuck up my home life?" he said. " You ought to know by now I'm far too proud for that. And anyway, it isn't his problem. Even if he is madly stuck on you. It's *your* problem. And maybe mine."

Lucky got into her side of the two big beds and under the sheet without answering this. " I guess that's correct," she said finally from the bed " And anyway, it wasn't Jim who ' fucked up your home life ', as you so delicately put it."

If she expected this to be a hard parting shot, there was no

T

visible evidence that it worked. If she expected an answer, she did not get one. True to his word, they went out the next day again, spearfishing from the catamaran. Ben and this time again Irma too both went along. Lucky occupied herself once again with her binoculars, studying the naked native fishermen, more to make Ron angry than for any other reason. She did love him a little sometimes—or, at least, once in a while some small tendril of what she had once felt for him touched at her lightly somewhere inside. And that was why she wanted to hurt him.

Bonham (and his sidekick Orloffski) did not show up at the hotel all that day, and they did not appear that night either. They had apparently disappeared into the interior of the schooner and intended to stay there. So they dined alone that night, with Jim Grointon naturally, and with Ben and Irma, who appeared almost visibly disturbed. Not so Jim. He apparently couldn't have been happier. And he insisted on picking up the check. He spent most of the evening loudly extolling Ron's increasing prowess as a free-diver and spear-fisherman.

It was after two more days and nights like this, days spent out on the catamaran, nights spent eating and drinking with Jim and the Spicehandlers, that Lucky, fuming and boiling inside with the tension and at the same time extreme boredom of it all, made her little proposition. She didn't want this kind of life, hadn't ever wanted it, with this kind of people, and she hadn't expected to have this kind of life when she married Ron Grant. She had thought that eventually they would live in New York, maybe spend a year or two in Europe. She was sick of it and of all of them.

She didn't know what " devil " in her made her do it. It was the same " devil " Jim had in him. Grant had had it too. Ron. Ron had had it, the " devil ", in him when she first had met him. But now that had changed somehow. After the dinner and a couple of drinks at the bar, Ben and Irma had said they felt like going into town to the illegal " casino " for a little roulette and chemin de fer. Ron had said no. He wanted to get to bed early to-night, he was tired from the day's spear-fishing and diving, and he didn't feel like going out gambling.

It was then that Lucky heard herself, almost as if it

were some totally different person, another voice, offering a counter proposition.

" But it's only twelve-thirty. Everybody else wants to go. Why don't you just go to bed, and I'll go on in and gamble a while with Ben and Irma and Jim. Jim'll look after me." The voice she heard was a little giggly, and about half, or less than half, say thirty per cent, teasing.

Grant's, Ron's voice was totally calm when he answered. But a tiny tickle of intense warning somewhere in her made her intensely aware that beneath the calm was a lot more of something entirely else.

" No, I think I'd rather have you stay with me," he said. " And you really do look pretty tired yourself, as a matter of fact." He smiled at her friendlily, lovingly.

" All right. If you say so," Lucky said.

" I don't think I'll go either," Jim Grointon smiled. " If we want to get a full day's diving in to-morrow, I better get some sleep myself." But he hadn't said that before.

As she followed Grant, Ron, docilely to the suite she thought that at least she could now be reasonably sure he wasn't *pushing* her at Jim, anyway.

After they had undressed, he turned to her and spread his arms out slightly from his sides, palms toward her. " I want to make love to you to-night," he said in a voice that seemed quietly full of despair. " Not just *fuck*. Make *love* to you."

" All right, Ron. I want to make love to you too," she said. She moved toward him and toward the bed. " To-night," she heard herself add. To-night I want it, but of course " it " was him. He did not answer, as he lay down beside her. Then he moved over her. Next day the Finers arrived and everything changed again.

The advent of the Finers changed quite a lot of things, but it did not change Lucky's basic problem. She still didn't know. She - just - did - not - know. If she loved him at all, a little bit, once in a while, as when he had put his arm around her and given her that grin in his excitement over the schooner, it was still not enough to overcome the deep cold anger in her for him, not enough to melt at all the thick layer of dry ice she felt herself encased in. She could not love him as she had before. She could not forget that he lied to her, and there-fore would always be able to lie to her. She was *not* a whore! Distrust. And she had thought it was all pure. She had believed Carol Abernathy was important to his work, he had led her to believe that. Had told her that. The coming of the Finers could not change any of that.

The Finers had hit Kingston, Jamaica and the Grand Hotel Crount like one of the Caribbean's proverbial hurricanes. There was no hotel jeep for Sam Finer. He had wired ahead from New York for a private limousine, even though the Crount was only three miles from the airport. And that was the way the Finers arrived.

Grant, Ron, had briefed her on them long before they arrived, but she still did not expect what she saw when they came up the steps from that limousine, moved in, were introduced, and began making themselves at home. Ron had for instance told her how very much in love they were, and how good a thing it was for them, both of them, but the moment Lucky saw them together when they sat down on the veranda for their first drink while the houseboys carried up their bags, she knew instinctively and intuitively that they were not in love at all. Instead, they obviously hated each other's guts. There was a sullen, long-suffering look on Cathie Finer's face that made this plainly evident, at least to Lucky. And how anybody could be in love with Sam Finer anyway was more than she could figure. Grant, Ron, had also told her that she might in fact know, or at least have met, Cathie Finer around New York. Lucky found that she did indeed know her, and know her better than just a few casual meetings. Cathie Finer, or Cathie Chandler as her name had been then, was one of the bigger Writer-Fuckers of Manhatten Island. One of the biggest, though she had never been a member of the " The Club ". The old Club. All of this brought back all sorts of old memories to Lucky—memories that, in her present situation, with Grant, with Ron, left her feeling terribly low and depressed: to remember that old life she had thought she was through with forever. And she knew intuitively and surely, though she could not have said just how, that at some point or other Cathie Finer—Cathie *Chandler*—had fucked Ron Grant, or Grant, Ron, had fucked her. Now that complicated matters now, didn't it?

Ron had also briefed her on the " self-made-man " " diamond-in-the-rough " guy that was Sam Finer, who was putting up, who *had* put up, $10,000 to buy the *Naiad* and start the company, and who was very likely to put up

$10,000 more, or so Bonham had said. Even so she was not prepared for the crude, loud, totally selfish, hard-eyed, sly-faced tough-nut of a little guy who deliberately squeezed her hand too hard when he shook hands with her and grinned hello. She couldn't believe it. She had hoped that at least here, with the Finers, there would be somebody nice to be along with, if they had to go on this damned trip. Ron could seem to collect more creeps, oddballs, and generally unpleasant people around him than anybody she had ever met, or maybe it was just that this sort of life, of diving and sailing and all that junk, abounded with those types. In much the same way that Orloffski had looked around the hotel to see if there was one man there he couldn't whip, Sam Finer now looked all around the hotel to see if there might be one man there who might be richer than himself. He obviously found none. And this seemed to please him. After all, most clients of the Crount were artists or in the entertainment world in some form and while they all made good livings they were none of them millionaire financiers. Sam Finer, on the other hand, made no bones about his wealth. Sitting himself down very positively he ordered himself a double martini, and offered to buy drinks for every-body seated out on the long and fairly well-filled veranda. His wife Lucky noted took only a Campari-soda.

He was not, Sam Finer said, after ordering his second double martini, going to eat, to hell with lunch he was going right down to the boat yard to see the ship, he had retained the limousine and chauffeur for that purpose, and when he had tossed off the second double, he got up to go. Ron went with him. So did Jim Grointon. So did Ben. That left Lucky with Irma and Cathie Finer. The three of them spent the afternoon at the pool.

Almost immediately the three of them hit it off. Cathie Finer, once she was away from her husband, became kind, interested, full of fun, and charming. After their "boat-widows'" lunch together with a bottle of good Bordeaux and then three coupes of champagne each at the pool-side, it did not take her long to unburden herself of her troubles to the other two, who were both so much the smart, wise and out-spoken "imported-New-Yorkers" like herself. It was all simple enough. Her husband Sam had started stepping out on her with other women soon after they had met Grant, Ron, and that stepmother or foster-mother of his with Bonham and Orloffski in Grand Bank Island. She did not know if he had already been doing it before. But she herself had only caught him and became aware of it after they returned to New York from Grand Bank. She herself had married him in all good faith, and had been true to him—at least until she had found out for sure he was stepping out, she added with a sour smile—and while they perhaps had not loved each other like Clark Gable and Carole Lombard had, she had felt they had a serious and honourable marriage. But apparently they had not. As she talked about it that other look, which Lucky could only describe to herself as like a snail drawing in its horns and pulling back into its shell when it is scared and needs protection, came back over her sensitive and pretty face. But after a fourth coupe of champagne it passed on, went gradually away like a slow cloud moving along over someone's particular plot of land on a bright day. She didn't know what they were really going to do now, and she didn't much care, she said bitterly. Then she laughed. Yes, she remembered Lucky. Once that she had seen her. Grant, Ron, had spoken a lot about her in Grand Bank, a lot. Once she had seen her, she remembered her very well from the old days, the old New York days. Well at least Lucky was one of them who had made out, one who had married and had it actually work. She was glad, Cathie Finer said, and it was good to know.

"Yes, Lucky has," Irma put in quickly, "and it *is* a good thing to know. I guess Ben and I have too. But then Ben and I hardly ever knew anybody else—except that he ran off and left me for a year about six months after we were married. But now we're back together and happy. I've been lucky. And Lucky's been lucky too." Her fine sensitive face showed all the sensitivity and sympathy of which she was capable, and even her thin dark little body in its swimsuit seemed to lean forward on its own to express its and its owner's understanding.

Lucky had no choice but to follow Irma's lead. "Yes, I've finally made it," she said, and then looked at Irma. "I never really thought I would, I guess."

"I guess none of us did," Cathie said sourly. "Not after all those years of wear on the old New York mart. Well, let's talk about something else more pleasant, hey? So you and Ben are going along with all of us on this trip too, Irma?"

Irma nodded. Lucky stopped listening. She had been struck by something Cathie Chandler had said, and this had been about meeting Grant, Ron, on Grand Bank *with* his foster-mother. She searched back through her memory, and while she could not actually remember in fact that he had ever told her this, she was sure he had because whenever she thought of him in Grand Bank she thought of Carol Abernathy being there too. But he had never told her that Hunt Abernathy had not been along. He had never said Hunt *was* along, but he had never admitted Hunt was not along either. Lucky had always assumed in her mental picture of his Grand Bank trip that Hunt Abernathy had been there too. So he had lied to her again, indirectly anyway. Oh, how could he have screwed that dirty old woman all those years? There had to be something very sick about him to do a thing like that. A large dark cloud seemed to hang all over her.

When the other two girls got up to go and change, she tuned back in. " I just don't know, Irma," Cathie Chandler —Cathie *Finer*—was saying. " He's really awfully wealthy, out there in Wisconsin. He's a crude, loud man ; but, that didn't seem to make much difference when we had our marriage going. Oh, sometimes I *hate* him! " she said viciously. " He's a very violent man, too, you know. Sometimes. Sometimes when he's really drunk."

Lucky decided instantly, intuitively, she preferred to not have heard any of that last speech. She did not know why. " Well, girls! " she cried gaily, " off to the showers. The fucking boy scouts " (Irma's now generic term for all of the sailors) " will be coming home soon! "

It did not take very long for Sam Finer's violence to erupt. It did not take long for his wealth to show itself either. When the men returned from their afternoon with the schooner *Naiad* and had showered and joined the women downstairs in the bar for drinks, everything was on Sam Finer. Drinks on Sam for everybody in the whole damn' bar ; nobody was allowed to pay for one single cocktail before dinner. Dinner was on Finer too, not for the entire clientele of course, but for everybody in their group, which now again included Bonham and Orloffski whom he had brought back with him, and of course the now ever-present

Jim—who smiled his slow evilly attractive "devil's" smile at Lucky and gave her one solemn wink behind Finer's back. Not only that, Sam Finer announced in his loud duck's voice to all and sundry, he had definitely decided after to-day to put another whole $10,000 into Bonham's corporation and the schooner. The money would be coming along as soon as he got around to it. There was no doubt he meant it. René obviously didn't like Sam Finer at all, and Lucky didn't either. On the other hand, it was clear that Grant, that Ron, was no longer going to be the "big spender" and the payer for everybody's dinners and drinks. Sam Finer was taking over Grant's, Ron's, role unto himself; and Lucky didn't mind at all. It was about time somebody did. And it was not, when the next day came around, just to stop there, either. For the next two days Sam and his wife and the entire group (minus Bonham and Orloffski, of course, who had to work on the ship) went out spearfishing with Jim Grointon in his catamaran, and Sam Finer paid for everything. Everything, and everybody, everybody's boat fees, and even including the sandwiches and beer they took along from the hotel. He had flown down his Scott Hydro-Pak aqualung with its three sets of tanks, and he used this while the others free-dove. He was volubly impressed by Grant's, by Ron's, progress, but he had never done much free-diving himself, and he didn't much like it, and besides he did not believe in being sporting to fish since fish were not sports themselves, and anyway Jim had a compressor to refill his tanks. It was on the evening of the third day that the violence erupted.

Lucky never did find out what the initial cause of it all was. Neither did anybody else that she talked to. She had already talked to Grant, to Ron, about the Finers and about her intuition that they were not at all in love like he had said.— "Well, I don't know anything about that," he said defensively, "and I certainly didn't notice it. I'm not saying you're not right. All I know is that when I first met them in Grand Bank they were as much in love as we—" and then he stopped. He had obviously meant to say "as we are." Then, as the pause went on, he plainly thought of saying "as we were." But he clearly didn't want to say that either. And finally he left the sentence as it was. It was correct enough grammatically: "as much in love as we." But it had not been his original intention, and the drop at sentence's end had

not been emphatic. Still he carried it off well, she thought—
" That's all I know," he finished, not lamely at all. She had
gone on then to tell him about the conversation they, she and
Irma, had had with Cathie at the pool. She did not tell him
her intuition that he, Grant, Ron, had screwed Cathie
Chandler at some time or other himself. " So I guess it's all
because he started cheating on her," she summed up finally.
—" Well, at least that's something you can't accuse me of,"
he had come back with, " by God."—" Can't I?" she said.
" Oh, but I can."—" Listen, if you're going to start that
again!" he said. " I explained all . . ." It was one of their
more typical evenings alone before bed.

In any case, Sam Finer had not gone out with them on
the catamaran on that third day's diving since his arrival
and had gone in town to the schooner, though he had insisted
that Cathie go along on the catamaran and had informed them
all—and informed Jim—that even though he wasn't going
they were all his guests and he was paying anyway. He had
returned that evening about six-thirty with Al Bonham, but
not with Orloffski, both of them looking a good bit the
worse for wear, René said later. They had obviously been
touring the bars in town.—And why not to a couple of whorehouses too? Lucky thought to herself when she heard it
later ; there was, from what she already knew about Bonham,
no reason to think not.

Perhaps it was only, and just simply, the drink. And not any
guilt. None of them had been in the bar—where they were all
supposed to meet him for cocktails—and perhaps if one or
two of them had been it might never have happened. She
and Grant, Ron, were still upstairs just finishing changing to
come down. So were the Spicehandlers. Cathie, who was upstairs too, apparently had heard his voice as he and Bonham
had come through the gate and along the drive and up the
steep stairs, and recognising the sound of trouble in it had
come running down. But she was either too late, or too inconsequential. He and Bonham had ordered a drink at the
end of the bar, and after knocking back half of his first one
Finer had ordered a second. The bar was already crowded
with cocktail-hour drinkers, guests in the hotel and customers
from town, and when Sam the barman had not served his
drink immediately. Sam Finer had hurled, slid, his low-slung
heavy still-half-filled glass down the long bar like one of those

pucks in those mechanical ten-cent bowling machines, sending bottles and stemmed martini glasses flying and smashing among the startled and convivially drinking cocktail customers. "I ordered a goddamned drink down here! And when I order a goddamned drink down here I expect to be goddamned served down here! And fast!" Bonham had had hold of him by this time, but this did not erase or dry the stains and drippings from the shirt-fronts and dresses down the long length of the bar. René kept two big Jamaican bouncers around the place, although they had almost never been needed in the history of the hotel, and as usual now when they were needed neither was around. René had got there as quickly as he could. "You bet-tair get your frien' out of'ere fast, Al!" he said. He was furious. "I call ze cops ozzerwise."—"Whatta you think I'm tryin' to do?" Bonham had said, still holding on to the struggling and cursing Finer who was trying desperately to get back at the bar and the barman where he felt he had been so roundly insulted. Finally Bonham had got him out on to the veranda and to the steep set of steps, where René's Jamaican "doorman" in his Haitian general's uniform came running up them to help Bonham get Sam Finer down them. Finally the two of them had got him down the steps on to the driveway, but there he had broken away from them.

By this time just about everybody in the hotel had heard the racket and come running, among them Ron and Ben who had recognised Finer's voice and hoped to help, Lucky and Irma coming right behind them. The Jamaican doorman was a big man, almost as big as Bonham if not as big around, but he was startled and off his pace because he had never had to handle anything like this. Attacking the doorman at the Grand Hotel Crount was as unheard of as someone attacking the doorman at Sardi's or Pavillon, but that was just what Sam Finer was doing. After breaking away from the two of them, he stood breathing a second or two, then rushed straight for the big doorman who had moved to stand like a guardian in front of his stairs. Finer trying to get back up the stairs and punching at him with all his power, and there was a lot of power in his stocky broad-shouldered body. The first time the doorman just pushed him back away, taking a couple of hard punches to the head while doing it. Finer came in again, and this time the doorman started punching back, although it was plain he wasn't much of a real fighter and did not appear to be particularly enjoying himself. He still looked as if he couldn't believe what was happening as he wiped some blood off a cut on his cheek.

In all Finer came at him four or five times, cursing and yelling almost incoherently all the time and actually appearing to be enjoying himself hugely. And all the time Bonham was standing back behind him saying, " Sam, Sam. You don't know what you're doing. This is the *Crount*. For God's sake, stop it. This is *the Crount*! This isn't the docks. Stop it." Up on the veranda all the bar customers had crowded to the railing to watch, even those with still-wet shirtfronts and damaged dresses. Nobody had ever seen anything like it at the Grant Hotel Crount. When Ron, who was standing right beside her, tried to push his way through to get down the steps to help stop it, Lucky grabbed his arm, but she needn't have. He was stopped by a famous New York columnist who was staying at the Crount, and who had been a good friend of his in New York for many years. " You know those people?" Lucky heard him say in a low voice.

" Yes. They're friends of mine. I want to stop it."

" Stay out of it," the columnist said in the same low voice. Though not a big man he shouldered himself in front of Ron.—" He's right," Lucky said from behind her husband.

His columnist friend nodded. " There's nearly a dozen newspaper guys and columnists and *Time*-guys around here, locals as well as New Yorkers. This'll be all over New York —as well as Kingston—by the morning edition. Keep your name out of it, for God's sake. They'd love to drag your name into it. Especially those *Time*-guys."

" He's right," Lucky said again, and felt relieved when Grant's, Ron's, her husband's arm relaxed within her hand.

Down below Sam Finer had backed off and was preparing to charge the big but befuddled doorman once again, still shouting his almost incoherent, hysterical phrases about they couldn't kick him out of this fucking place, who the fuck did they think they were, he had a suite in this fucking place ; and it was here that Bonham finally took a hand. With that infinitely patient, dogged look of a man in a rainstorm with no place to go that Lucky had seen on his face so many times before, he stepped in and half-turned Sam Finer around and as delicately as a ballet dancer clipped him, very

lightly, on the side of the jaw. Finer went down like a sack
of cement. Bonham stood looking at him sadly for a
moment as if he had just done something he had promised
himself he would never do and then, ignoring the excited
crowd up on the veranda completely, bent and picked up the
short but heavy Finer as if he were a child, flung him over
his shoulder lightly and started walking out down the curving
drive toward the gate where the taxis were. For perhaps
the second or third time since she had known him Lucky's
heart went out to him completely. Around her the excited
talking people, herself and Ron, and Ben and Irma included,
started to move back inside to their interrupted drinking,
several still complaining about their wet shirts or dresses.
Cathie Finer wasn't talking. Lucky got her by the arm and
made sure she came with them. Just as she turned to go in
she saw Jim Grointon coming up the drive looking puzzled.
As he passed Bonham who was still carrying the insensate
Finer, he stopped and said something, but the giant Bonham
did not pause or say one single word to him and trudged on
stolidly, patiently with his burden in that man-in-a-rainstorm
way toward the waiting taxis.

The upshot of all the next day was almost inconsequential.
Bonham did not show up at all, nor did Orloffski, as if they
felt this a better policy. But around eleven Sam Finer showed
up looking sheepish and wearing a big blue knot on the side
of his jaw that Bonham had given him and a very slight black
eye the doorman had managed to inflict, and went straight to
his suite where Cathie was waiting for him. He immediately
called up Ron and Ben on the hotel intercom phone, and so
the six of them congregated in Sam Finer's suite. Sam could
not go and speak to René himself, he was too embarrassed,
so Ben and Ron were to be the intermediaries for him with
René.

" I just can't," he said, " I'm just too damned embarrassed.
Anyway, he'll listen to you guys much better than he'd listen
to me. The very sight of me would probably make him throw
me out before I could even say a word. Boy, did you ever see
such a wallop?" he said proudly, fingering the lump on his
jaw. " It was perfect. Just absolutely perfect. Just hard
enough to do the job, not hard enough to hurt anything. A
perfect punch. Christ, he could of killed me if he'd wanted.
Him? It was just exactly perfect." His hero-worship for

Bonham, which Lucky knew from Ron that he had had at least since Grand Bank, had not at all diminished but rather, had increased. So that if Bonham had had any fears about losing his further $10,000 investment (which was what Lucky had suspected, in her anti-Bonham heart) he need not have worried; more likely, his action had only further insured the additional investment. " What a guy, hunh? Did you ever see such a guy, hunh?" Sam said with his eyes that glowed with admiration.

So Ron and Ben were the intermediaries for Sam Finer with René. Lucky went along because Ron asked her to, she being René's oldest friend amongst them. And because she consented to go, she asked Irma to come along too. So the four of them accosted René—trapped him, was the more likely word—in the quiet, noontime-deserted bar. Ron was the spokesman.

But Lucky was sick of all of it, and sick of all of them. Except maybe for Ben and Irma. Kids' games: hitting and fighting and apologising and going out sailing and trying deliberately to kill sharks: fucking damned kids' games. These were not any of them, these sailing-diving people, the kind of people she wanted even to spend even a small part of her precious future life with. And Cathie Chandler—Cathie *Finer*—could look after her own damn' problems; she had got herself into them. Lucky Videndi—Lucky *Grant*—had her own goddamned problems to cope with. But in any case Ron was the spokesman.

" Ronnie, I 'ave nev-air 'ave such a t'ing 'appen in my place!" René came back furiously. " Nev-*air!* Not in zee 'ole seven years I am 'ere! W'at you expec' me do?"

" Look," Ron said doggedly. " All I'm saying is it isn't going to do you any good to throw him out. That's all. We'll all be leaving here in a very few days on the cruise anyway."

" Zees guy is mishuga," René said stubbornly. " I mean her. A real mishugena. I never like 'eem. From zee firs' second 'ee harrive. Nev-air. Oy a bruch! I know 'eem that he make only tsorres w'en I firs' time see heem. I honly let 'eem in zee 'otel because eet's you. You an' Lucky."

Ron—whose methods and modes of play Lucky knew as well as her own by now—nodded solemnly and sympathetically. Then he turned over his holecard ace, as she had already figured out he would. " It will only make you more bad publicity if you throw him out, though, René. As it is, it might be a small item in a couple of columns. You throw him out and it'll get at least twice the play. Some of them could drag it on for a whole week of items if you do that."

" Zat's true," René said thoughtfully. " H'I not theenk of heem zat."

" Especially those *Time*-guys. You know how they love to knock anybody off who's up on top. And you're up on the *very* top now, with the Grand Hotel Crount." Then he added, as she had also just anticipated, his clincher. " And I can promise you, *promise* you, that my friend Leonard won't even mention it. Not one word in his column. That I can promise you. But if you kick him out— . . ."

" Hokay," René said. He made a vastly Gallic shrug of defeat, of rather admiring defeat. " You win zee 'and. You 'ave zee ass in zee 'ole. Like always. I know you, Ronnie." He tapped his temple with a forefinger several times, significantly. " You always 'ave zee ass. Hor you don' play. Hokay. But you tell zat mishugena 'ee stay out of zee bar at cocktail 'our. Hafter dinner, maybe hokay. But not hat cocktail 'our. H'I can't 'ave 'eem zere hat cocktail 'our now, hafter zat. Hand not hafter dinner eezair, prefer-ably. But certainement pas not zee cocktail time."

" Okay, I'll tell him," Ron said. " And thank you, René." He grinned. The delegation bought a drink all around to celebrate. Then they left.

The funny thing was that it, the confrontation with René, could all have been avoided, because the next day Sam Finer got a call from New York that he was needed urgently in New York on business, business that simply would not wait or he stood to lose—Sam did not tell them how much he stood to lose. But it was clearly a vastly greater sum than the $10,000 he still intended to invest with Bonham. He left that night.

They had been out nearly all day on Jim's boat, going west and south as far as Wreck Reef and the Hotch Kyn Patches to dive on both of these, nearly eighteen miles out in all, so they had left at 10.30 in the morning, taking a packed-up lunch with them, everything once again all paid for by Sam Finer. When they returned at nearly seven in the evening, the call had been coming in regularly every half-hour since noon for

Mr. Finer. After he had taken it in his suite he and Cathie had drinks with all of them (including Bonham and Orloffski whom he had telephoned at the boatyard) at one of the farthest tables down the big veranda, so as not to intrude on the to him off-limits bar. There simply wasn't any choice. He had to go. The next plane out was the nine o'clock jet direct to New York, and he had already had René get him on it. There was no possibility that he could get back before the cruise began. He would have to be in New York at least a week, and possibly two weeks. Even if he could get out of New York in one week, it would be impossible to try and meet them in the Nelsons since there were no jet flights to the Nelsons' one tiny airport. And if they left in two or three days as planned, by the time he island-hopped down in an ordinary plane they would already be on their way back to Ganado Bay. "And I know you guys, Ron and Ben, are just hangin' around here now, waitin' to start," he said in his gruff, so often thoughtful, kindly way. So it looked like he would have to miss the trip—*this* trip—altogether. "But there'll be others" he said sadly. "*God*, how I hate to miss this maiden trip! But there's no reason you should miss it, Cathie. There ain't no earthly reason on earth for you to go back to New York with me. You'll just spend your time hangin' around some damned hotel. If you want to, I think you ought to go ahead and go."

Lucky thought she had detected a slightly sly note in Sam Finer's proposition to his wife, but she was not at all prepared for Cathie's answer.

"All right, I will!" Cathie Finer said cheerfully. "I've been looking forward to this trip almost as much as you have, Sam darling. And as you say, there's nothing for me to do in New York."

So that was settled. And Sam Finer didn't seem surprised. But Lucky was surprised, and she thought most of the others were too, certainly Ron was, and Ben and Irma. Al Bonham on the other hand had a strangely noncommittal look on his big moon-face.

They all saw him off on the nine o'clock jet. Sam Finer had already ordered up his big private limousine, but even that wasn't big enough for all of them. So, after telling René to hold dinner for them, Lucky once again found herself riding in the middle of the front seat of Jim's old jeep, between Jim and Ron, once again with an arm across the back of both their seats to hold on against the jouncing. This time she was wearing a skirt. Ben and Irma—once again—rode, and hung on wildly, in the back. The others rode in the limousine with Finer.

Once the big jet was off the ground and had disappeared off into the brightly moonlit night-time sky, they all—all except Sam Finer—had a drink in the airport bar. A slightly sad, but nonetheless gay, celebratory drink over poor old Sam's departure. It was then, during this drink, that Cathie Finer informed the Grants and the Spicehandlers that she would not be coming back to the hotel to dine with them. She was sick and tired of the hotel food and she had eaten so much fish the past few days she didn't want to look at fish again. She would take the limousine into town and have dinner at one of the two or three better restaurants in town with Bonham and Orloffski—with Al and Mo, was the way she said it. After, they might go and gamble a little. So there was no point in them waiting up for her. Unless, of course, they should all want to meet them later at the little, illegal, "casino". None of them did want to. So yet once again Lucky found herself riding homeward—hotelward—in the middle of the front seat of Jim's jeep, with one arm holding on behind Jim's seat and back and the other clutching on behind her husband's.

And that was the pattern that things took, in the next days. Somehow she always seemed to find herself between Jim and Grant—Jim and Ron. Bonham and Orloffski did not finish up the schooner in two days as they had expected when Sam Finer left (later Lucky thought she guessed why), and said it would be at least two more days of work, say five days in all, before they could pull out and put to sea. Cathie Finer stopped going out on the catamaran, and spent her days in town, presumably at the schooner. She stopped eating at the hotel too and took her meals in town, presumably with Bonham and Orloffski, although in fact Orloffski did not seem to be much in evidence, whenever she did appear at the hotel with Bonham, in the car she had rented in place of the limousine. And Ben and Irma, having only these few final days left in Kingston before leaving it for good since the return from the cruise would be to the north shore and GaBay, decided to rent a car and take a three days' trip around to see some of the remaining sights they had not seen. So that left just the three of them, going out in the catamaran in that same hot baking sun every day. Herself and Jim and Ron. Herself, between Jim and Grant, Jim and Ron, Jim and her husband. And Grant, Ron, had not changed his stubborn mind or his method, had not changed his attitude toward—or his self-appointed role of open friendship for—Jim Grointon. Sometimes Lucky was sure that the people in the hotel were talking. Especially with the reputation Jim enjoyed locally. She had been proud of Grant, of Ron, when he had handled René like he had over Finer. Even though it had all been over such a poorly, low-ass, low-class gang and group of people, she had still been proud of him and the suave way he had handled it. But at the same time it had reminded her once again of the equally suave, smooth, tricky poker-player's way he had as easily handled herself over the matter of Carol Abernathy. As René had said, 'ee always 'ad zee ass in zee 'ole. He did, by God. And lways had had. That had infuriated her anew, and she found herself for perhaps the third time now looking at her husband—whom she once had thought, had *believed* she knew—with new eyes.

She had meant to invite Ben and Irma on the night she gave her spaghetti dinner. She herself had gotten as sick of fish in the past weeks as Cathie Finer had. Fish had always been her favourite food, and she had always claimed she had never had enough—could never *get* enough—of it. But now she had to admit this claim could no longer be maintained. And she had had the idea to cook up a good old serious Italian sauce that she knew so well how to make well, and have a good old spaghetti dinner. All of the better suites at the Crount were equipped with tiny kitchens, René's idea, in case any of the more select guests were gourmets and amateur chefs who might want to cook in for themselves, so there was no problem there. René and Lisa of course could not come as they had to be with and supervise the hotel's dinner. But she had certainly meant to have Irma and Ben. However, the day—the night—she had planned it for, and invited them all for, was the night they were supposed to return from their three-day trip. And they did not come back that night. She didn't know why. Naturally, she did not invite Cathie Finer, mainly because she did not want to invite Bonham, and she did not want to invite Bonham because she did not want to have to invite Orloffski. Anyway, her feeling for Cathie Finer had changed considerably in the past few days since she had become convinced that Cathie was sleeping with Al Bonham. (*That* was why the boat work had slowed up.) How in *hell* could anybody, even a bitter Cathie Chandler—Cathie *Finer*—sleep with Al Bonham? Jim Grointon maybe: yes. But Bonham? or Orloffski?

So in the end there were only the three of them again. Herself and Grant, herself and Ron, and Jim.

They had been out nearly all day that day on the catamaran, and since there were now only the two of them diving they had gone down to the place near Morant Bay, shark-fishing. Naturally she did not approve of it, but there was nothing at all that she could do about it. Nothing except go along and hope something bad would not happen. The tide was right for it to-day, Jim had said, since it would be an outgoing tide nearly all the afternoon, so they had gone. They had taken almost no fish, just enough to bleed for shark-bait, and had hunted most of the remainder of the morning and all the afternoon. Finally they, the two of them—using a Brazilian rig and two extra spearguns—had taken an almost twelve-foot tiger shark that had come nosing around and had boated it. Boated it! They had had to lash it alongside the dinghy behind the boat to get it home! Lucky could not understand them, either of them. Why did they want to do it? In any case, Ron had been drinking beer almost all day, from almost the very moment they had started. When they got home—where the shark caused a big sensation—he was plainly exhausted, if not half-drunk. He said he was going to take a nap for an hour or so until eight-thirty when Jim came. When Jim did come at eight-thirty, looking fresh and hungry, and she made them both their first serious before-dinner drink, talking and laughing loudly and clinking ice and glasses furiously, Grant, Ron, her husband, was still asleep. And he did not wake up.

Lucky was furious. He *knew* Jim was coming. And that Jim was coming alone. There wouldn't *be* anybody else. With Irma and Ben not back. She decided to let him just damned well fucking sleep. Or was that just her damned mind tricking her? Anyway, the dinner was practically ready. Her sauce had been simmering all day. All she had to do was

dump the spaghetti into the already boiling water and cook
it seven minutes. After two drinks and he still didn't wake up
she did this, and then she served it and she and Jim ate it all
alone. " Ron is terribly exhausted from that shark-fishing to-
day," was how she explained it. " I think I'll just let him
sleep. He'll probably wake up after a while. But he's awfully
tired. And I can always heat it up for him." It was after the
dinner (at which Jim ate heartily and kept up a running
pleasant conversation), when it had become pretty obvious
to everybody that Grant, that Ron, was *not* going to wake
up—it was after the dinner that Jim Grointon propositioned
her again. And this time he asked her to leave Grant and
marry *him*.

She could hardly believe it. With her husband lying asleep
(or was he asleep?) right in the next room. Instinctively,
after eating, she had gotten up and left the dining area with
her final glass of wine in her hand and moved away from him
to a chair in the corner clear across the sitting-room, so that
it was from there that she heard his proposition.

In spite of the crazy audacity of it, or because of it, Lucky
had to admit to herself it excited her a little. He was really
a real dirty-Irish-cop " devil ", this one.

" You must be crazy," she said finally. " You've already
got a wife."

" But I'm in the process of getting a divorce."

" But you've got two kids by her."

" I've got two kids by my first wife, too. She can have
them."

" She'll want your money."

" Her parents can take care of them. And her. They're
nothing but in-bred Jamaican peasants anyhow."

" *I'd* take you for every last goddamned nickel that you
had," Lucky said.

" I know you would," Jim said, and grinned. " I guess that's
one reason I'm not in love with her and am in love with you."

" Can you see me as the wife of a Jamaican skindiver in
Kingston, Jamaica?"

" Oh, I haven't always been a skindiver. And I've got a
pretty good business head. I've got plenty of contacts in New
York. I know several places I could start in at ten or fifteen
thou' a year. I'd even do that for you. To have you."

" You really would?"

"I sure would. I told you. I'm in love with you. I want you."

"Do you realise that my husband, my *husband*, might be lying awake listening to all this in the next room?"

"I know that. And I'm sorry about that. But it's the truth I'm telling you. I'd tell him too."

"He'd knock your block off," Lucky said, wondering if he would, wondering if he *could*.

"He might. And then he might not. Even then it wouldn't change anything."

"You're incredible!" she said.

"I guess I am. I can't help it. Why don't you shut the door?"

"I think I'd better," Lucky said. She did. Ron did not seem to have moved since she had last looked in at him. And only then did she realise she had placed herself in a trap, a compromising position. Jim was grinning at her from the dining-table as she sat back down in her distant chair.

'How many other wives have you told that to since you've been taking their husbands out skindiving down here?" she said sharply.

"Well," Jim said with his easy, cop's smile, "none, really. Not that. Not *exactly* that."

"You are incredible," Lucky said. "Well, the answer is no. And the reason the answer is no is that I'm not in love with you."

"Well. All right." He grinned. "Fair enough. That's straight. That's straight enough. But you'd like to sleep with me."

Lucky could feel her ears getting hot. She didn't answer. How dare he lie in there like that, asleep, or not asleep, while this went on out here, *allowing* this to go on out here. He deserved whatever he got, by God.

"Wouldn't you?" Jim grinned.

"Not especially," she said. "Not particularly."

"But maybe just a little bit? A teensy bit?" Jim grinned. Then he erased his grin. "Well, I want to sleep with you. I want you. Now. To-night. And I want you as bad as any man ever wanted any woman."

"I get all the sex I want at home," Lucky said. "More, in fact. More than I can handle almost, in fact."

Jim Grointon nodded. "I bet you do at that."

"You really are incredible," Lucky said. "I can't understand you. Here you are, openly and baldly propositioning the wife of a man you profess to like and admire. And in his own house. You've done nothing but brag him up for the past two weeks, every chance you got it seems to me, and now here you are trying to fuck his wife. I can't understand that."

"Well, I'm sorry about that," Jim grinned. "I really am. But I can't help the way I feel. I do like him. And I think I am his friend. Seriously. Better than most; as friends go. I think I even love Ron—straight, I mean—in the way some men, brave men, can love each other. It's just bad luck that I'm in love with, and want, his wife."

"I can't understand that," Lucky said, giving him the most open, coldest stare she could muster up. He really was an evil devil. An evil dirty-cop devil. Why did it excite her so? It always had. "I think that's just about the dirtiest, lowest, rottenest thing I ever heard of."

"I guess it is," Jim smiled. "I guess I'm just dirty. Hunh? I apologise for that. But I think you want me too. And I'm right here. I'm available. Just tell me—honestly—that you don't want me too, and I'll fold my tent and quietly take off."

"Whether I would want you or don't want you hasn't got anything to do with it," she said, a little desperately. "Can't you see that?"

"Okay, then. Then tell me. Just tell me."

He was still smiling that smile and his eyebrows were up with a sort of amused confidence, an amused supreme confidence. Her ears must be fiery red by now from the way they felt.

"Do you realise what you're suggesting could change *my* entire life?" Lucky said. "It wouldn't change yours."

"Oh, come on now. Isn't that just a little bit dramatic? Anyway, wasn't that what I offered you, that change, at the very start? Come on, what the hell?" he grinned. "You're always talkin' about all those four hundred men you've had, always studyin' those native fishermen's big whangs. You've been flirting with me for weeks. You think *I'd* be in there asleep if *my* broad was out here with *ME?* Now's the time to put up or shut up, Mrs. Grant."

"Are you mad?" Lucky said. "Here?"

"My car's right outside," Jim grinned. "There's even a

blanket in it. He's not about to wake up, not for a long time."

Lucky stared at him and thought about it. That flirting remark, that hurt her pride. But of course that was why he was doing it.

"'Do you realise I could take you and break you up into little pieces and throw you away? Like a busted chandelier?" she said coldly.

" Maybe," Jim Grointon grinned. " Maybe I do." Slowly he poured himself another glass of red wine out of the straw-wrapped Chianti bottle. " And maybe that's just what I'm lookin' for, Mrs. Grant," he grinned at her.

Lucky stared at him again and thought about it some more. You couldn't get away from that dirty-Irish-cop, black-leather-jacket-smelly-motorcycle thing about him. She *was* still attracted to him. And he was certainly honest enough. Considering. Oh, would she lead *him* a merry chase, a merry chase and farewell. Of course he would never marry her, and never meant to. But even so— And there was that *son* of a *bitch* lying in there asleep on his damned ass. Asleep! And who had fucked that dirty old woman after he had known her, had actually stuck his thing in that old bitch, after knowing her, after knowing her *intimately*. And had lied to her about it. He damned well deserved it. Asleep! Like Jim had said. Suddenly it was all like all those years in New York again. Suddenly it was. If they were sometimes lonely, they were certainly carefree. Responsibility-free. She was tired of responsibility.

Yet on the other hand she knew it would be all over with Grant, with Ron, if she did go ahead and do it. Wanting to was one thing, doing it another. And what kind of profit was there in that? Certainly no *money* profit in it, by God! Even if he did marry her, and did go to New York, and all that jazz he had tried to con her with. And yet—Asleep! lying in there *asleep!* If she did it and didn't tell, it would all be over anyway. What she had wanted to make of it. What she had wanted it to be. But it—that—*that* was already all over with anyway, wasn't it? It sure was. That dirty old woman. Even if he never found out, and he could be a stupid jerk sometimes even for a playwright, it would still all be all over. But it already was. All over. It *was* just like back in New York. She wished she knew what his thing looked like, she thought in a kind of crazy way, she wished she could see it. She bet it was a pretty one. Like Ron's.

Lucky stood up and smoothed her skirt and arranged herself, arranged herself to walk over to the dining table, or to go open the bedroom door. It was, it had to be, one or the other. She walked across half-way to the cocktail table against the wall to get herself a good stiff scotch, and to tell Jim Grointon the decision, her decision, that even she herself didn't yet know the answer to.

THIRTY-THREE

Grant awoke at around two-thirty. His luminous Spirotechnique diving watch with its two big brightly luminous dials, which Bonham once had sold him in the what now seemed so long ago, said two-thirty-eight when he looked at it on his naked wrist. A kind of panic had gripped him from the first second he had awakened even before he glanced at the watch, and he had waked up with that total alertness and total instant full possession of all his faculties that he had used to always wake with during the war but had not done for a long time now. Bright chartreuse moonlight flooded into the corner room from the windows on two sides, and he could see everything clearly except the four darkened corners. But there couldn't be anything there? Lucky lay quietly asleep in her own big bed placed right alongside of his own.

What could have happened? They were supposed to have a spaghetti dinner? Jim was coming? Jim! After a moment's reassurance, he got up and slipped into his robe and walked around the two double beds to look at Lucky. She was sleeping soundly, deeply, peacefully (repletely, even?), sleeping on her stomach with her head turned away from his bed and toward where he now stood, the champagne-coloured hair spread out in the moonlight like a halo. She was breathing softly and evenly, deliciously through her mouth. Totally relaxed. Like after sex. Everything seemed to be becoming a symbol, a Symbol, crazy Symbols, suddenly. Was everything what it really seemed to be, or was it all his imagination? He rubbed his hand hard over his face several times and then looked at it and saw that it was blue-coloured in the chartreuse moonlight. That was scary enough in itself. A blue hand?

Had he lost her? But why say *had*. *Was*? he losing her, was what he meant to say.

Lucky did not wake, and seemed perfectly content to go right on sleeping, perhaps forever. He did not touch her, or try in any way to wake her. Without knowing quite why, he was afraid to. So instead he walked out into the living-room of the suite. One night light, a stand-up floorlamp, was burning; but it was entirely unnecessary in that moonlight. He could never remember having looked at *things* and seen them so clearly, so distinctly, as if they were all separate and disparate universes, instead of fairly reasonably connected objects in the same room. He felt, quite suddenly and for no reason, the terrible way he had used to feel as a very little boy when he had been told, informed, that he had done a very bad thing. He went into the kitchen.

In the kitchen, which had only a very tiny window—and that covered up with those horrible chintz curtains—he was forced to turn the light on. Immediately he saw in the sink: two spaghetti plates, two salad plates, two wineglasses, three highball glasses. All had been put to soak for the house-maid in the morning. When he opened the refrigerator, so violently the door banged back against the too-close wall barking his knuckles, he did not even curse. In the refrigerator, seen under its own interior light, was a large earthen-ware bowl of spaghetti and sauce—and of course all the other normal stuff: beer, Seven-up, Coke, a dried-up piece of old salami. Each of them, each object and each group, looked as though he had never seen them before. Grant was suddenly and simultaneously ravenously hungry, and sick at his stomach and unable to eat.

Forcing himself, he got out the bowl and getting a fork out of the drawer, wolfed down the cold spaghetti and meat sauce until his belly felt full. It did not take a lot of spaghetti to achieve this. Then he put back the bowl, switched off the light, went back into the moonlit sitting-room, got a full bottle of whisky and sat down with it and a bottle of soda. He drank the nearly straight whisky until he was drunk enough, groggy enough, dopey enough to go back to bed and be sure that he could sleep. It took a while.

All sorts of terrible thoughts passed through his head, through all of him, as he sat there drinking the therapeutic whisky. Terror, fear, murder, a sense of foolish idiocy, and a sense of castration all boiled together in him until it was impossible to separate one ingredient from another in the infernal stew. Green, flaming jealousy hurt him worse than it ever had, hurt him close to yelling. But he wasn't going to yell. And all the old half-formed, only half-examined masochistic fantasies exploded and disappeared totally in the blaze of actual possibility. He would *kill* her. No, of course he wouldn't kill her. Finally drunk enough, he went back to bed. For a moment he stood looking down at her again as she slept in the chartreuse moonlight on her own side of the pushed-together double beds, the golden, champagne-coloured hair spread all about her on the pillow. She was so beautiful.

Maybe she *hadn't* done it. But then, why hadn't she waked him?

In the morning he determinedly determined to say nothing. And, strangely enough, Lucky suddenly displayed for him a love the like of which she had not shown since possibly their very earliest days in New York. Before they were even fully awake she came into his bed of her own volition, something she almost never did, even when they were on the best of terms. And when they had gotten up, and had had coffee, and then made love yet once again, and then dressed to go down and meet Ben and Irma at the pool to hang around till lunch, she had said before descending that she did not want to go out on the catamaran to-day, this afternoon, she wanted instead to spend the afternoon with him, in bed. " And I promise you you won't regret it," she whispered. She had clung to him like a frightened child in the bed ; on the stairs going down she took his arm, took it close, and said : " It's taken me a long time to get over it. And don't think I don't know how patient you have been. But I am over it now." Then she added softly, " Don't forget this afternoon." Grant accepted, hungrily. How could she possibly be treating *him* this way, now, if she had just cuckolded him with Grointon the very night before ? This was what he had always dreamed since the beginning of their trouble, that their reconciliation would be like. Then his heart stopped totally still for a long moment when he thought that if she had cuckolded him this might be just exactly the way she might act in her guilt. She would have gotten even with him over Carol Abernathy, and now she would be both guilty and frightened and trying to make it up, make amends. But, my God, wouldn't that be too damned obvious? Could she possibly be that naïve? She couldn't be.

"Why didn't you wake me up last night?" he asked calmly, conversationally, at the bottom of the stairs. Ben and Irma were waving at them from the pool. They had called this morning the moment they had got in.

"You were so beat, poor darling," Lucky said. "I just thought I'd let you sleep. You looked so really beat."

That much was certainly true enough. He had been beat. He had run out of guts again, run out of courage, run out of nerve. It was the bottle with the tiny hole in the bottom all over again, and he had watched his courage-level sink in it again day by day. It had taken every absolute ounce of nerve he had, plus all the beer, to go shark-shooting yesterday. Go shark-shooting deliberately. Why had he done it? Why did Jim do it? Why did Jim *like* to do it? He had hated it. Afterwards of course he had loved it, loved having done it, loved the stir it made when they anchored off the hotel and hauled the big shark ashore. It had looked really monstrous. Eleven feet, ten inches, give or take a couple inches gained or lost in the measuring. You could with all honesty call it a twelve-footer. And it had been so easy to kill. The problem was to catch it, not to run away from it. After it had come in to the blood spoor and started circling and nosing around, they had had to actually *chase* it, to get the Brazilian-rig spear into it! But he knew damn' well *all* sharks weren't like that. They were almost at the pool by now, Ben and Irma were getting up, grinning and waiting to say hello after their absence. Why couldn't they have stayed around? They'd said they'd wanted to help, hadn't they? God damn them. He grinned and stuck out his hand and said nothing further to Lucky.

But he watched closely all through lunch. Jim was there of course, and of course ate with them, as usual. The catamaran was still anchored off the hotel beach on the still calm sea, where they had left it yesterday when they'd swum the dead shark in. The shark itself had already been taken away, by Jim. Maybe he'd sold it. For the liver. Jim seemed, as far as he could tell, exactly as he had seemed yesterday. He got up and smiled his smile and shook hands with Lucky as he always did. Grant avoided shaking hands with him, but without making it at all obvious. When they told him they wouldn't be going out to-day, Lucky added in her normal voice with a sweet smile at Grant, "We've got an engagement this afternoon. That we just have to keep."

"Yesterday make you a little nervous, hunh?" Jim grinned at Grant.

"I have to admit that it did," Grant said. "In spite of all the beer I drank. But I guess I'd still go to-day. Except that we have this appointment we can't break." He smiled lovingly at Lucky. He was determined, certainly at least around Jim Grointon, not to show, not to let on, not even in the faintest way indicate, that he had any suspicions about last night. Good God! he thought suddenly. Poor Hunt Abernathy!

But then, that had all been different.

Watch as he might, he could not throughout the normally long lunch find any symptoms, any look, any indication at all of anything in either Jim or Lucky. Christ, if it was true, what would he do? Beat him up? He thought he probably could. What *could* he do? Beat *her* up? And what good would any of that do? Why did Americans take this thing of being cuckolded so much more seriously and as so much more un-manning than Europeans did? Europeans didn't even care, didn't give a damn. Or so people said. Europeans just went out and got *themselves* a girl. Or so people said. Immediately after the lunch the two of them retired.

They did everything. Just about everything two human beings could do together sexually, assuming that one of them was a male and that the other one was a female, they did that afternoon. And they spent the entire afternoon at it. Not even in the early days of their love affair in New York had they ever made love any more passionately, furiously, tend-erly, lovingly, rupturingly, than they did this afternoon. And in most of the new things Lucky was the instigator, the aggressor. Grant had always been too shy. It was Grant's dream of what a love affair—of what *all* love affairs for *all* people *every*where—ought to be like. And yet deep in his mind his suspicions of her, of Lucky, of his wife, were not allayed. Could she do a thing like that to him? Could she? And then be like this?

"Why did you suddenly change so suddenly?" he asked

once when they were resting between bouts on the bed. Lucky
was lying nude in the bed beside him and fingering his chest.
Suddenly he had a mental picture of another man lying here
with her, doing all these things with her, that they had been
doing. The man in the picture was faceless, but he appeared
to be built suspiciously like Jim Grointon. " I mean, yesterday you were still furious at me. What *caused* you to
change?"

" I just decided it had gone far enough," Lucky said lightly.
" I just realised that it could really wreck our marriage. And
I find I don't want our marriage wrecked."

You don't, hunh? was what Grant thought. But what was
it suddenly made you find that out, hunh?

" You're quite a man, you know," Lucky said lightly. " Not
only in the sack, a good lover. But in other ways. I realise
you had serious integrity problems. With all that Carol
Abernathy business. I accept that you had to take me up
there. I wish you hadn't had to. I wish you hadn't lied to
me. I wish most of all you hadn't actually fucked that dirty
old woman, after me."

" I tried to explain about that," he said in a low voice. " I
didn't want to hurt her."

" So instead you hurt me," Lucky said lightly. " But it's
all over. I'm willing to forget it. It's under the bridge. And
I find that I do need you, darling. Darling Ron." She began
to tickle him where it counted.

Grant said nothing. The thought of it, of that other, faceless, man, was more than he could bear to think about. Had
Hunt Abernathy ever thought like that? But Hunt and Carol
hadn't been making love for years by that time. After a
moment he began to tickle Lucky where it counted, too.
How, why, when did she *suddenly* discover so suddenly that
she needed him? was what he was thinking and asking himself.

He watched again, all through dinner (at which Jim
Grointon ate again with them, at Grant's own express invitation; he would have died rather than not invite him), and he
watched all through the drinking and fun and talking in the
bar that followed after dinner. He could not find one single
look, or glance, not one innuendo, that he could point to,
use to prove to himself that she—*that she and Jim*—were
lying to him, living a lie out *for* him. Ben and Irma, who ate

with them of course, were both visibly relieved and elated over their so sudden making up, becoming again the early lovers they had known. Not one thing could he find.

It had to come out. Later he would wonder just *why* it had to come out. But at the time there was no wondering. His manhood was affected here and he had to find out. After all of it, though, he did not find out.

He waited until they had retired for the night. After Lucky had crawled over into his bed beside him, nude, and lay hugging him (almost desperately, it seemed to Grant), he brought it up again.

" I still don't understand why you didn't wake me up last night," he said.

" I told you all that, darling," Lucky murmured against his shoulder.

" But it doesn't make sense," Grant persisted. " It just doesn't make sense, unless of course you wanted to be alone with Jim Grointon."

Lucky pulled away from him and half sat up. " What?"

" You heard me."

" What would I want to be alone with Jim Grointon for?"

" What for? For Christ's sake, the other night you asked me pointblank, outright, if *I* wanted you to have an affair with him, didn't you?"

Lucky's voice was now no longer soft, or loving. " Only because you embarrassed me by saying, right in front of him and in front of me, in front of everybody, that he was in love with me."

" Well, he was. Is."

" Yes," Lucky said. " He is. And I'll tell you one thing: he asked me to leave you and marry *him*. Are you trying to imply that you think I slept with him last night?"

" No, but you could have. I'm asking you did you."

" Do you think I could do something like that to you, and right here in your own house?"

" Yes, I think you might have. You've been furious with me since I told you about Carol Abernathy. You might have done it to get even. And you could have gone out. Out somewhere with him. I would never have known." The picture of that faceless man and Lucky together nude, nude and doing things together, would not go out of his head.

"Do you think I could do something like that with him, and then be with you the way I've been to-day?"

"Yes, I think you might. If you found it wasn't very good, and found you were still in love with me after all, and then were guilty and afraid. Yes, I think that."

"I think *you're* crazy," Lucky said coldly. "I think you *want* me to fuck Jim Grointon. I think you're some kind of a crazy half fag."

"You already told me he asked you to marry him," Grant said just as coldly. "What did you say to him?"

"I told him no. That I was in love with my husband."

"All I'm asking is that you tell me that you didn't fuck him last night, that's all."

"All right. I will. *No!* No, I didn't fuck him last night, or any other time. And furthermore do you think I would ever admit it to you if I did? The answer is no. I didn't fuck him. Okay?"

"Then how do I know you're not lying?"

"You don't. You don't, do you? You just don't. All you have is my word for it, and that's all you're ever going to get. Ha, ha, you son of a bitch. No, I didn't do it. Okay?"

"I could ask him," Grant heard himself say.

"He wouldn't tell you either," Lucky said. "If he had."

"If I thought you had," Grant began.

"What would you do? And I'll tell you something else, Mister Smart-Ass, Mister Smart-Ass-Fag,—because I swear I think you are—I'll tell you something else." She had gotten out of bed by now, and had put on her robe, and was calmly and coldly tying its thick corded belt around her. "I'll tell you something else. I'm not going on your goddamned crazy cruise with you. I happen to still be in love with you, and never mind how or why, and I'm not at all sure that you deserve for me to be in love *with*. But I am. But I'm not going on your crazy cruise with you, in a boat that's un-insurable. I'll go back to New York and wait for you; or I'll stay here and wait for you (but I know you wouldn't want that): or I'll go to Ganado Bay and wait for you in a hotel; I'll even go to Miami and wait for you there in a hotel. But I'm not going on your fucking cruise."

"You're going on that cruise," Grant said. "You're my wife, and you're going on that cruise with me. Or else."

" Or else what?"

" Or else you won't be my wife any more. It's as simple as that. I'll just be long-gone. And you'll never see me again. And you won't collect a fucking nickel off me either. I'll go to gaol first."

Lucky stood staring at him a long time, her fine Italian nostrils flaring and flattening as she breathed deeply over and over. " All right, I'll go," she said finally, in a thin hard voice. " But you better get us the fuck out of here, and fast."

" You're *warning* me?" Grant said coldly.

" Yes. Get Bonham off of fucking Cathie Chandler—Cathie Finer—and get him to get his damned boat ready. I want to get out of here and fast. I can't stand this place and I can't stand these people. They're all sick. Except René and Lisa. I am warning you. Get moving. Or maybe *I'll* leave *you*."

" I hear you," Grant said. " How did you know Bonham was fucking Cathie Finer?"

" How did you know it yourself? I've got eyes too. I'll tell you something else. You used to fuck her yourself. Didn't you?"

" Yes, I did as a matter of fact," Grant said and grinned. He could feel it was not a pleasant grin. " A long long time ago. You're complaining? *You?*"

" No," she said, and grinned herself, an equally unpleasant one, " I'm not complaining. I'm just pointing it out to you that I'm not the stupid broad you think I am."

" I don't think you're a stupid broad," Grant said thinly, " far, far from it."

" And just what do you mean by that?"

" Take it any way you like," he said.

" And I'm telling you once again No, I didn't fuck Jim Grointon! And that's all I'll ever tell you: No. No, I didn't fuck Jim Grointon."

" I hear you," Grant said, and rolled over.

That ended it for that night. And he still didn't know. Maybe he would *never* know. What a thought. But in the next morning, early, while Lucky slept on obliviously and once again back in her own big bed, Grant was up early and downstairs, where he called Bonham at the boatyard.

" I want to see you, Al," he said authoritatively, " and I want to see you right now. Here."

" Hey-hey," Bonham said calmly from the other end. " What's up?"

" You may not have any goddam' cruise, that's what's up. And if you don't have any cruise, you don't have any mortgage from me, that's what's up. Now damn well get in here."

There was a long pause on the other end of the phone, it seemed to go on and on. " All right," Bonham said calmly, finally. " I'll be right there."

When he arrived, in his paint-spattered working clothes, Grant took him into the deserted bar for a morning drink.

" I don't know what's up with you," he said, " and it's none of my business——"

" What do you mean, ' what's up with me '?"

" With you and Cathie Finer, that's what I mean. But that's none of my business. What is my business is that you're not getting the schooner ready, and you should be. If the schooner isn't ready to pull out of here by to-morrow or next day at the very latest, *I'm* pulling out of here for New York. And if I pull out of here, Ben and Irma will pull out of here with me. And all you'll have left of your cruise is your surgeon friend and Cathie Finer." At the very last moment he decided, he did not quite know why, not to mention the threat of the mortgage again.

Bonham stared at him, rather coolly Grant thought, for a long moment. Then he took a slow drink from his glass. Grant had never spoken to him this way before, and it was clear to Grant that it was unexpected. " It must be pretty important," Bonham said coolly, " whatever it is, to make you suddenly decide to leave like that so quick."

"' Why I want to leave is my business and nobody else's," Grant said, and watched Bonham's level cool look turn into a shrewdly speculative one, but he went on. " You've been neglecting getting that work done on the ship, I think. For whatever reasons of your own. If we can't leave here day after to-morrow at the latest, I'm through. Don't forget. I've got play rehearsals I've got to look after in New York," he added just to confuse.

Bonham waited again, coolly, a long time before he answered. He took another slow thoughtful swallow of his drink. Grant had never spoken to him so. Up to now Grant had always deferred to him. Sam the bartender had tactfully faded away out of earshot. When Bonham did finally speak, it was in a voice of decision. Of cool decision. " All right. We can leave here to-morrow. But late. We'll leave at dusk, just before dusk, and make it a night sail. We should make the Nelsons by 2.30 p.m. the next day and we can look Georgetown over and start diving that afternoon. Is that okay? That okay by you?"

" That's fine," Grant said crisply. " But I wish you'd said that two days ago." He added hastily. " Or three." Then added again, to further confuse, " Or four."

Bonham looked at him again for a long time. " We've had a lot more interior work to do than I expected."

" I don't care," Grant said. " As long as we can get out of here according to the way you've just said."

" We can," Bonham said. " Is that all you wanted to talk about? I better be gettin' back to the ship."

" Yes, that's all. So long, Al," Grant said, relenting a little. Bonham did not seem to accept this yielding.—" See you later on," he said laconically.

What auspices to be starting a week or ten days' cruise under! And in close quarters yet! Hell, he thought suddenly, they couldn't even make it ten days now, if that surgeon had to be back in GaBay on the eleventh. What must that Bonham be *thinking* about? Grant had himself another drink and then went back upstairs where he found Lucky up and just dressing. There didn't seem to be much to talk about, so he didn't talk.—" No, I didn't fuck Jim Grointon!" Lucky said, bitterly.—" We're leaving to-morrow evening for the Nelsons," Grant countered.—" At night!" Lucky said. " A night cruise, or sailing, or whatever they call it? Jesus! And on that old uninsurable tub! With all those big freighters and ships out there?"—" Bonham knows his business," Grant said shortly.—" God! I hope he does. I sure hope he does," Lucky said viciously. But when they went downstairs to see the others she suddenly became her old loving self of yesterday again with him. She sat by him, she clung on to him, she kept touching him. Lucky had changed again. This was not like last night, and not like those days and nights before. She had just changed again, that was all. Why? The image of the faceless man and her rose up again. What if she had really done it? What would he do? What could he do?

He insisted on going out in the catamaran again that after-

noon after lunch. Ben and Irma, when they learned departure
was to-morrow night, did not want to go out and wanted to
stay in instead and work on their packing, choosing what to
take, what to send on ahead back to New York, since *Naiad*
would not come back here. They had bought a lot of stuff
down here. So once again it was the three of them, the three
of them alone, himself and Lucky and Jim out on the boat.
And once again they went down to the place near Morant
Bay, shark-fishing, although this time, though they put out
good bloody baitfish and the same outgoing tide had hardly
changed but a few minutes since two days ago, they saw nary
a single shark. In spite of that it seemed to Grant, the whole
thing, crazily, as if it were some perpetual experience he might
have to go through forever, some perennial penance, like
Sisyphus and the rock, that he would never again be released
from: himself and Lucky and Jim, only just the three of
them alone on the boat, going down near Morant Bay, shark-
fishing.

The new change in Lucky manifested itself on the boat
equally as much as it had back at the hotel, when they had
come down into and amongst the others. On the catamaran
with just the three of them alone she was just as loving, just
as solicitous, kept touching him just as much, even clung to
him a little bit, like kissing him on the shoulder once or twice,
whenever they moved the boat about to try slightly different
places. When he would come back on board from a dive, she
always had a towel ready for him, even lovingly dried his
back for him. She got him beer whenever he wanted it, or
poured him coffee from the Thermos if he preferred that.
This time he drank more coffee than he did beer, for some
reason. But Lucky's ministrations knew no limit. A couple
of times he wanted to slap her; and a couple of times he
wanted to kiss her. But he did neither. He accepted all her
attentions in silence and with a loving smile, into which he
tried to put a faint overtone of amusement, male amusement,
of cynicism even. If there was any interior effect upon Jim
Grointon, either pro or con, by these actions of Lucky's, it was
certainly not at all visible anywhere on his normally amiable
and workmanlike exterior.

But her attentions did not stop there, with the boat, or with
the bar where they had a couple of celebratory drinks with
the others to libate their final trip on the catamaran. It did

not, in other words, stop when the presence of others was removed. Because when they went up to rest, bathe and dress for The Dinner, she lay down nude on the two big beds and stretched her arms deliciously as far as she could reach above her head and those delicious breasts and smiled, "Wouldn't you like to make love to me?"—"I would," he said; and did. Her way. First. He did not mention whether she had fucked Jim Grointon, and she did not mention whether she had fucked Jim Grointon. She just had changed. She had just changed, that was all. But once again, Why? was what he could not help thinking. And the faceless spectre, with the somewhat short, somewhat Irish-cop's build—the image of the spectre and her together—rose up again. Christ, he was getting so he almost couldn't tell which one he was, himself Grant, or the spectre. How did you kill a spectre? He knew how to fight men, fairly well. But how did you beat up, left hook and cross the right on, a spectre?

The Dinner was magnificent. It would be their last dinner at the Grand Hotel Crount, since *Naiad* would be pulling out at evening, although they'd have the whole day and lunch there to-morrow, and René actively and frenetically outdid himself. He planned it, supervised it, stood over his chefs with it, even cooked part of it himself. And it was all on him. Everything was on René, and the entire gang was there—all of them as René's guests. All because of Lucky, mainly, their Lucky, and her husband Ron, who had been *married* in his place and who now had the Ron Grant Honeymoon Suite named after them, and of course for Ben and Irma too, who had stayed with him so long. But mainly it was Lucky, their old Lucky, and the marriage. "We nevair forget him zat, my Ronnie," he said as he clapped him on the back and tears came into his expressive Gallic eyes. "Nev-*air!*" Bonham and Orloffski were there from the ship, and Bonham's surgeon and his girl, Cathie Finer, Jim Grointon (and a handsome lovely Jamaican girl he had brought for the occasion), Paule Gordon the black swan, the Spicehandlers, the Grants, the Halders and all three of the kids. He even threw in the movie star and his wife and a couple of other of his more special couples. All on him, all on René. The long table extended from one end of the long room of the bar fully to the other end. René's celebrated fish soufflé first (that was the part he actually cooked himself), then huge platters of golden fried fish served with frenchfries, fish of the most superior type in a place where good fish was commonplace, and after that duck à l'orange that actually physically melted apart in your mouth before you could begin to chew it, then cheeses, all his best imported reblochon, pont l'évêque, camembert, brie, all exactly perfectly aged, and finally ices, ices made on the premises, mirabelle and cassis, made from syrups especially imported to him from La Belle France. The long table groaned with it all, and so, finally, did the guests. Lucky sat on his left at the head end and Ron on his right, and René led off each apéritif, wine and liqueur served by a huge standing toast to the pair of them, to the *Mariage*, pronounced the French way. And after this, after The Dinner, the drinks at the bar were also on the house, on René, for the evening. And it was a long evening.—" Eeet eez al-most im-poss-ible, Ronnie, almost im-poss-ible to see you go, toi et elle," René told him with his arm around him at the bar later on, much much later on. Tears ran unashamedly down the sides of his sharp Gallic nose on his round face. " But you come back. Eez certain you come back, hein? We always 'ave ze Ron Grant Honeymoon Suite ready for you, h'any time. H'any h'any time."— " Sure," Grant said. " Of course we'll come back, René. How could we not come back?" Like hell, he thought, brutally. Like hell we will. As long as you got that fucking skindiver hanging around your place to catch his customers. Like hell. And then suddenly like a small silent explosion in his drunken mind, he thought of Raoul, Raoul-the-South-American, and that—whatever his name was—he couldn't even remember his name now—that Jacques Edgar. And how Raoul-the-South-American had whisked Lucky out of here and back to New York so fast. The thing, the very thing that he Ron Grant had said he would never permit himself to do, never permit his pride to *allow* him to do.

When they finally got to their room, their suite, at what hour nobody ever knew, Lucky stretched out lazily, sleepily, on the two big beds for him again. " I couldn't come," she whispered. " I couldn't possibly. I'm far too drunk. But maybe you could?"—" I can sure as hell give it a try," Grant heard himself say. He did not ask. She did not offer. Ask any questions, offer any answers.

After the packing, most of the next day—by just about

everybody—was spent lying around the pool trying to get over the night before. Then at around three-thirty Bonham came to collect them—in Cathie Finer's rented car—and the exodus began. The great party of René had to a large extent removed the onus feeling about the cruise for Grant, but when he saw Cathie Finer installing her gear and herself in the little rented car with Big Al Bonham, the bad feeling came back.

They made quite a caravan. There was Cathie's car with herself and Bonham, Jim Grointon's jeep, the hotel jeep and because Lisa and Ti-René and the littler kids wanted to go down too the hotel's big car, and finally two more cars of hotel guests who wanted to see the ship off just for a lark. One of these included (with his wife) the movie star, who had taken a great shine to Grant since the serious commencement of the shark-shooting. Grant had asked René that he and Lucky ride in the hotel's jeep (" I think we ought to ride with old René, don't you?" was the way he explained it to Lucky), so Irma and Ben rode with Jim. Lisa and Ti-René and the other kids came, with a good deal of the luggage, in the big car with a driver, since Lisa couldn't drive and Ti-René was still too young to. Bonham led off, and at the rear came the two extra cars of the hotel guests. They had to go all the way in on the spit and around the Windward Road to the anchorage, in convoy. From both of the open jeeps, and from the windows of the two guests' cars, bottles were occasionally brandished at passers-by and the traffic.

In the very end, after all the good-byes and farewells and handshakes and quick little personal toasts, Jim Grointon came forward grinning and brought from behind his back where he'd been hiding it the big shark's mouth of the twelve-foot tiger they had caught together. He had had it cut out when he removed the carcass at the hotel and it had been drying, and now he presented it to Grant.

" I thought you might like to have it," he smiled with that slow, so slow smile of his. " This one you can nearly for damn sure get your head through. It's true you didn't take it entirely by yourself, but you did do at least half the work of taking it. And I'll have plenty chances to take others. And since we did take it together, I also thought you might like to have it to remember me—us—" he gestured at the crowd "—by. It ain't quite dry yet but you put it up on deck where the spray won't hit it, it'll be bone-dry in a couple more days."

Grant took the still-leathery cartilage in his hand and felt along the sharp teeth with a fingertip. It meant absolutely nothing to him. He had been trying to avoid Grointon since they had arrived at the dock—without making it at all obvious —so that he would not have to shake hands good-bye with him. And now here he was apparently going to be forced to. And yet he couldn't. He remembered Jacques Edgar and the touch of his hand. He simply couldn't.

Then he remembered something. It was how on the trip home from the Morants, after Jim had made his so generous and so flattering eulogy of himself (the same because of which he had had to sit down quickly because he was afraid of showing wet eyes! ha!)—how after that eulogy Jim had clapped him hard across the shoulders, for all the world like one Roman soldier saying hello or good-bye to another Roman soldier. The resemblance to Romans had to have been deliberate? And even if he were wrong about them, the two of them, Jim and Lucky, he still simply could not shake his hand.

He looked up from the shark mouth. Jim, grinning, was just sticking out his hand. Taking a quick step forward, Grant reached quickly inside, and clasped Jim by his fore-arm muscle through the long-sleeved shirt.—"This is how *we* shake hands!" he grinned. Jim got the analogy, the reference, and clasped him, Grant, by his forearm in the Roman greeting. Then, grinning, he clapped Grant on the back with his other arm. Grant clapped him on the back. Then they broke apart, and Grant turned away.

All the gear and luggage had already been stowed away aboard, and Orloffski stood on the dock by the big mooring cleat forward, ready to lift off the big eye splice of the bowline. Almost all of the people were already aboard. All except Lucky who, he noted from an eye-corner, was shaking hands good-bye with a smiling Jim Grointon. Well, what the hell? Why shouldn't he be smiling? at a good-bye, at an *ordinary* good-bye? Grant turned and ran for the sternline. René, Papa René, handed Lucky aboard. When Bonham bellowed, they two, he and Orloffski, lifted off the big eye splices, pushed off with a foot each fore and aft, and then leaped on board. They were away.

"Hurry back to the hotel!" Bonham bellowed in his loudest voice. "Hurry back! We'll signal you!"

They went out of the harbour under motor, hotels and cranes and tanks and buildings wheeling around them and changing their relative positions as they moved. It was much easier to go out under motor, if you had one, especially in a big boat, Bonham said, and especially in a long narrow harbour as crowded with shipping as this one was. Ben and Grant hung on to the shrouds watching everything in the harbour move and change. The girls all sat in the cockpit, where Bonham behind the wheel looked as solid and as indestructible as one of those ages-old ninety-ton Indian Buddhas.

As soon as he rounded the Port Royal Point, he cut the motor—why waste expensive fuel, girls, 'ey?—and yelled forward for Orloffski to hoist the mainsail, then when it was up to hoist the jib. The surgeon helped Orloffski to heave on the halyards. Ben and Grant stood around watching excitedly, but afraid to try to help for fear they'd do more harm than good. Now they were under sail alone, and Bonham headed east-southeast down the Main East Channel. When he had passed between Rackham's Cay and Gun Cay— where they had all dived so many times now, before moving on to better spots—he turned inshore a little. Soon the bulk of the hotel appeared to all of them, standing only slightly above the spit itself.

"Dip the mainsail!" Bonham yelled forward. Orloffski and the surgeon let go the halyard, and the big sail sank down slowly, edge flapping in the breeze until her head was half-way down the mast. They ran on like that on the jib alone past the hotel for a full minute. It was impossible to see any signals, waves, or people on the shore. "Hoist her!" Bonham called. Orloffski and the surgeon hauled on the halyard till the mainsail was full up. It had been a beautiful gesture, and although there was no answering signal visible from the hotel Grant for one was sure they had all seen it and appreciated it, and suddenly his heart came up into his throat. *Good-bye Kingston!* he wanted to yell foolishly. *Good-bye, Jamaica!* He looked over at Ben with a sheepish grin, and saw that Ben felt exactly the same way. It was all going to be all right, he felt suddenly. It was going to be a fine trip, now. It was all going to have been worth it!

Naiad, Bonham guiding her, came offshore a little and then ran on down the East Channel east-southeast until they had passed Plumb Point Light. It was almost dark by now. A little farther on Bonham swung her around to southwest by south.

Then the long night sail began, and with it the first of the trouble. It was just seven o'clock.

THIRTY-FOUR

In ten or twelve minutes the tiny white breakers of East Middle Ground showed up to starboard, then the low bushes of South East Cay beyond. First reference, Bonham grinned. When he had passed these, he swung her over half a point to the west and settled back.

Bonham was a different man on board ship. On board *his* ship, because there was no doubt that it was *his* ship. He had his Master's papers to prove it, and he actually seemed to sink into the ship and become a wood or rope or metal part of it. At the same time, his Authority with a capital A increased several hundred per cent. Although he made no overt effort to display this. Rather the reverse. But you could not help but feel it. He had been distant and much more reserved with Grant since Grant's " bearding " of him that day in the hotel, but this on board ship had nothing to do with that. He had always been authoritative with anything having to do with the diving or his pupils and his charges, but this new " Ship's Master's " Authority was different totally in kind and texture.

For the first hour, two hours after their departure the excitement of leaving and of actually being at sea kept them all up high, and they all clustered around Bonham in the cockpit where he sat like that granite Buddha moving the wheel almost not at all, steering a course a few degrees west of southwest by south, taking advantage of the evening land breeze, the wind on his starboard quarter. He would, he explained to them all, sail that course for around eight hours or so to the Pedro Cays. They would hit these at around three a.m. in the morning. Then he would bring her around almost due west to pass inside the Pedros, crossing the end of the Pedro Bank, and then just sail her on a few degrees north of west to the Nelsons. They should sight the Nelsons arounds 2.15 to-morrow afternoon, anchor around 2.40. In the morning the trades would come up again. He was sailing by dead reckoning, but he would get a fix when he sighted Pedros Light. The currents here were all northwesterly, and he could guess the drift. He didn't feel like sleeping, he loved to sail at night, but if he got tired Orloffski could spell him. Grant listened to all this fascinated, and it was then that he made up his mind that he would stay up all night, learning, listening.

He would learn, of course, later, that there really wasn't all that much to learn. It was mainly just staying awake and sitting behind that binnacle and wheel.

The breeze was good. It was amazing how quiet, how *seemingly* silent, it could be without the sound of motors forever present on a ship. The breeze was good, and so were the drinks that they had lounging around the cockpit which despite its size wasn't really big enough to hold all of them. Orloffski therefore stood in the saloon hatchway, its slide pushed all the way back, his feet on the little companionway, grinning and holding his bottle of Seven-Up laced with gin. The surgeon and his girl lay side by side—or rather, belly to belly—on the little side deck beside the cockpit, about as close together as two bodies could get, and murmuring. Yes, the breeze was good, the drinks were good; but the food was lousy. It consisted solely of cans of tuna fish and cans of Spam—take your choice or have both—with a couple of loaves of bread that had been fairly seriously squashed. And a jar of mustard. Grant didn't mind it too much, and in fact enjoyed it. More than enjoyed it. He was an old camper, an old Navy man (though he knew next to nothing about sailing and navigation) he was ravenous, the sea air was great, and he ate like a pig. But the ladies didn't take to it too much. Except for Cathie Finer who didn't seem to mind what she ate as long as she drank and stayed near Bonham. A couple of murmured complaints like " Jesus, is this *it?*" from Lucky, Irma and the surgeon's girl-friend, brought from Bonham the comment that Orloffski notoriously could not cook, and that he himself did not feel at this stage of the trip like turning the sailing over to Orloffski and going below to cook up a hot meal. He could do it, under way like this, though it was difficult a little bit, but he didn't want to and to-morrow when they made landfall they would be eating their own catches incomparably cooked by himself. This statement, given in his new Authoritative manner, ended all complaints.

But it wasn't the food which started the trouble part, everybody could stomach (if the word applied) that. It was the accommodations. After a couple of hours or so the excitement of departure wore off for most of them, though not for Grant. Orloffski and the surgeon had long ago hoisted the staysail and foresail, and there was little to do but sit in the cockpit, watch the dimly lighted binnacle, listen to the sea slip by, listen to the cordage slapping and the wind move past the sails, and look at the stars. This sufficed for Grant, but not for any of the others, even including Ben. And when finally the excitement of leave-taking and being at sea left them, and they decided to bed down, this was when the execrable conditions of the accommodations below-deck became only too openly apparent. This terrible condition of the accommodations was compounded by several factors.

When there was trouble, when trouble finally came, and it always did come, it was never the ship, never the weather, never the sea—it was always the people who brought it on, and carried it through, and kept it going. Always the people. On this voyage at any rate it was never the elements that were at fault; it was the people.

In the first place, the surgeon and his girl had decided to sleep on deck. Lucky and Grant had been given the master cabin that with its one-third-open bulkhead on the little companionway was on the starboard side just forward of the saloon. The surgeon (whose name was Richard Finestein, but who was hardly ever called anything but Surgeon during the whole of the trip) and his girl had been given the portside open bed that opened out just across the little companionway from the main cabin. When they decided to sleep on deck, they very kindly offered their space to Ben and Irma, who then could move aft and not have to sleep in the cramped crew's bunks in the bows. They themselves, they said, would use these if it rained. This was fine, but it soon turned out that the reason they wanted to sleep on deck was to secure for themselves a certain bare minimal amount of privacy in order to drink and screw. By the time everybody was bedded down such rustlings and thumpings, whispering, scrapings and thuddings were coming from the forward deck near the bow that it pervaded the entire belowdecks. This both irritated and angered both Irma and Lucky, both because of the (they felt) inexorably low-class bad taste of it, and because they themselves had no such privacy below. Neither of them, they told Ben and Grant, could have done it even up there on deck, the "minimal" privacy was just too minimal, but down here it—and just about everything else—was impossible.

In fact, anybody with any brains should want to sleep up on deck—provided of course that it didn't rain. There was the smell of paint below, uncomfortable in itself, but none of Bonham's much-talked-about cleanings and freshenings-up were anywhere visible. Two walls of the saloon appeared to have been painted, but everywhere else the same old peeling paint and cracking varnish prevailed. The mattresses must have been, almost certainly had been, aired ; but they did not smell like it. No sheets had been provided. So it was sleep on the old stained mattress-covers, with a blanket over you. Grant the camper (Grant the Great Sailor) didn't care for himself, but Irma and Lucky, and even Ben, certainly did.

He went below with them, when they finally first decided to go down, and helped to get them straightened out as best he could. He had already informed her of his intention to stay up all night and sail with Bonham, and Lucky had not objected and apparently understood, though she obviously didn't like it. Now he pointed out to her with a smile that it was a good thing he was staying up, at least she could sleep some in the too narrow bed. Lucky sniffed the paint-ridden musty air.—" If I *can* sleep," was all she said, and then added, " Hunh, you and your heroes." A sudden inexplicable needle of rage shot through Grant, but he bit it off before it reached his mouth and talk. He turned to go.—" Don't go," Lucky said. " Stay with me for a minute." He turned back, and sat down on the bunk's edge. After a moment Lucky took his hand. Another moment she pulled him to her. He stretched out on the bed beside her.—" Hold me," she whispered after still another moment. He put his arms around her.—" I'm scared on this damned boat," she said after a while. Then, " Love me," she whispered. " Please love me."—"I do love you," he said.—"There's nothing we can do on this damned old boat. Everybody can hear everything everybody does. Can't even go to the john without being heard. I hate that. Listen to them up there!" They listened for a while to the scrapings and thumpings coming from the deck up in the bows.—"Hold me more," Lucky said, whispered. He did, squeezed her closer, although he was beginning to get hot, get a hard-on. Suddenly he thought of that little Jamaican house where they had had the room close by Bonham's house. They had had to whisper there too, and make love quietly because of the thin wall. Suddenly he wanted to cry. Really weep. He had to cough and choke it back down. Lucky kissed his cheek. She hadn't noticed.— "There. Go now," she said and pushed him away. "Go on back up on deck."

In the hatchway up out of the saloon he stopped on the little stairs, rested both arms at shoulder height on the coach-roof and looked up at the sky, the stars. There it was. She had just completely changed. And so suddenly. But why, *why*, WHY? *Why* so suddenly? The faceless spectre rose up before him again, nude, with a tremendous hard-on. He was convinced now that she had done it. She really had; and was trying to make it up. How could he ever forgive her?

Suddenly he realised, in a totally cold objective analytic way, that the knife of rage he had felt below (and had swallowed) a moment ago, when she had said something about *Hunh, your heroes*, had been caused by the *plural*, her *plural* usage, which of course included Grointon. He continued to stand, still resting on his arms on the coach-roof, still looking up at the clear sky and the stars.

"Hello, kid," Bonham said from behind the wheel, in the light from the binnacle.

Grant sat down beside him behind the wheel, on the bench there with its new plastic cushions. It had gotten colder and Bonham had put on a jacket. Orloffski had made up his bed on the coachroof, apparently as far aft as possible to give the surgeon privacy, and Grant could see him lying there crossways in his bag just aft of the mainmast under the boom. Cathie Finer, also in a big jacket now, was asleep tucked up in a stern corner of the cockpit near to Bonham, a whisky bottle beside her. "You didn't do very damned much

with the downstairs, the 'belowdecks'," he said after a
moment. One particular day he himself and Lucky had seen
Bonham in town with Cathie and the surgeon and his girl
having a long leisurely lunch at the most expensive restaurant
in town, which meant of course that Cathie was paying.

"I told you we had a lot more interior work than expected," Bonham said.

"It doesn't look like you did *anything*," Grant said.

"Painted two walls of the saloon," Bonham said. He
moved the big wheel one spoke, one exact spoke handle, to
the starboard from where he slouched easily behind it.

Grant looked at the lighted compass in its binnacle. They
were still running a little bit west of southwest by south.

"We're passing over Mackerel Bank," Bonham said.
"Dived there couple of times. Fourteen to nineteen fathoms."
Grant automatically translated this into feet: eighty-four to
a hundred and fourteen. "There's nothing but open water
between us and the Pedros now," Bonham went on.

Grant looked at the compass again. "You're playing with
fire," he said after a moment or two.

"Always have played with fire."

"What if Sam finds out?"

"How'll he find out?"

"She might tell him."

"No. Why would she tell him?"

"Christ, man!" Grant exclaimed angrily, but softly.
"Sam *loves* you! You're his *hero!*"

"So?"

"But that makes you the best choice, you dumbhead. And
then she'd tell him to hurt him!"

Bonham turned his great head to look at him and screwed
up his eyes. "I never thought of *that!*"

"Because you don't think much. Why'd you have to pick
on her?"

"Didn't pick, I *was* picked."

"Even so. You ought to *like* Sam."

"Like Sam! Hell, I *love* Sam! I wouldn't be here running this sweet smooth lady along like this if it wasn't for
Sam!"

"Then how can you do his old lady?"

"Every man has got to look after, handle, and take care
of his own pussy," Bonham said.

"Is that the rule? Is that the way the big he-men do it?"

"That's the way *life* does it."

"Well, I sure wish you hadn't picked on her. You're liable to lose your whole—"

"I told you, I didn't pick, I *was* picked."

"Well, I wish you'd of *un*picked yourself, then. You're liable to lose schooner and all. Can he call in that loan? Foreclose it?"

"I don't know. Have to look. When we get back to GaBay. But I don't think so."

"Then there's that other $10,000 coming up," Grant said, shaking his head. "What about Orloffski? Does he know?"

"He might suspect it. What about your wife?"

"She was the one who told me first," Grant said with a sad smile. "But I already suspected it myself. You weren't too terribly careful, Big Al."

Bonham turned his head away again from the binnacle, and looked at Grant, and suddenly those murky strange storm-cloud eyes of his actually blazed. "There are times in a man's life when he just doesn't give a *damn*. About anything. Consequences, or anything else. And I guess that's the way I am now."

"—But you've worked all your life for this; this ship, the company," Grant put in. "It's been your dream."

"I know it. But I like this too." He inclined his head down toward the sleeping Cathie. "I like it a lot. And I'm gonna keep on with it. For the rest of this trip certainly. And afterwards, now and then, if I can."

He looked back at the compass. Suddenly, but easily, from his slouch, the big man moved the big wheel again, two spoke handles, then a further half spoke handle, to the starboard.

"Well, if it's like that," Grant said. He was thinking about what Bonham's wife Letta had told Lucky that time about Bonham. How did it all fit? How did it all hang together? He wished he knew. But he couldn't see through it.

"I could talk to her about it," Bonham said in a very low voice. "Telling him, I mean."

"I wouldn't *talk* to her. Openly. But you could feel her out about it a little bit. Of course, you could always quit. Now. Right now."

"It's all done," Bonham said in that same low voice.

" Once is enough. So why quit? Anyway, like I told you—"

" I know," Grant said. " As an old painter friend of mine used to say, Man, I've been there."

" You want to take the wheel a while?" Bonham said with a grin, but he spoke in that same low, beat-down voice.

" You think I could?" Grant said. He felt beat down and sad too, but the prospect of actually taking the wheel excited him anyway.

" Sure. Nothing to it. Just keep her as she goes. Wind's changing slowly so she'll move off to port on you a little bit. Let her. Just bring her back with a spoke or two once in a while. Try to keep her right on that littlest marker. That's southwest three-quarters south. Don't worry about the degree markings, they're too small to bother with." Before moving he slackened the mainsheet a little bit, easing the mainsail a little, then the foresail sheets which led back to the cockpit. " Wind's moving a little north now, but she won't get so far north we'll have to run dead off. Or jibe her. At least not for a while." Then he moved over slowly, passing Grant the wheel, and then hunched over with elbows on his knees, looking down. Where he was looking was where Cathie Finer was hunched up sleeping. He looked in that same direction a long time. Then he reared up and leaned back on the cushioned bench against the stern decking with a long sigh that seemed to go on a very long time before he stopped it, let it die, kill itself to emptiness, a free-diver's sigh. Grant recognised it.

After a half-hour's steering he turned the wheel back over to Bonham and got one of the heavy jackets and sat back down on the stern bench. Finally, though, after a couple of good stiff drinks (against the cold? ah, yes ; but which *cold?*) he slid down on to the cockpit floor and stretched out.

He was asleep when they passed the Pedros. But all the action of jibing to bring the wind on the other quarter waked him easily enough. Bonham was still at the wheel, where he had been when Grant dozed off. The wind had swung all the way around, slowly, from north by west almost to northeast, freshening as it hauled, and Bonham had already jibed once while he was asleep because they were now jibing back from port to starboard. From up front Orloffski and the surgeon hollered back.

"Is there anything I can do?" Grant asked, sitting up. "Can I help?"

"It's all done," Bonham said, a little thickly. A gin bottle was clamped between his feet. But his eyes and hands were as bright and fast as ever. "We've made the jibe."

"But you jibed once when I was asleep, and it didn't even wake me," Grant said, feeling foolish, or guilty, or both.

"No," Bonham said in his slightly thicker voice. "No, because I did that one myself."

"Oh," Grant said.

"This one was a little harder. What the hell! Let the bums work a little. Know they're on a cruise, that way. Do you think she would really tell him about it?"

"I don't know," Grant said. "I honestly don't know. I hope not. Maybe she won't."

Bonham didn't answer. And from up front Orloffski and the surgeon came back cheerfully sleepy to have a shot of Bonham's gin, and that ended the conversation.—"Well, I don't give a damn anyway," Bonham said to Grant. "*Not anyway*." He said it in the others' presence, but they of course didn't know what it referred to."

"You want me to spell you?" Orloffski asked cheerfully in his brutal way.

"No," Bonham said. "Maybe I'll wake you later." The wind had fallen off, but they still were moving along pretty good, he said, and anyway when morning came, they'd finally begin to get the Trades. "Might have to come about again, when the Trades come up. But then again, maybe not."

That must have been two-thirty or three. Grant had himself a shot too and went back to sleep, as did the surgeon and Orloffski. Bonham was still at the wheel.

Grant woke at three-thirty. It was at four-thirty in the morning that the two women, Irma and Lucky, came running up into the cockpit from the saloon, both of them totally hysterical. More slowly, reluctantly, Ben came along behind them.

Grant had half-dozed off. He realised right away, as soon as he was full awake, which took four or five seconds, that he must have totally underestimated Lucky's fear at being at sea aboard the sailing ship. She had told him she was scared, but he had thought she had meant it only rhetorically, or half-rhetorically. Now he ran to meet her as she came up

out of the saloon hatchway hollering " Stop!" with Irma
right behind her and yelling " Stop!" too. Grant grabbed her
at the head of the little ladder, forcing Irma—and the dis-
traught-looking Ben behind her—to stop in the narrow hatchway.

" Cut it out! Cut it out!" Grant yelled, shaking her a
little. " Now what the hell's the matter?"

" Look! Look!" she yelled back, pointing. Her eyes
were so wide as to seem almost sightless. Grant followed her
pointing arm, turning around and seeing as he did so Bonham still behind the wheel, and watching them—and as he
turned saw what he and Bonham had been looking at for
almost an hour: about a mile off their port bow a big
freighter or tanker, a veritable Christmas tree of running
lights, was slowly moving toward crossing their bows toward
the north. They were in one of the main North and South
American shipping lanes now, and had seen two other such
vessels in the past hour, although both of these were much
farther north and had already crossed them before being
sighted.

" I told you this goddamned Bonham was crazy!" Lucky
cried. " We're going to hit that ship! We're going to hit it!"

" We're not," Grant yelled at her. " It'll be a long time
past us by the time we get to it, cross its course. Now sit
down," he said more quietly. " Sit down, all of you, and tell
me what started all this off." He was thinking privately that
he wished she had not said that about Bonham. It should
not have been said, not in Bonham's hearing anyway. It
would almost certainly make for trouble later on. For the
moment anyway, Bonham said nothing. He continued on his
course. The freighter (or tanker) continued on its, approaching the line of their course somewhere off in front of them.

It was easy to see how it could have frightened them, even
Ben too. They knew nothing about sailing, and did not
realise that, with the relative movement of the two vessels,
and the schooner's slow speed, the ship would have crossed
their course a long long time before they got to its course.
Finally he got a drink down them, and heard their story.
Lucky had waked up, for no particular reason, and in getting
out of her tiny cabin door had disturbed and waked up
Irma, and naturally Ben. The three of them had come up to
sit in the saloon for a while (Cathie's bunk there had not

even been made up)—and of course the first thing they
had seen through the large ports was the lighted freighter
(they could make out that it was a freighter now, not a
tanker) appearing big as all hell, and looking as though it
would run into them. It had panicked them all.

" Well, it won't," Grant said. " Trust my word. And
trust Bonham's—Al's—knowledge. And ability." From the
wheel Bonham spoke for the first time. But before he did he
gave Lucky a long, burning look which, while it did or said
nothing actually, made Grant nervous about the future of the
cruise. He didn't like it.—" I hate to have to remind *anybody*
of this," Bonham said mildly, " but I am *actually, legally*
the captain of this ship. Any decisions that are to be made
are my responsibility, and in fact—in law—*are my* decisions.
And any orders that I give to anybody *are* orders, and have
to be carried out. At least while we're at sea."

" That wouldn't help us if we ran into that great big goddamned ship," Lucky said pertly.

" No. But it would still be *my* responsibility," Bonham
said. " And it would also be *my* responsibility to save you,
at the risk of—at the *cost* of—my own life. That's my
honour and my duty as a sea captain, as master of this
vessel." He moved the wheel a spoke or two to starboard,
actually turning in the collision direction of the approaching
freighter. " That freighter will have passed our course at least
a half an hour before we reach his course. And in fact will
probably be damn' near out of sight to the north by the time
we do reach his course."

" Well, I'm sorry," Lucky said, in a crestfallen, sincerely
contrite voice.

" That's okay," Bonham said mildly. But there was an
increased distance, coldness, in his voice. The damage, Grant
thought, the damage of Lucky's first—even if hysterical—
remark, had been done. He got another drink down the three
of them, pouring the whisky into the already used, slightly
muggy plastic cups in the cockpit. Cathie Finer had waked
up with all the commotion and was now sitting up, and accepted a drink herself, but she said nothing except a hello
with a small smile.

" Well, I think I'll go back down," Lucky said, after a little
while.

" Me too," Irma said.

" Me too," Ben said.

Grant went down with Lucky and, in the cabin, kissed her. " It's all right," he said.—" I shouldn't have said that first thing I said," she said right away. " I *really* shouldn't have. Not where he could hear it. But I don't like him. He really bothers me. He scares me. He really is accident-prone. And he doesn't like *me*."—" He's not accident-prone in sailing and diving," Grant said. " He's a great sailor. But I guess you were right in saying that about his ' personal life ' that time." Lucky looked at him quickly and he nodded, but put his finger to his lips and motioned he would tell her later. Then he went back up on deck.

Dawn began coming up very soon after, and with the dawn everything and everybody freshened up immediately. The sight of daylight, and then of the sun itself, washed away all of the fatigue Grant had accumulated during an almost sleepless night. It affected Bonham, who had not slept at all, the same way. The wind which had turned to the northeast during the night stayed in the northeast and as the day warmed up began to freshen until it actually became, gradually, the true trade wind. Bonham relinquished the wheel to Orloffski, giving him the course, and went below to the galley and fried up huge plastic platters of bacon and eggs for everybody which made doubly enjoyable the coming of day. The surgeon and his girl-friend came back aft to eat laughing happily and looking none the worse for wear, after spreading out their air mattress the surgeon had thought so wisely to bring along, putting it out on the coachroof in the sun. The morning was very pleasant in the bright sun and the freshening wind. Lucky and Irma sunned themselves in their swimsuits up forward in the bow, where last night's " orgy " (as they two now referred to it between themselves) had taken place. Bonham put out two trolling lines from the stern, and they hauled in two good-sized bonito when they apparently passed though a school of them, which they threw back, since bonito was too bloody a fish to really be good eating. Bonham cooked them lunch at noon, and while it was only fried Spam and German-fried potatoes, it was better than the cold tuna fish and cold Spam of last night. Then at two p.m. the Nelsons hove into view dead ahead on the horizon as Bonham had promised they would, and by two-thirty they were sailing slowly under shortened sail past North Nelson and Georgetown the tiny capital, where they could see a trim handsome-looking yacht docked at the little wharf.

"But aren't we going to put in there?" Lucky asked.

"Yes," Irma said. "I thought— . . ."

"We will later," said Bonham, who had taken over the wheel again after they sighted the land. "Maybe to-morrow. It's too late now. What the hell, they charge you thirty-five bucks a day docking charges there if you stay overnight. I thought we'd go on to another island I know, a little one. I'ts got good reef and we can dive there this afternoon, catch our supper, and anchor off the island for the night."

This was what they did, and it was fine for the rest of the daytime. Bonham anchored the *Naiad* in close to the lee shore, and everybody put on aqualungs and went spear-fishing. This was strictly a lung-diving cruise, and since Ben had never used a lung, Bonham spent the afternoon with him in shallow water patiently checking him out in the lung until he was satisfied Ben could use it safely. The others fished. Except of course for Lucky, who snorkelled a little, Irma who of course couldn't swim, and the surgeon's girl-friend who it turned out was an excellent lung-diver but who didn't feel like it to-day. Lobster—langouste really, since they were crayfish and had no claws—were plentiful everywhere, and by evening they had more than enough fish and lobster tails to fill everybody up, as Bonham had planned. These lobster tails (although Bonham fried them *that* night) were immediately dubbed " piss-marinated lobster " by Lucky and the equally irreverent Irma. This was because the men—only Orloffski, Grant and the surgeon this particular afternoon—rather than swim all the way back to the ship with it every time they took one, simply pulled off the heads and bodies and threw them away, and deposited the tails in the crotches of their swimtrunks or bikinis and carried them there until the suits would hold no more.—" Can you imagine eating a lobster tail that that Orloffski's been peeing through for an hour or so?" Lucky demanded of Irma and Grant, fortunately out of hearing of that Polish gentleman. In spite of that, the lobster tails made great eating when Bonham fried them in his cornmeal batter. And the lobster-fishing was great sport, peering in under the rocks and corals for them, fish were plentiful also, and at one point—looking for a lobster—Grant killed a five-foot moray eel, his first, which he boated. Although Bonham maintained that the moray made excellent eating, the ugly, slimy, vicious-looking creature was finally thrown overboard by the combined vote of everybody except the crew, which meant Bonham and Orloffski. Yes, the daytime was fine. The sun was bright, the sea was beautiful, the breeze fresh and lovely. It was only when night came that it wasn't fine. Then it was the same old thing. The accommodations.

Since this *was* a lung-diving cruise, most of the entire deck space was crammed with single tanks, sets of double tanks, regulators, all sorts of gear, and Bonham had naturally brought along his portable Cornelius air compressor and this took up a good deal of space all by itself. The surgeon and his girl had staked out their claim first to the only available space in the bow, and nobody felt like asking them to trade off, so it was either sleep below or sit cramped up in or beside the cockpit, which anyway had by now somehow become the province of Bonham and Cathie, whose bunk had not yet once been made up for her in the saloon, and whose blankets Bonham brought up for her in the cockpit.

This was all really Bonham's fault, too, Grant was well aware. Like not having finished the accommodations. He had just brought along too many paying customers. He should either—with all the diving gear he was carrying—have left the surgeon and his girl at home, or else not have asked Ben and Irma along. He had just been greedy, because of having no ready money, as Lucky had commented (and Grant had noted) before. Grant had told her all this during the afternoon, as well as all about his private conversation with Bonham about Cathie Finer the night before. " Some outfit," Lucky said with an I-told-you-so air. " Some cruise it's turning out to be!"

And in the morning Lucky (who probably would not have done it had she not been backed up by Irma, and even Ben) rebelled. She would not spend one more damned miserable night on that damned boat.—" Hell, I can't even sleep with you, with my own husband," she said to Grant privately before. " I just won't. And neither will Irma," So they took it to the captain.

" Why can't we put into Georgetown and dock there at night? There's a hotel there, and those of us who want to can rent ourselves a room, and have at least a little comfort. I swear I simply can't sleep down in this hole any more. And we can eat dinner there. We're all fed up with fish. And then there's that other place you told us about, that Dog Cay? That ritzy place? Aren't we going to go there?" She made an ardent, and excellent, spokesman.

"Yes, we can go there,' Bonham said slowly, very slowly. It was plain he was angry, and when he was angry he got slower and slower. "But there ain't any *sleeping* accommodations there for us. Only free dockage. It's all private houses there. And only the free dockage for only a night or two. Longer would be abusin' their hospitality."

"Then why can't we dock every night at Georgetown, and just go out from there every day in the boat?"

"Well, for one thing," Bonham said, "I didn't plan on paying thirty-five or fifty bucks dockage charges every night when I calculated the cost of this trip. And I certainly didn't count on buying any *dinners* ashore."

"I'll take care of the dinners," Grant put in. "Don't worry about that."

"Another thing is," Bonham said stubbornly, "is that we can't get to all the places I've got it planned for us to visit and dive on, if we have to travel twenty miles to thirty-five miles to get there and twenty to thirty-five miles to get back. That's sixty to seventy miles' sailing. Would take us all day just to get there and back."

Now Irma spoke up. "Then why don't we just dive and explore around here? And down at that Dog Cay? Couldn't we sleep out on their dock?"

"It wouldn't look very high-class," Bonham said. "They're British."

"To hell with high-class," Irma said. "A dock's better than down in this boat. And Christ, it's no damn' difference to me where we go. Here or there. I can't even swim. You were going to teach me to swim."

"And I will," Bonham said. He was looking more and more harassed. "I was planning to start with you to-day for an hour, now Ben can use the lung. But— . . ." It tapered off.

"I just can't spend another night on this boat," Lucky said.

"Ship! *Ship*, damn it!" Bonham said, his voice rising. "This is not a damned *boat!*" Then he brought it back down to slow again. " I just didn't plan that kind of a trip when I quoted you people the daily charges—"

" You never quoted me any daily charges," Ben said.

Bonham went right on. " All these extras will be comin' out of my expenses. I won't make a nickel on the trip. Do *you* want to pay those dockage charges?"

" What the hell? No," Ben said, with some asperity. " You got that other ten thousand dollars coming from Sam Finer, don't you?"

" Maybe," Bonham said. He sighed. " Anyway, I haven't seen any of it yet. God, what a bunch of lubbers you are!" he exploded suddenly.

But in the end he gave in. And it was Cathie Finer who caused it. Cathie had been standing and listening—with that new soured, bitter face of hers, so different from the happy face she'd had in Grand Bank that Grant remembered, when she'd been happy with Sam. And now she stood and listened and said nothing, and then she gave her vote in favour. With a rather special look at Bonham, and a particular smile, she said she too would much rather spend the nights ashore, and Bonham looked at her once and acceded. He got the point. So did Grant; and so did Lucky, from her face. So did just about everybody. But Cathie Finer didn't seem to care. And so it was that at the end of the day's diving they quit early and hoisted sail for Georgetown. And that was how they met the Texans.

The Texans were incredible. There were three well-larded couples of them—at least the men were well-larded; the women were lean and stringy-dieted-thin, and they it soon turned out were the actual *men* in the whole group. It was their trim handsome yacht they had seen from the *Naiad* when they first passed by Georgetown, and when *Naiad* pulled in and docked at the wooden and not-at-all-brand-new wharf right behind her, her beautifully white-painted hull and well-painted, well-varnished spick-and-span abovedecks made the *Naiad* look like some creaky old derelict bum that had just managed to pull into port. She, the *Lady Suzanne*, out of Houston (Suzanne being the name of the wife of the owner, who immediately introduced herself as such), was a 98-foot-overall two-masted schooner and in addition to the three rich Texas couples carried four in crew, and she made the *Naiad* look like plain shit, as Lucky said. This was especially evident when they saw her beautiful, spacious, well-cared-for accommodations belowdecks, as they immediately did—were shown—when they were all invited over for drinks, which they immediately were.

It was this, that immediate and quite early invitation over for drinks, that started off the catastrophic chain of events that went on and on—getting more and more horribly nightmarish—on and on into the night. " Yawl lak bubbon, honey?" Grant heard one of the ladies say to Lucky as soon as they were aboard.—" Well, no," Lucky answered. " I'm really a scotch drinker, but—"—" Thas awwwl rat, honey! We got scotch. We got bubbon, scotch, giun, ruum. Honey, we got anything. We got it awl!" And they did. And they put it away too.—" Then I'll have scotch," Lucky had said; " scotch and soda,"—" Ferd!" the lady Suzanne screeched her command. " Lady'll haave a scotch!" Her husband turned immediately from whatever he was doing and saying to Bonham and Grant and went to fulfil the command. Ferd, the *Lady Suzanne*'s obviously rich owner, with his well-larded paunch, was the total slave of his thin wife, and so apparently were the male members of the other two couples. This was all right, but as the evening wore on it got worse, rougher, much much rougher. " Weall bubbon driinkers," Suzanne continued to Lucky, " bean suthren. Bubbon and braanchwater, y'know. Ha, ha. Thas aways the way to teull a Suthrener f'om a Nothrener." This part would get worse too as the night—the unbelievable night—wore on.

It started off nicely enough. Conversation. More drinks. More and *more* drinks. It was pleasant in the cooling sea air as the dusk came on. " This is a lovely ship you have," Grant had said sincerely, very sincerely, considering, to Suzanne. " Yaas, it's a nas o'l boat," Suzanne smiled. " We got a betteh boat back haome in Hewston. It's much begger. But it's a motoh one, y'know. A motoh yacht. So we neveh breng it down thiis fa'. We call thiis one ouur maarlynn-fiishin' boat." Had they been down to the famous Dod Cay with it yet? Yaas, they haad. But they didn't much like those Anglish. They were much more parashul to the Greens, here. She said it " Greeyans ". They loved the Greens.

Now the Greens, as Bonham had explained to all his group some time back, were a Bahamian Negro family who had somehow got themselves transplanted down here into the Nelsons. And except for two or three closed-down houses owned by Miami marlin-fishermen and one big luxury hotel that was just in the process of being built by Florida speculators, the Greens owned practically all of North Nelson including the town itself, which was tiny and was inhabited mainly by other Greens who were brothers, sons, cousins, or nephews. They owned the wharf, and they owned the one functioning hotel, and they owned the one and only restaurant. Certain of them also maintained a sort of home-made-guitar and steel-drum calypso band which would play on the dock for a certain fixed fee. And the *Lady Suzanne* party was partial to these Greens. " They'uh awful smaart niggas," Suzanne smiled. " And they jest lo-ove us."

And apparently—unbelievably, incredibly—they did. " 'Course Ferd aways tiips them good. An' he paays the steel ban' double wheneveh they play," Suzanne smiled. " 'Couse they won' haave a reaal codlock on thiis plaace, anymoare, when the new *ho*tel open uup in a month or so. It's too baad. It's a reaal shaame for uus."

One of Ferd's guests (called Bert), hearing the calypso band being mentioned, said, " The ban'? The steel ban'? Sho!" and strode to the ship's rail and shoved his own larded paunch (though not as larded, and not as paunchy as Ferd's) against the lifeline. " Hey, boa!" he called at a small Negro boy who was sitting against one of the jetty buildings back on the shore with his knees drawn up, watching the " party " with large white eyes. "Hey, boa! Hey, nigga!" Bert didn't even say " nigger." " Heah's a quarter!" He flipped it ashore. " Run up an' tell that nigga steel ban' get theah black ass down heah play some music."

The boy ran off.

" You call them all nigger like that?" Grant asked him curiously.

" What? Sho! Why not? They ahr niggas, ain't they?"

" Don't they mind it?"

" Why should a nigga min' bein' called a nigga?" Bert wanted to know.

That set the tone. Pretty soon a straggling group of Greens straggled out on to the dock dragging their straggly looking instruments and began to play some very bad calypso music.
—" Hey!" Bert called. " You niggas come awn up hea closeh.

We ca-yunt even hea you with the noise f'om this hea damned
party." The group of Greens straggled in closer and straggled
off some more bad calypso. "Thas enuf," Harry who was
the other guest, said finally, "Ca-yunt heah yo'self think!
Ferd?" Ferd distributed largesse happily amongst the band,
and they straggled off smiling just as happily.

Grant could hardly believe it.—"They rially do jest lo-ve
us!" Suzanne said from beside him on the hatch, and then
put her hand kindly on his knee. "Don't you jest lak uus a lil
too?" she added.—"Hey!" Grant grinned. "Cut that out!
My old lady'll beat me up!"—"I jest bet she would,"
Suzanne purred.—"And what about your old man?" Grant
asked. "Oah, they'ull awl be deaad drunk and aslee-up
'fore very long," Suzanne smiled, and then gave him an
openly suggestive look.

It was quite true that everybody was swiftly getting drunk.
Grant was himself. For quite a few days now, since René's
farewell dinner, and even before, he had been drinking fairly
heavily all through the day, and even more heavily in the
night, and after that night—that first night out—when he
had stood in the open saloon hatchway looking at the stars
and had decided, had become convinced, that Lucky actually
had done it with Jim Grointon, had actually *fucked* him, that
crazy night, since then he had been drinking even more
heavily, daily *and* nightly, and why not? Most of the time—
sailing or diving—he had not had to think about that, but
now he did think about it. And why not? Why not drink?
Damn them. God damn them. All of them. And God
damn this miserable lousy cruise. Even that wasn't any good,
like all the rest. He carefully removed Suzanne's hand from
his knee, and got up to go get another drink. Somebody had
decided that they must, they *must*, all eat together in Georgetown's single restaurant. In the Green's restaurant.

The ensemble dinner in the restaurant was a catastrophe. A
further catastrophe. But even worse was to follow. But at
the dinner, Lucky finally blew up. There was a good deal of
that Nothren-Suthren talk, at the dinner. It wasn't really all
that bad really, either. Grant had lived in the South, half of
his blood had come from there, up into Indiana, though it
was back before "The War", and in fact he had two great-
uncles buried at Gettysburg, one with the 19th Indiana and
one with the 47th Virginia. He had always been proud of

that, and Texas accents—any Southern accents—had never bothered him. On the contrary he rather liked them. But then, with his ear, he liked all accents. But when Harry (which was the name of Ferd's other guest; he was the husband of Lois; Bert's wife's name was Betty-Lou) began to feel he had not been served fast enough, and hollered, "Hey, boa! Hey, nigga! Git that damn nigga wayteh ova hea, hea'? Ah'm *hongry!*", even Grant was embarrassed. The Greens apparently, though, were not embarrassed at all. The waiter came. But Lucky was more than embarrassed.

"Can't you say Negro?" she demanded crisply. "Or say coloured? Or, even better yet, just say waiter?"

"Whut the heull?" Harry said. "So whut if Ah do say nigra—"

"Not 'nigra', *Negro*," Lucky interrupted crisply.

"Thas whut Ah said," Harry said. "But whut the heull? Nigra, nigga, it's awl the sa-ume thang, fo' Chrast's saike!"

"Harry, don't sweah!" Lois his wife commanded.

"Yeaus, lo-ove," Harry said without pausing for breath and continued. "A nigga's a nigga, Mrs. Gra-unt. He'ull aways be black. Bean black is bean a nigga."

"I won't sit and eat with people like this," Lucky said and got up.

"Sit down, for God's sake," Grant said. He was already drunk-mad at her anyway. Jim Grointon!

The situation was saved by lady Suzanne. "Aw, come on, honey. Siit dowwn. Eaat. We all lo-ove ouur niggas, *nigros*. We lo-ove the Greans, and the Greans lo-ove uus. It's awl raat. The Wa-ah's oveh. I was only kiddin yiou abaat all thaat. Say, what ahre yawl? A bunch of New York Jee-ews?"

"Yes," said Lucky. "And please don't you forget we have a rabbi with us!" She indicated Ben. This impressed the Texans. And it wasn't so far from the truth at that, Grant thought with an interior giggle, remembering Ben's earlier rabbinical studies. Only where the hell was the happy rabbi when he had needed him back in Kingston? Jim Grointon!

Dinner was resumed, but at considerable nervous expense. Lucky was a dyed-in-the-wool New York liberal if she was anything, and she spoke not a further word. But it was the Greens that Grant couldn't understand. They obviously

must hate these people's guts, and were only taking it because
they wanted their money and to hell with them, was the only
way he could figure it. But later he was disabused of even
this theory, or partially disabused of it. Later when the
Great Diving Contest arrived.

A lot of space, and a lot of time, came and went before
that. And most of it he couldn't remember. He was really
very drunk by now. So was everybody else. After the
dinner, outside on the cool walk, Lucky got him together with
Ben and Irma privately, and suggested that they all just fade
away and go to bed. " I can't stand another minute with
those drunks, those *people!*" she said.—" Yeah," said Ben
in his so-Midwest accent. " I guess me'n Irm'll hit the old
sack." He was subdued. They had already inspected their
rooms in the rickety hotel, taken in whatever they would need
in the way of luggage and equipment to bathe, get clean, and
change clothes. All they had to do was disappear and use
their keys.

" Well, I'm not! " Grant raged, suddenly. He *was* raging.
Jim Grointon! " A'm gonna git mase'f darunnk," he added
in his best Southern accent. " Wif ma frien's theah, and wif
ma ol' paal, Bunnum. You guys do whatever you want to
do."

He did not remember when they left him. There seemed to
have been a bit more argument, mostly from Lucky, before
that occurred. He ran into, literally ran into, Bonham some
yards farther on down the walk to the wharf. He did not
remember getting there.

" They've all went to bed," he said. Strangely enough, his
head was clear as a bell.

" So's Cathie," Bonham said noncommittally. He had
hardly spoken a word throughout the catastrophic dinner, trying mainly to keep people from attacking, fighting each other.
A 320-pound peacemaker.

" Well, I'm goin' back to our boat," Grant said, " and get
drunk. *Really* drunk. I don't care if I never see those
asshole Texans again."

Bonham grinned his big storm-cloud grin. " Well, I could
always use a couple drinks more myself. I'll come with
you. They're really something, those Texans, hunh?"

" They're rich," Grant said, apropos of nothing. " I can't
stand them."

But it was not to be. Since they would not go on board the Texans' lovely yacht, the Texans came on their own crummy one. Poor old *Naiad*. A lot of time got lost here too. He seemed to remember some horrible thing about the Texas women, one or more, more he thought, going down belowdecks in the *Naiad* ostensibly to use the head but in fact sitting there on the yachtsman's sea-going pump-up john and inviting them, the strangers, himself, Bonham, Orloffski, to come down and see them, *do* them. He was shocked and then horrified. One of them sat there with her skirt up around her waist, her legs spread wide, on that john in the head, motioning. At least one of them. As Suzanne had told him earlier—and truthfully—the Texan men would soon be dead drunk and asleep. However, while they *were* dead drunk, they were not asleep. They were standing there on board the *Naiad* discussing something loudly, between themselves. Skindiving, he thought. And down below the woman, whichever one it was, was motioning. Grant did not go. His self-imposed condition never to step out on his wife was still in effect despite Jim Grointon, apparently. Bonham did not go either. Orloffski went. Then some more time was lost somewhere, and then with a totally clear head again he found himself already engaged in the Great Diving Contest.

Bonham was already collecting the money. They had apparently been able to get up eighty dollars cash between them, and Ferd the owner of the *Lady Suzanne* matched it, in cash. Bert, who was perhaps the most aggressive of the Texans (if such a word could even be applied to them, after their women), fancied himself as a springboard diver. In his youth, of course, he pointed out. He was perhaps a year or two older than Grant. The bet was who could do the best back flip off the side of the *Naiad*. Bonham was holding the stakes. One of the younger Greens, the boss of the restaurant in fact, had been selected to be the judge, apparently after great argument that Grant did not at all remember. Bonham knew how good a springboard diver he was, had seen him dive in GaBay once, and gave him a wink: it was a cinch bet. Of course, Grant realised that the Texans thought that he was drunk. But at the moment he was in fact not drunk at all. His head was again clear as a bell. On the outskirts of the murmuring mob, which now—on the dock—included a raft of Greens, he saw Irma standing in the background,

realised instantly that Lucky had certainly sent her down as
a spy. He waved at her. Then the Great Diving Contest
began.

Grant went first. Bert had demurred about going first, so
Grant offered. Bert, quite obviously, slyly wanted to watch the
competition and see what he was up against. Grant, on the
other hand, was not worried at all. So he offered. " Sure.
I'll be glad to go first."

When he went off the rail outside the lifeline and into the
air, the free air only springboard divers and trampoline
artists ever really know, he went up straight, remembering to
lean back just a little and flatten his arc. Unlike a springboard, the side of the ship ran straight down to the water, even
bulged out a little. A tight backflip could throw him into the
side of the ship. At the top he pulled up, his legs together
and against his chest, feet pointed, made the head throw,
and calmly watched the starry sky, the lights of the hotel
then the water itself under him, all rotate around his open
eyes. When the water's edge of the ship appeared he made
the snapout, hands straight at sides, feet together, then shut
his eyes and blew out through his nose as he went under. It
was a good dive, but it wasn't perfect because he went in at
a slight angle leaning a little backward. That was because
he had flattened his arc that little bit to avoid hitting the ship.
But it was a good dive. Then he surfaced and swam off a
ways to wait for Bert, treading water. The Texans were
obviously impressed.

Then Bert made his dive, and it was a pretty bad one. He
did not get his knees more than half-way up to his chest. His
feet were at least a foot apart. And at his entry his right arm
flailed out as if for balance before he was fully under. He
went under almost sitting down.

Grant swam lazily back to the boat pleased with himself,
knowing he had won, the water feeling freshening and sobering. He climbed up the ladder, feeling good, to a lot of
noise going on on board—and to find to his disbelief that
the young Negro Green had already awarded the prize, the
bet, to Bert. Ferd's guest aboard the *Lady Suzanne*. Ferd
was chortling. At first Grant couldn't really believe it. He
knew he had won it, and won it hands down. But the young
Negro Green insisted the man from *Lady Suzanne* had made
the better dive. And he was the judge. And he remained

adamant. A great deal of argument began. Grant got himself another drink, and after a while—though the argument seemed to go on a long time—he lost some more time somewhere. To hell with it. Finally he left. As he walked up the wharf toward the hotel, all his for-a-while-forgotten misery about Jim Grointon coming back on him, Bonham was just in process of throwing the wadded $160 over the side into the water. "You want it, you pricks, you go and get it," Bonham was saying blazingly. "You're all a bunch of fucking thieves. And rich thieves at that! You obviously paid that punk kid off to say what he said. Now get off my ship. All of you! Now!" Not even a raft of Greens, plus all the Texans, were about to dispute with Bonham. It must be great to be a really *big* man, a really *big* man physically, sometimes. Well, he wasn't. And he would never be. He listened to the feet of the crowd on the wharf behind him.

The hotel room door was locked when he got to it and tried to open it, though the light was on. He knocked. "Go away," Lucky said from inside. "Go away forever." Grant threw his shoulder against the door, shaking most of the rickety, jerry-built hotel.—"Open this door, or I'll break it in," he said, and meant it.

This apparently influenced her. Lucky opened it. She was in her robe, a bottle of scotch and a half-filled glass were on the bed table. A book lay opened up and turned face down on the bed. She was pretty drunk herself, her eyes having that strange, mean, concentrated look they got when she was loaded. "You fool! You poor slobbering idiot fool! I'm ashamed to know you! I'm ashamed to be seen as your wife! You might have known those Texas bastards would cheat you, try to cheat you!"

"You saw it then," Grant said heavily. "Gimme a drink."

"*No!* Irma saw it. I wouldn't be caught *dead* seeing you make such a ridiculous spectacle of yourself!"

"Sure," Grant said and sat down heavily on the bed. "But you'd send old Irm out as your spy to come and tell you. Oh, boy. What a happy marriage we've brought ourselves around to, hunh? What a happy marriage. I said gimme a drink."

"You've had enough to drink," Lucky said viciously. "Far, far too much."

"That is not for you to decide," Grant said. "Pass me that fucking bottle or I'll tear this place apart! And I mean it!" Lucky handed it to him. "You're drunk yourself, for God's sake," he said. "I can tell by that mean look you get in your eyes."

"You should see yourself."

"Yeah. I bet. I don't want to." Grant tipped the bottle back and drank down the straight scotch in what he knew was only a gesture, a bad, unhealthy, and stupid gesture, even as he did it.

Some more time got lost somewhere. He knew only that he accused her openly, this time, accused her flatly of having slept with Jim Grointon. She fought back, saying she hadn't, but he couldn't remember her exact words or her arguments. Once in there somewhere she said, "I didn't! I told you I'd never tell you anything else, didn't I? So worry about it! No, I didn't fuck Jim Grointon! But whether I did or not, I should have! As far as you're concerned."

Then more time got itself lost. The last thing he remembered was her saying, "Get out! For God's sake get out! Out of my sight! They're going to throw us out of here! I can promise you!"

"Listen, I'm leaving! I've had it up to here with you! If this is what being married to a great artist is, I don't want it! I'm leaving! To-morrow! There's a seaplane from Kingston I can radio for! I inquired! I want to order that plane and leave on it to-morrow!"

"Then go," he said. "Go, Captain Willis, and may God be with you on your journey downward! Go! *Go!*"

"I need money," Lucky said.

"Ha!" Grant said and grinned a deeply drunken grin. "No money. *You* get the money. Get it anyway you can. But you'll not get it from me!"—"You son of a bitch!" was the answer he got. "Just get out. Just get out of my sight." —"Gladly," was his own answer.

Then he was walking alone down along the beach under those beautiful royal palms, plodding heavily in the deep sand. Where to go? There was a beautiful moon. A lover's moon. Finally after walking until he was tired, he lay down on the sand fully clothed and went to sleep. When the cold night air woke him in the deep dark after the moon had gone down, shuddering and deep-frozen to the bone, he covered himself with sand. Where to go? *What* to do? Thirty-six years old and already a cuckold! Thirty-six years old, and *two months married*, and already a cuckold. Still a cuckold. As the sand he had covered himself with in self-defence against the cold slowly warmed him, he drifted off to sleep.

When the first light of dawn woke him, he trudged back through all that deep sand (how in God's name had he ever made it this far down here, for God's sake!), and found Al Bonham already up and about on the *Naiad*, preparing to don an aqualung and go search for the $160 he had with such a magnificent gesture thrown away last night.

THIRTY-FIVE

When Al Bonham saw Grant trudging up the beach, he realised he was caught. That was his first thought. He was caught and he knew it. Caught right in the act. And since there didn't seem to be any way to get out of it, lie himself out of it, he decided to do what all them military and political types did when they got in that situation: take the other side in on it, take the enemy—no, not enemy: antagonist; opposition—take the opposition in on the conspiracy. He grinned as Grant trudged up and came on board. —" Get yourself a lung and come on along." he winked. " There's one all rigged there. If we find it, we'll split it fifty-fifty. You won it. And anyway there's nothing like a good thirty, forty-foot dive early in the morning when you got a hangover," he added.

Because Grant looked like the wrath of God. His white ducks which had been so white last night were grimy all over, and although he had obviously tried to brush himself off, sand clung to him everywhere. It was in his hair. He had come trudging along from the direction of the beach that led down to South Point, the southern end of North Nelson, where the new luxury hotel was being built, was in fact nearly completed. And that will settle those goddamned sons of bitching Greens, Bonham thought with happy meanness. Those bastards.

Bonham had, of course, expected Grant—or anybody—to come from the direction of the hotel. That was what had fooled him. He would have expected especially Grant to come from the direction of the hotel, where his room—and his wife—were. Lucky. Lucky, hell. Lucky my ass. She was about the most *un*Lucky thing that had ever happened to Bonham.

Orloffski, of course, was sound asleep below, sleeping off his hangover and his night of humping with that—or was it *those ;* Bonham didn't even know how many—Texas woman or women. And the Texans were now all quiet on their own ship, sleeping off their big drunk. They had still been " revelling " wasn't it they called it? on their own boat, when he had sneaked off to Cathie Finer's room in the hotel. Naturally, he had to be back on board by daybreak. That meant his second white night without sleep—though he had dozed a little upstairs it was true, between times, until she would wake him up again—(God, what a broad!). But since he did not have to be back at daylight, what was a better idea than to have a look on all that sand bottom for that money at dawn when everybody else would still be sleeping off their booze, or sex—or both? He had, actually, folded it all up together last night with that express idea in mind.

And now goddam Grant had to come trudging along at the very crack of dawn, looking like death warmed over. He did not quite know whether to ignore the way Grant looked or not. And he decided not to mention it. But then, since it was so very damned obvious, he decided it was better to mention it than not.

" Where the hell've *you* been, and what happened to you?" he grinned. " You look like one of our proverbial hurricanes wiped up the island with you, but I don't see no palm trees down anywhere." He'd fallen completely back into his bad-grammar style again, he noted. Sometimes, of course, he did it on purpose, for business. But something about Grant made him do it, do that. Maybe it was because he was literary and a famous playwright. Or maybe it was because he, Grant, wrote plays about people who talked like that. Well, hell. What difference did it make?

" My old lady threw me out. Told me to get out. So I did." Grant managed a feeble grin. But it was a very thin one. " Slept on the beach. Slept on the beach before. In my time."

" In the old Navy days, hunh?" Bonham grinned. " She

mad at you over 'The Great Diving Contest', hunh? Well, come on and get out of those godawful lookin' clothes and into that bikini of yours and we'll see if we can find that dough. It might just still be down there. If it didn't float off."

He waited while Grant changed; if they did find it, now, he would certainly have to split it with him, damn it. Then they slipped over the side quietly, using the ladder and putting their flippers on underwater so as not to wake anybody, grinning conspirators together. Though it was just after dawn and the sun itself had not yet risen above the horizon, there was still plenty of light to see by in the thirty-to-thirty-five-feet-deep clear green water. And as he swam over the weedless, clean, rippled sand bottom marred only by an occasional rusting beer can or old whisky bottle, looking for the wad of money, Bonham thought about Cathie Finer and his problem, his problems. His problems and what Grant had said about them, that night during the all-night sail.

That Grant was certainly smart about people. Course, that was probably why he was a playwright. Sam's hero. Of course, that was why she had picked him. And he knew it. Just because he *was* Sam's hero. But it was smart of Grant to figure that out. On the other hand, Bonham didn't care much why she'd picked him. And, in the true fact of it, she hadn't really done all that much " picking ", he had to admit. Not as much as he had let on to Grant that night at the wheel. He'd been in there doing a little picking himself. He'd been looking at her as far back as that first trip to Grand Bank, he suddenly remembered. But he hadn't thought there'd been any chance, back then. And there hadn't been. But he'd still had a little hots for her then, even so. He had thought even then that she'd be quite a piece of tail. But God! he hadn't bargained for what he'd finally got! When he finally did get it! Wow! Hell! Peering this way and that through his mask among the sparse beer cans and whisky bottles as he swam but seeing no wad of money, or even one bill, he thought back to the first night, that very same night Sam had left.

There had been some sort of something, some sort of unseen—ungiving and unreceived but still there—signal between them ever since that same afternoon, when Sam had suggested that she stay on and make the cruise and she had so cheerfully agreed. Bonham hadn't looked at her. She

hadn't looked at him. But it had been there, and he had let
her know it. Let her know it in some unseen, unsmelled
animal way he couldn't even describe. He only hoped Sam
hadn't seen or smelled it himself. It had made him hot right
then and there, *doubly* hot, with Sam sitting right there
beside him. Why was that? The intrigue, of course. Wasn't
it? It had to be that. Suddenly for the first time in a very
long time, adjusting his mask, Bonham thought about that
old highschool pingpong buddy who, after they both had returned from the war, had without ever actually saying it
offered him his wife and him, he had taken him up on it. He
had been ashamed of *that*; *then*. But not this. This Cathie
Finer brought something out in him he could never remember
having felt before. Except once or twice. He could never
have that kind of hots for that Lucky, now—that *un*Lucky
—not like this hots. But *un*Lucky really loved her man. Or
at least Bonham thought she did. Worse luck for his cruise,
and his corporation.

   She really was a cool customer. That Cathie. That night,
that same night after Sam had only just left how many
minutes after? just one drink, anyway, she had coolly dis-
invited herself from dinner at the hotel with the Grants and
the Spicehandlers, and taken that same, Sam's self-same
limousine and driven him and Orloffski into town for dinner.
And then, then, after the dinner, for which she'd slipped him
the money to pay, she had just as coolly had the limousine
(which she had coolly told off to wait) drive Orloffski back
to the docks.—" I want to do a little gambling," she told him
quite calmly and coolly, " and you're not really dressed for
going to a place like that, so Al will look after me." She had
told him that, that coolly, while quite plainly Bonham himself wasn't dressed a damn bit better than Orloffski was.
Orloffski had got out quietly.

   " Well, what'll it be?" she smiled at him coolly from her
corner without even touching him, without even touching
his hand, after the chauffeur had driven them off from the
dock. " Are you game to try the hotel?"

   " Well, won't they still all be up, there?"

   " If they are, they'll certainly be in the bar. And there's a
back way in, around by the beach."

   " It's kind of risky, isn't it?" he had said.

   " Oh, aren't you the scaredy-cat though!" she'd said. " All

right then, the Myrtle Beach it is!" and had leaned forward and told the chauffeur to go there. When they got out, she told the chauffeur she would not need him until five-thirty in the morning, and when he had tried to argue, told him not to worry she'd pay him double but just be there. And then she had walked into that lobby as if she owned it and registered them as man and wife and coolly told the clerk she wanted to leave a call for five-fifteen sharp because they were going out fishing; and the clerk had treated her like a queen. So did the bellboys. He had followed her to the elevator, speechless. It paid to have money. You knew how to use it. You learned. In the room she had said, " I'm only doing this because of Sam, you know. Because he loves and admires you so."—" I don't really care why you're doing it, Mrs. Finer," he had answered.—" I didn't think you would. Well, just so that you know," she had smiled and begun to take her clothes off. And what a body. She was the kind of rich man's wife Bonham had dreamed of ever since he had first gotten into this profession, way back there in the States. He had done things with her that night he had never done with any woman, had sworn he never *would* do. It was just a shame he had to be her husband's friend, was all.—" I just wish Sam was here, tied to that chair, watching all this," she had smiled sweetly once. " Then it would be *per*fect. Of course," she added sadly, " if he were, once he ever got loose he'd kill me."—" You mean he takes a dim view of this sort of thing?" Bonham said.—" He most certainly does," Cathie Finer had smiled. " Why else would I be doing it?"

Through his mask, from maybe thirty feet in front of him, Bonham saw Grant swimming toward him with spread-out arms and shaking his head. He made a despairing shrug. Bonham stopped thinking about his love life, and stopped looking too. The money just wasn't there. Being light, it might just have drifted off, especially if it had come un-wadded into separate bills. It was just bad luck. He shook his head also, back at Grant, and pointed upstairs, and back at the boat which by now was a good ways away from them. They hadn't found it. And if they hadn't found it by now, they wouldn't.

Mo Orloffski was already up, and waiting for them, when they climbed back on board. " Well, ain't you the couple of smart-ass types though," he grinned in his brutal, so unpleasant way but which Bonham had gotten pretty much used to by now. " Had the same idea myself. But you beat me to it. Okay, fork over."

" Except we didn't find it," Bonham said. " Not a wad, not nary a bill even."

" Come on," Orloffski growled. " Don't try to con *me*! I had eight bucks in that pot myself!"

" And if we'd of found it, you'd of gotten your sixteen. You don't think I'd leave you out, do you?"

" Not as long as I caught you. I don't. Come on! There ain't hardly any current down there at all. And you know it."

" Then some damn fish ate it or something," Bonham grinned. " You want us to stand search?"

" I sure as hell do," Orloffski said.

Bonham moved his head. " Okay, come on, Ron." He hooked his thumbs into his big boxer-type trunks and pulled them down to his knees, turning them inside-out so that he now stood bare-assed—and bare-peckered—on the open deck in the now bright sun and air, the aqualung tank still on his back. Grinning, he even lifted up with a finger the little inside pants, so Orloffski could see between them and the suit. Beside him, after watching, Grant grinned and did the same with his bikini, which however had no little inside pants. Now they both stood there in the full daylight and morning breeze bare-assed and bare-peckered. Anyone coming down the wharf, or even the path, could have seen clearly everything they had.

" Okay?" he grinned. " You want to look between the tank and my back for Christ's sake?" He moved his head again and both of them pulled back up their suits. Then they began to shuck out of the gear.

" Okay," Orloffski said dubiously. " But I sure don't understand it. Maybe you hid it somewhere."

" Aw, come on," Bonham said, irritably. " There wasn't nothing down there except old beer cans and whisky bottles." He put his own tank, then Grant's, into the tie racks he had rigged up for them along the side of the coachroof. " We'll have to fill those. But when we're under way. Not now. Compressor's noisy.

" Because," he said, particularly emphasizing each word, " I think we better get under way as soon as possible. As soon as possible before those Texans wake up over there. Or we're liable really to have some trouble with them. And those fucking Greens. We'll want to come back here some day," he explained, "on other trips."

That was the second time, he realised, that he had used the word—fucking—within twenty-four hours, the other being last night when he had kicked the Texans off his ship. That Cathie Finer was certainly changing him! Well, what the hell? "And that means," he added, "that somebody better be gettin' up to the hotel and wakin' up the deep sleepers."

"I'll do that," Grant offered.

When they were all congregated aboard and the hotel bills all settled, Bonham laid out his plan for them. They would pull out right now, before the Texans got up, eat later under way, and head down for the famous, ritzy Dog Cay. It was a little over half a day's sail. They could lay up there to-night —lubbers sleep'ng on the damned dock if they must—fish around those waters all next day, and then if they wanted, come back here—because he knew, had found out from them, that the Texans were definitely leaving out, the next day. To-morrow. For the States. They had been here over a week now this trip, Ferd had told him before the trouble started, and that was about as long as any one man's stomach could stand that much boozing. Were there any disagreements or other suggestions from those on board the *Naiad?* There were not. It was great, absolutely great, standing there in the afterdeck and cockpit in that chill blue after-light of just after dawn, all larded over with—but completely separate from— the yellow and red light of the sun itself, all of them barefooted and in their shorts and trunks and thin shirts and the girls' round thighs all covered with goosebumps. "Okay," he said, "then the sooner we get under way the better."

It was in getting under way that an incident occurred that gave him a further insight into the strange and double-natured character of Grant, which Bonham had never been able to understand anyway. They were lying portside to the dock, and Grant was up forward to cast off with Ben Spice-handler standing behind him there back on the deck to "help" him. After he had started the motor and they'd cast off bow and sternlines and were moving, a sudden puff of breeze came up from nowhere, as they will do, blowing the bow against the wharf. No harm in that, except that Grant was standing there after casting off, and as the ship moved rearward with the motor in reverse, backing away from the stern of the Texas yacht, Bonham saw they were going to strike just where one of the ancient waist-high, outward-leaning old wooden wharf-posts stood. The ship wouldn't be hurt, the rope fenders he had woven up himself so carefully would protect the ship, but the jutting wharf-post would strike just where Grant was standing, and almost certainly crush him, crush one or both of his legs against the heavily braced, wire-rope shrouds. There was nothing Bonham could do, and his heart leaped up in his throat. To change helm would take far too long to affect anything before they struck. There wasn't even time to throw the motor into forward out of reverse. There was only seconds. And if he tried to jump and missed, he'd get it between the dock and the hull. All Bonham could do was hope and holler, " Ron!"

But Grant, who had already tossed the big eye-splice of the bowline back behind him to Ben Spicehandler, was already alerted. As coolly, calmly and sweetly as a professional ballet dancer who had been practising a particular movement all his life, he watched the dangerous post approaching him, calculating his distance, and then skipped to his left around the shrouds back to deck, and standing on his left leg withdrew his right leg from in front of the wharf-post just half a second before it met the shrouds. And Grant was safe. Bonham had never seen as cool a calculation followed by the completed action in his life, and he'd seen some good ones.

But then the other part of this strange guy's strange character took over. Grant began to shake. That he was actually shaking was not visible from as far back as the wheel at the stern, but Bonham could tell that he was. Now that the guy was safe, after as cool an act as Bonham had ever seen, he got scared! And not only that, *was not ashamed to show it!* After a moment Grant sat down on the coach-roof top and put his head between his hands. Bonham would *never* have let himself do that! Bonham immediately jerked his chin at Orloffski, and Mo sauntered forward grinning, with a bottle of gin. " Pretty cool, there, pretty cool!" he heard Orloffski say admiringly. " I think I would have jumped for the dock." Grinning a little sickly, Grant downed a healthy slug of the gin.—" I was afraid I might miss the dock," he heard Grant answer. After a moment the playwright got up and came aft grinning and still a little shaky.

" Close shave," Bonham said, making it deliberately laconic.

" Sure was," Grant said.

" I'm sorry about that," Bonham went on calmly, " but there wasn't a damn thing I could do after that breeze blew up. Just wasn't any time."

" You think it hurt the shrouds?" Grant said. His wife, who had seen it all from up in the starboard bow, came and stood beside him. Her face was white.

" Naw-w," Bonham said. " No, sir. They're strong. Anyway, it hardly even touched them. It was you between the two there that was bad. But tell me: why afterwards—why after it's all over and you know you're safe—why did you get scared *then*? Once it's over, and you're okay, it's all done!"

" Nerves, I guess," Grant grinned. " Too much imagination." He made suddenly as if to put his arm around his wife, then did not do it; Bonham could not tell if it was because they were still mad, or whether on his second thought the playwright thought it might seem unmanly. In any case, his wife, Lucky, turned and walked away, right back up to the bow where she'd been with Irma and Cathie, without a word.

Anyway, they were away with no harm done. Bonham headed up into the breeze and had the boys set the mainsail easing off just a little on the mainsheet. After they were out a few more hundred yards he cut the motor and had them set the jib. Then after things had settled down a little, he sent Orloffski below to cook up bacon and eggs and coffee. Even Orloffski could make bacon and eggs and coffee. They ate outside clustered around the saloon hatch, near the cockpit, sitting on the coachroof. He ate his own plate of eggs at the wheel. Then they all went forward, except himself at the wheel, to what little deck and coachroof space there was left open. He supposed he had overloaded her a little for this trip. But he hadn't known what damned lubbers they all were! He had asked Ben and Irma that day at the Crount just on the spur of the moment. The wind was from the east-southeast to-day and fresh, and since they were heading almost due south he could put her on a close reach and she would practically sail herself. God, what a sweet old gal. There was no need to navigate or sail by compass since the string of uninhabited little islets were all clearly visible off the starboard beam. Bonham put her on the port tack and, sitting all alone back at the wheel by himself, let himself think some more about his new lady-friend, Cathie Finer.

She was sitting up front with the others, all of them in their swimsuits and bikinis naturally, and every now and then, when some one or other of them moved, he could catch a glimpse or long look at one or both of those beautiful long slim legs he knew so well now. He couldn't tell much about the Grants. They certainly didn't seem to be staying so very close together to-day. They certainly weren't acting love-birds. Lucky—*un*Lucky—was spending all of her time forward with the girls, apparently, Irma and Cathie. The surgeon and his girl were off by themselves. That left Grant and Ben together, with Orloffski. He probably had overloaded her by one couple, probably. But what the hell? Paying dockage charges!

Grant was probably right about the dangerousness of what he was doing. What he was doing with Cathie. And he was well aware, now, and had been, that Cathie's taking up with him was deliberately because he *was* Sam's big hero, and that that was her *only* reason. She had told him, over the days—and the nights—all about Sam's philanderings back in New York after Grand Bank. But it was also clear, from what she had said the very first night in Kingston—as well as things she'd said later—that Sam, philanderer even so, was no upholder of no Single Standard. Sam was obviously a Double Standard man—as of course he was himself—so there certainly was danger in what he was doing, like Grant had said. But on the other hand, he was pretty surely convinced that Cathie was not at all thinking about telling Sam she had slept with his hero Bonham. To do it was apparently enough, without having to tell him. Mean. Very mean. And yet in some perverse way that Bonham didn't really fully understand it added to the very attraction for him. Dirty. She was really dirty. But she wasn't *his*, wasn't Bonham's wife. No, she wouldn't tell. Not unless perhaps at some long now-unforeseen time in the future when she and Sam divorced. She liked having access to Sam's money pretty obviously. She *liked* having it to spend. She probably would never divorce him. No, she wouldn't tell. And if he did catch her with some guy, at some indefinite future date, and she did tell him about Al Bonham, the schooner's corporation, Bonham's and Orloffski's Corporation, would be such a going concern by then the withdrawal of his $10,000—of his *twenty* thousand—wouldn't destroy it or even hurt it. No, she wouldn't tell. Grant was wrong about that. And who the hell was there to tell on them? Ben and Irma? The surgeon? Grant? Orloffski? None of them had any reason to tell, and Orloffski stood to lose as much as Bonham if he told.

But, even so, there was more to it than that. There was that body, for one thing! And what she knew how to do with it. But there was still something else. There was the dirtiness. The very dirtiness of what they were doing was at least fifty per cent of the attractiveness of it. She was dirty, really *dirty*. To be doing to Sam what she was doing, and doing it deliberately. And so was he. So was Bonham. Even if Sam was philandering and stepping out on her, she was dirty, especially dirty, to go out with Sam's hero Bonham. And Bonham was especially dirty too, to be screwing the wife of Sam, knowing that he *was* Sam's hero. Bonham flexed one of his big arms, the one that was not holding the wheel. Strength, size was no credit to a man. You were born with it or you weren't. But people *would* heroise it. So they were both dirty. And that was exactly why he wanted her. He wanted Cathie, he realised, because she *was* dirty and she brought out all the dirtiness in him, all the dirtiness that had always been there but he'd never been able to free, to bring up and out of himself. And she wasn't *his* wife. Poor old Sam. Christ, if she was *his* wife, he'd—

Anyway, he wanted it. Whatever reasons. He wanted it and he was having it, and he meant to keep on having it. It had brought out things in him he had never even suspected were there. And he liked those things. Sometimes a man just didn't give a damn, like he had told Grant that first night out, just didn't give a *damn*. And Christ, it could go on for years, off and on, if they were careful—with Sam partly in the business, and coming down for cruises, maybe even buying a place in GaBay. It could go on for *years*. Maybe. He had not tried to feel her out about telling Sam, as Grant had suggested he do, but he was reasonably sure she wouldn't. Well— He stopped thinking about it and looked

at his watch. It was just past noon, and that meant they had
another hour's sail or so to Dog Cay. If they stopped now
and spearfished up their lunch and ate, they could be there
by two-thirty or three in plenty of time to see all the island.
Calling forward to Orloffski to handle the jib if necessary,
he brought her slowly around, jibing slowly, until the wind
was on his starboard quarter and headed in toward one of the
little islets where he had fished before and knew there was
plenty of stuff to catch.

It was while he was cooking the lunch from the fish they'd
caught after going around the islet and anchoring in the lee,
that he—standing in the galley sweating and working—overheard the conversation between Lucky and Irma, who happened to be sitting alone together on the coachroof just above
the galley's long rectangular port.

He had not listened much to what they were saying until
he heard first the seaplane and then his own name mentioned. Then he looked up and started to listen. Right in
front of him, touching distance, less than touching distance,
through the rectangular port, hung these two lovely pairs of
female legs, easy enough to recognise even without the voices,
Irma's slighter and of course much the darker, being Jewish,
and the others—Lucky's—nervously and continuously crossing and uncrossing their ankles. What he heard so infuriated
him that he very nearly burned the lunch.

"Well, I _know_ I can get one from North Nelson," Lucky
was saying. "So I don't see why, if they have a resident
manager and all that, they won't also have radio equipment at
Dog Cay too."

"I'm not saying they _don't_ have it," Irma answered. "I'm
only saying you better think twice, think _several_ times,
before you really decide to do it."

"I told you I've had it," Grant's wife answered quickly.
"Up to here."

"And I'm saying you're very seriously endangering your
marriage if you do it," Irma said, just as hotly. "Think about
that. If you ruin this cruise for Ron—"

"It's already ruined," Lucky Grant said. "And as for the
marriage . . ." She added, "I sometimes wonder if I even
care."

"You care. And I don't think the cruise is all that terrible.
I'm enjoying myself. And if it's that one drunken night

with those horrible Texans, and that drunken diving contest, I can't understand it," Irma said. "That's not worth going *home* over—especially if it means your marriage maybe goes *too*?"

It ended on a sort of plaintive question. Lucky Grant did not answer.

"And I know it isn't still over that old thing about that old Mrs. Abernathy ex-girl-friend of his," Irma said. "You forgave him for that. I heard you say so. And you *acted* it. You *acted, showed* that you'd forgiven him. I can't understand, Lucky, I really can't."

There then came a long, curiously long, sort of suspicious (Bonham felt), almost guilty, pause which he could not make out the meaning of.

"So what is it?" Irma said, finally.

"Well, for one thing it's that goddamned Bonham," Lucky Grant said, but in a changed, rather strange voice. "He's horrible. That gross fat huge ugly creature. And he's not safe. I know he isn't."

"Well, he's done everything well so far," Irma said. "And everything he's said has come right out on the dot."

"And he's cheap," Lucky Grant said. "A big cheap lard-ass bastard. Not wanting to pay docking charges. Not wanting to allow dinners ashore and only eating the fish we catch. What kind of cheap cruise is that? With all the money he's charging you people."

"He never actually quoted us any prices, really," Irma Spicehandler said. "Ben figured maybe twenty, twenty-five dollars a day per person."

"I'll tell you something else," Lucky Grant said. "I think he's fucking Cathie Finer."

"Oh, hell, I've known that since the night Sam Finer left Kingston," Irma said. "But that's not any of our business."

"It is if *your* husband had happened to have loaned him four thousand five hundred dollars to get his schooner out of hock! Even if he does fix up the insides, which are really truly horrible now, he's so damn low-class he's never going to make it with this yacht and company. Not with any *high-class* clients. And if he loses Sam Finer's support . . ."

It trailed off significantly. Bonham suddenly remembered to look at his fish, and turned them with a spatula that was trembling with fury in his hand.

"But I still don't see what all of that has to do with you deciding to order a *seaplane* over here to take you *home*," Irma insisted.

"He hates my guts," Lucky Grant said. Which was true enough, Bonham thought from down below. "He hates me because I've got Ron. And he *wants* Ron. I've taken his beloved Ron away from him. I think he's some kind of a half-fag. Latent fag. Or something."

"Still," Irma insisted stubbornly, "Ron—"

"Oh, Ron!" Lucky said furiously. "He's at least as bad as them! He loves all these guys as much as they love him! As much as Bonham loves him. That's another thing that makes me—And I'll tell you something else," Lucky said in a much lowered voice, and her pair of legs leaned away from Irma's, as her invisible upper body leaned toward her. And Bonham knew, surely, with a kind of transfixing horror, what she was just about to say. And if she did say that—to Irma—to *Irma Spicehandler*—or *anybody*—everything would be over. It would tear the whole damned cruise, the whole damned thing. He *himself* wouldn't be able to go on with it. Letta *had* told her. "He—"

"*Ladies!*" Bonham boomed, in his best and loudest "Sea Captain's" voice. "Ladies! Luncheon is now being served in the saloon and on the afterdeck and cockpit! Lunch is served!"

The two pairs of legs jerked. Then they disappeared sideways and two upside-down faces replaced them. "Oh, hello!" Bonham said. He gave them his very best smile (though he feared it wasn't much good, the way he felt), and at the same time tried to put into his eyes the total and extreme contempt he felt for the both of them. Women! "Lunch is served," he said softly. The faces disappeared, then the legs disappeared, too, walking aft.

While they ate the fish, Lucky Grant came over to him where he was perched alone on the lifeline with his plate.— "I suppose you heard what I said about you," she said in a subdued, but strangely stubbornly proud enough voice to indicate she would repeat every word of it to his face if he asked her to.

"Heard?" he said pleasantly. "Were you saying something about me? I wish I *had* heard. I was far too busy cooking. I thought all of you were over on the starboard foredeck. That's why I yelled so loud." He smiled at her pleasantly, while at the same time putting back into his eyes all he really felt about her. The long look he got in return was enigmatic in the extreme, then she took her plate and walked away.

An hour later, after the plates and pots had been dropped overboard and thoroughly washed in sand and sea water by Orloffski in an aqualung, they were under way for Dog Cay, and an hour after that they were docked there.

Now Dog Cay really was ritzy. The Duke and Duchess of Windsor had often stayed there a few weeks during the season, that was how ritzy it was, and Bonham knew how unship-shape, how un-ritzy-ship-shape, and gypsy-like poor old *Naiad* looked pulling in there, with all her diving gear and stuff strewn all over. But the British were great sticklers for all forms of sea-hospitality, being an old race of sailors. And fortunately (he had inquired about this at North Nelson) Dog Cay still had the same resident manager they'd had when Bonham had sailed here two years ago. Bonham had sailed in here as assistant Master (though actually acting as Master) two years before on a *very*-ritzy-ship-shape private yacht, and the resident manager recognised him instantly and happily. What the hell, it was lonely for him, living here as the only white Britisher during the off season. He came out on to the dock in very white, very starched ducks and wearing a very handsome white yachting cap with its own big gold *Mgr* insignia on it, and welcomed them practically with open arms. First off, they must come to the office where he would break out a *new* bottle of scotch in their honour, have a drink, and then he would give them all a tour of the island in the " house " Land-Rover. " Long time no see!" he said to Bonham. " Long time no see! And how *is* Commodore Inspane?" The " Commodore " Inspane had been the rich owner and " Master " of the ritzy yacht Bonham had sailed for him. He was fine, Bonham said—though he had not seen him since, since then. And they all trooped to the office for the *new* scotch bottle.

Bonham however had a swimming lesson to give. To Irma. So while the others made the tour of the island with the so hospitable resident manager, he himself took Irma into the shallow water off the lovely sand beach right beside the wharf where the schooner was docked. He himself had already seen the island anyway, with its big lovely well-made homes, handsome walled-in gardens, groves of tall royal and coco palms all over. If anywhere was a true " island paradise ", it was here at Dog Cay, but Bonham didn't give a damn if he saw it again. None of it was his. And Irma would much rather have her swimming lesson than tour the island, she said happily.

Bonham believed in the old-fashioned method of teaching swimming to rank neophytes. Give them the old frogkick and breastroke with the head entirely out of water first. Then teach them a good solid sidestroke. The crawl was no damn good for anything really, except somebody who wanted to be a speed swimmer, or wanted to do it for exercise. He had already given Irma one lesson for an hour or so yesterday, and had got her so she could do the old frogkick-breastroke for fifty yards or so without putting her feet down. To-day he concentrated on the sidestroke, and before very long had her so she was swimming two hundred yards out and two hundred yards back. Irma was a good, and eager, pupil. But then he was a damn good teacher. After she could do around four hundred yards sidestroke in water over her head without panicking, he decided to put her through the mask and snorkel routines—which she picked up quickly, using his method—and then took her out with the mask, snorkel and flippers since the tour party wasn't back. The flippers of course delighted—and surprised—her with how easy they made everything, as they always did everyone. So did the mask, naturally, when she realised she could actually *see* underwater. It always delighted every pupil. Unfortunately here there was nothing but pure white sand for as far out as you could swim, so there was no shallow reef or small fish for her to look at, but he took her alongside the hull of the schooner to look at it and at the few barnacles that had already attached to it. Then, finally, holding their breath together and him holding her by the hand, they swam under the schooner together—but belly up—for her to look at it—and come up on the other side under the dock. After that he let her explore along the dock, where there were a few—a very few—sergeant-majors for her to look at, and let her swim down along the wooden dock posts to the twelve-foot bottom to look at the sea growths which had attached to them. Of course she was delighted. And by the time the others returned from their tour of the lovely tropical island, full of praise for it and for the resident manager, who was beaming, he had Irma ready to try her first little aqualung dive.

" This would cost you twenty-five or thirty bucks back in Kingston, or in my place at Ganado Bay," he told her with a sour grin, " at the very least. But just to show you how cheap I'm really not, I'm not even going to charge you a nickel for any of it."

Grant and Ben went with them, starting off the sand beach so that she could wade out and go under first in water that wasn't over her head. Then, when she was used to that, they all four of them swam along the bottom and under the schooner and back and forth along the bottom under the wharf, he himself holding her hand (something he had learned always gave a lady beginner confidence), Grant and Ben swimming along on both sides, both of them gesticulating their pleasure to her. When he brought her up finally, he grinned and said, " So now you're a diver!" Little Irma was delighted. It was partially a lie, of course, because he hadn't shown her any of the lung techniques except the essential one of clearing the mask underwater. It was too shallow here to teach her ear-clearing, but he could show her that to-morrow, and it was true that she could then probably dive on the shallow reefs they were likely to be seeing on the rest of the cruise, as long as she had himself or Grant—or Orloffski—with her. But when Lucky Grant was asked if she wouldn't like to go through the same routine, she steadfastly and stubbornly refused.

There was enough fish and lobster tails left from the noon-time spear-fishing to make plenty of food for dinner, but the resident manager (hungry, as he must always be this time of year, for company) invited them ashore for dinner, where he broke out excellent deep-freeze steaks that had been flown in by seaplane from the States, and even went so far as to bring out several bottles of good Bordeaux wine. Everybody was a little tight when they finally said good night to him and went back to the wharf and the ship by flashlight.

" Any of you damned landlubbers who want to sleep on the dock can," Bonham told them when they were back on board. " I spoke to the manager about it and explained that we were just on our shakedown cruise and were also a little overcrowded. And he's so damned glad to see some people he'd agree to damn near anything! But I just want you to know that it embarrasses me to do it, to have had to do it. The private houses here are all closed up, of course.

"So you can sleep up here if you want, but I'm damned if I'm going to carry any mattresses off for anybody. You'll just have to sleep in your blankets."

"Well, I'm going to sleep on the dock," Lucky Grant said immediately.—"Then so will I, of course," Ron said. Ben and Irma also both elected to sleep out on the dock. The surgeon and his girl said they might as well keep their same old place on the forward deck, and naturally later on the same scramblings and thumpings were heard by all.

"Well, I'm gonna sleep below," Bonham said. "Like a proper cruising yachtsman ought to."

"I think I'll sleep below too," Cathie Finer said coolly.

"Then you can have the master cabin," Bonham said blank-faced. "And I'll take the portside bunk. That way you'll have more privacy."

"That's fine, Cathie said coolly.

"I can even sleep up in crew's quarters in the forepeak, if you want more privacy," Bonham said.

"Oh, no," she said. "You won't bother me there."

"I guess I'll sleep on the dock too," Orloffski said with a cynical grin at the both of them. "I'm gettin' a little tired of the curve of the damned coachroof."

And that was the way it was settled and arranged.

Of course Bonham did not sleep in the portside bunk at all. And when they were in the not-large master cabin bed together he found he could not help but ask Cathie if she didn't think her so open decision to sleep below was not maybe a bit incautious.

"What the hell?" she said calmly. "I don't care if they know. I don't care if anybody knows. Excepting Sam, of course.

He told her what—or part of what—he had overheard between Lucky Grant and Irma to-day.

"I'm sure they all know," Cathie said calmly.

"But don't you think it might get back to Sam from somebody?" Bonham half-whispered.

"From some of them? Why?" she said. "What difference

does it make to any of them? Why would any of them want to tell Sam?"

"I don't know," he said. "No reason that I know. But gossip travels. And it still seems to me that that—what you did to-night—might be just the slightest bit incautious."

Cathie didn't answer him—"Aren't we going to play?" she asked after a moment or two.

"We sure as hell are," he said huskily.

They had an invitational breakfast ashore the next morning with the resident manager, a superb breakfast at which even kippered herring was served in typical British style, and after a late start spearfished most of the day in the waters near Dog Cay and during which little Irma actually managed to spear a small grouper while diving in a lung with Bonham and Grant beside her. She was quite a kiddie, that Irma. Then they set sail once again for North Nelson. North Nelson, and the Greens. Lucky Grant had apparently decided to do nothing about radioing for a seaplane to come and pick her up. They pulled in just at dusk. The Greens treated them just as if nothing had ever happened. The Texans were gone. Only the young Green who had been the judge of the Great Diving Contest, the one who ran the restaurant, seemed a little bit surly. They ate there anyway.

After all the rooms had been arranged, and all the others had retired to them, Bonham hung around the ship a while and had a few drinks with Orloffski. Then he said he was going to take himself a walk and went off down the beach. After he was out of sight of the port he circled back and sneaked up to Cathie Finer's room, where of course she was waiting for him. She had become like dope to him. Real dope. Real dirty, self-abandoned dope. God, was she dirty. He was glad she wasn't *his* wife. Poor old Sam. Poor old *idiot* Sam. It made him even hotter.

THIRTY-SIX

Final calamity came the next day. Or rather, in the evening, the night, of the next day. They had all of them, or just about all, suffered minor or major calamities, minor or near-major (even major) catastrophes, Grant mused, since the beginning of this adventure way back in November or December of last year when he had first gotten this crazy (or peculiar, strange) idea to learn skindiving, and when he had not yet even met Lucky Videndi. Lucia Angelina Videndi. All of them, all of them except maybe Ben and Irma (who were not really involved and who anyway had apparently gone through theirs a long time back that time when Ben had run off for a year, before finally returning), all of them had suffered some misery or other. But this calamity was real, true catastrophe. Terminal catastrophe. Like " Terminal Cancer ", as the euphemists of stage, screen, radio and *Pravda* were so fond of saying now. Terminal catastrophe. End of cruise catastrophe. Five nights out of Kingston, on what could only be a seven or possibly eight-day cruise now anyway, because of inordinate (and perhaps unnecessary?) delays in getting the ship outfitted and ready to leave, catastrophe happened. So that, with only two days to go, at the *very* best two and a half, it came before the final sail back to Ganado Bay could even be begun and save it from the total, the bad-taste-in-the-mouth, feel-of-ruin catastrophe with which it ended.

And as always on this trip, nature, the sea, bad winds, storms, hurricanes, nothing, no other natural phenomenon such as even the Greens, nothing could be held responsible except the people.

It ended with Ron Grant having a broken nose (and being thus totally unable to dive any more at all anyway for at least a month, or two), and it ended with just about everybody on board not speaking to everybody else on board. Thinking back on it, as he always liked to do, though he rarely gained anything, any knowledge at all from such practice, Grant thought that perhaps—during the middle of the day while they were out spearfishing still—he had had a

premonition of it, when he did something so outrageous
(though only to himself) that it made him suspect he was
getting close to being insane. But like with all his poor
premonitions he could—unlike Lucky—only view them as
such a long time after events had proven them out, thus
obviating them as any real premonitions.

The day began auspiciously enough, at dawn again—though
the night before, the night of their return from Dog Cay, had
not been all that fine, admirable.

Grant had tried very hard not to drink much that day, and
that night, the night they returned to North Nelson, and had
succeeded quite well. In spite of that, after dinner, when they
had all retired early, he and Lucky had spent the best part
of—the *whole* of—the night on the very opposite edges of the
regular-sized double bed they had in the thin-walled, rickety,
jerry-built hotel room supplied (at premium, naturally) by
the Greens.

Whatever pleasant sexual practices were going on between Bonham and Cathie in her room, or in the room of
the Spicehandlers, or between the surgeon and his girl who—
like hamsters in their chosen-corner rutting place of a
rather unprivate cage—were still in their same old spot on the
deck ; whatever was going on with any of these, there was
nothing going on in the Ron Grant's room.

Lucky had tried a couple of times, tentatively, earlier on,
to make up with him from their big fight and accusation of
two nights before, but Grant, self-convinced, self-*convicted*
cuckold since the night he had stood in the coachroof hatch
during the long sail had been polite but distant. He simply
could not get that curiously faceless, though obviously Jim
Grointon, image out of his mind. And now when they lay in
the bed, and she made a half-tentative gesture toward him, he
repulsed her almost savagely. Because of the first night's sail,
the next night's sleeping aboard at the islet anchorage, the
third night's big fight, then the night on the dock at Dog
Cay, they had not had any sex at all for five nights ; but
Grant did not care.—" I'm too damned tired from all that
spearfishing to-day to think about making love," he said,
almost brutally. Silently she had turned away toward the
wall and her own bed edge. As a reciprocal gesture, Grant
had moved himself over to his own bed edge.—" It's funny,"
he said after a while, " I find now that I'm much braver

underwater, much more courageous now, since we've become
'estranged', as they say. Isn't that funny?" He made it
heavily ironic. Lucky did not answer. And so that was the
way they lay. It was no hardship at all for them to get up
at dawn when the first light came into the room, and dress
to go down to the *Naiad*.—" I think," Lucky said thinly as
they were dressing, but in a strangely tired voice, " that when
we come in to-day, I'm going to wire for that Kingston seaplane to come get me to-morrow. You'd better be prepared
to give me the money. If you don't, I'll get it from Ben."
Grant merely nodded. But by the time she really could have
done that, gone all the way through with it, it—" the cruise " ;
as cruise—was already all over, and there was no need.
Bonham was happily cooking bacon and eggs on *Naiad* with
the bright red disc of the sun just letting go its last touch of
the horizon as they came down. There was the delicious,
normally so happy-making, homey, friendly smell of coffee
in the fresh morning air.

And so the final day began.

He took them, Bonham took them, to a place about a half
an hour's sail from the dock out through the pass between
North and South Nelson and off to the north-northwest,
where there was a large collection of fairly small reefs over
an area of several hundred yards, all separated by pure white
sand, and all ranging in depth from fifteen to never more
than forty or forty-five feet. It was a superb spot. And Bonham obviously knew it well, from before. And yet he had
never brought them here. It was clear to Grant, at least, that
Bonham could easily have docked them on every night at
North Nelson for two or even three weeks and never have
run out of new and interesting, superb diving spots. And if
that was so, it was clear that Bonham's only reason for not
wanting to was just simply to save himself money on dockage charges. And that was no way to run a ritzy, luxury,
" rich-man's " cruise (especially with *Naiad*'s present accommodations!), which was the type of reputation, and clientele,
Bonham wanted to acquire. Grant made a mental note to talk
to him about this.

In any case, Bonham anchored them squarely in the centre
of this large patch of separated reefs, all richly teeming with
all sorts of fish and under-sea life large and small. Everybody at once put on free-diving gear and within a few

minutes had collected enough fish and lobster tails to feed them all lunch, a huge lunch, and even dinner, a huge dinner—if any of them wanted it for dinner. After that they—those of them who wanted; those of them who could—all put on aqualungs and went off exploring the farther, slightly deeper reefs.

And it was then that there occurred the strange experience, act, outrageous act, which Grant was later to rather lamely and half-heartedly refer to as what he *should* have recognised as his " premonition ". The ship as she lay was heading southeast, and Grant had swum off to the southwest where he had noticed a reef a hundred yards or so away. Orloffski had come off on that side too, but had turned off toward the southeast. It was true that it was not customary, or even accepted or recommended practice, to go off alone like that, but on dives as shallow and as short as these nobody well-acquainted with diving and the lung ever paid any attention to this " buddy " principle—except of course in the case of little Irma, and even Ben, though Ben had now begun to go off by himself on little forays. But this was Bonham's job, of course. This particular time he had taken Irma and Ben off to the northeast clear over on the other side of the ship, where the surgeon and his girl-friend were also diving. So Grant was really alone when he came up to his little reef.

The first thing he noted was that it was almost circular in shape. For some reason the coral had grown that way, and while there were a few irregular entrances into it here and there, it made an almost perfect circle of coral, with a clean white sand field completely bare of any growth: weed, gorgonia, anything: in its centre. A really strange formation in any case, something he had never seen before. It wasn't deep; to the sand bottom in the centre was maybe thirty to thirty-five feet, while the circle of coral around it rose up to maybe twenty and in places fifteen feet from the surface. Rather adventurously, or at least feeling rather adventurous, he decided to swim in over the coral and go down into the centre and have a look.

It was true, as he had told Lucky last night, that since their " estrangement " (what a word!) he had curiously grown more brave, more courageous underwater, in his diving. It had started back when she had gotten angry and had " estranged " herself from him over Carol Abernathy. It had

grown stronger, considerably stronger, after that horrifying
" spaghetti dinner " night—although he had not—or had he?
—yet begun to " estrange " himself from her. But after that
moment during the all-night sail (he would never forget that
moment), when he had stood in the open hatchway, one armpit resting on each side of the coachroof while the ship communicated its so-delicious lilting movement to his body as it
moved through the water, and him looking up at the so-
bright stars and the masthead that moved back and forth
in a great arc amongst them, and had suddenly known,
realised, become convinced that she *had* in fact cuckolded
him—after *that* moment, his courage, bravery (whatever you
wanted to call it) underwater had suddenly grown at least
two hundred per cent. At least. Maybe more. It was not
that he was reckless. Or at least he didn't think it was:
recklessness. It was just that he had become more aggressive,
more belligerent, and being more aggressive became less
thoughtful, and being less thoughtful was less cautious. It was
as if in the diving he was relieving himself of some terribly
intense, and yet at the same time equally terrible un*know*-
able, frustration over her and over all of it. Bonham and
Ben had both commented on it, this new aggressiveness,
during the cruise. And, well what the hell? why not? But
just the same, and in spite of all that, what he saw—on his
right—when he swam slowly down into the sand centre of
the coral ring, made his heart literally stop beating. For
several seconds. Or at least it seemed that long.

On his right in that part of the coral ring that ran all
around him was a large deep overhang, like so many that
you saw continually down on the reefs, but under it, just
lying there, was the hugest fish he had ever seen in his life—
including the giant snapper Jim Grointon had once shown to
him and Ben from a distance. It was so big that it was as if
his eyes refused to believe it for several seconds. They kept
travelling up along it from tail to head strangely, as if trying
to convince him not to believe what they were seeing for him.

It was partially hidden by parts of the overhang which
drooped lower in some places than others, and he swam
down farther and levelled off, being careful not to disturb
the sand and make a cloud, and then he saw that it was a
shark. And at that moment he decided to shoot it.

He didn't know why he decided to shoot it, and could not

even have said. There was no audience. To perform for. He was totally alone. But so much the better. He did not know what it was doing there. He knew sharks could not float and sometimes were said to take rests on the bottom, but sharks of this size were supposed to live only out in the deep ocean. Weren't they? He could not even make out what kind of shark it was. He could see enough of the snout, as he swam carefully and very slowly a few yards off, to see that it had no barbels and was no nurse shark, but then nurse sharks never got that big. It did not have the characteristic spots that mark the tiger shark, but tigers never got that big, either, did they? It was at least three times his own length, and more. Maybe four times. Maybe even more. What would that be? Three times his own length, was about seventeen feet. Four times was about twenty-three feet. The tail was almost entirely covered by an especially long over-hang so that he could not see if it was the " lunate " type tail which characterised the white shark and the mako, but the white shark—the real " man-eater "—was the only shark he had ever heard of that attained such lengths. It was sort of reddish brown in colour, and the huge dorsal fin, like a damned sail, was only two-thirds visible under the over-hang. How the damned thing had managed to wriggle itself in under there was incredible anyway. And all the time all this was running through his mind, in really only a very few seconds, he was preparing to shoot it.

He did not know why he wanted to shoot it, or why he had to shoot it. But he knew he did want to, and knew he did have to. He really didn't expect to kill it. The way it was, under the overhang, he couldn't get a real brain shot. But if he hit it right, so that the spear went forward through the mouth he was pretty sure it wouldn't attack him. It prob-ably wouldn't anyway. As a precautionary move, he slowly and stealthily drew his knife from his leg sheath and cut the heavy cord that attached the spear to the gun. The gun was already cocked, both rubbers. Then, holding the knife in his left hand, he swam slowly toward it.

The beast had not moved at all during the time, say ten or twelve seconds, that he had been there. He had swum away a few yards, now he approached it from the tail (which he still could not see), swimming up along its length from behind until he could see the gill slits. It was at least four times his length, he was pretty sure. Then, when he had the gill slits in view, he reversed his position slowly and with very careful movements, so that his feet were toward the shark. Aiming from between his feet at the gill slits, from almost on the very sand bottom now, he tried to aim upward, forward, toward where the brain would be, trying for a brain shot. When he pulled the trigger and felt the jolt in his arm—that finality—he was already swimming backward along the bottom as hard as he could swim.

It was well that he did. The shark erupted out of the overhang like some kind of projectile, taking most of the overhang with it when it did. It was as if an underwater explosion had occurred. Pieces and chunks of sharp coral sailed slowly through the water, turning in slow motion, exactly the way debris from a topside explosion would have flown more swiftly through the air, and was followed more slowly by a great cloud of sand and coral dust. Pieces of sharp coral stung Grant's arms and legs and chest, but even so he swam up until at least his head was out of the dust-sand cloud. The shark, whose snout had been almost at one of the little entryways into the coral ring, had swum, plunged, out through this, and—his head above the sand cloud—Grant watched it, gyrating wildly and frenetically, disappear off into the sea into the green fog of the visibility range. The spear had seemed to go on in, and on in, and on in until it disappeared completely through the gills. The head of it must certainly have come out through the top of the head somewhere after travelling through the mouth cavity. Even though it had not been a true killing shot (it had been an awfully tough position to shoot from), that shark was certainly not going to eat anything for quite some time to come. It sure was a damn good thing he had cut that line! Feeling an exquisite satisfaction he could not have explained, and in fact had rarely ever felt in his life except in bed with some woman which of course he could explain, Grant swam on up out of the sand and dust cloud and looked himself over. He had certainly been stung plenty, but he had only actually been nicked, cut a little, by the coral in only four or five places. All the fish around the reef had suddenly disappeared. It was as if a giant electric shock had suddenly shot through the reef making the entire underwater world jump. Grant finally, now, took the time to look around—and off to his right, to the south since he was facing the ship, saw Mo Orloffski lying half-way between the surface and the sand bottom about forty yards away, making incredulous and horrified gesticulations at him.

Grant swam over to him. Orloffski continued his gesticulations. Grant wiggled his eyebrows and bunched his nose inside his mask to show that he was grinning. But Orloffski would not accept this. They swam slowly back to the ship together, and Orloffski did not cease his remonstrations, using his hands and arms and shoulders and head, and even his back. The first thing he said when they had handed up their rigs and climbed up the diving ladder was, " You're *crazy!* You must be out of your ever-lovin' fucking *mind!*" And he said it in just about as loud a voice as he could.

The others who were on board, which now included Bonham, Ben and Irma, as well as Lucky naturally, clustered around.—" You know what this guy just did! You know what this dumb son of a bitch just did!" He proceeded to tell them. " At *least* twenty feet, twenty-*five* feet! He's a nut!" he concluded. " He's some kind of a crazy ravin' fucking nut, I tell you!" Then he turned on Grant. " Have you done things like that before when you was out alone?" He turned to Bonham, shaking his head. " Really, Al! I don't think you ought to let this guy go out all alone by hisself no more! I mean it! Really!"

All this, from the tough, big, brutal, insensitive, totally unimaginative Orloffski! Grant began to have his first doubt.

Grant had not, of course, known Orloffski had been watching all the time. He had thought he had drifted on off to the southeast and had been totally unaware that he had doubled back south and then farther, southeast to the strangely circular reef. He had not wanted to make a fuss. And he had not done what he'd done for any audience. He had done it for some grinding, gnashing, screeching something in himself. And he was sorry Orloffski had seen it. And if he had known that he was there, watching, he almost certainly would *not* have done it. But now it *was* done. And they all knew about it.

Bonham questioned him about it. He explained the situation as it had been, and his plan and his theory, embarrassed now, and beginning to get angry.

" What if he had come at you?" Bonham asked.

" I figured he would go the other way. Go in the direction

away from whatever it was had hit him, hurt him. Which, in fact, was what he did."

" But under that ledge, that overhang. In that position, in total panic, he might just as easily of turned back toward you. What would you have done then?"

" I figured with that spear running through his mouth out the top of his head he wasn't in any position to bite anything."

" Bite, hell! He wouldn't have to bite you. All he'd have to do would be just run into you. Or even hit you with his tail. By accident."

" I was swimming backward from the second I shot. Swimming backward, upside down on my back, right down on the bottom. Would he be likely to hit me there?"

" I don't know."

" Wouldn't he be much more likely to take off upward, to get out of there?" Grant persisted. He was beginning to get even more angry.

" I don't know," Bonham said. " Yes, that's true. He would," he admitted thoughtfully. " But I still think you made a serious mistake in judgment."

" Where?"

" By even deciding to go after him at all alone like that in the first place! You should have had help around."

" Help wouldn't have helped. He was off and out of there so fast you couldn't— Another diver up above backin' me up would have had more chance to get hurt than me!"

" The shot was too tough. Shooting from behind and below and forward, like that. Your own position was bad: for the shot. There was almost no real chance for a killing shot."

" But I told you I anticipated that. I planned for that."

" He was too big. He was just too big."

" Big!" Orloffski interposed. " I ain't never seen a shark that big in my whole fucking *life!* Not even in a damned marineland aquarium! It had to be a white."

" Tigers can get that big," Bonham said. " You say he was sort of brown, reddish brown?"

" That's right," Grant said, angrily.

" Tigers that get that big lose their spots that give them that so-called ' striped ' look, but they're usually greyish brown, not reddish brown. And you didn't see his tail?"

" I told you. I—"

" And you didn't see it?" Bonham asked Orloffski.

" Hell, he was up and out of there so fast— And that cloud, you couldn't see anything for that cloud—except this crazy guy sticking his head up outta the top of it lookin' aroun' like some damned tourist!"

" Well, this is all pretty academic anyway," Bonham said. " I think you made a serious mistake in judgment. I'll get some merthiolate for those nicks."

" Well, I say I didn't. I say I didn't because it all turned out exactly like I anticipated it would and like I planned it." He was really mad now. All this _fuss_. He hadn't _wanted_ anybody to know about it. Orloffski had ruined his whole satisfaction that he had had.

Bonham was staring at him. There had been a grave quality about his manner all this time, the captain and leader doing his job, his excellent leadership job ; and yet at the same time underneath that there had been another quality, a sort of silent, secret, proud and pleased understanding of Grant's act that somehow Grant didn't like, didn't like at all. It was a sort of feeling of approval and of brotherhood— unstated, and passing only between the two of them—and it had made Grant think while they were all talking—curiously enough—of Letta Bonham and what she had told Lucky about her husband, and naturally forced an immediate comparison with his own relationship with Lucky. Now Bonham suddenly grinned, and both bad feelings in Grant got stronger.—" Look," the big man said, " I like to shoot sharks myself. I love shootin' them. But there's just certain chances that you don't take, see? In that situation, and in that position, with that big a shark and that kind of a shot, you went just a little bit over the edge. You should have come back and got me. We could have taken a Brazilian rig and—"

" Look," Grant said thinly, " am I being punished? I mean, I know you're the captain of the ship and that when you give orders we all obey at sea. But does that apply to the diving too? I mean, am I being confined to quarters? Am I not to have another lung? Or must I go in the big class with teacher?"

" Oh, for Christ's sake, of course not," Bonham grinned. " I only just—"

"Then can I have the lung?" Grant said. "Because I'd like to get back in the water."

"Help yourself," Bonham said, and then grinned that grin again.

Grant nodded; "Thanks," and went to get the lung.

Lucky of course was furious with him. Over the shark incident. She had followed closely all the talk about it. Now she came over to him as he was getting another, full tank out of the row of tie racks. "I think you're really crazy," she said. Grant went on set-faced with the work, and she walked away. She went up forward where Irma was waiting for her, looking very much like the good Jewish mother who wants to help but can't. He refused to even look after her.

But when he was back in the water, speargun in hand, knife strapped to leg, he thought about what she had said. His first doubt had come when he heard all that Orloffski—whom up to now Grant had always thought of as totally brave, totally *physically* brave, if stupid—had had to say about what he had done. What he had done with the shark. Now Lucky's remark compounded the doubt. Was he really maybe going off his rocker a little? Some way? How did one know? If one was going off? Maybe he was; maybe he was going a little kooky with all his woman troubles, wife troubles, cuckold troubles, cruise troubles, skindiving troubles, Bonham troubles. Maybe he was. He felt totally reckless now, really reckless, fuck-it-all reckless, as he swam out toward another reef, farther to the west than the circular one where he had seen the shark. He felt recklessly ready for anything, just about anything. Unfortunately, or perhaps fortunately, he found nothing. Or nothing of much importance. He did shoot four lobsters (four tails was all his little bikini could hold) and one large grouper, which he left dead on the bottom under a small rock while he himself went on. That was all though, and finally when his air began to run a little low, he came back and picked up the big grouper and dragged it by the eyeball sockets back to the ship. The others were all just returning. In a short time they were under way under sail, and in an hour they were back at the dock of all the Greens at North Nelson, all tied up, all sail secured, all ready to relax, drink, have fun, eat and the rest of it.

"I'm going up to the Weather Station to send that radiogram," Lucky said to him as soon as they were off the wharf and on the white crushed-coral path up to the hotel.

Grant stopped, in the middle of the path. Ben and Irma were in front of them and moving on. Nobody was behind them. In spite of the tone of her words, which was tough, quite tough, there was a strange look of appeal on her face, her lovely Italian face. Grant felt suddenly as though he had never even seen her before. He suddenly felt like, suddenly had the wild idea of, introducing himself to her. Instead he said nothing.

"The Station is just up beyond the hotel," Lucky said, as if he didn't know where it was, "and I'm going to send it."

Grant nodded. "You do that," he said with a set face. "And I, *I*, am going back down to the boat—to the *ship*— and have a few drinks with the boys." He turned on his heel. —"*No*, I didn't fuck Jim Grointon!" Lucky said after him. Without answering he went back on down the path toward the wharf. When he reached the ship's rail across the long wooden length of the wharf without having turned his head one millimetre to look back once, and then stepped on board turning naturally as he did so and looked back up the path, she was no longer anywhere in sight.

He had said he was going to have a few drinks with the boys, and that he did. That he did, in spades. The surgeon and his girl were still there on board, with Bonham and Orloffski, and they had a few with them but soon they wandered off toward the restaurant. Then there were only the three of them, himself, Bonham, and Orloffski. Cathie had already gone up to the hotel to shower. In the end the three of them did not even eat dinner with the others at the hotel restaurant, but stayed aboard drinking while Bonham fried them up some of the fish that he could cook so deliciously, and after they ate they went on drinking.— "What the hell!" Bonham growled a little drunkenly, in the first even partially open reference Grant had ever heard him make to his relationship with Cathie. He lolled back in the cockpit. "I deserve a night off once in a while. With the boys. Even *I* deserve that!"

Grant had done a fair amount of drinking all through the day of spearfishing, more certainly than he had the day before, and of course it was all accumulative: that drinking, the drinking before the fish, the drinking with the fish, the drinking after the fish. He was unable to remember later just when he became drunk. The three of them sat on board with the bottle—before long it was bottles—exchanging skindiving stories (a few of which of his own Grant now had from his days with Grointon)—ha! *old Jim Grointon*—talking about the old days in the war, in which Mo Orloffski had been a S/Sgt in the Quarter-master Corps and Bonham had been (because of his previous sailing training) a navigator on first a Flying Fortress and then a Superfort. Finally it got around to talking about women they had laid. Back in their youth of course, and all present company totally excepted.

Grant never did know just when it got around to the point where Orloffski brought up the cache of whisky which he had discovered on the island, on the island of North Nelson.

Somewhere in there Ben came down to talk to him. He did remember that. Good old Ben.—" You mind if I talk to Ron?" he asked Bonham quietly. "In private?"—" Sure, hell, why not for Christsake?" Bonham grinned. But he gave it somehow the feeling that Ben was his enemy.—" Thanks," Ben said, Ben in his old Middlewestern accent. He took Grant forward, almost to the bowsprit.—" Lucky sent the wire," he said. Grant nodded. " I figured."—" She asked me for the money to pay for the plane," Ben said. " I told her I'd give it to her. But that I wanted to come down to talk to you first."—" You don't have to," Grant said. " I'll give it to her myself."

" Are you *sure* you know what you're doing?" Ben said. He then began a long rambling, and painful, effort to tell the story of the year he had spent away from Irma, right after they themselves had gotten married. It was all very inarticulate and pretty incoherent, Grant thought with that crystalline drunken clarity his mind sometimes achieved when loaded. The upshot of it all was that Ben had studied and studied and analysed finally in himself that it was all really because he had been terrified of the *responsibility* of marriage and all that it entailed, and he thought that maybe that was Grant's problem too. It was all so far from the truth that Grant found it almost laughable, although he did not laugh, and then he suddenly found himself telling Ben the whole story, incredibly. He had never thought he would ever tell anyone, the flirting with Jim Grointon (" But Lucky flirts with everybody," Ben interjected, " it's her nature, it's

her style, it don't mean anything."), Jim Grointon's proposition to her in the Morants (" Christ, everybody—every
fool—propositions *Lucky!*" Ben said.), Jim Grointon's offer
to *marry* her she had even told him (" But she didn't take
him up on it, did she?" Ben said.), and finally that horrible
horribly terrible " spaghetti dinner " night, when she had not
waked him, *inconceivably* had not waked him. She *had* to
have cuckolded him. Though she claimed, said, *shouted* that
she didn't, hadn't.

(" And where were you then, Ben old fren, old buddy,
with all your big offers of help?"—" I'm sorry about that,"
Ben said, " we shouldn't have taken that trip, but we didn't
know.")

Well, all that didn't matter. What did that part matter?
That was all just horse-shit. No, the way he saw it, she *had*
to have cuckolded him. She just *had* to have.

" Well, maybe she didn't," Ben said. " Have you thought
of that? Maybe she's tellin' the truth?"

" Sure," Grant said. " And do you think she'd tell if she
had? Shit, man."

Ben did not say anything for a moment. " Well, you know
I don't know anythin' about what all the men Irm might
have slept with while I was gone that year," he said finally.
" And I've never asked."

" Come on! This isn't the same. Ain't the same at *all!*
I was right *there! Asleep!*"

" You know, I once wanted to write a book about that
time, a novel I mean, with me and Irm," Ben said thoughtfully.

Grant stared at him incredulously, and then suddenly
giggled. " Why not a play? Make it a play. Then we could
collaborate."

Ben's eyes brightened. " Gee, that's a great idea!" he said.
" You mean you really would?" Then he remembered his
serious role. "—Anyway, it's Lucky we're concerned about
right now."

" It sure is," Grant said.

" But are you *sure?*" Ben said seriously. " Are you really
sure?"

" You're damned right I'm sure. Why else wouldn't she
have waked me up?"

Y

"Maybe she just did it to hurt you," Ben said. "Because of uh because of that Mrs. Abernathy thing."

"And maybe she just screwed Jim Grointon for the same reason," Grant said sharply.

"Listen," Ben said slowly, and seriously. "I want to ask you something. Something maybe very serious. Take your time and think it over. Before you answer. Do you think that maybe it could all be in your head?"

"How do you mean?"

"I mean, do you maybe think that just maybe you're goin' through all this torment about Lucky cuckolding you with Jim because of your own guilt over havin' cuckolded Hunt Abernathy all those years with Mrs. Abernathy?" Quickly he raised his hand. "Think it over. Take your time."

"Hunh," Grant said.

"Just think it over," Ben said. "Do you think it might maybe be that? Or even *partly* that?"

Grant did think, for several minutes. "Let me say this," he said finally. "I would say that it might be that, might very well be that—*if it were not for that one night when she didn't wake me up.* Because, see, she had lots of other opportunities to cuckold me with Grointon. (Christ, she even told me she had a kind of hots for him," he put in parenthetically, "for Christ's sake!) And she could have, lots of times. Like in the Morants. Or at the hotel. But I never thought she did, even doubted, never even considered that she would. *Till that one night.* So I don't think your bright idea's the answer. You see what I mean."

"I see," Ben said. "But it's still something to think about."

"It sure is," Grant said. "How much are you charging me, Ben?"

"I'm only trying to save you something," Ben said. "You've got somethin' very precious there in Lucky."

"She's got something very precious—She *had* something very precious there in me," Grant said.

"I know," Ben said quietly.

"And she *threw* it away."

"Well," Ben said, "do you expect everything in life to come to you without paying for it. You're too big, too important, too *much*, not to know better than that. Are you too big and too important to even be willing to indulge in a little education? You refuse even to educate, teach a little? Of all you claim you know about life?"

"She fucked him," Grant said.

"Maybe not. That ain't for sure," Ben said. "But if she did—and I ain't *sayin'* that—maybe she's sorry. Maybe she learned something. Something about where the real importance lies. In things. That's sort of what happened to me. That time."

"I can't stand the thought that she could do that like that," Grant said. "I just can't stand it."

"But maybe she *didn't*," Ben Spicehandler said kindly. "There's always that possibility. And then look at what you'll be throwin' away. Look, you're a little drunk. Come on back up to the hotel with me, and go to bed. There's always the chance that she might cancel it, the wire."

"There is," Grant said. "And she can cancel it any time. Any time she wants to. But I sure as shit ain't gonna *ask her to!*"

"That's as much as admittin' that you want to keep her," Ben said.

"I don't know whether I do or not. Ben, that's the truth."

"Then come on back up with me," Ben said, "and see how it goes then."

"No," Grant said. "No, I won't. I'm going to stay here and have a few drinks with the boys. I think they understand more about women than you do, Ben.—What's that old saw?" He laughed. "That they say out in our country, Ben: "He's a hell of a guy around the poolroom, but he's a son of a bitch at home!'" Grant laughed again. The spectre! The spectre! That damned spectre! Faceless spectre!

"Don't ever say I didn't try," Ben said.

"I'll never say you didn't try, Ben," Grant said.

He walked back aft with him, to the opening through the lifeline railing against the wharf, and slapped him on the back as he stepped off the ship, then went on back to the cockpit. They were still talking about women they had fucked.

He never did remember just when the subject of the whisky cache came up. He did remember that when it did, Bonham growled, grinned, and accused Mo Orloffski of tailing him, "shadowing" him. This was because the whisky cache was located at South End, which was the route Bonham took when he went in his roundabout way to the hotel and Cathie Finer's room, apparently.

Orloffski only grinned. " What the fuck?" he growled back in his brutal way. " I got as much right to prowl around this fuckin' island as anybody else has, ain't I?"

It was by prowling that he had found the whisky cache. It was located in the " cellar " of the new not-quite-finished luxury hotel that was being built, and was almost finished, down at South End. They used the word " cellar " in quotes because to dig a real cellar on a sand island like this would be to have it seep itself full of water in a week. So the " cellar " was above-ground, and what was more was closed only by an old makeshift wooden door and a padlock because the final door itself had not yet been mounted on. Orloffski had peeped in through the one barred window and seen the whisky cache, and it was *enormous*. The owners, the new American syndicate, had apparently been shipping it in for quite some time for their gala opening which everybody aboard hoped would put the Greens, the entire clan of Greens, out of business.

They were all drunk. By now. And it did seem like a boyish prank. Then. But Grant remembered that it was Orloffski who really first suggested it. Orloffski, the thief, Orloffski, the kleptomaniac. Orloffski, who in fact had once stolen Grant's old Exacta V camera. It was Orloffski who suggested it, and he was high, high, high ; high as a kite over the idea. He looked exactly like a man hot after a broad.

It would be easier than anything for them to go up there right now, in the middle of the night, crack the old rusted padlock, and just help themselves to a couple, to a *gang* of cases? No one would ever miss them, there were so damned many. There were only a few workmen actually working on the final interior work up there right now. You fix the padlock back so it looked locked, and who would know? who would pay any attention? They could stow the several cases of whisky in the bilge under the sole in the schooner. Who was going to search them? Especially if they didn't notice the door, or lock, had been tampered with?

It seemed like a great idea. Bonham was all for it, and his eyes glittered stormily with acquisitiveness. And Grant thought why the hell not? It was no worse than stealing equipment from the Navy. Or Army. To steal whisky from a rich corporation syndicate was not dishonourable. More, it was even honourable. A sacred duty, almost. The old-timers in the Navy had called stealing gear " decorating yourself ". And it appealed in him to that same gnashing, grinding, screeching thing he carried now that had made him want to, have to, shoot that shark. The big shark.

He did not remember getting up there, though it was quite a long walk down the heavy sand of the beach and then inland up through more heavy sand to the deserted brand-new hotel itself. They hadn't yet laid the walks for the tourists. No, he didn't remember getting there, but he did remember Orloffski tearing off a good near-half of the door. In his excited enthusiasm Orloffski prised too hard with the little crowbar they had brought from the schooner's lazarette, and the rusty old padlock was a lot stronger than it looked. The result was that he broke away a good portion of the old half-rotten wood, lock and hasp and all.

That was when the arguments started. Orloffski was for going ahead anyway ; he was, in fact, nearly rabid. Bonham was not so sure. Grant himself said he would go along with whatever Bonham decided. Finally the acquisitiveness, the rich greed, in Bonham at all that whisky just lying there, that beautiful whisky, just lying there for the taking, decided him in favour of going on with it anyway.

They took five cases. Staggering bulkily down through the heavy sand Bonham carried a full case under each arm. Orloffski also carried a case under each arm. Grant could hardly manage to carry one case in both arms, and even then fell to his knees a couple of times in the deep sand. What if his goddamned wife could see him now? he thought with a kind of crazy exaltation. Finally they reached the beach itself, at the water's edge, and put them down to rest. The plan was to get the ship's dinghy and row them to the ship.

Perhaps it was the long struggling climb down through all that heavy sand that sobered him up, but when he put his single case down on the hard sand at the water's edge and sat down on it to rest his arms, Grant was suddenly sober, sober enough to realise what it was they were doing, what they had done.

Despite the offensive and ubiquitous Greens, this island was part of a British Protectorate, and it was British administrated, and there was a British Administrator, a white British Ad-

ministrator from England, who was the law on this island.
The Law. That was not the same thing as bucking heads
with the Greens, who were objectionable in any case, and
who also in any case had nothing to do with the new luxury
hotel. No, that was not the same thing at all.

"I think we better take it all back," he said bluntly. After
he got his breath back. "I think we should. I really mean
it." And then the arguments really started.

Orloffski was dead set against taking it back. He came up
with and developed a list of excuses and reasons as to why
they could get away with it that was as long as a tall giant's
arm. He seemed almost beside himself in his enthusiasm for
going ahead. Bonham and Grant listened to the end, all three
of them sitting on one or another of the disputed cases of
whisky, gesticulating back and forth at each other over this
point or that. In the end, after Orloffski's spiel, Bonham
appeared still undecided.

"Since you busted the whole door," Grant said, in rebuttal, "somebody's sure to see it to-morrow. Early. They'll
know that it was us. And they must certainly have an in-
ventory of the number of cases. They'll search the ship. And
don't think they won't look in the bilge under the sole,
either!"

"We can be away from here by dawn," Orloffski sneered.
"So who cares. You think they'll send the British Navy
Coast Guard after us? Fuck off!"

"No," Grant said, reasonably. "No, they won't do that.
But the *Naiad* will never be able to put in here again on any
future cruises. I can pretty well asure you that. Al?"

"That's right," Bonham said thoughtfully, and drunkenly.
"And this is a good place to bring hired cruises. On the
other hand," he added, "there's a lot of other places we can
go, too. Thousands."

"And the boat's reputation?" Grant said. "You don't
think word of this will get to Kingston? to MoBay? to
GaBay? all over the Caribbean?"

Bonham scratched his head. "That's all true. Of course,
if they don't actually catch us with it, they can't very well
accuse us. Not openly." He just, very plainly, hated to have
to give up those five cases of free whisky. "And in three or
four months I think we can put back in here. Safely enough.

Though it might not be pleasant. But in six or eight months, we could."

It all seemed to be getting ridiculous to Grant. All this, over five lousy cases of whisky.

"Of course we could!" Orloffski said contemptuously. And it was, quite suddenly, then that Grant knew the fight was coming. He started to prepare himself, both mentally, and physically the way he was sitting on his box. "Listen, you," Orloffski said with supreme, with insulting contempt, swinging back on to him as Grant had already anticipated he would. "What's the matter with you? If I didn't know you better, I'd be tempted to think that new broad of yours has cut off your balls and is wearin' them around her neck for a neck-lace. Where's your guts, prick?"

While he had anticipated the attack, he had not anticipated the virulence of it, or its direction. The direction of it made it even worse. He of course could not accept it. "You go and fuck yourself, Orloffski," he said calmly and deliberately. "And while we happen to be on the subject of stealing or not stealing, you fucking oaf, there's something else I wanted to take up with you also. I want to know when you are going to give me back my Exacta camera that you stole from me that time up in GaBay."

"You what?" Orloffski said. He sounded incredulous.

"You heard me," Grant said calmly. It was as if he were listening to another person talking. "I want back my camera that you stole. Or one like it, if you sold it. That stupid oafish little trick almost cost Al Bonham here the four thou' I loaned him to get your fucking schooner out of hock for you. When may I expect to have it back?" He was using good grammar, even. Deliberately.

"I don't know anything about your goddam fuckin' camera," Orloffski growled.

"And I say you stole it," Grant said. "It must be some-thing compulsive about you. I think maybe you're a klepto-maniac. That's a certain kind of sexual perversion that makes people have to steal. Though it's usually reserved to women. So I suppose you can't help it, in a way. But I say you're a plain, simple thief."

He was ready when Orloffski swung. Of course, Orloffski had to jump up off his own whisky case and cross the inter-vening space, about four or five feet, but that didn't take long. Still, being already prepared as he was, he was up, and even able to step out sideways away from the box into clear ground. Ground! Sand, deep heavy sand. He slipped the long looping right hand expertly and hooked hard with his left to the gut, which brought a satisfying grunt from Orloffski, and danced back away, back down toward the water where the sand was at least a little firmer.

Grant had never fought a man as big as Orloffski. When he had fought back in the old days in the Navy, he had fought first as a lightweight, then as a welter as he grew up and filled out. Now at thirty-six he weighed just exactly 165 pounds, which meant he was giving away just about 70 pounds in weight he figured, quite a lot, but for his age and what with all the diving and swimming he'd been doing he was in pretty good shape and wind. But so, of course, was Orloffski. There wasn't he calculated, the slightest chance of his winning—unless he could actually knock the big Polack ape out. Grant had always been an awfully hard hitter for his size. But the first time he connected with a hard good right hand exactly rightly and correctly just off the jaw point of Orloffski's jaw and the bigger man didn't even stagger at all, he knew there was no chance, as he had pretty much figured from the beginning. It was the neck. Those thick necks. He had one himself. He was beat.

But it took an awfully long time. Grant meant to make it take as long as possible. And he meant to inflict as much damage, do as much harm, as possible in that amount of time. Orloffski was certainly no boxer. He was a real sucker for a clean fast snapping left jab, of which Grant had a fine one. With it he managed to open up cuts over both eyes and on one cheek. Orloffski was also a great sucker for belly and heart hooks, left and right in combination, when he came lunging in. When he tried to grapple and go to the ground, where his weight and strength would make Grant even more helpless, Grant used the hook combinations and backed away, or jabbed him to a standstill and danced back. The two or three times Orloffski tried to kick him or knee him in the groin he evaded easily, and Orloffski stopped that. After that first good solid right to the jaw-point, he knew he could not knock him out, but he used his right hand to good advantage on the cut he had opened under the Pole's left eye on the cheek. He was also pretty sure Orloffski's ribs and belly were getting pretty sore.

But it couldn't go on forever. It was like hitting a heavy bag in the gym. Or punching at a big side of beef hung up in some slaughterhouse. It even sounded like that. And nothing stopped him All this time Bonham sat on his whisky case, watching calmly, drinking from a bottle from one of the cases which Orloffski had already prised open with the little crowbar. Grant's legs felt pretty good, and his wind hadn't gone. There was actually a moment or two when he actually thought it might go on forever, just go on ind on and on like it was going. He actually almost believed that for a little while. But of course he had not been hit yet. Not once. Not even once. And that of course could not continue forever.

Finally the angry Pole connected. It was a short right hand from in fairly close, which Grant could neither slip, nor catch and slap off with his left, and when it hit him he felt as though it had torn his head off. It hit him squarely in the nose, breaking it (he could actually hear it breaking there inside his head, slowly almost), and it felt as though his whole face had come unhinged and been pushed out through the back of his head exactly at that point where his skull met his spinal column. He staggered back a few steps and sat down in the wet seaside sand, blinded. Then he could see again. Orloffski had apparently stepped back a step or two himself, as if in surprise, surprise that he had actually connected. Then Orloffski, grinning, started to come in again.

Grant struggled to his feet to take his beating. His beating he had more or less expected from the start, from the moment he had insulted the Pole so severely that fight must follow. Blood was pouring from his nose all over his mouth and lips and jaw and down on to his chest. But he preferred to take as much of it as he could while still on his feet. He still couldn't see too good, but he still hoped to get in one or two or three good damaging hooks to the gut and heart. And there was always that old trick of blowing the blood in the other guy's eyes to confuse him. Ah, Lucky, he thought ruefully, if you could only see your heroic husband now!

Then suddenly in front of him was something else, something broad, something extremely broad. He realised after a moment it was Bonham's back. Whew! he thought, without feeling ashamed at all, Thank God!

"That's enough," he heard Bonham say. "Go and sit down. Have a drink. Take a rest. You certainly *earned* it, Mo." The last ironic touch rather pleased Grant.

"The jerk accused me of stealin' his camera," Orloffski snarled.

"I still say he stole it," Grant said, in a thick strange new voice he didn't recognise.

"You're not going to do anything," Bonham said. "You've done enough. Go and sit down. Unless you want to fight me, too."

Orloffski did not answer this and after a moment went to where the open bottle was and sat down with it on the torn-open case.

"Well, is he going to beat me up, or not?" Grant said in his strange new voice. "Because if he's not, I'd like to sit down."

"He's not going to beat you up," Bonham said. "Sit down. Here," he added and handed Grant his handkerchief.

In all he used up four of them, sitting on a whisky case. He always carried two handkerchiefs himself, because he sweat so much and it embarrassed him. And Bonham happened to have two with him also. He refused the offer of a fifth, which was Orloffski's, and which Bonham had more or less demanded. And while he tried with the four handkerchiefs to stem his pouring nose-bleed, Bonham and Orloffski went back to arguing over what to do with the whisky. Bonham was half for and half against keeping it. He couldn't quite make up his mind.

"I guess this puts me out from divin' for quite a while, hunh?" Grant said in his new voice he hardly recognised.

"I guess it does," Bonham said.

"Well, I guess that does in the trip."

"Yeah, I guess it does," Bonham said.

"Well, I still want you to know I think you stole my camera, Orloffski," Grant said. Orloffski leaped up as if to go for him again but Bonham blocked him off, and Grant got up off his whisky case.

"Gentlemen, I've had it," he said. "I'm going to bed. But if you've got any sense at all, you'll see that the whisky gets back where it belongs. Even if one case *is* busted open."

He did not bother to listen if there were any answers, and as he went off trudging slowly through the heavy deep sand with his four soaked handkerchiefs which still failed to stop his nose-bleed, he could hear them still arguing behind him. Somehow or other he had learned something this night, something he had needed to learn, something he had perhaps even come down here to the Caribbean deliberately to learn. Even though he didn't quite know what it was he had learned. All he knew was that he had learned it. But he couldn't quite say, even to himself, what it was. Well, maybe that would come, eventually, with reflection.

Back at the hotel, he tried quietly to sneak in with his key and sneak quietly into the bathroom. But of course Lucky waked up. If, even, she had ever been asleep.

THIRTY-SEVEN

In the dinghy, Bonham rowed. He loved rowing. He always had loved it, ever since a kid when he had first seen and gone on estuaries and open water. It was one of the few damn things in the world where strength and size in a man meant something, helped. And now he let his body and his back; his arms, and hands, and legs, and feet, *and* back, take over and do all the work. He concentrated on feeling his body row. He did not want to think. On the shore before him over the stern of the dinghy, Orloffski with his hands on his hips angrily and his back hunched in an even greater fury stood watching him row away. Well, fuck him. Fuck him, and his goddam klepto crazy idea, and everything. It was all over, it was all ruined. He had tried so hard, so very hard. And now, ruined. Bonham rowed.

He rowed well, with great experience, and even pleasure (even now), putting all his great strength into it, but the little dinghy didn't move very swiftly through the water just the same. The weight of the five cases of whisky in the boat with him, all around him, effectively prevented that.

They had compromised, finally. Orloffski was like some kind of mad man and absolutely refused to help carry any of the whisky back up to the hotel. He had even seized the little crowbar and busted the opened case even farther open, and then had smashed two bottles of whisky with it. Bonham, drunk as he was, had thought carefully about everything Grant had said, and had finally decided they ought to take it all back.

But it was all pretty academic anyway, with the one case so busted open, and with now three bottles of it—the one they'd mostly drunk, and the two Orloffski'd busted—gone. There wasn't much chance of it not being found out now.

So the compromise was that Bonham would go and get the dinghy, while Orloffski guarded the loot, and then row the whisky out to one of the little brush- and scrub-grown islets about three-quarters of a mile out in the big bent-up U-shaped " harbour " formation made by the two islands, by North and South Nelson, and there hide them in some fashion. Then some day they could come back and pick them up, all at once or one at a time. On the shore before him over the dinghy's stern Orloffski turned and started trudging through the sand toward the wharf. Bonham continued to row, liking it.

Ruined. Just damn, completely, bloody-well ruined. Everything. And all over five bloody lousy cases of whisky. God, he was beginning to talk like a damned Englishman, living down here in the Caribbean. Using bloody all the time. That Grant. What a cat, what a *chap*. Bonham had seen some courageous things in his life, some *damn* courageous things. But he had never seen anything quite as courageous as what Grant had done, when he cold-bloodedly and deliberately insulted Orloffski into a fist fight knowing all the time beforehand that there wasn't the faintest chance in hell that he could win, and that if he lost, which he must do, he would almost certainly be beaten to a bloody pulp afterwards. And this wasn't *bloody* in the Englishman's sense ; this was really *bloody*. He was glad he had been there to stop it. Being so big did have its advantages, once in a while.

The cruise was ruined of course. Grant wouldn't be able to dive any more for quite a while, with that busted nose. Apart from all the hard feelings all over the ship. There was no point in even attempting to go on with the cruise. They'd have to leave for Ga-Bay to-morrow. Sailing on a close reach all day and tacking all the time into the trade wind meant they'd make maybe four or five knots an hour, and it was a hundred and sixty sea miles to GaBay from here, which meant that with any luck at night after the land breeze came up, it would be just about a twenty-eight to thirty-hour sail. With all these fighting people aboard. With *Grant* and *Orloffski* both aboard!

Back on the shore, after they'd settled the big whisky problem, he had told Orloffski to stay forward to-morrow and keep out of the way. He had also suggested that Orloffski apologise to Grant to-morrow and that that might help some, a little bit. Orloffski had said sullenly he guessed he could apologise but he was damned if he would. Guy accusing him of stealing his damned camera! And for Bonham that had been too much. Just one hair too damned much. "Well, I think you stole it, too. What do you think of that?" he had said. "I always did think you stole it. Now, do you want to fight me?" Orloffski of course had not. But he wasn't going to forgive it for a long time, either. A long long time.

Ruined. Bonham rowed. Partnership ruined, or practically so. Relationship with Grant ruined—especially if that damned Lucky—*un*Lucky—had anything to say about it; and she would. And that meant that also ruined with it, also ruined was his big dream of getting the clientele he had so hoped Grant would bring him, the clientele of Celebrities and such (the "Chosen Ones" of his chosen ones theory). If that Lucky could put in any bad word for him-with all the rich and famous people that they knew, she would, he had no doubt of that. And in a strange way he admired her, too. She was certainly all for her man, anyway. Ruined. Bonham rowed. The wharf was almost out of sight by now. Bonham rowed on, feeling it pleasantly, harshly in his back. He felt that if he could only do that, just row, forever . . . But he was drunk, wasn't he? Loaded. Stoned.

About the only thing that wasn't lost was the schooner. He still had her. And Sam Finer. Sam Finer was not quite the clientele Bonham's dream had envisioned, but he had money. He would bring others like himself down for the cruises. So he did still have that. (And he could imagine the kind of crazy low-class drunken cruises Sam Finer and his friends would make up; it certainly wouldn't be any ritzy "Chosen Ones" type of cruises.) When he got back to the dock, he would go on up to Cathie's room and wake her up even if she *was* asleep. He needed *some*thing, *some* solace. Rhythmically, sweating a little now, Bonham rowed on. Ruined. Ruined. At least for what his dream had been.

But that Grant. What he had done. With Orloffski. Bonham still could hardly believe it. He must have known he couldn't win. He did know it. Bonham could tell, could smell it on him almost. And yet he went right ahead like that, cold-bloodedly, calculatedly, deliberately. And then to act nervous and scared all the time, like he did. What a strange guy! And smart. He had warned him off of Orloffski a long time back. A long long time back. No, he wasn't worried about Grant causing him trouble, calling in his mortgage or anything like that. But of course if Sam Finer put up that other—

When his bow scraped against the little rock islet, he jumped out in his Sperry " Topsider " sneakers into the sharp-rock, slippery shallows and tied the dinghy's painter on to a spur of rock, then began to unload the dinghy of its cargo. The only sand on this damn little rock was all inland, and he slipped a couple of times on the rock bottom of the shallows but he did not fall. Inland he found a couple of hollow places close together under rocks where he could put three of the cases. He did this and then covered the hollows over with sand. The other two cases he buried in the sand nearby. Then he smoothed out all the footprints. Nobody would ever find it. It took him, all told, almost an hour. He felt like some kind of a damned pirate, and wanted to laugh ; but he couldn't. Ruined. Ruin. Blackbeard! Henry Morgan! Captain Hook, even! After finishing, he stood astride the tiny rock (you could hardly even call it an islet) and looked shoreward. The island of North Nelson was clearly visible in the starlight, three-quarters of—or just about—a mile away. But he could not call back up any of the pirate feeling. There was no moon. Thank God. All for five lousy damned cases of free whisky!

The row back was easy, compared to the trip out with the weight of the whisky. He rowed easily, pulling powerfully, feathering, leafing the oars with his wrists precisely, on each back stroke. Ah, if he could just only do that, just row, forever . . . But he'd said that already, hadn't he? And he had other responsibilities to think of now.

The plan now, with the whisky not on the ship, was *not*

to leave early in the morning. Instead, he intended to wait until the Commissioner did come down, with his one gendarme (a Green, naturally) and did search the ship. Then they'd be in the clear.

He tied the dinghy's painter on to the stern of the schooner. For a moment he looked at her. At least, she, the schooner, was still there. He patted her a couple of times, on the bottom as it were, where her name *Naiad* had been painted on in good gold leaf, back at the yard in Kingston. He'd insisted on that.

Then he looked up at the hotel and saw what he had not noted before, that the light in the Grants' room was still on.

THIRTY-EIGHT

" Good *God!* What in the *name* of God happened to you!" was the first thing she had said, naturally.

Grant debated this internally for a little bit. He could make it funny (like, " I ran into a Pole!), or he could make it ironic (like—like what?), or he could even make it tragic and self-pitying—a considerable amount of which latter emotion he seemed to be suffering at the moment. He decided not to do any of these. " Orloffski broke my nose in a fist fight," he said tiredly. " I'll tell you all about it later. But first there's something else I want to tell you." He was aware, well aware, that with his busted nose he sounded exactly like a man who had accidentally swallowed a foghorn and then put a barrel over his head.

Lucky was already up and running around, like some distressed mother hen who has sighted or smelled a fox around, running into the bathroom, running out of the bathroom with a towel, running around to one side of the bed, running around to the other side. " God!" was all she said, and she said it bitterly.

" Hold on! Hold on!" Grant said in his croaking, strange, foreigner's voice. " I know how to handle this. I'm an old first-aid expert from the United States Navy, remember? It'll probably stop of itself pretty soon, anyway. Have we got any ice? If there's no ice, cold water from the tap will have to do. Soak the two washcloths—"

"There's ice," Lucky said, cool as ice herself now that he had taken over. "I had them send some up to have a few drinks with." She looked darling as ever in that shorty nightgown of hers that did not quite hide the view of her nipples or her triangle through it.

"Okay, then. Take two of my handkerchiefs. Put a couple ice-cubes in each of them and wrap them up. Only one layer of tissue, though. Twist the rest of the handkerchief around them. Okay?"

"Right," Lucky said.

He had sat down in the chair, with his four soaking handkerchiefs, through which blood still seeped to the floor. When she returned with his specific demands, he abandoned his four soaked handkerchiefs and pressed one handkerchief-wrapped pair of cubes against the back of his neck up near his skull. It felt damned good. Then, forcing himself, he pressed the other pair in against his upper lip just under his poor old nose. That action, as he had anticipated, caused him both to wince and to hiss with the pain. And bending his head forward, like the book said, he remained like that.

"I'll do that for you," Lucky offered. "I'd rather do it myself," he said, then added quickly, "not because of anything between me and you, or being mad. Just because I can feel it inside myself and feel how hard to push." Then he pulled the one away from the back of his neck. "Here, you can do this one, though, for me. Keep it up near the back of the skull. Press as hard as you want. You'll have to cancel the seaplane call early in the morning. We'll be leaving before it can get here even. For GaBay. I can't dive now. With this."

"I will," Lucky said. "First thing." She took the handkerchief-wrapped ice and pressed it to his neck exactly as he had told her. After a moment, almost automatically, as if it were the most natural thing in the world to do, though a little tentatively, she began to run her other hand through his hair. His thinning, even-at-thirty-six-thinning, hair. He could not remember having felt anything quite so nice in a very long time.—"Those sons of bitches," she said toughly after a moment. "That Polack. I'll slit his fucking belly open with a butcher knife. They may not know it but my family comes from Calabria."

"No, no. No, no," Grant said in his weird voice, even more muffled now with the ice-cubes against his mouth. "If anything, he did me a favour. Maybe one of the biggest favours anybody ever did me."

"That oaf," Lucky said. "That prick. Fist fighting with men half his size."

"That's not the point," Grant said in his muffled voice.

"How did you ever imagine you could whip him?"

"I didn't," Grant said in his mumble. "I knew I couldn't. But wait till you see him to-morrow. I promise you to-morrow he's going to look at least as bad as I do. But that's not the point. Listen, I can't talk now. With this damn thuff against my lip. But I've got loth to tell you."

Lucky changed the ice-cubes once, as they melted down. Then, as it began to let up and begin to settle down to a drip, Grant moved his ice-cubes—like the book said—from his upper lip to the bridge of his nose. Once again it made him wince and hiss with pain as he pressed, but then he could talk. And he had lots to say.

"Look. I learned something to-night. I don't quite know what I learned. But that's the new play. And when I've finished it, I think I'll know what I've learned."

Lucky ran her free hand through his hair, his thinning hair, again.

"Christ!" he said excitedly, though in that foghorn-in-a-barrel voice, "I can see the set now. A schooner, on stage. A schooner cut away in section, see? Not crossways, but from stem to stern, so you can see everything. Abovedecks and below! What a set!!"

"It'll take an awful big stage," Lucky said.

"We'll make it a small schooner," Grant said. "And everything takes place on board, see? Maybe we can even rig up some kind of a machine to give it movement when it's actually at sea. See? And have a rolling back-drop, painted, like when they come up to an island? Or just sea. Just seascape. But changing all the time. Christ, what a set!" He pressed with his ice-cubes against his nose bridge and hissed again. "It's stopping.

"But that's not the main thing," he said. "The main thing is I apologise to you for accusing you of fucking Jim Grointon the other night when I was loaded here. I don't

think you fucked Jim Grointon," he said. Ah, didn't he?
Didn't he? " I don't think you fucked him," he said again.
" It's just that I'm a very jealous man. See? Okay?"

" Ah, Ron," Lucky said. Her hand was actually stroking
his head now. Through the diminishing haze of his pain she
sounded tentatively, strangely, grateful. Or was that just
him?

" Will you accept my apology?" he asked. " Okay?"
Spectre! Spectre!

" Yes," she said, in a very low voice. " I'll accept your
apology."

" Okay. Now, about the play. I don't know what it is
exactly that I've learned. I can hardly say it to myself. I
probably won't be able to until I've finished it. If I ever can,
even then. But it's something like this. (You can take that
ice away from the back of my neck now," he added parenthetically, " it's about stopped now.) But he kept his own still
pressed against his nose bridge. " It's really awfully hard to
say. But it's like this: It's like they're not men. Any of
them. They're small boys, playing that they're men. And
that's what makes it all so dangerous, because they *are*
grown up, and what they do *counts*. *Nations* depend on it.
The whole world depends on it. But they, they can't *believe*
they're not small boys any more, that they're grown up, and
that there are not big people somewhere, real grown-ups,
somewhere around who can smack them, spank them and
make them do things. Not only in America, but everywhere! Grown-ups around to take over and make things
right. So they just *play*. And figure it don't *count*. If they
could only *believe* they're grown up!"

Lucky was still stroking his hair, though she had taken the
ice away now.

" An image came to me," he said, excitedly, in the
peculiar foghorn-barrel voice. " I don't know whether it was
while I was walkin' back through that damned sand, or just
now when I was talking. But I remember as a little boy when
I used to stand in the bathroom doorway and sort of covertly
watch my daddy making peepee. And this thing, his cock,
was so *big!* 'Course I was little. But it looked so big, and
mine was so little, and I knew mine, my thing, would never
be as big as that. Well, they're like that. All these guys. All
over the world. It doesn't matter what they *call* it: Com-

munism; Americanism; the Empire. They're small boys standing in the men's room watching their daddies make peepee and knowing that their things will never be that big: as big as his: their things will never be as big as Dad's. Because, see, the ratio of size gets fixed in their heads, the kids' heads, so that no matter how much they grow up, how big they get, the *proportion* keeps growing with them. The little kid's picture—memory picture—stays and grows *up* with the adult. So that, in the end, they can *never* grow up. They can never catch up, grow up to *Dad's*, and so they stay kids. Adult kids, *playing* at being men. But not believing it. I think maybe the whole world is all like that. Russians, Chinese, Americans; Presidents, Prime Ministers, Heads of State; everybody. All of them trying so hard to grow up to Dad's, Dad's thing. And remaining small boys inside because they just can't.

"So they take refuge in bravery. It becomes important to be brave. It is more important to them to be brave than to be anything. Only by being brave can they be what they think—hope—is manly, a man. *No other way*. Bravery. That proves they're men. So they make up games. The harder the game, the braver the man. Politics, war, football, polo, explorers. Skindiving. Shark-shooting. All to be brave. All to be men. All to grow up to Daddy's great huge cock they remember but can never match."

He paused, excitedly, and looked at Lucky, out from behind the two swollen sides of his nose which he could see along the insides of his eyes. Then he gave a lame shrug.

"I know it sounds a little kooky," he said after a moment. "But that was the way the image hit me. I can remember so well, when I was so little, and Dad's thing was so *huge*. I'd like to think, I think I maybe am, growing up to my father's cock. Anyway, that, that essentially, is the play. And it all takes place on board this schooner cut right in half down the middle, on the stage. We'll even haul up sail, and everything. Have a wind machine in the wings, see? Does it sound kooky? To you?"

"It doesn't sound kooky at all to me," Lucky said softly, in that same very low voice. "I think you're a fine man. And I always have. Except maybe for a little while there, when I was mad at you," she added, lowly.

" It's all right," he said, " it's all right. I *should* have told you."

" Would you like to make love to me?" Lucky asked in a low, almost apologetic voice.

" I sure as hell would," he said in his foghorn-barrel voice. " But I couldn't do it your way. I couldn't go down on you. Not with this sticking out of my face. But if it's fucking you want, I'll sure as hell give it a hell of a try."

" Fucking's fine," Lucky said.

It was just then that the quiet knock came, on the closed door ; and then the door, which Grant had deliberately not tried to lock, in order to make less noise, swung open. Bonham stood in it, filling it really, and he looked like a zombie. His eyes had the deep dark totally empty look of a zombie, largely because he was so drunk.

" May I come in a minute?" he asked politely.

" Sure, Al?" Grant said quickly, before Lucky could say anything. " What's up?"

It didn't take very long. Bonham explained, in a voice which sounded just about as zombie-ish as his face (and body) looked, about the whisky. It had not been returned. But it was well hidden. So instead of leaving out early to-morrow they were going to wait for the Commissioner to come and inspect them, which he absolutely for sure would. Then they would get under way, back to GaBay. So they didn't have to worry about getting up early. They could sleep late. Here Lucky laughed suddenly, a bitter laugh. Bonham turned his zombie eyes to look at her slowly, then just as slowly he turned them back to Grant. " How's your nose?"

" Not so bad. I've got the bleeding stopped. In a minute or two I'm going to try to shape it up a little bit, if we've got any adhesive tape around. If not, I'll sleep in the chair."

Without speaking, Bonham in his slow zombie manner reached into his hip pocket and came out with, and handed over, a one-inch roll of adhesive tape complete in its plastic clip-ring holder. Grant took it, and nodded. " Thanks."

" See you in the morning." Bonham turned to go out of the door. Then he turned back. He stared at the two of them zombie-like for several moments. " You've got yourself one hell of a man there, Mrs. Grant," he said in his zombie voice. " And you should appreciate him. But I know you do."

" Thank you," Lucky said politely, and Grant was vastly relieved. He did not really care what Bonham thought any more, about anything, though—in a childish way—he supposed he *was* pleased by what the big man had just said. It was a considerable compliment. But mainly, he was worried about Lucky, that with what Bonham had just said which was so utterly ridiculous, from her viewpoint—she might blow up, and begin to screech and holler like some angry fishwife. But she hadn't. She had said exactly the right thing to say, and he was immensely relieved.

" And though I know you don't like me much," Bonham went on, speaking to her, " I want you to know I admire you and I think you're some hell of a woman—hell of a *lady*," he corrected quickly. He turned away again. Then he turned back once more.

" I'm sorry about what's happened. I know it's dumb to say that. I guess it's all—all of it been pretty much my fault." Then in his zombie-ish way he was turned and gone before either of them could dispute, or agree with, this opinion.

Grant took the roll of adhesive tape (they had not had any themselves, he discovered) into the bathroom and worked on his nose before the mirror. That had been really thoughtful of Bonham, he thought, to bring tape. " I'd rather you didn't watch this," he said, " but you can if you want to."—" I want to," Lucky said. " I've never seen anybody make a nose out of a blob before." He glanced at her quickly. She had said it bitterly, but she wasn't *being* bitter. She was really interested.—" Okay. Come on," he said.

It took him about fifteen minutes. The pinching and squeezing, one forefinger pushing from each side. Then the tape, the first strip, up at the top of the bridge and the re-squeezing with the thumb and forefinger of one hand on the outside of the tape. Then the same thing lower down, the same process, always moving lower down, until there were four overlapping strips of the tape, spreading out across and over his cheekbones under his eyes. Thank God neither cheekbone or sinus had been busted. He had to stop several times because of the tears the pain of it brought into his eyes so he couldn't see, and also in order to relax his tensed-up diaphragm with a bit of the deep breathing that now came so naturally to him, as an experienced diver. Both nasal passages were all closed up naturally, with the coagulation, mucus, what-the-fuck-ever, and he had to breathe through his mouth.

"That's the best I can do," he said finally. "It'll be all right for to-night. And I'll have the surgeon take a look at it to-morrow."

"I think it's a pretty good job," Lucky said quite coolly. "It even almost looks like a nose again."

"Wait'll you see Orloffski to-morrow," Grant promised.

"To hell with Orloffski," Lucky said.

Then they went to bed together and made love in that skin-touching, electrical-skin-contact way they had once had, but had not now had together for quite a very long time.

The inspection went off quite well, perfectly, the next day, as Bonham had predicted. The Administrator, in his white suit and white topee that was almost a uniform, and his one Green constable in his blue uniform with its red trouser stripes and red cap band, came aboard after requesting formal permission from the Master of the Vessel. The Administrator was precise, pleasant, proper, and very polite. So was Constable Green, since he had been personally trained by the Administrator, or perhaps by his predecessor. The constable (while the Administrator stood by) looked everywhere—including in the bilge under the sole, the lazarette, everywhere.

"You understand of course that it was quite necessary," the Administrator said, shaking hands with the Master of the Vessel. "I'm quite sorry to have had to have done it. You understand? Quite."

"But of course, sir," Bonham said. "I wouldn't have had it any other way. I'd hate to have my vessel put to sea under any kind of a cloud. I'll want to return to the Nelsons, probably quite often, in the future."

"We will always look forward to seeing you here," the Administrator said, and smiled, "and your clients," he added, nodding pleasantly to the others. "We flatter ourselves that we have one of the future's better spots in the Caribbean. Especially for cruises such as yours." If he noticed the swollen taped-up nose of Grant or the cut swollen face of Orloffski he gave no indication of it.

Once they were under way and out at sea, the surgeon looked at Grant's nose.—"Not a bad job," he said with the grudging admiration of a professional, "not a bad job at all." In spite of that, he got out his little medical kit (he always carried it, he said, would feel naked without it, and especially on cruises) and redid the job, pulling off the tape, remoulding a little, and putting on his own new tape while Grant hissed and teared with the pain. Then he carefully swabbed the swollen nasal passages. " Of course, it all should be done again in a few days, as soon as that swelling goes down." Badly hungover, shaky, worn out with rutting, he still had good hands, great hands ; and when he had finished it was clearly a better job than Grant had done, or could have done.

In the case of Orloffski he found he had to take four stitches in the cut on the Pole's left cheek under the eye. He had all the gear and did it swiftly, sanitarily, and efficiently. For the smaller cuts above Orloffski's two eyes which were not so bad and didn't really need stitching, Grant took him aside and showed him how to make the boxer's and boxer's trainer's " adhesive bridges ", something the surgeon had for some reason never heard about, and again received his rather grudging admiration. The surgeon then made these and applied them to both cuts over Orloffski's eyes, but at no time did Grant or Orloffski speak to, or even come near, each other.

That was the kind of sail it was. Because of the Administrator's inspection, they did not get under way until pretty late, just about ten o'clock, so they did not sight Negril Point until around nine the next morning. Most of this time they were beating to windward into the Trades, tacking often, so Orloffski stayed up forward to handle the jib and staysail while Bonham from the cockpit handled the main and foresails. For this reason Grant chose to stay back near the cockpit. The land breeze at night did not help them much this time ; for some reason it had shifted and came to them off Jamaica only a little more easterly than the northeast daytime Trades. Grant and Lucky, who were together just about every minute now that they could be, tried to sleep a while below during the night but finally gave it up and came back up on deck, and Ben and Irm came up with them, where the sea and the sky of stars and the breeze were all so beautiful. Bonham remained at the wheel. Cathie Finer dozed in a corner of the cockpit. There was very little talk, now. At around ten in the morning when they rounded Negril Point they were two-thirds of the way home. Just about everybody was glad. Not too terribly long after, three or four hours,

they passed Montego Bay. By six in the evening they were
pulling into GaBay harbour and hauling down sail.

Ben and Irma of course had never been to GaBay, except
once for a day in a rented car, but Grant and Lucky knew
it well. The first thing Grant did was to telephone the West
Moon Over from the Yacht Club for reservations, for that
night, which they got quite easily when Grant used his name.
All any of them could think about right now was getting
away from these people, all of them, and—perhaps—resting
up a little, resting up from their " vacation cruise ".

But if there had been little talk during the long voyage
back, there was talk now when Bonham presented his charges
to Ben and Irma for the trip. He asked them forty dollars a
day per person. That made seven days, or so Bonham figured
—although they had finished the cruise at six p.m. and would
not be on board that night. The total came to just five
hundred and sixty dollars.

" Well, Jesus! " Ben said in a pained but embarrassed voice.
" You never did quote me charges, but I figured maybe
twenty to twenty-five bucks a day. Per person, of course. I
must say it seems kind of high to me."

" But don't forget I reminded you all of them dockage
charges," Bonham said calmly and evenly.

" But we only actually docked—I mean, docked where you
had to pay—two nights! " Ben protested, with embarrassment.

" Also," Grant put in, who was embarrassed also now,
" remember that Ben and Irm are pretty good friends of
mine."

Bonham's face remained totally inscrutable. " Them's my
charges," he said, " and I think they're fair. More than
fair." He had obviously fixed up his charges with the surgeon
and his girl before the voyage, and was sticking to them, but
of course the others could not know what this arrangement
was. And Bonham, in money matters, in *anything* having to
do with money, remained always as inscrutable and as un-
readable as a sphinx.

In the end Ben paid him, rather than suffer the embarrassment of argument, writing out a cheque right there on the
Yacht Club bar—just as Bonham (or so Grant suspected)
had figured ahead of time that he would. On the way to the
hotel in the taxi, Grant apologised for it. Ben only shrugged.

They made quite a sight at the West Moon Over Hotel,

Grant with his swollen taped-up nose, all of them sunburnt almost black with their salt-saturated hair askew and sticking out all over, and looking very " salty " indeed. But of course Grant was known there, by the manager as well as by just about everybody else, so there was no problem—especially when they learned they had just returned from a cruise to the Nelson Islands with Big Al Bonham in his new schooner, which of course everyone had heard all about. They bathed and cleaned up, swam and floated a while in the fresh-water pool, all of them glad to be away from salt water and the sea for a while. Then they dressed for dinner, had some drinks in the bar, ate an excellent dinner which included no sea-food at all, and went happily to bed, the two pairs of them.

It was at one-thirty in the morning when Bonham called Grant, waking him out of a sound sleep, making him get up to walk across the room to answer the phone.

It was about the worst thing in his life that could happen to him at the moment, he thought. For one insane, night-marish, dreamlike, sleep-drenched moment he thought Bonham was calling him to tell him about his wife and Jim Grointon, that he had seen them, had caught them, together. Vigorously, he rubbed one hand harshly back and forth across the back of his neck, and then slapped himself there several times. He had made that decision. It hadn't happened. It hadn't happened. He had analysed and judged all the evidence, and he knew it hadn't happened. " What?" he kept saying into the phone, " what? I don't understand. I don't understand. What?"

" I'm in trouble," Bonham's drink-thick voice said again. " I'm in real trouble. I need your help. Can you come? I'm at the Moonrise Motel. Can you come?"

" Okay, okay, I'll come," Grant said rubbing his neck some more. " I'll come."

" Are you sure you're awake?" Bonham said.

" No, as a matter of fact, I'm not," Grant said. " Now tell me again."

" The Moonrise Motel," Bonham said thickly. " It's about ten miles in toward town from where you are at the West Moon Over. Have you got a car?"

" Yeah, yeah, we rented a You-Drive here," Grant said. " I can be there in twenty minutes or so."

"Please come," Bonham said thickly. It was the first time Grant had ever heard him use that word ever. "Please."

"All right. I'll be there," Grant said, almost hating himself for saying it. "Twenty minutes. But what's the trouble."

"If you can't figure it out by the time you get here, you're not as smart as I think you are," Bonham said. "How many kinds of trouble are there if the weather's good?"

Grant was suddenly full awake. Cathie Finer! It had to be something to do with that. But *what?* "All right. I'll be there," he said and hung up.

"Honey," he said to Lucky in the bed.

"Don't wake me up," Lucky said, in her sleep. "Let me sleep. Please. Please let me sleep. Please don't wake me up. Is it hard? I'll hold it for you. But please don't wake me up. I promise I'll make love to him to-morrow the best he's ever had. I'll kiss it for you. But please don't wake me up. Now. I haven't slept in so long." And, in fact, she was still asleep. Even as she talked.

He had sat down on the bed edge again, nude, and now he rubbed her shoulder in the shorty nightie, and the back of her head beneath her hair. "I've got to go out. For a while. Will you be all right if you wake up and find me gone? Can you hear me? I've got to go out. But I'll be back. Hear? I'll be back."

"Go," she said, and turned herself violently over on to her side, away from him. "Go. I know you'll be back. I'll be all right. And I'll be here when you get back. What is it? Bonham?"

"Yes," he said.

"Cathie Finer?"

"I think so," he said.

"Go. I know you have to go. I'll be here when you get back," she said. She wiggled her shoulders and settled herself into the bed.

Grant sat looking at her for a moment. Then he reached for his bikini shorts. Had she? Hadn't she? Had she? Hadn't she? What couldn't Jerome Kern or Cole Porter have done with that refrain? *Had she? hadn't she? had she? hadn't she?* Had she? Hadn't she? He began collecting the rest of his clothes.

It was quite a scene when he got there. They were all sitting around the motel room looking embarrassed, except for

Cathie Finer, who was the most unclad of the group. She was still in her shorty nightie, not too different from Lucky's. Bonham had put his pants and shirt on, but was bare-footed. The others of course were fully clad. They were, altogether: Bonham, Cathie Finer, Orloffski, Letta Bonham, and an embarrassed-looking police sergeant in his uniform of very starched khaki shorts, khaki shirt and blouse, and the khaki cap with the red band.

" Hello, Cathie?" Grant said.

" Hello, Ron," she said, and then actually smiled. " Do you think you can do anything about this mess?"

" I'll try," he said. It was pretty obvious what had happened, and even Orloffski, with his ganged-up face, looked a little embarrassed. But he also looked bullheaded and stubborn as hell. Letta Bonham was not embarrassed at all. She was just plain mad. Orloffski had told her where Bonham and Cathie were stashed up for the night, and she had insisted on going there, with Orloffski, and she herself had called the police sergeant. The laws on adultery in Jamaica were stringent enough, but the elders of Ganado Bay had added their own wrinkle. A person caught in the act of adultery with witnesses was subject to immediate jailing. He could of course post bond.

Grant tried to reason with Letta Bonham, but she was indomitable. " How much is the bond?" Grant asked the sergeant finally.

" I don't know, Saar," the sergeant said. " We must have to go down to the Post and I will aither call the Inspector, or look it up in har book." Grant noted, with that peculiar quality of over-awareness of detail that so often crops up in tragedy, that he said " Post " and not " Station " or " Stationhouse ", and remembered that he was in fact a member of the Constabulary. " I had rahther hhate to call the Inspector, Saar," the sergeant added. " At this hour."

" Well, will three hundred dollars be enough?" Grant said.

" Oh, yes, Saar," the sergeant said, and grinned. " I am sure that it would."

Grant wrote out the cheque. " Now, let's all get out of this and get some sleep, what do you say?"

" I, Saar, ham in fact on duty," the sergeant grinned. " I can't." He said it " cahn't ", like an Englishman.

" It would be rather difficult for me to call a taxi now, at this hour," Cathie Finer said. " Would you mind giving me a lift back to my hotel, Sergeant? It's in town. You could drop me off on your way back to the Station—The Post." She was staying, in fact, it turned out, at the next ritziest hotel in GaBay, next ritziest to the West Moon Over.

" Sartainly not, Mom," the sergeant said gallantly. " I be most hhoppy to."

" Then would you all mind getting out of here for a few minutes so I can get dressed?" Cathie said.

They all stood outside in the court, including Bonham himself, while Cathie dressed. Grant tried once again to reason with Letta Bonham, but to no avail. The motel manager approached them, the group, for what was apparently the third or fourth time, and explained and protested that he was not responsible since they had registered as man and wife. How might he know? he asked with that flatted peculiar Jamaican-English accent.

" You heard that, Sergeant?" Letta Bonham said. " You noted it?"

" I did Mom," the sergeant said. " An' I noted him. Each time hair." Bonham said nothing. Neither did Orloffski.

When Cathie came out, she went off blithely with the police sergeant in the police car without saying good-bye to anyone particularly except Grant. Orloffski escorted Letta Bonham to her car, Bonham's old Buick, with all the solicitude of a man escorting a new widow. Which in a way, Grant supposed, she sort of, probably, was. Wanda Lou Orloffski, he noticed, was sitting in the back seat.—" I guess I'll sleep here," Bonham said. His half-drunken face was as sphinx-like, as cold and as stony, as it got when he talked about money. Grant nodded. He got in his You-Drive and drove back to the hotel. Lucky was still all curled up fast asleep. He looked at her for a long time after he got undressed, standing nude beside the bed. She really was so beautiful.

During the next two days before their flight out, Ben and Irma and Lucky disported themselves at the hotel with its tennis courts, its miniature golf, and its pool. None of them bathed in the sea off the pretty beach on whose edge the hotel was built. They had all had enough sea for quite a long while. Grant disported himself with them, when he could, feeling pretty much the same way. But a good deal of the time he was in town. He saw Letta Bonham three times.

Nothing he could say would move her, even when he carefully and very exactly explained to her what Orloffski was trying to do, had done. He saw Bonham once, and Bonham had nothing particular to say. He was still staying at the motel.

The day before they left a meeting of the Bonham-Orloffski-Grant-Finer-Schooner Corporation was held, with lawyers present. Grant did not attend. It was not necessary. There was nothing he could do. Orloffski had of course wired Sam Finer the news in New York, and quite legally and properly, the news also of the meeting. He had received back only an enigmatic wire saying only " WILL NOT VOTE TWO PER CENT." It did not matter. Orloffski with his 44 per cent and Letta Bonham with her 20 per cent Bonham had assigned to her had plenty more than a sufficient majority. Bonham was voted out as captain of the schooner *Naiad* and as President of the Corporation. Orloffski was voted in. Bonham, Grant understood (from the manager of the West Moon Over, who like everybody else in town was following the case closely), did attend the meeting. Grant did not know if he voted. In any case, Bonham was out.

In the taxi on the way to the airport the next day with all their luggage and Ben and Irma with them, they saw Bonham sitting on one of those dusty stone benches in the dusty square—the Parade, as it was called in Jamaica. He was looking at the dusty ground. Grant swung around in the front seat beside the driver, raised his hand, but then decided not to have the driver stop.

" You know," Lucky said to them all, in a rather sombre tone for her, " I hate to see it happen to him. Like that. Even though I didn't like him much, and even though I knew it, I really do hate to see it happen to him like that."

" I guess there's no reason really to stop and say good-bye," Grant said. " Is there?" he added.

Nobody answered and covertly Grant studied his wife, sitting there in the back seat with Ben and Irma, all of them looking out the back window at the square. She really was so beautiful. And for whatever reason, she did love him quite a lot, very much, he thought. Hansel and Gretel. The Babes in the Woods. Poor Hansel and Gretel and poor Babes in the Woods. They didn't have a chance . And alone, they didn't either one of them have even that much of a chance. In these woods. In these Orloffski and Bonham woods. Sam Finer woods. Maybe, if he hung on, if *they* hung on, they might someday again achieve that sort of strange wonderful Single Viewpoint they had once had, during those first few short days back at the Crount, and during that even shorter time at Evelyn's villa here in GaBay. Maybe they could. They had not even called or gone up to see Evelyn. Maybe they could: That feeling of looking at the world through the same, single, the one pair of eyes. In the two different heads. Maybe they could. God knew they needed it. Because they really were Hansel and Gretel. Grant studied her some more, intensely. Deeply, wonderingly, unknowingly. The back of her head and the champagne-coloured hair. Then when she turned back and looked at him, he smiled quickly; and then he thought he could see in her eyes that she had been thinking the same thing.

Cathie Finer was not on their plane. They did not know if she had left before or would be leaving after.

Nor did they hear of, or from, her afterwards.

They heard of him later, of Bonham; in New York. From friends who had been down to GaBay on vacation. Grant was into rehearsals by then, and also deep into the new play, the "schooner" play, as he called it. Bonham had got a job with the Ganado Bay Chamber of Commerce, conducting tourists. There were quite a few sights around, waterfalls, famous old bays, plantations back in the hills. He drove them around in one of the Chamber of Commerce's cars. Orloffski had, as captain and president of the schooner and the corporation, run the *Naiad* aground on reef and sand on a cruise to Grand Bank Island, and the cost of getting her off had bankrupted the corporation. Sam Finer had not put in another additional $10,000. Letta Bonham had gone back to her family in Kingston, and was teaching school there, a divorcee. Grant of course had been informed. His New York lawyers were quite pleased with the way René had handled his loan, because when the schooner was sold at auction in the liquidation of the corporation's assets, Grant's first mortgage on the schooner of $4,500 was the first thing to be paid.

James Jones

The Ice-Cream Headache *30p*
A collection of thirteen powerful stories by this best-selling author. 'Each story is perfectly constructed and rich in overtones.' *Times Educational Supplement*

Go to the Widow-Maker *60p*
A superb novel which dramatises a breed of men of action who are slowly being killed by twenty years of peace. In Jones's world of dangerous living, love is for men—women are for sex. 'Jones is the Hemingway of our time . . . There is savage poetry in his descriptions of spear-fishing and treasure-hunting.' *Spectator*

The Thin Red Line *40p*
His novel of the Marines on Guadalcanal—a gory, appallingly accurate description of men at war. 'Raw, violent, powerful and terrible, the most convincing account of battle experience I have ever read.' *Richard Lister, Evening Standard*

From Here to Eternity *60p*
The world famous novel of the men of the U.S. Army stationed at Pearl Harbour in the months immediately before America's entry into World War II. 'One reads every page persuaded that it is a remarkable, a *very* remarkable book indeed.' *Listener*

 *Fontana Books*

Fontana Books

Fontana is best known as one of the leading paperback publishers of popular fiction and non-fiction. It also includes an outstanding, and expanding section of books on history, natural history, religion and social sciences.

Most of the fiction authors need no introduction. They include Agatha Christie, Hammond Innes, Alistair MacLean, Catherine Gaskin, Victoria Holt and Lucy Walker. Desmond Bagley and Maureen Peters are among the relative newcomers.

The non-fiction list features a superb collection of animal books by such favourites as Gerald Durrell and Joy Adamson.

All Fontana books are available at your bookshop or newsagent; or can be ordered direct. Just fill in the form below and list the titles you want.

––––––––––––––––––––––––––––––––

FONTANA BOOKS, Cash Sales Department, P.O. Box 4, Godalming, Surrey. Please send purchase price plus 5p postage per book by cheque, postal or money order. No currency.

NAME (Block letters) _____

ADDRESS _____

_____

_____